James Clemens was born in Chicago, Illinois in 1961. He now has a veterinary practice in Sacramento, California, where he shares his home with two Dalmatians, a stray German Shepherd and a love-sick parrot named Igor.

Find out more about James Clemens and other Orbit authors by registering for the free monthly Orbit newsletter at www.orbitbooks.co.uk

WIT'CH WAR

Book Three of
The Banned and the Banished

JAMES CLEMENS

www.orbitbooks.co.uk

An *Orbit* Book

First published by The Ballantine Publishing Group, 2000
First published in Great Britain by Orbit 2002
Reprinted 2003 (twice), 2004, 2005

A CIP catalogue record for this book is available
from the British Library.

ISBN 1 84149 190 X

Printed and bound in Great Britain by
Mackays of Chatham plc, Chatham, Kent

Orbit
An imprint of
Time Warner Book Group UK
Brettenham House
Lancaster Place
London WC2E 7EN

For Carolyn McCray,
for friendship, guidance, and the gift of dragons

ACKNOWLEDGMENTS

No one writes in a vacuum. And I am no exception. This novel would not be possible without the valued and comprehensive assistance of many friends, colleagues, and enthusiastic readers.

Behind the production is one of the best editorial staffs in the business: Veronica Chapman, Jenni Smith, and Steve Saffel. I can't thank them enough for their skill. Also my ardent and tireless agent, Pesha Rubinstein.

Closer to home, a group of friends and experts whose keen eyes honed the first draft of this novel: Inger Aasen, Chris Crowe, Michael Gallowglass, Lee Garrett, Dennis Grayson, Debbie Nelson, Jane O'Riva, Chris Smith, Caroline Williams. And a special thanks to Judy and Steve Prey, for leading us forward, and Dave Meek, for the long talks across the pool table.

And no one can write without a strong foundation: Thanks, John, for always being there.

Lastly, to all the fans who have sent me notes, both praising and critiquing: You are heard . . . and appreciated!

FOREWORD TO WIT'CH WAR

(NOTE: The following is an open letter from Professor J. P. Clemens, the translator of **The Banned and the Banished** *series)*

Dear Students,

As the historian of this textbook, I welcome you back to this series of translated texts and beg a moment of your time to comment on my work and some of the rumors surrounding it.

As is well known, the original scrolls were lost to antiquity, and only crumbling handwritten copies discovered over five centuries ago in caves on the Isle of Kell yet remain of this most ancient tale. Because this language has been dead for over a millennium, hundreds of historians and linguistic experts have attempted to tackle the reconstruction and translation of these Kelvish Scrolls. Yet under my supervision at the University of Da' Borau, a team of distinguished colleagues finally accomplished the impossible: the complete and truest translation of the tale of Elena Morin'stal.

In your hands is my life's work. And I wanted to state that I believe my translations should stand on their own merits.

Yet, over my objections, my fellow scholar, Jir'rob Sordun, had been assigned to write forewords to the first two books, to warn readers about the devious nature of the scrolls' original author.

Now were these doleful warnings truly necessary? As much as I respect Professor Sordun, I believe these ancient histories of Alasea's 'black age' do not need embellishments or extravagant introductions. Though this ancient age of our land is cloaked in mystery and muddled by conflicting accounts, any person of sound mind will know the tales herein are just the twisted fictions of some ancient madman. Do we really need Sordun to point this out to us?

Let's look to the facts.

What do we truly know of this 'black age'? We know Elena was a true historical figure – there are too many contemporary references to deny this – but her role during the uprising against the Gul'gotha is obviously a whimsical tale. She was *not* a wit'ch. She did *not* have a fist stained with blood magicks. I wager that some charlatans had painted her hand crimson and propped her up as some anointed savior, milking the simple village folk of their hard-earned coppers. Among this troupe of tricksters was obviously a writer of some modest skill who created these wild stories to bolster their fake leader. I imagine he regaled the farmers with these fabrications, which he passed off as real events – and so the myth of the wit'ch was forged.

I can picture the gap-toothed farmers staring slack jawed as the story teller related tales of highland og'res, woodland nymphs, mountain nomads, and silver-haired elv'in. I can imagine their gasps as Elena wielded her magick of fire and ice. But surely in today's enlightened Alasean society, there is no need to warn readers so vocally that such things are fictions.

So with that said, I must make one confession. As I translated these series of scrolls, I began to believe them just a bit. Who wouldn't want to believe that a young girl from some remote apple orchard could end up changing the world? And what she accomplished at the end – what the author claimed occurred – who wouldn't want to believe that to be true?

Of course, being a scholar, I know better. Nature is nature, and what the author proposes at the very end of the scrolls is obviously a falsehood that can only weaken our society. For this reason, I have also come to accept that my translations should be banned and kept only for the few enlightened, for those who won't be duped by its final message.

However, even with these tight restrictions, I've begun to hear absurd rumors surrounding the required fingerprint that binds each text to its reader. It is whispered in certain circles that some readers – those who have marked each of the five textbooks with their fingerprints and bound the compiled series in silk ribbon, or so the story goes – have found themselves beguiled by ancient magicks that have reached out from my translated words. I believe the fault for this ridiculous notion lies with the university press that produces this series. The requirement to mark each of the five volumes with the print from a different finger of the right hand only fosters such foolishness. For a publisher to require such a thing, especially when the story in these books suggests that powerful magick can be wielded by a wit'ch's hand, is downright negligent on the part of the publisher.

Though I am flattered at such supposed power behind my work, I can't help but be shocked and befuddled by such blatant foolishness.

So perhaps I judge too harshly my illustrious colleague. Maybe it is best after all to warn all potential readers.

So let me repeat Jir'rob Sordun's final word of caution as printed in the foreword to the first text:

Remember, at all times,
in your waking hours and in your dreams,
The author is a liar.

Sincerely and humbly,

J. P. Clemens,
Professor of Ancient Histories

WIT'CH WAR

*Heralded by a dragon's roar
and born in a maelstrom of ice and flame,
this is the way the war began.*

Through my open window, I can hear the strum of a lyre's chords and the tinkle of a minstrel's voice rising like steam from the streets below. It is the height of the Midsummer Carnivale here in the city of Gelph. As the searing heat of the day winds down to the sultry hours of evening, townspeople gather in the square for the Feast of the Dragon, a time of merriment and rejoicing.

Yet I can't help but frown at the gaiety of the celebrants. How much the fools have forgotten! Even now as I sit with pen and paper and prepare once again to continue the wit'ch's tale, I can hear the screams of the slaughtered and the blood roar of dragons behind the music and happy voices outside my window.

The true meaning for this celebration has been lost over the ages. The *first* Midsummer Carnivale was a somber affair, meant to cheer the few survivors of the War of the Isles, a time for wounds to heal and for spirits torn by blade and betrayal to be restored. Even the meaning behind the ritual exchange of fake dragon's teeth and baubles painted like precious black pearls has been forgotten by the present revelers. It was once meant to signify the bond between—

Ah . . . but I get ahead of myself. After so many centuries, with my head so full of memories, I seem constantly to find myself unhooked from time's inevitable march. As I sit in this rented room, surrounded by my parchments and inks, it seems like only yesterday that Elena stood on the bluffs of Blisterberry and stared out across the twilight sea at her dragon army. Why is it that the older one gets, the more valuable the past becomes? What once I fled from is now what I dream about. Is this the true curse that the wit'ch has set upon my soul? To live forever, yet to forever dream of the past?

As I pick up my pen and dip it in the ink, I pray her final promise to me holds true. Let me finally die with the telling of her tale.

Though the day's heat still hides in my room as the evening cools, I close my window and my heart against the songs and merrymaking below. I cannot tell a tale of blood-shed and treachery while listening to the gay strains of the minstrels' instruments and the raucous laughter of the Carnivale's celebrants. This part of the story of Elena Morin'stal is best written with a cold heart.

So as the Feast of the Dragon begins outside among the streets of Gelph, I ask that you listen deeper. Can you hear another sort of music? As in many grand symphonies, the opening soft chords are often forgotten in the blare of the horn and the strike of the drum that follow; yet this forget-fulness does insult to the composer, for it is in these calm moments that the stage is set for the storm to come.

So listen and bend your ear – not to the lyre or the drums outside my window – but to the quieter music found in the beat of a morning surf as the tide recedes with the dawn's first light. There lies the beginning of the grand song I mean to sing.

Book One

TIDES AND TEARS

1

With only the crash of waves for company, Elena stood by the cliff's edge and stared out across the blue seas. At the horizon, the sun was just dawning, crowning the distant islands of the Archipelago with rosy halos of mist. Closer to the coast, a single-masted fishing trawler fought the tide to ply its trade among the many isles and reefs. Over its sails, gulls and terns argued while hunting the same generous waters. Nearer still, at the base of the steep bluff, the rocky shore was already occupied by the lounging bodies of camping sealions. The scolding barks of mothers to their pups and the occasional huffing roar of a territorial bull echoed up to her.

Sighing, Elena turned her back on the sight. Since the seadragons of the mer'ai had left fifteen days ago, the routines of the coastline were already returning to normal. Such was the resiliency of nature.

As if to remind her further of the natural world's strength, a stiff morning breeze tugged at her hair, blowing it into her eyes. Irritated, she pushed back the waving strands with gloved fingers and attempted to trap the stray locks behind her ears, but the winds fought her efforts. It had been over two moons since Er'ril had last cropped her hair, and the length had grown to be a nuisance – too short to fix with ribbons and pins, yet too long to easily manage, especially with her hair beginning to show its curl again. Still, she kept her complaints to herself, fearing Er'ril might take the shears to her once again.

She frowned at the thought. She was tired of looking like a boy.

Though she had readily accepted the necessity of the disguise while traveling the lands of Alasea, out here in the lonely wilds of the Blisterberry bluffs, there were no eyes to spy upon her and no need to continue the ruse as Er'ril's son – or so she kept telling herself. Yet she was not so sure her guardian held these same assumptions.

As a caution, Elena had gone to wearing caps and hats when around Er'ril, hoping he wouldn't notice the growing length of her locks or the fading black dye that had camouflaged her hair. The deep fire of her natural color was finally beginning to reappear at the roots.

She pulled out her cap from her belt and corralled her hair under it before hiking back up the coastal trail to the cottage. Why the appearance of her hair should matter so much to her she could not put into words. It was not mere vanity, though she could not deny that a pinch of pride did play a small role in her subterfuge with Er'ril. She was a young woman, after all, and why wouldn't she balk at appearing as a boy?

But there was more to it than that. And the true reason was marching down the path toward her with a deep frown. Dressed in a wool sweater against the morning's chill, her brother wore his fiery red hair pulled back from his face with a black leather strap. Reminded of her family by Joach's presence, Elena was ashamed to hide her own heritage under dyes any longer. It was like denying her own parents.

As Joach closed the distance between them, Elena recognized the character of the young man's exasperated grimace and his pained green eyes. She had seen it often enough on her father's face.

'Aunt My has been looking all over for you,' he said as greeting.

'My lessons!' Elena darted forward, closing the distance with her brother. 'I'd almost forgotten.'

'Almost?' he teased as she joined him.

She scowled at her brother but could not argue against his accusation. In fact, she *had* completely forgotten about this morning's lesson. It was to be her last instruction on the art of swordplay before Aunt Mycelle left for Port Rawl to rendezvous with the other half of their party. Kral, Tol'chuk, Mogweed, and Meric were due to meet with Mycelle there in two days' time. Elena wondered for the hundredth time how they had fared in Shadowbrook. She prayed they were all well.

As she and her brother marched back up the trail toward the cottage, Joach mumbled, 'El, your head's always in the clouds.'

She turned in irritation, then saw her brother's quirked smile. Those were the same words her father had used so often to scold Elena when time had slipped away from her. She took her brother's hand in her own. Here was all that was left of her family now.

Joach squeezed her gloved hand, and they walked in silence through the fringe forest of wind-whipped cypress and pine. As Flint's cottage appeared on the bluffs ahead, Joach cleared his throat. 'El, there's something I've been meaning to ask you.'

'Hmm?'

'When you go to the island . . .' he started.

Elena inwardly groaned. She did not want to think of the last leg of their journey to retrieve the Blood Diary from the island of A'loa Glen — especially given Joach's own accounting of the horrors that lay in wait.

'I'd like to go back with you. To the island.'

Elena stumbled a step. 'You know that's not possible. You heard Er'ril's plan, Joach.'

'Yes, but a word from you—'

'No,' she said. 'There's no reason for you to go.'

With a touch on her arm, Joach pulled her to a stop. 'El, I know you want to keep me from further danger, but I have to go back.'

Shaking free of his hand, she stared him in the eye. 'Why? Why do you think you need to go? To protect me?'

'No, I'm no fool.' Joach stared at his feet. He still would not meet her gaze. 'But I had a dream,' he whispered. 'A dream that has repeated twice over the past half moon since you arrived from the swamps.'

She stared at her brother. 'You think it's one of your weavings?'

'I think so.' He finally raised his eyes to hers, a slight blush on his cheeks. Joach had discovered he shared their family's heritage of elemental magicks. His skill was *dreamweaving*, a lost art preserved by only a select few of the Brotherhood. It was the ability to glimpse snatches of future events in the dream plane. Brother Flint and Brother Moris had been working with Joach on testing the level of his magick. Joach nodded toward the cottage ahead. 'I haven't told anyone else.'

'Maybe it's just an ordinary dream,' Elena offered. But the part of her that was a wit'ch stirred with her brother's words. *Magick*. Even the mere mention of it fired her blood. With both her fists fresh to the Rose, the magick all but sang in her heart. Swallowing hard, she closed her spirit against the call of the wit'ch. 'What made you think it was a weaving?'

Joach scrunched up his face. 'I . . . I get this feeling when I'm in a weaving. It's like a thrill in my veins, like my very being is afire with an inner storm. I felt it during this dream.'

An inner storm, Elena thought. She knew that sensation when she touched her own wild magick – a raging tempest trapped in her heart screaming with pent-up energy. She found her two hands wringing together with just the remembrance of past flows of raw magick. She forced her hands apart. 'Tell me about your dream.'

Joach bit his lower lip, suddenly reluctant.

'Go on,' Elena persisted.

His voice lowered. 'I saw you at the top of a tall spire in A'loa Glen. A black winged beast circled the parapets nearby—'

'Black winged? Was it the dragon Ragnar'k?' Elena asked, naming the ebony-scaled seadragon who shared flesh with the Bloodrider, Kast, and who was blood-bonded to the mer woman, Sy-wen.

Joach's fingers wandered to an ivory dragon's tooth that hung from a cord around his neck; it had been a gift from Sy-wen. 'No, this was no dragon.' His hands fought to describe the figure, but he gave up with an exasperated shrug of his shoulders. 'It was something more shadow than flesh. But that's not the important part of the dream. You see . . .' His voice died, and his eyes drifted away to stare out at the ocean. Her brother was hiding something from her, something that scared him deeply.

Elena licked her dry lips, suddenly wondering if she truly wanted to know the answer. 'What is it, Joach?'

'You were not alone on the tower.'

'Who else was there?'

He turned back to her. 'I was. I stood beside you bearing the poi'wood staff I stole from the darkmage. When the creature dove toward us, I raised the staff and smote the creature from the sky with a spellcast bolt.'

'Well, that proves it was only a nightmare. You're no practitioner of the black arts. You're just dreaming that I need your protection. It's probably worry and fear that "thrilled" your blood in the dream, not weaving magicks.'

Frowning, Joach shook his head. 'Truthfully, after the first dream, I supposed the same. Papa's last words to me were to protect you, and that has weighed heavily on my heart ever since. But when the dream came to me again, I was no longer so sure. After the second dream yesterday, I crept out at midnight – out here alone – and I ... I spoke the spell from the dream while holding the staff.'

Elena had a sick feeling in the root of her stomach. 'Joach ... ?'

He pointed behind her. Elena turned. Only a handful of steps away stood a lightning-split pine, its bark charred and its limbs cracked. 'The spell from my dream worked.'

Elena stared with her eyes wide, suddenly weak in her legs, not just from the thought that Joach's dream might be real, but also from the fact that Joach had called forth black magicks. She shivered. 'We must tell the others,' she said in hushed tones. 'Er'ril must be warned of this.'

'No,' he said. 'There's still more. It's the reason I've kept silent until now.'

'What?'

'In my dream, after I smote the beast from the sky, Er'ril appeared from the depths of the tower, sword in hand. He ran at us, and I swung the staff toward him and ... and I killed him, like the beast, in a blaze of darkfire.'

'Joach!'

Her brother could not be interrupted; the words tumbled from his mouth in a rush. 'In the dream, I knew he meant you harm. There was murder in his eyes. I had no choice.' Joach turned pained eyes toward her. 'If I don't go with you, Er'ril will kill you. I know it!'

Elena swung away from Joach's impossible words. Er'ril would never harm her. He had protected her across all the lands of Alasea. Joach had to be wrong. Still, she found her eyes staring at the charred ruin of the nearby pine. Joach's black spell – a spell he learned in a dream – had worked.

Her brother spoke behind her. 'Keep what I've told you secret, Elena. Do not trust Er'ril.'

Not far away, Er'ril woke with a start from his own troubled dreams. Nightmares of poisonous spiders and dead children chased him from his slumber. They left him restless and sore of muscle, as if he had held himself clenched all night long. He tossed aside the blanket and carefully eased himself from the goose-down bed.

Naked chested, dressed only in his linen underclothes, he shivered in the chill of the early morning coast. Summer waned toward autumn, and though the days still warmed to a moist heat, the mornings already whispered of the cold moons ahead. Barefooted, Er'ril crossed the slate floor to the washbasin and the small silvered mirror hanging on the wall behind it. He splashed cool water on his face as if to wash away the cobwebs of the night's dreams.

He had lived so many winters that his nights were always crowded with memories demanding his attention.

Straightening up, he stared at the black-stubbled planes that were his Standi heritage. His gray eyes stared back at him from a face he no longer knew. How could such a young

17

face hide so completely the old man inside?

He ran his one hand over the boyish features. Though he looked outwardly the same, he often wondered if his own long-dead father would recognize the man in the mirror now. The five centuries of winters had marked him in ways other than the usual graying hair or wrinkled skin. He let his fingers drift over the smooth scar on his empty shoulder. No ... time marked men in many ways.

Suddenly a voice rose from the corner of the room. 'If you're done admiring yourself, Er'ril, maybe we can get this day started.'

Er'ril knew the voice and did not startle. He merely turned and stepped to the chamber pail. He ignored the grizzled gray man seated in the thick pillowed chair in the shadowed corner. While relieving himself of his morning's water, Er'ril spoke. 'Flint, if you'd wanted me up earlier, you had merely to wake me.'

'From the grumbling and thrashing as you slept, I figured it best to let you work out whatever troubled your slumber without interruption.'

'Then you had best let me sleep another decade or two,' he answered sourly.

'Yes, yes. Poor Er'ril, the wandering knight. The eternal warden of A'loa Glen.' Flint nodded toward his old legs. 'Let your joints grow as hoary as mine, and we'll see who complains the louder.'

Er'ril made a scoffing sound at his words. Even without magick, time had eroded little of that older Brother's strength of limb; instead Flint's many winters spent on the sea had hardened his frame like a storm-swept oak. 'The day you slow down, old man, is the day I will hang up my own sword.'

Flint sighed. 'We all have our burdens to haul, Er'ril. So

if you're done feeling miserable, the morning is half over, and we still have the *Seaswift* to outfit for the coming voyage.'

'I'm well aware of the day's schedule,' Er'ril said bitingly as he dressed. His night's disturbed rest had left him short-tempered, and Flint's tongue was rubbing him especially raw this morning.

The Brother sensed Er'ril's irritation and softened his tone. 'I know you've borne a lot, Er'ril, what with hauling that lass across all the lands of Alasea while pursued by the hunters of the Gul'gotha. But if we are to ever free ourselves of that bastard's yoke, we cannot let our own despair weigh down our spirits. On the path ahead, the Dark Lord will give us plenty to plague our hearts, without the need to look to the past for more.'

Er'ril nodded his assent. He clapped the old man on the shoulder as he passed to the oak wardrobe in the corner. 'How did you grow so wise among these pirates and cutthroats of the Archipelago, old man?'

Flint grinned, fingering his silver earring. 'Among pirates and cutthroats, only the *wise* reach a ripe ol' age.'

Retrieving his clothes, Er'ril pulled on his pants and began working his shirt over his head. With only one arm, the chore of dressing was always a struggle. After so many centuries, time had not made some things easier. Finally, red faced, he accomplished his task and tucked his shirt in place. 'Any word from Sy-wen?' he finally said, searching for his boots.

'No, not yet.'

Er'ril raised his eyes at the worried tone in the old Brother's voice. Flint had grown protective of the small mer'ai girl since plucking her from the sea. Sy-wen, along with the mer'ai army, had been sent to the oceans south of the Blasted Shoals in search of the Dre'rendi fleet. Also named 'Bloodriders,' the Dre'rendi fleet were the cruelest of the dreaded Shoal's pirates. But old oaths bound the mer'ai and the Dre'rendi, and Flint hoped to gain the Bloodriders' aid in the war to come.

Flint continued. 'All I hear from my spies upon the seas is foul rumors of A'loa Glen. Perpetual black clouds cloak the island, sudden vicious squalls beat back boats, storm winds scream with the cries of tortured souls. Even farther out from the island now, trawling nets are pulling up strange pale creatures never seen before, beasts of twisted shapes and poisoned spines. Others whisper of flocks of winged demons seen far overhead—'

'Skal'tum,' Er'ril spat, his voice strained with tension as he picked up one of his leather boots. 'My brother gathers an army of dreadlords to him.'

Flint leaned forward and patted the plainsman's knee as Er'ril sat down on the bed. 'That creature masquerading as the Praetor of A'loa Glen is not your brother any longer, Er'ril. It is only a cruel illusion. Put such thoughts aside.'

Er'ril could not. He pictured the night five centuries ago when the Blood Diary had been bound in magick. That night, all that was just and noble in his brother Shorkan and the mage Greshym had gone into forging the cursed tome. But all that remained of the two – the corrupt and foul dregs of spirit – had been given to the Black Heart, to use as pawns in the Dark Lord's dire plans. Er'ril's jaws clenched. Someday he would destroy the foulness that walked in the shape of his beloved brother.

Flint cleared his throat, drawing Er'ril back to the present. 'But that is not all I have heard. Word from down the coast reached me this morning by pigeon. It's why I came to fetch you from your bed.'

'What is it?' Er'ril worked his boots on, his brow dark.

'More dire news, I'm afraid. Yesterday, a small fleet of hunting boats put in at Port Rawl, but the fishermen on board had been corrupted. The men were like wild dogs, attacking townsfolk, biting, slashing, raping. It took the entire garrison to fend them off. Though most of the berserkers were killed, one of the cursed ships managed to break anchor and escape, carrying off several women and a few children.'

Er'ril laced his boots, his voice strained. 'Black magick. Perhaps a spell of influence. I've seen its like before . . . long ago.'

'No, I know the magick you speak of. What was done to these fishermen was worse than a simple spell. Ordinary wounds would not kill these berserkers. Only decapitation would end their blood lust.'

Er'ril glanced up, his eyes hooded with concern.

'A healer examined the slain and discovered a thumb-sized hole bored into the base of each skull. Cracking the skulls open revealed a small tentacled creature curled inside. A few of the beasts were still alive, squirming and writhing. After that horrible discovery, the carcasses of the dead were immediately burned on the stone docks.'

'Sweet Mother,' Er'ril said sullenly, 'how many new horrors can the Black Heart birth?'

Flint shrugged. 'The entire town reeks of charred flesh. It has the townsfolk edgy and jumping at shadows. And in a town as rough as Port Rawl, that's a dangerous mix. Mycelle's journey there to search for your friends will be fraught with risk.'

Er'ril worked silently as he finished tying his boots. He pondered the news, then spoke. 'Mycelle knows how to take care of herself. But this news makes me worry if perhaps we shouldn't set sail on the *Seaswift* earlier than planned.'

He straightened to meet Flint's eyes. 'If the evil of A'loa Glen has reached all the way to the coast, perhaps it's best to leave now.'

'I've had similar thoughts. But if you want your friends to rejoin you, I see us leaving no earlier than the new moon. Besides, it'll take at least until then to man and outfit the *Seaswift*, and who can say if the seas will be any safer than where we are right now?'

Er'ril stood up. 'Still I don't like just sitting here idle, waiting for the Dark Lord to reach out for us.'

Flint held up a hand. 'But if we rush, we may find ourselves placing Elena right into his foul grip. I say we stick to our plan. Sail at the new moon, and rendezvous with the mer'ai army in the Doldrums at the appointed day. With the growing menace at A'loa Glen, we must give Sy-wen and Kast time to reach the Dre'rendi fleet and see if their old oaths will be honored. We need their strength.'

Er'ril shook his head. 'There is no honor among those pirates.'

Flint scowled. 'Kast is a Bloodrider. Though he now shares his spirit with the dragon Ragnar'k, he was always a man of honor, and his people, worn hard by storms and bloodshed, know the importance of duty and ancient debts.'

Er'ril still doubted the wisdom of the plan. 'It's like putting a wolf at our back when facing the Dark Lord's army.'

'Perhaps. But if we're to succeed, any teeth that can rip into the flank of our enemy should be welcome.'

Er'ril sighed and combed his stubborn hair into order with his fingers. 'Fine. We'll give Sy-wen and Kast until the new moon. But whether we hear word from them or not, we sail.'

Flint nodded and stood. With the matter decided, he

fished his pipe from a pocket. 'Enough talk,' he grumbled. 'Let's find a hot taper and welcome the morning with a bit of smoke.'

'Ah, once again proof of your wisdom,' Er'ril said. A smoke sounded like a perfect way to set aside the foul start of the morning. He followed willingly after the grizzled Brother.

Once they reached the kitchen, Er'ril heard a familiar scolding voice echo through the open window next to the cooking hearth. The shouted complaints were accompanied by the occasional clash of steel. Apparently, the swordswoman, Mycelle, was finding her pupil's last lesson to be less than exemplary.

It seemed everyone was having a sour morning.

Mycelle batted Elena's short sword aside. Then with the flick of a wrist, she sent her pupil's blade flying through the air. Stunned, Elena watched the small blade flip end over end across the yard. The move was so swift that Elena's gloved hand was still aloft as if bearing her sword. Elena slowly lowered her arm, her cheeks red.

The swordswoman gave her pupil a sorrowful shake of her head, fists resting on her hips. Mycelle stood as tall as most men and as broad of shoulder. Her coarse blond hair hung in a thick braid to her waist. Dressed in leathers and steel, she was a formidable swordswoman. 'Fetch your sword, child.'

'Sorry, Aunt My,' Elena said, chagrined. Mycelle was not truly Elena's blood relative, but the woman had been as much a part of her life as any real relations. The woman's true bloodlines traced back to the shape-shifters of the Western Reaches, the si'lura. But Mycelle had given up her birthright long ago when fate and circumstance had convinced her to 'settle' into human form, abandoning forever her ability to shift.

'Where's your mind at this morning, girl?'

Elena hurried over to her vagrant sword and grabbed its hilt. She knew the answer to her aunt's exasperated question. Her mind was still on Joach's earlier words, not on the dance of blades. Returning to her position, Elena held the sword at ready.

'We'll try the Scarecrow's Feint again. It's a simple move, but when mastered, it's one of the most effective methods to lure an opponent to drop his guard.'

Nodding, Elena tried to push back the nagging doubts that Joach had raised in her mind – but she failed. She could not imagine Er'ril ever betraying her. The Standi plainsman had been steadfast in his loyalty to both Elena and the quest. They had shared many a long afternoon together, heads bowed in study, as she learned simple manipulations of her power. But beyond their words and lessons, there was a deeper bond unspoken between them. Through sidelong glances, she occasionally caught the trace of a proud smile on his usually dour features as she concentrated on some aspect of her arcane arts. And other times, though his lips were frowning at some mistake of hers, she spied an amused glint in his gray eyes. Though he was a complex man, Elena suspected she knew his heart. He was a true knight in spirit as well as word. He would never betray her.

Suddenly Elena's fingers stung with fire, and she found herself again staring at an empty glove.

'Child,' her aunt said in a tone that bordered on fury, 'if your attention is not on this lesson, I could be saddling my mount for the journey to Port Rawl.'

'I'm sorry, Aunt My.' She crossed once again to her fallen sword.

'Magick is unpredictable, Elena, but a well-oiled sword will never lose its edge when you need it. Remember that. You must become proficient at both. Once skilled in magick and sword, you will be a two-edged weapon. Harder to stop, harder to kill. Remember, child, where magick fails, a sword prevails.'

'Yes, Aunt My,' Elena said dutifully. She had heard it all before. She raised the sword and cast aside any further doubts about Er'ril.

Mycelle approached across the packed dirt of the yard, feet poised, sword balanced easily in her left hand. Her aunt's other sword was still sheathed in one of the crossed scabbards on her back. When armed with both her twin swords, Mycelle was a demon of steel and muscle.

Still, her aunt's single sword was threat enough. Elena barely managed to stop a sudden feint and parry, and her aunt's follow-up thrust tipped Elena off balance. The girl struggled to keep upright, determined to show Mycelle that the fortnight of lessons had not been for naught.

Her aunt continued her furious assault. Elena dragged her sword up to block the next thrust. Mycelle's blade sang down the length of her pupil's steel to strike the sword's guard with a resounding blow. Every bone in Elena's hand felt the impact, her fingers numbing.

Elena watched Mycelle's wrist flick, a move meant to disarm her once more. Biting back her frustration, Elena forced her weak fingers to match her aunt's movement just in time, catching the edge of Mycelle's weapon across the meat of her thumb. Elena felt the blade slice through glove and skin, stinging like the bite of a wasp.

Ignoring the minor cut, Elena kept her sword up as Mycelle retreated a step before her next assault. 'Very good, ch—' Mycelle started to say when Elena brought the attack back to the master, taking the offensive for the first time.

Elena's blood suddenly sang with energies flowing from her wound. Holding her magick in check, Elena fought with renewed vigor. If her aunt wanted her to be a two-edged sword, so be it! Magick and steel now mixed in her blood.

Mycelle tested Elena's mettle for a few strikes, clearly surprised with her pupil's sudden skill and daring. Then the master set to break the pupil's attack and force her back to a more defensive posture.

Elena met each attack with a blow of her own. Steel rang clear across the yard. Elena, for the briefest twinkling, felt the true rhythm of the dance. For a crystalline moment, nothing else mattered in the world. It was a battle of perfect clarity, a poem of motion and synchronization. And behind it all, her wild magick sang in chorus.

Elena finished with a double feint and dropped her sword's point. She saw her aunt hesitate, then follow the bait. Elena turned her wrist and spun her sword's tip, trapping the other's blade at the guard. Elena flicked her wrist. In a flash of steel, it was over.

An empty hand was now raised between them – but not Elena's this time.

Mycelle lowered her outstretched arm, shaking the sting from her wrist. Her aunt bowed her head ever so slightly. 'Elena, that was the most perfect Scarecrow Feint that I've ever had the pleasure of witnessing. Even while knowing you were doing it, I couldn't resist.'

Elena grinned foolishly at her aunt's praise. Sudden clapping brought her attention to the others who had gathered at the sound of the clanging blades. Er'ril stood with Brother Flint in the rear doorway to the cottage. Both men's eyes were wide with appreciation. Even Joach stood speechless near the woodpile. 'Good show, El!' he finally blurted as the clapping subsided.

At her brother's feet crouched Fardale, the si'luran shape-shifter in his wolf form, his black fur showing its rust and copper highlights in the bright sunshine. He must have just come back from his usual morning hunt for rabbit and meadow mice. He barked his consent to the others' praise and sent a brief image in a flash of amber eyes: *A wolf pup wrestles its littermate to become pack leader.*

Elena accepted their praise while keeping a firm grip on her sword's hilt. The siren's song of her magick still rang in her ears, almost drowning out the others. 'Again,' Elena said lustily to Mycelle.

'I think this is a good place to stop,' Mycelle said with a small laugh. 'When I get back from Port Rawl, we'll take your lessons to the next level.'

Elena had to bite her lip to keep from begging for more. Magick had flamed her blood and urged her to continue. Elena felt ready to take on a battalion of swordsmen.

'Elena, you're bleeding,' Joach suddenly said. 'Your hand.'

Elena glanced down. Thick red drops of blood rolled from her sliced thumb and slid down the length of her lowered blade. She pulled her hand from the eyes of the others. 'It's just a scratch. I didn't even notice it.'

Er'ril crossed over to her. 'Those are the most dangerous injuries – the ones you ignore as minor. Let me see.'

Reluctantly, Elena passed her sword to her aunt, then pulled free her fouled glove, unsheathing her true weapon. Rich with wild magicks, ruby whorls slowly spun across the skin of her hand.

Er'ril held her palm and examined the thin slice. 'Just the skin. No muscle. Let's get inside, and we'll clean it up and bandage it.'

Elena nodded and followed the plainsman into the kitchen. Seated on a stool, she endured his ministrations quietly. He pressed a dab of sweetwort ointment to the wound, but even now her thumb was beginning to heal, her flow of magick knitting the wound together.

For a heartbeat, Er'ril studied the healing cut with narrowed eyes, then put a light wrap over it. By this time, the others had finished with their congratulations and had left to finish various chores of the day, leaving the two of them alone.

'With the bandage, you'll not be able to wear a glove for a few days,' Er'ril mumbled. Even with only one hand, he skillfully secured her wrap with a final snug pull, then sat back on his heels to stare her in the eyes. 'Pass me your other glove.'

'Why? I didn't injure that hand.'

'Your glove.' He held out his palm, his eyes suddenly dark.

Elena slowly slid her left hand free of the lambskin glove. She passed it to him, keeping her hand hidden.

'Show me.'

'I don't see what—'

'Your sword cut was already healing. That only happens when you've touched your magick.' Iron entered his voice. 'Now show me *both* of your hands.'

She would not meet his eyes as she reluctantly displayed her palms on her lap. She stared at the twin ruby hands. They were no longer mirror images of one another. Her right hand – her sword hand – was slightly less rich in whorling dark dyes. The magick spent during the swordplay had slightly drained the full richness of the ruby color. In the sunlight streaming through the window, her subterfuge was plain. Elena had used magick against Mycelle to sharpen her swordsmanship against her teacher.

'It's called a blood sword,' Er'ril said tiredly. 'A form of magick that I wish you'd never learned.'

Elena pulled away her hands back from his scrutiny. 'Why? It cost only a trace of magick.'

Placing a hand on her knee, Er'ril moved closer to her. 'It costs much more than that. I saw it in your eyes. You didn't want it to stop. In my time, mages also heard the siren's call of wild magicks. But it was only darkmages who heeded the cry without care for the harm it might cause.' He nodded toward her two hands. 'And you are doubly marked. I can only imagine how fierce this call must be in your blood. You must fight its temptation.'

'I understand,' Elena said. Since first using her magick, the song of the wit'ch had been a constant melody. She knew the danger in listening too closely and resisted the wit'ch in her, never relinquishing the woman. It was a fine line she walked. Over the past year, she had learned the art and importance of balance.

'That's why a blood sword is so dangerous,' Er'ril continued. 'You offer the magick a tool by which to escape your control. With enough blood, the sword itself becomes host to your magick – almost a living thing, a wild thing. It has no conscience, no morals, only an insatiable blood lust. It will eventually overwhelm its user. Only the strongest mage can master a blood sword and tame its will.'

Elena listened with horror at what she had almost done.

'But that is not the worst,' Er'ril said. 'Once fully blooded, the sword is forged forever. The magick fuses permanently with the steel. It can then be borne by anyone, and its magic-wrought skill is available to any wielder. There were tales of darkmages passing blood swords to ordinary men and women, people unable to resist the magick's call. They quickly became enthralled to the swords, slaves to their blood lust.'

Elena's face paled. 'What happened to them?'

'These swordslaves, as they were named, were hunted down and killed, and the blades were melted to raw ore, driving off the twisted magick. It cost many lives. So beware what you so casually forge, Elena. It may cause more sorrow than you can fathom.'

Elena slipped her one glove back on and fingered the wrap on the other hand. With her wound bandaged and healing, the call of the wit'ch subsided. 'I'll be more cautious. I promise.'

Er'ril studied her a moment as if testing her sincerity. Satisfied with whatever he saw, his eyes softened their stern glint. 'One other item, Elena. About that final exchange with your aunt, blood sword or not, it was not all magick that guided your arm. You've grown in skill.' His voice grew firmer. 'Never forget that there is a strength in you that has nothing to do with blood magicks.'

His quiet words, more than all the boisterous exclamations of the others, touched her deeply. Sudden tears welled up in her eyes.

Er'ril stood up, seeming to sense her emotions, and grew quickly awkward. 'I must be going. The sun is already high, and I promised Flint to take a look at the *Seaswift*'s outfitting. If we are to leave with the new moon, there is still much to be done.'

She nodded and scooted off her stool. 'Er'ril,' she said, sniffing a bit and forcing his eyes back to hers. 'Thanks. Not just for this—' She raised her bandaged hand. '—but for everything. I don't think I've actually told you how much you've come to mean to me.'

Er'ril's cheeks colored, and his eyes were suddenly shy. 'It's ... I ...' He cleared his throat, and his voice grew hoarse as he stumbled out of the room. 'You need not thank me. It's my duty.'

Elena stared at his back as he strode away.

Whether Joach's dream was prophetic or not, Er'ril was a knight she could never mistrust.

Never.

By the time Mycelle was ready to leave for the coastal city of Port Rawl, the afternoon sun had warmed the bluffs to a moist heat. Clothes clung to damp skin, and a shimmering glare shone off the ocean. Mycelle was anxious to be under way, cinching her saddle one final time and adjusting her packs.

Squinting and shading her eyes, Mycelle turned to the group gathered to bid her fair travels. Living mostly a solitary life, Mycelle did not care for these emotional partings. Sighing and determined to finish it quickly, she crossed to Elena and gave her niece a brief but firm hug. 'Practice while I am away,' she said. 'I expect you to perfect your Feather Parry by the time I'm back.'

'I will, Aunt My.'

Elena seemed to want to say more, but Mycelle crossed to Er'ril. 'Watch after my niece, plainsman. A storm is growing, and I'm trusting you to shelter her.'

'Always,' Er'ril said with a terse nod. 'And you watch your own step in Port Rawl. You've heard Flint's news.'

She nodded. 'I'm familiar with Swamptown,' she answered, using the nickname of the port city. Landlocked by vicious swamps and guarded from the sea by the tricky currents of the thousand isles of the nearby Archipelago, the town was a haven for those who skirted the law. Governed by a corrupt and cruel caste system, justice was an obscene word in Swamptown. Only one rule was obeyed by all in Port Rawl: *Guard your back.*

Before she could turn away, Er'ril stopped her. 'Are you

sure you'll know if any of the others have been corrupted by the Dark Lord?'

'For the thousandth time, yes!' she said in surly tones, ready to be off. 'Trust my talent! My elemental sense will judge if they are tainted by black magick. I am a seeker. It is what I do.' She scowled at the plainsman.

Er'ril bridled against the sudden anger.

Elena spoke in the plainsman's defense. 'Er'ril is just being cautious, Aunt My. If one of them has become an ill'-guard—'

'I will kill him myself,' she said, turning away and ending the discussion. She knew her duty. For hundreds of years, the Black Heart had been twisting the pure elemental magicks in innocent folk, creating an army of loathsome ill'-guard. In Port Rawl, Mycelle would search for their other mates – Kral, Mogweed, Meric, and her own son, Tol'chuk. She would judge if any of the four had been twisted by black magicks. Only if they were all clean would she reveal Elena's hidden location. If not . . . She settled her crossed scabbards more firmly in place. She would deal with that problem, too. But in her mind's eye, she pictured her son's craggy face. Even though half-bred with si'luran blood, he had grown to appear much like his og're father. Could she slay her own son if he had been corrupted?

Mycelle put aside those worries for now. There was one last member of their party who still awaited a farewell.

Joach stood nearby, shifting his feet, the black poi'wood staff clutched in one fist. Mycelle frowned at the scrap of gnarled wood. Over the past few days, the boy seemed to be always carrying the foul talisman. She crossed to her nephew and hugged him quickly, avoiding the touch of the staff. Mycelle's skin crawled whenever she neared it, and she did not like Joach's newfound fascination with the talisman. 'You'd best keep that ... that thing out of sight,' she said with a nod. 'It's bad luck.'

Joach moved the staff back from her. 'But it's a trophy from our victory over the darkmage Greshym. How is that bad luck?'

'It just is.' Scowling, she turned back to her mount, a piebald gelding with nervous eyes.

Well to the side of the horse, her companion on the journey ahead sat on his haunches, trying to keep his wolf scent from spooking her mount. Still, the piebald danced slightly as Mycelle approached, clearly anxious about its proximity to a huge treewolf. Mycelle pulled the lead taut. 'That's enough now. Settle down.' Since Fardale was coming along, the horse needed to get accustomed to the wolf's presence.

Fardale stretched and stood, clearly indicating his readiness to depart. Amusement shone in the slitted amber eyes that marked his true heritage as a shape-shifter. Though Mycelle had settled into human form voluntarily, forsaking her blood right forever, Fardale had had the choice stolen from him. It was a *curse* that had trapped Fardale in his current shape and his twin brother, Mogweed, in human form. They had ventured forth from the forests of the Western Reaches in search of a cure for their affliction, becoming entangled with the wit'ch on their way to A'loa Glen.

It seemed everyone, for varied reasons, was being drawn to the sunken island city.

Mycelle mounted the saddle and twisted to face the others. 'If all is well, I should be back before the new moon. If not ...' She shrugged and turned to face the road ahead. There was no reason to finish her sentence: If she was not back within six days, she would either be captured or dead.

'Be careful, Aunt My!' Elena called behind her.

She raised a hand in salute. Then, with a click of her tongue, she nudged the gelding down the coast road. The wolf trotted a few horse lengths to the side, passing through the meadow grass like a shadowed shark in a green sea. Mycelle did not look back at the others.

Soon horse and wolf passed around a high bluff, and the cottage was out of sight. Mycelle relaxed her shoulders slightly. The road was her true home. With the wolf trotting well to the side, it was easy to imagine herself alone. For most of her life, she had traveled the lands of Alasea, searching the countryside for those rare folk gifted with elemental magicks. It was a harsh, lonely life, but one to which she had grown well accustomed. A sword and a horse were enough companionship for her.

Putting aside her worries, she let the horse's easy, rolling gait lull her, settling into her old routine. The wagon-rutted road wove in and out of groves of cypress and pine. Occasionally small herds of tiny red deer darted away from their approach. Otherwise, the road remained empty.

Her plan was to reach the seaside hamlet of Graymarsh before dark. From there, it was an easy day's journey to Port Rawl.

As they traveled, the day wore on in easy strides. The roads remained empty, and the afternoon grew more pleasant as the midday heat faded to twilight breezes. Sooner than she had expected, the sun neared the horizon, and if her map was accurate, she suspected Graymarsh was only another league or two ahead. They had made good time that day.

Around them, the bluffs became more forested, and the hills became a little steeper. Suddenly a low growl from the wolf arose to the left of her path. Fardale came racing back to the road. Mycelle pulled her gelding to a stop. The si'luran wolf could speak to other shape-shifters mind to mind through locked gazes; but since Mycelle had settled in human form, she could no longer communicate in this manner. The only human she knew who could speak the si'luran tongue was Elena – another gift of the child's blood magicks. The wolf growled again and turned to stare ahead down the forest road.

'Is someone coming?' Mycelle asked.

The wolf nodded his head.

'Danger?'

Fardale whined warily. He was not sure, but he warned her to be careful.

Mycelle clucked her tongue to the horse and tapped the mount forward. She shifted so that the crossed scabbards on her back were free and the two sword hilts within easy reach. The wolf disappeared back into the wood. Fardale would stay hidden to attack if any threat arose, using the element of surprise. From the corner of her eye, Mycelle searched for any sign of the wolf. Earlier, she had easily been able to spot his dappled form trailing beside her, but now it was as if the huge treewolf had simply vanished. Not a twig snapped; not a shadow moved.

Mycelle began to hear a soft singing from up ahead. She edged her gelding around a curve in the rutted road. The trees grew denser, and the road ran straight for a good span. The singer stood to the right of the trail, half shadowed by the thick limbs of an old wind-carved cypress. The fellow traveler gave no acknowledgment of Mycelle's appearance and kept quietly singing an old ballad in an unknown language.

Wrapped in a motley cloak, seemingly sewn as a patch-work from rags, it was impossible to tell if the stranger was

35

a man or a woman. Mycelle searched the surrounding woods. There was no sign of any others. As Mycelle slowly approached, clopping along on the packed dirt of the road, the singer's song changed rhythm so subtly as almost to add the cadence of the horse's hooves to the music.

Once near enough, Mycelle raised up an arm in greeting, empty palm open, offering no threat. The singer still did not acknowledge her, just continued the haunting melody. Now closer, Mycelle should have been able to tell what manner of traveler this was: man or woman, young or old, threat or friend. Still, the hood of the patchwork cloak hid the singer's face. Not a speck of skin showed from beneath the motley attire.

'Ho, traveler,' Mycelle said. 'What news of the road ahead?' This was a standard roadside greeting from across almost all the lands of Alasea. It was an offer to share tidings of the land and swap both information and wares.

Still, the singer continued the song. But now the measure of the melody changed. It slowed and faded as if the voice drifted far from here. Yet, oddly, the effect of the music grew stronger in Mycelle. She seemed drawn to each fading note and strained for meaning behind the foreign words. Just as the song finally finished, Mycelle would have sworn she made out three whispered words there at the end: *'Seek my children . . .'*

Squinting her confusion, Mycelle drew nearer. Had she truly heard those words, or was it a trick of her own mind?

Mycelle pulled her horse even with the stranger, meaning to query the singer further. What had the stranger been trying to tell her? As her horse drew to a stop, the stranger vanished with her song. The patchwork cloak collapsed to the forest floor, as if the singer had never existed. And what Mycelle had thought was a mantle made from quilted rags

36

was now seen to be just gathered leaves of various hues, a patchwork of autumn foliage and spring greenery.

A sudden ocean breeze gusted through the wood and scattered the leaves out onto the path. What manner of magick was this?

Needing some proof that she had not slipped off into some world of phantoms, Mycelle called out. 'Fardale!'

The wolf proved his worth and appeared at her side, solid in muscle and dark fur. Mycelle climbed down from her horse, and the two of them sorted through the scattered leaves. Mycelle picked up a few: mountain oak, northern alder, western maple. Such trees grew nowhere near these lands. She let the strange leaves flutter from her fingers.

Nearby, Fardale nosed through the pile and worried something forth from the heart of the leafy mound. He rolled it out onto the road. Staring at it with his head cocked to the side, an odd mournful whine escaped his throat.

'What is it?' she asked, bending to inspect Fardale's discovery. She could not fathom what had so upset the wolf. It was just a plain thumb-sized nut, much like many others found commonly littering forests. This one, though, had sprouted a tiny green shoot.

Fardale gently picked up his treasure in his jaws and held it out toward Mycelle. She opened her palm to accept it. The wolf then nosed her pocket, indicating he wanted her to keep it safe.

Perplexed at his odd behavior, Mycelle did what he asked, and with a final frown she remounted her horse. Tapping her gelding forward, she continued down the road and wondered about the pinch of magick demonstrated here. She had sensed no evil in the apparition, no touch of black magick. So what did it mean? She shook her head and dismissed it for now. She had a mission to finish and no time to dwell on this mystery. As she continued toward the hamlet of Graymarsh, Fardale followed, but Mycelle noted that he kept glancing back down the path toward where the singer had stood.

Frowning at the wolf's behavior, she patted her pocket and felt the hard, firm nut. What was so important about an ordinary acorn?

The sixth drak'il slid from the surf and crawled across the still-warm sand of the midnight beach. With the sun long set, there were no eyes to watch as the last of the drak'ils joined the five others on the narrow strand between sea and cliff. He stood upon his clawed rear legs and stretched to his full height. Only slightly taller than their goblin brothers, the sea-dwelling drak'ils were a distant relation to their underground brethren, choosing instead to live among the sea caves of the remote Archipelago islands. Though crudely intelligent, the drak'il seldom had dealings with other creatures, preferring their isolation.

But necessity warranted their journey here to the coastline – necessity and old goblin oaths. Word had reached their clan that near here hid a wit'ch who had murdered hundreds of rock'goblins, their mountain brethren. She had brought the hungry light, the stealer of spirits. She was to be cobbled, blinded as the old ways spoke, and her magick taken back to their queen. It was the duty of the drak'il to seek vengeance for all the various goblin clans.

The honor of the drak'il, the blood of the goblins, would be satisfied.

It was the way.

The sixth drak'il joined the others, tail twitching and coiling around his ankles, nervous at these foreign shores. He greeted the dominant female of their pod, touching his forked tongue to the poisoned barb at the tip of her tail, and stayed bowed. Only the female drak'ils bore the poisonous *rhyst* upon their tails, the shark killer, the bringer of burning death. The other four males were already bowed before their leader, awaiting her bidding.

The female, larger and more massively muscled than the males, growled and hissed her orders. Her fangs reflected the moonlight, and her red eyes shone with the fire of her hatred. The males trembled at her words. None dared disobey one of the she-lords.

Once instructed, they hurried to the cliff wall and scurried up to take their positions, each male digging claws into rock, locking himself into place. The female still waited below. The male drak'ils could feel her burning eyes pass over them; none dared even to tremble, lest he draw her attention further. A low growl rose like steam from below.

In response, a familiar fire excited the skin of the five males. Soon each form blended perfectly with the rock face, disappearing so thoroughly that even the coming light of day would not reveal them from the surrounding reddish orange sandstone.

The males were to be the eyes and ears of the drak'il war party. Other pods and other she-lords were spread up and down the shoreline for hundreds of leagues. The coast would be watched by thousands of slitted black eyes, and thousands of sharp ears would listen for word of the wit'ch. Once this she-demon was found, the drak'il clan would move and claim their enemy. Her hungry light would die, and the magick would be theirs to wield and draw upon.

Even from his place on the cliff's face, the male drak'il sensed the lust for magick in the female below. His nose caught the scent of her excitement, a wisp of musk and spoor. It made him want to grovel before her, beg for her touch.

So he kept himself perfectly still; only by obedience did a male win the favor of a female. He would show her how motionless he could remain. Even when the hot sun came to sear his skin and dry his flesh, he would not move.

Below, he heard the female return to the surf's edge. He cracked one eye open and rotated it back to watch the thick-muscled she-lord scrabble across the rock. Her back was arched so seductively, and her full rump moved so invitingly. He imagined she displayed herself so handsomely just for him, but he knew better. The male drak'il knew who came next. It was the one who had first brought them word of the wit'ch's atrocities among the rock'goblins, he who walked with dread magicks in his heart. His power incited all the she-lords to flaunt for him, their flinty *rhysts* tapping the stone caverns hungrily, their eyes alight with lust. Even the drak'il queen could not resist the allure of this stranger's magicks. The foreigner had been assigned as war leader by their queen and was due to inspect their pod as he passed along the coast.

As the male drak'il hung on the sandstone wall, an ember of rage smoldered in his heart. It was wrong that a male *not* of their clan – *not* even of their heritage! – should lead them. Still, he knew better than to disobey.

Below, the female suddenly became even more excited. Her scent moistened the air with her thickening musk. The leader must be close.

The male's insight proved correct. A silvery bubble rose from the surf and rolled to shore, opening to reveal the man in its empty heart. Dry as if he had never been in the waters, he stepped onto the rocky shore. He ignored the squirming female at his knee, not even noticing the eager invitation of the she-lord's drumming *rhyst*. Instead, he stepped past the female to inspect the sandstone wall.

'She's close,' the man said in the common tongue.

Just hearing this language hurt the male drak'il's ears. How foul and twisted a language! The man opened his loose, billowing shirt and revealed his magickal heart. His pale chest was split open like a burst seapod, skin puckered and raw at its edge, cracked ribs poking forth. It was not the man that inspired the groveling female, but what lurked inside that dark chest — a thing of pure dire magicks.

From inside the dank cave of the ruptured chest, bloodred eyes stared out into the night. Magick flowed forth from the old wound, rich and twisted like the tangled tentacles of a deep-sea octopus. It quested up the cliff face. So powerful, so fetid.

A voice of the blackest, coldest seas echoed out from the chest wound. 'Be prepared. My ill'guard soldier, the one I named Legion, will flush her into our snare. Be ready, or suffer my wrath.'

The man suddenly convulsed with inner fires, gasping like a fish on hot sands. His tongue fought out words of renewed allegiance. 'I . . . I will not fail you . . . again.'

Then suddenly the magick was gone. The male drak'il glanced to the beach.

The man moaned and clutched his shirt closed and stumbled back to the sea. As his feet touched the surf, the bubble of dire magicks flowed up to surround him once again.

As it closed, the female drak'il made one last desperate attempt to attract the man. She spoke his name, using the foul common tongue. Her voice was rough with lust, and the split tongue of their people complicated the attempt. As the bubble and the man vanished below the waves, she struggled out the single word, his name: *'R-r-rockingham.'*

2

'You're just going to have to grow accustomed to it,' Er'ril said as he led Elena down the stone-and-timber dock. The morning sun was just cresting the waves at the horizon, casting its meager light toward them.

Ahead, the *Seaswift* rocked at the end of the stone quay. The winds had grown stiffer overnight, and the ship rolled back and forth in thick swells, its sternlines and bowlines creaking as oiled rope rubbed iron cleats. Sheltered in a shallow cove, the ship's twin masts and reefed sails were all but hidden from sight by the tall walls of sandstone that circled the tiny bay. Only if another boat, traveling close to shore, passed by the narrow inlet would the *Seaswift* ever be discovered. It was a safe and secret harbor, one of hundreds that dotted the coastlines. In this region of pirates and brigands, such bays were carefully groomed and valued.

With trepidation in her heart, Elena followed Er'ril down the long dock. While watching the ship tilt and rock, she again felt the queasy sensation that the dock was moving. The flow of bobbing waves past the stone pilings amplified this sensation. To further unsettle her belly, the reek of the dock's oiled planks competed with the overpowering stench of salt and algae. Elena swallowed hard, and her cheeks paled.

She had battled demons and monsters, wielded mighty magick, even traveled a poisonous swamp in a tiny punt, but she dreaded the coming sea voyage. Born and raised in the foothills of the mighty Teeth, lands built of granite and hard-packed soil, Elena had quickly learned during a short excursion to visit the seadragons that the rolling motion of the ocean swells sickened her stomach and weakened her balance. She had no defense against this assault, no magick to give her sea legs. Here was an obstacle she had to face on her own.

To assist her, Er'ril had decided to move them both down to the boat and set Elena up in a neighboring cabin on board. He meant to get her over her sea weakness by simple exposure. 'A few days belowdecks,' he had instructed her, 'will harden your stomach against the sea's motion.'

She had reluctantly agreed.

Aboard the *Seaswift*, a huge man dressed in a dark sealskin jacket, his skin the color of burnished mahogany, raised a hand in greeting as they approached the boat's gangplank. As he turned to face them, his silver earring glinted in the first rays of the morning sun. It marked him as a member of Brother Flint's order. But where Brother Flint spoke with wry humor and scolding jests, Brother Moris was taciturn and stoic. Elena had never felt completely comfortable around the brooding, dark-skinned stranger. His hulking size, his strange complexion, his perpetually penetrating stare – all made Elena feel like shrinking and slipping away.

Even now, as Er'ril waved her first onto the gangplank, Elena found Moris studying her intensely, as if he were trying to peer into her bones. Elena glanced away but only found her eyes settling on the surging swells. She stumbled a step as her balance was rocked. Er'ril caught her from a fall into the choppy waves.

'Elena, what did I tell you?'

Her cheeks reddened as she reached the deck. She raised a gloved palm and rested it on the oak rail. 'Grip a firm handhold at all times.'

Moris interrupted any further lecture from the plainsman. 'Er'ril, I have two rooms in the foredeck aired out with fresh linens prepared. Once you've settled the child in, we must finalize the plans for the approaching new moon.'

Er'ril nodded. 'Where's Flint?'

'In the galley preparing porridge and cured potfish. We're to meet down there when you're ready.'

Elena's stomach churned at the thought of salty fish and thick porridge. Under her legs, the boat heaved in slow rolls; the two masts swung back and forth as if pointing out the sweep of seagulls overhead. Elena kept her grip on the ship's port rail, but her palms grew clammy.

Er'ril nudged her from her reverie of the ship's movements. 'Let's get you to your bunk where you can lie down. Let your belly calm.'

'That's not very likely,' Elena mumbled, but she trudged after the plainsman across the middeck. Underfoot, coils of thick ropes threatened to betray her steps, but she followed Er'ril's instructions and traveled from handhold to handhold.

Once they reached the raised foredeck, Er'ril held open a heavy ironwood door. Lantern light beyond revealed a short passage leading to the upper cabins and a set of dark stairs descending steeply to the lower decks. As Er'ril nodded her inside, Elena noted there were no windows in the hatch, and three heavy iron crossbars lined the inner surface. It reminded Elena of a portal to some dank dungeon.

Er'ril must have noted her nervous glance. 'During

storms, heavy waves can crash across the deck. The iron bars can be thrown to batten down the door and keep the lower decks dry.'

Elena stared at how high the middeck sat above the waters. She could not imagine the size of waves that could crest tall enough to swamp the ship. With her heart beating in her throat, she ducked through the portal into the fore-deck.

Immediately, the sharp odor of kerosene and oak resins assaulted her senses. In the dim passage, the rocking lantern and tilting floor dizzied her further. Leaning on the wall for support, Elena followed Er'ril toward a small door near the passage's end.

'Here's your cabin,' he said, pushing the door open. It bumped into the tiny bed bolted to the far wall.

Elena's heart sank. The room was no larger than a medium-sized wardrobe. Even with just a narrow bed, a small chest, and a single lantern, the cabin seemed cramped and crowded.

'We'll have your things brought up from the cottage this afternoon.'

'Where would I put them?' she mumbled.

Er'ril nodded to the bed. 'Have a seat. There's something I want to talk to you about.'

Elena dropped to the creaking bed. The lantern swung gently overhead, dancing their shadows on the walls. Though seated, the motion weakened her stomach. She concentrated on the tips of her sandals.

Before her, Er'ril stood stooped, his head bowed away from the low rafters. He kept his legs slightly apart and used his knees to keep easy balance in the rocking cabin. 'It's about Joach,' he started. 'Last night, he approached Flint again about accompanying us.'

This news drew her eyes back up. Even though she had

pulled Joach aside and had insisted that his dream had to be false, her brother obviously persisted in his belief and would not leave the matter be.

Er'ril waved his hand at the room. 'As you can see, the *Seaswift* is not generous of space. Flint has arranged for a handful of seamen loyal to our cause to man the boat's rigging. Otherwise, the ship has no room to spare for a boy who's worried about his sister.'

'It's more than that,' she mumbled, hesitant about betraying Joach's trust concerning the dream.

Er'ril knelt beside her and rested his hand on her knee. 'Then what? Are you afraid to leave him behind? Are you encouraging him?'

'No!' she said, aghast. 'I'd rather he stayed at the cottage, too – well away from me.' She smiled wanly at the plainsman. 'My family members don't fare well around me.'

Er'ril squeezed her knee. 'So we're agreed. Perhaps if you spoke to him.'

She stared the plainsman in the eye. Though she knew Joach's dream of betrayal could not be true, her brother believed it. His heart would not let him stay, and no words of hers would sway him and calm his fears. 'I've already tried talking him out of coming,' she said in a tired voice. 'He won't listen, and I don't think—'

The boat suddenly lurched under a heavy wave, churning Elena's stomach violently. She barely made it to the chamber pail before her belly emptied its contents in a sloppy splash. Still bent over the pail, Elena breathed heavily. Once her gut had calmed sufficiently, she pushed back, red cheeked and unable to meet Er'ril's eyes.

The plainsman had moved back a bit. 'It'll take time to get your sea legs,' he offered as consolation.

'I don't care about sea legs. I just hope the Mother above will soon grant me a sea belly.'

'I'll fetch you some water and bread crusts. It helps. We can talk more of Joach later.'

Er'ril turned to leave, but Elena stopped him. 'No, this worry of Joach's has gone on long enough.' Elena was suddenly tired of all these secrets. Whom to trust? It was nonsense, and before the voyage started, she wanted this matter settled. With her stomach temporarily appeased, she firmed her resolve and spoke bluntly. 'Er'ril, Joach doesn't trust you. He had a dream in which you betrayed me.'

Er'ril swung back to face her, a combination of anger and hurt flashing in his eyes. 'What! What is this foolishness?'

'He believes his dream was a weaving, a prophecy of the future.' Elena related all that Joach had told her the previous morning.

'He called forth black magick from the staff?' Er'ril asked under black brows.

'Using words from his dream,' Elena added. 'So now you know why he is so convinced of his dream's prophecy.'

Er'ril shook his head. 'The staff is a foul talisman. I would never trust black magick as proof of anything. Even the most able mind can be fooled by the dark art's trickery.'

'But how do we convince Joach of that?'

'I don't know. I know little of dreamweaving, but Flint and Moris are experts. We must let them know of your brother's dream.'

Elena winced. She had already betrayed her brother's trust by telling Er'ril and was reluctant, but the truth of Joach's dream must be tested by more than the use of black magick. She nodded her agreement.

'I'll have Moris fetch Joach to the ship this evening. We'll settle this matter then,' Er'ril said and turned to the door.

As he slipped out of the cabin, he added, 'You were right to tell me, Elena.'

Once the door closed, Elena studied the twisting grain of the wood. Was the plainsman correct? Was she truly right in betraying Joach's confidence? As she bit her lip, the queasiness again rose in her gut, but this time her churning belly wasn't entirely the result of the ship's motion. Since when had her faith in Er'ril overwhelmed the trust in her own family? She pictured Joach's face when he had first spoken of his suspicion of Er'ril and had sworn her to secrecy: the urgency and love in his eyes, the wordless trust of a brother for a sister.

For the second time, Elena rushed to the chamber pail.

'Stand fast, traveler!' the gatesman called. He stood atop the wall, half hidden by a stone parapet.

Mycelle stepped her gelding back to better eye the guard. Fardale stood tense at her horse's side, seeming to sense Mycelle's wariness.

After spending a night at a Graymarsh inn, Mycelle had left with the first rays of the sun, knowing it best to reach Port Rawl in daylight. Now here, she was surprised to find Port Rawl's south gate closed and locked. To the west, the late afternoon sun was still well above the horizon – and in a town notorious for its nightly carousing, the southern and northern gates were seldom barred before the moon rose, if at all. The two-story stone barricade, nicknamed the Swampwall by the natives, encircled the entire city, except for the section of the town that fronted the bay. The wall's function was not to protect its inhabitants from marauders but simply to act as a stone dike between the town and the poisonous denizens of the nearby swamps. As such, the gates were seldom lowered and rarely manned. In Port Rawl, the townspeople did not like locked doors between them and a quick escape when needed.

Mycelle leaned back in her saddle. 'I've business to attend and need to enter,' she called up. 'Why are the gates secured?'

'What business have you in Port Rawl?' the guard called back. He was a portly fellow whose hard-earned coppers apparently were spent quickly on ale and good food. A wicked scar – another feature most likely earned in those same hard pubs – trailed from his right ear to his nose. 'Which caste vouches for you?'

His inquiry surprised Mycelle. In Port Rawl, no one asked another's business, not if one meant to live until the day's end. Curiosity was not a healthy pastime in Port Rawl.

'Of what concern is my business to the town's garrison?' she returned, putting proper threat in her voice.

'Since the attack on the docks two morns ago,' the guardsman answered, 'all who seek entry must be registered and vouched for by one of the town's sixteen castes.'

'This is news to me,' she said. 'I've been hired as a guide by a group of travelers due to arrive in the city, and I am here to meet them.'

'A hired guide?' He seemed to check a list near his elbow. 'That would put you under the mercenary caste. You'll need to register with their caste's leader as soon as you enter and agree to their authority.'

'I belong to no caste. I seek only to—'

'Without a caste's allegiance, you'll be jailed if found on the streets without the proper papers.'

Mycelle frowned. Such a requirement went against all that Port Rawl once upheld. The sanctity of anonymity was one of the unwritten rules that guided all commerce in the port city. The attack by the possessed fishermen had shaken the town worse than Flint or Er'ril could have suspected. Her eyes narrowed as she considered her options. She suspected the new laws were not for the safety and protection of the citizenry but were devised simply as another way to eke bribes and tariffs from travelers. Knowing she had no choice, she straightened in her saddle. 'Fine,' she called back up. 'Open the gates!'

The man nodded and signaled someone hidden below. The clink of chains and creak of rope marked the raising gate. As soon as the bars had risen high enough, Mycelle tapped her gelding forward. Fardale followed, padding in the shadow of her mount.

Two other guards flanked the inside of the gate. The one closest to the wolf backed a step and began to unsheathe his sword.

'Harm my dog,' Mycelle warned, 'and you'll find the point of my sword buried in your belly before my dog can howl.'

The man lowered his blade back into its scabbard and took another step away as Fardale passed.

The guard to the other side of her mount cleared his throat. He had the bowed legs of a sailor, but his missing left arm and sullen features suggested the injury had grounded him from decent work aboard any ship. He now earned his coppers with whatever duties he could scrounge, like manning the city's gates.

The guard's gaze wandered appreciatively over Mycelle's physique. 'I belong to the mercenary caste,' he said with a thick tongue, his eyes slightly hooded. 'You'll find Master Fallen on Drury Lane in the Eastern Quarter. For a fee, I can guide you there.' He held out papers toward her.

Mycelle suspected any coin offered would only get her led to a blind alley where others of his ilk would jump her.

'I know the city,' she said, taking the papers. 'I can find my way.'

'That's only a temporary pass. By twilight, it'll expire.' His voice lowered in conspiratorial tones. 'If you've not found Master Fallen by then and gained his seal on your papers, you'll be taken by the watchmen. But with my help, I can get you to the mercenary's lodge in plenty of time.'

Sure, Mycelle thought silently, he'd get her there – but bound in chains and ready for sale in the slave pits. She grinned at the man. Only menace shone from her lips. 'I'll manage.'

She kicked her horse and entered the Southern Quarter of the city. Here, the craftsmen and artisans took up their residence. Even in Port Rawl, certain basic needs had to be met. She passed a small cobbler's shop on the right. Her nose was greeted with the familiar smell of leather dyes and curing hides. It seemed even pirates needed sound footwear.

Farther along, the ringing of hammer on anvil announced the presence of a smithy well before the open doorway revealed the smoldering forge and the burly blacksmith. Other shops included a chandlery with candles of every size and shape displayed in the window, a tailor's shop with bolts of cloth leaning in the doorway, and even a silversmith whose work most likely involved melting ill-gotten gains into untraceable new contours.

Yet as common as these shops appeared, no one could mistake this for any ordinary town. Here the shopkeepers all carried conspicuous swords, and their expressions were anything but inviting. Even the slender tailor, whose tiny hands were well suited for his craft, had a muscled guard posted by his stoop. It seemed trust was not offered with the wares sold here. And from the demeanor of the patrons who frequented these fine establishments, trust was in little demand.

A clutch of gaunt women gathered their cloaks about them as she neared. Then seeing the rider was a woman, they dropped their guarded stances and stared openly at her. A few whispered behind palms at each other and pointed at the huge treewolf at her side. Mycelle knew the townswomen must think her daft to travel alone through the streets of Port Rawl, even here in the tamest section of the town. Few women dared risk the streets without someone to guard their backs. Mycelle suspected each woman here was armed with a dagger or a crooked dirk under her cloak. And if any were attacked, all would come to the victim's aid in a mutual bond of survival.

As Mycelle passed, she stared at the feral eyes of these hard women. Pact or not, Mycelle also knew that for the right price any of the women here would turn on another. In Port Rawl, truces were short-lived and only born of immediate necessity. The solidarity shown here was as insubstantial as the morning's fog.

Mycelle continued on through the Southern Quarter, aiming for the central bazaar named Four Corners, where all four sections of the city converged. As she rode, no one gave her much attention besides the occasional furtive stare. Mycelle, though, kept up her guard. She knew the presence of the huge wolf and her two crossed scabbards were giving any attackers momentary pause.

Still, Mycelle kept both eyes and ears attuned to the flow of traffic around her. Even Fardale's hackles were raised in wary attention. Occasional growls flowed from his throat when anyone approached too near.

Walking her horse past an apothecary, Mycelle's senses were suddenly struck by a melange of elemental magicks.

Her seeking skill thrummed strongly. She slowed her mount. Through the doorway, Mycelle spotted shelf after shelf stocked with tiny jars and bottles of various herbs and medicines. This was no ordinary apothecary dispensing willow's bark and dandelion tea. Whoever ran this shop was skilled in the elemental art of healing. And from the way Mycelle's own senses were responding, the healer here was a strong one.

Mycelle pulled her horse to a stop, intrigued.

Inside, the practitioner could be seen in the shadowed interior behind a counter. A cluster of candles lit her features. Dressed in a simple gray frock and black shawl, she was an old woman of wrinkled visage. Her snow-white hair was bound in a single braid and coiled like a nesting serpent atop her head. Though the small woman was old, Mycelle sensed that the winters had hardened her like a wind-burned cypress. Even her skin was the hue of burnished wood.

From behind the counter, the healer seemed to be staring back at Mycelle, apparently curious of the stranger on horseback by her door. But Mycelle knew this was only a trick of light. There was no way the woman could see her. The healer had no eyes. Under her brows was only smooth skin. No empty sockets nor thick scars marred her face. Mycelle guessed that the healer must have been born this way. Poor woman.

To add to the illusion that the woman could see her, the old healer straightened and waved to her, indicating that Mycelle should come inside.

Fardale suddenly growled, drawing Mycelle's attention away from the woman. From the top of the door frame, a small face appeared, hanging upside down. The beast's head was the size of a ripe pomegranate. Though framed in fur the color of a dying fire, its face was as bare as any human's, dominated by two bright black eyes and wide grinning lips. It chittered at them and crawled lower down the door frame, revealing small clawed hands and feet that gripped the wood as efficiently as its hands. Even a long tail, furred in rings of black and gold, helped hold its place in the doorway.

'His name is Tikal,' the old woman behind the counter said. She had a melodious accent that Mycelle could not place. 'He is from my jungle country of Yrendl.'

Mycelle's eyebrows rose. She had heard tales of the thick jungles far to the south of the Wastes but had never met anyone who claimed to have traveled there. Even by sea, it was easily an entire winter's journey.

'What brought you so far from your homelands, healer?' she asked. She knew she must get to the mercenary caste soon, but curiosity detained her.

'Slavers.' Her reply was matter-of-fact, not bitter or angry. 'A long time ago.'

Mycelle, embarrassed by her prying question, was ready to bid the woman a good day and be on her way, but the old woman again waved her inside, more persistently.

'Come inside.'

'I have no need of a healer.'

'And I don't have all day.' The healer turned her back on Mycelle and began running her fingers along the shelves behind her, as if searching for something. 'I know about the friends you *seek*.' The healer stressed the last word, making clear she knew Mycelle was a seeker.

What was this? Wary but curious, Mycelle climbed from her horse. She felt no taint of black magick here. Just what did this old healer know? 'Fardale, guard the gelding.'

The wolf moved to stand between the street and the horse, hackles raised. Satisfied, Mycelle slipped through the doorway. The fiery-maned beast still hung from the frame by its tail and chittered at her as she passed. Mycelle checked the corners of the room for anything suspicious before she approached the counter. She sensed no other presence. 'What do you know of my business?' Mycelle asked as she stepped forward.

The woman did not answer.

Behind Mycelle, the door to the apothecary swung closed and latched with a loud click. Mycelle suddenly remembered that curiosity was not a healthy pastime in Port Rawl and recalled the tiny tailor with the hulking guard. Since when in this city did a blind woman operate a shop all by herself?

A gruff voice rose behind her. 'Touch your sword and die.'

'Too often an ordinary dream is confused with a weaving,' the huge ebony-skinned Brother explained to Joach, 'even by those skilled in the art.'

In the galley of the *Seaswift*, Moris and Er'ril sat on the bench across the pine-planked table from Joach, both wearing dour expressions. Joach was not going to let the presence of the plainsman sway him. 'It *was* a weaving,' Joach said with determination. 'Er'ril will betray us.'

By the galley's hearth, Flint tasted the stew's broth. He sighed with satisfaction, then spoke. 'Joach, you're a blasted fool.'

Joach's cheeks burned at the bluntness of the fisherman.

Flint gave his stew one final stir and settled the lid on his brewing pot. 'You should have come to us first. Bringing this to the attention of your sister and burdening her with your secret was just damn wrong. She has enough to bear without you worrying her with false weavings.'

Joach's blood still burned with the knowledge that Elena

had broken her promise to him and spoke of his dream to the plainsman. Elena had not even come to this meeting, too sick to leave her bunk, but Joach suspected shame also kept her hidden. His fists clenched on the poi'wood staff that lay across his knees. Here was all the proof he needed. Under his palms, he felt the dire magicks in the wood flow like oil on skin. 'The spell from the dream worked,' he argued. 'How could this *not* be a true weaving?'

Er'ril answered. 'At its heart, black magick deceives. That foul staff of Greshym's should've been burned long ago.'

'You'd like that,' Joach spat, 'since in my dream, it was the staff that kept you from my sister.'

Er'ril's brows darkened and lowered over his eyes in threat. 'I would never betray Elena. *Never.*'

'As you said,' Joach mumbled, repeating the plainsman's words, 'black magick deceives.'

Joach and Er'ril glared at each other.

'Enough!' Flint said, punctuating his word with a strike of his ladle on the table. 'I've heard enough of this nonsense. Black magick or not, your dream's truth can be weighed in another way.'

'How?' Joach asked.

Flint pointed his spoon to Moris. 'Tell them. I've a stew to stir before it burns. I won't have this nonsense ruin my meal.'

Moris had remained silent during the exchange, apparently content to let the fire of their words die down before imparting his knowledge. 'Now that I have your attentions again,' he said, fingering his silver earring, 'I will finish explaining what I started. First, Joach does have a sound argument for initially believing the truth of his dream. The black spell *did* work.'

Joach sat straighter on his bench. At least someone here was talking sense.

Moris continued. 'All aspects of a weaving, when studied closely, must prove true for the dream to be called a weaving. The spell did work, but that is only one element of the dreamscape. And as Er'ril said, black magick is tricky. Perhaps it was not the words of the spell learned in the dream that ignited the magick in the staff, but simply your own will wishing it to happen. Your dream must be examined further before you put such fervid faith in it.'

A seed of doubt found its way into Joach's heart. He trusted Moris – the dark-skinned Brother had saved his life in A'loa Glen – and his words now were compelling. 'How can we judge the truth of my dream when the events are yet to happen?'

'It is in the details,' Moris said.

'*All* the details,' Flint echoed from the hearth.

Moris nodded. 'Tell us your dream again, but I will query you further on certain aspects of your story, attempting to find anything false. If even one element is found to be wrong, then your dream was not a weaving.'

Joach removed his hands from the staff and placed them atop the table. 'I see. So everything must be true – or none of it is.'

Flint snorted. 'Finally the boy is thinking with his head and not his gut.'

Joach chewed his lower lip. Maybe they were right. He reached and fiddled with the dragon's tooth that hung around his neck. 'The dream began with Elena and me atop a tower in A'loa Glen. We were—'

'Stop right there,' Moris interrupted. 'Describe the tower.'

Joach closed his eyes and pictured the spire. 'It was narrow ... coming to a point no wider than two horse lengths. I couldn't make out much else, since I never peered over the parapet's edge.'

'What else? What color were the stones? What towers neighbored it?'

Joach brightened, remembering. 'The stones were a burnt orange, and there was a huge statue of a woman bearing a sprig from a flowering tree across the way from the tower.'

'The statue of Lady Sylla, bearing the branch of unity,' Flint said.

'Hmm ... And beside her,' Moris added, 'the Spire of the Departed is a reddish orange.' The two Brothers stared at each other meaningfully. 'Perhaps the boy had a passing glimpse from one of the Edifice's windows while imprisoned there.'

Flint grunted noncommittally. 'Go on, Joach.'

He continued to describe the attack by the black winged monster.

'Sounds almost like a wyvern,' Moris said, 'but none of its foul ilk have been seen in ages.'

'But who knows what the Gul'gothal lord has dredged up to protect the island?' Flint mumbled, his brows pinched together with concern. He now ignored the stew beginning to steam from around the pot's lid. Joach caught the quick glance toward Er'ril. Was that doubt in the old man's eyes? Flint waved his ladle at Joach. 'Tell us about Er'ril's attack on your sister.'

In Joach's chest, twisting emotions roiled. He had initially feared that they would *not* believe him. Now he was more afraid they would. If Er'ril was a traitor, whom could they trust? Joach stared at Er'ril, who still wore the same stoic expression. Joach swallowed hard before continuing his story. 'After dispatching the beast, I heard the creak of wood behind me. I turned and saw Er'ril pushing open the door, his face half crazed, his arm already raised with sword in hand. I knew he meant us harm. He slammed the door and latched it, blocking our only means of escape.'

'I would never harm either of you,' Er'ril said fiercely. 'This dream is ridiculous.'

Flint approached the table, abandoning both the hearth and his bubbling stew. 'So far his dream images do bear the truth, Er'ril. Maybe you were under the influence of some black spell.'

Er'ril glowered but could not speak against it.

But Moris did. 'No, Joach's dream is false. We can now put this matter safely aside.'

'How so?' Flint asked.

'Joach, tell us again how Er'ril locked you from the only means of escape from the tower.'

Confused, Joach repeated this portion of his dream. 'The plainsman held his sword against us, and then reached behind to key the door's lock.' Suddenly, like a sun appearing from between storm clouds, Joach understood. 'Sweet Mother, maybe the dream *is* false!'

'What?' Flint asked, still in the dark.

'Er'ril had two arms in my dream! One held the sword; the other locked the door. And it was no phantom arm, but flesh and bone!'

'Two arms.' Flint's tensed shoulders sagged. 'Thank the Mother above! That detail is obviously false, so all of it must be. That's the law of weaving.'

Joach was still skeptical. 'But are you sure?'

Moris' deep voice answered. 'Not even the strongest magick can grow a new limb. And Flint is quite correct: A true weaving contains no false items.'

'Then maybe I'm remembering it wrong,' Joach persisted. 'Maybe in the dream, he had only one arm, but in the light of day, my mind changed this one minor detail.'

Moris shook his head and stood. 'That would be further

proof that your dream was not prophetic,' he said. 'A true weaving will lock into your memory, enduring forever.'

Joach sighed and stared at the two determined Brothers. So the dream was just an ordinary nightmare. He turned toward Er'ril. The plainsman had remained silent during the entire exchange. His stoic features had developed a sick bent to them.

Flint continued. 'So if it was only a foul dream, I guess there is no need to bring the boy with us. He can stay and keep my livestock fed.'

Er'ril spoke, his voice oddly strained. 'No, the boy should come with us . . . as a precaution.'

'Whatever for?' Moris asked. 'He only had a bad dream dredged up from buried memories of his imprisonment on the island. Just old worries coming to a head.'

'Nevertheless, he should come.' Er'ril shoved back from the table, clearly indicating the matter settled and the discussion ended.

Before anyone could question him further, a piercing scream split through the ship.

Joach flew up, staff in hand. 'Elena!'

3

'Turn around ... slowly,' the harsh voice behind Mycelle ordered.

By now, the old healer had turned from her study of her laden shelves of medicines and balms. She had a bottle of some herb in hand. Mycelle had a hard time reading the expression on the ancient woman's face; the healer's missing eyes made her hard to fathom. Still, Mycelle caught a hint of amusement crinkling the corner of the woman's thin lips.

'Tikal,' she scolded, 'leave the poor woman alone.'

Mycelle slowly turned. No one stood behind her. She saw the tiny furred beast hanging from the door's latch. His weight must have shut the door. But who spoke? Mycelle glanced around. No one else was here.

Tikal climbed farther up the door, his large black eyes staring at her. 'Touch your sword and die,' he said in that same gruff voice.

Mycelle's eyes grew wide.

The old healer spoke up behind her. 'Don't mind him. Tikal doesn't know what he's saying. Just mimicking what he's heard from the streets.'

'How much for oranges?' Tikal continued, his voice changing to that of a shrill woman. 'For these prices, I could buy three bushels!' The little creature clambered up to a swing hanging from the ceiling and hung upside down from his tail and one foot. He stared directly at Mycelle and in a child's voice said, 'I like horsies.'

Mycelle blinked a few times at the odd creature, her heart still pounding from the scare. 'What type of beast is that?'

'A tamrink. A golden-maned tamrink, to be precise, from the jungles of Yrendl. His art of mimicry is one of the tamrink's many talents, though I'd call it more a nuisance than a talent.'

With a slight shake of her head, Mycelle turned to the woman.

'My name is Mama Freda,' the old woman said, nodding in greeting. Though blind, she reached accurately to a short cane leaning against the wall and used it to march around her counter.

'You mentioned something about my friends.'

'Yes, they just arrived yesterday. They needed a healer.'

Worry nestled into Mycelle's chest. Who had been injured? 'Do you know where my friends are lodging?'

The old woman glanced over her shoulder, as if to study Mycelle's expression. 'Of course. Come.' Freda led the way to a back door and swung it open. A dark stairway led up.

Tikal landed with a small thud behind Mycelle. 'Tikal . . . Tikal . . . Tikal . . .' he chanted, racing ahead of them up the stairs.

Mycelle studied the dark steps. She probed with her senses and felt nothing wrong. Still, she remembered her lack of proper caution before and voiced her previous worry. 'Freda, please don't take offense at my next words, but just how does a blind woman protect herself in as hard a town as Port Rawl?'

Mama Freda turned to Mycelle with a snort. 'Protect

myself? I'm the only healer worth her salt here in Swamptown, and they all know it.' She waved the tip of her cane. 'The whole town watches over my shop. Without me, who would heal their sword cuts or poisoned bellies? These folks may be hard and crude, but never think them stupid.' She glanced over her shoulder and seemed to be studying Mycelle again, as if judging her. 'Besides, who said I was blind?'

With those words, Mama Freda climbed the stairs. 'Follow me.'

Mycelle hesitated a breath, then obeyed. This strange woman knew more than she said. Doubt and wariness followed her up the stairs.

At the top, they came upon a short hall with a few doors off the passage. As Mama Freda led the way toward the room farthest back, Mycelle eyed the other doorways. It would be easy to set up an ambush here. One of the doors was cracked open, and Mycelle got a peek of shelves stocked with crates and bushels. She caught a glimpse of a drying rack where stalks and leaves of various herbs were desiccating. The rich smell of spices and an earthy aroma from the room scented the hall. It was merely a storeroom and not worth further attention.

Still, as Mycelle passed, her senses tingled with a brush of magick, raising the tiniest hairs on her arms. Not strong magick, but a touch of something elemental, something she had never felt before – and as a seeker who had crisscrossed through the many lands of Alasea, to come across a magick she could not identify slowed her footsteps. It scented of loam and deep-buried ore – coal perhaps.

Mama Freda must have heard her boot heels faltering. 'Come. Do not tarry.'

Mycelle hurried to catch up. Many mysteries surrounded

this woman, but for now, Mycelle had more urgent concerns.

Reaching the last door, the old healer tapped the crown of her cane on the oaken frame – *crack, crack, crack* – clearly a signal to someone within.

The tiny tamrink danced around the woman's feet excitedly. 'Tikal ... Oh, Tikal is a good puppy.'

Mama Freda scooted the small beast aside with the tip of her cane. 'He loves guests,' she said.

Mycelle felt, more than heard, a stirring from the next room. She tensed her arms, ready to free her swords. As the door swung open, a rush of elemental magicks washed out, like a window opened on a whirlwind. The assault on her senses was so sudden that her knees almost buckled. *A rush of wind, the rumble of storm clouds, the keening cry of a falcon. And mixed with these tastes was a lingering hint of granite and the low rumbling of grinding boulders.* She recognized these torrents. Her legs regained their strength.

In the doorway stood a familiar figure.

'Mother?'

'Tol'chuk!' Mycelle hurried past the old woman as she stepped aside. She hugged her son fiercely as Tikal clambered up the og're's leg as easily as up a tree trunk. 'Thank the Mother, you're safe,' she whispered to his chest. Mycelle could not get her arms fully around the thick torso of her son. He towered over her, even when slightly stooped in the usual og're fashion. She raised her face to stare at him. So like his dead father, she thought. Same splayed nose and thick, overhanging brows, even the similar hint of fangs raising his upper lip a bit and a spiked ridge of fur that ran from the rocky crown of his head down in a small crest along his spine.

Only his eyes, large golden orbs slitted like a cat's, told of a heritage that was not og're but si'lura, like his mother.

Tol'chuk returned Mycelle's affection with equal enthusiasm but broke their embrace sooner than she would have preferred. 'You made it through the swamps,' he said. 'How be Elena and Er'ril?'

Wary of how much to reveal in Mama Freda's presence, Mycelle spoke carefully. 'My *niece* is fine. We all are. A few scratches and scars, but otherwise intact.'

Tol'chuk's voice grew grim. 'I wish we had fared as well. Come inside.'

Her son's somber tones reminded her of her own duties. She probed with her own skills, sniffing after any taint in the room. Even under close scrutiny, the elemental magicks in the room felt pure, untainted by corruption. Still, she also sensed the pain in the room. She followed Tol'chuk into the chamber.

The room surprised Mycelle. She had expected a dark gloomy cell but instead found a room, though windowless, shining cheerily with lamps and a small hearth glowing with coals. Adding to the sense of warmth and invitation, a thick wool rug covered the oak-planked floor. A pair of sturdy beds stood against either wall, and three pillowed chairs stood before the hearth.

In one of the chairs, a familiar spindly fellow dressed in road-worn clothes pushed up to greet her. His features were pinched, and his lips thin and prone to frowning. Under mousy brown hair, his slitted amber eyes matched his twin brother's. 'Mogweed,' Mycelle said, seeking to change the man's frown into something more hopeful. 'Your brother Fardale is downstairs guarding my horse. He'll be thrilled to see you safe.'

The news did little to change the man's expression. If anything, the shape-shifter's expression grew more dour. 'It will be good to see my brother again,' he said plainly.

Mycelle raised questioning eyes toward Tol'chuk. The og're drew his mother toward one of the two beds. 'Don't mind Mogweed,' he grumbled under his breath, trying his best to keep his voice quiet. 'All of our hearts are heavy.'

As she neared, she saw the bed was not empty, and her senses tingled stronger with the billowing scent of elemental wind magick. She knew who must lie in the bed – Meric, the elv'in lord. Still, as she reached his bedside, she failed to recognize him. Meric, his lanky frame half hidden by linen sheets, was not the man she had last seen in Shadowbrook. His chest was burned in thick swaths; the reek of charred flesh clung to him as tight as the medicinal wraps that bound his chest. His lips were swollen and cracked, his handsome silver hair burned to the scalp. Thankfully, he seemed to be resting, his eyes closed and his breathing regular and deep. Mycelle sensed that even these small blessings were only due to the skill in Mama Freda's balms and elixirs.

Mycelle could look at him no longer. 'What happened?'

'He was caught and tortured by one of the Dark Lord's seekers.' Tol'chuk then continued to recount the events that led them here: Meric's last-minute rescue by Tol'chuk from a foul d'warf lord and Mogweed's outwitting of a pair of ill'guard twins in the great castle of the city. 'We all escaped to the barges as the towers of the Keep crumbled and fell. But Meric sickened rapidly from his injuries. Though we saved him from corruption, we could not keep his tainted wounds from festering and growing foul. It be great luck that an innkeeper directed us to Mama Freda soon after we entered Port Rawl.'

'I don't think it was luck, Tol'chuk,' Mycelle mumbled, knowing that generosity was rare in the port city and often came with a price. The innkeep had probably feared contagion and had been glad to send the group off to a healer rather than risk his own inn with disease.

'Luck or not, here we came.' Tol'chuk slipped a bit of biscuit to Tikal, who was searching through the og're's pockets. The tamrink swallowed it whole, then licked each finger clean.

'Luck it was,' Mama Freda said. 'The Sweet Mother herself must be watching over you all.' She took Tikal from the og're's shoulder and carried him to a chair, where she sat down. 'It took an herb grown only in Yrendl – a rare supply I still cultivate – to break his fever. Another day and he'd have been dead for sure.'

Tol'chuk nodded. 'Already Meric fares much better.'

Mycelle frowned. If the elv'in was better, she dreaded to think how Meric must have looked yesterday. She stared around the room. 'And what of Kral? Where is he?' The mountain man was the only member of the group still unaccounted for.

Mogweed answered. 'He watches the north gate of the city for you. We did not know which gate you would enter Port Rawl through.'

'He usually does not return until well after dark,' Tol'chuk added.

'Ever since Shadowbrook,' Mogweed continued, 'the big man has grown more and more restless. He is out almost every night, prowling, watching for signs of the enemy.'

'Well, there was no need for him to search for me,' Mycelle said. 'My skill at sensing elemental magick would have hunted you down. I thought that was clear.'

Mogweed backed to the chair beside Mama Freda and sat down, a condescending smile on his lips. 'Did you sense Meric from the street?' he asked. 'Or even when you were in the shop downstairs?'

67

Mycelle's brows drew tight together. The shape-shifter's words proved of concern. She had not felt even a whisper of Meric's unique wind magick, not until the door to the room had opened. 'How . . . ? I should have been able to . . .' Mycelle turned to Mama Freda.

The old healer was smiling at her. 'There is much you don't know, young lady. In my jungle lands, where the land's magick is as fertile as the forests themselves, we have learned ways to protect what is ours. I painted these walls long ago with an aromatic oil of banesroot. It hides my elemental skills from prying eyes.'

Mycelle studied the oiled planks of the wall. She tried to send her senses beyond the room and failed. It was as if nothing existed beyond those four walls. 'That must be why I never sensed Mama Freda's presence when I was last through the city,' she muttered. 'And how you've managed to escape the corrupting touch of the ill'guard up to now. You've created a safe haven.'

Mama Freda snorted. 'There's no such thing as a safe haven in Port Rawl. Swamptown would never stand for it. But it is my home.'

Mycelle grew suspicious. Every moment she spent with this old woman seemed to bring forth new discoveries – and Mycelle did not like it! She felt as if she were fighting on quicksand, and Mama Freda had the longer sword. 'It was mighty generous of you to open your own home to my friends. But—'

Mama Freda finished her thought. '—but generosity in Port Rawl never comes without a price.'

Mycelle's features grew stony.

Mama Freda settled deeper in her seat and waved a hand to the last free chair. 'If your face becomes any darker, I'll need a lantern to see it. Sit . . . sit.'

Mycelle remained standing and spoke bluntly. 'Enough with this foolishness. Speak plain. You can't possibly see my face. You have no eyes.'

'What are eyes? I can see that speck of dried mud on your cheek and a tiny bit of hay caught in the hair above your left ear.'

Mycelle's fingers wandered to wipe the mud from her cheek and pick the hay from her hair. 'How?'

Mama Freda tousled the golden mane of her pet and tickled him behind an ear. The tamrink batted at the teasing fingers, then settled in her lap and sucked at one of his toes. During all this time, Tikal's eyes never left Mycelle's face. 'The tamrinks,' Mama Freda began, 'have unique talents, other than mere mimicry. In our jungles, they travel in large groups – bonded families. They're raised so intimately among one another that each becomes a part of the whole. What one tamrink hears, they all hear. What one tamrink sees, they all see. In a sense, the pack becomes one living creature, hearing all, seeing all.'

'Sense bonded?' Mycelle asked, shocked. She had read of such a talent in texts kept by the Sisterhood.

Mama Freda ignored Mycelle's question. 'I was born without eyes, and among my tribe such a deformity was considered an ill omen. To appease the gods, I was left as a babe in the jungle to die.'

Mycelle's horrified expression must have been noted.

'Don't fret, child,' Mama Freda said. 'I remember little of that time. The first memory I truly had was of flying through the trees, seeing through the eyes of a huge female tamrink. She was swinging through the branches overhead, curious about the bawling naked creature near her nest.'

'You?'

She nodded. 'Her band took me in and nursed me. With

time, I became more firmly bonded to the tamrinks and saw through their many eyes.'

'These creatures actually raised you?'

Mama Freda laughed at such a preposterous thought. 'No, I doubt I was with the group more than a single moon. One day, one of my tribe's hunters found me near the tamrink's nest and discovered that I was still alive. I was returned to the village and worshiped. They believed the jungle gods had marked me and kept me safe. So I grew among my own people, yet I never lost my bond to the tamrinks. Over time, I grew to be a skilled healer among the many tribes of Yrendl.' Mama Freda glanced away and her voice quieted. 'But one day, our village was attacked by slavers. I think they were attracted by the rumors of a blind woman who could see. I was stolen, along with the baby tamrink I had been hand raising.'

'Tikal?'

'Yes. Over the course of three winters, we were brought north to your lands, stopping at coastal towns and ports to display my *talent*.'

'But how did you escape?' The slavers were notorious for holding tight to their merchandise.

A fierceness entered Mama Freda's voice. She faced Mycelle again. 'Some tales are best forgotten, locked forever in one's own heart.'

Mycelle respected the woman's words. There were parts of her own life she did not wish ever spoken aloud. 'So you ended up in Port Rawl. But why my companions? Why did you take them in?'

'As I said, generosity does not come without a price in Port Rawl.'

'What do you want? I have silver, even a gold coin.'

'No.'

'Then what?'

'When your companion is hale enough to travel, I ask that you take me with you when you leave.'

Mycelle stiffened. This was a price higher than she was willing to pay. 'Why? Why do you wish to come with us?'

'I wish to meet this wit'ch of yours. This young girl Elena.'

Mycelle backed a step. She stared at her companions, searching for the traitor, for the one who spoke their secrets so freely.

Tol'chuk straightened from where he crouched, like a boulder shifting. 'We said not a word,' he grumbled.

Mogweed just sat in his chair, his eyes wide with shock. Only a small squeak of denial passed his lips as Mycelle turned in his direction.

Mama Freda scolded Mycelle. 'Leave the others be. None spoke out of turn or betrayed the trust given them.'

'Then how do you know our business?'

The old healer scratched her pet's mane. The small tamrink burrowed closer, making soft cooing sounds of contentment. 'I left Tikal in the shop yesterday when I prepared the medicinal tea for your burned friend. I know my way around my storeroom and kitchen without the need of his eyes. While I was gone, the others spoke in private about you, about Elena, and about the book you seek, the Blood Diary.'

'Still, how did you —?'

'Tikal and I are not only bonded by sight.' She wiggled one of Tikal's ears. 'What one tamrink hears, they all hear.'

In a back alley of Port Rawl, the creature slaked its blood lust upon the dying heart of its young prey, a girl-child just new to her first bleed. Once finished, the beast raised its

71

black muzzle from her ravaged chest and howled to the rising moon. Its call of hunger echoed down the rows of seedy bars and brothels. Slipping into the dark shadows, the creature crept on all fours, claws digging into the filth of the alley. It wished to hunt all night – but it knew its master's will.

None must grow suspicious ...

The beast whimpered slightly at the thought of its master's touch. Somewhere deep in its hungry mind, it remembered the burn of black flames and the boil of blood. It would obey. The monstrous creature scented the street beyond the alley: *empty*. Only the foolhardy or the drunk braved the roads of Port Rawl after the sun had set. Doors were barred and windows boarded up. The massive creature bounded across the muddy road. Though the moon was just beginning to rise, the hunt was over for this night. To delay any longer would risk awakening suspicion in those the beast hid from.

It sped across the street, catching a glimpse of itself in the moon's reflection in a barroom window. Slathering jaws, rows of shredding teeth, bunched and corded muscles, naked skin the color of a deep bruise. Flaps to either side of its nose spread wide to drink in the sea wind. So much blood, so many beating hearts.

It dashed into the alley and followed the narrow passage to its darkest corner. The tight space reeked of urine and excrement. Finding the pile of discarded clothes, it burrowed through them to find the object hidden underneath. Using teeth, it dragged its treasure forth. It studied the object, first with one cold black eye, then the other. A shudder passed over its flesh. It resisted returning to its hiding place, wanting only to run and feast on flesh and bone. It howled once again into the night.

From out in the street, someone yelled, 'Shut your damn dog up, or I'll come down there and slice its stinking throat.'

Skin prickling with hunger, the beast took a step back toward the road, but the memory of black flames stayed its paws. It could not refuse its master's will. The monstrous beast returned to the clothes and the long object it had dragged forth. Bending over, it ripped the cured hide off the iron of the weapon. Once exposed, the hunt ended for this night.

The beast felt the burn of flowing flesh and the warp of bone. It collapsed in the trash of the alley and writhed, its jaws stretching wide in a silent scream as its muzzle sank back to flesh and fangs receded into gums. Paws spread into fingers as claws pulled back to yellowed nails. In only a few gasping breaths, the transformation was complete.

Naked, Kral crawled up from the mud and debris. He rubbed his chin where his black beard still continued to fill in cheek and neck, then stood. His heart still throbbed with the blood of the young slain girl. He grinned in the dark alley and stepped toward his discarded clothes. His huge white teeth were aglow in the moonlight. It had been a good hunt.

Still, the moon continued to climb the night sky, and he had to hurry lest the others grow suspicious. He bent and retrieved his discarded ax. The scraps that had bound the ax head fell away: bits of purplish hide from a slain sniffer. Kral collected them up. He had found the cured skin at a fur trader's booth in the Four Corners bazaar and had been anxious to sample its power. He had not been disappointed. The night spent hunting as a sniffer of the Great Western Reaches had stirred Kral's blood like no other hunt. Even now his heart beat faster, and his manhood stirred with the memory. Before this night, he had used the hides and skins of dogs and wolves to incite his transformation. And though those previous hunts were exciting, none compared to this evening. The scents had been so much clearer, his muscles so much stronger, his teeth so much sharper. Kral folded the scraps of hide carefully, saving them for another hunt.

He licked the trace of blood from his lips. Kral had also spotted the silver fur of a snow panther among the wares of the trader in Four Corners bazaar. Kral's fist clenched at the thought of wrapping his ax with that rich fur and hunting the night as a monstrous cat. His manhood throbbed with the thought. His master had been generous the night he burned away Kral's craven spirit and forged him into one of his ill'guard soldiers. On the night of his new birth, the Gul'gothal lord had named him *Legion*, granting him a generous gift of black magick. Whatever skin or fur he cloaked around the black heart of his ax, Kral could assume that beast's form and abilities. He was not one creature, but a *legion*!

With his blood still surging, Kral gathered his clothes and dressed.

As he hitched his ax, he ran his fingers over the newly smelted iron. His original weapon had been destroyed, shattered upon the stone skin of the Dark Lord's demon in Shadowbrook. That night, in the cellar, he had collected the shards of iron from the mud floor, and at a riverside smithy, he had forged his ax anew. Yet there was more than just iron in his new ax. From the mud of the cellar, Kral had also retrieved a chunk of ebon'stone. Blood from his severed finger had anointed the stone that night. Even now, his four-fingered hand caressed his ax with the memory of the stone's oily touch. Guided by the Dark Lord's instructions, he had melted the sliver of ebon'stone into his ax, forging a new black heart for his weapon. The original iron of his ax, still tainted with the blood of a slain skal'tum, would mask Kral's secret from the prying eyes of any seekers, including Mycelle.

Unknowing, the swordswoman would guide him to his final prey.

Now fully dressed and armed, Kral began the long walk across the city. Disguised as a friend, he was a trap set to kill a wit'ch. His heart thundered in his ears with the thought of burying his teeth in Elena's tender heart. She would never suspect until his claws were at her soft throat.

Be it dog, bear, sniffer, or panther – Legion would have its prey.

4

Elena scrambled for the door to her cabin. Through the tiny porthole above her bed, she stared back at the pair of glowing red eyes. Even through the distortion of the crude glass, hatred and hunger seemed to flow from those slitted orbs.

Just a moment ago, she had awakened from a weak slumber to find those fiery orbs studying her. Like an itch on the skin, the gaze had drawn her from sleep. For half a breath, she had stared transfixed, frozen, until sharp claws dug at the glass. The keening scrape had ignited Elena's heart. She had rolled out of bed, a scream bursting from her chest.

Her fingers fought the door's lock. For a moment, she believed Er'ril had locked her inside. Then as quick as that thought came, the latch gave way, and the oaken door fell open. Elena tumbled into the passage as the scraping became fiercer, frantic. It knew its prey was escaping. Suddenly the scratching stopped. Elena glanced back into the cabin. Her eyes met those of the beast; then a sharp hissing, sibilant and furious, arose from beyond the porthole.

Elena paused in midstep. She knew that sound. She had heard it long ago and could never mistake it. It was like the hissing of a thousand serpents. Again their gazes locked, this time in shared recognition. Elena named the beast clinging to the hull of the *Seaswift*, her lips cold. 'Goblin.'

The single whispered word broke the spell. The eyes of the beast vanished in a blink, as if it were but a fragment of a nightmare dissolving back into the land of dreams. But the echo of its hiss still filled Elena's ears. This was no nightmare.

She ran down the short corridor, the rolling of the boat forcing her to keep one hand bumping along the wall. She reached the triple-barred hatch to the middeck and grabbed at the latch, but the door suddenly sprang open on its own. A hulking creature blocked the portal, filling the doorway.

'Elena?'

It was just Er'ril. With a gasp, she flew into the plainsman's embrace, hugging him tight. 'At my window ... outside ...' She fought to control her breathing and panic. 'I awoke ... and ... and ...'

Er'ril pulled her away from his chest, holding her shoulder gripped in one hand. 'Slow down, Elena. What happened? Are you hurt?'

Elena finally noticed Joach, and the two Brothers, Flint and Moris, nearby. All were armed: Joach with his long staff and the two Brothers with short swords. The show of strength slowed her tongue and heart.

'Goblins,' she said. 'I saw a goblin outside my cabin, through the porthole, staring in at me.'

'Goblins?' Er'ril relaxed his grip on her. 'Elena, there's no goblins near here.'

The two Brothers lowered their swords, glancing at each other. 'Drak'il?' Moris mumbled.

'Maybe deep in the Archipelago,' Flint answered, 'but not near here.'

Er'ril glanced over his shoulder, studying the empty deck

and seas. 'Maybe it was just the motion, the play of moonlight on the water playing tricks on you. The sound of the hull rubbing on the dock can echo strangely through a ship's belly.'

Elena pulled free from the plainsman's grip. 'It wasn't that!'

Moris crossed to the starboard rail and leaned over to check the side of the boat.

'It was no figment,' she continued, but did not know how to explain the strange sense of recognition shared between her and the beast. 'It seeks revenge for my slaughter of all those rock'goblins in the caves below Uncle Bol's cottage. It *knew* me!'

As if to confirm her words, a soft hissing suddenly arose from all around the boat. Everyone froze. It was like the seas themselves were steaming.

'On the dock!' Moris shouted. His sword was out once again. He ran to the head of the gangplank and began savagely working a winch to haul the planking away from the jetty.

Er'ril gathered Elena to him and crossed to the rail. Small dark bodies clambered from the sea onto the stone quay, tails lashing like angry snakes about their clawed legs. Though larger than ordinary rock'goblins, there was no mistaking their forms: huge eyes, clawed toes, gray skin.

'The shore,' Flint mumbled and pointed

There, too, the dark creatures gathered, as if the rocks of the shoreline had come to life. Hunched forms scrabbled in the surf. Some climbed to join their brethren on the dock; others slipped into the surf to vanish under the black waves.

'What are they?' Er'ril asked.

'Drak'il,' Flint said. 'Sea kin of the goblins.'

On the far side of the boat, a crash drew their eyes.

Swinging around, Elena saw a huge sea goblin land on the deck. Crouched on all fours, it hissed and bared its needled teeth at them. A long tail waved in front of it threateningly. In the moonlight, a black barb as long as an outspread hand tipped its whipping tail.

Er'ril pushed Elena toward Joach. 'Get her belowdecks!' Er'ril drew his silver sword and swept toward the creature.

'Beware its spiked tail,' Flint warned. 'It's poisoned!'

Joach drew Elena toward the raised foredeck, one hand on her elbow, the other on his staff. As she watched, more goblins spilled over the rails to assault the middeck. Most were smaller than the one Er'ril attacked. They seemed to lack the poisoned barbs but were heavily muscled and armed with claws and teeth.

Er'ril knocked aside the spike of his attacker and fought the beast back toward the rail.

'Release the bow- and sternlines!' Flint called to Moris, slashing with his sword. 'The cove is a death trap if we stay.'

The huge black man flew toward the rear of the ship, cutting smaller goblins from his path. Flint worked to the main mast and snatched a hand ax. Keeping the goblins at bay with his sword, he attacked the ropes snugly tied to iron stanchions. As each rope was cut, its ends snapped away. Counterweights crashed to the deck as the main sails unfurled with loud pops of sailcloth and the wind grabbed hold of them.

Er'ril dispatched his adversary with a sudden savage jab. He twisted the sword and danced back as the beast gave one final lunge with its tail before falling dead to the planks. But before he could even turn away, two more of the larger drak'il clambered over the rail.

One hissed and garbled something to a group of smaller goblins that were making toward Flint. They turned to harry Er'ril from the rear as the two threatened the plainsman from the front.

'C'mon, El!' Joach urged. Elena and her brother had reached the door to the ship's lower decks. He had let go of her elbow to shoulder the door open and now held it wide. 'We need to barricade inside.'

'No.' She already had her gloves off. Her ruby hands glowed in the moonlight. 'If the others fail here, we'll be trapped.'

Suddenly the boat lurched under her feet, and she fell back into Joach. He also lost his footing, and with a yell, the pair tumbled in a tangle of limbs into the open passageway. Joach regained his footing first and reached to slam the door to the middeck.

Before the door closed, Elena heard Flint call out. 'We're adrift! I have to reach the wheel, or we'll hit the reefs!'

Elena fought to her feet. 'Don't, Joach! They need help!'

He ignored her plea and slammed the door. Throwing the latches, he turned to her. 'No, you know nothing about ships.'

Elena touched the wild magicks in her blood and raised her palms. Her hands burst with wit'chlight, bathing the passage in a ruby glow. 'But I am not useless.'

Joach raised his staff against her. 'I'll not let you leave. It's too dangerous.'

With wild magick singing in her blood, she reached for Joach's staff, meaning to thrust it aside. Where her fingers brushed wood, her flesh burned as if she touched molten rock, and in a blinding flash, her fists flew back with such force that her knuckles crashed to either oaken wall. Gasping, she stepped away.

'Elena?'

She rubbed her fingers, making sure they had not been

charred away by the flash and burn. They were still there —
but not unharmed. Where her fingers had touched the wood,
the ruby stain had been scoured from her hands. Patches of
white skin marred the deep ruby surface. As she watched,
the stain flowed to fill in these gaps, but the overall richness
of the scarlet dimmed as the white skin was vanquished.

Elena raised her eyes.

Joach was staring at his staff with wonder.

It was as if his staff had absorbed a part of her magick.

Over her shoulder, Elena heard a faint scrape of claw on
wood. Hissing arose from directly behind her.

'Elena! Look out!'

Before she could even turn, Elena felt the jab of a flaming
dagger bury itself deep into her back.

As Mycelle assisted Mama Freda with Meric's bandages,
heavy footfalls sounded on the stair outside their room.
Without a word, Mycelle unsheathed one of her swords and
crossed to the door.

'Calm yourself, lass,' Mama Freda said. 'It's just your missing
companion. The man from the mountains.'

Mycelle ignored the old healer's words. Pulling a sword too
soon never harmed the wary . . .

A loud rapping announced the visitor at the door.

As if in answer, the elv'in moaned behind Mycelle,
thrashing weakly at his thin sheets. Mycelle leaned closer to
the door. She probed beyond with her senses, but the planks
coated with banesroot oil blocked her senses. 'Who is it?'
she hissed at the door.

After a short pause, a gruff but familiar voice answered.
'Is that you, Mycelle?' There was no mistaking that grumbled voice; his throaty highland accent flavored the few
spoken words.

'It be Kral,' Tol'chuk said needlessly.

Still cautious, Mycelle kept her sword in one hand as she unlatched the lock. Who was to say Kral was alone on the stair? With her senses muffled by the banesroot, Mycelle's edginess remained keen. She swung the door open.

The huge mountain man greeted her with a broad grin. He was alone on the stair. She quickly studied him. His black beard had grown thicker and longer since she had last seen him, almost a wild tangle, but the flinty eyes and scent of rock magick were unmistakable. Mycelle stood aside to let him enter. She sensed no foulness tainting the man. Even the injured hand where the demon rat had ripped off a middle finger had healed cleanly, leaving only a pinkish scar.

Kral had to stoop his head and twist his wide shoulders to push through the doorway. 'I thought you must be up here. I met Fardale down below guarding your mount.' As he straightened, his gaze passed over Mycelle's unsheathed sword. 'Not a very warm welcome,' he commented, but before Mycelle could even scowl, he softened his rebuke. 'But considering what I've seen this day on the streets of Port Rawl, perhaps you'd best keep steel in both hands, even while you sleep.' He patted the ax hanging on his belt. 'Among the scavengers of Swamptown, a weapon is always the safest greeting.'

Mycelle closed the door and latched it before turning around. 'Is Fardale still with the horse?'

Kral slipped off a cloak coated in road dust and hung it on a hook. 'I had a groomsman from a neighboring inn take your horse to where my warcharger is stabled. Fardale followed after him to insure the fellow's honesty. I expect the shape-shifter will be bedding down at the stables to keep a watch over your horse and gear.'

'Good,' Mycelle said. 'I want to be off at the first light.'

'Or sooner,' Mama Freda said. She had finished with Meric's wraps and pulled the thin sheet higher across the thin elv'in's chest. She faced the others. 'The town grows more tense with each passing day. The foul incident on the docks has everyone clutching their swords tighter. It would take only the tiniest spark to ignite this tinderbox.'

'Still, before we leave,' Mycelle said, 'I must check the Watershed Trading Post. A friend was due to arrive this past day from the swamps with the supplies and mounts we had abandoned in Drywater.'

Mama Freda shook her head. 'Are these other horses worth the risk of spending more time on the streets of Port Rawl?'

'It is to Elena,' Mycelle said.

'Then I guess Mist must be with them,' Kral said.

Mycelle nodded. 'The small gray mare means much to the girl. To know the horse is safe will hearten her for the journey ahead. A small delay to check the trading post could bring Elena great cheer.'

Mama Freda shrugged. 'Or get us all killed.'

Mycelle frowned. 'Perhaps it's best we all try to get some rest. We've a long journey still ahead of us.'

Mogweed spoke up. The shape-shifter still sat slumped in the chair by the feeble fire. 'And just where are we going?'

Mycelle straightened and glanced around the room. Though the elemental magick in the room struck her senses like a clear draught of spring water, a small part of her still balked at revealing Elena's location. There was no taint of the Dark Lord's touch here. But something else made her wary – something she could not name.

'It'd be best if that secret still remains close to my heart,' she mumbled, suddenly red faced at the clear lack of trust in her words.

Mogweed, though, persisted. He shifted higher up in his chair. 'But what if something were to happen to you tomorrow? How would we find Elena and the others?'

Mycelle glanced to the rug. The shape-shifter was correct. These were Elena's friends and had proven themselves countless times. And what if she *were* injured or captured? The others could still journey ahead to add their skills and strength of arms to Elena's defense. Was she being overly cautious in this instance?

She opened her mouth, ready to admit her folly and share with the others Elena's location along the coast, when suddenly an angry voice interrupted. 'No.'

All their faces turned to the bed, where Meric stared back at them. His sky-blue eyes were open, his gaze edged by lightning and thunderclouds. 'Do not speak,' he warned her, his voice no more than a whisper, his eyes drilling at her.

Mycelle crossed to his bedside. 'Why, Meric? A secret shared among those you trust is safer in many hearts.'

Before Meric could say another word, a loud pounding suddenly burst from the door. They all jumped and swung to face the only exit. The stout door shook in its frame. A loud, commanding voice followed the pounding: 'By the order of the caste master of the city of Port Rawl, you are hereby commanded to turn yourselves over to the watch. Any resistance will be met with the point of our swords.'

There was a pause; then a resounding crash smashed into the door. Its planks split and cracked. One more blow and the door would be open. But even before the next blow struck, Mycelle sensed it: elemental magick flowing into the room from between the panels of split oak – not the pure elemental weavings that were pent up here, but something twisted and black.

Mycelle had both her swords out. Curse the healer's

coating of banesroot! Though it had helped hide the others, now it betrayed them, masking the evil that had crept so silently up the steps until it was too late. Mycelle stretched her senses. She recognized the foulness beyond the doorway. Only the ill'guard monsters gave off such a stench. She knew what she had to do.

Mycelle dropped both her swords. The steel blades rang as they struck the floor. 'I must not be taken,' Mycelle whispered. She reached to her neck and pulled free the tiny jade vial that swung on a coarse thread.

'No,' Kral said, noticing what she was doing. He tried to reach for her arm.

She skipped free. 'An ill'guard leads this assault,' she said to Kral. 'I cannot risk capture. The Black Heart must never learn from me where Elena hides.' She pulled free the sliver of jade that plugged the tiny vial. 'Thank the Mother, Meric kept me from speaking my secret.'

A second crash shattered through the room. The door flew wide, pieces of oak tumbling across the floor. Dark shapes rushed through the ragged opening.

'Save yourselves as best you can,' Mycelle yelled to the others, 'but Elena's secret dies with me!' She raised the vial to her lips and poured the poison down her throat. It was a burn that quickly spread from her belly to her limbs. 'I'm sorry, Elena.' She dropped the empty vial to the floor.

Tol'chuk rushed forward. 'Mother!'

As darkness swallowed Mycelle away, she fell into her son's thick arms.

Elena collapsed to her knees in the passageway. Behind his sister's shoulder, Joach spotted the monster. Near the stair that led to the lower decks, one of the larger sea goblins crouched, skin the color of sour milk, eyes a baleful red. Its breath stank of rotted fish as it hissed at him, claws raking the air. It took a step closer, toward his sister.

'Get back, demon!' With fury narrowing his vision to a point, Joach slammed the butt of his staff into the face of the drak'il. His aim was sure. Bone cracked, and the beast howled. The force of the blow tumbled it down the stairs to the lower decks.

'Joach?' Elena moaned.

He hurried to his sister's side as she swooned toward the deck. 'El, I'm here.'

'It burns . . .' Elena collapsed into his arms. The back of her thin shift was hot and slick to his touch. In the lamplight, he spied the spreading pool of blackness across her lower back. So much blood! 'Elena!' Joach pulled her tight to him and dropped his staff to press his palm against her wound, attempting to stem the flow of blood.

Drifting up the stairs from the lower deck, a low hissing began to gather again. Whether from the injured drak'il or a new foe, Joach did not know. He hauled Elena up in his arms and half carried, half dragged her to the large stateroom in back. He dropped her onto the narrow bed, ripped a sheet into long strips, and wrapped the linen bandage snug around her midsection, tying it tight to keep pressure on the wound.

Once done, he hurried to the door, glancing back, a prayer on his lips. Then he did the hardest thing he had ever done in his life: He abandoned his sister. He left the stateroom and closed the door behind him. Elena needed help, more than he could offer. He must fetch the others.

Down the dim passage, he spotted his staff on the deck, like a black snake stretched across the passage. But beyond the weapon, between Joach and the hatch that led to the open deck, crouched his foe. Red eyes glowed in the shadows; claws gleamed silver in the lamplight. Its tail, whipping and stabbing at him, was black with his sister's blood. From its splayed nose, blood still dripped from where his staff had struck.

Weaponless now, Joach had little chance of defeating the well-muscled predator, not unless he could reach his staff. Instinctively, he reached out with a bloody hand toward the gnarled scrap of wood. As if in answer to his silent wish, the staff shifted a handspan closer to him, the scrape of bark on planking loud in the narrow passage. The goblin noticed the movement and took a step closer, lowering its injured nose to the black talisman. It cocked its head and reached a claw forward, apparently curious and drawn to the magick.

Joach clenched his fists. He must not let the drak'il reach his only weapon. 'No!' he spat loudly, meaning only to draw the beast's attention. The result, though, was more dramatic.

The staff jumped into the air, as if startled by his loud command. A scintillation of black flames blew across its surface. The drak'il froze in place. So did Joach. He had never seen the staff behave in such a manner. Was this display powered from the energies drawn earlier from Elena or simply a reflection of his own urgency? Joach's eyes narrowed. He did not care. He needed a weapon – any weapon!

He thrust his arm out farther toward the floating staff. 'Come to me!' he yelled with all his heart. But nothing happened. The gnarled wood just continued to float.

Though ineffectual, his shouted words had at least managed to scare back the drak'il. It cowered a step away, slinking from the flames of the staff, wary of these black magicks. Maybe he could use this to his advantage.

With no plan, he simply pounced toward the goblin, arms raised in the air, a scream of rage and hate flowing from his lips. The beast jumped back from his abrupt display, retreating until its rump pressed against the deck hatch.

Joach reached the staff, and using both hands, he grabbed its length. He cringed slightly, expecting to be burned by the dark flames. But at his touch, the fire dimmed until the flames were vanquished, leaving only a deep rosy glow, as if the staff were a glowing ember just removed from a hearth. Yet its heat did not burn; instead it was frosty to his touch, as if his hands gripped a shard of icicle from the coldest peak. The iciness spread into his fingers and seemed to sink into the vessels of his arms. As he gripped the wood, he could feel the frostiness travel up through his veins as if the staff were some cold heart pumping its ice into him.

Ignoring this effect, he swung the staff toward the beast who still blocked his escape. The words of power he had learned in the dream came again to his mind, unbidden, rising like steam to his lips. His tongue moved with the first words of the spell.

The drak'il dropped to its knees and splayed itself before him, forehead pressed to the planks. A soft mewling rose from its throat. It clearly begged for mercy.

But the magick's ice had reached Joach's heart – now was not the time for tender feelings, not when his sister lay bleeding from a wound inflicted by this same beast. As his lips grew cold with the ancient spell, the end of the staff bloomed into a rose of black flame. Smiling without warmth, Joach finished the last garbled syllable and thrust his staff at the goblin.

The petals of the black rose burst open, and balefire lanced from its heart in a furious storm. At the last moment, the goblin must have sensed its death. It raised its face, eyes reflecting the flames. Then the fire struck. The beast was thrown back with such force that its flailing body crashed through the bolted hatch behind it. Iron rods tore loose, and storm-hardened wood splintered like dry twigs. The carcass of the sea goblin, licked by hungry flames, skidded across the open deck. In the time it took Joach to climb through the debris of the hatch, only the charred bones of the drak'il remained.

Joach straightened as he reached the deck. All eyes were on him, both goblin and man. The air reeked of burned flesh and charred bone. The deck was awash with goblin blood, and everywhere Joach looked the hacked remains of the small predators covered the deck. Joach's eyes were wide with horror. The *Seaswift* had become a foul charnel house.

Joach stared at the burned remains of the sea goblin on the deck. Its bones lay contorted into a small ball, smoking in the cool night air. Every bone seemed to speak the pain of the flame he had unleashed. The sight reminded him of another time, another night, when fire had consumed his mother and father, leaving only blackened bone then, too. Only this night he was the wielder of death. Oh, Sweet Mother, what had he done?

Joach raised the staff over his head and cried his pain into the night. The ice in his blood fled his veins, and flames blew from both ends of his staff, like the last licks of a dying hearth.

The fiery display ignited the frozen drak'il army. The beasts fled in fear to the rails, leaping and diving into the black seas. Soon the deck was empty, except for the three men and the many dead goblins.

'Joach!' Er'ril crossed to him. A bloody raking of claws marked his left cheek. 'What have you done?' Both wonder and horror etched the plainsman's words. He had sheathed his sword and now reached toward Joach.

Joach stepped back. He could not bear to be touched right now. He simply shook his head and pointed through the ruins of the door. 'Elena ... she ... she's badly hurt. In the rear stateroom.'

Er'ril lowered his arm, his eyes wide. He dashed into the passage without another word.

Joach knew he should follow. Elena was his sister. But his legs were numb. He could not move.

Flint strode briskly across the fouled deck. His eyes were fixed on Joach, but his words were for his fellow Brother. 'Moris, take the wheel! Guide us out the mouth of the cove, but mind the reefs to port in these shallow tides. We need to reach the open seas. The boy's performance will cow the drak'il for only so long.'

In response to his shouted orders, the sails billowed and snapped overhead as the black-skinned Brother brought the ship about.

Flint reached Joach and grabbed his shoulder. 'Listen, boy, I appreciate what you did. The drak'il had us pinned down, and we were lucky not to have the keel torn out from under us on the rocks. But I know the magick you wielded. It—'

'Balefire,' Joach mumbled, naming the flames he had called forth.

Flint knelt down to stare Joach in the eyes. 'Yes, and the fact you can utter its name means it's touched you – marked you. It's one of the darkest of the black arts, and I'd rather lose the ship than see you succumb to its allure.'

'I had to,' Joach answered. 'I needed to protect Elena.'

Flint sighed. 'Your sister has enough defenders. She needs a brother more than another guardian. Remember that.'

Joach shook free of Flint's grip on his shoulder. 'A sister who is murdered has no need for a brother.' He backed a step and positioned the black staff between him and the grizzled seaman.

Flint stood up, his eyes on the staff. 'Be that as it may, look to your heart, boy. Study it closely. Soon the staff will become more important than your sister.'

'That will never happen!' he said fiercely. 'I can—'

A call echoed up from inside the foredeck. 'Flint, get down here! Now!'

Flint stepped toward the opening but spoke over his shoulder. 'Are you so sure of your heart, Joach? Why are you still up here when your sister lies injured below?' Flint ducked into the passage.

Joach stared at the black poi'wood gripped in his fist. He remembered its frigid touch and the ice in his veins. Though the wood was no longer cold and the ice in his blood had thawed with the realization of what he had done, he sensed that somewhere deep in his heart a seed had taken root. A small shard of ice still lay imbedded there.

The power will *mark* you, Flint had warned. Joach glanced to the ruins of the doorway. Maybe it already had. But black or not, he would risk his own spirit to keep Elena safe.

Joach bowed his way into the narrow passage, keeping a firm grip on the poi'wood staff.

Kral lunged at the soldier of the watch. His ax sliced the man's arm off at the shoulder; blood sprayed his face as he swung the edge of his weapon into the side of the next assailant. Fury fed his rage. He had been so close to learning the secret his master craved: the whereabouts of the wit'ch. Now, the only person who knew Elena's hiding place lay dead on the rug of the room. Curse the blind loyalty of the damned swordswoman! Only a moment more and she would have betrayed her niece to the Dark Lord.

Spinning on a heel, Kral tossed his ax from one hand to the other and swung his blade with practiced skill into the face of another attacker. But as quickly as he moved, other armed men still swarmed into the room. He parried a sword thrust at his belly, then used the wooden haft of his ax to club the man aside.

A quick glance over his shoulder showed that he fought alone. Tol'chuk stood guard over both his mother's body and the bedridden elv'in. Mogweed had fled his chair and now cowered in the farthest corner. If Kral was to free their party, he would have to carve a path out of here by himself.

'Tol'chuk! Grab Meric and follow me!' Kral yelled.

In a flurry of blade and muscle, he hacked his way toward the door. Men fell in tortured screams and writhing limbs to both sides of him, his beard soaked in their life's blood, his white smile a beacon in the ruin of his face. An old war song came to his lips as he sliced his way through the city's watchers.

None could defeat him! His blood lust almost ignited the black magick buried in his ax. He craved to bury his teeth into the throats of these rough men. But he knew that with the others looking on, he had best rein in this lust and satisfy his desires with the edge of his blade. His heart thundered in his ears, deaf to the wails or cries for help.

He would have easily dispatched the last handful of soldiers if not for the sudden appearance of the leader of this watch. Standing shorter than most of his fellow soldiers and appearing frail of limb, the man was not outwardly intimidating as he stepped through the battered door. But he stopped Kral with a glance: Foul magick danced behind those tiny eyes. Kral recognized the man's nature – ill'guard, an elemental twisted by the black magicks of his master. But the leader of the watch did not recognize Kral's kinship. The Black Heart had hidden Kral's secret too deep for even another ill'guard to recognize.

As Kral paused, the ill'guard leader raised a clawlike hand and raked it in his direction. At this signal, a furious black cloud burst into the room from the hall outside. Wings and claws ripped through the air toward Kral. A flock of monstrous ravens and deadeye crows! Swinging his ax, Kral fought the demon birds. Such a weapon was little protection against such numerous small foes; still, he used blade, haft, and fist to beat back the assault.

For a moment, Meric added his support from the bed. The elv'in used what little skill he could muster to send sharp gusts of magickal wind to attack the flock. The cloud of birds was battered ragged by the unexpected attack. Even the leader of the watch stumbled a step away, wary of this sudden gale.

Kral pressed his attack, defense becoming offense, hoping to reach the ill'guard and dispatch the fool who had so foully interfered with his own plans. Yet suddenly, one of the crows slipped past Kral's ax and dove toward his leg. It buried its sharp beak into the meat of his thigh. The pain was but a pinch, and Kral crushed the beast under the butt of his ax. But the damage was already done. Kral's left leg went instantly numb. Unsupported, he toppled to the floor.

The black cloud fell upon him, keening squawks accompanying their assault. Beaks and claws tore at him. In moments, he felt the ax kicked from his numb fingers.

'Enough!' the leader screeched through the howl of the birds. 'I need them alive!'

The birds squawked their displeasure but obeyed their master, hopping and flapping away from Kral. Unable to move, paralyzed by the black magick, Kral could not even turn his head as he heard the footfalls of the ill'guard leader. From the corner of his eyes, Kral noted that Tol'chuk had fared no better. He lay sprawled across the rug, unmoving. It seemed even the og're could not resist the numbing magick of the demon crows.

The man's pinched face leaned over to peer into Kral's eyes. 'No one hides from me in Port Rawl.'

Kral suppressed a groan. Damn ill'guard fool! The man had no idea how artfully he had blocked his master's true desires. Kral found small comfort in knowing how this man would suffer when the Black Heart learned of this interference.

The leader of the watch straightened up, towering over Kral. 'Shackle that monster and haul the lot of them to the garrison.'

'Sir,' one of the soldiers asked, 'what about this dead woman?' Kral saw the soldier's boots kick Mycelle's body.

'My birds are still hungry for meat,' he said with a wave of his hand. 'She'll make a fitting meal.' At his signal, the flock swarmed over Mycelle.

'Master Parak . . .' It was Mama Freda, naming the ill'-guard leader. 'I should warn you that the woman consumed poison. She killed herself. If your handsome birds feed on her flesh and blood, they could be poisoned, too.'

Kral could just make out the startled look on the man's face. Parak snapped his fingers and drove his birds from Mycelle's carcass. Just then men grabbed Kral's arms and began hauling him up. Half sitting in their grips, Kral had a better view of the room. Several men worked over Tol'chuk with iron shackles, while Mogweed already lay trussed in ropes.

Mama Freda, her head bowed, stood beside the scrawny Parak. Her pet tamrink, Tikal, crouched on her shoulder, tail wrapped around the old woman's neck. It stared with wide black eyes, shivering in restrained panic and making the tiniest whining noises in the back of its throat.

'Thank you, Mama Freda,' the leader of the watch said. 'As a fellow lover of beasts of the field, I'm sure you understand how dear my birds are to me.'

Mama Freda absently scratched her tamrink behind an ear, calming the beast. 'Of course. My duty is always to the city and the well-being of its citizenry.'

'Still, you should have warned us of these strangers. You know the new statutes. None of them registered with their respective castes or paid their tithes. If it wasn't for our one-armed friend over there—' Parak pointed to where a rough soldier dressed in colors of the town's gatekeepers lay dead. '—who so skillfully shadowed the swordswoman and reported her location, we would never have discovered this clutch of criminals. As such, they are now slaves of the watch.'

Kral's blood thundered in his ears. So this assault was for no other reason but to gain slaves. As in all matters of Port Rawl, it seemed even the ill'guard were guided by the shine of gold coins.

'Your pardons, Master Parak. But you know my rule: I *heal*; I don't ask questions.'

Parak snorted in amusement. 'Yes. That is why you are so valued a citizen.' He turned to face his men as they finished lashing Kral's arms behind him. 'Take them to the garrison.'

'What about the sick one in bed?' one of the soldiers asked.

'Leave him. From the looks of him, he's already half in his grave. He'll fetch no good coin.' Parak glanced around the room. 'The rest of this lot, though, should bring us a nice price on the slaver's block.'

The soldiers began hauling their bounty toward the door. Kral's arms were yanked cruelly behind him as he was dragged away, but the numbness in his limbs masked any pain.

Parak faced Mama Freda and waved an arm to encompass the room. 'I apologize for the intrusion, Mama Freda. I'll send someone to clean this mess on the morrow.'

Mama Freda stood among the many dead, amid the stench of blood and excrement. She bowed her head. 'As always, you are too kind.'

Er'ril knelt beside Elena's bed. Aromatic oils of the woods scented the air of the cabin, but under the sharp odor was the tang of blood and medicines. Soiled bandages were piled at the foot of the narrow cot, and pots of willow bark and woundswort lined the planks.

As Elena slumbered, Er'ril held the girl's hand in his own. She was so cold, her lips so pale. She did not respond as he rubbed her wrist – only a whispered mumble, nothing more.

'She does not wake,' he said to Flint. The old Brother had applied what little healing skill he knew to save Elena. The two of them were alone in the cabin. Joach and Moris were doing their best to man the sails and rigging while guiding the boat along the coast.

'Perhaps it's best she sleeps,' Flint finally said as he pulled a thick wool blanket up to her neck. 'Her body needs its energy to heal. Even as I stitched, the edges of her wound were knitting together on their own. Her magick protects her.'

'Then she'll live,' Er'ril said.

'She should already be dead,' Flint answered. He sat back on his heels on the far side of the bed. He stared somberly at Er'ril. 'The poison of a drak'il's tail kills with the barest scratch. I suspect her slumber is her body's attempt to rally its meager resources to keep her alive. But there are limits to which even her magick can protect her.' Flint slipped one of Elena's ruby-stained hands free of the blanket. 'See how her Rose slowly fades as she lies here. Her magick feeds her spirit, sustaining her.'

The deep crimson of Elena's hands had waned to a sallow pink. Er'ril raised his eyes to Flint. 'And when the girl's magick fades completely away ... ?'

Flint met Er'ril's gaze unflinchingly, then simply shook his head sadly.

'Then what are we to do?'

'I've done all I can. The healers who once studied in A'loa Glen may have been able to aid her, but ...' Flint shrugged. The island had been lost to the Dark Lord's minions.

'What about dragon's blood?' The healing properties of a seadragon were well known. 'If we reach the rendezvous site with the mer'ai ... ?'

'She'll be long dead by then,' Flint said. 'But you've given me an idea. There's a skilled healer in Port Rawl. Her apothecary is well stocked with herbs and potions. I don't know if she carries dragon's blood; it's scarce and expensive. But she is a wise healer.'

'Port Rawl?' Er'ril asked skeptically. Little good was ever gained by a visit to that swamp city.

'I also know a few good men in Port Rawl who can help crew the ship. Alone, we are too few to properly sail the *Seaswift* into the tricky currents of the Archipelago. And if we should be attacked again ...' Flint shrugged. Only luck and black magick had saved them this time.

Er'ril pulled a chair closer to the bed as he weighed their options. Sitting down, he raised a palm to Elena's cheek. Her flesh was like ice. Around his own heart, a similar coldness settled. He could not watch her die. 'We'll have to risk it.'

Flint nodded and stood. 'Then I'd better alert Moris to our new plans and let the boy know of his sister's condition.'

'The boy ...' Er'ril said, stopping Flint. 'About that magick ...'

'I know,' Flint said. 'Joach shouldn't have been able to wield such might. Therein lies something worth closer study. But either way, I think that staff should be burned and its ashes cast into the sea.'

'No,' Er'ril said. 'Leave the boy his staff.'

Flint's eyebrows rose in doubtful acceptance. 'Whatever you say.' The old man reached for the latch to the door.

'Flint ...'

The grizzled Brother glanced over his shoulder.

'Keep a close watch on the boy,' Er'ril finished.

Flint's face grew grim. Both men knew the stranglehold that the black magicks could have on a man. Even a pure spirit could be choked by the black arts' grip. With a sharp nod, Flint ducked out of the room and closed the door behind him.

Alone with Elena, Er'ril leaned back in his chair. He pushed aside his worries about Joach. His immediate concern lay wrapped in woolen blankets before him.

Er'ril studied the small girl, his fingers clenched with worry. If she died, so died the last chance to free Alasea. But in his heart, Er'ril knew it was not the fate of his lands that clenched his fist, but a simpler fear – the fear of losing Elena herself. In his long life, he'd never had a younger sister to watch over, nor a daughter to dote upon, but somewhere on the dark journey here, Elena had become both to him – and perhaps more.

But who was she really – *wit'ch, woman, or savior*?

Er'ril sighed. He had no answer.

Upon her pale features, the first signs of womanhood were just beginning to shine through the roundness of childhood: the soft curve of cheekbone, the fullness of lips. He reached forward and combed back a strand of fiery curl from her smooth brow. And when had the black dye faded from her hair? She must have been hiding it from him, hoping he wouldn't notice. A ghost of a smile shadowed his lips. Even with the fate of Alasea hanging over her head, the simple vanities of a young girl still weighed her heart. This thought gave him some small cheer.

But as he leaned back in his chair, Er'ril's smile dimmed. His eyes wandered to the moon shining through the small porthole. 'Savior or not,' he muttered to the empty room, 'I will not see you die, Elena.'

5

Breaking from darkness, Mycelle woke to streaming light so bright that it blinded her. She blinked against the glare. Was this the Grand Bridge to the next life? If so, she had never suspected the transition would be so painful. Her entire form was afire with an intense itch that burned both inside and outside – but inside and outside *what*? She had no true awareness of a body, only of pain defining the boundaries of her form.

'Lie still, child,' a bodiless voice murmured in her head.

'Wh-where am I?' she asked, unsure if she spoke with her lips or with her thoughts.

Either way, the speaker heard her question. 'You're safe – at least for the moment.'

That voice . . . She knew that voice. 'Mother . . . ?' As soon as she spoke the word, Mycelle knew this was not correct. 'Mama . . . ?' Then her memories returned in a babbling torrent – images, sounds, smells, all falling back into order. Mycelle remembered the warm room, the burned elv'in, and the small golden-maned pet of the old healer. 'Mama Freda.'

'That's correct, child. Now don't struggle. The paka'golo is not finished with its work yet.'

Mycelle still felt no awareness of her body. Was she lying

on her back or belly? The blinding light filled her entire mind. Suddenly a violent spasm wracked through the core of her being. She retched violently.

'Keep her head turned,' Mama Freda said. 'She'll choke if you're not careful. Yes, like that . . . Very good.'

Mycelle coughed and spat. What was happening? The last she remembered was swallowing the poison in her jade vial. She recalled slumping to the floor, glad to protect Elena with her own death, relieved that the poison was painless, tasteless. Why was she still alive? For a horrifying moment, the thought of failure wormed through her mind. She still lived. Could the secret of Elena's location still be wrested from her?

'No . . . I must not . . . Elena . . .'

'Stop struggling!' Mama Freda ordered. 'I said you're safe. The soldiers of the watch have left with their trophies. They thought you were dead from poison.'

A new voice intruded. 'She *was* dead.'

'Hush. Death is not as final as most would suppose. It is like a child's croup. If caught early, it's curable.'

A derisive snort. 'She still looks dead to me.' Mycelle suddenly knew that voice, the snide arrogance. It was Meric. 'How long does this process take?'

'The sun is just dawning. It's almost over. She'll either rally now, or we'll lose her forever.'

The voices faded into the background as a roaring suddenly filled Mycelle's ears. If she could have found her hands, she would have clapped them over her ears. What was happening? She had a thousand questions, but the noise, the blinding light, and the fiery burn made it hard to think. With all her senses overwhelmed, she became aware of something beyond all the pain and confusion.

She reached out to it, like a drowning woman for a floating log, something to hang on to, something solid in this intangible plane. It scintillated and sparked like a jewel in sunlight, moving slowly through the core of her being. What was it? She sensed magick surrounding it, radiating from it like heat from a hearth. It seemed to suffuse through her, cooling the burn slightly with its passage.

A vague sense of recognition drifted in her mind. She struggled to clear the fog from her awareness, reaching toward this new magick with her seeking talent. What was this strangely familiar scent? She sniffed at it with her talent. The elemental signature was unusual: mold, dirt, and a touch of black coal. Suddenly she knew why it was familiar. It was the elemental magick she had sensed in Mama Freda's store-room earlier, among the drying herbs and shelves of medicines. Something from beyond the lands of Alasea.

As she studied it, the magick swelled, becoming a part of her. The source of the elemental power climbed closer, as if from some abyss, sliding and curling toward where her mind hid. Its magick grew stronger as it approached. Hues of blue and green whorled about it, pushing back the blinding light. Then it was upon her, burning her magick, drowning her. Mycelle felt something vital being ripped from her.

Mycelle choked; she could not breathe. It filled and enveloped her. She writhed as awareness of her body returned in a searing rush.

'Hold her limbs! Pin her down!'

'I can't—'

'Curse you! Sit on her if you have to, you scrawny bird!'

Mycelle fought for air! She struggled to gasp, choking.

'Tikal . . . Tikal . . . Tikal . . .'

'Get your tail out of my way!' The squeal of an upset beast. 'Now's the moment, Meric! The paka'golo climbs up from her throat. She lives or dies on this moment.'

'Sweet Mother!'

'Help me hold her jaws open. Get me that mouth gag. No, not that! Over there!' A curse under mumbled breath. Then Mycelle felt lips at her ear. 'Don't fight it. Let it pass.'

Mycelle did not know what the old woman meant. Her back suddenly convulsed in a contorting spasm. Tears burst from her eyes.

'Hold her!'

Then Mycelle screamed – a ripping cry as if she were casting the very life itself from her body. And in a way she was. Mycelle felt something squirm and coil out from inside her throat, sliding out through her stretched lips as she screamed. She choked and gasped as what she gave birth to slipped over her tongue and out of her body.

Once her throat was unblocked, her spasming body collapsed down and rattling gasps tumbled from her lips. Darkness resolved into watery images: blurred faces, movement, wavering light. She raised a hand to her face. She was soaked in sweat. With each breath, her eyes continued to focus.

'Lie back, child. Rest. Keep your eyes closed.'

Mycelle did not resist her words, too weak to argue. She simply obeyed. She sensed a table under her back. No soft bed, but bare planks. Still, she did not move. She let the tremors and mild twitching calm in her limbs. Her breathing became less ragged, and her moist skin cooled. Someone opened a window nearby, and a cool breeze raised gooseflesh on her legs and arms. She was suddenly conscious of her own nakedness.

Embarrassment and shyness finally moved her to open her eyes. She blinked against the brightness, but it was only the soft light from a rising sun that lit the room. Voices could be heard nearby, muffled in whispers: '. . . live, but the bite of a paka'golo will be needed to sustain her.'

Mycelle pushed up to her elbows on the table. A groan escaped her lips. Her muscles were as sore as if she had been battling with both swords all night.

Glancing around, Mycelle saw that she was in the storeroom of the healer's apothecary. Lines of wooden shelves stocked with bottles, flasks, and pouches filled the room, except for the back section where she lay atop an oaken table. A row of small wire cages lined the nearby wall. Strange beasts peered out from these small cells, eyes glinting in the light of the new sun. The assortment was amazing: wingless feathered creatures, lizards with ridged spikes down their backs, small furred rodents that swelled up with air and hissed at her movement. From her wanderings, Mycelle knew these beasts were not of Alasea, but from lands beyond.

Mycelle sat up as Mama Freda approached from the bank of cages. Meric, swaddled in bandages, limped after her with the use of a crutch. Fardale padded beside the elv'in. At least the wolf, holed up in the stables with the horses, had managed to escape the clutches of the ill'guard, too.

Reaching the table, Mama Freda wrapped a blanket around Mycelle's nakedness and helped her sit up on the edge of the table. 'Your strength should quickly return.'

'H-how?' Mycelle asked, fighting her tongue. 'The poison . . .'

'Extract of nightshade,' Mama Freda answered. 'A common enough poison . . . but I have my ways.'

Mycelle knew the old woman was hedging. 'Tell me.'

Mama Freda glanced at Meric, who nodded. 'She'll need to know eventually,' the elv'in said.

The healer turned to a nearby cage behind the table. Still feeling dull and disjointed, Mycelle twisted to see.

'In Yrendl,' Mama Freda said as she worked the latch on

the tiny cage, 'the jungles teem with many poisons, but as in all things, there is always a balance. The gods of the jungle created a special creature to help protect our tribes against these poisons.' Mama Freda turned. Coiling around her wrist and about her fingers was a purplish snake striped in blues and greens. 'We call them paka'golo. In the language of my people, it means "breath of life." The serpents are steeped in elemental magicks. Where most snakes carry venom in their fangs, the bite of a paka'golo draws poisons out.'

Mama Freda offered Mycelle the snake to examine closer. Mycelle reached out her hand, curious at such an odd beast. A small red tongue flickered out from its scaled jaws to investigate one of her fingers. Then slowly the serpent stretched its body to slide from the old healer's fingers onto Mycelle's palm. She had expected it to be cold and slimy but found its scaled skin to be oddly warm and smooth. It writhed in slow movements up her forearm, then seemed to settle there like a fanciful piece of jewelry.

Fardale slipped closer to sniff at the snake.

Mycelle raised her eyes from the serpent. Something did not make sense. 'I concocted my own poison,' she said. 'I know its potency. It often kills before the poison even reaches the belly – too fast for any cure.'

Mama Freda sighed and nodded. 'Yes, you are right. But the paka'golo were aptly named by my people. They truly carry the "breath of life." Besides curing the poisoned, they can bring back those recently killed by the touch of venoms.'

'How is that possible?'

Mama Freda shrugged. 'It takes more than just their bite. The serpent itself must *enter* the poisoned body of the deceased.'

Mycelle's eyes narrowed, but she did not flinch. She was

never one to shy from hard realities. She recalled the squirming she had felt in her belly, the sickness, the sense of its magick pulsing through her flesh. The snake had been inside her. She even recalled the sensation of it sliding and writhing up her throat and out her lips.

'Inside you, they use their magick to rid your tissues of poison and suffuse your body with their spirit. They become part of you.' This last part seemed to worry Mama Freda. She glanced away from Mycelle.

Meric hobbled forward. 'Tell her all of it.'

Mama Freda turned, her thin lips drawn tight. 'The serpent and you are now one. Bonded. The two of you share a single life.'

'What does that mean?' Mycelle asked, suddenly afraid of the answer.

'You are now linked forever with this paka'golo. During the first night of each full moon, the serpent must bite you. Once life bonded, you need the magick of its fangs to sustain you, and it needs your blood to survive. Without its magick, you will die.'

Mycelle glanced to the snake, her eyes wide. Surely the old woman was mad. Reaching out with her elemental talent, she probed for the serpent's magick inside her. She felt nothing. Relieved, she pushed harder, just to be sure – and again only emptiness. She glanced to the snake, meaning to study its magick. As she delved into it, a frown appeared on her lips. Nothing.

Raising her gaze, she glanced to Meric and sent her senses out toward him, searching for his scent of lightning and storm. Her eyes grew wide with horror. Again she felt nothing. She sat up straighter, shocked. 'I . . . I'm blind,' she whispered.

Meric stepped closer, eyes crinkled with concern.

For the first time, Mycelle realized the dull sensation in her head was not just the fuzziness from the cure, but a deadness in her spirit. She turned frightened eyes first toward Mama Freda, then Meric. 'I can no longer seek,' she mumbled. 'My elemental ability is gone.'

Mama Freda spoke quietly. 'There is always a price to be paid.'

Meric stepped to the table's edge, raising a hand to comfort her, then suddenly froze. He leaned nearer, studying Mycelle's face. 'Your eyes!' he exclaimed. 'They've changed.'

Mycelle's hands rose to her face, checking what new horror awaited her. The snake at her wrist hissed slightly at the sudden motion.

'They're now golden and slitted,' Meric said, glancing at the wolf who sat nearby, 'like Fardale's eyes.'

Mycelle's fists clenched on her cheeks. It could not be. She dared not hope.

'I've never witnessed such a change,' Mama Freda said. 'She—'

Mycelle stopped listening. Warily, cautiously, she reached deep inside her heart and touched a part of her spirit that had withered and died long ago. Where once there had been nothing, she now felt a familiar resistance. She pushed gently and felt bone and sinew, long trapped in one form, shift and bend. Like an iced pond in spring, frozen flesh melted. She stood on legs of clay beside the table, the blanket falling from her shoulders as bone gave way.

The paka'golo hissed and writhed tighter on her arm as its perch melted underneath it.

Mycelle raised the serpent before her eyes. What miracle was this? The paka'golo had not only returned her own life, but it had revitalized her dead heritage. Mycelle willed her flesh back to solidity, returning to the form with which she was most familiar. 'I . . . I can shape-shift again,' she explained to the stunned group. Tears of joy ran down her cheeks as her voice cracked. 'I'm not only alive, I am si'lura!'

Fardale's eyes glowed toward her, a deep amber, and for the first time in countless winters, images flowed into Mycelle's mind, the spirit talk of her people: *A dead wolf, nuzzled by a mourning pack, comes back to life. The pack howls their joy.*

Joach stood at the starboard rail of the *Seaswift* as the sun rose out of the oceans in the east. He studied the western-most edge of the Archipelago as the ship sailed north along the coast. Around him, dawn transformed the distant islands from menacing black humps into towering green mountains. Mists draped the peaks, glowing a soft rose in the morning sunlight. Even from here, Joach caught the sweet scent of the islands' lush foliage carried on the sea's early breezes.

'There is much beauty here,' a stern voice said behind him.

Joach did not have to turn to know it was Moris, the tall dark-skinned Brother. 'And much danger,' Joach added sourly.

'Such is always the way of life,' the Brother mumbled. Moris stepped to the rail beside Joach. 'I've just come from your sister's bedside. She remains the same. Alive, but a prisoner to the poisons.'

Joach remained silent, fear for his sister clenching his throat. 'Why did those goblins attack her? Were they sent by the Dark Lord?'

Moris' brows bunched together with concern. 'We're not sure. Goblins are notorious for carrying a blood grudge. When your sister destroyed the clutch of rock'goblins in the ruins of the ancient school near your home, word must have spread to other of their foul ilk, even to the coastal clans of the drak'il.'

'And they've been hunting for her ever since?'

'So it would seem, but I still suspect the Black Heart's hand in this attack. It was too coordinated, too well orchestrated. Someone guides these beasts.'

Joach tightened his grip on the poi'wood staff in his left hand. 'How much longer until we reach Port Rawl?'

Moris turned to study the passing coastline, then examined the billowed sails. 'If the winds keep up, we'll reach port just before sunset.'

Joach turned to face the tall Brother. 'Will Elena hold on until then?'

Moris placed a hand on his shoulder. At first, Joach shied away from the comforting touch, but then his brave resolve crumbled and he leaned into the man's support, only a boy again. 'Elena's magick is strong,' Moris consoled him, 'and her will even stronger.'

'I can't let her die,' Joach moaned into the Brother's shoulder. 'I promised my father that I'd watch over her. And at the first sign of danger, she's almost slain at my side.'

'Do not blame yourself. By calling forth your magick, you drove off the drak'il and allowed us to escape. At least now she has a chance.'

Joach grasped at this thin straw. Perhaps Moris was correct; his black magick *had* at least helped protect his sister. That had to mean something. He pushed free of Moris' hand and stood straighter, wiping his forearm across his nose and sniffing.

'Still,' Moris continued, 'beware the lure of the staff. It is a foul talisman, and its magick seductive.'

Joach studied the length of poi'wood. Its oily touch felt slick under his fingers. Seductive? That was not a word he would use to describe it. Only the urgency of protecting his sister had forced him to call forth the staff's black arts. He ran one finger along its polished surface. But was he being totally honest? A part of him knew that it had been *fury* more than brotherly love that had fueled his attack on the murderous sea goblins.

'Be careful, boy,' Moris added. 'A weapon sometimes comes with too high a price.'

Joach remained silent, neither agreeing nor disagreeing. But in his heart, he knew that he would pay any price to keep Elena safe. He still remembered his father's earnest eyes as the large man placed the burden of Elena's safety onto his son's smaller shoulders. It had been his father's last charge to him: *Guard your sister.*

Joach would not dishonor his father's memory by failing.

Moris clapped him on the shoulder before returning to his duties. 'You and your sister are both strong willed. It's in the strength of your young hearts that I find hope.'

Joach blushed at his words and tried to stutter a thanks, but only managed an embarrassed gurgle.

Moris strode from his side and crossed toward the stern. Alone with his thoughts, Joach turned back to the oceans. Leaning over the rails, he stared into the blue waters. Dolphins occasionally followed in the bow's wake, but this morning the waters were as empty as his spirit.

'How far we've both traveled, Elena,' he mumbled to the passing seas.

It was then Joach saw a face staring back up at him from under the waves. At first, he thought it but his own reflection in the glass-clear swells. But then his throat clenched as he realized his mistake. The vision was not his own reflection, but someone rising up out of the sea, suspended in a bubble that scintillated with magicks.

Joach had opened his mouth to yell a warning when the shock of recognition stilled his tongue. He knew this man: the narrow face, the thin brown mustache under a hawkish nose, even the sneering eyes. The face had haunted his nightmares for many moons.

It was the butcher of his parents!

The smiling face rose from the waves, his lankish brown hair sliding dry from the sea, untouched by the salty spray. Beyond the man, the seas boiled with the twisting forms of hundreds of drak'il.

'So you think you've traveled far, have you, my boy?' Rockingham said with a jeer, obviously having eavesdropped on Joach's private words. 'Unfortunately, not far enough to escape me.'

Kral stalked across the length of his cramped cell, scowling through the thick iron bars at the guards. The place reeked of sour bodies, and the clink of chains echoed from other cells. Somewhere farther down the row, a prisoner was softly sobbing. Kral ignored all this, his hands itching for the hickory handle of his ax. Curse the interference of these blasted fools! He smashed his fist into the timbered wall.

'Cracking the bones in your hand will not free us,' Tol'chuk said behind him. Tol'chuk's voice was like the grinding of a granite millstone: harsh and unyielding. The other two occupants of his cell had been so silent all night that Kral had almost forgotten their presence. Sharing his cramped cell, the og're sat hunched on the straw-littered floor, arms and legs in huge shackles used to hobble draft horses, while Mogweed lay sprawled on the narrow cot, an arm over his eyes.

'But we were so close,' Kral said between clenched teeth. He let his anger show but disguised the true reason for his fury. 'Elena needs as much protection as we can muster, and now not only are we kept from her side, but her aunt is dead. If only they hadn't discovered us, we would've been gone by morning.'

'We all lost much this past night,' Tol'chuk said, his voice mournful.

Kral suddenly remembered that Mycelle, besides being Elena's foster aunt, was also the og're's mother. He had not considered how the loss of Mycelle, dead by her own hand, must affect the huge creature. He forced his features to a calmer demeanor, one of sympathy. 'I'm sorry, Tol'chuk. I was not thinking. Your mother did what she had to do to protect the child.'

'We will find a way to rejoin the others,' Tol'chuk said, still dour.

'How?'

'We must retrieve my pouch. If freed, the Heart of my people will guide me to her.'

Kral's eyes narrowed. He had forgotten the tool of the og're, a chunk of precious heartstone that bound the og're's spirit to the magick in its heart. The crystal was a vessel for the deceased spirits of Tol'chuk's people. It normally acted as a spiritual channel, carrying the deceased over to the next world. But the stone had been cursed by the land itself for an ancient atrocity committed by one of Tol'chuk's ancestors. The curse was given form in the shape of a black worm in the core of the crystal. The Bane, as it was named, trapped the spirits of the og're clans within the stone, consuming the spirits and not allowing them to ascend to the next world.

Tol'chuk had been given the duty to break his ancestor's curse. But how the og're might accomplish this was unknown. Tol'chuk had only the urging of the magick in the stone to guide him.

'And you think the crystal could guide us to where Elena hides?' Kral asked. 'Even without Mycelle's knowledge?'

Tol'chuk shifted his huge bulk farther from the bars, slightly turning his back on Kral. His iron chains clanked. 'If we can escape,' he added.

Kral turned from the others and crossed to the barred door. He pounded a fist on the bars to draw the eyes of the pair of guards at the end of the hall. 'Yo, guardsmen. I must speak to your leader.'

One of the two guards, a stout fellow with bristled black hair, broken nose, and squinted eyes, waved a hand dismissively back at Kral. 'Pipe down, or I'll use my knife to carve your tongue out.' The guard returned to whatever conversation he'd been having with his partner, a shaven-headed ruffian with a severely pocked face.

Mogweed spoke up behind Kral. 'Just what do you think you're doing?'

Kral glanced over his shoulder. The pale shape-shifter had pushed up onto his elbows and was staring at him. 'I'm trying to see if I can bully our way out of here,' the mountain man answered.

'With one of the ill'guard? Are you daft? Our best hope is that they simply forget about us.'

'Not likely. Slavers are not lax about their property.'

'Then maybe it'd be best if we let them sell us. Once we're out of this prison and away from that ill'guard creature and his cursed birds, we'll stand a better chance of escaping.'

Kral would have normally nodded at the wisdom of Mogweed's advice. But he could not risk the og're being taken from his side. Tol'chuk was now his only lead to the wit'ch. 'No, we stay together,' he said. 'Besides, we don't have the time. Er'ril will leave at the new moon if we don't show up.'

Mogweed lowered himself back to the bed and put an arm back over his tired eyes. 'Maybe that's best,' he mumbled.

Kral scowled at the shape-shifter's cowardice. He turned back to the door and banged his fist again on the frame. The iron bars rattled in their hinges. 'I have news for your leader,' he yelled back to the guards. 'Information that'll fetch more than my price on the slaver's block.'

The bristle-haired guard growled at the interruption and reached for his sheathed dagger, but the other sentry placed a hand on the fellow's elbow.

'What news?' the pock-faced guard asked, still holding back his partner.

'I'll only tell it to your leader, the man with the trained crows.'

A spurt of profanities flowed from the stout guard with the dagger. He wrestled free of the other's grip, but the other sentry persisted. Though they spoke in whispers, Kral's ears, trained by many winters of tracking in the mountains, picked out their words. 'Hold on there, Jakor. Let's hear what the bearded fool has to say. Lord Parak may pay us a nice finder's fee.'

Twisting his lips into a sneer, Jakor slammed his dagger back into its sheath. 'You're a fool, Bass. He's got nothing. Only trying to save his own skin. He probably heard that the Sect of Yuli is looking for a few new eunuchs and is trying to keep from being clipped.'

'I don't blame him,' Bass said with a snicker. 'But what do we have to lose? Let's shake him down before the branders come with their irons. Maybe he knows something we can use.'

Jakor shrugged. 'Grab a set of shackles.'

Bass obeyed, still snickering as he grabbed a pair of rusted restraints from hooks on the wall. The shackles jangled as the guards approached the door.

Jakor nodded to his partner. 'Toss 'em to him.' Bass kept his distance from the bars as he flung the set of irons toward Kral. Jakor then stepped closer to the door, throwing his chest out to show his authority. 'Put 'em on.'

Kral leaned closer to the bars. He allowed a bit of his inner black beast to shine in his narrowed eyes. Jakor's face blanched, and the guard retreated a step. Kral grinned savagely. He would love to tear this one's throat out. But instead, he shoved away from the bars and collected the shackles from the soiled hay.

'Lock 'em behind your b-back,' Jakor stuttered. He already had his short sword out. Kral suspected the guard was beginning to regret his decision to bother with this prisoner yet was unable to retreat now without losing face before his fellow sentry.

Worried that Jakor's craven heart might break, Kral complied with the guard's direction. Once done, Kral turned to face the door, waiting.

Jakor fumbled a set of keys from his belt, unlocked the door, and waved the mountain man out.

Kral offered no resistance, stepping from the cell and into the hall. Jakor's sword was pressed so firmly into Kral's ribs that a trickle of blood ran down his side.

After securing the door, Bass took the lead. 'Follow me, prisoner.'

Jakor kept his blade at Kral's back as they proceeded down the line of cells. Two other snoring men occupied the neighboring cell, and in the next, a woman with two ragged children lay huddled together on the one cot. The thin woman looked at Kral with hopeless eyes as he passed.

Then they were past the cells and entering the guard-room. It was empty, and the hearth was long cold. It seemed these two were the only guards stationed here this morning.

With the sun's rising, the garrison would most likely fill with other members of the watch. If he was to break free, it would have to be now.

Bass glanced over his shoulder. 'I just had an idea. Instead of disturbing Lord Parak, how about we chain this bastard in the inquisitor's chamber? The room's always empty this early. That old sot never arrives until the sun is fully up.'

Jakor laughed but could not fully mask the nervous strain. 'Fine idea, Bass. It'll give us a chance to get this fellow's tongue wagging.'

Kral scowled. So the guards thought to torture the secret out of him. In Port Rawl, opportunity was carved by those with the quickest steel and the shrewdest cunning.

Kral allowed himself to be goaded at swordpoint into a neighboring warren of halls. The metallic stink of dried blood and a fetid reek of decay filled the passages. Stone cells closed with iron-banded oaken doors marked the length of the passage. Kral could discern low moans and the faint clink of chains from inside the sealed cells. Here, terror and torture were the coin of the inquisitor, paid out handsomely to buy the secrets from the prisoners here.

At the end of the hall, a windowless chamber opened. No doors closed off this room; the screams of the tortured served to weaken the will of the other prisoners. In the center of the room, a large brazier lay open and cold. Branding irons hung neatly overhead, ready for flame and flesh. Along the far wall were displayed knives and other sharp tools used to strip skin from a man and bore holes in bone. A rack with neatly coiled straps of leather stood nearby, the wood of the device stained a deep black from ages of shed blood.

Kral hid a smile in his beard. He enjoyed the scent of horror and fear that permeated the stones of this room. It aroused him, made his mouth grow dry with lust.

The pock-faced guard crossed to the wall on Kral's right. Chains hung from bolts pounded deep into the blocks of stone. Bass yanked on a length of chain, clanking the links loudly. 'These will hold even a bull like you,' Bass said to Kral.

Kral fought his face back to a neutral disposition, hiding how the room excited the black magicks in his blood. 'No knife will free my tongue.'

Jakor dug the point of his sword into Kral's side. 'If you don't talk, then my knife will free your tongue – permanently. I have a dog at home who likes it when I bring home scraps.'

Kral allowed himself to be herded toward the length of chain. He did not fear the tortures that these two might inflict. Deep in his mind, he remembered writhing under the searing flames of darkfire as his master granted him the gift of Legion in the cellars below the Keep of Shadowbrook. Neither the sharpest blade nor the hottest flame could compare to the agony of his spirit being forged into a tool of the Black Heart.

Kral leaned against the cool rock as the pair of guards locked his ankles and wrists to the new chains, then removed the old shackles. Jakor stepped away from the mountain man, the guard's shoulders visibly relaxing, clearly relieved to have the prisoner secured in links of forged iron.

Bass crossed to a winch and worked its handle round and round. The chains at Kral's feet and hands pulled and stretched his form across the stone, his wrists pulled so high that the toes of his scuffed boots only brushed the grate on the floor. Kral glanced down the black throat of the well at his feet. How many tortured spirits had bled down this very hole? A thrill passed over his skin, prickling his hairs. But now was not the time to dwell on such pleasant thoughts.

He raised his eyes toward the two guards. The sun must be fully up by now, and he was done playing with these two fools.

Jakor made the mistake of looking into Kral's eyes at this moment and must have sensed his own death, like a deer being run down by a wolf. Jakor's mouth opened as if to warn his partner. But what could he say?

Kral let his eyes drift closed as he bit his lower lip to draw blood. Its sweet tang burst on his tongue like the finest Arturan wine. He reached out to the ebon'stone that bound him. Attuned to his rock magick, Kral could smell the iron ore of his ax. He knew where it lay hidden, stashed in a nearby storeroom, in among the bounty collected by the watch this past night. He sensed the wolf hide that covered its stained blade. No one had bothered to unsheathe so common a weapon.

Now, well away from the eyes of his companions, Kral had no need to fear unmasking his secret. He spoke the words needed to call forth his magick. With a bloody tongue, he spoke the spell.

Bass must have heard him. 'What's that he's saying?'

Jakor's boot heels scraped, backing away. 'I don't like this.'

Kral smiled. No, the man would not *like* it at all. Kral's blood burned with the spell, his flesh melting in the flames, his bones bowing and stretching like heated iron.

'Mother above!' Bass screamed.

Kral fell from his shackles onto all fours, hands clubbing into paws, nails sharpening into claws. Fur sprouted thickly from his pores as his beard drew back into his cheeks and his jaw stretched open in a silent howl.

The guards were already fleeing.

Kral loped after them, his sense of smell guiding him more than his eyes now. Tangles of clothes slowed his pursuit until he used his teeth to rip loose the leathers and wools. As he ran, the transformation still continued. The muscles of his legs bunched and found new attachments on bone. His throat contracted, his larynx warped. He opened his muzzle and spoke with his new voice, announcing the hunt.

The demon wolf's howl chased the guards down the hall.

Once again he was Legion.

The beast eyed its prey as the pair sped down the passage. It could smell the blood, hear the panicked beat of the two men's hearts. A thick tongue tested its fangs, sharp and aching to rip into flesh.

Then the wolf was upon the first of its prey, the pock-faced guard. The beast ran at the man's heels, and with a slash and a growl, it tore out the man's hamstrings. The guard howled in pain and shock, tumbling to the hard stone. Bone cracked as he fell. Still Legion did not stop. It let the man writhe and moan, leaping over the fallen prey and pursuing the other. The beast knew its master's will. No word of warning must leave these halls, for Legion still had a greater quarry to flush from this place: a creature who shared his black magick, another ill'guard, but one who stood between Legion and the trail of his final prey, the wit'ch child Elena.

The guard turned at the last moment, threatening with steel. But Legion in his wolf form feared nothing made of folds of metal. It leaped and impaled itself on the short blade. The man stumbled to the side, lunging away with his bloodied blade, a look of triumph and satisfaction on his face.

Legion ignored the savage wound as the magick repaired the rent tissues. Twisting, Legion burst toward the man's throat. Terror swelled in the prey's eyes. Legion's lips rose up in a wolfish smile, exposing a length of fangs. Then it was upon the man. Hot blood spurted and filled the demon's hungry throat. A low cry escaped the guard as he died, thrashing weakly under the wolf's bulk. The lust to rip open the man's belly and feast on the tender organs inside had to be fought aside. Legion spun on a paw and returned to the other wounded prey.

'No, please Mother, no!' The pock-faced guard raised an arm across his face and screamed. Legion tore away the arm with one huge bite. Nothing would stand between it and the throat of its prey. The man's scream of pain and terror echoed up and down the passage. Legion did not worry as it ripped into the man's face. Here in the chambers of skinning knives and burning flesh, wailing was a common song.

As life fled the warm body, Legion pounced away. It bounded down the last of the passage and pawed open the latch to the door. Cautiously, it stalked into the empty guardroom, nose raised to the air. From somewhere distant, it caught the spoor of crow and black magicks.

It followed the scent.

The demon wolf was a flowing black shadow as it raced down the dim halls. Occasional lamps, set to a low flame, marked the passages, but otherwise the darkness was a cloak that Legion wore as it ran down the scent. Stairs flashed under its paws; it slinked past an open chamber where the clanking of pots and shouted orders revealed that the morning's meal was well under way. It ignored the tantalizing scents. If it was to escape with the og're and the shapeshifter, it could not have this craven ill'guard at its back. Besides, Legion remembered the paralyzing touch of the ravens' beaks, and revenge honed the edges of its lusts.

In only a short time, the demon wolf wound its way

through the garrison to the northeast corner. It sniffed at the bottom of the door. Spoor of bird. It had reached its prey. Ears pricked up at the faint sounds of snoring.

Legion tested the latch with a paw. Locked. In Port Rawl, no one slept behind an unbarred door, not even in the heart of the town's garrison.

Raising up on its paws, Legion unleashed a howl that shook the very stones of the structure and dug at the hardwood door. From beyond the door, Legion heard its prey awaken with a startled snort. Further in the garrison, men awoke in cold sweats. The blackness of the deep forest had crept into their rooms.

The ill'guard beyond the door would recognize his master's voice in this howl – and could not refuse to answer it. Legion heard the approach of bare feet on stone. The door peeked open. One eye, then another, peered out.

Legion did not wait for an invitation. It burst through the door, throwing Lord Parak back on his scrawny bottom. Ravens and crows, perched all along the room, burst up in a black cloud of feathers and screeches.

Before the ill'guard lord could react, Legion's teeth were at his throat. Finally, Lord Parak seemed to recognize his kindred spirit. 'No,' the man moaned, 'we serve the same master.'

As answer, a hungry growl escaped the demon wolf's throat. Then, with a howl that ripped through the halls of the garrison, Legion ripped out the throat of Lord Parak. For the first time, it feasted on the black blood of another ill'guard. As the blood flowed down its throat, so did the magick of its prey. Legion had thought its blood lust could know no greater depth than during a hunt – but it was mistaken! The magick it consumed as teeth rended flesh and tendon made even a virgin's blood seem but a pale drink.

The arcane power flowed into Legion. It raised its muzzle from the ruined throat and wailed its lust from strong lungs.

Fire and pleasure ravaged Legion.

The wolf's limbs quaked under the onslaught as its blood absorbed the other's magick. Mirroring this inner transformation, the cloud of ravens and crows descended upon the demon wolf. But instead of landing on Legion's back, the flock dove into the flesh of the wolf, disappearing like hunting seabirds into the watery depths. And Legion knew this to be right. Just as its blood had absorbed the ill'guard's magick, its flesh now consumed the other's demons.

Legion howled a cry of power and hunger as its magick grew.

It now had an inkling of what it would be like to feast on the wit'ch, to absorb her magick, too. With this thought, it bounded away and out into the halls. Nothing would stop it from tasting such an experience.

As it sped, all who heard its howl fell numb to the floor. The paralyzing magick of the other ill'guard was now Legion's to employ. With such power, it was a simple thing to reach the storeroom and retrieve its master's talisman. Bloody teeth ripped the wolfhide from the ax's blade and ended the spell. Its body flowed and twisted back into the naked form of a man.

Standing on bare feet on the cold stone, Kral grabbed one of the guard's gold-and-black uniforms hanging in the storeroom. It fit poorly on his huge frame, but a cloak over his shoulders hid the worst of it. Among the pile of collected items were his companions' bags, waiting to be searched with the morning light. Barefoot, Kral tossed the bags over one shoulder, then secured the ax to his belt. Satisfied, he fled the room.

Chaos ruled the halls of the garrison. Like an overturned

anthill, men charged this way and that. One guard ran up to him. 'Grab a sword! There's a pack of wolves loose here!' Then the armsman was gone.

Kral marched through the roiling confusion.

He reached the hall of cells holding his imprisoned companions. Luckily, no guards had come to replace the two he had slain. He grabbed a key ring from a hook and crossed to the barred door.

Both Mogweed and Tol'chuk were at the entrance, roused by the commotion. Mogweed's eyes grew wide when he recognized the huge guard crossing toward them. 'Kral!'

The mountain man keyed the rusted lock and pulled open the door, freeing Tol'chuk of his shackles.

The og're lumbered out of the cell. 'How did you –?'

'Now's not the time for tales,' Kral said simply. 'Come, while the way still lies open.' Kral passed Tol'chuk his thigh pouch and Mogweed his cumbersome pack.

The og're clawed open his satchel and, after delving deep inside, retrieved the chunk of heartstone hidden in an inner pocket. Tol'chuk pulled it free. 'It's still here.'

'Luck is with us,' Kral said. He nodded toward the ruby crystal. 'Are you sure that can lead us back to Elena?'

Tol'chuk raised the stone. Its faceted surface bloomed a deep inner rose. Tol'chuk swung it slightly eastward; the stone flashed like a small ruby sun. 'Yes,' the og're said, pointing the way. 'The Heart will guide us to her.'

Kral smiled, still tasting blood and magick in his throat. 'Good. Then let the hunt begin.'

6

Joach flew back from the ship's rail, scrambling to raise his staff. He screamed for aid, his voice a howl on the morning breeze. 'Moris! Flint! We're under attack!'

From beyond the boat's edge, laughter answered his call. 'Protecting your sister again, I see.' The smiling apparition rose from the sea, gliding smoothly atop a tower of solid water. Once high enough, the figure of Rockingham, the butcher and foul traitor, stepped over the rail and onto the deck. He wore a pair of brown leggings and a billowing linen shirt, open across the front. Down his pale chest, a jagged black scar could be seen in snatches as the wind tugged at his unbuttoned shirt.

Already, Moris was rushing to the boy's side from the rear deck. He bore a long sword in one hand and a cudgel in the other. Behind the black-skinned Brother, near the stern, Flint was tying off the wheel, readying the ship for the battle to come. The scrabbling of claws could be heard climbing the sides of the boat, accompanied by hundreds of hissing goblin throats. The beasts were about to swarm the ship.

Joach stared into Rockingham's eyes. He sensed that this was the hand that led the legions of drak'il, the fist that sought to destroy his sister. He raised the staff higher before him.

Rockingham eyed the length of poi'wood, his brows momentarily crinkling in confusion. 'Isn't that Dismarum's cane?'

'You mean your old master's staff? Yes, I defeated him, wresting the weapon from his dead fingers,' Joach said boldly, hoping his lie would worry the fiend, buy extra moments for the others to arm themselves. 'And now I'll defeat you.' Joach whispered words of power to his staff, the spell dredged from the lands of dream. The staff's polished surface ignited with black flames.

Moris skidded to a halt beside Joach, adding his sword to the flaming defense of the *Seaswift*.

Rockingham ignored their threatening stances and greeted Moris with a calm nod. Beyond the demon, goblins clambered over the ship's rail, hissing and thrashing, clearly waiting for a signal from their leader. Rockingham turned his attention back to Joach. 'That old darkmage – Dismarum, Greshym, or whatever you want to call him – was never my master. Let me show you my true lord.'

Rockingham reached to his shirtfront just as Flint ran forward from the stern. 'Don't look!' the old seaman hollered across the deck.

But the warning came too late. Rockingham pulled back the drapes of his shirt to expose the ragged scar that split the center of his pale chest. As Joach stared, the wound opened like the mouth of a shark, lined by shards of broken ribs. From inside, an oily darkness flowed out of the man's chest, living tendrils of shadow. The stench of an open crypt followed.

'Here is my true master.'

Behind this monster, the goblins had grown in number;

claws dug at the deck, and spiked tails rattled like old bones. Still, the beasts held their wary ground, awed and fearful of the black magick.

'Beware,' Moris growled to Joach. 'The man's a golem. A hollow seed. It is only black magick that sustains his flesh.'

Joach, his breath frozen in horror, coughed on the words of his spell. The black flames died on his staff. He now clutched only mere wood, little protection against the evil that pulsed from the core of Rockingham.

From up out of the depths of the open chest, howls of twisted spirits echoed forth, and from deeper still came the cold laughter of the torturer.

'I was left moldering in the grave after the battle with the skal'tum in the highlands above Winterfell,' Rockingham said. 'Left for dead. Until servants of the Black Heart clawed me from the cold dirt and gave me back my life.'

'It is not your life that was returned,' Moris argued, his voice booming. 'It is a foul spirit that possesses you, hides the truth from you, and smothers your true spirit. Remember who you once were!'

Joach saw Rockingham's left eye twitch slightly with Moris' words. 'Remember what? Who do you think I was?'

By now, Flint had reached them. Bearing an ax, he stood as a third against their enemy. The old sea-hardened Brother added his own words. 'We know your ilk. Long ago, before the Dark Lord claimed you, you were a suicide. Only from such sorry souls are golems forged. When you forsook your own life, you gave up the right to your body.'

Moris lowered his blade slightly, his manner urgent and consoling. 'And the Dark Lord claimed what you discarded and enslaved it. But remember that other life! Remember the pain that drove you to such black depths that you would end your own life. Even the most dire magicks can't wipe away so sharp a memory. Look to your waking dreams. *Remember!*'

Joach studied his adversary. He saw the man glancing inward, suspicious but searching for any truth in these two Brothers' words. Joach scowled at him. What, besides black magicks, could be found inside this fiend? But something was found – Joach could see it in the man's face, muscles twitching as a war waged to dredge up a forgotten past.

Words tumbled from Rockingham's lips. 'I remember . . . a dream . . . a cliff with pounding surf . . . someone . . . hair the color of the sun at noon . . . and lilacs . . . no, the scent of honeysuckle, or something much like it . . .' His eyes grew suddenly wide, staring blind at the horizon. Fingers that held open his shirt lost their hold on the fabric. Even the wound began to close on the darkness. 'And a name . . . *Linora!*'

A harsh voice suddenly rose behind Joach, startling everyone. 'Yes, I remember that name, too, Rockingham. You screamed it out the last time we killed you. The time you betrayed us all.'

Rockingham's eyes snapped back into focus. 'Er'ril!' he hissed.

The swelling legion of goblins roared, echoing their master's anger. Behind Rockingham, the beasts hissed and thrashed, a mass of claws and poisoned tails, scrambling and piling atop one another in frustration.

'Damn his timing,' Flint muttered, glancing fire at Er'ril.

Er'ril ignored the others, his eyes only on Rockingham. He stepped forward, his sword of magickal silver held in his one arm, his face a mask of red fury. 'We helped you escape the claws of the skal'tum, and you repaid us with treachery! Whatever life you once lived – foul or fair – it is now forfeit.'

'Bold words for someone who is going to finally die after five hundred winters.' Rockingham ripped his shirt from his shoulders; his chest wound cracked wide open, a gaping maw from which darkness spilled forth.

Joach stared transfixed into the flowing shadows. Deep in the core of the golem, crimson eyes stared back out at him, filled with balefire and dread magicks.

Accompanied by the howl of goblins, the Black Heart had come to watch the slaughter.

Elena stood bathed in light. Somewhere far off she heard shouting and the cries of strange beasts, but here was an island of peace and stillness. The faint tinkle of crystal chimes filled her ears and a scent not unlike spiced cloves swelled around her. Where was she? She had a hard time remembering how or why she stood here. She took a step cautiously forward. 'Hello!' she called out into the brightness. 'Is anyone there?'

Before her, a figure appeared; a woman draped in swirls of light coalesced into existence. 'Mycelle should have taught you better to watch your back,' the figure scolded. The features of the woman solidified into a familiar stern expression.

'Aunt Fila?' Elena rushed forward, meaning to sweep her dead aunt up in her arms. But when she reached the apparition, her arms passed through her. Dismayed, Elena stepped back.

Aunt Fila raised a shimmering hand and brushed it along Elena's cheek. Only a soft warmth marked the passage of the ghostly fingers. 'You should not be here, child.'

Elena glanced around her. In the past, through the use of a magickal amulet, Elena had occasionally been able to speak to the shade of her dead aunt. But what was happening now? Around her, the featureless world of blinding light eddied, revealing vague glimpses into other lands and swirling images of other people. Snatches of conversation from far off whispered in her ears. 'Where am I?' she finally asked.

'You've crossed the Bridge of Spirits, child. The goblin's poisons drain your life. With death so near, your spirit can flow between the worlds of the living and the dead.'

'Am I going to die?'

Aunt Fila was never one to pamper with falsehoods. 'Perhaps.'

Tears rose in Elena's eyes, blurring her vision. 'But I have to save Alasea.' She raised her palms to show Aunt Fila the twin ruby stains of power. But her hands were pale and white. Her power had vanished!

'You've spent all your magick sustaining your life,' Aunt Fila explained. 'But fear not, child. Even here you can renew. Any light, even ghostly, can ignite the magick in you. Remember your ancestor Sisa'kofa – there was a true reason she was named the wit'ch of *spirit* and stone. But you must hurry.' Aunt Fila again brushed Elena's cheek with her fingers, but this time, Elena actually felt her aunt's hand. 'With your magick spent, death grows closer, and we grow closer together.'

Elena stepped away, horrified.

'You must renew, Elena. Hurry.'

As Elena raised her right arm high, she prayed for the gift, wishing with all her spirit. Before her, Aunt Fila's face began to grow clearer; small details Elena had forgotten – the small dimple on her aunt's chin, the fine wrinkles at the corners of her eyes – began to appear. Time was running out.

Elena stretched her arm fully up. Her hand vanished in a cool rush.

'Hurry, child! From this light, a new magick will be born into the world. Sunlight brought you fire; moonlight brought you ice. Ghostlight will bring you—'

Elena lowered her arm; the spirit world vanished around her. She crashed back into a world filled with bloody screams and the cries of the dying. Raising her arm from where it rested on a blanket, she stared at her hand.

Her eyes grew wide with horror. Her own scream drowned out all the others: '*No!*'

Meric hobbled on his crutch across the empty storeroom. The others had all left to prepare their packs and mounts for the journey out of Port Rawl. His injuries, though healing, had left him of little use to the others as they hauled and packed various supplies from Mama Freda's apothecary. Alone in the storeroom, he crossed to the bank of cages that housed the assortment of creatures the old healer used in her arts.

Quickly, he opened the cage that housed a trillhawk. The bird's bright green plumage marked it as a jungle bird, from lands far away, but Meric intended to send it even farther. The bird spread its wings threateningly and hissed at him as he reached toward it. But Meric sent a wisp of his elemental magick to twine around the wild creature. Reined by his magicks, the hawk calmed and mounted his offered wrist.

With the bird in hand, Meric limped toward the small open window of the storeroom. He held the hawk up toward the window. As the bird perched, Meric worked his elemental magick on it. The elv'in were masters of the air and all creatures of the wing. None could refuse the call of an elv'in lord. The trillhawk cocked its head, listening as Meric instructed it.

Mycelle had related to Meric all that had befallen Elena and the others: the swamp journey, the battle with the blackguard d'warf, the downfall of A'loa Glen. It was clear the Dark Lord had dug his forces deeply into the sunken city, and any attempt to reach the Blood Diary would surely fail. How could the others even think of taking Elena into such danger?

Meric knew his duty. He would protect the girl, even if it meant the death of Alasea. Of what concern was it to his people if this land should fall? His people had long been banished. All that mattered was the mission his queen had sent him on – to return the king's lost bloodline to his people.

In this, he would not fail.

'Go,' he whispered to the hawk. 'Go to Stormhaven. Seek my queen. Let her know that time runs short. She must free her Thunderclouds and let loose her ships of war.'

He tossed the hawk up through the window. With a screeching cry, it sailed on wide wings out into the sea breezes. Turning on a wing tip, it arced over the slate rooftops of Port Rawl and disappeared into the sun.

Meric followed its flight with his sky-blue eyes, his final words no more than an expelled breath. 'We must stop Elena.'

With a rock-heavy heart, Tol'chuk followed the others through the streets of Port Rawl as the morning sun climbed toward midday.

He had spent the entire night grieving for his mother. Like a candle, she had come so briefly to enlighten his empty life, only to be snuffed away before he could appreciate the warmth and true glow of family. But now was not the time for regret and melancholy. He hardened himself against the hollowness in his spirit and continued on the course set upon him by the ancients of his people. And the next step in his sworn duty was to escape this foul city. He'd had enough of its stink and the wretched souls that slinked through its oily shadows.

Cloaked in the black-and-gold colors of the city's watch, the og're hunkered down to disguise his size and keep his face hidden as he traversed the streets. But in such a corrupt city, Tol'chuk doubted that even the monstrous presence of a highland og're would warrant more of a reaction than a cautious appraisal of the price for his skinned hide.

Kral led the party, keeping his ax well displayed. Mogweed clung to Tol'chuk's shadow like a mouse beside a bull. After a bit, Kral stopped at an intersection of two narrow streets and glared in all directions. The roads here were wagon-rutted mud tracks, thick with horse dung and refuse from the houses to either side. Overhead, a few sullen women leaned on elbows out of second-story windows.

One of the women spat at Kral. Her aim was good. He wiped his cheek with the edge of his cloak. 'Get your arses away from here,' she said boldly. 'We don't need no watch breathing down our backs. We paid our tithes this past moon. So be gone from our stoop.'

Tol'chuk pulled his cloak farther over his head. The watch, it seemed, was poorly thought of by its people.

Kral ignored the commotion, glancing back to Tol'chuk. 'I don't think we're far from the southern gate.' But doubt weakened his voice.

Mogweed crept warily forward, his eyes constantly darting toward the openings to dark alleys and the women above. 'What about my brother?' he asked. 'Fardale must be still with the horses.'

'I know,' Kral said. 'My own mount, Rorshaf, is stabled

at the same inn. But the garrison is already in a fierce uproar. We were lucky to escape in the chaos. It won't take long for someone to order the city's gates locked down and a search for the escaped slaves to begin. We must be gone before that happens.'

'But Fardale . . . ?'

'He's a wolf. At night, it'll be a simple thing for him to escape on his own. He knows where Elena hides and can easily return to her side. For all we know, he may already have run off after we were captured.'

Tol'chuk placed a clawed hand on Mogweed's shoulders. 'I know you fear for your brother, but Kral be right. A wolf alone will attract less attention.'

Mogweed slipped from under Tol'chuk's grip with a sour grumble and simply waved Kral onward, but the mountain man had already turned back to the road. He stood, scratching his head, clearly unsure which crossroad to take.

Just then, a bent-backed old crone using a crooked cane angled around the corner, almost running flat into Kral's wide chest. She backed a step, wiping a few stray gray hairs to glance surreptitiously at what blocked her way forward.

Scowling, she waved her cane in Kral's general direction. 'Get outta my way, you big oaf.'

Kral stood his ground against the meager threat. 'Grandmother,' he said politely, 'I would gladly step aside if you'd be so kind as to point us toward the southern gate.'

'Leaving the city, are you?' She cocked her head like a warybird, eying Tol'chuk, then Mogweed. She swung toward the left and shambled in that direction. 'I know a shortcut. I'll show you, but on the condition that you large gentlemen keep me company. I've a daughter and son-in-law who live out that way and was meaning to visit them anyways.'

Kral studied her slow-moving form. 'Really, we just need the directions. If you could—'

Tol'chuk nudged the mountain man's elbow. 'Traveling with the old woman will give us some camouflage,' he whispered. 'They won't be looking for an old woman and her guards.'

Kral sighed, puffing out his beard, but followed after the woman's bent back. She doddered slowly down the street. 'Maybe you could carry her,' the mountain man mumbled through his beard at Tol'chuk.

'I heard that!' the old woman cackled without looking back. 'Just 'cause my eyes are thick with the cataract, don't think my ears aren't keen. And my two old legs have lasted near on to a century. They'll get me to the gates.'

The group drudged onward, keeping company with the thin-boned old crone, who whistled as she marched through the backstreets, grinning back at them occasionally with a mouth barren of all but a few teeth.

Tol'chuk eyed the woman. He suspected she little needed their strength of arms; as old and worn as she was, even the most cunning pirate in the city would have a hard time finding any value in her frail figure. He supposed she just enjoyed their company, someone to chatter with and nod at as if they were all old friends.

'If you like candied swampweed and kaffee,' she commented to Mogweed as he shambled next to her, 'there's a shop not far from here. We could stop for a rest.'

'No, thank you,' Mogweed said.

'We really must reach the gates,' Kral added, his impatience beginning to show on his stony features.

'Oh, it's not far, not far at all,' she mumbled. She turned another corner into a further maze of narrow streets, still whistling.

Here the shabby homes were stacked high and close together. To add to the sense of confinement, the foundations of the surrounding buildings were so rotted by age and salt that some of the homes leaned forward as if studying them as they passed, while others rested against neighboring structures like drunken men wandering home. Kral grumbled.

By now, the old woman had so entangled them among these ramshackle homes that Tol'chuk guessed the mountain man was as thoroughly lost as himself. 'Do you know the way to the gate from here?' he whispered hoarsely to Kral.

'I could find my way out of here ... eventually.' The mountain man kept a wary watch on doorways and side streets, expecting an ambush at any moment.

Soon the sun glared down from directly overhead, and the morning's cool breezes died away. Yet the group's path still lay entangled in the labyrinth of backstreets. Kral kept clutching at his ax, first with one hand, then the other. The heat of the afternoon reminded them all that summer still reigned here in the filth and stench of Port Rawl's alleys. The reek of spoiled fish competed with the stench of human waste, as if countless winters had passed since a breath of clean air had freshened these streets.

'Enough!' Kral finally barked, stopping them all.

The old woman leaned heavily on her cane as she swung around. 'What?' she said irritably.

'I thought you said you knew a shortcut to the gate?'

The crone sighed loudly. 'If you want to avoid the eyes of the watchmen, this is the shortest route.'

Tol'chuk's scraggled brows rose higher up his forehead. This woman knew more than she let on.

She continued before anyone could say a word. 'You come

prancing in ill-fitting garb of the watch, yet don't know the route to the city's gate? Do you think me a fool? I heard about the commotion at the garrison, and I suspect you're all involved in that mess.'

'Old woman,' Kral said, the kindliness gone from his voice, 'if you seek to betray us—'

'Betray you? If it wasn't for me, you all would've been recaptured by the watch by now. The town is riddled with those who would've sold you back to them cutpurses for a single dull copper. And what do I get as payment for my troubles?' She scowled at them all. 'A rude tongue and threats.'

Tol'chuk stepped forward. 'Excuse us. We be indebted to you and mean you no disrespect. But it be urgent we leave this city.'

She snorted at his words and swung around. 'Then come,' she said and sidled around the next corner.

They all followed her. As Tol'chuk rounded the dilapidated building that housed a cobbler's shop, he stumbled in shock. The towering Swampwall lay only a stone's throw away, and its gate lay open.

'We're here,' Kral said, amazed.

The old woman kept urging them on with a wave of her hand as she hobbled onward. 'If you mean to escape, quit gawking and get walking.'

They continued after her. The old woman seemed to sense their growing urgency as their goal was in sight. Though Tol'chuk was stepping quickly to close the gap to the gate, with Kral and Mogweed marching briskly beside him, the crone kept well ahead of them.

She was the first to reach the gate and nod to the gatekeeper atop the wall's walk. The sandy-haired lad who manned the gate's wheel barely paid her any attention, his eyes toward the center of town. 'Have you heard any word?'

he asked as Kral approached, his young eager eyes full of excitement. 'What's happened at the garrison?'

Dressed in the black and the gold, Tol'chuk realized the gatekeeper must think them fellow watchmen. Kral answered the youth. 'That's none of your concern. Keep your eyes on your duty.'

A deep-throated horn suddenly echoed up from town, its mournful tones resounding eerily off the nearby bay. Three long notes stretched over the city's shingled roofs. 'Them's the signal to lock down the city,' the young man said with amazement. He turned excited eyes to the trio. 'Do you think it's another of those cursed boats come to plague the docks?'

Kral spat a curse at the boy. 'Just mind your own post. We're to check the lay of the land south of here. You just lock those gates after us and let no one – and I mean *no one* – past your post.'

'Yes, sir!' The lad saluted smartly and went to his gate's wheel.

Tol'chuk kept his cloak drawn fully over his form as he passed under the walk and through the tunnel in the wall. The others were at his heels. Beyond the gate, the old woman still waited for them, leaning on her cane. Tol'chuk scrunched up his features and came closer. 'Should you not be getting back into the city before you're locked out?'

Behind him, Tol'chuk already heard the winches and pulleys lowering the iron gate to the city.

The old woman shrugged and hobbled away from him, aiming toward the line of coastal woods in the near distance. Tol'chuk found himself following her as he had done all morning.

Kral joined him. 'Just where in the Sweet Mother does that old crone think she's going?'

As they chased after her, the woman's pace increased. Near the edge of the wood, she tossed aside her cane; her back seemed to straighten with each step. She seemed to grow taller, broader in shoulder, as if the years had melted off her crooked figure and returned her lost youth.

'I don't like this,' Mogweed muttered, fear bright in his eyes.

Once under the eaves of the trees, the old woman turned toward them, now standing tall and straight. She tossed back her drab shawl and shook out lengths of hair that shone the color of spun gold in the patches of sunlight. Other figures moved in the shadows of the wood behind her. Near her heels, a large dog – no, a wolf – climbed around the bole of a thick cypress and sat on his haunches by the woman's heels.

Tol'chuk stepped closer.

'It can't be,' Mogweed said, stunned.

Kral echoed his words. 'Impossible.'

Tol'chuk took another shaky step forward. Surely this was some cruel trick, a phantom come to torment him.

Standing under the green branches of the cypress was no longer the bent-backed crone but Mycelle, beaming broadly toward her son. She raised her arms toward him. Her eyes shone amber in the shadows.

Words formed in Tol'chuk's head. *Come, my son. See your true heritage.*

'Mother?' he said aloud and stumbled toward her.

Mycelle sighed, the glow in her eyes dimming. She switched back to normal speech, a smile still playing about her lips. 'Oh, just come over here, Tol'chuk, and give me a hug.'

With the sounds of battle echoing down through the ship, Elena stared at her right hand, her eyes wide with horror.

Instead of the usual deep ruby stain, her fingers and palms swirled and glowed with a soft rosy azure, but the pale hue was not what disturbed her. What clutched her heart with an icy grip was how insubstantial her hand now appeared. Instead of stained flesh, her hand was translucent. She could see through her palm to the antique sextant hanging on the far wall. It was as if her hand were that of a ghost.

'Wit'ch of spirit and stone,' she mumbled, remembering Aunt Fila's words. As ethereal as her flesh appeared, Elena sensed the magick pent up in her glassy skin. It sang and thrummed as strong as any magick born of sun or moon. But what aspect did this new magick bear?

As her heart's beating slowed slightly, the echoing screams and bloody cries reached her ears. She heard Er'ril's commanding voice shout orders, but his words were too muffled by the ship's wood to be discernible. Were they still fighting the drak'il? She reached and fingered the wrap around her belly, suddenly remembering the thrust of the goblin's spike and the burn of poison. She somehow sensed that its venoms had finally been vanquished from her body.

Elena pushed up.

Through a porthole to the side, the sun now shined brightly. Had the fight raged all night? She slipped to her feet and stood shakily, still weak from the residual effects of the venom.

She leaned on a wall and crossed to the porthole. Beyond the glass lay only the empty seas. In the far distance, she spotted a few islands dotting the horizons. They were no longer docked but were sailing through the Archipelago!

The din of battle rattled down to her.

Weak or not, she had to help. Elena stared at her ghostly hand. Not understanding this new magick, she feared touching it. But with the sun this bright, she could always renew the power of wit'ch fire in her other hand and chase the foul creatures from the ship's decks with flames.

She raised her left hand and placed it upon the coarse glass of the porthole. Sunlight streamed past her white fingers. She willed the gift of fire, praying to the Mother above for power. Her eyelids sank slightly as she opened herself to the rite of renewal.

Standing still as stone, she waited – but nothing happened.

Elena's eyes widened. Her left hand still lay on the port-hole in the glare of the sun, as pale as ever. Frowning, she concentrated. In the past, her mere desire was all that had been necessary to ignite the transformation, to fill her with power. Tears began to well. Desperation began to creep into her chest. She had never wanted to renew more than she did right now, so why wasn't it happening?

She continued to wait. Still nothing. The battle raged on overhead; the hissing grew louder in her ears. She could delay no longer.

Turning away, she lowered her arm and again studied the eddying swirls of rosy light that outlined her ghost hand. She balled her fingers into a fist. It felt like normal flesh. But if she cut herself what magick would be unleashed?

With a shake of her head, she thrust her arm away. There was only one way to find out. She crossed to the door. With a hard swallow, she swung the latch free and creaked open the old hinges. The cries of battle swelled around her like a visible presence. The reek of blood and fear struck her senses like a cold wind. She heard the mad laughter of someone from just up ahead. What was happening?

Darting into the passage, she quickly ducked through a door to the left and entered her own cabin. She crossed to her pack of personal items and snatched out her wit'ch's dagger. The silver blade shone in the splinter of sunlight lancing from this cabin's porthole. Whatever magick she bore, she would practice it upon the goblins.

Swinging around, she caught a glimpse of herself in a small looking glass hanging from a nail in the wall. She gasped and stopped. It was as if her clothes, even the dagger, floated across the room on their own. She raised the knife higher. It just floated before the mirror. No hand bore it aloft. She leaned closer to the looking glass and traced her cheek with the tip of her blade. In the mirror, the dagger just floated before empty air.

She stood straighter, touching her face and staring at her hands. To her, she seemed ordinary flesh, but her form did not reflect in the glass. It was as if she had become a true spirit. 'Wit'ch of spirit and stone,' she repeated in a whisper. Was this an aspect of her new magick? Did it grant her the ability to move unseen?

She remembered her inability to renew a moment before. It took sunlight upon her skin to ignite the power. Had the renewal failed because her flesh had become invisible to the sun?

The implications of such a gift were clear. She shed her clothes and used the dagger to free the bandages from around her waist. She stood naked now, but her bare skin no longer reflected in the looking glass. Only the dagger floated in the mirror, gripped in the ghostly fingers of her right hand.

She tightened her hold on the hilt of the blade and touched this new magick in her heart, letting it roll through her being, testing it, tasting it like a fine wine on her tongue. She let it build in her clenched fingers. Not too fast. She would not let it rule her. As the magicks swelled, the rosy light burst out from her fist, swallowing the dagger in its cold light. As Elena stared, the image of the blade slowly faded away in the mirror, consumed by her magick.

In the looking glass, the cabin now appeared empty. At her feet, her clothes lay crumpled on the floor, like the discarded shell of a newly hatched chick. Elena stepped free of the clutter.

A cold smile of the wit'ch formed on her lips. She did not fight it. She would not deny that part of her spirit. Like everyone, she had a dark side that lusted for power; hers sought to unleash the wild magick without restraints. She named this dark side *wit'ch*, and it was as much a part of her as the woman who tempered and controlled these lusts. Elena had learned that to deny the two sides of her heart – wit'ch and woman – only gave the darkness in her more power. So she let the energies in her blood sing while holding a tight rein.

As she reached toward the door to her cabin, the chorus of raw magick cried to be unleashed, screamed for her to use her ghost blade to puncture her skin and let it rip into the world.

'Not yet,' she answered their cries. It was easy to ignore their call – for a quieter voice had caught Elena's attention.

In her ears, the whisper of the wit'ch held her enthralled.

Elena listened, but only one word was heard: *ghostfire*.

7

As Er'ril crouched, his clothes and skin torn from countless claws, he studied the wall of goblins before him. His silver blade ran red with blood as he raised its tip for the hundredth time, awaiting the next assault. He and the others guarded the square of deck in front of the demolished hatch to the lower cabins. None must pass to the girl below.

'How many of these friggin' beasts are there?' Flint complained, breathing hard between clenched teeth. 'For every one we cut down, two more pile over the rail to swell their ranks.'

'Keep alert,' Er'ril grumbled back, but he was tiring, too. He now regretted not retrieving the iron ward from his bags when he had rushed to the deck from Elena's bedside. He could have used the extra strength of his phantom arm. He eyed the others, judging their exhaustion.

Flint and Moris guarded his right flank while the boy Joach proved that even black magick had its uses. His staff had spouted jets of dire energies, holding back the horde from Er'ril's other flank. Occasional wails and the reek of charred flesh had marked the boy's post.

'My staff is losing power,' Joach said, his face pale, his

voice frightened. 'I don't know how much longer I can keep the magick flowing.'

Er'ril nodded. 'Do your best. Once the magick is spent, get down below and guard over your sister.' With narrowed eyes, Er'ril kept watch on the legion before him. For the brief moment, the battle had ebbed away as the goblins regrouped, some dragging their dead and wounded brethren from underfoot and tossing them overboard. Around the boat circled hundreds of shark fins, drawn by the meat and blood.

Er'ril's chest ached, and sweat drenched his frame, slicking his grip on the sword's hilt. A glance at the others revealed they fared no better. The sun had risen close to midday, and the cool morning had warmed to a moist heat, further sapping their strength. It would not be long before the endless drak'il horde overwhelmed them. Er'ril used the back of his wrist to wipe blood from his cheek – mostly drak'il blood. But for how long? Even if they withstood the drak'il army, beyond the press of cold goblin flesh stood their true adversary.

Rockingham leaned on the mast of the mainsail. Bare chested, his gaping wound seeped black shadows, and a pair of feral crimson eyes stared back at their group from the hollow golem. Er'ril shied from that gaze; it seemed to sap his will and darken his own vision. By now, Er'ril suspected the demon's true strategy here. He wasted the lives of these drak'il. The demon did not truly expect this horde to succeed but simply used the beasts to wear the defenders down, to weaken their strength and resolve.

Er'ril stared at their true enemy. The fiery eyes seemed to be laughing at him. The demon knew Er'ril understood the situation. But what could the plainsman do? Even if the drak'il were mere fodder to erode the group's defenses, Er'ril could not stay his sword. He would slay the entire drak'il tribe to protect Elena.

The hissing among the goblins rose to a fevered pitch – a signal for their next attack. Upon the deck massed a force larger than any so far. Er'ril suspected this would be the final volley. They would stand or fall on this moment.

'Ready yourselves, men,' Er'ril commanded.

A massive goblin wielding a poisoned spike on its tail stalked out from the writhing pile. The creature bore bands of polished coral around its upper arms and a circlet of woven pearls around its crown. It also held a long spear tipped with a filed shark's tooth. Clearly, here stood one of the beasts' leaders. Its tail slashed and writhed; garbled sounds choked from its throat.

'May I introduce you to the goblin queen?' Rockingham called over the hissing of the others. 'She is explaining how you all will be meat to feed her children, and how she'll use the skull and leg bones of the wit'ch as a drum to sound her victory to all the other goblin clans.'

'At least our corpses won't be wasted,' Flint mumbled.

In a final signal to her army, the she-goblin shook her spear above her head and screamed in bloody rage.

Er'ril tensed his legs, sword poised for the assault to come.

Then the she-goblin's wail suddenly cut off, as if sliced from the air itself – which as Er'ril stared, he realized was true. The queen's neck, which had been stretched taut as she howled, now opened in a wicked gash. It appeared like a bloody smile, spilling forth her life blood.

The huge beast stood quivering, all eyes upon her, then toppled to the deck.

A hush descended over both sides. Only the cries of hungry gulls fighting for scraps disturbed the stillness. What had happened? Er'ril glanced at Joach, who shook his head. It had been no magick from his staff.

Beyond the spreading pool of black blood, the drak'il

force stood frozen, stunned by the sudden death of their queen. Even Rockingham stood straighter, his eyes crinkled with suspicion. Deep in the chest of the golem, the crimson eyes flared brighter, as if the being there disbelieved what it saw. Shadows poured thickly from the ragged wound, spilling in a growing lake around the golem's feet.

Elena stood over the corpse of the goblin queen. In her shaking hand, she clutched her dagger; its rose hilt dripped blood onto the deck as her whole body tremored.

The goblin queen had been the first creature she had ever slain by her own hand. In the past, she had destroyed foul beasts of the Dark Lord with her magick, but this battle had been different. There had been no thrust of wit'ch fire, coldfire, or stormfire – it had been simple butchery.

A moment ago, Elena had slipped past Er'ril and the others and simply walked up to the goblin queen. She had stood with her silver dagger raised, staring into the furious eyes of the beast. It took no skill, no dance of blades nor art of magick. As the goblin wailed, Elena had merely reached forward and slashed the beast's throat. Only the hot blood spraying her arm and face had marked the murder.

Elena stared now at the crumpled form of the slain creature.

As the beast garbled its last breath, one of its clawed hands clutched at its belly. Only now did Elena see a characteristic swelling there.

The goblin queen was with child!

Oh, Sweet Mother, what had she done? In one fell stroke, she had murdered both mother and innocent child. What was she becoming? Elena swung away, facing her guardians. She held out the dagger toward Er'ril, silently begging him to take it from her. But no one saw her. All their gazes were still fixed on the crumpled form of the goblin queen.

Her legs began to tremble. Her magick sang louder in her ears, drowning all else out. Shock at what she had done quickly weakened the tenuous hold she had on her magick. Taking advantage of her weakness, the wit'ch in her broke free of its shackles and swept through her blood. Elena could not resist the darkness in her spirit, her will too shaken by the murder. And deep inside, a part of her did not even want to fight it.

Elena fell to her knees in the pool of goblin's blood and opened herself to the wit'ch, letting that icy part of her spirit soothe her hot shame and guilt.

Free at last, the wit'ch rejoiced, and uncontrolled laughter burst from Elena's lips – a mixture of lust, horror, and madness. The thin line between woman and wit'ch blurred. Elena found herself rising to her feet. The wicked glee poured forth from her throat, as the life's blood had flowed from the slashed throat of the she-goblin.

Elena struggled to add as much of her own voice to this outburst as she could. She cried her horror and regret, her loss and her pain; she screamed for someone to take this all from her. But her voice was but a whisper before a gale. The delight of the wit'ch bubbled forth from her heart, singing of release and the glory of power.

Elena could not stop it.

She watched her left hand take the dagger and prepare to slice the palm that glowed a deep rosy azure. The wit'ch meant to let loose the magick pent up in her hand, to free the *ghostfire* in her blood and let it run wild over the ship.

No, Elena moaned, *that must not happen!* Hiding in her heart, Elena was not so lost to her grief and sorrow that she had forgotten the others who were still on board: Er'ril, Joach, Flint, and Moris. They would all be slain!

Elena fought against the wit'ch. The dagger trembled in her hand. But it was like fighting against a raging river. She could make no headway as she was buffeted back by the strong currents now racing in her blood. The wit'ch refused to relinquish control.

Throughout her inner battle, mad laughter flowed out from her throat. Behind the glee, no one heard Elena's cry for help.

'What's happening?' Flint asked.

'I'm not sure,' Er'ril said, keeping an eye on the goblin horde. A moment ago, he and the others had faced the beasts over the slain body of their queen, both sides clearly baffled. No one had moved; no one had dared speak.

Then, wicked laughter had suddenly erupted into the tense silence from the center of the deck – first softly, then more feverishly. It now echoed off the sails and water. The quality of the voice spoke of madness and something more – something hungry.

The drak'il horde squirmed and hissed, unsure of this strange phenomenon. A few goblins sniffed at the air. Then a handful of the beasts fled – and that was all it took. Soon the whole army retreated, writhing over one another, claws scrabbling at the deck. The splashes of fleeing drak'ils sounded from all around the boat.

Er'ril and the others kept their posts. Though the laughter raised the hairs on the plainsman's arm and tortured his ears, he knew the battle was not over. Rockingham, and the demon spirit he carried, still stood by the mast of the mainsail. Like a raging flood over a rock, the goblins fled past the golem.

Still, it was not the presence of Rockingham that kept Er'ril from moving. For just the briefest moment, he thought he had recognized a certain lilt to the disembodied voice.

'Joach, go check on your sister,' he ordered quickly.

'But—' The boy's eyes remained fixed on the fleeing goblins.

Er'ril elbowed the boy toward the damaged hatch. 'Get below!'

Joach hesitated, then dodged through the doorway, his heels flying down the wooden steps. Er'ril listened to the wicked laughter, his eyes narrowed. The maddening glee bubbled over the ship, seeming to rise from the wood itself.

'What is that?' Flint asked.

Er'ril swallowed hard but remained silent.

By now, only the goblin dead still remained atop the deck. Even the direly wounded drak'ils had dragged themselves overboard, taking their chances among the sharks rather than risk the wrath of the ghost who had slain their queen.

Amid the laughter, Elena continued to battle the wit'ch, struggling to wrest control of the wild magicks. The point of the dagger now scraped against the flesh of her palm. Elena fought savagely.

Around her, the goblins had seemed to sense the menace about to be unleashed and had fled in all directions, leaving the deck empty except for the dead.

Elena struggled harder. With the drak'ils gone, there was no need to free her magicks. The deaths of her companions would be for nothing.

Still, Elena could not stop what was about to happen. Mad laughter poured uncontrolled from her throat.

Elena searched for help – and found it in the most unlikely place.

Across the deck, standing by one of the masts, stood a figure she had barely noticed among the press of goblins.

Black magicks surrounded him like a foggy mist. With the deck now clear, she had a better view of him. At first, Elena's eyes grew wide with slow recognition; then her lids narrowed with hatred.

It could not be! Yet, there was no denying it. *Rockingham!*

A fire in Elena's belly that had long gone to ash flamed anew. He still lived! A scream of rage escaped her heart, bursting through her blood.

The laughter of the wit'ch suddenly died in her throat as the woman in her flamed up with hate and fury. Wit'ch and woman were no longer blurred – no longer fought. The twin sides of her spirit fused in the fiery forge of her rage.

Silence descended upon the deck. With the dagger still poised above her palm, Elena once again had control of her limbs, but now the coldness of the wit'ch was not something to be resisted, but embraced.

The murderer would not escape her again.

She dug the point of her dagger into her palm.

The laughter died as quickly as it had come.

Er'ril strained for any hint of the mad glee, but the ship was dead silent. Even the gulls had fled. Nothing stirred, not even the sails. The winds themselves seemed to be avoiding the ship.

The two parties – Rockingham and the wit'ch's guardians – stared at each other across the corpse-strewn deck.

Rockingham had not moved. He still stood steadfast in a spreading pool of shadows, a smirk on his face. 'Now that all that foolishness is done,' he said casually, 'maybe we can get back to the matter of the wit'ch.' Rockingham stretched his arms out wide, his eyes flaring to match the crimson glow in his chest. The golem was being possessed by its master. Its voice became ancient ice. 'Enough play. Now it's time to die.'

Through the jagged tear in its chest, shadows rolled like oily thunderclouds from some black well. But instead of thunder, the screams of tortured spirits and the howl of demons accompanied this storm front. Out of these clouds, snaking ropes of darkness spread in all directions – not toward Er'ril or the others, but toward the dozens of dead goblins strewn on the deck.

Where these tendrils of shadow touched cold skin, the corpses convulsed, as if repulsed by the black caresses. Then all across the ship's deck, goblin flesh sank to bone, the darkness sucking the very substance from the corpses. In only a few heartbeats, all that was left of the goblins were leathery skeletons, all knobbed joints and poking bone. With their flesh winnowed away, their teeth and claws seemed more prominent, shining bone-white in the sunlight.

But soon it was clear that what appeared as *illusion* was in fact *real*.

The fangs grew longer on the shadow-touched dead. Daggered claws stretched into sickles longer than a man's forearms. Soon the beasts were nothing but teeth and claws connected by leathery bone.

'Now what?' Flint asked in a hushed voice.

Moris answered, his voice deep with doom. 'I've read of these creatures. The golem creates ravers – demons of the underworld who inhabit dead flesh to hunt the living.'

'How do we fight them?' Er'ril asked.

Moris only shook his head.

The sound of footsteps behind them interrupted their words. Joach's frightened face appeared in the shadowed doorway. 'Elena . . . She's gone!' he said, his cheeks red with panic. 'I found her clothes . . . and . . . and this!' Joach held forth a handful of bloody bandages.

Er'ril took a deep breath, his fist closing tight on his sword hilt. So he had not imagined the familiar lilt in the mad laughter. 'Elena . . .'

Before them, the fanged beasts rose up on razored claws, like huge spiders of teeth and horn. They chattered at Er'ril, the noise like a jagged knife dragged up his spine. Eyes stared at him, hollow sockets that glowed a sickly yellow, as if glowing fungus filled their skulls.

But Er'ril knew the demons were the least of his worries.

'Elena,' he mumbled to the empty air, 'what have you done?'

Holding her bloody right fist clenched to her chest, Elena crouched and watched as the snaking shadows spread out from the core of Rockingham's chest. Before her, the flesh of the goblin queen had withered to leathery bones, claws and teeth sprouting like weeds in a barren field. Beyond it, others took form.

Ravers, she had heard Moris name these creatures.

The corpse of the goblin queen grew to be the largest of these foul demons, its fangs dragging on the deck. Now, with its possession complete, the raver lifted its head. Baleful yellow eyes sought the life essence of its prey. All across the deck, its foul brethren rose and scrambled to flank this huge monster. While the others chattered and hissed, the raver who inhabited the goblin queen remained as still as a cold grave.

Elena sensed that here stood the leader of this pack; the goblin *queen* had been possessed by the ravers' *king*. This largest of the demons raised its hungry eyes and stared straight at Elena.

It somehow was able to see her.

Good, Elena thought. Let the demon see who was about

to tear its spirit to shreds and feast on its energies.

Elena thrust out her fist and slowly opened it, exposing the bloody slice across the palm of her right hand. Silver flames rose from the wound, as if her blood were afire. Dancing like whirlwinds, the flames spread up her arm and over her naked skin. Elena somehow knew this fire would burn away her spell of invisibility, but she was past caring.

She heard gasps from the guardians behind her and ignored them.

The wit'ch in her smiled at the raver king, stretching Elena's lips into the wicked rictus of a naked skull.

Let demon fight demon.

Er'ril watched the fiery apparition materialize between him and the gathered raver demons. First a silvery flame, the size of a small torch, blew into existence, floating waist-high above the deck. Then from this seed of flame, the blaze billowed out in sheets and runnels, growing into a pyre of silvery fire.

'Get back,' Flint yelled, urging them all toward the hatch.

Only Er'ril refused to budge. He stood before the growing conflagration, his sword raised. Unlike Flint, Er'ril knew this was not a new manifestation of black magick, but something . . . something else.

As the others gathered behind him, the flames flared higher. Silver and azure hues writhed in the wild blaze. Then, from the heart of the inferno, a figure was born. She stepped forth from the flames naked as any squalling infant; yet this was no newborn babe, but a woman of stark beauty. And it was no cry that issued from her lips, but wild laughter.

Er'ril's skin prickled at the mad sound. It ate at his mind, worming like maggots into his skull. He retreated a step, instinct urging him to flee. But instead he tightened his grip on his sword's hilt and held his ground. He knew that what stalked from these flames was not entirely of this world, but something from the darkness between the stars. Yet, as foreign and strange as the figure seemed, Er'ril's heart recognized the woman behind the savage magick and feral laughter.

He spoke her name. 'Elena.'

The woman glanced fleetingly toward him. Flames still trickled across her naked skin as she stepped fully from the conflagration. Once free of the blaze, the fire that gave birth to the woman died away, sucked back into the void from which it came. Now only the woman remained on the deck, naked except for traceries of fire running like oil across her skin.

Er'ril found his eyes meeting her gaze. What stood before him was not Elena, at least not entirely. The contours of her body, though familiar, now seemed carved of pale moonstone, as if the figure were only a sculpture of the girl he once knew.

But what dwelt inside her now?

As their gazes locked and the wild laughter died away, Er'ril saw his answer. He gasped and stumbled back. It was as if he were staring into a maelstrom of wild energies, a storm of such ferocity that it threatened to burn the very spirit from his flesh. But that was not the worst, not what squeezed a gasp from his chest. He now spied what sat in the center of this vortex of magicks. It was no demonic intelligence that guided these colossal forces. *It was only Elena.*

'Child, what have you done?' he moaned.

'Stand back, Er'ril,' she commanded him, her words echoing with both human rage and a power as immense as the flow of tides. 'This is my fight.' She swung away to face the ravers.

'No! Leave them! This is not the way!'

She ignored him. Her flames flared higher as she faced the demons.

'What's going on?' Flint said near his ear.

Er'ril's brows darkened like thunderclouds. 'The wit'ch in Elena has broken its chains. It now runs wild in her blood.'

Joach pushed up closer, his staff still in hand. 'What does that mean?'

'It means Elena has given part of her spirit over to the wit'ch. A part of her is now a force as strong and wild as any cyclone and with as little heart.'

As if to demonstrate his words, Elena's form blew forth with silvery flames, driving away the raver pack except for the largest of its foul ilk, which still stood with its claws dug deep into the storm-hardened wood. As Elena approached, its yellow eyes did not reflect the wit'ch's flames but seemed to consume them. Finally, the monstrous raver beast raised its leathery head and screamed at the wit'ch.

Elena met its challenge with her own wild laughter.

Beyond them both, Rockingham stood with the raver demons capering about his shadowed feet. A smile of victory etched his lips. Er'ril knew why the monster smiled. Even if Elena defeated the Dark Lord's beasts, a small victory had already been achieved. A fraction of the girl's spirit had died today, not killed by the drak'il's poison but given freely to a force that did not belong to this world.

Elena was no longer fully human.

Er'ril felt ice settle around his heart. If the wit'ch ever wrested full control, all would be lost. Elena would become as dark and heartless a creature as the Black Beast himself. Er'ril raised his sword.

Moris stepped beside Er'ril. 'She balances on a thin wire,'

the dark-skinned Brother warned. 'If she does not rein in her magick soon . . .'

Er'ril only nodded, his eyes still on Rockingham's gloating smile. He suddenly understood the true ploy here. He now understood why Rockingham had been dragged out of his moldering grave and back into the world of the living. Just as the Dark Lord had used the drak'ils to wear the men down, now he used the visage of her parents' murderer to strike where Elena was most weak – at her spirit, at her heart.

The Dark Lord meant to goad Elena into a blind fury, forcing her to touch such titanic forces that she would be consumed by her own passion, leaving only a burned-out husk of a girl – someone filled with magick but no longer tempered by human emotion.

Er'ril knew what he must do. He waved the others toward him as he circled around the flaming figure of Elena. 'We must stop her from confronting the golem,' he urged.

'Why?' Joach asked. 'She's the only one with the power to destroy him.'

'No. That's just what the Black Heart wants. To Elena, Rockingham is as much an inner demon as a physical one. She risks destroying herself as much as harming him.'

Flint and Moris flanked his other side. Moris spoke. 'What do you propose we do?'

'Leave her to attack the ravers, while we deal with Rockingham.'

As if hearing his words, the pack of ravers scrambled across the deck toward Elena like moths to her silvery flames, leaving a path open to the shadow-shrouded golem.

Joach's eyes were on his sister. 'She'll be swamped by them all.'

'Good,' Er'ril said, drawing the shocked eyes of Joach

and the others. 'Let them keep her distracted from the true demon here. It's better that she die among the ravers than lose her soul to the Black Heart.'

The others had no words, too stunned by his cold statement.

By now, the scrape of their boots on the deck had drawn the attention of Rockingham, still rooted by the main mast. 'So the tiny rats think to take down the lion,' he said with venom. 'I thought you wiser than that, Er'ril.'

'Even the fiercest lion has a weak spot,' he answered and raised his sword. 'A well-placed spear thrust to its heart will still kill.'

'Ah, that might be true,' Rockingham said as he cast aside the shreds of his linen shirt, revealing fully the gaping black well in his chest. 'But, you see, I have no heart.'

Elena let the smaller demons circle her. The scrabble of their claws filled her ears, but she ignored them. Her eyes remained fixed on the largest of the beasts, the raver king. She sensed that here was the heart of the pack. Defeat it, and the rest would fall.

Sheets of flame spread in small waves from her body, flowing across the deck around her bare feet. The smaller ravers kept wary guard on these flames, scurrying forward when her magick waned, then dancing back on sharp claws when the waves of silvery flame approached.

Yet so far the king of the demons had kept its post upon the deck, claws dug deep in the hard boards. It seemed little daunted by her display of ghostfire.

One of the smaller ravers clacked its fangs in menace and made a bold move. It leaped over Elena's spreading pool of ghostfire, hurdling through the air. It dove toward her throat, razored claws stretched out like an iron bear trap.

Ignoring its threat, Elena turned away. The wit'ch would guard her back. Elena's right hand rose on its own and pointed toward the hurtling raver in a warding gesture. A spurt of magick lanced out from her palm to strike the demon, ending the raver's attack in midleap.

From the corner of an eye, Elena watched as the demon beast was consumed in ghostfire. Its flesh was burned from its spirit. All that was left was an outline of the raver etched in silver flame. Her ghostfire held the writhing spirit trapped. Then the magicks burned deeper, branding the demon spirit with her mark. Elena could hear its wail as the wit'ch took possession and bent it to her will.

No spirit could resist the burning touch of her ghostfire.

Elena smiled as the demon spirit was spat away. It struck the deck and scrambled back up, shining now like a silver ghost. The spirit, still in its beast form, turned and attacked a neighboring raver. It dove atop its unsuspecting prey and latched onto its new mount. Then slowly it sank into the heart of the demon, disappearing inside it. Assaulted, the raver writhed in silent agony, claws skittering on the deck. Its neck arched back, and a horrendous scream tore from its throat, casting the invading spirit out through its black gullet. The silver spirit rolled across the deck, and with a shake, stretched back onto its ghostly claws unharmed.

The other raver had not fared as well. It quaked and quivered on its claws. The moldy glow in its yellow eyes flared to silver. Then, from its shell of leathery flesh, its own spirit sprang forth, crackling with ghostfire. Behind it, the vacant body collapsed into a ruin of hollow bone and sagging flesh. Abandoning its old roost, the new ghost stalked across the deck to join its twin. Then the pair of demon spirits continued their attack on the other ravers, spreading her touch of ghostfire like flames in dry grass.

Soon a ghost army grew around her as the wit'ch fed them more of her magick.

Elena paid them no heed. She knew that this was only the opening volley in the battle to come; the main fight beckoned. The raver king waited across the deck for her, drooling black blood. Her assault upon the other demons had not fazed it. It just stared at her.

Elena suspected the raver king would not be so easily swayed by her ghostfire. Here was a creature forged in the deepest pits of the netherworld. Fires of molten rock were its home, and the other ravers were mere pawns. To defeat this beast would require more than just the raw power of a wit'ch. The raver king was a cunning demon, and it would require both a wit'ch's strength and Elena's wisdom to carve a victory here.

Suddenly one lone raver scrambled between her and its king. Its claws danced in terror as it was set upon by her ghost pack and brought down like a frightened rabbit under hungry hounds. Then, in a moment, its spirit, too, joined her army.

Now no other ravers were left aboard the *Seaswift* – except for their king.

Satisfied, Elena reined back her magick, gathering it from the decks like the fiery hems of a long robe. For the battle ahead, she would need all her remaining power. Already her right hand had lost much of its rosy hue. She could waste no more.

Before her, one of her ghost soldiers approached its king. The others followed. It was as if the spirits sensed the last of their quarry. In a burst of silver ghostfire, the army lunged at their king, meaning to rip its spirit free.

But the king stood its ground. It rose on its clawed limbs among the horde, a black stone in a maelstrom of silver spirits. Finally, the king opened his fanged maw and attacked the others, slashing and hacking with razored teeth. Just as its eyes had spotted Elena when she was invisible, now its fangs found purchase where none should be found. Its teeth ripped and tore her ghost army to flaming shreds. A black tongue snaked from its throat and consumed the scraps of spirit, lapping like a hungry cat.

As it fed, the beast grew, using Elena's own magick to swell its size. Legs, jointed and armored like a spider, spread under it. Fangs grew to the length of an outstretched arm. Its eyes sank deep under thickening brows, while horns of glistening spikes sprouted over its leathered skin.

Elena did not wait. Thrusting out her arm, she lanced out with her magick. Silver flames arced across the deck to hit the demon. She pumped all her magick toward the beast.

For the first time, the raver king howled as raw ghost-fire enveloped it. It fought her hold, scrabbling across the deck toward her, meaning to snuff out the source of the searing flames.

Elena danced back from it, her arm still outstretched. 'Begone, demon,' she screamed as her blood sang with the release of her energies. 'I send you back from whence you came!'

Unfortunately, the raver king did not obey. Where the smaller ravers had succumbed quickly, the demon king fought on.

From somewhere beyond the pyre of ghostfire, a cry reached her. 'El, hang on! I'll help you!'

Her right eyebrow crinkled. It took her half a heartbeat to recognize Joach's voice. Finally, she noticed Er'ril and the others gathered across the deck, swords raised toward Rockingham. She spotted Joach's boyish form, armed only with his staff, dashing across the planks toward her — toward the flaming figure of the raver king.

'Joach! No!' Elena fought against the hold of the wit'ch. That cold part of her spirit wished only for the battle between demons to continue. It cared nothing for a sister's love for a brother: Such emotions had no role in the dance of magicks. Still, as the wit'ch cast her magicks at the struggling demon lord, draining the wild energies from her blood, Elena found the wit'ch's call less seductive. She found herself able to think more clearly.

Elena remembered her earlier awareness — that to defeat the raver king would require more than just raw power. A moment ago, she had lashed out without thinking, but little had been gained from such rash action. She had wounded the beast, nothing more.

With her magick waning, Elena wrested control from the wit'ch. Quickly she stanched the flow of ghostfire, drawing the last of her magick back to herself before it was foolishly spent.

Before her, the raver king still burned with the touch of her flames, but her ghostfire would not last much longer. She had only a moment. She glanced to her pale hand. What could she do? This demon spirit seemed immune to what little of her magick there was left.

'Stand back, El!' Joach called back from the far side of the writhing demon. He bore his staff over his head as if he meant to club the beast with the stout wood.

Elena stared at her brother's weapon. A seed of an idea bloomed in her mind. *Where magick fails* . . . She suddenly remembered Aunt Mycelle's lesson from just the other day: *Where magick fails, a sword prevails.*

Elena sprang straighter. 'Joach! Don't!' she yelled to him, but she knew that no word of hers would keep him away.

He would die defending her. 'Join me over here!' Holding her magick clenched in her right fist, she circled the writhing demon as it stamped out the last of her silvery flames.

Brother and sister sped toward each other's side.

Noticing the motion, the raver king spun on its claws, gouging deep channels in the wood. It roared at them, confused, but failed to keep them apart. Joach skidded to a stop beside his sister, raising his staff like a shield between the beast and Elena.

The raver king stretched up from its pained crouch, towering over the two of them. The stench of charred flesh curled from its blackened shell as two yellow eyes spat vengeance at them.

'Finish her!' Rockingham yelled to his demon creation.

Across the deck, Er'ril swiped his sword at Rockingham's head, driving her tormentor back from the mast. 'Elena!' he called to her. 'Flee belowdecks! Use the last of your magick to hide yourself!'

Elena considered the sense in his words. She *did* have enough magick in her blood to fade from sight.

At her silence, Joach half turned to her. 'Do it,' he urged quietly.

Elena shook her head. Here was her place. Beside them all.

As brother and sister silently communicated their determination and love, the beast attacked in a flurry of sharp edges. Fangs slashed at Joach while razored claws speared toward Elena.

Without flinching, Elena reached up beside her brother and grabbed his staff with her bloody right fist. As in the ship's hallway, white and black magick clashed. An explosion of energies burst out from them, knocking the beast back a step. Where before the concussion had also flung

Elena away, this time she was ready. She locked an iron grip on the staff and held tight. Joach gasped beside her, feeling the surge of power as her blood and magick absorbed into the staff.

As she clenched the rod, more and more of her energies fed into the hungry wood. She swooned as she was drawn into the staff. For a moment, she experienced the fibers and channels of the wood. Even a whisper of forest song echoed in her ears. Still, the staff fed on her – and not all the energies it absorbed were mere magicks.

Some of her own life essence flowed, too.

'No,' she moaned, suddenly understanding what was asked of her. Clutching the staff, she watched her fingernails lengthen, curling and yellowing with age. This price was too high!

'Elena! Watch out!' Joach's frantic words drew her back from losing herself completely in the wood. He knocked her away, breaking her contact with the staff. Her arms fell limp to her side. Not only was her magick spent, so was her strength.

'El, what . . . what did you do to my staff?'

Elena fought to focus her eyes. The black poi'wood of Joach's staff now shone silver, like the polished wood of a snowy maple. But marring its pristine surface were flowing streaks of scarlet, as if blood pumped through the heart of the wood. 'Use it,' she said aloud.

'The magick?'

She shook her head, sagging against the rail. She pushed him toward the monster as she fainted. 'Use it the way Father taught you.'

Joach's brow crinkled in confusion, but he was given no chance to argue. The raver king sensed the weakening of its prey and attacked. It jabbed a claw at Joach, meaning to impale him. But Joach blocked the deadly blow with a crack of his staff. He had only hoped to parry its thrust, but the results shocked both beast and boy.

The smote claw exploded under the staff into a shower of stinging shards. The demon yanked away its maimed limb and hissed as it retreated a step. It crouched lower on its armored limbs and studied Joach with sick yellow eyes. It had underestimated its prey.

Warily watching the beast, Joach glanced to the staff in his fist. The snowy white of the wood now glowed, and streaks of red flowed through the wood like thin rivers. As he stared, his eyes flew wide. The red rivers did not end with the wood but continued on into his own flesh. Through his pale skin, Joach watched the flowing channels creep over his knuckles and up his wrist. From there, the rivulets spread in curls and twists up the length of his arm, disappearing under the cuff of his shirt.

What was happening?

Before he could ponder it further, a hissing growl woke him to the more immediate danger.

Joach raised the magick-wrought staff. The thick wood was now as light as a willow branch in his fingers. It took only the slightest dance of his fingers and twist of wrist to manipulate the whirling length of wood. Joach swung the staff before him in a wicked arc, a blur of polished wood. His father had once told him that a wooden stave in skilled hands could be deadlier than the sharpest sword. He had doubted him then, but not now. He spun the staff over his wrist, catching it cleanly. He had never felt such control, such an understanding of wood and force. It was almost as if the staff were an extension of his own arm, a deadly statement of his own will.

Boy and staff were now one.

The raver king leaped, intending to rip them apart. Joach responded. With only a thought, the staff spun, and Joach drove its butt end into the face of the hurdling demon, stopping it in its tracks. The shivering impact shot up the wood and into his shoulder. Such a blow should have knocked the stave from numb fingers. But Joach hardly felt it. With a deft twist of his wrist, he twirled the staff and slammed its other end square atop the demon lord's skull.

Bone cracked, and the raver king crashed to the planks, splintering a section of decking. The blow had been fierce enough to kill a bull – but this beast still lived. Clawed limbs dug for purchase, first weakly, dazedly, then with renewed determination.

Joach did not wait for it to regain its footing. He dashed forward, planting his staff on the deck, and vaulted up over the flaying storm of razored claws. He landed atop the back of the demon. Without pausing, he positioned the butt end of his staff against the center of the monster's back, both fists clamped on its upper end. Joach dragged the staff straight up, then using all his weight and will, drove its end through the core of the demon. Wood cleaved cleanly through leather and bone, stabbing at last into the wood of the deck under the raver king.

The beast writhed like a pinned spider on corkboard.

Joach danced to keep his footing, but the threat of claws and fangs was too near. Using his planted staff as a purchase, Joach again vaulted over the flailing limbs and tumbled across the deck. He caught up against the rail, only an arm's length from his sister.

Rolling over, Joach watched the end result of his attack. The raver king's struggles weakened with each shudder. The silver spike of wood held it trapped. Claws rattled to the deck, then lay still. In a wail that split the clouds and tore away a section of sail, the black spirit fled, steaming from around the impaling wood, and was gone.

All that was left were the hollow remains of the goblin queen, twisted and burned. The staff, still imbedded in the deck, had returned to its dark hue, the white magick spent.

Joach sat up and reached for his sister's limp form. His hand froze as his eyes finally recognized her condition. 'Sweet Mother ... El ...'

Elena lay sprawled, unconscious, in a crumpled heap at the bottom of the ship's rail. Though she still breathed, her skin was as pale as the first snow. Yet her weak pallor was not what trapped Joach's breath. His sister's hair, once cropped short, now lay like a thick pillow of fiery curls under her head. Only the very tips still showed the black dye that had once disguised her.

Joach scrambled toward her, too stunned to call to the others. As he neared, he saw that even the nails of her fingers and toes showed the same miraculous growth. Her fingernails had spread into twisted corkscrews across her palms.

Yet her hair and nails were not all that had grown out. Joach tried not to stare at her naked form, but the changes were too shocking to look away. Elena no longer bore the physique of a young girl whose womanhood beckoned. Her figure had blossomed and stretched into the full curves of a beautiful maiden. It was as if four winters of age had swept over her in mere heartbeats.

Joach quickly shrugged out of his shirt and wrapped her nakedness in the thick wool. It barely covered her. She must now be a good head taller than him.

The motion stirred her. 'J-Joach?' she mumbled. Her eyelids fluttered with fatigue.

'Hush, El. Sleep,' he whispered, unsure what to say. 'You're safe.'

Across the deck, a voice argued otherwise. 'You'd best deliver her to me, boy,' Rockingham called. 'Perhaps I'll even let you live.'

With eyes narrowed in hate, Joach turned and stalked across the planks until he stood beside the impaled staff, his only weapon.

On the far side of the deck, Er'ril and the others still held Rockingham in a temporary standoff. Swords circled the monster, but the golem lay nestled in his protective shadows. Flint warned against stepping into that oily darkness.

Joach raised his own voice, fierce with vengeance. 'Send the entire demon horde of the netherworld against us, you monster. But you will *never* touch Elena.'

'Strong words for someone now bereft of his sister's magick.'

'I will fight you with any weapon,' he spat back. He reached for his staff. As his fingers wrapped around the wood, a shock arced through his body. His knees gave way.

Using the staff as a crutch, he barely kept his footing.

Where his fist gripped the wood, red channels flowed out from his flesh into the staff. Black wood became white again as rivulets ofscarlet spread through the staff. Each thudding beat of his heart pushed the darkness farther away. Joach's eyes grew wide, but he could not deny what he sensed. It was his own blood now that flowed through the wood, feeding the hungry staff. He had thought Elena's magick spent, but now he understood that it had only gone *dormant*, awaiting his blood to rekindle it. As the magick reignited, he heard a distant chorus deep in his ears: a hum of magick, gleeful and wicked. Strength returned to his limbs.

'El, what have you done?' he muttered.

'I had no choice,' a weak voice answered from near the rail.

Startled, Joach glanced and noticed that his sister's eyes were open. She stared transfixed as his blood filled the staff. It now shone white from tip to tip.

'I needed a weapon,' she continued, tired and forlorn.

'So you forged this.' Joach yanked the staff from the deck. It was as easy as if he were removing a fork from warm butter.

'No,' she said. Her eyes met his for the first time. 'I forged *you*.'

Er'ril kept his sword raised between Rockingham and the wit'ch. He did not glance back as Joach and Elena whispered. He feared giving the golem any chance to better its position on the deck.

So far, he and the two Brothers had played a cautious game of cat and mouse with the demon across the deck of the vessel. After the creation of the raver horde, the magick in the golem had seemed to weaken. It had retreated to a defensive position, casting a protective ring of shadows around its ankles. While their swords had kept it from nearing Elena, its shadows still held them at bay.

Er'ril tightened his grip on his sword's hilt. Shadows or not, they must act soon. They could not give the monster a chance to gather its strength for another assault.

It was at this moment that fate took hold of destiny.

A grinding roar ripped through the bowels of the *Seaswift*. The decks tremored underfoot; the crunch and crack of timber echoed over the waters. Er'ril guessed it to be another black trick of the golem. But from the pinched, surprised expression on Rockingham's face, Er'ril suspected he might be mistaken.

Flint answered the mystery. 'Reef!' he yelled. The seaman's face was a mixture of indecision. From the worried glance to the stern, he obviously feared abandoning the demon's flank, but he knew a hand was needed on the lashed wheel if they were to survive.

Before either Brother could act, the ship lurched and a deep growl shook through the vessel. The masts tilted drunkenly; the canvas sails snapped in protest.

'We're stoved!' Flint yelled.

The ship ground to a battered stop. Surprised, Er'ril fell backward, even as the deadly shadows swept over the very spot where he had been standing. Rockingham, no more experienced at keeping his footing atop the bucking planks than Er'ril, had stumbled nearer, falling to his knees.

Er'ril started to roll farther away across the deck when he stopped in horror.

Moris, well seasoned by the rough seas of the Archipelago, had ridden out the sudden halt with one hand on the mast, only to be consumed by the passing wave of shadows as Rockingham stumbled. The dark-skinned Brother stared in disbelief as the shadows swept up his legs.

Flint took a step nearer.

Moris must have seen him. 'No! Man the wheel!' he ordered, raising his head. His voice was thick with pain. The black-skinned Brother raised his sword. 'Save the ship! I'll dispatch this fiend.'

Already the darkness consumed his body. Flashes of white femur shone through snatches of parting shadows.

Rockingham, still on his knees, tried to crawl away, but Moris towered over him. As the shadows ate away the man's thick legs, the large Brother dropped like an axed tree. He bore his short sword gripped in both fists, his face a mask of pain. Still, his strength of will could not be tainted by the spreading darkness. Moris made sure as he fell that he toppled toward the cowering figure of Rockingham, his sword aiming true.

Rockingham swept an arm up in useless defense, a cry on his lips. It was to no avail. Moris struck the demon clean through the chest with his sword, collapsing atop the golem as the shadows swallowed them both away.

'Moris!' Flint cried.

Er'ril rolled to his feet as the shadows swirled in on themselves, whirling tighter and tighter like water down an unseen drain. A shrieking wail echoed out from the shadows, growing shriller and more piercing as the pool of darkness shrank. Then, in another breath, the darkness was sucked away.

Joach joined them. No one spoke.

Atop the deck was a long, bleached skeleton, a short sword still gripped in the tangle of finger bones. Moris.

Everyone stared in shock, too exhausted to find their tongues. Relief at the monster's defeat fought in their hearts with horror at the final cost.

Joach finally broke the silence with a whispered prayer. 'Sweet Mother, take our friend safe to your bosom.'

Er'ril found no words to add, struggling with rage and sorrow. How many such warriors would have to die before Alasea could be free?

Flint bent and reached to the skeleton. He touched the white skull reverently, then retrieved a glint of silver from the deck. He stood up and held out his hand to Joach. The boy accepted the gift.

Er'ril stared at the silver star in Joach's palm. It was Moris' earring, the symbol of his old order.

'He would've wanted you to have it,' Flint said, his voice hoarse with emotion.

'I'll wear it with honor.'

Flint wiped at his eyes, then straightened. His gaze was still full of tears. 'I must check the ship,' he said to Er'ril. Already the boat had begun to list in the water.

Er'ril nodded, sensing that the old man also needed a moment to himself. He had lost a dear friend this day, and some grieving could only be done alone.

Once Flint was gone, Joach pointed to the skeleton. 'What of Rockingham? Where are that monster's bones?'

Er'ril remembered the tortured scream fading away with the shadows. 'I don't know. I fear even here he might have again escaped death.'

'Then Moris' sacrifice was in vain.'

'No, his attack, even if not fatal, drove the monster from our decks. I don't think we could have withstood another magickal assault.'

Joach nodded, his fist tight around the silver star. 'Next time,' the boy said with such venom that his words drew Er'ril's eye, 'I'll rip his heart out with my own hands.'

Er'ril gripped Joach's shoulder consolingly, then noticed the length of white staff in the boy's other hand for the first time. He could not miss the threads of crimson flowing in the wood. 'Joach, let me see your staff.'

Joach pulled out of his grip and held the staff away from Er'ril suspiciously. 'Why?'

Er'ril studied Joach, noting the streams of scarlet linking boy to staff. 'Never mind. You've already answered my question.' Er'ril started to turn away, then added over his shoulder, 'I suggest in the future, if you're not in battle, that you wear a glove whenever handling the staff. You only have so much blood, boy.'

Er'ril ignored Joach's wrinkled brow and turned away, searching the far side of the deck. He finally spotted Elena seated by the starboard rail. She sat with her knees pulled up, hugging her legs, her face buried in her arms. From her quaking shoulders, he knew she was weeping.

He crossed to her with a heavy heart, noting the cascade of red curls hiding her face. He was as much to blame for Elena's rash action and its result as the girl herself. The other day in Flint's kitchen, he should have explained to Elena in more detail about the spell. But at the time he had feared frightening her too much. She had been shaken up enough already. Er'ril sighed and stepped nearer.

Elena must have heard his tread. She kept her head bowed, and her words were muffled by her arms. 'I'm sorry about Moris,' she said. 'I hardly knew him, and yet he gave his life to protect me. I should have ... I could have ...'

'No,' he said sternly. 'We lost a good man this day, but it's not right for you to assume any blame. If you do, you dishonor my friend. He gave his life to protect you, and you should accept his sacrifice with good grace. Honor Moris by knowing he saved you and that there was nothing you could do to prevent it.'

Her sobbing worsened for a few moments. Er'ril let her cry. They still had much to discuss, and he let her grief run its course. Finally, he spoke again. 'About Joach ... and the staff.'

Elena flinched visibly at his words. She seemed to shrink farther in on herself, pulling her face away. 'I thought I had no choice,' she mumbled, her voice full of pain.

'And perhaps you didn't. But your decision didn't allow Joach any choice either. You took that from him.'

She remained silent.

'Do you understand what you did?' he asked. 'Do you know what you created?'

She nodded, her face still covered. 'I ... I forged a blood

weapon. Like those blood swords you told me about. And
... and I linked it to Joach.'

'Yes,' Er'ril said, glad at least that she recognized what
her magick had wrought. He had feared that perhaps the
wit'ch had controlled her actions. 'He is a strong boy, and
your whole family has an affinity for magick. There is a
possibility that he can control the weapon with training. But
he is also rash and quick to temper. These qualities could
lead him to become enthralled to the staff's magick. Only
time will tell.'

Elena pulled tighter into a ball. 'I'm destroying my entire
family.'

Er'ril knelt beside her. 'Freedom is always costly.'

'But must my whole family bear the debt?'

Er'ril reached and pulled her into his one-armed embrace.
'I'm sorry, Elena,' he said as he held her tight. 'It's a heavy
burden, but it's not just your family that bears it. All of
Alasea bleeds.'

She trembled against him, leaning deeper into his chest.
'I know,' she whispered, her voice so hopeless that Er'ril
wanted to shelter her like this forever. They sat silently in
each other's embrace for several breaths more. Finally,
Elena's trembles died away, and she raised a hand. 'And
what of this?' she said, indicating the overgrown fingernails. 'Why did this happen?'

At last, she turned to stare Er'ril full in the face. Her eyes
were puffy from grief, her cheeks pale and stained by tears.
For the first time, he saw the woman who had hidden behind
the softness of a young girl's features.

Framed by curls the color of fire, Elena's green eyes were
now flecked with a commanding gold. Her cheekbones were
arched high and begged a finger to trace the long curve past
her strong chin to her slender neck. Her lips were slightly

parted as she stared up at him, and they had fully bloomed into the heavy bud of a rose.

'Er'ril?'

He blinked a few times and pushed slightly away, clearing his throat. He had known the cost of forging a blood weapon and knew there would be changes in the girl. Still, he was momentarily shocked by her visage. He had not expected this woman to be staring back at him.

Sensing his sudden discomfort, Elena glanced down at herself and tugged the woolen edges of Joach's shirt tighter around her physique. 'What's happened to me?'

Swallowing, he pried his tongue loose. 'To forge a blood sword, or any such magick-wrought weapon, a part of the mage has to be given freely. A part of his life must be granted.'

Her brows wrinkled together. 'What do you mean?'

He sought to speak more plainly but found his thoughts hard to organize. He could not keep his mind from dwelling on the changes in her. 'Years were stolen from you and given to the staff. You've aged, Elena. In the moment it took you to create Joach's blood staff, I estimate that you've aged at least four or five winters.'

Her hands fumbled to her face, as if she wanted to feel the truth of his words, but her long nails made it difficult. 'My hair ... my nails ...'

'It's as if you've slept for four winters and just now awoke.'

Her face paled further, and again tears began to well.

Before either could speak, Joach interrupted. The boy called across the deck, waving his staff to urge them up. Behind him, the grizzled figure of Flint could be seen crawling out of the stern hatch. He was soaked from top to bottom. Joach's words flew to them. 'We're completely stoved in! Seawater's swamped the lower holds. We must abandon the boat!' He finally reached them, out of breath, his leggings soaked with seawater. 'We're to gather our belongings and retreat to the skiff.'

As if accenting his words, the ship suddenly rolled and a shuddering rip reverberated through the planks of the deck. Er'ril helped Elena stand, then passed her to Joach. She seemed wobbly on her legs. Er'ril was not sure how much was due to exhaustion and how much was due to the sudden increase in her height. She would have to grow accustomed to her longer limbs and new physique.

Joach eyed his sister's height, then took her arm. He now had to glance up at his sister, where before it had been the other way around. The boy of fourteen winters now stood beside a woman of eighteen or nineteen.

'Get her to the skiff,' Er'ril ordered. 'Then help me gather our gear.'

Nodding, Joach led her away.

Er'ril crossed quickly to where Flint stood near the stern wheel, a spyglass fixed to his eye.

'How long until she sinks?' Er'ril asked.

'Depends,' Flint answered, still studying the surrounding seas with his glass. 'If she rolls off the reef she's caught on, we could sink in moments. If she stays hooked, she might stay above water until sundown. But that's the least of our worries.' He lowered the spyglass.

'What do you mean?'

'Another boat's spotted our tilted masts. It just changed course toward us.'

Er'ril frowned. 'In these waters . . .'

Flint finished his thought. 'Pirates for sure, looking for a quick and easy bounty.' Flint shook his head as he stared at the approaching ship.

'What?'

'I know the colors of that ship. The captain and I were once friends.'

'So why isn't this good fortune?'

Flint scrunched his face sourly. 'I said we were *once* friends. No longer. The approaching ship is Captain Jarplin's shark-beamed hunter.'

'Captain Jarplin?' The name rang familiar in Er'ril's ear.

'I told you about him. He's the fellow from whom I stole Sy-wen's dragon. A treasure of a lifetime. So I don't think he'll take kindly to meeting up with me again.' Flint glanced significantly at Er'ril. 'Or anyone I'm with.'

'Can we escape in time in the skiff?'

'Not in these currents.'

'Any other ideas?' Er'ril knew their party was too bone-tired from the day-long battle with demons to handle a shipload of fresh pirates. Elena, especially, was too worn and shaken by her transformation. To use any more magick without a proper rest would threaten her control and her spirit.

Er'ril eyed Flint, silently asking for help.

Flint nodded, letting out a long sigh. 'I have a plan.' He turned to stare over the waters, quiet for a moment, then shrugged. 'But we'll have to give the hunter what he wants.'

Book Two

OLD DEBTS

8

Walking in silence, Mogweed followed the others deeper into the coastal forest. Up ahead, Mycelle led the way down a faint deer path, guiding them toward where she had hidden their horses and to where Meric awaited them. Mycelle had already explained her sudden change of fate: from death to full revitalization. She had also explained that Mama Freda would be joining them on the journey to meet the wit'ch. But Mogweed had heard little of this, too stunned by Mycelle's sudden demonstration of her shape-shifting ability.

Ahead, Tol'chuk marched beside Mycelle. He stuck close to his mother's side, reaching to touch her every now and then as if he feared she would melt away into the surrounding wood.

Behind Mogweed, Kral and Fardale guarded their rear. They had left the gates of Port Rawl far behind, but there were still bandits who frequented these woods, so caution was needed. Though well guarded, Mogweed still jumped at every crack of twig or rustle of brush.

Not all of his edginess was simple fear.

As he stared at Mycelle, odd feelings worried his belly. He could not deny that a sliver of joy thrilled his blood at seeing a full si'luran after so many seasons, someone who had complete use of her shape-shifting abilities. But mostly a gnawing anger and frustration burned in him.

Why her?

A slight scowl etched his hard mouth as he hiked. It wasn't fair! The swordswoman had chosen to settle into human form. It had been her own choice – unlike Mogweed and his brother. Their shifting abilities had been stolen from them through the abuse of an ancient spell. In search of a cure, the two brothers had traveled far, through so many dangers. If anyone should be free of this curse, it should be them.

Fardale padded quietly through the brush to join Mogweed, as if sensing the strong emotions warring in his brother's breast. The wolf nudged Mogweed's tight fist.

'What do you want?' he snapped sourly, glancing toward his brother.

The wolf's eyes glowed a deep amber in the darkening wood. Images formed: *A flower growing from desert sand. A small bird hatching from a cold nest. A stillborn pup revived by a wolf bitch's warm tongue.* All were glimpses of new life springing forth from hard circumstances.

Mogweed knew what his brother was trying to communicate. Fardale's images all spoke of *hope*. If Mycelle could regain her abilities, then so could they. Mogweed grasped at this thin prospect. He reached for Fardale, hoping to share this sliver of renewed hope. But Fardale was already gone, twisting on a paw and slipping back to join Kral.

Pulling back his hand, Mogweed tried to hold onto his renewed faith, but like smoke, it faded away. Mogweed knew better. Mycelle had had to die to regain her abilities. Was he willing to go that far? In his breast, Mogweed knew the answer. Frustration and despair swelled through him.

But there was even more reason for consternation.

Fardale had always been an eloquent speaker, whether by tongue or mind. But this last sending had been coarse, the images rough and blurred at the edges. Perhaps it was just Fardale's excitement, but Mogweed doubted this simple explanation. He had sensed something wilder behind his brother's amber eyes, like the howling of a feral wolf. Fardale was beginning to lose his ability to spirit speak as the wild wood claimed him. Time was running out. In less than three moons, the curse would consume them both, freezing them permanently into their current forms. Both brothers' eyes would lose their amber glow, and any chance of regaining their si'luran heritage would be gone forever. Fardale would become another wolf in the wood, and Mogweed would become another man among many. They would forever forget their heritage.

Mogweed's legs trembled under him. *Never!* Even if it meant betraying everyone here to the Dark Lord of this land, including his own brother, then so be it. He glanced to where Mycelle smiled warmly at Tol'chuk. Mogweed's eyes narrowed with determination. *One day I will again enjoy my own freedom. I swear it!*

As he scowled at the unfairness of fate, he failed to notice the motion to the right of the path until too late.

A figure stepped silently out of the neighboring cluster of skreebushes. Mogweed gasped and stumbled, not only from the shock of the man's sudden appearance but also because of the figure's monstrous countenance. Half his face was eaten away by a roil of pinkish scar tissue, consuming one ear and half his black-bristled scalp.

Swords and axes appeared up and down the deer path. Tol'chuk lunged toward the intruder, moving surprisingly fast for such a bulky creature. The man's eyes grew wide at the onrushing og're. He backed deeper into the surrounding brush. Behind him, Mogweed spotted other shadowy figures and the glint of steel farther back in the wood.

'Stop!' Mycelle suddenly cried harshly. Her command split through the woods like a thrown ax.

Tol'chuk obeyed his mother and skidded to a halt on his thick, clawed legs. The og're leaned one huge fist in the loam of the wood, panting and baring his fangs at the man.

Mycelle pushed to join them. As she elbowed forward, she shoved down Kral's ax with her palm, then crossed to stand between Tol'chuk and the bandit. 'He's a friend,' she scolded them all. 'I had left word in the city for him to join us here.'

Kral's voice was more growl than human. 'Who is he?'

Mycelle scowled and dismissed Kral's question for a moment. She stepped forward and embraced the man warmly. 'How is Cassa Dar?' she asked as she released him.

He smiled at the swordswoman, a most gruesome sight due to the twist of scarred flesh. 'She rests in Castle Drak. The attack last moon drained her, but she recuperates.' The man suddenly squinted at Mycelle, frowned a moment, then held her at arm's length, studying her. 'Your eyes . . . They've changed! What happened?'

Mycelle seemed to shrink back from him, lowering her gaze.

Mogweed realized that the stranger must know nothing about her true si'luran heritage. Mycelle finally spoke, not lying but dancing around the truth. 'I died,' she said, then exposed the snake on her arm. 'A healer and the magick in a snake brought me back. My eyes were like this afterward.'

The man leaned closer. 'The way they're slitted, they could almost be snake eyes.'

Before the situation grew more awkward, Fardale danced

forward, tail wagging furiously. The man greeted the wolf with a scratch behind an ear and a friendly thump on the side. 'I see your burns are healing well, Fardale,' the man said.

Fardale barked his agreement.

Kral interrupted the reunion. 'Could someone explain who this is?'

Mycelle turned. 'His name is Jaston. He helped guide Elena through the swamp.' Mycelle gave them a quick version of the tale of their journey through the Drowned Lands.

'So this swamp wit'ch is a d'warf,' Kral mumbled, his eyes filled with a red fury Mogweed had never seen before.

'Yes,' Mycelle answered. 'But I know what you think . . .'

'You know nothing about what I *think*.' Kral's voice had frosted to ice. 'You know not how her foul brethren drove my clans from our ancestral homelands near Tor Amon. It was d'warf armies that destroyed our homes, slaughtered our women and babes on their pikes, and made nomads of my people.'

'Cassa Dar is not like that,' Mycelle insisted. 'She saved our lives in the swamps.'

'Your lives would not have needed saving if the wit'ch hadn't cursed Elena and forced you all into the foul bogs.'

'Sir,' Jaston said coldly. His face had grown flushed during the exchange. 'You know not what you speak. Cassa Dar does not deserve your wrath.'

Tol'chuk grumbled his agreement, seeking to end the tension. 'If Er'ril and Elena trusted her, so should we.'

Kral was not swayed. 'A d'warf is a d'warf,' he said angrily and turned, marching a few steps away.

Mycelle watched Kral's back with tight lips, then let out a long sigh. 'Men,' she grumbled and turned back to Jaston. 'So you got my message?'

'Just at dawn,' Jaston said. His angry flush faded. 'I just managed to escape the city before it was locked down.'

'And Mist? Does the child's mare fare well?'

He frowned. 'Yes, but perhaps I should've done you all a favor and fed that piece of stubborn horseflesh to a hungry kroc'an. That is the laziest, most ornery mare I've ever led.' He started ticking off items on his fingers. 'On the trek here, she almost colicked on swampweed, then bit Sammers on the elbow when he doused her with herbs to settle her belly. She kicked the lead stallion who pulled our wagon, laming the beast for a fortnight. Because of that, we had to abandon one of the wagons with a quarter of our wares. And just last night, she chewed through her lead, and we had to hunt her down through the streets of Port Rawl. We found her at an apple vendor. She had cracked his stall and eaten half his wares. It cost me a steep fee to compensate him.'

Mycelle grinned at his story, and by the end, Jaston's scarred features also shone with the ghost of a smile, the tension from a moment ago fading. 'So I guess,' Mycelle said, 'you'll be glad to be rid of her.'

He rolled his eyes. 'You don't know how pleased I was to find your note this morning at the Watershed Trading Post.' Jaston waved his companions forward.

The rustle of hooves and whispered words announced their approach through the wood. Mogweed counted six men and one hard-looking woman among the swampers. They led three horses. The largest was a striking dappled stallion with lines that clearly led to the horse clans of the Northern Steppes. The next was a golden-skinned gelding with a stately gait and quick, intelligent eyes.

Mycelle reached a hand to this horse's nose. 'Grisson,' she said in greeting. This horse was obviously hers. The gelding snuffed at her offered palm and nudged her.

The last to be led forward was Elena's small gray mare. Her big brown eyes studied the gathered troupe with indifference, and she dug one hoof in the dirt in irritation. Mogweed thought this horse's belly seemed a bit fuller than the rest.

Mycelle must have noticed this, too. 'I see you've been feeding Mist well.'

'As if we had any choice.'

Mycelle crossed and ran a hand along Mist's flanks. 'She looks in good shape otherwise.'

'Well . . .' Jaston's voice sounded hesitant. 'She's in even better shape than you might imagine.'

'What do you mean?'

Jaston ran a hand over his cropped hair, a strained look in his eye. 'You know that stallion she kicked? Well, she kicked him when he tried to breed her a *second* time; she wouldn't stand for him again.'

Mycelle's hand still rested on Mist's flank. She ran her hand over the mare's full belly. 'You're not telling me . . . ?'

'He mounted her the first time at the last moon. I think she may already be with foal, but it's too early to say for sure.'

Mycelle sighed and stepped back, appraising the horse, then shrugged. 'That's why I always ride a gelding. Come, Grisson,' she said, taking the lead of the golden-maned horse. 'We've another half league to cover before reaching camp.'

Jaston stood his ground and eyed Kral. 'We've still wares to sell in Port Rawl. So maybe it's best to part ways here.'

Mogweed noticed a hurt glint in Mycelle's eyes. 'Nonsense,' she argued. 'The gates to the city are already locked down.'

'They'll let us through. The watch never refuses entry to swamp traders.'

'Then at least enjoy a hot meal with us.'

Jaston, still hesitant, slowly nodded. 'I guess we could use a moment among friends before tackling the traders of Port Rawl.'

'Then it's settled.' Before anyone else could argue, Mycelle led her gelding to the front of the group.

In a short time, the troupe marched through the last of the twisting wood and came upon a clearing atop a craggy bluff. Sheltered back under the eaves of the trees, a small campfire burned cheerily in the approaching gloam of sunset. A few horses stood nestled and roped to one side, while two frail figures stood limned in the firelight staring back at the group warily.

Mogweed recognized the wizened figure of the old healer, Mama Freda. Beside her stood Meric. Apparently, the elv'in lord had finally healed enough from the attack in Shadowbrook to be out of bed. But as they crossed the clearing, Mogweed noticed how heavily Meric leaned on a thick cane as he strode forward to meet them.

'Who are these others?' Meric said with a scowl, clearly not happy with the additional members of the party.

Tol'chuk took the elv'in aside and explained while Mycelle directed the others to settle the horses. Mogweed ended up standing beside Fardale as the flurry of activity rolled around them.

Mogweed turned to his brother. 'What do you make of this Jaston fellow?'

Fardale's eyes glowed toward Mogweed. An image formed in his mind, a picture of a past event. Mogweed saw Fardale being snatched aloft by the white tentacles of a winged beast, his fur burning with the creature's grip. Jaston leaped from a small boat, a knife clenched in his teeth, and rescued the wolf.

Mogweed nodded with these images. Jaston had saved Fardale's life, and among the si'luran, there was now a blood debt between the wolf and the man. As kin to Fardale, Mogweed shared the debt, whether he liked it or not.

Fardale nudged his brother's hand, then wandered over toward the hearth. Mogweed hung back, still uncomfortable around all these humans – especially the strangers.

From behind him, Kral suddenly stepped next to Mogweed, startling the erstwhile shape-shifter. Glancing up to his huge companion, Mogweed saw the sour expression on Kral's face as he contemplated the others, as if sharing the shape-shifter's sentiments about the strangers. Mogweed also noticed how the mountain man's fist rested hard on the hilt of his ax. But at least his weapon was still sheathed in leather.

Mogweed started to turn away when a flare of firelight revealed the purplish, bruised hue of the leather that sheathed Kral's ax. Disgust curled the corner of Mogweed's lip. As a si'luran, he recognized the source of that leather. It was the skin of a sniffer, the slavering beasts who hunted the deep forests of the Western Reaches. Mogweed recalled the sniffer who had attacked him and his brother among the lands of the og're.

Before Mogweed could comment on Kral's choice of leathers, the mountain man's brows lowered, and he spoke, his voice as deep and vicious as the hunting growl of a sniffer. 'I don't trust these others, especially that scarred man, Jaston.'

Kral eyed Mogweed, who could only nod under his intense gaze. Mogweed fought to keep from trembling. Maybe it was just the sudden memory of the sniffer's attack in the mountains, but for a moment, Mogweed felt a hungry menace in Kral's gaze, like that of a predator from the blackest forest. He was relieved when Kral finally glanced away and stalked across the clearing toward the campfire.

After several shuddering breaths, Mogweed followed on numb legs. He had never seen this side of Kral. He joined the others, making sure the campfire was between him and the mountain man. In the firelight, Kral's eyes glowed a deep crimson, his face an unreadable mask.

Mogweed studied him a moment longer, one eyebrow crinkling. He watched Kral's right hand reach and rub at the leathered skin that hid his ax blade. He was sure the mountain man was unaware of how his fingers caressed the leathers with such fervid intensity, the movement slow and almost hungry, like a man caressing a lover's breast . . .

Mogweed looked away and swallowed hard. An icicle of fear slid through his innards. How *had* the mountain man managed their escape from Port Rawl's garrison? He had never explained.

Interrupting his reverie, Mama Freda hobbled up to Mogweed, a platter of venison and wild onions in her hands. Tikal, her pet tamrink, sat perched on her shoulder and stared at him with huge eyes. The tiny beast held a small onion in one fist and nibbled at it. Mama Freda offered a fork to Mogweed. 'Help yourself, little man,' she offered.

He waved her off, his stomach suddenly sick at the thought of food.

'You should eat,' she insisted. 'We've a long way to travel.'

'Thank you,' he said softly. 'Maybe later.'

Shrugging, she wandered off as Tol'chuk settled next to Mogweed. 'It must be good to see your brother safe,' he said, waving a hunk of meat toward where Fardale sniffed around the horses. The og're's fingers were greasy from the meat.

Mogweed answered by nodding toward where Mycelle

stood talking with Jaston. 'Nothing like family to hearten the spirits, eh?'

Tol'chuk clapped Mogweed on the shoulder. 'Besides my mother, you be my family, too,' he said. 'Among my clans, I was a half-bred outcast. Since leaving my lands, I've found my two half brothers – maybe not in blood, but at least in spirit.'

Mogweed studied the og're to see if he was jesting with him.

But Tol'chuk's features were warm and relaxed as he stared around the camp. He was sincere. 'You both be now my clan,' he finished.

Mogweed stared into the flames. For the oddest reason, he found himself wiping at an eye. Surely it was just the burn of the campfire's smoke.

Tol'chuk suddenly clutched at his chest, a groan flowing from his lips.

'Tol'chuk?' Mogweed stood abruptly, leaning over the og're.

Straightening back up, Tol'chuk sighed deeply, a sheen of perspiration on his brow. 'It be all right. I just never felt it this strong.'

'What happened?'

Tol'chuk just shook his head. 'Trouble, I think.'

From where he stood guard near the wood's edge, Kral watched the others eat.

By the time everyone was finally seated near the campfire and digging into their meals, the sun had touched the western horizon, striping the clearing with the long shadows of tree trunks. Kral enjoyed the approach of evening. His senses, already keen, had been heightened by dark magicks. The night's black cloak hid nothing from his sight, and his sharp ears could pick out the pounding heart of prey from a hundred paces.

Still, the rumbled conversation and occasional spate of laughter from around the camp kept him distracted. He hated these newcomers, with their strange smells and alert eyes. They were hunters like himself, and he distrusted them – not that he expected any foul betrayal on their part, but simply because they were an unknown element in his careful plans. Kral watched them warily.

For this reason, he didn't sense the presence of the spy until the crack of a twig alerted him to the intruder.

He spun around to the shadowed wood. 'Who goes there?' he barked loudly. Behind him, the camp instantly went silent with his call. His ax lay already bared in his four-fingered fist, the iron shining in the last rays of the sun.

Nothing lay out there. He saw no movement among the black shadows. He narrowed his eyes and cocked his head, listening. Deeper in the wood, off to the left, he heard the fluttering beat of a buck's heart, but nothing else. He relaxed his grip on the hickory handle of his ax. Nothing was out there.

Suddenly a small voice intruded, just a few paces away. 'I'm hungry.' Kral's eyes grew wide as the speaker, a small naked child, stepped from around the bole of a cypress. The boy scratched behind a filthy ear and shyly moved closer. 'Do you have any sweetcakes?'

Kral was taken aback by the child's sudden appearance. 'Who are you?' he asked harshly, feeling slightly foolish brandishing his ax before a child barely tall enough to reach his knee. Still, Kral sensed that this was no ordinary urchin. He heard no rush of blood or beat of heart from the boy.

'You're a big man,' the child said, craning his neck back, hiseyes wide with awe. He seemed little threatened by the ax. The boy crossed to Kral and held up his hand for the mountain man to take it.

Instead Kral backed a step away.

Mycelle, by now, had crossed to him. She was putting away her twin swords. 'It's all right, Kral.'

Kral kept his ax in hand. 'That is no ordinary boy.'

'Fear not. It's just one of Cassa Dar's swamp children, a magickal construct of moss, mud, and swampweed.' Mycelle knelt down beside the child. 'Well, little one, why have you come all the way here?'

Behind Kral, the scarred swamper joined them, trailed by the rest of the camp.

The boy eyed the others, one hand rising to suck a thumb. When he spotted the towering og're, his face grew scared. He slid closer to Mycelle and pointed toward Tol'chuk. 'A m-monster!'

Mycelle smiled and gathered him up in her arms. 'There are no monsters here.'

The boy kept his eyes glued on Tol'chuk, clearly unconvinced. Kral followed the others back to the campfire.

A few more dry branches were added to the fire as the sun finished setting. The camp gathered around the fresh flames.

Meric leaned both hands on his cane as he stood. 'What does this mean?' the elv'in asked. 'Why did he come?'

Jaston held up a hand and leaned close to the boy as Mycelle cradled him in her lap. 'Cassa?'

The boy stuck out his tongue at the scarred man. 'You're an ugly, stinky man.'

Jaston ignored his insult. 'Cassa, are you there?' he persisted.

Kral watched the boy squirm and stiffen in Mycelle's embrace, then grow still. The child's eyes glazed and no longer seemed to reflect the fire's light.

'The distance is great,' the boy said, his words a whisper as if from another world. 'I had a hard time tracking you this far from the swamp's edge.'

Kral's nose curled at the demonstration. He had to restrain himself from sneaking closer and sniffing at the boy. It was as if someone else spoke through the child's lips.

'Why have you come?' Jaston asked.

'I sense a great evil moving toward Port Rawl and came to warn you. It has something to do with the girl.'

Mycelle approached closer. 'Why do you say that?'

'She still carries the Try'sil. The magick in the warhammer is like a beacon to me, calling to my d'warf heritage. It has rested along the coast for the past many days, but this prior night, it vanished beyond my ability to sense, swallowed up in a magick as foul as the heart of a blackguard demon. I fear the worst. Not just for the Try'sil, but for the child.'

Kral's blood raged. He suspected some d'warfish trick here, a ruse to guide him astray from his prey. Though forged by the Black Heart and unable to deny his master's true will, Kral was still a mountain man whose clan had a long memory. Like the ill'guard lord of Port Rawl whose thievish nature could not be completely wiped away, Kral could not deny the cry of revenge for the atrocities committed by the d'warf armies. He would one day have that revenge.

The beast in his blood lusted to tear this rag of a child into bloody ribbons. When finished with Elena, he knew whom next he would hunt. Not even the monsters of the swamp could keep him from this d'warf's throat.

'Cassa,' Jaston continued, 'can you tell us anything else?'

'No, only that you must all hurry. The evil sweeps toward Port Rawl.' The boy began to shiver in Mycelle's lap. 'I can't hold on much longer. Too weak still. Hurry!'

With this last word, the figure of the boy swirled with a

moldy luminescence and vanished. In the child's place was a dank pile of moist weed and mud. Mycelle stood, wiping the debris from her lap in disgust.

Once clean, she faced the others. 'We leave now. It is still a hard day's journey to reach Flint's cottage. If Elena is in danger, we dare not spare the horses. We'll ride the entire night and day.'

'No.' Tol'chuk straightened up. 'We be deceived.'

His words drew Kral's attention. 'So this d'warf lied to us,' he said with clear indignation.

'No,' the og're said. 'I think she speaks true. Only we interpret her words falsely.'

Mycelle's features were taut with worry and impatience. 'Speak, Tol'chuk. What are you saying?'

The og're fumbled to his thigh pouch and removed the chunk of ruby heartstone. A murmur of awe at the sight of the precious jewel arose among the swampers. Tol'chuk held the stone toward the southern edge of the wood. Though a handsome stone, it only glittered in the final rays of the sun. 'A moment ago, I felt the call of the stone shift, like my heart be suddenly torn from my chest. The call be sure and strong. We should heed the swamp wit'ch. We *must* hurry. But not south. Elena no longer be there.'

Mycelle's brow crinkled. 'What are you saying?'

'Elena flees toward Port Rawl,' Tol'chuk insisted.

'How –?' Kral began to say.

The og're swung his arm behind him, pointing north, back toward Port Rawl. The chunk of heartstone flared to a brilliance that outshone the setting sun. Kral held up a hand against the aching glare.

Tol'chuk gasped in pain, as if the jewel's radiance burned his claws. 'The stone demands we go.'

* * *

Atop her tall gelding, Mycelle led the 'caravan' toward the gates of Port Rawl. She no longer wore her usual leather and steel but, like the others, had disguised herself in the sturdy and plain gear of the swamp traders: coarse shirt, worn trousers woven of boghemp, a hooded snakeskin slicker, and kroc'an boots that reached above her knees. It seemed this day was full of masquerades.

As she rode, Mycelle reached to her arm and stroked the small snake wound around her wrist. The paka'golo's tiny tongue flickered over her fingertip, almost thanking her for the attention; then it settled back to rest. Mycelle found herself smiling slightly at its affection. How odd that such a small gesture should warm her heart.

Pulling her sleeve over the snake to keep it warm, she glanced to the rising moon, a sliver of brilliance among the cloud-swept stars. They had made good time, but were they fast enough? Based on the omens of a glowing stone, they were rushing headlong into unknown danger. But Mycelle trusted her son's auguries. Having lived among the og're tribes for a time, she had come to respect the stone called the Heart of the Clans. If Tol'chuk sensed danger for Elena, Mycelle would follow the stone's guidance – even if it meant returning to this black-hearted city.

A grumble drew her attention to the right. Beside her, Jaston rode atop Er'ril's dappled stallion. The tall man fought the reins of the fiery-spirited horse. Watching his difficulty, Mycelle had a new respect for Er'ril's horsemanship. The stallion, purchased in Shadowbrook, had given Er'ril little trouble on the journey to the swamps.

'Curse this mount,' Jaston grumbled. His stallion rolled its sharp black eyes and tossed its head, huffing a white stream into the cooling night.

'Then let him have his head. He's a smart beast, and a lighter touch may suit you better.'

'I've had less trouble with a rutting bull kroc'an,' he mumbled. But he tried her suggestion, and the stallion seemed to respond accordingly.

Satisfied, Mycelle craned around in her seat and studied the long line of their swamp caravan. They were all mounted, except for Meric and Mama Freda, who guided the open wagon, and Tol'chuk and Fardale, who kept pace on their own legs. She sighed. With Jaston's swampers, they numbered fifteen. Too small a number for a serious assault, but it would have to do.

Swinging around, she faced the Swampwall as it came into view around a bend in the trail. Unlike the previous evening, the gates now blazed with torches. Mycelle slowed her horse to a walk and, with a wave, slowed the entire troupe. At least twenty men manned those gates. Clearly the city had been spooked by the deaths at the garrison and was roiled up like a hornet's nest now.

'Get Tol'chuk in the wagon and covered,' she hissed back at them. There was no way to disguise Tol'chuk with mere clothes. Too many townspeople would have heard of the escaped og're by now, and his presence would raise suspicions.

Once her son was loaded in the back of the wagon and covered with a thick tarp, Mycelle tightened her grip on her reins and continued toward the blazing gates. The air stung her eyes with oily smoke from all the torches. Off toward the coast, a thick fog rolled from the shrouded seas. Mycelle noted its approach approvingly. The masking mist could weave a fine cloak to hide their movements and numbers as the night wore on.

Jaston kicked his stallion a step ahead of Mycelle. 'Maybe

I'd better do the talking,' he offered. 'Swamp caravans are Port Rawl's only means of trading with the neighboring landlocked towns, and the guards know better than to inter-fere with us.'

Mycelle waved him on. She had no great wish to confront the rough men guarding the gates. Besides, without shape-shifting, there was even a good chance the gatekeeper might recognize her from last night. Though she could always change faces, Mycelle only wanted to touch her si'luran abilities if absolutely necessary. She was still tired from wearing the old crone's form earlier. Changing too frequently taxed a shape-shifter. There were limits to which even a si'luran's flesh could be stressed. Time was needed to rest the body.

Yet, exhausted or not, Mycelle could not deny the true reason for her reluctance. She stared as Jaston trotted ahead and rode toward the gates. She had failed to mention to him about her ability to shape-shift. She had told herself there was no need to tell him and had convinced herself that the fewer folks who knew the better – especially when a shape-shifter's nature was so repugnant to most men. It was purely a logical decision. Still, deep in her heart, Mycelle felt shame – not at her heritage, but at the secret she kept from a man she had once loved. She remembered the looks of fear and loathing that her shifting had once evoked in men. She could not bear to see it in Jaston's eyes, too.

Irritated, she kicked her horse to close the gap with Jaston's stallion.

Already the swamp man was pulling to a stop before the thick iron portcullis. He threw back the hood of his slicker, exposing his scarred face to the torches' glow. No longer shying from the eyes of others, he did not flinch from the unforgiving light. The trials of the swamp and the love of a wit'ch had gone a long way toward healing his shame. His boldness only made Mycelle's own shame seem that much larger.

'Ho! Gatekeep!' Jaston called.

From the walkway above, a shadowy figure leaned over. 'Who goes there?' a guard called stridently.

Jaston waved at the band of swampers and wagon. 'Who does it look like? We've come a long way to do some trading. Open the gates. We've had a hard day of travel and wish to wash the road dust from our throats with the swill you call ale here.'

The guard chuckled harshly. 'Swill? Just 'cause your mama burned your mouth with swampbeer, don't insult the ales of our fine inns.'

'Then open your gates and prove us wrong!' Jaston patted a small cask lashed behind his saddle. 'I've a sample of swampbeer so you and the other boys can taste the drink of real men.'

Mycelle watched the familiar ceremony: the ritual exchange of insults and carefully proffered bribes.

Jaston knew what he was doing. There was nothing like the offer of free spirits to oil many a tight doorway. The gates were already creaking open. Jaston waved his thanks to the gatekeep and led the others toward the opening.

Once through, Jaston took up a position by the lead guard. He stayed saddled but stood in his stirrups, barking harsh orders at the caravan, haranguing them with his tongue, acting the part of the tough troupe leader.

A young guard, no more than a boy, tried to peek under the tarp as the wagon passed. But Jaston lashed at him. 'Leave our wares be. If you want to trade, see us in the morning at Four Corners.' Mycelle saw the sweat pebbling Jaston's forehead. Their plans would be ruined if Tol'chuk was discovered. Mycelle's fingers wandered to the hilt of a dagger at her waist.

'I thought I saw something move,' the boy squeaked.

Suddenly the head of a large snake slid from under the wagon's covering and hissed at the boy, only a handspan from his nose, exposing long fangs. The youth danced back, white faced.

The other guards laughed and ridiculed the boy as he backed farther away. 'Like the man said, Brunt,' the lead guard scolded the boy, 'don't poke your nose where it don't belong.'

The wagon was allowed to pass without further investigation.

Once the entire caravan was through and winding toward the darkened streets, Jaston cut free the cask and let it roll off his horse's rump into the hands of the thirsty guard. 'With the compliments of the traders of Drywater.'

The guard nodded. 'We'll raise our first mug to your good trading.'

Jaston snorted. 'I hope it's the first mug. Remember, this is swampbeer. By the last mug, you won't even remember your own names.' Amid the appreciative guffaws, he kicked his horse toward where Mycelle waited at the head of the caravan.

'That wasn't too hard,' he said, wiping the nervous sweat from his brow.

Mycelle nodded him forward with her. 'It's always easy putting your head in a noose. It's getting *out* that's hard.'

The two led the others through the outskirts of the town's narrowing streets. Tension kept the company quiet. Only the tromp of hoof and creak of wagon wheel marked their progress through the dark avenues. Once well away from the gates, Tol'chuk rolled from the wagon, shoving the innocuous swamp python back into its cage under the tarp.

Mycelle smiled at him as he lumbered up to the front. 'Quick wits, Son. Now I know you've got more than just your father's good looks.'

He wiped his clawed hands on his thighs. 'I hate snakes,' he said with a shiver.

Mycelle exposed the 'bracelet' wound around her wrist. 'Even this tiny one who saved your mother from poison?'

'That be not a snake anymore. It be a part of you. That I can never hate.'

She reached and touched his cheek, sharing a moment of familial warmth.

'So where do we go from here?' Jaston asked.

Tol'chuk fished his chunk of heartstone from his pocket and slowly swung it in a circle. It bloomed to a sharp brilliance when pointed in only one direction.

Mycelle sighed in exasperation.

'What?' Jaston asked.

'It points toward the docks.'

Jaston's face grew grim. Like her, he knew the town well. The port section of the city was its roughest and meanest quarter, thick with pirates and their crews. Even the most wily denizens of Port Rawl knew better than to wander into that lair without an invitation, and no sane person *ever* went there at night.

'What are we to do?' Jaston asked.

Mycelle nodded toward the glowing stone. 'Follow the light, keep a hand on your sword, and pray.'

9

Elena tested the ropes that bound her. Tied by experienced sailors, the knots were secure. Her struggling only succeeded in tightening them further. She stared at the other two prisoners who shared the tiny cabin. Across the narrow room, Er'ril lay on his belly, his one arm tied to his ankles. He had yet to awaken from the club to the back of his head. Even from here, Elena could see the blood welling through his black hair and down his cheek.

'He shouldn't have tried so hard to resist when they took Flint away,' Joach said, noticing where Elena stared. Her brother was also trussed tight: ankles bound to a chair, and wrists tied behind him.

'He was just trying to make it look authentic.'

'That cudgel they used on him looked authentic enough.'

Elena chewed at her lower lip. It had taken all of Elena's restraint not to lash out at the one-eyed sailor who had struck Er'ril. It would have been only a minor magick to burn through the ropes and flame his cudgel to ash, but Flint's stern eyes and furtive shake of his head had stayed her hand. They all had to play their parts if they hoped the ruse to succeed.

Flint's plan was for Er'ril and Elena to pose as husband

and wife, an upland couple accompanying their lame nephew, Joach, on their way to Port Rawl's healer. After renewing her power, Elena had trimmed her overgrown hair and nails and donned a set of Er'ril's clothes. With the change in her body, she could no longer pose as a boy. Elena glanced down at the ample swellings upon her chest – that was definitely a ploy that could never work again. Still, Flint's ruse had proven sound, especially since the captain seemed more interested in the older Brother than in his passengers. Their ultimate goal was for the captain to deliver them to Port Rawl, and once on land, they'd use Elena's magick to make their escape.

Before her, Er'ril groaned and began to push himself from the floor. Elena found herself able to breathe again. Though she was somewhat sure the blow was far from fatal, she was glad to hear him grumble and move.

'Sweet Mother, that man had more of an arm than I suspected,' Er'ril said, rolling to his side. The move was difficult with his trussed limbs. 'I didn't think he'd strike so hard.'

'You fell like an axed tree,' Joach quipped. 'You should've seen Flint's face.'

'Elena, are you all right? Did they harm you?' The concern on Er'ril's face seemed misplaced as blood dripped from his own cheek.

'I only wish they *had* tried to touch me,' she said blackly, murder clear in her words. 'But they were only interested in Flint.'

Er'ril smiled at her expression. 'Now I know why I married you.'

She appreciated his attempt at levity. He clearly sought to ease her tension, but it did no good. She hated this waiting, especially when the fate of their friend was still unknown.

'Where did they take Flint?' Er'ril said, voicing their common concern.

Elena looked to her toes.

Joach answered. 'They dragged him off to the captain's cabin for a "private" talk. We heard Flint cry out once, but nothing since.'

'Don't worry. These pirates wouldn't kill him,' Er'ril argued. 'He's the only one who supposedly knows the fate of the seadragon.'

'Unless they believe he lost it,' Elena said, raising her eyes. 'I overheard a sailor talking. He was sure Flint's dragon had somehow escaped. According to the sailor, the price of dragon's blood should've bought Flint a whole fleet.' Elena stared Er'ril in the eyes. 'If this question arose in a simple sailor, it'll also be on Captain Jarplin's mind.' She let the rest remain unspoken. Flint's last scream still echoed in her ears.

After a worried moment of silence, Er'ril spoke up. 'Elena, can you free yourself?'

'Not without magick. The knots are snug.'

'Then use your power.'

Joach sat straighter. 'What about Flint's plan?'

'I don't have as much trust as Flint does in the logic of pirates.' Er'ril rolled to face Elena more fully. 'Free yourself; then untie us. Conserve your magick as much as possible.'

Elena nodded. She needed no further encouragement. Touching her magick, she directed it to her right fist. With her hands gloved and tied behind her, Elena could not see if her fist glowed with magicks, but in her heart, she knew it. She sensed the power concentrating, waiting for release. She was ready, too.

The head of a copper nail protruded from the seatback of her chair. Using her fingers, she slipped her glove down a bit, then gouged the soft flesh of her wrist on the nail's sharp edge. Pain lanced up, quick and sharp, but before she could even wince, the fire in the wound was washed away by a flow of magick and blood. The chorus of power sang in her ears.

'Easy, Elena.'

She scowled. Did no one have confidence in her? For countless nights, she had practiced controlling her wit'ch fire, and if she concentrated, she had learned how to flame the wick of a candle without even melting its wax tip.

Using that skill now, Elena loosened a thread of her magick and wove it into the ropes that bound her. Once it was wound through the entire length of cord, she ignited the filament. There was a bright flash, and the ropes fell to ash.

With an aching protest from her shoulders, Elena brought her arms around and dusted ash from her wrists.

'Are you hurt?' Er'ril asked. 'Did you burn yourself?'

Frowning, she shook her head. She raised her gloved fist before him and loosened another thread of magick. The glove that hid her hand vanished in a brief flicker of flame. Ash rained down, exposing her glowing fist beneath. Her hidden Rose bloomed bright in the room, driving back the gloom.

Er'ril and Joach's eyes grew huge at her display.

It was so simple. Elena glanced to the ropes that bound her legs. Cocking her head, she cast out a strand; the ropes vanished from her ankles. With smoke curling around her, Elena stood up.

She began to point toward Joach.

Er'ril interrupted her. 'No!' he spat out.

She turned to him. 'Why?' This fine weaving of magick was more exhilarating in some ways than her blasts of wild fury. Here was not just raw power, but a fierce strength that was hers to control. It was like riding a muscled stallion attuned to her every movement.

'Just untie us,' Er'ril ordered.

'But magick is quicker,' she mumbled, still a bit breathless.

'Do it!'

Reluctantly, she crossed to Er'ril and fingered his knots loose. In a few tugs, he was free. Er'ril rocked onto his knees and shook feeling into his fingers. Before she could move to free Joach, Er'ril stopped her with a hand on her shoulder.

'Listen, child,' he said. 'One of the first lessons a mage was taught during my times was to learn *restraint*. It is also one of the hardest lessons for most mages. As my brother's liegeman, it was my sworn duty to warn Shorkan against using his powers when ordinary means were at hand. To waste magick to light a cold hearth when tinder and flint are available is wrong. Magick is a gift not to be squandered, but to be used thoughtfully and only when necessary.'

She nodded, drawing back her power, and crossed to Joach. She freed her brother as she pondered the plainsman's words. Once done, she turned to face Er'ril. 'But if a mage can renew his strength, why should it matter how he uses it?'

Er'ril stood and helped Joach from his chair. 'We can talk more of this later. For now, just know that to use your powers indiscriminately only makes you more and more dependent on them. You become a tool of your magick, rather than the other way around.'

Joach rubbed at his wrists and nervously straightened the dragon tooth that hung at the hollow of his neck. 'What now?'

Nodding toward the door, Er'ril said, 'I don't like our position here. It's time we armed ourselves.'

Joach retrieved his staff from where it had been tossed in the corner. His ruse as a lame boy had convinced the pirates to let him keep his wooden stave. While he was wearing his gloves, the wood remained dark as Joach gripped it. 'I already have my weapon,' he said, raising the stout rod.

Elena watched as Joach ignited a whisper of black flames along its length. They had learned that as long as Joach kept the skin of his right palm from contacting the wood, the staff remained a tool of black magick. Otherwise, without the glove, her brother's blood would be called into the wood, and the staff would again become a weapon of white magick. Twin weapons in one length of wood.

'Did they post a guard?' Er'ril asked.

'No,' Elena answered. 'In that regard, Flint was right. After locking us up, they've ignored us.' She crossed to the small door and leaned her ear against it. 'I don't hear anyone in the hall either.'

Er'ril moved beside her, his breath warm on her cheek as he leaned to check, too. 'Can you melt the lock without setting fire to the door?'

Pushing back a stray curl of hair from her eyes, she glanced at Er'ril. It was so strange to stand almost eye to eye with him now. In his gaze, she saw him appraising her – in more ways than just magickal. She suddenly felt very conscious of the changes in her body. The fullness in hips and chest, the length and curl of her hair. Even her responses to him were no longer the same. His gray eyes, the touch of his hand, even the brush of his breath on her cheek a moment ago – all stirred something deep inside her, a spreading warmth that both strengthened and weakened her at the same time. She stared into his eyes and knew she must succeed. 'I think I can,' she murmured softly.

He stepped back, clearing the way for her.

Licking her dry lips, Elena turned to the door and raised her hand. She wove several strands of magick out from her palm. Fiery filaments rose from her fingertips, wrapping and writhing into a thicker cord. With a thought, she guided the crimson strands into the door's lock, suddenly sensing the old iron. She felt its cold touch wrap around her heart. For a strained moment, she thought she might drown in the ancient stillness of the ore. But she fought the iron's cold touch, her blood becoming a forge, fierce and hot.

Somewhere beyond her senses, she heard Joach gasp.

'It's working,' Er'ril mumbled as if from far away.

Her magick pumped with each fiery beat of her heart against the old iron. Like a reluctant lover, the cold ore gave way slowly, warming to her touch, yielding to her.

'You've done it, Elena.' Er'ril gripped her shoulder. 'Now stop your magick before its wit'ch fire spreads.'

Elena blinked back to clear focus, shivering under Er'ril's touch. She closed her fist, severing the strands that linked her to the molten lock. She stared as red-hot iron ran in rivulets down the planks of the door, leaving scorched and smoking trails. Without her magick's touch, the iron cooled rapidly.

'Careful now,' Er'ril warned. 'From here, we stick close together.' He nodded toward Joach.

Her brother pushed the door slowly open with the end of his staff. The creak of salt-encrusted hinges seemed like the screams of the dying as they all held their breaths.

Crouching and cautious of the pools of cooling molten iron, Er'ril peeked out the door, looking first one way, then the other. 'Follow close,' he whispered and led them into a short, dark companionway. Only a single lantern lit the hall with its tiny flame.

Somewhere a few men were singing bawdily, out of tune. Harsh laughter accompanied the singer's efforts. It sounded like it came from directly overhead. Elena found herself crouching away from the noise.

Er'ril slipped to the only other room exiting the hall and peered within. 'Bilge pump and crates,' he whispered. 'We must be in the lowest bowels of the ship.'

'Where now?' Joach asked, his eyes shining with fear.

'I need a weapon first. A sword, an ax, something.' Er'ril's hand balled into a fist in frustration. 'Then we free Flint.'

With Joach at her side, Elena followed behind the plainsman as he crept down the short hall. A narrow ladder led up to a closed hatch.

'We came down this way,' Elena whispered. 'There's a kitchen above us.'

The singing of the men had died down, but murmurs and occasional loud guffaws could be heard beyond the hatch. Er'ril paused at the foot of the ladder. From his dour expression, Elena could almost read Er'ril's thoughts. Escape this way would lead them directly into the midst of the pirates.

'There must be another way,' Joach whispered.

Er'ril's brows bunched together as he plotted.

Suddenly, something tickled Elena's ankle. She started slightly, jumping back a bit. A huge rat squeaked in protest and scurried down the hall. Its oily fur stank of rotted fish.

'Follow it,' Er'ril urged. 'This is a fishing boat. Its hold must somehow connect with these lower decks.'

Joach hurried after the rat as it ducked into the bilge cabin. 'We need light!' he whispered urgently.

Elena raised her hand, beginning to call forth a flame.

Er'ril knocked her arm down and snatched the lantern from the wall hook. He raised the lamp before her eyes, glancing at her meaningfully, then ducked after Joach.

Blushing, Elena followed. Er'ril's earlier warning rang in her ears. Maybe there *was* a threat in the indiscriminate use of her magicks. Already her first instinct when called to action was to reach for her power, ignoring her own ingenuity and resources. In this way, she narrowed herself, defining her worth only with magick. She shook her head. She was more than a red fist and was determined to stay that way.

In the cabin, she found Joach kneeling by a large crate. Er'ril hovered over him with the lantern. 'It dashed behind here,' Joach said.

Er'ril lowered his lantern closer to light the cramped space between crate and wall. 'Move aside, boy.' Joach rolled to the side to let Er'ril lean nearer. 'I don't see the bugger back there,' the plainsman said.

'I'm sure that's where it went.' Joach made to poke at the space with his staff, as if to flush the beast out.

Er'ril waved him back and stood up. Passing the lamp to Elena, Er'ril waved Joach to the corner of the box. 'Help me move it.'

Joach used his staff as a lever to pry the heavy crate from the wall while Er'ril pushed with his shoulder. The crate shifted with a scraping protest across the rough planks. 'What's in this thing anyway?' Joach complained as he strained.

One of the crate's pine slats cracked under Joach's staff. Elena's brother stumbled at the sudden release of his hold. He caught himself up against the wall, cringing at the noise. The sharp crack of the board had sounded like a thunderclap in the tight space.

Everyone froze. No one moved until a new bawdy chorus echoed down from above. They had not been heard. Elena moved closer to the others, reminding herself to keep breathing.

Near the crate now, Elena raised the lantern to the broken section of the box, not so much curious of its contents as seeking something to distract her from their peril. Like her brother, she had heard tales of the gold coins and jeweled treasures plundered from the seas and hoarded by pirates.

She lifted the lantern higher and peered closer.

No treasure lay inside. From the black heart of the crate, a pair of bloodred eyes stared out at her.

A splash of cold seawater shocked Flint back to full awareness. He gasped and choked, throwing his head back with a crack against the high-backed chair to which he was bound. The salt in the water burned the cut below his eye and stung the abrasion on his cheek, both injuries courtesy of his hard-knuckled captors.

Captain Jarplin leaned closer to Flint's bloody face. He was a large-shouldered man with silver hair and green eyes. Winters at sea had weathered him hard as stone. Flint had once respected the man's firm resolve. He had been a tough but fair captain. Yet something in him had changed. Though outwardly the same, if not a bit paler of skin, something about the captain struck Flint as wrong, like a whiff of rot.

Flint had noticed it as soon as he was dragged into the captain's cabin. The usual orderliness to his chamber was no longer evident. Maps and charts were strewn about the room. Unwashed clothes lay piled where they had been dropped. Clearly, Jarplin seldom left his cabin now, where before it was impossible to keep him off his ship's decks.

Flint licked the blood from his split lower lip. Had his

theft of the seadragon so shaken up his former captain? No, something else was wrong here. He should never have convinced the others to step aboard this ship.

Jarplin used a finger to raise Flint's chin. 'Have Master Vael's fists freed your tongue yet?' he asked in mocking tones, so unlike the man Flint once knew.

Flint spat blood. 'I ain't tellin' ya nothin' about the dragon until we reach Rawl,' he said, employing the old slang he had once used when he was first mate on this rig.

Jarplin's green eyes pierced through his disguise. 'Don't play the poor fisherman with me, Flint. There's more to you than I once suspected, but my eyes have since been opened.' He laughed harshly. 'Oh, yes, they're wide open now.'

Flint found himself staring at the trace of spittle hanging from the man's lips. What had happened to the man he knew, a man he had once considered a friend?

Jarplin pushed away and turned to his new first mate. Flint did not recognize Master Vael as any member of the *Skipjack*. It was clear Master Vael hailed from lands far from here. The man's head was shaven smooth, his skin like yellowed parchment. His eyes were the oddest hue – a deep purple, like a bad bruise. Even the whites of his eyes were tinted, as if the color had bled outward.

Jarplin nodded toward an ornate chest. 'Maybe there is another way to free Flint's tongue.'

The only acknowledgment from Master Vael was a barely perceptible bow of his head, almost as if the first mate were giving his approval to the captain. Flint's brow crinkled. Who was the true leader here?

The captain slipped a silver key from a chain around his neck and crossed to the gold filigreed box. 'This is my last one,' he said as he unlocked the chest. 'You should feel honored that I want to share it with you.'

Jarplin's wide back blocked Flint's view of the chest. Still, Flint sensed when the box's lid opened. The cabin suddenly swelled with the reek of entrails bloating in the summer's sun. But the smell was not the worst of it. It was as if someone had raised the tiny hairs all over Flint's body. The very air seemed charged with lightning.

Whatever lay inside that box, Flint had no desire to lay eyes on it. But he was not given any choice. Jarplin swung back around. In his hand, he held a mass of gelatinous slime. At first, Flint thought it looked like some fetid scum scooped out of the bilge pipes, but when Jarplin approached closer, Flint saw it was actually alive. Thin tentacles writhed out from its main bulk. Each tip ended in a tiny mouth, sucking blindly at the air.

Flint could not help himself. The pain, the tension, the smell – and now this new horror. It all overwhelmed him. His stomach churned, and he spewed bile across his lap. In his heart, he knew what Jarplin carried. He remembered the tales he had heard of the raiding ship that had assaulted the docks of Port Rawl, of the tentacled creatures found curled inside the cleaved skulls of the berserkers. Oh Sweet Mother, not here, too.

It seemed forever until the spasms in his belly stopped. Afterward, his head hung heavy as he gulped air.

Jarplin laughed. 'Ah, Flint, it's nothing to fear. This little darlin' will make you look at life in a whole new light.'

Raising his head, Flint discovered he could think more clearly now. It was as if his body had needed to cast out all the poisons built up since stepping aboard the ship. 'Jarplin,' he said, throwing aside any pretenses, 'I don't know what has happened to you. But listen to me. This is wrong. Somewhere inside you must know this.'

'Somewhere inside?' Jarplin knelt down and brushed

back the silver hair that draped his neck. Twisting around, he exposed the base of his skull to Flint. 'Why don't you check what's inside me?'

A small neat hole lay at the top of his neck. Bloodless, it looked like an old, healed wound. Then, from the hole, a pale tentacle slid out, its small mouth swelling and puckering as it drew fresh air to the creature hidden deep inside Jarplin's skull.

'What was done to you?' Flint mumbled in horror.

Jarplin let his hair drape back over the wound. 'Let me show you.' He turned to Master Vael. 'Fetch the bone drill.'

Flint finally noticed Master Vael again. The stranger no longer remained expressionless. His lips were stretched in a hungry grin, exposing large teeth, each filed to a sharp point.

There was nothing human in that smile.

Elena gasped and danced back from the crate. She almost dropped the lantern.

Er'ril was immediately at her side. 'What is it?' he asked.

Joach backed nervously toward them, staff raised against the unknown menace.

'I ... I'm not sure,' Elena mumbled. 'I thought I saw something.' She had expected some monstrosity, something with fiery eyes, to crash out of the crate and pursue her. When it had failed to happen, she was less sure of exactly what she had seen. Her hand fluttered toward her face. 'I saw a pair of eyes.'

Er'ril squeezed her elbow. 'Stay here.' He took the lantern from her shaking fingers and approached the box.

'Be careful,' she whispered.

Joach kept guard at his sister's side.

The two watched Er'ril raise the lantern toward the split section of the crate's planking. He, too, seemed to jump slightly at what he found. But instead of fleeing, he stood his ground and slipped the lantern deeper toward the hole, peering after it.

'Well?' Joach asked.

'I'm not sure. A sculpture of some sort,' he said. 'I think the eyes are two rubies.'

Joach approached, followed by Elena. Her brother raised on his toes to stare into the dark crate. 'There's something—'

Er'ril waved him away. 'We don't have time to waste on this.'

'No,' Joach said, glancing over his shoulder at Er'ril. 'There's a power coming off it. My staff grows warm as I near it. We should at least see what lies here.'

Er'ril hesitated, then nodded. 'But let's be quick about it. We can't risk the crewmen discovering our escape.'

They used Joach's staff and pried at the side, but it refused to budge. The planks were nailed tight.

Elena stepped forward. 'Let me help.' Before either could argue, she sent forth flaming tendrils of wit'ch fire toward the crate. Joach and Er'ril ducked, fearing the strands' touch. They need not have worried. The strands were like extensions of her own thought. Threads of energy drew to the nails, like iron to lodestone. With the merest push, she melted the fasteners. Unhinged, the side of the crate fell open. Er'ril and her brother caught the wall of planks and settled it gently to the floor.

Once done, the three gathered before the open crate. Elena had retrieved the lantern from the floor. They all stared in silence at the revealed sculpture.

'It looks like some big blackbird,' Joach commented.

The statue was finely crafted, standing taller than Er'ril. Only an artisan of considerable skill could have sculpted the huge stone in such detail. Each feather was in clear relief; the sharp beak looked ready to tear. Its eyes, twin crystalline rubies, sparked hungrily in the lamplight. Its claws seemed to dig into the floor of the crate as if the winged beast had just come to roost.

'Not a bird,' Er'ril said mournfully.

Elena did not argue with his assessment. Though feathered and winged, there was something distinctly reptilian about the beast. The neck was a bit too long and the joints of its legs seemed to bend the wrong way. 'What is it?'

Er'ril turned to Joach, a dark expression on his face. 'It's a wyvern.'

Joach gripped his staff and backed a step. 'Like from my dream.'

'What are you talking about?' Elena asked.

Er'ril just shook his head. Her brother and Er'ril stared at each other, wearing strangely guarded expressions, as if each were hiding something from the other.

Joach finally broke the awkward silence. 'But I dreamed nothing about a statue. In my nightmare, the beast *flew*.'

The plainsman just continued to stare at the stone beast, little comforted by Joach's words. His rugged features had paled. 'I don't like this.'

Neither did Elena. She had seen too many statues come to life during the long journey here. She could not keep the worry from her voice. 'You mentioned power, Joach. Maybe it's like the crystal statue of the boy Denal. Maybe it'll come to life.'

Joach drifted nearer, stepping atop the fallen planks. He reached a hand toward the statue.

'Get back!' Er'ril scolded.

Wearing a frown, Joach slid his hand away. 'This stone is strange. Even polished, it doesn't seem to cast any reflection.'

Er'ril and Elena stepped nearer, but they maintained a safe distance.

'What do you think?' Joach asked Er'ril.

Elena was the one to answer. 'We need to destroy this. Now.'

'Why?' Joach asked. 'My dream was false. Moris and Flint said so. This bird is not coming to life.' He tapped at it with his staff.

Both Elena and Er'ril yelled a frantic 'No!' But nothing seemed to happen. Only a hollow *thunk* marked where wood met stone. The statue remained the same.

Er'ril shoved Joach away. 'Are you daft, boy? You don't fool with black magick like that.'

'What black magick? It's only ordinary stone.'

'No,' Elena argued, 'it's *ebon'stone*.' She pointed to the veins of silver running through the black rock. She had recognized the sculptor's medium. 'This stone drinks blood.'

Flint knew he had to hurry. The first mate, Master Vael, had left to fetch the bone drill and would be back in a few moments. If Flint wished to remain his own man, he had no time to waste.

His original plan had been to endure the tortures aboard the *Seaswift* until the boat reached Port Rawl. What was a broken nose and a bit of lost blood compared to the safe passage of the girl to the port city? But as Flint watched Captain Jarplin caress the tentacled creature in his palm, he knew his original scheme had to be scrapped.

Evil rode these waves, and no amount of fancy talking would get them safely to port. If he should succumb and become a thrall to that foul creature, Elena's secret would be revealed.

A new strategy was needed. And the first step was escape with his skull intact.

With his arms tied behind him, Flint worried the cuff of his battered coat with deft fingers. A small knife, no more than a sliver of steel, had been sewn into the fabric. Among pirates, it was always good to have weapons hidden where they couldn't be found. Once he had it gripped firmly, he pushed the blade through the ragged hemp. It popped through the material, and for a heart-shuddering moment it almost fumbled from his frantic fingers. Flint bit his split lip, using the pain to focus his attention. If he should drop the knife, he would be lost forever to the evil here.

Eying his former captain, Flint watched for any sign that his secretive movements had been noticed. Jarplin had always been sharp eyed and had seldom succumbed to trickery. Even with the monster in the captain's head, Flint could not trust that his instincts had dulled.

Licking the blood from his lips, Flint spoke, hoping to keep Jarplin distracted as he began working at the ropes. 'So just when did you become this creature's slave, Jarplin? How long has it been your master?'

As expected, the captain's face bloomed with color and his brows grew dark. Possessed by a monster or not, a part of Jarplin's personality persisted. He had been captain of his own fleet for twelve winters, and to suggest that Jarplin was no longer in control was a sore insult. Blustering for half a moment, Jarplin finally freed his angry tongue. 'I am and always will be *captain* of this vessel!' He waved at the back of his head with his free hand. 'I am not this thing's slave; it is a mere tool. It allows me to finally see the play of life for what it really is – a game of power where there is only one winner. And I mean to be on the right side.'

'And how did you acquire such a wonderful "tool"?'

'It was a gift.'

'Yes, I'm sure. One you accepted willingly,' Flint said, letting the sarcasm drip. He watched Jarplin's face twist with frustration.

Flint drove his words deeper as sweat built up on his own brow. 'So who was master when this was done to you? Master Vael perhaps? Does he pull your strings like a mummer's foppish puppet?'

Jarplin jerked with anger, almost tossing the tentacled creature from his palm. 'You know nothing! You can't possibly comprehend—'

'All I know is that the captain I once respected now bows and scrapes to the bidding of his jaundiced first mate – and a stinking foreigner at that.'

Jarplin had always had a hard prejudicial streak for non-Alaseans. By now, his cheeks were black with anger. And if Flint was not mistaken, there was also a bit of confusion in that expression.

Flint worked feverishly at his ropes. Time was running short.

The captain blinked a few times, doubt in his eyes, and a hand went to finger the back of his skull. 'What have I –?' Suddenly Jarplin doubled over in pain. A short, choked scream escaped his lips.

Flint almost stopped working at the ropes. Once, during a savage storm, Jarplin had taken a loose harpoon through the leg and had still managed to captain his crew through the gale, stomping around with a length of whaling blade through his thigh. Not a single cry had marked the injury then. But now . . . For Jarplin to show this much pain, Flint could not imagine the agony he must be experiencing.

'Captain?' Flint said, concerned, dropping his attempt at needling the man.

Jarplin fell on the edge of his bed, knees buckling. He sat there with his head bowed, shuddering gasps still shaking from him. Flint noticed that during this whole time Jarplin had never let loose of the tentacled beast. Even now, he held it cradled to his chest like a small infant. This could not be good.

Flint continued sawing at his bindings with the knife as Jarplin finally raised his head. Blood dribbled from where he had bit through his lip in pain. 'You . . . you'll soon learn,' he said weakly. 'It's a wonderful gift.'

Flint's eyes grew wide – not at the absurd statement, but at what he found in Jarplin's gaze. He had sailed through many hardships with the captain and knew him well. Right now, Jarplin not only believed his words, but there was the light of exultation in his eyes.

Mother above, what manner of beast or black magick could succeed in creating that worshipful response after such torture? Flint was determined *never* to find out. He almost gasped aloud when his knife finally sliced through the ropes that bound his hands.

Using his fingers, he kept a firm grasp on the freed ropes and knife. He could not risk letting them fall to the floor and be seen. Not yet. He must wait for the right moment.

A sudden creak of the door startled them both. The thin first mate pushed through the door. In one hand, he held a long drill that was used to core into whale skulls, a common tool aboard hunting vessels. The steel bit looked well used, its shaft glinting brightly in the lantern light.

Jarplin smiled at Flint, almost warmly. 'You'll soon see.'

Flint closed his eyes. His time had just run out.

Elena bunched her hand into a red fist. She could almost sense the malevolence pulsing from the ebon'stone statue.

'How do we destroy it?' Joach asked. 'It looks like it would take sledges and several strong men to crack that stone.'

Elena frowned. 'No, I doubt even the full force of my wit'ch fire could scratch its surface.'

'Then what can we do?' Joach asked. 'Maybe we should just leave it.'

Er'ril, who still stood silently eying the wyvern statue, shook his head. 'We can't leave this thing at our backs. There's no telling what menace broods here.'

Lowering the lantern, Elena turned to Er'ril. 'If the Try'sil is still packed in one of my trunks . . .'

Er'ril nodded, his features turning contemplative.

'What's that?' Joach asked with a touch to Elena's elbow.

'It's the sacred hammer of the d'warf clans, a hammer whose iron was forged in lightning.'

Er'ril finally spoke, straightening his stance. 'I know Cassa Dar places much reverence on the rune-carved talisman, but we don't know for certain that the Thunder Hammer could damage the statue.'

'It succeeded in cracking the ebon'stone armor of the blackguard demon,' Elena argued, referring to the battle at Castle Drak.

'But that was only a shell of ebon'stone. This appears to be cast from a single massive chunk of the foul ore.'

'Still, what other choice do we have? It's impervious to my magick, and I fear having Joach strike at it with his black magick.'

Er'ril glanced at her brother, silently. The plainsman's eyes revealed that he agreed with her statement. 'Did you see where they took our gear?'

Joach spoke up behind him. 'After they clubbed and dragged you off, I saw them hauling our supplies into the main hold.'

'Then we must find a way to get there without being seen.'

Elena held up her pale left hand. 'If I could regain my ghost magick, it would be a simple thing to sneak there.'

'But to do that, you'd first have to reach the spirit realm and renew,' Er'ril said, 'and I'd rather not have you that close to death again.'

She nodded. In truth, she had no wish to travel there again either.

By now, Joach had wandered to the crate's back side, peering into the crack between wall and box. 'Well, the rat that led us here wasn't in the crate, so it must have gone somewhere.'

'Good point, Joach. The beast reeked of fish, as if it had been nesting near the hold. Following it may be our best chance.' The plainsman waved Joach out of his way, then crawled within the narrow space between the wall and the crate. As they watched, Er'ril braced his back against the wall and pushed. Muscles bunched and strained against his wool breeches.

Joach moved to help, but Er'ril held up a hand. 'I don't want you near this cursed thing,' he said, his teeth clenched with effort, his face reddened to a ruddy fire. Still he strained harder. Finally, with a huffing gasp, he shoved with his whole body, and the crate slid across the floor with a low grind of wood.

Sighing from the exertion, Er'ril rolled out of the cramped space and stood up on his weakened legs. He used a hand on the wall to steady himself. 'Bring the lantern,' he said to Elena.

She crossed to him and lifted the lamp toward the darkness behind the crate. Near the base of the wall was a gnawed hole about the size of a ripe pumpkin. She squeezed past

Er'ril and knelt slightly to better illuminate the hole. As Elena got closer, she caught the whiff of an awful reek. She blinked against the smell, her nose curling. It stank of offal and the sting of salt.

'Do you see anything?' Er'ril asked.

'No,' she said, 'but I do smell something.' Fighting against the stench, she pressed into the cramped space, knelt with the lantern set beside her head, and peered through the ragged hole.

Just beyond the opening, she spotted the bottoms of barrels and nothing much else. Still, even through the reek, she sensed that the neighboring chamber was much larger. The slight drip of water from deeper in the room echoed hollowly, like the trickle of rainwater in a cavern. 'I think you were right. There's a large chamber, and from the smell, it might be the fish hold.'

'Let me take a look.' Er'ril and she exchanged places. He peered silently. 'Brine and fish. If this isn't the main hold, it must be close.'

'Then stand back,' Elena warned. She cast out threads of fire from her outstretched fingers.

Er'ril ducked away as she set about melting the nails and screws that secured a section of the wooden wall. Planks fell away, clattering against a row of barrels in the next room. Joach and Er'ril hurried to secure the falling boards before the noise should alert the crew.

'Mother above, that stench!' Joach choked.

'It's only salted fish,' Er'ril commented, but Elena noticed the slight curling of his nose. The reeking smell seemed to seep into their very skin. 'It's not as bad if you breathe through your mouth.'

With Joach's assistance, Er'ril tilted and rolled a barrel of oil out of the way, clearing a path into the next chamber.

They hurried, sticking close to the shadows by the wall. Er'ril ordered Elena to shutter the lantern's flame to a mere flicker. Now was not the time to be spotted.

They edged forward to where the floor of the chamber opened into a wide hole. Staring over the edge, they saw a sea of dead fish awash in thick crusts of salt. The smell stung their eyes, raising tears.

Er'ril pointed for Elena to shine the light above. 'If that's the fish hold, the main hatch of the ship must be directly above us.'

'What about our packs?' Joach asked. 'They must be stored somewhere on this level.'

Er'ril nodded. 'You two search for our things,' he answered. 'I'm going to find the crew hatch to the decks above.'

Elena hated the idea of splitting up. The main hold encompassed the entire midsection of the ship and was divvied up into smaller cubbyholes and side chambers. They would surely lose sight of each other as they explored, and that frightened her more than a pack of ravers. But she knew better than to complain. She sensed that time was running thin for all of them.

Joach took her hand as Er'ril disappeared into the shadows along the wall. 'Let's check over by those stacks of dry goods,' her brother whispered. He began to lead her along the edge of the deep hold.

Glancing forward, she spotted the section of decking where sacks of flour and grain lay piled like cords of wood. Once there, Joach pushed among the stacked barrels and burlap sacks. Elena followed, lantern raised before her like a shield.

They searched the short rows, the scent of rye and pepper almost masking the reek of fish here, but there was no sign of their gear.

'We'd better move on,' Joach said, his eyes darting all around.

She nodded just as one of the sacks near her elbow shifted, the rustle of burlap as loud as a scream in her tense ears. She almost bobbled the lantern from her fingers in her hurry to jump away.

Joach was immediately at her side. 'What –?'

Already Elena was swinging her lantern toward the displaced sack, using the lamp as both a weapon and as a means of illuminating any hidden menace. Beyond the far edge of the sack, toward the middle of this particular pile of stored goods, a small reddish-furred creature lay nestled.

Elena's first thought was that it was the back of a huge rat, but a small frightened sob suddenly arose from there. Raising the lantern higher, she realized her mistake. It was not a rat. It was the top of somebody's head – someone hidden in a castle of flour.

A small boy's face rose into the light, his features filthy and tearstained. Horror and fear reflected in the lamplight. 'Don't hurt me,' he moaned.

'Who are you?' Joach asked a bit harshly, his throat still obviously tight with his own fear.

Elena placed a hand on Joach's wrist. 'It's just a boy.' The lad could not be any older than ten or eleven winters. She lowered the lamp away from the boy's face and crept slowly nearer. He cringed back. 'We mean you no harm,' she whispered kindly. 'What are you doing down here?'

He seemed on the verge of tears. 'Hiding,' he finally said, half whimpering.

She continued in soothing tones. 'It's all right. You're with friends now. Why are you hiding here in the dark?'

'It's the only safe place. The smells keep the monsters from sniffing me out.'

Elena looked with concern at Joach. She did not like what his words implied.

Joach motioned for her to continue coaxing information from the boy.

She stepped nearer. 'Monsters?'

Nodding, the small lad shivered and hugged his arms around his belly. 'I've been hiding down here since the ship was bewit'ched by Master Vael. Him and the creatures that was with him. They made ... They did ...' The boy suddenly sobbed and buried his face in his hands. 'I ran and hid with the rats. They didn't find me.'

She placed the lantern on the floor and reached to his cheek, resting a palm there. He was so cold. 'We won't let anything happen to you,' she whispered. She waved Joach over to move some of the sacks out of the way.

'What's your name?' she asked as Joach began freeing the boy.

'Tok,' he said, wiping at his eyes. 'I was the ship's cabin boy.'

Joach and Elena helped him from his hiding place. The lad wore scraps of torn and soiled clothes. As he stood, his limbs twitched, and his hands kept picking at his shirt in nervousness.

She knelt to be at eye level with him and took his tremoring hands in her own. 'How long have you been hiding down here?'

'Almost a full moon,' he said. 'I been picking at the supplies when no one was around. I was hoping we'd reach some port. Then maybe I could run away.'

Now that he seemed calmer, Elena finally turned to the more important question. 'What happened here?'

His eyes grew round with her question. He obviously feared even talking about it. But she stroked his arm and squeezed his hands until his tongue finally freed. 'On the far side of the Archipelago, Captain Jarplin spotted an island that we never seen before. He ordered the ship to turn about and go explore it.'

Elena glanced significantly at Joach. The island of A'loa Glen.

'But as we neared,' Tok continued, his voice growing smaller as he recounted the tale, 'a horrible storm blew in. Lightning seemed to crawl across the sky after us. We thought we were dead for sure. Then a ship came up out of the darkness — a ship like you never seen before, all lit up with blue and green crackles in her sails, like the storm itself were powering her. We could not escape. Creatures came at us. Beasts with bony wings and skin so pale you could see their bellies churning.' He raised his eyes, as if checking to see if he was believed.

'Skal'tum,' Elena whispered to Joach.

Tok continued. 'There was a foreigner with sick-looking skin and teeth filed sharp as a shark. His name was Vael. And after what he did to the captain and the others, Jarplin made him his first mate.'

'What did they do to the crew?' Joach asked.

Tok shook his head and bit his lower lip. 'It were so horrible.' The lad slipped his hands from hers and covered his eyes as he spoke, as if to lessen his view on this horrible event. 'They marched all the men on deck. They bent them over the butcher's block and drilled into the back of their heads with the whale pinner. And the screams ... They went on for a day and a night. Some of the crew tried to leap overboard, but the winged monsters snatched them back.' Tok suddenly lowered his hand from his face. His eyes were half mad. 'I saw them eat Mister Fasson. Tore him in half and ate him while he still screamed.'

Elena pulled the boy into her embrace. He shook for the longest time. Maybe she shouldn't have pushed him so soon.

After a few more shuddering breaths, he pushed out of her embrace. 'But that weren't the worst of it. After they drilled them holes in the men's heads, they shoved in these creatures that looked like squids, but they weren't nothing like anything I ever seen netted from the sea. The men twitched and moaned on the deck for near part of a full day. Afterward, they'd do whatever Master Vael said. At his order, they even butchered some of the men that didn't wake up fast enough from the drilling. They chopped them up and fed 'em to the winged monsters.' Tok stared Elena in the eye. 'And the crew didn't even care. They laughed while they worked on their friends with the axes and saws.'

Elena's stomach churned at this story. Mother above, how did this boy survive this horror? She hugged him tight as he began crying again.

'I couldn't do nothin' but hide,' he moaned into her chest. 'I spied when they captured you, too, but still didn't do nothing. I'm such a coward. I should've warned you away. Told you to leap into the sea and drown rather than come aboard this cursed ship.'

She wrapped her arms tighter and rocked him as her own mother had rocked her after a nightmare. But it was little comfort. This was no night figment. 'Get Er'ril,' she mouthed to Joach over the boy's head.

Her brother nodded and slipped away.

Once he was gone, Elena spoke words to calm the boy. The lad had faced horrors that would break most men. 'You could not stop such evil by yourself,' she whispered to him consolingly. 'You would only have been killed. By living, you were able to warn us of the evil.'

He finally raised his face again, sniffing back tears. 'But

what can you do? There are so many of them.'

She placed a finger on his lips. 'Hush. There are ways.' An idea suddenly occurred to her. If the boy had spied on their capture . . . 'Tok, do you happen to know where they took our supplies?'

He nodded. 'It's just down the ways from here. I could show you.'

Suddenly he tensed in her arms – then she heard it, too: the approaching scuff of heel on wood. He tried to wriggle and bolt, but she calmed him. She had recognized the muttered voices accompanying the footsteps. 'Fear not. It's just my brother returning with a friend.'

Er'ril stepped from the darkness into the tiny pool of lamplight. He eyed the young lad as if appraising a piece of horseflesh. 'Joach told me his story,' he said gruffly.

'He also knows where our packs are,' Elena added.

'Good,' the plainsman said, 'maybe he can show us a better way through the ship.'

Elena turned to question the boy, but he was already nodding. 'I know many ways.'

Er'ril crossed to the boy. Elena thought he meant to comfort the lad in some way, but instead, he bent the boy's head down and brusquely ran his fingers over the boy's neck. 'He does not seem contaminated.'

Elena's breath caught in her throat. After all the boy'd been through, how could Er'ril be so callous, so cold? But at the same time, another part of her quailed that she had never considered the boy a danger. She had even gone so far as to send Joach away, leaving herself alone with this stranger.

The same assessment could be seen in Er'ril's angry features as he stared at Elena. Even Joach seemed sheepish, eyes downcast. Her brother must have heard a few hard words from Er'ril about abandoning his sister.

'We dare not delay any further,' Er'ril finally said.

Suddenly a shrieking scream burst through the ship's bulkheads, echoing across the cavernous hold.

Tok moaned in her embrace, ducking his head away. 'Not again.'

Elena eyed Er'ril over the top of the boy's head. There was recognition also in the plainsman's stare.

Flint.

10

'Who goes there?' a voice thundered from the darkness near the inn's stoop.

The fog hid the guard well in the shadowed alcove. Behind him, the beat of a drum and the twang of a poorly tuned lyre accompanied the raucous laughter from beyond the inn's closed door. Above the lintel, a single lantern illuminated a faded sign that read *The Wolfshide Inn*.

'We come to speak with Tyrus,' Jaston said. Mycelle stood at Jaston's side. They had left the rest of the troupe near the docks, with Tol'chuk and Kral acting as guards. Her son's heartstone had led them to the water's edge, still urging them onward with its fiery glow, but to follow the stone any further would require hiring a boat. After a heated debate, it had been decided to contact the dock's caste master and arrange for a crew and a small ship. But the title *caste master* was only a thin veneer of respectability that, in fact, masked the bloody leader of Port Rawl's pirates. And no transaction was done at the docks without a proper 'fee' paid to this brigand.

'What business have you with Lord Tyrus at this late hour?'

Mycelle snorted. In Port Rawl, the cloak of midnight was

when all pirates struck their deals, usually in smoky taverns like this one over many tall flasks of ale. 'Our business is our own,' she answered sullenly.

'Fine. Keep your tongue to yourself then. But if you bother Tyrus with matters that don't concern him, he'll cut out your tongue and hand it back to you for your troubles. He is not a man to be trifled with.'

'Your warning is well appreciated,' Mycelle said and tossed a silver coin into the shadowed alcove. The coin vanished but never struck stone. Silver always caught the eye of pirates.

A loud knocking erupted from the stoop, sword hilt on wood. The pattern rapped was clearly a code. A small peephole opened in the door. 'Tyrus has visitors,' the guard said. 'Strangers . . . with silver.'

The tiny door snapped closed, and the larger door swung open. Laughter and music rolled out from the inn's heart, leaving a trail of pipe smoke and the odor of unwashed bodies. 'Go on in,' the guard said. In the flare of torches, the guard's features were seen for the first time. He was a swarthy man whose face was not much less scarred than Jaston's. He winked salaciously at Mycelle as she passed.

She smiled at him – not in a friendly manner, but to reveal the steel behind her handsome features. His eyes darted away as he quickly closed the door.

Glancing ahead, Mycelle studied the room. The commons was crammed with crude tables constructed from what looked like planks from shipwrecks. A few tables even had the old names of the original ships still painted on them: the *Singing Swan*, the *Esymethra*, the *Shark's Fin*. Mycelle suspected it wasn't all storms that sank these ships. They seemed more like trophies, and she was sure the stories that went with them were bloody.

Seated at the tables were hard men from every land of Alasea and beyond. Mycelle spotted dark-skinned warriors from the Southern Wastes, tattooed Steppemen with rings through their noses, thick-browed giants who normally roamed the Crumbling Mounds, even a pair of pale, spindly-limbed Yunk tribesmen from as far away as the Isles of Kell. It seemed the filth from every land ended up washing ashore here in Port Rawl.

Yet as varied as these men appeared, they all shared two things in common: a hard, calculating glance in their eyes, even when their lips were laughing, and scars. Not a single face was free of a disfiguring sword cut or torch burn, and some injuries looked fresh.

As Mycelle followed Jaston, she realized that it wasn't only men who sat at these tables. Mycelle was so startled that she tripped over her own toe. The small snake at her wrist hissed at her sudden movement.

In a shadowed corner, she spotted a trio of women wearing matching black leathers and cloaks. Three sets of twin crossed swords rested on the table amidst their mugs of steaming kaffee. Each wore her blond hair long and braided in back. Mycelle could have been one of their sisters – and in a way, she was. The trio were mercenary Dro from Castle Mryl, where she herself had been trained in the art of the sword so long ago. At the time, Mycelle had shifted her shape to match the blond, tall women of the northern forests while undertaking her training. It was this form she had settled upon forever. It suited her well.

But what was a Dro trio doing here, among these pirates? True, a Dro's sword was always for hire, but it was only granted to serve a cause considered noble enough for their sacred training, not to lend their strength and skill to pirates.

One of the trio noticed Mycelle. The woman's blue eyes

opened slightly wider, her only reaction – but for a Dro, it might as well have been a scream.

Jaston stepped beside Mycelle and touched her elbow. 'I learned that Tyrus is in the back room. We're in luck. He'll see us right away.'

Mycelle nodded. She had been so shocked by her discovery that she had not even noticed that the swamp man had left. The man to whom Jaston had spoken still stood nearby, an officious-looking fellow who wore the coned hat of a scribe. Tapping a toe in impatience, the scribe waved a battered ledger to get them to hurry. Mycelle noticed the man's fingertips were stained black with ink. It seemed even pirates needed to keep track of their accumulated plunders.

Mycelle pushed aside the mysteries of the Dro. For now, she needed a ship to hire. If Elena was in danger, as Cassa Dar sensed and Tol'chuk's heartstone supported, they did not have time to ponder the reasons for the trio of trained warriors appearing in a seedy Port Rawl inn.

'Let's find this pirate and get out of here,' Mycelle grumbled.

Jaston followed the back of the tiny scribe as he led them through a curtain into a private hall, then down to a small door at the end. The skinny man kept tucking stray strands of brown hair back under his scribe's hat. He knocked on the door.

'Enter!' was hollered back at him.

The scribe turned, smiled sickly at them, and opened the door. 'Lord Tyrus will see you now.'

Jaston entered first. With the slightest hand signal, a common gesture used among the hunters of the deadly swamps, he indicated that it looked safe to continue, but to watch their backs.

Mycelle could feel the weight of steel riding on her back. She was slightly surprised that the guards had not asked them to leave their weapons behind – not that she wouldn't have managed to slip a dagger or two past any search of her person. Still, this lack of simple precaution made her more uneasy than if the guards had removed every weapon she had. Just how formidable an adversary were they about to encounter?

Mycelle entered the room and was stunned by what she discovered. Lord Tyrus sat at a table by himself, a half-finished meal before him, with an open book at his elbow. No guards. Yet Mycelle knew the man was well protected. She sensed the danger emanating from him like heat off a hearth. Even with the loss of her seeking ability, she sensed that his power was not born of black magick, but of simple skill and training. He was his own protection and feared nothing from them.

Licking her dry lips, she found his eyes weighing her every move, judging her for weaknesses and strengths. He smiled at her, a simple nod. She returned the nod, two warriors acknowledging one another.

Dangerous or not, she was unprepared for how truly handsome Lord Tyrus was. He was younger than she would have imagined, no older than thirty winters, with broad shoulders and an even broader smile. Under thick sandy hair, brushed and oiled back behind his ears, with a neatly trimmed mustache and small clipped beard, he could have been a handsome prince from one of the many kingships of Alasea.

'Please, come and be seated,' he said with plain civility. 'I've taken the liberty of ordering a mug of swampbeer for the gentleman, and I believe the Dro have a preference for kaffee. You have no reason to fear for the others in your party by the dock. They are under my protection while we chat.'

Jaston glanced at Mycelle. The man already knew so much about them.

Clearing her throat, Mycelle thanked him for his graciousness, and the two took the offered seats. 'If you know so much already, then you must also know we seek to hire a ship.'

'Indeed, to rescue some girl . . .' He paused, inviting them to fill in any additional details. With their silence, his smile grew wider.

As he smiled, Mycelle noticed one other detail about this handsome king of the pirates. He bore no scars – and this worried her most of all. How did he fight his way to the top of these hard men and show no sign of the battle? Just how skilled a fighter was he?

She found the question asked aloud before she could stop it. 'Where did you learn to fight so well?'

His smile dimmed slightly. He had not expected a question from such an unusual direction. But he brightened quickly. 'Ah, you are perceptive . . . Though long gone from Castle Mryl, you keep your skills well honed. "A keen eye for detail is often more important than the keenest-edged sword."'

Mycelle started at his words. This last was an old adage taught to her by the mistress of the sword during her training long ago.

Lord Tyrus reached for his glass of red wine, and faster than Mycelle could follow, a long sword appeared in his other hand. She jumped back, knocking her chair away and sweeping out her two swords. But she was too late. The sword tip already lay in the hollow of Jaston's throat. The swamper had not even had time to raise a hand.

The king of the pirates laughed, hearty and gay, and pulled his sword away. 'Just judging your speed. I'm sorry, but I could not resist testing your Dro training.'

Mycelle still shook from the sudden threat. The man moved with the grace and speed of a striking serpent. She kept her swords at ready, figuring she could negotiate just as well armed. She would not be caught unprepared again.

Tyrus eyed her swords, his eyes still laughing. There was no hard, calculating glint to his gaze, just plain amusement. He had not resheathed his sword either, she noted. Instead, he rested the blade on the table. Judging from the luster of the steel, the weapon was ancient. If she was not mistaken, it looked as if the steel had been folded at least a hundred times during its forging. Such a skill had been lost to blade-smiths for countless centuries. All in all, the sword was as handsome as its current wielder. She wondered from what rich owner this pirate had plundered such an exquisite weapon.

His hand finally slipped free of the hilt, exposing its design. Plain in form, it held no jewels, no gilt or filigree, just an arc of steel in the shape of a striking snow leopard.

Mycelle's mouth dropped open. Sweet Mother! She remembered the trio of Dro in the common room. Sudden understanding lit her face. She fell to her knees and crossed her swords before her, bowing her head between the blades.

'Mycelle?' Jaston's voice was full of confusion.

'Your Grace,' she said, ignoring the swamp man's inquiry.

'Oh, on your feet, woman!' Tyrus ordered. 'I'll not have you bowing and scraping before me. You owe me no allegiance. You swore fealty to my father, not me.'

Mycelle raised her face and sheathed her swords. Blindly, she fumbled behind to retrieve her chair and pulled it upright.

Sitting, she stared again into his face and amused eyes. She now saw the father in the son's face. When last she had laid eyes upon Tyrus, he had been only a young boy. Old memories roiled in her mind. 'Prince Tylamon Royson,' she named him truly.

'Please, here I simply go by Tyrus.'

Mycelle's mind spun off in a hundred different directions. 'What ... what happened? Why are you here?'

'The Northwall has been sundered,' he said. 'Castle Mryl has fallen.'

'What!' Mycelle could not have been more shocked than if the man had said the sun would never rise again. Castle Mryl overlooked the great Northwall, an ancient barricade of solid granite, built not by man or any hands, but simply thrust up by the land itself. A league in height and a thousand leagues in length, it marked the northernmost border of the Western Reaches. Its impregnable bulk separated the black forest, the Dire Fell, from the green of the Reaches. If the Northwall had fallen ...

'How long ago did this happen?'

Tyrus' features grew grim for the first time. 'Almost a decade.'

Her face paled. 'And the Dire Fell?'

'My Dro spies report to me regularly. The Grim of Dire Fell have spread as far as the Stone of Tor.'

'So fast? That's already a quarter of the way into the great forest.'

He just stared at her, letting her absorb it all.

Her mind turned toward her own people, the si'lura. The Western Reaches was their home, their green bower. If the Grim of the Fell should continue their foul reach into the forest, soon the tribes of her people would be doomed to flee the forest's safety, likely to die in the mountains of the Teeth.

'H-how did Castle Mryl fall?'

'For many winters, our scouts had been sent into the Fell and had returned with reports of strange lights and blighted creatures seen roaming the heights near the ancient homelands of the Mountain People, near Tor Amon and the Citadel. Then one winter, our scouts stopped returning.'

'The d'warves?' Mycelle could not help glancing at Jaston, who only wore a stoic expression.

Tyrus nodded. 'The entrenched d'warf armies had been so quiet for so long that we didn't know what to expect. But my father called back all his Dro-trained warriors, calling for them to honor their oaths.'

'I heard nothing of this,' Mycelle said, shame burning her face.

Tyrus ignored her words. His eyes seemed lost in the past. 'That winter, something came out of the deep mountains – something from the black core of Tor Amon. The Grim of the Fell grew stronger, fed and goaded by black magicks. My father's Dro armies could not resist such strength, and my father died defending the last tower.' His eyes filled with tears and anger.

'I'm sorry,' Mycelle said, but even in her own ears, the words sounded hollow. 'Your father was a great man.'

Still, Tyrus did not acknowledge her. His story seemed to spill from him like a torrent down a dry gully. 'The night before he died, he sent me out with the last of the Dro. He knew he would die the next day and did not want our bloodline to end. If there was ever to be a chance to regain our lands and repair the Northwall, one of the Blood must survive.'

Mycelle understood the necessary caution. The Northwall was not a cold slab of granite. She herself had placed both palms on the great wall as she swore fealty to the Snow Leopard, Tyrus' father, the king of Castle Mryl. The stone had warmed with her words until the granite almost burned her palms. The Northwall was a living creature – she had even sensed its heart with her seeking ability. The granite heart was not in the stone, but in the man to whom she swore fealty – in the king of Mryl. The two were forever linked. Blood and Stone.

She stared at Tyrus. Here stood the new Blood of the Wall.

'So I fled,' he said, the words all but spat out, 'leaving my father to die under the roots of the Grim. I fled as fast and far as I could – to here. Once I could flee no farther, my anger exploded and knew no bounds. I let my heated blood boil through these streets and out into the cold seas. Not all I did during that time was noble or even good. No man could stand in my way.' He laughed harshly, nothing like the amusement from a few moments ago. 'After two years of such raving, my blood finally cooled, and I discovered I was lord of these pirates.'

He stopped talking, picked up the ancient blade of his family, and sheathed it. The silence loomed like a fourth member of the conversation.

Finally, Mycelle spoke. 'I should've been there.'

'No,' he said plainly. His eyes were no longer heated or amused, just tired and drained. 'Contrary to appearances, you are not Dro.'

His words wounded her, but she could not blame him. Though she had never heard the summons to the Northwall, she still felt as if she had betrayed her oaths. 'Why did you end up here?'

'It's where my father told me to go,' he answered. 'As Blood of the Wall, the land spoke to him and instructed him to send me here, to languish for near a decade among these heartless men.'

'But why?'

'To wait for the return of she who would give her blood to save the Western Reaches.'

Mycelle knew he spoke of Elena and her blood magicks. The prophecies surrounding the child seemed to grow with each passing day, from all the lands of Alasea.

Tyrus turned hard eyes toward Mycelle and dashed away her assumptions. 'I came to wait for she who was Dro but not Dro, for she who could change faces as easily as the seasons.'

Mycelle's heart grew to ice in her chest.

'I came to wait for you.'

She stammered and fought to speak. 'B-but that's impossible.'

'You are si'luran,' he said plainly, ignoring her shock.

Jaston startled in the chair beside her, a gasp on his lips. 'You're mad,' he said. 'I've known Mycelle since before she was—'

Mycelle placed a hand on his elbow and shook her head, silencing him and acknowledging the truth in Tyrus' claim. As the realization dawned in Jaston, she did not see the horror she had expected in his eyes, but simply wounded betrayal.

'I'm sorry, Jaston . . .'

He shook free of her touch.

Mycelle turned back to Tyrus. 'What do you expect of me?'

'To come with me – back to Castle Mryl.'

A rustle of cloaks announced the presence of others stationed behind her. Jaston turned, but Mycelle did not. She knew the rustle was done purposely to signal their presence. The Dro could move silently as ghosts. The trio of women warriors had probably been standing there all along.

'Old oaths or not, I cannot abandon Elena,' she said succinctly.

Tyrus smiled, all amusement again. 'I'm afraid you must, or the wit'ch you guard will die.' He stood up, and she saw the granite behind his gaze. 'Thus the Wall has spoken.'

Tol'chuk worried about his mother. She had been gone only a short time, and though he imagined that dealing with pirates was best not rushed, he could not keep his heart from calling out to her. He had lost her when he was a mere babe, only to find her again and see her die. Now that he had her back once again, he feared having her leave his side for even the shortest time or the gravest necessity.

Fardale approached from where the wolf patrolled their encampment along the docks. His eyes glowed amber in the foggy darkness. As he approached, the wolf sent a fuzzy image toward the og're: *A wolf cub nestled in the curl of its mother's belly.* All was safe, the wolf reported, but the maternal picture of mother and child only made Tol'chuk's heart ache more.

Tol'chuk stretched atop his clawed legs and followed Fardale as he passed along the troupe's edge. He needed to keep moving, keep distracted. He was glad when Mogweed stepped out of the shadows toward them.

The tiny shape-shifter greeted his brother with a nod as the wolf continued his sentry. Tol'chuk stayed at Mogweed's side. It was clear the man wanted to talk. 'I'm sure Mycelle is fine,' Mogweed said.

'I know,' Tol'chuk said. 'She be skilled with both swords and has little to fear from pirates.'

Mogweed stared down the fog-choked alleys that led out from the docks. 'But still you worry.'

Tol'chuk remained silent. There were times when the shape-shifter rubbed Tol'chuk's bristles the wrong way, but every now and then, the man surprised him with his empathy.

'You need not fear for her, Tol'chuk. Besides her swordsmanship, Mycelle is a skilled shape-shifter. With the return of her heritage, she can slip away from any tight noose – even fly away if she needs to.'

Tol'chuk rested a hand on Mogweed's shoulder. He heard the longing in the shape-shifter's words. For a brief flicker, he sensed how trapped Mogweed must feel in this one form. Escape for him was impossible. Tol'chuk offered him hope. 'If my mother could regain her abilities—'

'It's not the same,' Mogweed cut him off sourly. 'To cure me – I mean both Fardale and myself – it'll take more than a magick snake.'

'We'll find a way.'

Mogweed turned moist eyes toward Tol'chuk. 'I truly want to trust your words, but time runs short.'

Fardale suddenly raced back into their midst. His images were rushed, vague, but the meaning clear. A large group approached.

Tol'chuk followed the wolf back toward where a dark street delved into the black heart of the port. Kral appeared at his side, blade in hand. Meric, Mama Freda, and the others hung back. Mogweed retreated to join them by the horses and wagon.

From out of the fog, a large, shadowy group took form. As they approached, the ghostly silhouettes became solid flesh. Tol'chuk recognized his mother leading the group with the swamp man on one side and a tall stranger on the other. Mycelle raised a hand in greeting, empty palm forward, indicating that those she led meant them no harm. Still, Tol'chuk noted that Kral kept his ax in hand.

Mycelle had no smiles of greeting as she joined them. She came with grim news. Over her shoulder, Tol'chuk spotted a trio of dark shadows: women with braids as golden as his mother's, all outfitted with the characteristic crossed swords. They could have been his mother's sisters.

Tol'chuk finally noticed a similar resemblance in the stranger who stood beside her. Like the women, this stranger could also pass as a relation to his mother – a younger brother perhaps. Even his clothes were the same mixture of worn leather and steel, but instead of twin swords crossed on his back, he bore a long sword at his waist.

'We have a ship,' Mycelle stated plainly, drawing all their attentions from the strangers. There was no satisfaction in her voice.

Kral spoke next. 'And who are all these others?'

'Crew and fighters sworn to take you safe to Elena's side,' she answered, her voice tight.

Tol'chuk heard the extra meaning in her words. 'What do you mean "*take you*"?' he asked.

She would not meet his eyes. 'I don't intend to travel with you all. I have been called to pursue another path.'

The shock ran like lightning through the group.

'What?' Tol'chuk could not keep the wound from his voice.

The stranger stepped forward. 'We've arranged a small sloop that is well worn to the straits of the Archipelago, and a crew of four.' The man waved to a group of four tall black-skinned men who stood behind him. They wore feathers in their hair and had eyes of piercing jade. Scars marked their brows – not from battle but from some old ritual. A criss-crossing of pale scars formed a different pattern on each man's forehead. They're marked with runes, Tol'chuk thought.

The stranger continued speaking. 'This crew will serve you well on the journey ahead. The zo'ol are skilled warriors and seamen, and well familiar with the channels of the Archipelago.'

Kral growled at the stranger. 'But just who are *you*?'

Mycelle stepped forward. 'This is Lord Tyrus,' she said as introduction.

'The leader of this city's cutthroats?' Kral asked with clear disdain.

'Also a prince of Castle Mryl,' she said significantly.

This statement quieted the mountain man. 'Mryl? Below the Dire Fells?'

'Yes,' she said, still not meeting Tol'chuk's eyes. 'You must know of the castle. It once housed your people as they fled the d'warf armies.'

Kral finally hooked his ax to his belt. 'Yes, during the Scattering of our clans. We owe the Blood of the castle a debt that can never be repaid.'

Tyrus strode forward. '*Never* is too final a word, man of the mountains.'

Kral crinkled his brow at this mysterious statement, but no further elaboration was offered. Tyrus turned to survey the others in their troupe while Mycelle and Jaston started organizing for their departure. Tol'chuk could only stare numbly at his mother. She was leaving? The thought still had not fully reached his heart – and he feared what would happen when it did. Sighing, he busied himself with loading the wagon and hitching the horses.

Once outfitted, Tyrus led his pirates and their group along the docks to a long pier. Berthed near the end was a twin-masted sloop. The name, *Pale Stallion,* was painted in red on the blond wood. It was not a big ship, but it would fit their company and house the horses.

With all the extra hands, the boat was loaded quickly. They would depart with the morning's tide. Already birds were stirring from their nests under the boards of the pier, greeting the dawn's approach with song and noisy squawks.

Once all was ready, the group gathered on the pier. Mycelle had her back to Tol'chuk, talking to Jaston. Tol'chuk slid closer to overhear them.

'. . . I should have told you,' she said. 'I'm sorry.'

'No, you owe me no apology. When we were together, there was always a part of you that was kept hidden from me. I knew it then, and it was probably that reason more than any I knew that we could never fully share a life together. I knew you cared for me, and I did you. But there was never a sharing of hearts that is true love, a love that will last until gray marks our hair.'

Tears were in his mother's eyes. 'And Cassa Dar?'

Jaston smiled and kissed Mycelle on the cheek. 'Some things only the fullness of time will reveal truly. In many ways, she is as wounded as you.'

Mycelle returned the kiss. 'Something tells me you will find a way to heal her.'

He smiled, a bit sadly, and bowed his head. 'I should see to our wagon and horses.'

She nodded, touching his arm one last time as he turned away and left. Mycelle stared for a few moments, then turned around to find Tol'chuk standing behind her. She met his eyes finally. The pain was clear in her face.

Before any word could be spoken, Tyrus intruded. He had stridden to Mycelle. 'Something is wrong here,' he stated.

'What?' she snapped, venting her pain and frustration at him.

The prince's eyes widened a bit, but he seemed to

understand her tension and spoke a bit softer. 'There are other shape-shifters here,' he said, nodding toward Fardale and Mogweed. 'Their eyes give them away.' He stared closer at Tol'chuk's eyes. 'And I'm not sure about this large fellow.'

'He's my son. A half-breed og're,' Mycelle said sullenly, the fire blown out of her. 'What does it matter about the other two?'

'They must come with us,' he stated firmly.

'Why?' By now, the content of their words must have reached the wolf's keen ears. Fardale and Mogweed approached nearer.

Tyrus acknowledged their presence. 'My father's prophecy spoke of two other parties who must come to Castle Mryl. I thought we'd meet them on the journey home, in the Western Reaches, not find them all here with you.'

'Who?'

'First, a pair of shape-shifting brothers – twins, I believe?'

Mogweed's startled eyes revealed the truth in Tyrus' assessment. 'How did you . . . ?'

Tyrus faced them. 'Twins frozen by a curse.'

Mogweed stepped closer to Tol'chuk. This was the first time either of the shape-shifters had been mentioned in any prophecy. The thought seemed to frighten Mogweed. A low growl even rattled in Fardale's throat. 'D-did your prophecy mention a cure?' Mogweed whispered, hope hushing his voice.

'"Two will come frozen; one will leave whole."'

The brothers glanced at each other. Hope and doom were mixed in these words. It sounded like only one of the twins would survive the lifting of their curse. A silent exchange passed between brothers. Tol'chuk caught a glimmer of it. One was better than none.

By now, the entire party had gathered around them.

Mogweed touched his brother's shoulder. Fardale turned and sat on his haunches, the matter settled. Mogweed spoke. 'We will come with you.'

Their decision upset Mycelle. 'We can't all go with you, Tyrus. They're needed to lend their strength to defend Elena.'

Tyrus' brows drew up doubtfully. 'A spindly man like him and a large dog? If the fate of this girl rests on this pair, then she is already doomed.' He turned away. 'Besides, their decision has been made.'

Mycelle was left red faced and frustrated.

Tol'chuk was calmer. He spoke at Tyrus' back. The stranger was leaving something still unsaid. 'You mentioned two parties. The pair of twin shape-shifters and one other. Who?'

'Another shape-shifter,' Tyrus said, not turning around.

Tol'chuk's heart leaped, believing the prince meant him. Even Mycelle glanced to her son, a glint of hope lighting her eyes. He winced from her gaze. He could not go with her. Even now, the heartstone called to him to continue out into the Archipelago, an ache in his heart and bones that he could never refuse – not even to stay with his mother.

But the choice was taken from him. Tyrus turned, swinging his sword out in a smooth pull and pointing it square into the chest of Kral. 'You, mountain man, are the last shape-shifter.'

All eyes turned to Kral. He fought to keep the shock from his features. Although forged in darkfire, he was still one with the Rock. His features maintained a stony countenance. 'You've been too deep in your cups, pirate,' he said with a dark glower. 'I'm no more a shape-shifter than you are.'

'The mountain man speaks the truth,' Mycelle spoke up. 'He has no si'luran blood. My son—'

'No,' Tyrus said, dismissing the swordswoman with a flash of fire in his eyes. 'Blood does not always show its true color. I am pirate and prince. You are Dro and not Dro.' He waved his arm at Fardale and Mogweed. 'They are shape-shifters, but then again not. In life, few people are whom they appear to be. We all wear masks.'

'Not I,' Kral said boldly.

'Is that so?' Tyrus continued his condescending grin. 'Then tell me, Are you a mountain nomad ... or an heir to the throne of Tor Amon?'

These words stunned Kral. Even among his own people, few remembered that his clan, the Senta flame, had once composed the royal house, and his family, a'Darvun, still bore a direct line to their abandoned throne. This secret was both his family's honor and shame, for it had been Kral's own ancestor who had lost their homelands ten generations ago to the d'warves, cursing their clans forever to their nomadic trails. Even now, the memory inflamed Kral's blood, the beast in him snarling for revenge.

Tyrus must have read his thoughts. 'Does your heart still cry to reclaim your homelands, to return your clan fires once again to the Citadel's watchtowers?'

Kral fought his cracking voice. 'Do not provoke me, small man. What is this you rant about?'

Tyrus partially closed his eyes, reciting from long memory. '"With the twins, there shall come a mountain of a man who wears many faces, forms shifting like snowdrifts in a gale. You will know him by his hard eyes and a beard as black as his heart. But do not be fooled. In him, you will find a king who will bear a broken crown upon his brow and sit again the throne of the Citadel."'

Kral dared not hope the pirate's words held any truth. It was too cruel a dream. After being driven off by the d'warf hordes, his people had become nomads – not because they enjoyed the wandering life, but simply because they refused to give up the belief that someday their lands would be returned to them. Could Kral make this hope come true? Could he end his people's centuries-long journey and take them home again?

Mycelle explained why not. 'He needs to join Elena.'

The mention of the wit'ch's name pushed aside Kral's dreams of thrones and crowns. He could not deny his master's will.

'If the mountain man seeks Elena, he will kill her,' Tyrus said simply.

No one moved. Eyes glanced at Kral. From their worried gazes, they expected blood to be spilled for the insulting words. Little did they know how true Tyrus spoke; not even the pirate himself was aware of it.

Tyrus continued, revealing the limits to his prophetic knowledge. 'I don't mean to imply that Kral would betray your young friend and slay her with his ax, but if he does not come with us, she will die just as surely. My father's words were exact: "Three must come, or the wit'ch will die." ' Tyrus sheathed his sword and crossed his arms.

Mycelle turned to Kral. 'The Northwall is rich in elemental magicks; it is a pure font of power direct from the land's heart. When I could still seek, its power was like a lodestone. Its call drew me north, where I eventually learned the sword from the wardens of Castle Mryl. There I also learned of King Ry's scrying powers when he linked to the stone. Though the old man's prophecies were rare, they never proved wrong.' Mycelle glanced back at Tyrus. 'But sometimes the interpretations were. So beware of making your decision based on these words, mountain man.'

Kral felt pulled within himself, two choices warring in his

heart. The part of his spirit forged in darkfire refused to give up its quest for the wit'ch, such was the Dark Lord's brand upon his blood. But as in all ill'guard, a shard of his true self persisted, a spark of elemental fire that fed the Black Heart's spell. And this sliver of spirit could not ignore the call of his homeland. It swelled with the hopes of all his clans.

In any other person, such a fight would have failed, for the Dark Heart's brand was set with a fierce flame that none could erase. But Kral was not just a man. In his blood ran the magick that flowed through a mountain's granite roots. And granite withstood even the fiercest flames. Though scorched by darkfire, the brand had not burned deep enough into Kral's stony determination to make him ignore the cries from generations of his ancestors.

The Ice Throne was his family's seat, and he would claim his heritage once again! Beware any who would stand in his way!

Turning to Tyrus, Kral ran a hand through his rough beard and eyed the pirate. 'I will come with you,' he growled hoarsely.

Tyrus smiled and nodded, as if he had expected no other decision.

Kral's brows darkened. The Black Heart's compulsion still nagged at him, gnawing at his resolve. But he calmed the last of its heated demands with a soothing thought, a balm on the friction within: After he reclaimed his throne, he would hunt Elena down as a reward and shred her young heart. He would not forget his duty to the Black Heart — only delay it.

Kral hid a hard smile in his black beard.

Nothing would be denied Legion — not a throne, not even the sweet blood of a wit'ch.

* * *

The *Pale Stallion* had been made ready, and the group now stood split into two parties – those on the docks wishing the others a fair journey and those on the boats watching friends ready themselves for a trek halfway across Alasea. Neither party was in good cheer. Faces were sullen at best, heartsick at worst.

Mycelle stared into the eyes of the one who seemed the most lost and alone. Before her, Tol'chuk stood at the foot of the gangway, his features damaged. Most thought og'res stoic and of little emotion. But Mycelle knew the signs that spoke otherwise. Tol'chuk's fangs were fully draped by his down-turned lip; his eyes had lost their subtle shine; even his shoulders had fallen like shattered mountain cliffs after a devastating quake. 'You could come with me,' Mycelle said softly, a hushed plea from her heart.

Tol'chuk sighed, a rattle of boulders. 'You know I cannot,' he finally said. 'The Heart of my people will allow me no other path.'

She touched his cheek. 'I know. But I just wanted you to understand that I'd even snatch your strength from Elena for a chance of us staying together. Now that I have you in my life again, I'd give the land over to darkness to keep you at my side.'

Her words finally brought a sad smile to his lips. 'Mother, you lie so well,' he said warmly, 'and I love you the more for it.'

Mycelle stepped forward and placed her palms on his cheeks. She pulled him down and kissed him. 'Do not be so sure what you know, my son.'

A voice intruded into their privacy. It was Meric calling from the ship's rail. 'The captain says we must be off with the tide. We can wait no longer.'

Mycelle waved her acknowledgment to the elv'in. Meric,

his duty discharged, hobbled away on his cane with Mama Freda and her pet tamrink in tow. Aboard the ship, the small crew blew into purposeful activity as lines were stowed and the sails readied.

She did not have much time, but she could spare one moment more with her son. She and Tyrus had already organized their party, and they stood ready. Her gelding, Grisson, was saddled and tacked. Mogweed and Fardale sat atop the small wagon loaded with their supplies, flanked by Tyrus and his trio of Dro warriors mounted on their own horses. Kral already sat upon his black warcharger, Rorshaf, both horse and rider clearly anxious to depart with the coming dawn.

The other two horses, Er'ril's steppe stallion and Elena's small mare, had been loaded and housed in small livestock stalls in the boat's hold. All was in readiness.

Except for a final good-bye.

Mycelle turned to gaze one last time into her son's eyes. No words could lessen this pain. Mother and son simply collapsed into each other's arms. It was like hugging a rough boulder, but Mycelle pulled her son harder into her embrace. She never wanted to forget this moment.

As she drew him tighter, memories of holding him as an infant clouded her vision, and a part of her responded. She felt the melt of flesh and bend of bone and soon found her arms reaching fully around his bulk. She remembered his father and the joy they once shared, and her body still continued to transform. The rip of cloth and leather whispered in her ears. She ignored it, unashamed.

Soon it was not woman and og're who embraced, but mother and son, two ogres. Tol'chuk pulled back slightly, sensing the change. He stared, eyes wide and shining with tears. 'Mother?'

Mycelle knew what he saw. A small og're female. His true mother. Clawed and fanged, she smiled. Her voice was the grumble of the mountains. 'You *are* my son. Never forget you are my heart. You are my proudest accomplishment. I look at you and know my hard life meant something.'

They embraced again as the dawn's glow warmed the horizon and gulls cried to the rising sun. It seemed even the birds felt the pain in her heart – for somehow Mycelle knew this was the last time she would ever hug her son.

11

Panting from the pain, Flint knew he would have only one chance. He needed both Master Vael and Captain Jarplin close beside him. As they prepared the bone drill, Flint flexed his fingers in secret to work circulation past his unbound wrists. Sparks of agony danced before his eyes.

He had endured the first step in their treatment with only a single scream. A moment ago, Captain Jarplin had come at Flint with a dagger. Flint had cursed and spat at Jarplin, feigning that he was still securely tied. It would do little good to take out just the captain. So Flint had endured the agony when Jarplin had sliced the skin over the base of his skull, dragging the point cruelly against the bone. It had been no false act when Flint had screamed. For a moment, his vision had blacked, but he had fought the encroaching darkness, biting his lip and clutching his ropes.

Even now, he felt the blood running in thick rivulets down his neck, and the room threatened to spin if he moved his head too fast. 'Jarplin, don't do this,' he gasped out. 'Be your own man!'

The captain only smiled.

His first mate, the yellow-skinned Master Vael, turned

to Jarplin. 'We're ready.' His voice had a slight lisp through his filed teeth.

Flint had read of tribes on the islands off the coast of Gul'gotha where the savages fed on the flesh of other men, where they filed their teeth like beasts to better rip into raw flesh. It was said they worshipped the skal'tum, eating human meat and grinding their teeth to fangs to be more like the winged demons of the Dark Lord. Flint suspected here stood one of those foul islanders. He had already noticed that the man bore no hole at the back of his shaven head. No tentacled beast guided his will. The atrocities Vael performed were done freely by his own hand.

He was the true enemy.

Jarplin passed the fetid creature into Vael's open palm. The first mate crossed to Flint and wiped the blood from his neck. Flint's skin crawled with the cold touch of the man's fingers. Vael then bathed the creature with Flint's blood. The motion seemed to excite the tiny beast. Tentacles and blind, groping feelers tangled with Vael's fingers as he continued the caress. 'Prepare him,' Vael ordered.

Jarplin followed after Vael with the long steel drill. They now stood to either side of Flint. He could wait no longer.

Gripping his small hidden knife in one hand and the wooden struts of the chair in the other, Flint screamed and attacked. Leaping up, he swung the chair out from under him and slammed it into Vael. The scrawny man went flying. Without pausing, Flint spun upon the startled captain. Before Jarplin could raise the drill as a weapon, Flint lunged and struck out with a fist. Jarplin spun with the blow, but Flint continued his assault, leaping atop the captain's back.

They crashed to the plank floor, an old board cracking under their weight. Flint grabbed a handful of Jarplin's steel-gray hair. He used it as a grip to smash his face against the floor, panting as he repeatedly cracked the man's head into the boards. He needed to win soon, for he was weakening rapidly. 'Submit, Jarplin!' he yelled in the captain's ear.

But the captain refused. He lashed back with an elbow that caught Flint on the chin, sending twirling sparks across his vision. Flint lost his grip on Jarplin's hair. The captain pushed up under him, Flint now riding his back like a wild horse. If Jarplin should get loose ...

Flint raised his other hand; old instincts had kept the sliver of a knife still clutched in his tight grip. He had lived among pirates too long to ever lose hold of a weapon during a fight.

Without considering his next action, Flint again grabbed a handful of Jarplin's silver hair and yanked it up, exposing the puckered hole at the base of the captain's skull. He slammed the slim knife through the hole, then used the heel of his hand to slam the butt of the knife deeper into the skull.

Under him, Jarplin spasmed and threw Flint off his back. Flint rolled across the cabin's floor, coming to rest beside a small desk. Jarplin convulsed a second time while still fighting to push onto his hands and knees. Blood bubbled up around the knife's hilt. Agony stretched the captain's face.

Then, as if some taut string had been cut, Jarplin fell limply to the floor. Facing Flint, his tortured features were once again relaxed as death neared. His lips moved, but no sound came out. Yet Flint knew the words his former captain formed: 'I'm sorry.' At least for his last breath, Jarplin was once again a free man.

Flint went to reach a hand to Jarplin when something struck a numbing blow to his own skull. Flint's vision blacked, and he fell forward to the floor. For a single heartbeat, his vision cleared. Dazed, he watched Vael step around from behind, cudgel in one hand, tentacled beast in the other.

'No,' Flint moaned as Vael retrieved the drill.

'You will be my new dog, and I your master,' Vael lisped in his ear as he knelt atop Flint's back, pinning him to the floorboards. 'When I am done, you will lick my boots.'

Too weak and dazed to resist, Flint could only groan as he felt the drill's sharp point dig into the wound at the back of his neck.

Again he heard the sibilant voice of his torturer. 'Since you will receive the last ul'jinn on board this ship, your friends below will serve in another manner. I believe that young girl will carve up nicely into several tender roasts.'

Flint tried to struggle, but he was still too addled. He felt his forehead pressed into the floorboards.

'Now hold still, my grizzled dog.'

Then steel bit into bone, grinding away the last of Flint's consciousness.

Holding the d'warf hammer in hand, Elena stood over the collapsed body of the ship's cook. His stained apron lay half ripped from where Er'ril had swung and slammed him into the wall. Like a sack of potatoes, the pudgy man had crumpled to the deck. Afterward, Er'ril and Joach had crept into the neighboring passage to check for other pirates, leaving Elena to stand guard over the cook. If he should awaken, she was to ensure the man's continued silence with the hammer.

The boy, Tok, stood near the galley's entrance, a fist tight with worry at his throat. 'Is Gimli dead?'

Watching the cook's chest rise and fall, Elena shook her head. 'Just a bad bump on the head.' She fingered the hammer, running her hand over the carved runes on its long ironwood handle. If necessity warranted her using this weapon, the cook would have more than just a bad headache. She prayed he stayed unconscious.

Nearby, a pot on the hearth popped and gurgled with a thick stew, a fish porridge. Her own stomach responded to the warm smells. It had been a while since any of them had eaten. But they didn't have time to tarry on such minor concerns – Flint's single scream earlier had been all that had sounded. The silence afterward had worn on all their nerves as Tok had led them to their stored gear and then through crawlways and down cramped chutes to reach the galley.

From the doorway, her brother Joach appeared. 'All clear,' he whispered. 'Tok, lead us to the captain's stateroom.'

The boy nodded, ripping his wide eyes away from the snoring cook. 'It's just a little farther.' He darted out of the kitchen.

Elena followed with Joach at her side. They found Er'ril a short way down the passage. He knelt over the body of another pirate, but this one was not breathing. Elena saw the reason why. A small sculptured iron fist had latched around his scrawny neck, throttling the man. As they approached, the iron fingers opened and released. It floated up as Er'ril stood. As the plainsman turned to them, he flexed the fist as if it were his own, which Elena knew it was in a way. The iron talisman had been imbued with the spirit of the boy-mage Denal and was linked to the plainsman. Er'ril could use it as well as his real hand when his need was great and his concentration focused.

'He came at me from around a corner. Surprised me,' Er'ril said, shrugging at the death he had caused. 'I lashed out harder than I should have.'

'It's Samel,' Tok said softly, eyes wide as he stared at the dead man. 'He used to share his ration of sweetcake with me.'

'I'm sorry,' Elena said.

Tok shook his head. 'After th-they put that thing in his head, I saw him kill Jeffers. Slit his throat without a thought, even though they were once the best of chums.' The boy turned to Er'ril. 'Maybe it's best he's dead now. I don't think he could live with what he's done.'

Suddenly the man's corpse jerked with a contorting spasm. Something pale and thick with trailing tentacles slid from under his head. It crawled like a slug across the planks.

Face twisted in disgust, Er'ril stamped his boot down upon the beast, grinding it under his heel. Its snaking appendages tangled and writhed at the leather of his boot, finding no purchase, then went limp. The stench of rotted meat filled the hallway.

Er'ril glanced at Tok. 'Take us to the captain's stateroom.'

Keeping his eyes averted, Tok stepped over the corpse. 'This way.'

Hefting the hammer, Elena followed. Joach kept to his sister's side in the narrow passage, his staff clutched in a tight fist.

After a short climb up a ladder and a turn in another hallway, they came upon a double set of doors opening into a larger cabin. Tok stood before the door. The boy pointed and mouthed the words, *In there*.

Er'ril nodded, eying the others for a moment to ensure their readiness. He raised a fist and knocked. The rapping seemed so loud in the cramped passage.

A voice arose from inside. 'Begone! I ordered us not to be disturbed!'

'Master Vael,' Tok whispered, naming the speaker.

Er'ril raised his voice. 'Master Vael, sir! We've captured a stowaway! I think you'd better come see!'

'Curse you all! I'm almost finished here and will be on deck shortly! Secure the prisoner with the others!'

'Yes, sir!'

Er'ril nodded to Elena. She stepped forward and swung the hammer overhead. Due to the magick in the weapon's haft, it was as light as a broom. She brought it smashing down upon the oaken door.

Wood splintered and exploded away, clearing the doorway. Er'ril was through the flying debris before Elena completed the arc of her swing. Joach was quick on the plainsman's heels.

Elena stepped through the ruined threshold. Tok shadowed behind her. Inside she saw too much blood. The captain lay facedown in a pool of his own blood. The strange first mate sat atop Flint's back, drill in hand, sweat upon his brow. His eyes were open with surprise as he stared at the rushing newcomers.

Er'ril had his sword at the man's throat before he could blink. 'Sound a word, and you'll taste my steel,' he glowered. 'Now get off my friend.'

Elena rushed to Flint's side. He still breathed, but there was so much blood. The wound at the back of his neck still bled fiercely. She went to stanch it with her gloved palm when a long pale snake arose from the wound, sucking at the air. With a look of horror, she tore her hand away.

'You're too late,' the yellow-skinned first mate said, wearing a smile that exposed a row of filed teeth. 'The ul'jinn is already rooted. The man is mine. If I die, so does he. So does the entire crew.'

'So be it,' Er'ril said, his face deadly. He tensed as he prepared to impale the Dark Lord's lackey.

'Wait,' Joach yelled. 'The man may know something. Something we can use.'

Vael spat. 'I'll tell you nothing.'

Er'ril's sword arm trembled, its point dragging a red line across the man's throat. Elena could read the plainsman's thoughts. He wanted so desperately to kill this fiend who had tortured and molested his friend, but Joach's words contained too much truth. As long as they held this one at bay, the rest of the pirates no longer posed a serious threat. If this yellow-skinned monster spoke the truth, a quick slash of his throat would kill the entire crew.

'Joach, tie this bastard's arms behind his back. Tight.'

'What about Flint?' Elena asked. The old seaman had not moved. He just lay dead still. The tentacle of the beast probed like a blind worm through the grizzled gray hair at the back of his neck.

Tok answered. 'It takes half a day for th-the thing to take control. He will either awaken then or die with the shaking fits.'

Elena lifted her gloved hand. 'Er'ril?'

The plainsman knew what she asked. He nodded. What could it harm to try her magick to heal him?

Elena stripped off her glove and exposed her ruby stain.

Vael hissed at the sight and struggled in Er'ril's grip. But Joach already had him lashed securely, and the plainsman had his sword tight at the man's throat. 'You!' Vael cried out. 'You're the wit'ch!'

Elena ignored him and turned to Flint.

Vael's voice became confused, lost. 'My master instructed me to watch for a small girl, hair shorn short and died black, not ... not a woman.' Vael groaned. 'If the Black Heart discovers how I've failed him ...'

It heartened Elena to know that the Dark Lord's

resources were not infallible. But this current ruse would only work this once. If Rockingham had lived after the assault aboard the *Seaswift*, the Gul'gothal lord would soon know of her transformation. Elena shook her head. She would worry about that later.

Setting aside the hammer, she slipped the silver wit'ch dagger from its sheath, cut into her thumb, and cast aside her worries. She had a friend to save.

Elena held her bleeding thumb over the wound at the back of Flint's neck. A thick red droplet rolled off her finger and fell upon the snaking appendage of the monster. It writhed as if her blood scalded it. Satisfied, Elena's lips grew tight. So the trace of magick in the droplet could harm it. Injured, the beast retreated inside Flint's skull with a snap of its tentacle.

'Not so quick, my little pet,' she mumbled and called forth her magicks. She was confident now that she could slay the monster hidden in Flint. But could she do it without also killing their friend? Such a healing would require the deftest touch.

Leashing her magick to her will, tendrils of fire climbed from her wounded thumb and reached out toward Flint. 'Careful,' she whispered to herself and her magick.

Closing her eyes slightly, she used her magick's senses to explore the edges of torn skin. Where they touched, the rent tissues healed. Elena sensed the flow of blood slowing to a trickle. Cautiously, she sent the barest thread of fire deeper into the wound, hunting the lurker below.

Now she had to proceed on her magickal instinct alone. She sent her senses along the thread of fire, like a spider down a web after a hidden fly. Holding her breath, she closed her eyes fully and cut off any further distractions. Around her, even the soft sounds of whispers and the rustle of woolen garments faded. All she heeded were patterns of light and darkness. She entered a world of warm phosphorescence and knew it for Flint's essence. She sensed that it usually shone stronger than it did right now, but the injuries and assault had worn away his brightness. Her own thread of magick was like a silvery red torch; she had to be careful that it did not overwhelm the glow around her. With too fierce a touch, she could burn away all that was her friend, leaving him an empty shell. This horrible thought helped her hone her penetration to the thinnest spark.

As she cast deeper into this strange world, her magick a beacon before her, she spotted her enemy ahead: a dark blemish upon Flint's gentle radiance. The ul'jinn. It sat hunched, a tangle of blackness, like snarled roots in the luminescent soil. Rootlets and fine traceries of darkness were already spreading out from it.

At its foul sight, an angry fire was stoked in her heart. The darkness felt so *wrong*. It was more than just a threat to her friend; it was as if it tainted life itself. It sickened her just to see it. An urge to blast it away, burn it to ashes, trembled her control. Her torch of wit'ch fire flared brighter.

No!

She fought it back down. She would not let this hideous creature control her actions. Her flame died away to a sharp spark again as she delved toward the lurker. Now closer, she realized that not all the black roots ended at the edge of Flint's spirit; two went beyond. She sensed power flowing strongly in these cords and cast her awareness nearer. Menace and disease throbbed out from them. Sickened, Elena lashed out and burned through them, severing both roots with a flash of wit'ch fire.

As she did so, she noted two things. In one root, she sensed a twisted mind linked through it and somehow knew it was Vael. Her hatred for him bloomed. The momentary brush with his spirit was so corrupt that even this brief touch made her want to scrub her skin raw. But this short peek into Vael's mind was nothing compared to the impression she received as she severed the second root. It was as if she drowned in a sea of evil. It swept at her as she cut through the root, almost latching onto her own spirit. She railed against it, her magick flaring brighter.

Luckily, as quick as the assault came, it vanished – but not before she sensed the pair of baleful red eyes staring back at her, eyes carved of ruby. Eyes of the wyvern. Elena suddenly understood the statue's presence on board the ship.

She reeled back from the cut cords, watching the roots shrivel away. Dread and panic gripped her, but she kept her magick reined in. Turning to the remaining mass of darkness, she quickly thrust out a net of fiery threads and enveloped the ul'jinn with her magick. In short order, she burned away all traces of the darkness, leaving Flint's spirit unblemished. She lingered no further to appreciate her handiwork. A bigger battle loomed ahead before any of them could be considered free.

As she withdrew her magick, Elena's awareness followed. She blinked her eyes open, taking a moment to orient herself to the real world. Once fully free of Flint's spirit, she loosened her pent-up magick, and her fist blew forth with flames.

The others backed from her abrupt display.

Elena did not care. Pushing to her feet, she stalked to where Vael stood with Er'ril's sword at his throat.

Tok spoke up behind her. 'Is Flint . . . ? Is he going to live?'

'The ul'jinn is gone,' she answered, her voice cold with anger.

'What is it, Elena?' Er'ril asked. He knew her too well.

As answer, Elena grabbed Vael by the throat, her flaming fingers burning into his skin. He screamed as the smoke of his charred flesh scented the air. It would be a simple thing to burn through his scrawny neck, and for a moment, she even considered it.

Vael must have sensed her thoughts. 'No!' he croaked.

'Why?' she hissed at him. 'Why would you do it?'

He knew what she asked, terror clear in his eyes. She cared nothing for the tentacled ul'jinn and the slaves they made of these pirates. It was inconsequential compared to the larger menace hidden in the bowels of the ship. Vael tremored in her grip.

She lifted him by his throat, the magick giving her the strength of ten men. 'Answer me!'

With his sword numb in his fist, Er'ril watched Elena shake the man like a dog with a rabbit, fury flaming her green eyes. Er'ril had never seen her so angry.

Elena leaned closer to her prisoner. 'Why did you bring it here?'

Tears rained down Vael's cheeks as smoke curled up from his neck. 'The Dark Master's servant . . . the one in the tower . . . the Praetor . . . he demanded it.'

Er'ril knew to whom he referred. He stepped closer. 'My brother.'

Elena held up her free hand to silence him. She continued her interrogation of Vael. 'Where were you taking it? To Port Rawl?'

Vael tried to nod as he hung in her flaming grip. 'Yes, and from there inland by river barge.'

Er'ril could wait no longer. 'Elena, what is it that you know?' He waved to where Joach and Tok stood guard by the door. 'Speak plain. The other pirates aboard will soon grow wise to our escape.'

As answer, Elena tossed the thin man across the cabin. Vael struck the far wall and collapsed in a pile of jumbled limbs. He cowered as flames of wit'ch fire climbed up her arm in an angry blaze, but Elena ignored the man's terror and turned to Er'ril. 'The statue in the hold – it's not just ebon'stone. While inside Flint's mind, I sensed the statue's link to the ul'jinn and caught an inkling of its true heart, the darker secret in the stone.' Elena began to tremble with fury.

Joach stepped closer toward his sister. 'What is it, El?'

'The stone is a womb,' she answered. 'Its belly brews an evil so foul that just the thinnest wisp of its spirit almost snuffed out my own.' Elena crossed and retrieved the Try'sil from the cabin's floor. With the rune-carved hammer in hand, she faced Vael again. 'Even if the hammer could crack the stone shell, I fear that what grows inside is already too strong for me to handle. If it should be unleashed now, it would destroy us all.'

'But what manner of beast is it?' Joach asked, his voice dry with fear.

Elena shook her head and crouched down beside Vael, who still lay curled in a ball by the wall's base. 'But *he* knows.'

Vael tried to press farther into the wall.

Raising her ruby hand, Elena's fingertips sprouted fresh flames, thin streamers of fire. Like outstretched claws, she threatened the man. 'Tell us what lurks inside the ebon'-stone statue.'

'I . . . I don't know . . . truly. The Dark Lord's servant bound my blood to its power so I could control the ul'jinn. I was to deliver the statue to Port Rawl, then inland to the mountains. I was told nothing else. I know nothing else.'

Elena drew back her magick, her anger waning with her growing exhaustion. Deep lines marked her tired face. 'He speaks the truth,' she said forlornly.

'Not entirely,' Er'ril argued. 'He leaves out more than he says.' Er'ril crouched beside the yellow-skinned foreigner. The man smelled of fear and dried blood. Er'ril used his sword tip to raise the man's chin until he stared into the man's odd violet eyes. 'Where in the mountains were you to deliver this stone womb?'

Vael quivered under the point of the sword and under the intensity of their gazes. 'A small town . . . near the highlands.'

'Name it.'

'Winterfell.'

Elena and Joach both gasped. Er'ril just stared, trying to fathom a reason for this choice of location. Why the town where Elena grew up? What did that matter?

Flint interrupted their shock with a rattling groan. Eyes swung in his direction. The old man rolled to his side, too weak to rise. Er'ril kept his sword on Vael as Joach crossed and helped the older man sit up. Flint's eyes, bleary and red, searched the room. He seemed quickly to take in the scenario. One hand fluttered to the back of his head.

Joach spoke. 'Fear not. Elena rid you of the beast.'

He groaned again. 'Still it . . . it feels like my head's been cleaved.'

Er'ril turned his attention back upon Vael. 'The statue – what were you to do with it once you reached Winterfell?'

Vael shrank away. 'Haul it to some old ruins and just leave it there. That's all I know.'

Flint struggled straighter in Joach's arms. 'What is this statue?'

Joach explained the discovery of the ebon'stone sculpture and the Dark Lord's plans for it. Flint's face grew grimmer with the telling. Er'ril let the older Brother ponder the information, trusting to his friend's keen mind.

'I must see it,' Flint finally said. He fussed against Joach's assistance and pushed unsteadily to his feet. Once up, he faced Elena. 'Can you clear a path to the hold?'

Elena slowly nodded.

Tok suddenly spoke up from near the ruined doorway. 'Someone comes!' he hissed at them. He stepped to the hall for a brief moment, then darted back inside. A fierce clanging of a bell sounded from atop the ship. 'They know you've escaped!'

'Elena?'

'You want a path?' Her eyes swung to Vael. 'By his own admission, he is the hand that guides these men.' Before anyone could react, Elena raised her arm, and flames coursed out in a thick stream.

Er'ril ducked away, feeling the scorch as the wit'ch fire passed. Vael scrabbled along the wall, attempting to escape the flames. He failed.

The end of Elena's stream of fire bloomed into a tangle of fiery filaments. They trapped Vael as surely as a spiderweb snags a fly. He screamed as he writhed in her web, clothes smoking, flesh burning.

Joach had joined Tok by the door. 'There's at least five men at the end of the passage,' he warned. 'They've swords and torches. And more are coming. They must know we hide here.'

'Elena, what are you doing?' Er'ril asked.

'The man knows nothing more. I sense it with my magick,' she intoned, the words dull in her mouth. What she did next was done without passion. The flaming filaments snaked past

Vael's stretched lips, flowing inside him. 'But he is bound to all the ul'jinn here.'

Elena thrust out her hand, clenched a fist, and twisted her wrist. Vael jerked as if his neck had been snapped, and his body went limp. 'Cut off the head of a snake and the body will die,' Elena mumbled and lowered her hand. The fires vanished like a snuffed candle.

Er'ril crossed toward Vael. Smoke still curled from his body. The girl had killed him.

He turned in horror to Elena.

She merely stared at Er'ril for several breaths, then spoke. 'You did not touch his mind. I did.' She turned away.

Joach reported from the doorway. 'All the pirates just collapsed in the hall,' he said in astonishment.

Flint nodded. 'Vael was the blood link. With his death, the ul'jinn die, too.'

Tok, who had again crept into the passage to investigate, danced back into the cabin. His face was flushed with panic. 'The fallen torches and lanterns are starting a fire! Half the passage is already aflame!'

Er'ril straightened up from his crouch and hurried them toward the door. This was an old ship, its timbers ripe for the flame. A strong fire could burn the ship down to the waterline in mere moments.

Joach helped Flint, lending his shoulder for support.

Tok hung back, eying Vael's body, then suddenly ran and kicked the man's corpse, spitting on it. Tears streamed down the boy's cheeks. 'They were my family,' he yelled at the burned body.

Er'ril crossed and gathered the boy up under his arm. Tok latched onto him like a drowning sailor. They did not have time to waste on tears or comfort. Still, Er'ril sheathed his sword and pulled the lad up to his chest.

As he carried the boy toward the door, Er'ril caught Elena staring at him from the doorway. Her expression was one of sorrow and hopelessness. If he had had another arm, he would have gladly given it to her to lean on. But instead he could only softly urge, 'We must hurry.'

She nodded. Her lost look hardened to steel again as she stared at the sobbing boy. She mumbled something as she moved to march alongside him.

Er'ril pretended not to hear the words, but he had. It was his own early words to her.

'. . . all of Alasea bleeds.'

Elena climbed with the others out of the smoke-choked passages onto the middeck. Behind them, flames already lapped skyward, lighting the early dawn with their own fire. Bodies lay strewn across the deck like scattered rag dolls, crumpled and forgotten. Even from the rigging, three men hung from tangled ropes after falling from where they had been working the sails.

As she watched, a lick of flame touched the foresail, and in a whispery rush, the fire raced up the sailcloth to the ropes and masts overhead. Hot ash rained down on them. Elena looked away as one of the bodies, hanging like a lantern far above, took flame.

To her side, Er'ril lowered Tok to the deck. 'We must abandon the boat. Now,' the plainsman said. 'The fire spreads wildly.'

As if accenting his words, an explosion belowdecks blew a flaming barrel of ignited oil up through the planks. It arced over the water in a blazing trail.

Ducking, Elena followed Er'ril aft. 'What about the ebon'stone statue?' Elena asked. 'We can't just leave it here.'

Er'ril waved Flint and Joach to their side as he answered

her. 'Whatever evil it broods, the seas will claim it now. That is the best we can manage.'

Elena was unconvinced. Such evil would not so easily drown, even in a burning boat. With hammer in hand, she eyed the main hatch.

Er'ril must have read her thoughts. 'No, Elena. Whatever its foul purpose in being hauled to Winterfell, we've at least stopped that part of the Dark Lord's plan.'

Flint, ashen in complexion and still leaning on Joach, hobbled to them. He coughed the smoke and ash from his lungs before speaking. 'Trouble,' he said between gasps. 'There is no way off this ship, except over the rail.'

Er'ril scowled and glanced through the smoke to the neighboring seas. Elena searched, too. They were far from the coastline and even farther from any of the Archipelago's islands.

Flint pointed toward the distant coast. 'There. See those lights?'

Elena squinted. 'Where –?' she began to say, then spotted the scatter of lamps lighting the rocky shore just north of their position.

'It's Port Rawl,' Flint explained, stopping to cough on a gust of smoke. 'The currents here are strong, but with flotsam from the ship, we might be able to kick toward shore and make it overland to the city.'

Er'ril glanced at the others. Elena knew he weighed their strength against the cold and currents of the surrounding waters. He frowned at the exhaustion he found in all their faces, but it mirrored his own.

Flint persisted. 'We may not even have to swim all the way to shore. This close to Port Rawl, our fire will surely be spotted. Scavenging ships will be sent out.'

'More pirates?' Joach asked.

Flint shrugged and fingered the healing wound on his neck. 'As long as they're *just* pirates, I'll kiss their salty feet.'

Suddenly, the mainsail blew aflame, brightening the smoky gloom. Elena even felt the heat through her boots as the fires hidden below began to cook the planks.

'We don't have much time,' Flint said needlessly.

'Stay here,' Er'ril ordered them all. Covering his nose and mouth with a scrap of sailcloth, he dashed across the smoky deck. Flint and Tok took up position by the rail.

Joach sidled next to her. She took his offered hand in her own, a touch of family. 'Always flames,' he mumbled.

'Hmm?'

He smiled weakly at her. 'Whenever we get together, we're always chased by fires.'

She returned a tired grin, knowing he referred to the orchard blaze that had first driven them from their homes. Her brother was right. It seemed flames always marked her path.

Er'ril suddenly appeared out of the smoke, coughing, a small wooden door clutched under his one arm. 'We can use this to keep afloat,' he said as he leaned the door against the rail and turned away. 'I'm going to fetch something more. I spotted a broken table in the galley.'

Before anyone could comment, Er'ril vanished back into the thickening haze.

At the rail, nobody spoke, worry and fear clear in all their eyes. Elena studied the choppy waves. Could she manage such a swim? She searched the waters for signs of shark fins or other hidden menaces.

From somewhere far away, a horn began to wail – at first softly, then stridently, echoing over the waters. It sounded like the mournful cry of a dying seabeast.

'Port Rawl has spotted us,' Flint explained, his voice a

mixture of relief and worry. 'They sound the alarm. If we can—'

Suddenly the deck jolted under their feet. Tok was knocked to his knees. A shuddering roar burst from deep within the boat, as if the ship bellowed its death rattle. The yardarm of the mast, half charred, crashed midship, taking out the far rail. The ship listed and rolled, seawater hissing as flames were consumed.

Flint was at Elena's shoulder. 'We dare not wait any longer. We must abandon ship. Now! She's breaking apart.' The old seaman pushed her toward the scrap of door. 'Stay with your brother. I'll keep with the young lad. Strike out as best you can. Watch for any ships.'

Elena stepped away from the starboard rail. 'But Er'ril ...?'

Flint gripped her shoulder with fingers of iron and pulled her back. 'He'll manage on his own. He's been in worse scrapes and survived.'

Joach stepped in front of her. 'Brother Flint is right, El. Help me toss the door overboard.'

Elena frowned but obeyed. The two heaved the chunk of wood over the rail. It struck the water, bobbed up, then quickly began to glide away. The current was strong.

Flint had managed to scrounge a section of broken rail from somewhere, and he and the boy were prepared to leap with it in their arms. 'Hurry,' he urged.

Joach helped his sister atop the rail. 'Go, old man,' he yelled to Flint. 'We'll manage.'

Tok's face was frozen in fear, but Flint gave the young lad's arm a final squeeze and over they went.

Joach turned to Elena. 'Ready?'

'Yes,' she answered and shoved Joach overboard.

He hit the water hard but floundered up, sputtering

seawater. Elena leaned over the rail and pointed to the floating door. 'Fetch the door! Wait for me! I'm not leaving without searching for Er'ril!'

'Elena! No!'

She was already gone. She would not abandon Er'ril. With the ship crashing around their ears, the plainsman might be trapped under debris, and with her magick, she could quickly free him.

Racing through the smoke, she aimed for the hatch in the stern deck. Er'ril had mentioned something about the galley. Holding her arm over her nose and mouth, she sped through the hatch. Her eyes burned with ash and smoke. Tears washed down her cheeks.

She clattered down the steep stair, almost knocking her head when a step gave way under her. Without waiting, she fought her way to the kitchens. Through the smoke, she spotted a body, covered in ash. With her heart in her throat, she rushed over only to discover it was just the cook.

Elena straightened. The galley was small, but the smoke still made it difficult to see all its corners clearly. The sting of tears compounded the problem. For this reason, Elena did not spot the open trapdoor until she almost fell headlong down it.

Crouching, she stared into the darkness. Lit by a vague reddish glow, a ladder descended. She knew to where these steps led. Elena, Er'ril, and Joach had once stood at the foot of these same steps and listened to the bawdy singing of pirates. Down there was where they had been imprisoned – and where the wyvern statue was stored.

'Er'ril!' she yelled down the trapdoor. 'Can you hear me?'

She waited, holding her breath. Nothing.

Before she could convince herself otherwise, Elena swung around onto the ladder. She scrambled down the steps into the hot bowels of the ship. The glow, she discovered, was not from a lantern, but from a smoldering fire near the back of the short passage. The heat singed her lungs as she breathed. She would have to hurry.

Cautious but moving quickly, she darted down the hall toward the fire, its heat more searing with every step. But in five paces, she was at the door that led to the bilge cabin. She ducked into the room, fist raised before her and already afire with blood magicks.

What she found there so startled her that she froze in place. In the center of the room were the remains of the crate – broken boards and charred remnants – and nothing else. The statue was gone.

From the scatter of wooden pieces, it was almost like something had exploded out from it. Elena glanced around as if expecting to see the wyvern statue lurking in a corner or hanging from the ceiling. But there was no sign of it.

Elena took a step closer. Her toe nudged a piece of debris that rolled across the floorboards. It drew her eye. A gasp escaped her throat as she recognized it. She hurried over and retrieved the small iron fist from the debris. It was the ward of A'loa Glen. So Er'ril had been down here!

Wiping the tears and sweat from her eyes, she searched closer, on hands and knees. She found Er'ril's weapon, the silver sword he had obtained from Denal. In horror, she realized the scatter of cloth scraps strewn about were actually the remains of Er'ril's breeches and shirt. They had been shredded to ribbons. She lifted her hand. It held the leather tie that bound the plainsman's hair. It was singed black.

Shock pushed Elena to her feet.

Her limbs shook. The grief and horror were too large for her to grip. 'No,' she finally moaned and backed away, stopping only to collect the iron ward and the silver sword from the floor. Elena ran from the room. Her mind was too shaken to manage the ladder, especially encumbered by Er'ril's items. But even if it meant her life, she could not discard them.

Elena struggled upward, her clothes and skin beginning to burn from the growing heat. She rolled out of the trapdoor and into the kitchen, sprawling across the deck. After the cramped oven of the lower hall, the kitchen felt almost icy. She closed her eyes, meaning to rest only a moment, but instead slipped into a numb daze. When next she was aware, the galley was thick with smoke, choking her. Coughing, she leaned up.

Fires surrounded her.

Overhead, planks suddenly crashed down. Craning her neck, Elena saw a monstrous, dark shape reach toward her. 'No,' she moaned, too grief-stricken to resist. Sharp claws grabbed Elena as her vision blackened.

Beyond caring, beyond hope, darkness claimed her.

12

Elena awoke slowly. She struggled against the bonds that held her trapped until she realized it was just heavy blankets, snugged securely around her.

'Hush, dear. You're safe.'

Turning her head, Elena watched an old woman move about the small room. Elena gasped as the elder swung back toward the bed. Above the woman's small nose was only a plane of dark skin. No eyes. Elena shuddered at the sight. 'Who . . . ? Where . . . ?' Elena fought to sit up. From the roll in her belly, she sensed she was in some ship's cabin. She glanced around the small chamber. A sea chest, a stout table, and the bed. There was not even a porthole.

Elena tried to speak, but a sudden fit of coughing choked her. She hacked and gasped for several breaths, spitting up a black phlegm from her throat. Afterward, with tears in her eyes, she slumped deeper into the thick goose down of the bed, too weak limbed for any real resistance.

The old woman, her gray hair bound in a coil atop her head, turned toward Elena, stirring a steaming mug with a twig of willow. It smelled of cinnamon and a tang of medicinals. 'Drink this.' The old woman held out the cup. 'I know your magick will help you heal eventually, but never turn down additional aid.'

Elena leaned away warily. As she did so, she felt something burrowing under the blankets near the foot of the bed. She yanked her feet away just as a fiery-maned face popped from under a fold of blanket. Its huge black eyes blinked at her; then a tail ringed in gold and rich brown fur wriggled free.

'Tikal . . . Tikal . . . bad puppy,' it intoned mournfully.

Elena caught a pungent whiff arising from that end of the bed. The beast looked oddly chagrined, head bowed, tail tucking around its neck.

The old woman scolded the animal and shooed him away. 'I'm sorry, dear,' she said and sat on the edge of the bed, still holding the cup. 'Tikal is still upset by the sea voyage. Normally he knows to use a chamberpot. I'll fetch a dry set of bedclothes in a moment.' She grimaced in the creature's direction, sending it scurrying to perch atop the nearby table. The old woman then turned to Elena. 'He's upset because the last time either of us were aboard a sailing vessel was when we were first caught by the slavers.'

Elena sensed no threat from the woman, but while naked under the sheets, she felt vulnerable. 'Am I with slavers now?' she asked hoarsely, her throat raw.

The woman smiled. 'Oh, my dear, don't you remember anything?' She laughed a quick note, a friendly sound. 'We rescued you from the flaming ship. Well, Tol'chuk did, that is. He found you nearly blacked out in the lower decks. Luckily, an og're's eyes are sharp in dim light, and with his stone guiding him, he found you quickly. Any longer and the smoke would have killed you.'

Elena remembered the sharp claws and the dark shape looming over her after climbing from the trapdoor. 'Tol'chuk?'

'Yes.' She patted Elena's blanket-covered knee. 'Luckily,

we were already under sail when we spotted your smoke, giving us a jump on any other ship from Port Rawl. Now drink this elixir of fellroot and bitterwort. It'll help clear your chest of the smoke. The coughing may get worse over the next hour, but the herbs will loosen the phlegm so you can clear it.' She smiled kindly and held out the mug again. 'Mostly you just need rest.'

This time Elena took it. The stone of the mug felt warm and soothing in her clammy hands. Elena could almost sense the healing properties through the stone. 'My brother?' she asked fearfully over the cup's rim.

'We fished everyone from the sea, except—'

A knock at the door interrupted them.

'Come!' the old woman called out.

A familiar figure strode into the room. The slender limbs, the hawkish nose – even with his hair but a silver stubble, she could not mistake the elv'in Meric. 'I have an extra pot of hot water—' he began to say. Then his eyes grew wide as he spotted Elena. 'You're awake!' he said with delight, such strong emotion rare in the haughty fellow. Elena noted that he needed a cane now to hobble across the floorboards to join them. 'I see you've met Mama Freda,' he said as he leaned on the foot of her bed. 'Without her healing skills, neither of us would be here now.'

'What happened to you?' she asked, noting the fading scars on his face.

He opened his mouth to answer, but Mama Freda cut him off. 'There is time for the exchange of tales later. Right now, I'd like to get this child up and moving a bit. She's been bedridden near on an entire day. And I think a short walk in fresh air will help her lungs.'

Meric nodded his agreement but did not move, still staring at Elena.

Mama Freda just sighed. 'A bit of privacy, sir.'

The elv'in's eyes grew wide. 'Of course . . . I'm sorry . . .' he mumbled, straightening up. 'It's just that she's changed so much. Flint warned us, but with her awake like this, it's just so much more . . . more astounding.'

Mama Freda shooed him away. 'Let her finish her drink in peace.'

Meric glanced one last time before slipping out of the room. 'She could be ancient King Dresdin's first child,' he mumbled as he left. 'The resemblance to the old tapestries is amazing.'

Once the elv'in was gone, Mama Freda removed a thick robe from the sea chest. 'After you finish with the herbs, I'll take you above.'

Elena nodded. She sipped the elixir slowly. The cinnamon's flavor could not completely mask the bitter tang of the medicinals. Still, it was hot and soothed the raw ache in her throat. As she closed her eyes and inhaled the scent into her sore lungs, she tried not to think about Er'ril and what she had discovered below the decks of the tainted *Skipjack*. The memory was too tender, and no elixir in all the lands could soothe that pain.

'Are you all right?' Mama Freda asked. 'Is the medicine too hot?'

Elena opened her eyes and realized tears had blurred her vision. 'No, the herb tea is fine,' she muttered. How had the eyeless woman noted her few tears? Pushing aside such mysteries, Elena sighed and drained the last of the mug's contents. 'I'm done,' she started to say, but the healer was already reaching for her empty cup.

'Then let's get you some fresh air.' Mama Freda helped her stand and slipped the robe over her shoulders. The old woman gave her a quick hug and whispered in her ear.

'Time alone is the best healer of some wounds.'

Elena knew the woman sensed the ache in her heart. She returned the hug. 'I pray you're right,' she whispered.

Mama Freda touched Elena's cheek with a warm palm, then turned to guide her out of the room. Tikal rode on the healer's shoulder. Elena was glad the old woman's cane kept her from moving too quickly. Elena's own limbs felt like those of a newborn, shaky and weak. Luckily, they did not have far to go — only down a short passage and up an impossibly steep set of stairs.

Holding the upper deck hatch open, Mama Freda helped Elena up into the clean air of late morning. The fresh breezes felt like ice in her lungs. Coughing a bit, she stood in place, taking in the bright sunlight and soft winds. Already she felt vigor returning in her limbs.

'You be looking much better,' a graveled voice said behind her.

Elena turned and spotted Tol'chuk standing by the ship's rail. He wore an awkward smile, yellowed fangs glinting in the sun. She crossed to the huge og're and hugged him. 'Thank you for risking your life to save me.'

Once free of the embrace, Tol'chuk patted his thigh pouch. 'The stone would allow me no other choice. Besides, a bit of flame be little threat to an og're's thick skin.'

She patted his arm. 'Well, thank you anyway,' she said, smiling at his humility. She glanced around the deck. 'Where's Mycelle?'

Tol'chuk's features clouded over with sorrow. 'She be gone.'

Elena's heart clenched. She could not face more death. 'Is she . . . is she dead?'

Tol'chuk touched her with an apologetic claw and corrected Elena's misinterpretation. 'Sometimes I be thick in the head. Mycelle be fine. She and Kral, along with the shape-shifters, have gone to stop the Dark Lord's armies in the north. She left a letter for you, explaining it all.'

Elena breathed again, relieved. They were not dead, but her mind was too fuddled to deal with the implications of the others' departure. She would ponder the loss later, but right now, she simply did not want to feel. Her heart was too raw.

From the stern, another familiar voice arose. Glancing back, she spotted Flint with a few black-skinned sailors by the wheel. From the flush to the old Brother's cheeks, he seemed to be in the middle of an argument with them. He waved to her, then returned to his discussion.

'El!' Joach rushed at her from where he and the boy Tok had been sparring with staffs on the deck. 'You're up!'

She endured his embrace, glad to see they were all safe. All this attention was beginning to tax her.

Joach straightened, a stern look on his face. 'If you ever shove me overboard again . . .' he scolded, but he could not maintain the ruse of anger. A foolish smile bloomed on his lips. 'Thank the Mother you're safe, El.'

Mama Freda must have sensed her growing exhaustion. 'Come, leave her be,' she clucked at Joach and scooted him back with her cane. From her shoulder, Tikal also scolded the boy with sharp squeaks. Once Joach relented, Mama Freda turned to Elena. 'Let's walk a bit, then back down you go.'

Elena nodded. She crossed the deck, coughing every now and then. Mama Freda placed a palm on her forehead at one point, but the healer seemed content with whatever she felt.

They ended up standing by the rail, staring over the open seas. Green islands with shores of steep cliffs rode the waves all around them. They must have entered the Archipelago while she slept. Elena scanned all the horizons. Not a smudge of dark smoke marked the sky anywhere.

'The boat sank quickly,' Mama Freda said. 'We searched the waters for half a day but found no sign of him.'

'He was already gone,' she muttered.

Mama Freda remained silent, just placed her hand atop Elena's.

Across the sky, gulls called to one another. Elena listened, her eyes staring at the swells as the boat rode the currents and winds.

Suddenly, Mama Freda's pet, who had been chittering softly and trying to unwind the healer's braid, erupted with loud screeches. Elena's gaze darted up just as the gulls overhead began their own angry cries. Tikal clutched tightly to the thin neck of the healer, the beast's eyes wide with fright. He stared toward the skies above.

'What's wrong with him?' Elena asked.

Mama Freda's blind face also stared upward. 'I see what Tikal sees,' she said in worried tones. 'His eyes are sharper than those of a man. It's some strange bird flying this way.'

'The wyvern.' Elena searched the skies for a black speck. 'It must be coming back.'

'It's odd . . .' the healer mumbled.

Then Elena saw it. It dove out of the sun's glare, as if birthed by its fires. As it shot across the blue skies, scudding under white clouds, its plumage shone like fire.

Elena and Mama Freda scrambled back as the bird plummeted directly toward them. Tripping on the old woman's cane, Elena fell. A commotion arose behind her as others spotted the attacker, but Elena's eyes were fixed on the plunge of the winged predator.

It was much too small to be the wyvern. But what was it?

She raised her red hand against it, scrambling for something to poke her skin to release a flow of fire.

Then it was too late.

She ducked back as the bird swooped at her. Elena gasped as its bright wings suddenly flashed wide. Its plummet ended as it landed gracefully on the ship's rail. It perched, panting through its open beak, wings held slightly open to cool its flight.

The sharp fiery brilliance of its plumage faded enough to reveal the snowy white of its feathers. Its black eyes studied Elena, head slightly cocked.

'It's the sunhawk,' Meric said, awe in his voice.

The elv'in stepped around Elena as she carefully stood up, cautious of any sudden movement in front of the huge bird. It had to stand at least four hands tall. 'A sunhawk?' she asked. Elena remembered the smaller moon'falcon that had led Meric to her so long ago.

'It's Queen Tratal's bird,' he answered. 'The herald of the House of the Morning Star.'

Flint had joined them by now. 'But why is it here?' he asked.

Meric turned to them all. 'She comes. The queen herself has left Stormhaven.'

'But why?' Elena asked.

He turned to her, his eyes full of worry. 'She comes to reclaim the lands from which our ancestors have been banished.' He waved toward the bird. 'The flight of her sunhawk heralds the eve of war.'

Sensations returned like an old nightmare.

First, a whisper across his skin, a touch so cold that it felt more like a burn. Then sound: a chorus of wails, distant but also as near as a lover's breath. The cries echoed inside his skull, begging him back to oblivion. He fought against this urge, swimming up from the drowning blackness. His reward for his effort was a final explosion of senses: a choking stench that reeked of death, and a burst of white light that shattered the darkness into fragments.

'He wakes,' a voice spoke from beyond the blinding brilliance.

Floundering in the sea of sensations, the drowning victim finally surfaced. Fragments of vision collected back together like a child's puzzle. He lay on his back atop a slab of stone: hard, unyielding, as cold as the marble of a crypt. The brush of icy air across his skin revealed his nakedness.

As his head lolled to the side, he saw walls of stacked granite blocks. Slitted windows, high up the walls, brought in little sunlight, only cold breezes.

Again the coarse voice spoke from behind him. 'He resists.'

Another voice answered. It was oddly familiar, a whisper from some long-dead past. 'His magick still protects him. He'll not be turned by the black arts.'

The listener fought to understand these words, but for now, he only lived in his senses; who spoke was of no concern. Even who he was himself was a question that had yet to arise in his fuddled mind.

'What do we do with him then? He should've died when he entered the Weir.'

'His iron ward,' the naggingly familiar voice answered. 'The talisman had the power to open it. As to surviving that dark path, again the magick in the Blood Diary protects him.'

As the sleeper continued to wake fully, his mind began noting more than just smells and shivering skin. He began to focus again on more important concerns. Who were these others? His hand rose to touch his face, to run a fingertip over his lips. *Who am I?*

'Forget this new plan. We should just kill him,' the coarse voice insisted. The listener now sensed it was an old man who spoke, his voice harsh with many winters.

'No,' the other answered. This was a young voice, full of youth's strength.

'Why? What difference does it make? The wit'ch will still come. She will believe him dead. Why not make it true?'

'Whether the child comes or not does not bear on my decision.'

'But Elena should be . . .'

Around him, the voices and room faded. One word rose to shine like a torch before his awareness: *Elena*. An image bloomed to replace the single word: eyes of commanding green, cheek and neck softly curved, hair the color of a fiery sunset. With this one memory, the rest began to return.

At first just a trickle of images: An iron hand raised toward a black sculpture . . . The rip of reality as the stone of the statue became a pool of black energies . . . His struggling body caught and dragged by a fierce tidal pull toward the pool's black maw . . . Then . . . then . . . a darkness so deep and ancient that there were no words to describe it.

He shuddered against the memory, pushing it away.

As he did so, other memories rushed back in, a raging torrent of old faces, old tales. Five centuries of memories quickly refilled the yawning void in his awareness.

Mother above, what had he done?

Er'ril gasped as his thoughts were again his own. He struggled to sit up, anger and pain heating his naked skin. 'Elena . . .' he mumbled in apology.

To either side of him, two figures stepped into sight.

He knew well the dark-robed elder, his hoary face

ravaged by time, his eyes gone cloudy from centuries of passing winters. 'Greshym.'

The old darkmage bowed his head mockingly and raised his stumped right wrist in a crude salute. 'So I see your mind finally wakes, too.'

Er'ril ignored him and turned to the other man. Where the darkmage was bent-backed and crooked, this other stood tall, straight, and broad of shoulder. Under black hair neatly cropped, eyes that matched Er'ril's own stared back at him. They were the gray of a snowy winter morn, the mark of a true Standi plainsman. But instead of finding the warmth of a shared heritage in the other's gaze, only coldness and blackness shone forth, as if Er'ril stared into an open grave. Too shocked, he found no words to speak.

The other was not so incapacitated. 'Welcome, dear brother,' he said, 'it's been a long time.'

'Shorkan,' Er'ril finally croaked out.

His brother's smile held no warmth, only the promise of pain. 'It's about time we were reacquainted.'

Er'ril spat in his face. 'You are *not* my brother, only a beast who wears his face.'

Shorkan did not bother to wipe the spittle from his cheek. He only sighed. 'You will learn to love me again. That I promise.'

'Never!' he answered with a snarl.

Raising a hand, Shorkan signaled with his fingers. From behind Er'ril, a third spectator stepped forward, a spy who had so far remained silent.

As Er'ril recognized this other, the shock almost thrust him back into dark oblivion. 'No!' he said, remembering that night in the inn so long ago, his sword thrust through the back of the boy, pinning him to the planks. 'I slew you!'

The small lad shrugged, his eyes bright with a feral light.

'Don't worry, plainsman. I don't hold it against you. It would take more than an ordinary sword to sever my ties to this world.'

It was Denal, the boy mage – and the third and final member of the coven who had forged the Blood Diary five centuries ago. Or at least it was what was left of him, the evil that had been freed by the spell. At the time, Er'ril had thought he had slain the boy's evil half.

Shorkan stepped forward. 'Now that we have all the parties reunited from that fateful night in Winterfell, we can proceed.'

Er'ril stared at the coven. 'I will not let any of you harm Elena.'

'You mistake my intentions, Brother. With you finally here, the wit'ch hardly matters. If we succeed, she will be but a plaything of the master.'

'Succeed at what?'

Greshym answered, his voice cracking. 'At correcting our mistake.'

Er'ril glanced around the group of heartless faces and brutal eyes.

Shorkan finished the explanation. 'Together again, with your help, we mean to recast the spell and unbind the book. To destroy forever the Blood Diary.'

Book Three

DRAGONFOLK

13

Deep within the belly of the leviathan, Kast felt trapped. Living walls surrounded him. As he followed Sy-wen, he ran a hand along the twisting corridor. The sea creature's leathery skin was drawn taut between struts of bone. Under his palm, he felt the tremor of the giant beast's heartbeat.

With a small shudder, he withdrew his hand. To live and make a home inside another creature was a concept too foreign for his Dre'rendi mind to fully grasp or accept. As a Bloodrider, the open air and the wide sea were his true home, not this world of cramped corridors and tiny cells burrowed under the skin of a gigantic beast that swam leagues under the sea.

Sy-wen seemed to sense his discomfort. She glanced back over a slim shoulder at him. Wiping back strands of flowing green hair, she spoke to him with a worried set to her lips. 'It's only a little farther. The council chamber is just ahead.'

Kast nodded, little comforted, and continued after the small mer'ai girl. Around him, the eternal soft phosphorescent glow from the walls had begun to strain his eyes with its weak light. Under his bare feet, the living floor yielded with each step, adding to his sense of disorientation and unease. It took practice to walk on this spongy footing.

As he concentrated on his steps, he noted that even the air felt wrong. It was too moist. He had learned that the giant leviathans somehow harvested fresh air from the sea's waters and used it to fill these chambers and corridors they shared with the mer'ai.

Kast shuddered and closed the distance with Sy-wen. He sought to distract himself from these distasteful surroundings. 'Do you think your mother will agree to your plan?' he asked as he reached her side.

Sy-wen shrugged. 'It does not matter. Mother is just one of five elders. We must convince them all.'

'But if we could sway her, the others might come in line. She may be our best chance of getting a foothold in the council on this matter.'

Sy-wen's pace slowed. 'I fear my mother may be the hardest to convince. After I almost got Conch killed ...' Her voice trailed off.

'But you also saved your mother's dragon's life.'

'No. It was the blood of Ragnar'k that healed his deep wounds.' Sy-wen stopped and turned to Kast. 'Since I returned from A'loa Glen, my mother will hardly look me in the eye, let alone speak to me. Even though she and the council have agreed to help in the battle to come, she still bears a hatred for all things associated with the lan'dwellers – and now that includes me. She fears me lost to the world of rock and dirt. So do not place much trust on our blood relations to sway her opinion.'

'But she and the council did agree to join forces in the coming battle.'

'Yes, to honor our people's ancient debts to the mages of A'loa Glen for aiding our escape from the Gul'gotha, not from any real feeling of loyalty or concern for the people of Alasea.' Sy-wen turned away and continued down the narrow corridor. 'My mother bears no love for any lan'd-wellers.'

They continued the rest of the way in silence. Kast did not know how to end this melancholy in Sy-wen. Ever since they had left the coast to search for the Bloodriders and their dragon-prowed warships, she had sunk into a deep somberness that could not be shaken. Kast could blame his own sour feelings on the surroundings; almost a moon had passed since he had last seen the sky, and he grew more and more anxious as each day wore on. But this was Sy-wen's home. To be here should make her happy.

As Kast followed the young woman, his eyes traced the curve of her bare back and the smooth lines under her snug sharkskin breeches. He had yet to grow accustomed to the concept that he and this mer'ai girl were bonded. His fingers wandered to his cheek and brushed across the tattoo inked in magick and poisonous dyes that ran from neck to ear. He knew what lay there: a coiled dragon of black scale and red eyes, the seadragon Ragnar'k. Here was Sy-wen's true bonded: the dragon that hid under his own skin.

Kast felt a slight warmth heat his skin as his fingers touched the tattoo. Emotions warred in his breast. A part of him raged against the curse that had been laid upon him – to be forever half dragon, half man. But another part only wished for Sy-wen to stare him in the eye and reach to his cheek, to once again feel the burn and ecstasy of her touch on his skin, to once again become her full bonded. But was this his own wish or the dream of the dragon Ragnar'k, striving to be released again?

Shaking his head, Kast followed Sy-wen. Dragon or not, he was also a man. And though his thoughts were swirled, one thing was clear. Since first they had met, his blood had stirred with the sight of her. Not from ancient blood debts or whispers of magickal bonds; it was as if a hole in his heart, an emptiness that he had never known was even there, had been filled. He knew in some way she completed him – and there lay most of his resentment for his curse. Kast did not want to share her with the dragon that hid inside him. But this, in turn, led to even more questions, worries that kept him awake long into the night as he tried to sleep: Just who was Sy-wen truly bonded to? Kast or Ragnar'k? And if the dragon was not present, would she still even acknowledge Kast or welcome him?

Kast sensed that these same worries wrestled in Sy-wen, too. He caught her sidelong glances at him when she thought he wasn't looking, her silver eyes appraising him. He also saw the confusion in her gaze. It was clear she mistrusted her feelings. How much of her desire for him was magick-born? And how much came from her true heart?

Kast wished he had the answers. But ever since their trials on the island of A'loa Glen, Sy-wen had kept a wary distance from him, refusing to discuss it. She was not ready to explore those answers yet.

'We're here,' Sy-wen said, a flicker of anxiety in her voice. She had stopped and now pointed to where the passage ended. 'The council chamber.'

Ahead, a mer'ai guard stood stiffly by a blockage in the corridor. Like Sy-wen, he wore only a pair of sharkskin breeches, his oiled and hairless chest almost aglow in the shine from the walls. His hair, a mane of light green with hues of copper, was loose and draped to his waist. In his hand, he bore a long spear of shark tooth.

As they approached, he spoke. 'Mistress Sy-wen, welcome. Your mother and the others await you.'

The guard did not even bother to glance Kast's way. By now, Kast was used to such an affront: the mer'ai had little warmth for those who lived above the waves. The name *lan'dwellers* was used as a vicious slur among these people.

Sy-wen, though, bristled at every barb thrown at him. Even now, her cheeks reddened and she stared the guard down, not acknowledging his greeting until he corrected this slight in courtesy.

Finally, through clenched teeth, the guard spoke. 'And of course, Master Kast. The council awaits you both.'

Sy-wen nodded, unsmiling and cold. 'Thank you, Bridlyn. If you would announce us to the elders – *both* of us . . .'

He bowed again and pressed the center of the flap of ruffled leathery tissue that blocked the way further. Instead of swinging clear like a hinged door, the way ahead opened like a puckered mouth, the thick tissue spreading open from the center to bunch along the walls and floor.

Though a common sight, it still made Kast queasy. There was no mistaking this passage as an ordinary corridor.

Stepping through the 'doorway,' the guard led the way into the chamber beyond. Bridlyn made their formal introductions, but Kast was too stunned by his view of the room to even hear him.

The chamber, though relatively small, appeared huge. This illusion was created by the wall to one side. Here the leviathan's skin was as clear as blown crystal. The deep blue of the ocean seemed to spread forever. Around and above, schools of yellowfin and waving strands of kelp swept past the slowly swimming behemoth. Below, the landscape of rock and coral was festooned with anemones like living jewels, some aglow with their own inner light. In the distance, Kast even spotted several mer'ai patrols atop their seadragons, mounts of every color: jade, alabaster, copper, gold.

The view trapped Kast's breath. He did not even know his feet had stopped until Sy-wen touched his elbow and drew him down a set of bone stairs. Still he could only follow slowly, his eyes wide, drinking in the sights.

Once he reached the floor of the chamber, his initial shock faded to simple wonder. He found himself able to concentrate again on the conversations around him. Bridlyn was already heading back up the stairs; he wore a disdainful smirk at Kast's reaction to the view. The guard's scorn helped sober Kast further. Kast was done acting the awestruck child.

Turning his back on the window, Kast focused on the remainder of the chamber. Before him, seated along a curved table of polished coral, were the five elders of the council. Sy-wen already stood before the table, facing the elders.

Kast recognized Sy-wen's mother among them, a stately woman with her daughter's features. But the warmth and spark in Sy-wen's eyes had long gone to ash in the gaze of her mother. 'It was the death of my father,' Sy-wen had explained earlier. 'Something in my mother died then, too.'

Even now, the presence of her daughter failed to bring any familial glow to the woman's cold eyes.

Kast could sense Sy-wen's hurt, the way her shoulders were not as straight and the way her hands, clamped behind her back, clutched with whitened knuckles. She refused to speak directly to her mother, instead speaking to the senior elder of the council, Master Edyll.

'We come with a request,' she stated briskly to the old man.

'So it would seem, child,' he answered her. Master Edyll was ancient for a mer'ai. His hair had gone to full silver, but there was no mistaking the sharp intelligence in his old eyes or the gentle humor in the bend of his lips. 'But what has you so stiff and formal? Have you already forgotten how I once bounced you on my knee?'

'Of course not, Uncle ... um, I mean *Master* Edyll.'

Kast stepped beside the now blushing girl and placed a hand on Sy-wen's shoulder. He spoke into her awkwardness. 'If I might speak ... ?'

Some of the humor faded from the elder's lips, but not all. 'Please elaborate then, Master Kast.'

'Sy-wen and I request permission to leave the leviathan.'

'To what purpose?'

'The mer'ai legions have scoured the Shoals now for nearly a full moon. And as of yet, the Bloodriders escape us. Time runs short.'

'And do you know where your people might be hiding out there?'

Kast licked his dry lips. 'No, sir. But the mer'ai move too slowly through these seas.'

These words raised heated murmurs among the other elders. The mer'ai were not wont to hear their shortcomings. Only Sy-wen's mother and Master Edyll remained quiet.

'Once again, Master Kast, what do you propose?' Edyll asked after the others calmed down.

'I propose that Sy-wen ignite the bond in me and release Ragnar'k. The dragon's ability to fly will greatly enhance the search and—'

Sy-wen's mother spoke for the first time. 'No. We already discussed this when we left the coast. It is not safe. One dragon is no match against the fleets of the Dre'rendi. Unless the Bloodriders have grown lax, they will easily spot a huge black flying past their sails. Even if an arrow does not take you down, you will alert them to our presence. If we hope to pin down the Dre'rendi and bend them to our wills—'

Now it was Kast's turn to bridle. 'Bend them to your wills? Do you believe yourselves still our slave masters? The Dre'rendi cast their blood upon the seas so the mer'ai could escape to the Deep. It was our ships that held off the Gul'gothal forces so you might live. And do you come back now and think to take us again as slaves? We won our freedom in blood!'

His words had no effect on the cold features of the woman. 'We know our histories. We also know that the Dre'rendi have one more debt to pay before they can be truly free.' She waved a hand toward her own cheek. 'Do you still mark your sons with the tattoo of the seahawk?'

'Yes, we have not forgotten our old oaths.'

'But do you know why we asked this of you?'

Kast remembered when Sy-wen had bonded to him. During the spell, they had shared a glimpse of an ancient sea and a deal struck upon a dragon-prowed boat. His ancestor had agreed to mark each male when of proper age with the tattoo of a hunting seahawk drawn in the dyes of the blowfish and reef octopi. Kast's fingers brushed his own cheek and neck where once such a seahawk tattoo had rested. He remembered Sy-wen's first touch, before the dragon had claimed him and changed his tattoo. It had been a brand upon his skin, binding him to her will, enslaving him for as long as they touched.

Kast glanced at the row of elders. 'Why?' Kast asked harshly. 'What more do you want of my people? I'm sure they will freely come to fight the Gul'gotha. You do not need to enslave us again.'

Master Edyll answered. 'You misunderstand, Master Kast.'

'How so?'

The humor had returned to the elder's lips. 'Have you

never suspected?' When Kast did not respond, Master Edyll continued. 'In the old tongue, your very name declares your secret. Dre'rendi means *dragonfolk*.' Master Edyll waited for his words to sink in and for Kast to understand.

Kast just shook his head.

The ancient elder finally sighed. 'The seahawk tattoo is not to enslave your people to us, Master Kast, but to bring them back home. Our two peoples must be united again.'

Kast found it hard to breathe. 'What are you saying?'

'I am saying, Master Kast, that you are mer'ai.'

Pinorr di'Ra, the ancient shaman of the *Dragonspur*, stood by the bowsprit and stared out over the empty seas. The morning breezes tousled his long white hair. He combed the loose strands back from his eyes. Once, when his hair was still black, he had worn it in a warrior's braid, but that was long ago, before the *rajor maga* had come upon him. Claimed by the sea gods, his sword had been taken from him, and he had had to untie his braid and don the robes of a shaman. It had been a day of both shame and honor. His lips grew hard at the memory. May he never suffer such a day again.

Pinorr sighed and studied the endless waves. Since he had woken this morning, the sea had called to him, summoning him with a nagging ache in his skull. At this age, he was well familiar with the call. 'What is it you want?' he mumbled to the empty water. 'Can't you leave an old man to his warm bed and dreams of the past?' But he knew better. The seas could never be refused.

Closing his eyes, he reached out with his senses. He pushed aside the salty scents from his nose and ignored the soft breezes that brushed his shaven cheeks. He searched much farther than his own skin. Reaching over the horizon, he found it at last – a hint of lightning in the air, the distant wail of wind. He knew the warnings. A fierce storm brewed, rising from the south.

He frowned and opened his eyes. Though the day was clear and the sky blue, by nightfall, the seas would roar and the winds would scream. These southern storms were the worst, whipping the rain-laden clouds of the tropics to crash and tear at the boats of the Shoals. With the boom of thunder in his ears, Pinorr stared at where the ocean met the sky. What brewed over the horizon was one of the worst southern squalls – a true ship killer.

Grim news for the fleet.

Pinorr spat into the sea, adding his water and salt to the great ocean, thanking the gods below for their warning.

'Papa,' a small voice said at his knee, 'they're coming.'

Pinorr continued to stare out at the sea. The child who sat by his ankles was not his own, but the daughter of his eldest son, whose spirit had returned to the waves before the babe was even born. And with her mother dying in childbirth, the youngster had known no other guardian but himself. Pinorr had at first tried to correct Sheeshon's perception that he was her 'papa,' but the poor child was weak inthe mind and had never understood. Eventually he had given up trying.

'Sheeshon, who's coming?' he asked softly, coddling her delusions. He knelt beside the child. Sheeshon was almost ten winters of age, but she still had the wide-open eyes of an infant. When her mother had died in the midwife's arms, the poor child had had to be cut free from her cooling belly. Unfortunately, the healers had not been quick enough. The child had already been touched by death, her mind damaged.

Pinorr wiped the drool from the girl's chin with the sleeve of his robe and smoothed back the drapes of black hair. Her face, though innocent, could never be considered pretty. The lids of one eye sagged, and she only had partial use of her lips on that same side. It was as if half her face had melted and drooped. He touched her cheek. *Who will watch after you when I am gone?* he wondered sadly.

Sheeshon continued to ignore his question and his touch. She concentrated on the piece of whalebone in her tiny fingers, working it this way and that. Her small carving tool continued to dig and scrape at the bone. 'I'm almost done, Papa.'

Pinorr smiled at her serious expression as she worked. Though she was addled in the mind, her fingers were skilled; they flew over the bone, feeling, digging, rubbing. With such skill, she might have been able to be apprentice to a master carver, but her dull wits made such a dream impossible. He leaned closer. 'What is it you're carving, dear?'

She waved him away. 'No peeking, Papa! I must hurry. They're coming!' She was so earnest, her brows wrinkling together, her eyes pinched as she worked.

'Come, dear, I must go see the keelchief. A storm rides down on us.' He reached for her shoulder.

'No!' Sheeshon stabbed at him with her small knife, driving him away. 'I must finish!'

Pinorr rubbed at the long scratch where the tool had caught the back of his hand. He frowned – not in anger, but surprise. Normally, Sheeshon was so pliable, so easy to direct here or there. This new strident behavior concerned him. He matched it with his own stern words, in a voice that made many keelchiefs cower. 'Sheeshon, leave your carvings till after your meal. I've work to do. Do you wish to be left with Mader Geel?'

The child's fingers paused. She finally raised sad eyes toward him, tears streaking her cheeks. 'No, Papa.'

He instantly felt like the lowest mud wader. He sighed and leaned closer to Sheeshon, enveloping her tiny hands in his large and bony fingers. Her hands were like embers in his palm. A sickness must be coming on the girl, her skin feverish. Was this the reason for her sudden temper? He regretted his words even more.

'I'm sorry, Sheeshon,' he said. 'You are my heart.' He pulled the damaged child to his chest. He kissed her on the top of the head.

She mumbled something softly to his chest.

Leaning away, he asked, 'What was that, my dear?'

'They're almost here,' she said, not meeting his eye. Her fingers clutched the figure she had been carving, but she no longer worked at it.

'May I see?' he asked softly, indicating the carving.

She hesitated, then slowly released her grip on the piece of whalebone. 'I wasn't done,' she said in a half pout. 'I can't see them clearly until I'm done.'

'That's all right. You'll have time after the high sun meal.' He took the offered chunk of carved bone and tilted back on his heels, raising the figurine to the sun.

He blinked at her work, stunned. Her skill was breathtaking – and she considered this unfinished. The detail work, the smooth curves, even the spread of fragile whalebone into thin wings – all was in such perfect symmetry. He rotated the sculpture in the sunlight. This could be a master's work.

'I wanted to paint the dragon black, Papa. It's supposed to be black!' She slammed her tiny fist on the deck planks. The child's frustration tremored her voice. 'And her hair is supposed to be seaweed green!'

'Whose hair?' Then he tilted the sculpture and realized that a small figure rode the back of this handsomely rendered dragon. He had overlooked the tiny rider; she was dwarfed by the huge dragon. 'Who is this?' he asked the child.

Sheeshon wore a crooked frown, one side of her lips slack. 'Papa, it's who's coming. Aren't you listening?'

He smiled at her imagination. 'Ah, so these two are flying here to see you?' He handed back the figurine. 'Where are they coming from?'

Clutching the figurine to her chest, Sheeshon glanced around the empty deck to make sure no one was eavesdropping. Once satisfied that they were alone, she turned wide eyes toward him. 'From under the waves.'

'Ah, so it's a seadragon then, like from the stories of the mer'ai.'

'But this one flies through the skies, too.' She lifted the chunk of scrimshaw and dove and glided it about the air.

'I see,' he humored her. 'Are they going to take you up with them on fine adventures?'

She stopped flying her dragon and turned to stare him in the eye. Her look was shocked. 'Oh, no, Papa, they're gonna kill us.' She then went back to flying her dragon about the air.

He sat back farther on his heels, watching his son's poor child. Pinorr rubbed his palms together as if to remove the clinging dust of whalebone from his skin. Mostly, though, he wanted to warm the chill that had suddenly set in with the girl's words.

Just the ramblings of an addled mind, he told himself as he stood up. But in his ears, he still heard the distant boom of a storm from over the horizon. He stared again at the peaceful seas while lightning and thunder echoed in his skull.

He was now certain.

Whether upon the winds of a squall or the wings of a dragon, doom raced toward them all.

Sy-wen stared at Kast's stunned expression, sharing his shock. How could Kast be mer'ai? The large man stepped away from the coral table as if to escape the elder's words. Blood drained from Kast's face, making the tattoo of Ragnar'k stand out like a black blaze on his neck and cheek. 'What is this nonsense you speak?' Kast muttered.

Sy-wen turned to face the council. Surely Master Edyll was making some joke at the poor man's expense. Kast shared none of the aspects of her people – no webbed fingers, no inner eyelid. Even his dark complexion was so unlike the pale and luminescent features of the mer'ai.

It was these very differences that had first attracted Sy-wen to the brooding man. Even now, the sight of him stirred her heart. His wind-hardened features, ruddy skin, and hair as dark as midnight waters were so *unlike* her own people. He was like a granite island in a tepid sea.

Master Edyll sat silently, a ghost of a smile on his lips as he recognized her confusion. Sy-wen's mother remained perched like a stone statue beside him. The other council members muttered amongst themselves, clearly upset with their senior member's revelation.

Mistress Rupeli, a small brash woman who painted her cheeks in florid hues, twisted in her seat to face down Master Edyll. 'You speak our secrets too freely,' she warned the old man. 'You may be the head of the council, but that does not give you the right to reveal mer'ai secrets to ... to this ... this outsider.'

'He is not an outsider,' Master Edyll said. 'He is a man of the sea, as are all Dre'rendi. And more than that, though you may wish to believe otherwise, he is also mer'ai.'

Sy-wen could keep silent no longer. 'But Kast is nothing like us. Just look at him! How could you name him mer'ai?' Sy-wen felt the Bloodrider's eyes swing in her direction. His gaze burned her cheeks. She had not meant her words to sound so dismissive of Kast, as if the man were somehow unworthy to be classified as a mer'ai.

Glancing a quick apology his way, Sy-wen noticed the hurt in his eyes. Her blurted words had wounded him deeply. She should have known better. In the days prior, she had sensed the feelings the man had for her – emotions she had dared not acknowledge, not until she knew her own true heart. Kast had waited these many days for any word from her, some sign that she shared his feelings. But for his patience and kindness, she now only rewarded him with her disdain.

Kast turned stiffly back to the council. 'Sy-wen is correct.' He raised his hands and splayed his fingers, revealing the lack of webbing. 'None of my people are marked with the signs of the mer'ai. You are deluded.'

Master Edyll's face grew grim. 'If you are so sure of mer'ai history, Bloodrider, then tell me yours. Where did the Dre'rendi come from? What land gave birth to your clans?'

Sy-wen turned to Kast, awaiting his answer. His feet shifted under him. After a long silence, he answered. 'We have no homeland. It is said we were birthed from the seas themselves. But the land grew jealous at our birth and cursed us, transforming us into ordinary men so that we might never return to the sea. Exiled from our mother's bosom, we forever ride the waves, seeking a way back home.'

As Kast spoke, Master Edyll's smile returned.

'It is just a hearthside story,' Kast stated, glowering at the senior elder. 'A myth. But in your eyes, I can see what you're thinking. You believe the story of our ocean birth to be some sign that our two people share a common heritage. Well, I say again: You are deluded! We share nothing with you, except a history of slavery.'

'Even there you are wrong,' Master Edyll said.

'Then speak plainly, old man,' Kast said, a worried glint in his eye.

Master Edyll turned to Sy-wen instead. 'I'm sorry, my dear. With the exception of a few scholars and the council itself, what you are about to hear has been kept hidden from our people. I must ask you to keep this secret.'

Sy-wen glanced at her mother, but again the woman had grown distant, not meeting her eye. Swallowing hard, Sy-wen turned back to Master Edyll and nodded. 'Wh-what secret has been kept from us?'

'The true history of our people,' he stated plainly.

Sy-wen's brow wrinkled. 'But I know our histories.'

'You know what we taught you, not the truth. Shame can make one do foolish things, even hide the truth from one's self.' He glanced significantly toward the other elders.

'I don't understand.'

'First, I ask that you listen with an open heart,' Master Edyll said. He eyed the large Bloodrider beside her. 'You too, Master Kast. Then judge if I am truly deluded.'

Kast simply nodded, his features gone hard, arms crossed.

Master Edyll settled back in his seat. 'Long ago, before the lands of Alasea were even settled by man, the mer'ai were fisherfolk. We lived on islands far out in the Great Ocean.'

Sy-wen interrupted. 'You mean we lived in the seas *near* these islands.'

'No, my dear, *on* the islands. We were once lan'dwellers.'

A shock passed through Sy-wen. Even though she had spent time among the men and women of the coasts and had learned of their nobility and courage, a shred of old prejudices still sickened her blood at such an idea. She raised and displayed her webbed fingers, as if to disprove the elder's words. 'How could we have ever been lan'dwellers?'

'We were,' Master Edyll stated plainly.

'Or so the ancient texts claim,' the youngest of the elders added, speaking for the first time. Master Talon wore his pale green hair tied with bits of polished coral and mother-of-pearl. As he spoke, he fingered a strand of beaded and braided hair that draped over his shoulder. 'Not *all* of us accept these old tales as our *true* histories.'

Mistress Rupeli nodded her support. 'Some of us know these old tales to be fabrications. I, for one, don't accept your assumptions, Master Edyll.'

'Assumptions? The scholars, one and all, agree with the validity of the written histories,' Master Edyll countered.

'Scholars can be wrong,' Talon said, throwing back his thin braid.

'And even if the texts *were* written at the time of our origin,' Mistress Rupeli continued, 'that does not mean what was scribed in ink was true. I say we—'

'Enough!' declared the final member of the council, the somber-eyed Master Heron. He slammed his fist on the table for emphasis. 'The past is past,' he stated sourly, his bald pate shining in the wall's glow. 'We waste our time on this foolishness. What does our past matter? We should address the current situation. The Gul'gotha mass at A'loa Glen, and the Dark Lord's minions scour the seas. It is only so long until they discover us and attempt to subjugate us, as they did Alasea. That is the issue we should be addressing.'

Sy-wen watched Master Edyll during this outburst. He just sat quietly, fingers folded on his lap. Finally, he spoke again once the others were quiet again. 'The man has a right to know,' he stated softly. He waved a couple of fingers at Kast. 'You cannot deny the truth that stands before you.'

The elders' eyes all swung toward the Bloodrider.

'What?' Kast asked, irritation and growing impatience clear in his tight lips and squinted eyes.

They ignored him. Sy-wen's mother turned to the senior elder. 'Go on, Edyll. Finish the foul tale and be done with it. I, for one, have little stomach to dwell on this matter any further.'

Master Edyll bowed his head slightly in acknowledgment and returned to Sy-wen and Kast. 'As I was saying, the islands were once our home, but it was not idyllic. On the contrary, the harsh seas of the distant ocean hardened our people. We started as a savage nation, attacking neighboring islands and ruling the conquered tribes like tyrants. We sacrificed children to our gods and drank from the skulls of our defeated. Our ancestors' hearts were as cold as the ice floes of the north.'

'That cannot be,' Sy-wen moaned. She had never heard these histories before. As she searched the elders' faces, she saw a spark of sympathy for her distress enter her mother's eyes. The other council members kept their heads bowed, a mix of shame and anger clear in all their postures.

'One winter, a man appeared among our people. Some say he was born from one of our conquered tribes; some say he was the bastard son of our king. He declared our ways wrong and spoke words of peace. The downtrodden flocked to him, attracted by his words of kindness and compassion. He traveled among our many islands, and his flock grew larger and more vocal. The mer'ai ruler at that time, King Raff, sent his warriors out to slaughter these followers and bring back the head of this man.'

'Who was he?' Sy-wen asked.

Master Edyll sipped from a cup of kelp tea. 'He bore several names: Spiritwalker, Dragonkin, Peacespeaker. But his true name was lost in history.'

'Further proof that the tales were mere myth,' Master Talon scoffed.

Sy-wen did not want a new argument to ensue. 'So what happened to this man?' she asked.

Master Edyll's gaze drifted away, into the past. 'It was a long hunt. Entire islands were wiped out. It was said that the seas remained bloody for an entire moon. Finally, to end the massacres, the man came forward on his own, appearing in the throne room at the height of the slaughter. "Let this end now," he declared, and gave himself over to King Raff's guards. They tortured the man for seven days and nights. They blinded him with flaming irons, they crushed his hands and feet, and finally they cut his manhood from him.'

Sy-wen cringed from these words. How could this horrible tale be true? How could this be her people's heritage?

Master Edyll continued in the same tone of voice. 'They lashed his bloody and broken body, still alive, onto a raft and sent him out to the sharks. He sang as his body floated away – not a song of vengeance and hate, but one of forgiveness. Those of his flock who still lived, and many who heard his song for the first time, followed his raft into the seas. Even the king's own daughter entered the waves after this man. Some say she had been his lover; some say she was simply touched by his song. Either way, one thing was clear – she bore magick in her voice. As she entered the waters, she added her song to his, and from the seas, the mighty dragons arose, answering her calls. They claimed these exiles and took them safely from the islands.' Master Edyll paused and reached for his cup of tea with trembling fingers. The old man clearly grew tired with the telling of this tale.

'And so the mer'ai were born,' Kast finished for him, a sour set to his lips. 'Seadragon and mer'ai united. How noble!'

'No,' Master Edyll said, shaking his head slowly. 'You don't listen closely enough. The tale is not yet done.' Master Edyll let his words sink in before continuing. 'After the rescue by the dragons, King Raff sent ships out to hunt his escaping people. He meant to slaughter them all, dragons included. But again, the broken man would not let him. Atop a great white dragon, he met King Raff's armada and asked for the bloodshed to stop. "Take my life in exchange for your people," he had yelled across the waves, his battered body barely able to stay seated atop his mount. King Raff laughed at the blind man and ordered the warriors' spears and harpoons loosed. Dragon and man were pierced with a hundred blades. Dying, they sank under the waves, their blood mixing in the saltwater.'

Master Edyll's voice grew grim. 'But with the savage slaughter of their leader, the man's flock grew wild. Aided by the dragons, they attacked King Raff's armada and washed the decks with the blood of the slain, sparing no one. King Raff's head was spiked atop the prow of the lead ship, put there by his own daughter, and the fleet returned to their home islands. It is said not a single islander escaped their wrath. These wild warriors were cursed by the islanders as dragonfolk – or in the old tongue, *Dre'rendi*.'

'My people,' Kast said, horror in his voice.

'Yes. Led by your first leader.'

Kast's eyes grew wide. 'The warrior queen Raffel.' Sy-wen saw the look of recognition in the large man.

'Raff-*el*,' Master Edyll elaborated. 'Daughter of Raff. One and the same.'

Into the stunned silence, Sy-wen spoke. 'But how does this lead to our people's origin?'

Master Edyll sighed. 'As the seas ran red with the blood of the slain, we were already being born. The leader who preached of peace, he who had sunk under the weight of a hundred spears, did not die with his great white. For three days, under the waves, the blood of dragon and man mixed with the salt of the sea. The healing properties inherent in the dragon's blood began to transform in the swirl of mixed bloods. Magick began to blur the line between man and dragon. The man became a little like the dragon, the dragon a little like the man. The two were forever fused and bonded.'

'He became the first true mer'ai,' Sy-wen said with a tinge of wonder in her voice.

Master Edyll nodded. 'Once fully recovered, the man rose from the seas atop his white dragon. His dark hair had gone white to match the dragon's scale; his fingers and toes had become webbed like the great beast's. Dragon and man could now speak to one another as kin. But with all the changes, one aspect of the man remained untouched by the magick – his heart. When he saw the slaughter done in his name, he cried to the cruel skies above and cast his gaze forever from the world of sunlight and rock. But before he fled, he went to his followers on their bloody ships and commanded them to end their murderous ways. The Dre'rendi bowed before his miracle and begged to join him. "Not until the blood is washed from your hands," he told them. "Serve the children of the dragon to come. Protect them well, and one day I will call you back home!" With those words, the man left, taking the seadragons with him.'

Kast cleared his throat. 'But he was only one man. How could he be the father of your sea-dwelling clans?'

'Our forefather was more than a man. He was part dragon now.' Master Edyll stared Kast in the eye. 'And his white dragon was a female. From their union, the mer'ai clans were born.'

Now it was Sy-wen's turn to struggle to speak, her voice grown incredulous. 'You mean we descend from the dragons themselves? We were once actual mates with the great beasts?'

'Yes, long ago. Though we can no longer conceive with dragons, we still share a blood bond with the great creatures that harkens back to such a time. Over the passing winters, other men and women, people from many lands, added their blood to our lines, expanding our clans. But then we fled with the coming of the Gul'gotha, exiling ourselves forever from the rock and coast.' As he finished, Master Edyll glanced significantly at Sy-wen's mother.

To Sy-wen's surprise, her mother swung away from the elder's gaze, almost in shame, but not before Sy-wen noted the flicker of pain and sorrow in her mother's eyes. Something unspoken had passed between them. Another secret.

Kast scowled. 'You expect me to believe all this?'

Master Edyll turned back to the Bloodrider. 'Believe what you will, but one thing is certain. Our two fates are tied – mer'ai and Dre'rendi.'

'And you have something to prove the truth of your words?'

Before the old man could answer, Talon interrupted. 'Just dusty relics from the past. He puts too much potency in ancient scraps.'

Master Edyll turned to the young elder. Sy-wen had never seen the old man's eyes flash so fiercely. 'You malign the past at your own risk, young Talon. You have lived too few winters to appreciate how quickly the past can bite you from behind if you stare only toward the future.'

Talon grumbled but could not meet Master Edyll's furious gaze.

Kast clearly grew tired of this bickering. 'What is this proof, then?'

Turning to face the Bloodrider, Master Edyll's brows rose slightly. He nodded toward Kast. 'Why, you yourself are my proof, Master Kast.'

'What do you mean?'

'It is time you learned who you truly are.' The old man waved a hand, and a fold of wall pulled away to reveal an ancient painting hanging behind the council table. It was of a white-haired man seated atop a great dragon whose scale was the color of pearl.

'Dragonkin,' Master Edyll named the figure. 'Our fore-father.'

Sy-wen gasped, unable to restrain her outburst. She took a step closer to the painting. Even with the man's strange hair, Sy-wen could not mistake the familiar features. The man was Kast's twin – even down to the dragon tattoo dyed on the skin of the man's throat.

Master Edyll spoke into their shock. 'You are our fore-father reborn! Dragon and man united once again by magick.'

'It cannot be,' Kast mumbled, his eyes fixed on the painting.

As the sun crested high in the blue sky, Pinorr stood behind the keelchief of the *Dragonspur*. The old shaman waited patiently for the ship's chieftain to finish whipping one of the boat's crewmen. The punished man's cries competed with the crack of the rawhide. Ten lashes was the common punishment for being found asleep on a watch.

The remainder of the crew went about the decks as if the screams of pain were nothing more than the cries of angry gulls. On a ship run by a hard keelchief, Pinorr had learned that such a chorus was routine. Still, as Pinorr watched Ulster soak the leathers of his whip in seawater, he noted the glint of hunger and pleasure in the young keelchief's eyes. Not all chiefs soaked their leathers in salt to heighten the burn of their whip's touch.

On this ship, the current keelchief always did.

Ulster caught Pinorr's gaze as he soaked the whip for the final lash. '"Add salt to a wound to help them remember,"' the keelchief said, quoting the old codes of the Dre'rendi, as if to justify the added harshness to his punishment. But the hard grin on the man's lips belied this excuse – Ulster truly enjoyed the pain he caused.

Pinorr simply nodded at the keelchief's statement. He let no sign of his true feeling show on his face. It was not his place to question a chief's punishment. Besides, Ulster was new to his chiefdom. After serving on many ships under countless keelchiefs, Pinorr had known many such young chiefs who had tried to prove their toughness and strength by brutalizing their crew, striving to earn respect through fear. Only the passing of many winters would teach such young men that terror never won a crew's respect; only honor and a chief's firm compassion earned a ship's loyalty.

Still, Pinorr suspected it was more than a lack of experience that spurred Ulster's cruelty. With the whip, the man exposed his true heart. Even now, Pinorr noted how Ulster had to shift himself in his breeches to hide how pleasurable he found these punishments.

As the keelchief turned away to deliver his last blow, the scowl that Pinorr had kept hidden rose to the surface for a brief flash, then retreated again under his placid expression. He hated this young chief – not just for his easy cruelty, but for everything about him. He hated Ulster's continually smug expression and his habit of weaving his warrior's braid in a pattern normally reserved for the survivors of mighty battles.

Even Ulster's chiefdom had not been earned through any triumphs of his own, but from the respect that the Dre'rendi had had for his dead father. Ulster's sire had been the fleet's high keel for almost two decades and had led the fleets to their current dominance in the Shoals. During this time of glory, Pinorr had been the high keel's shaman aboard the mighty *Dragonsheart*. But more than chief, Pinorr had considered Ulster's father a close friend. They had weathered triumphs and tragedies together: the death of Pinorr's dear wife, the loss of the high keel's first son to the madness of the sea, the victory of the fleet over the Bloody Wights. After all this shared blood, Pinorr could refuse his friend nothing.

On the man's deathbed, with an arrow still sprouting like a weed from his bloody chest, the high keel had begged only two requests of his people. First, before he died, he wanted to see his son receive the dragon's tooth brand of chiefdom. And second, he wanted Pinorr to serve his son as shaman. Nobody could dishonor the man by refusing. Before the sun had set that day, Ulster received the chiefdom of the *Dragonspur*, and Pinorr followed him to this smaller ship.

A scream of agony broke through Pinorr's reverie. He watched the whipped crewman collapse in his shackles to the deck. Bloody stripes scarred his back. The cuts were deep. Pinorr spotted the white of bone through one of the strokes. Pinorr's face grew ashen. There was no excuse for such force. A lashing was meant to discourage and punish, not kill.

Ulster crossed to the prone man, carrying the bucket of seawater in which he had soaked his whip. As the chief drew near, the man moaned and tried to curl into a ball, as if expecting another blow. The pain had long driven the count of lashes from his poor mind. He was now just an animal in agony. Ulster stood over the pathetic man and slowly poured the salty waters over the man's wounded back. His screams began anew, stretching across the deck, flowing over the sea.

Pinorr tried not to cringe. He kept his features bland as Ulster finally dropped the bucket, now empty, and turned to Pinorr. The old shaman saw the look of satisfaction in the young man's eyes.

Clenching fists behind his back, Pinorr kept silent. How could this petty creature ever have been spat from the loins of such a fine man as the high keel?

Wiping his damp hands, Ulster stepped beside Pinorr. 'Now what news have you for me?'

Pinorr fought to keep his tone even and respectful. 'I sense a storm coming from the south. A large one.'

Ulster glanced at the clear skies and calm winds.

The doubt in the keelchief's eyes almost drove Pinorr to throttle the man. No one disrespected the word of a shaman, especially not when that shaman was Pinorr di'Ra. All knew his *rajor maga*, his sea senses, were the most regarded of any shaman's. The sea gods had richly blessed Pinorr, and for this scrap of a man to doubt not only the shaman, but also the gods, was a dishonor that could only be cut away with the edge of a sword. Still, Pinorr kept silent. Ulster was the son of his friend, and he would honor the dead man's memory by serving this fool as best he could manage.

'So what should we do?' Ulster asked, facing Pinorr again.

'The storm that comes will strike with the night. We must flag warnings to the other ships of the fleet. We must seek—'

Ulster waved Pinorr's words away in impatience. 'Of course, of course. I'll have them signaled before the sun sets. What else do you have to report? My meal awaits.'

Pinorr bowed his head slightly. 'I apologize for not making myself clear from the start, Keelchief Ulster. What rides down upon us is no ordinary storm that requires only the reefing of sails, the laying of storm lines, and the battening of hatches. This squall hails from the deep *south*. A ship killer.'

Again doubt shone in the man's eyes. 'What are you saying?'

'I'm saying,' Pinorr stated coldly, letting a bit of anger slip into his voice, 'that the fleet needs to be alerted *now*. To protect the ships, we must seek a sheltered harbor before the squall strikes.'

Ulster shook his head, stiffening slightly at Pinorr's harsh tones. 'The Dre'rendi don't run from storms like so many thick-bellied merchant ships. Our keels will ride any squall.'

Pinorr gave up any pretense of obeisance to this fool. 'You're wrong, Ulster. You're too young to have seen the worst that can blow out of the south. I've seen storms that split boats in half, waves so high that boats topple end over end down their roaring troughs, skies so dense with lightning that night becomes day from their glow. What rides toward us now is worse than anything I've sensed before.' Pinorr leaned closer to Ulster. 'Send my warnings or die with the setting sun. It is your choice, *Keelchief*.' He spat the honorific so it sounded more a curse than a respected title.

Ulster's face had grown red with Pinorr's spouting anger. The tattoo of a diving seahawk blazed on his jaw. 'You overstep your station, Shaman. Don't rely on your old friendship with my dead father to keep you from my whips.'

Pinorr did not back down, not from this mud crawler. 'Send my warnings, Ulster, or I'll rip the blessing of the gods from this ship's keel and no shaman will ever walk these cursed decks again. See then what crew remain aboard your ship!'

The blood drained from Ulster's cheeks. 'You dare threaten me!'

'You are a keelchief here, Ulster, *not a god*. The order of shamans will not tolerate any disrespect, not even from the high keel himself. By ignoring my vision, you insult the sea gods who have sent us this warning. That I will not tolerate! I will not let a fool like you bring the wrath of the gods down upon the Dre'rendi.'

By now, other crewmen had gathered nearby, feigning work: coiling rope, dry scrubbing the deck, mending nets. They sensed the storm brewing here and had come to see the play of thunder.

Ulster was well aware of the others' gazes. His back grew straight and his shoulders square. 'I will not dishonor the gods,' he said stiffly. 'But that does not mean I have to suffer your tongue either, Shaman. You know the law: "Shaman will guide, but keelchief will *lead*."'

'Then heed my *guidance*, Keelchief Ulster. Send the warning, and *lead* our fleet to a safe harbor – before it's too late.'

Shaman and keelchief stood now only a handspan apart, neither ready to back down. Pinorr smelled a hint of spryweed on the other's breath. So Ulster partook of the potent herb that heightened a man's pleasure while bedding a woman. Here was further proof of the man's foolish nature. Not only did the weed dull one's wit and judgment, but with continued use, the lust for spryweed could eventually outgrow even the desire for the bed of a woman. Only a fool would dabble with such a foul herb.

Suddenly a bell clanged from deep within the ship, announcing the midday meal. Ulster's ear bent to its clangor. 'I will flag the other boats with your warning,' he conceded finally, his voice cold with the promise of revenge, 'but only *after* I sample the cook's grilled potfish.'

Pinorr knew the delay was Ulster's attempt to soothe his wounded pride, some way to snub Pinorr's nose without directly disregarding a shaman's vision. Pinorr allowed Ulster to have his little show. Why should he care as long as the keelchief spread the warning? He would not put his own honor above the safety of the fleet.

Bowing his head, Pinorr took a step back. 'So be it,' he said, the fire gone from his voice and manner. '"May the gods grant you stiff winds."'

Ulster nodded his approval and turned away, flipping his warrior's braid for all to note his victory.

Pinorr shook his head as the man left. The dolt had missed the clear insult in Pinorr's final words. The quoted passage – 'May the gods grant you stiff winds' – came from an ancient shaman prayer, a request to the gods to help a man who could no longer keep hard for a woman.

With tight lips, Pinorr turned away. For now, he let his anger fade from his blood and spent a long time staring across the expanse of blue sky.

As he studied the far horizon, Pinorr again sensed the brewing storm clouds, but closer now. He scented rain, lightning, and a whisper of something else, something that he could not name. He raised his fingers to the seahawk tattoo on his neck. Whatever the source of the foreign smell, even just a whisper of its scent made the dyes of his tattoo burn like a torch.

As he traced the wings of the hawk with a finger, Pinorr remembered little Sheeshon's seadragon carving and the small rider who rode the whalebone. 'They're coming,' she had claimed.

But who? Were her fancies of dragons more than just the dreams of an addled mind? Had the child inherited the gift of the *rajor maga*? Was there some truth to her words?

Suddenly an urgent voice arose behind him, coarse and rasping. 'Shaman Pinorr, you must come.'

Pinorr snapped from his reverie, surprised to find the sun lower in the sky. How long had be been standing in this trance? Turning from the sea, Pinorr found the crooked form of Mader Geel standing behind him. Her silver hair was tied in a severe braid, marking her prior years as a mistress of the sword. 'What is it?' he asked with irritation.

'It is Sheeshon,' the old woman hissed, then beckoned him to follow.

'What happened?'

'Keelchief Ulster tired of her mumbling in the kitchens and—'

Pinorr's heart clenched in his chest. *'What did he do?'*

Mader Geel continued to urge him across the deck. 'The child's unharmed. The keelchief only threw her little carving against the wall and smashed it to bits. But the child . . . She screamed, flying into a frothing rage, and attacked the keelchief. Even cut his hand deep with her little knife. I bustled her out of there before any worse could arise, but I can't calm her. And I fear Ulster's response.'

Pinorr was now racing ahead of the bent-backed woman, toward his cabins, his vision narrowed with hate. Ulster had finally gone too far. Sheeshon was the last of Pinorr's family, and he would not see her harmed by the keelchief's petty vindictiveness. Pinorr ripped open the hatch to the lower deck. If Ulster wanted this war, so be it!

As he dashed below, he made a promise to all the gods of the sea: *Before the sun rose again, either he or Ulster would be dead.*

14

Kast pushed away the platter of steamed clams. He had no appetite. His mind still reeled from all he had heard this morning. Across from him, Sy-wen rolled some type of boiled sea tuber across her plate, clearly just as uninterested in her own meal. They eyed each other over their respective plates. Neither was ready to speak.

After the meeting with the elders and the unveiling of the ancient painting, the council had disbanded for a midday repast before any further debate was allowed. Sy-wen and Kast had been bustled off by the guard, Bridlyn, to this private dining room.

The chamber was comfortably outfitted with a small table of polished coral and chairs cushioned with pillows of soft sea moss, while the walls were adorned with woven reed tapestries depicting various sea views. As handsomely as the chamber was appointed, it still felt cramped to Kast. It seemed more a cell than a room, especially after the morning spent in the council chamber, with its expansive views of the wide ocean. And it did not help that Bridlyn made it clear he would stay posted at the door.

Kast rubbed the stubble on his chin. He needed to break the growing silence before it drowned them both. Nodding toward the tapestry-covered wall, he asked a question that had nagged at him since arriving. 'So just how did the mer'ai ever train these leviathans to house your clans?'

Sy-wen shrugged. 'The dragons can communicate with the great beasts. Leviathans supply the seadragons with sources of fresh air, and in turn, the dragons help protect and feed the larger creatures. The mer'ai were just incorporated into this mutual relationship. The Leviathans house us, and as payment, we help keep them healthy and clean.' A small smile played on Sy-wen's lips. 'But then again, who knows for sure? For all I know, maybe we mer'ai were mates with these beasts, too. Who knows what your great grandfather fancied back then?'

Kast blushed at Sy-wen's frank talk. 'The Dragonkin was not my ancestor,' he insisted.

'Maybe not directly, but still, the resemblance . . .'

'As Master Talon said, it's probably just a coincidence. Most Dre'rendi have similar features.'

'Even the dragon tattoo?'

Kast had no way to dismiss this last statement. The males of his people were always marked with a *seahawk* tattoo, not a *dragon*. Under A'loa Glen, Kast's hawk tattoo had been transformed by the magick of Ragnar'k into a coiled black dragon, a twin to the design found on the painting of the Dragonkin. It made no sense.

Sy-wen seemed to sense his discomfort on this topic and switched to new matters – or *old* matters, rather: to the very reason they had sought the council this morning. 'Whatever history is true, maybe we should put aside such talk for now and consider again our idea about leaving here to search for your people. We're due to rendezvous with the others in only six days. Even if we left now, it would still take two days just to return to the point in the Doldrums where we were expected to meet. With time against us, I don't see any way of accomplishing our task successfully unless we commit to searching on our own.' She glanced to the sealed door. 'With or without the council's approval.'

'You would defy your elders? Even go against your mother's wishes?'

Sy-wen stared at Kast. 'How do you think I met you? Do you think I had permission to travel to the islands with Conch, or to pursue the ships that caught him? Besides, over time, my mother and I have developed an arrangement: She gives me orders, and I follow only those I agree with.'

'I see.' Kast had a hard time not matching the ghost of a smile that wavered about the mer'ai girl's lips. Her silver eyes seemed to light up with mischief. 'So you're saying, one way or another, we make a run for the surface.'

Her eyebrows rose. 'And why not? Have you not grown tired of breathing the stale air of the leviathan?'

'I guess I could use a bit of fresh air,' he conceded, his smile growing wider. He would love to feel the draw of a breeze through his hair, the touch of ocean spray upon his face. He had been cramped for too long within the belly of this seabeast. He straightened in his seat. 'When you're ready, I'll be more than happy to fly away from here.'

Sy-wen matched his expression, showing true joy at the thought of escape. 'I imagine Ragnar'k will be glad to stretch his wings, too.'

At the mention of the dragon's name, Kast's growing smile froze. He had forgotten that it was not he who would escape with Sy-wen, but Ragnar'k. Even if the two of them fled the belly of the leviathan, Kast would still be trapped – this time under the scales of a monstrous black dragon.

Sy-wen seemed to recognize his change of mood. She

reached a hand to him and touched his arm. He could not meet her eye.

'I am not like my ancient ancestor,' she said softly to him.

'What do you mean?' he grumbled.

'I mean that I don't share my forefather's passion for dragons.' She squeezed his wrist. 'When I choose a husband, he won't be covered in scales and bear wings.'

Kast glanced up to Sy-wen. 'But you're bonded to Ragnar'k?'

'So? Bonded to a dragon does not mean the beast consumes your whole heart. In truth, I have stronger feelings for my mother's dragon, Conch, than for Ragnar'k. In many ways, the dragon inside you frightens me. There is a wildness in him that can never be tamed, touched, nor drawn near to – not even by me.'

'But Ragnar'k will always be a part of me, even his wildness.'

She smiled sadly at his words. 'I have studied you, Bloodrider. You may bear a dragon inside you, but your heart is your own. That I know.'

'How?' he asked, his voice cracking.

She reached and touched his cheek, the one without the dragon emblazoned on it. 'I know your heart, Bloodrider.'

Kast wished he could say the same of her. Was Sy-wen just consoling him, or was there more meaning behind her words? He dared to lean into her touch, just a little, letting her palm warm his skin. But she pulled away as murmuring voices arose from beyond the room's door.

The portal puckered open, and Master Edyll stepped through the entry. 'I hope I'm not disturbing your meal,' he said and waved Bridlyn away.

'N-no, Uncle,' Sy-wen stuttered.

Kast glanced at her, but again he could not read the

woman. Was that relief or embarrassment that rattled her?

Master Edyll signaled the door closed, then crossed to join them. Kast stood and pulled another chair to the table, only sitting after the old elder had settled into his own seat.

'Thank you, Master Kast,' he said, patting the Bloodrider's wrist as Kast resumed his place. Master Edyll eyed them both silently for a moment, then spoke. 'So what's this about you two leaving?'

Kast glanced nervously at Sy-wen, whose expression remained placid. 'What do you mean, Uncle?' Sy-wen asked.

'I thought we'd discuss in *private* the reason the two of you approached the council this morning.'

Kast slowly let out his breath. He had been sure the elder had been privy to their secret plans. 'Should we not broach this before the full council?'

Master Edyll scrunched up his old features and shook his head sourly. 'They'll still be bickering for the next three days about me spouting mer'ai secrets. For a group so adamant that my words were false, they get quite heated when the subject is spoken aloud.'

'But why were these histories kept hidden anyway?' Sy-wen asked.

Master Edyll sighed. 'It is what the Dragonkin wanted. It was our forefather's first dictate. After fleeing under the sea and starting the mer'ai clans, he immediately banned any ties with surface dwellers. He thought to create a peaceful, idyllic society under the waves and wanted his people to believe the seas had always been their home.' Master Edyll finished with a derisive snort.

'So what went wrong?' Kast asked.

'Ah, so you happened to notice that his grand plans failed?' he said with a chortle, but then grew more pensive.

Kast saw the true pain in the elder's eyes. 'In some ways, our forefather was a fool.'

Sy-wen gasped a bit at such open disparagement of their ancestor.

Master Edyll sat quietly for a moment, then continued. 'He had thought to escape our heritage by fleeing under the sea. But it is never that easy. He just ended up dragging our violent heritage along behind him. Whether he hid the fact or not, our blood still rose from a people with a fiery temperament, and future generations were cursed with this same inner fire, a mixture of willfulness and an intense suspicion of others. To make matters worse, the merging of dragon blood in our bloodlines only added logs to this blaze, inflaming a fierce pride in our ancestors' veins. We grew to consider ourselves superior to the foul lan'dwellers. Why else should we hide from them? We came to think ourselves rulers of the sea.'

Master Edyll shook his head and gave a slight shudder. 'Even among our own people, before we fled the coasts, we used to cast out those who broke our rules. It was a cruel act. Away from the dragons, the sea magic would wear off those poor souls, and they would walk again like ordinary men, their mer'ai features fading away forever, damning them from ever returning to the sea. It was our greatest punishment – eternal banishment.'

Kast saw the horror on Sy-wen's face and caught an inkling of what such a punishment would mean to such a close-knit, insular people.

Master Edyll let them absorb his words in silence before he finished. When next he spoke, his voice was granite. 'I tell you all this as a warning. You must be careful what you plot. Since fleeing the Gul'gotha, the "banishments" were stopped in order to keep ourselves hidden from the Dark

Lord, but that does not mean we have grown less strict. For those who won't abide by our rules—' He glanced first at Sy-wen, then at Kast. '—our punishments are still severe.'

'You now slay them,' Sy-wen said heatedly.

Her words startled Master Edyll, his pale face reddening. 'So you know already?'

'While among the people of the coast, I learned that I was the first mer'ai to step from the sea in over five hundred years. It seems the stories of banishment were meant to hide an uglier truth.'

'Lies are often less painful than the truth.'

'Like our people's true histories,' Sy-wen said sullenly.

'As I said before, we could not escape our heritage so easily. The past has a way of strangling you when you ignore it.'

Silence settled over the room.

Finally, Master Edyll stood up with a slight groan, rubbing his old knees. 'Enough talk. It's time we were under way.'

Kast stood up reflexively, respecting the old man. Sy-wen remained seated, her face closed. But her anger could not be completely hidden. 'I have had enough of council meetings.'

Master Edyll nodded. 'So have I, some days ... Luckily that is not where we're going.'

His words drew Sy-wen's eyes. 'Then where?' she asked warily.

'It's time I helped you escape.'

Kast stumbled as he stepped toward the door. 'What?'

'The council has already met again and has banned you from leaving. I didn't agree.' He shrugged. 'We must hurry and get you both out of here.'

Sy-wen was on her feet and following. 'But, Uncle, you're one of the elders!'

'No, I'm just an old man – some would say a *foolish* old man. But in this matter, the council is clouded by a fear of the unknown. They would rather hide under the sea than risk change.'

Kast spoke as Master Edyll turned toward the door. 'What are we to do?'

The old man turned tired eyes toward him. 'Find your people. Finish the dream our forefather started.'

'What do you mean? How?'

'A time of bloodshed and slaughter has come upon us again, as during the reign of King Raff.' Master Edyll placed a hand on Kast's chest. 'But in your warrior's body beats the heart of a man of peace. Free our people, both our peoples, from our heritage of hate and war. Show us the path to a lasting peace.' With those words, Master Edyll turned and waved the doorway open.

As they followed, Sy-wen stepped beside Kast, and for the first time, she took his hand in her own. 'It seems I'm not the only one who knows your true heart,' she mumbled.

Kast stared at her hand as it rested like a soft peach in his granite grip. He was shocked and amazed – and for a brief moment, he imagined even the improbable was possible.

Even love.

Pinorr found Sheeshon rolled up in a ball upon her bed, arms locked around her legs, rocking back and forth. He crossed to her, sat on the bed, and held her. Words tumbled from her lips in chaotic fashion: bursts of lucid words as if she were having a conversation with an unseen partner, then bouts of unintelligible phrases, even moments when her voice would suddenly change, going deep, sounding nothing like a young girl. Pinorr knew from past events that it was best to just let these ramblings run their course.

Nearby, Mader Geel's granddaughter, little Ami, stood transfixed, eyes wide, fear clear in her unblinking gaze. Finally, Mader Geel shuffled in behind him and scooped her granddaughter under an arm.

Pinorr glowered at the old woman, his eyes indicating Ami. The frightened child should not have been left as sole attendant to Sheeshon when Mader Geel had gone to fetch him. Sheeshon's bouts could be frightening to behold, even for an adult.

Mader Geel made no apology, her face solid. 'I do not hide Ami from life's harshness . . . nor madness.'

Combing his fingers through Sheeshon's hair, Pinorr's eyes narrowed. 'Sheeshon is not mad. She is only a little weak in the head.' His voice lowered as he stroked the child. 'I have even begun to suspect her bouts worsen lately because . . .' He raised his eyes toward Mader Geel. 'Because she approaches a quickening.'

These last words broke the woman's usual stony expression. 'Her madness must be catching,' she stated dismissively. 'Why would the gods quicken such a broken child to the *rajor maga*?'

'I never assumed to understand the mind of any of the seven sea gods. Their choice in bestowing their gifts has never been fathomable.' In Pinorr's arms, Sheeshon seemed to calm with his voice and touch. Her flow of words died down to a trickle, and her rocking stopped.

'What makes you think she's touched by the sight?'

'You have seen her carving.'

Mader Geel's face darkened. 'She is skilled, I'll grant you that,' she answered with clear reluctance. 'But many of the mad, even those who eventually have to be walked into the sea, are often possessed by a specific talent. I once knew an addled fellow who was so skilled in the working of sails that he could walk a ship's ropes without using his hands, even in a fierce gale, as if he were strolling across a wide steady deck.' She finally waved her hand to dismiss these accomplishments. 'But beyond these single skills, these folk were still broken. You look too closely at Sheeshon's one talent and call her touched by the gods.'

'But it is not only her skill with scrimshaw,' he persisted. For a reason he could not name, he needed someone else to understand his growing realization. 'Until this morn, I myself never suspected her skill was tied to the *rajor maga*. But now I know!'

Mader Geel scooted Ami toward some playthings piled in the corner. Most were bone figures carved by Sheeshon when she was younger. Ami sat down and picked up a tiny scrimshaw piece carved into the likeness of a handsome girl. For some reason, Sheeshon had insisted on painting the doll's hands with red dyes.

With Ami settled, Mader Geel approached the bed. She sat on the far side of Sheeshon. 'I know you fear for her, Pinorr . . .'

Mader Geel's attempt at sympathy only goaded him further. 'We should all fear for her,' he spat out. 'A danger approaches the fleet. It rides a storm that will strike this night. And I believe Sheeshon is the key to understanding it.'

'What do you mean?'

'Have you ever suspected falseness in my visions?' he asked.

She pulled back a bit. 'Never! Do not forget I served with Ulster's father, the high keel. I know how your sea senses saved many a battle.'

'Then know this, Mader. Sheeshon carved the dragon

331

and babbled to me about a threat that approaches, something about dragons and doom.'

'Just a child's fancies,' the old woman insisted, but doubt now flecked her words.

'So I supposed as well. I had already sensed a great southern squall aiming our way and was impatient of her ramblings. But after I argued with Ulster, I again checked the seas. I sensed something new in the breezes.' He paused and pulled Sheeshon up into his arms. The child seemed to be coming out of her trance. Her eyes tracked around her tiny room, a thumb planted in her mouth. She leaned into Pinorr, needing warmth and reassurance.

'What?' Mader Geel finally asked. 'What did you sense?'

'I scented dragons in the air.'

Horror washed across her features. 'Perhaps you were influenced by Sheeshon's words more than you had first suspected.'

Pinorr stared over Sheeshon's head. 'So you *do* doubt my abilities.'

Mader Geel remained silent. The war inside her played across her face. She did not want to believe his words but could not dismiss the accuracy of his *rajor maga*. 'Are you sure?' she finally whispered.

He simply nodded. 'Sheeshon saw it first, then I. The mer'ai come for us.'

'Our ancient slave masters,' Mader Geel mumbled. For as long as Pinorr had known the hard woman, she had never shown a weak heart, even in fierce battle when the odds were severely against them. But fear now glinted brightly from her eyes.

Ami spoke up from where she played in the corner. She never looked up from her game, her voice plain. 'Sheeshie says we're all going to die.'

Mader Geel and Pinorr glanced to the girl, then back at each other.

'Sheeshon is the key,' Pinorr said and pulled his granddaughter closer. 'Locked in her head is the knowledge to free us from our doom.'

A loud booming rattled the door to Pinorr's set of rooms. Both Pinorr and Mader Geel jumped. Ami looked up from her play, and Sheeshon merely moaned. 'They're coming,' Sheeshon mumbled into Pinorr's chest.

'Open the door!' a voice ordered from beyond the latch. 'By order of the keelchief, the child Sheeshon must answer for her attack upon a member of the crew.'

Pinorr passed Sheeshon to Mader Geel. 'She must not be harmed,' he hissed at her. 'Do you understand this? Not just for the sake of my heart, but for the fate of the Dre'rendi.'

Mader Geel stared at him for a full breath, then slowly nodded. 'I believe you.'

The knocking resumed, less booming, more nervous. Pinorr knew the guards would not dare burst through, not even if the way was unlatched. The fear of a shaman's wrath would keep them at bay for a bit longer.

Pinorr turned to Mader Geel. 'Then you know what we must do.'

'We fight.'

Even with fear in his heart, he smiled at the fire in the old woman's words, two gray-haired elders ready to take on a ship of warriors. 'Ulster thinks his youth and strength make him strong. We will teach him that only the passing of winters forges a true warrior.' He pointed to his forehead. 'The true weapons of victory are wits, not swords.'

Mader Geel nodded. 'I always said you were wise.'

Pinorr bustled across the room, gathering the items Sheeshon would need. 'When did you ever admit that?'

Mader Geel's eyes sparked with amusement. 'Well, never to your face. A shaman's nose should not rise too high above the horizon.'

He stared daggers at her.

'Oh, enough of this false humility, Pinorr. You always were headstrong and insistent on your views. Even Ulster's father often wondered who truly led the fleet.'

'Be that as it may, we must hurry.'

The pounding resumed more boldly. 'Do not make us break down your door, Shaman!' a new voice bellowed. It was Ulster. The keelchief must have grown impatient with his lackeys' cowardice. 'Your son's daughter is not above the law. She has passed ten winters and is answerable for her actions. So open this door – *now!*'

Pinorr knew Ulster's speech was more for the benefit of the guards than for Pinorr. Once again, Ulster tried to hide behind the letter of the law to justify his cruelties. Everyone knew Sheeshon was far from ten winters of age in judgment, and Ulster's attack was not to mete justice but to hurt Pinorr. Yet wrong or not, the keelchief could not be disobeyed.

Shaking his head, Pinorr turned to Mader Geel, who had already gathered Sheeshon and Ami to her side. He crossed and hurriedly whispered his plans to the old woman. Once finished, he stood back and passed over the items he had gathered from Sheeshon's room. 'Can you handle your end?'

Mader Geel nodded, a hard smile on her lips. 'I'll watch over the girl. No harm will come to her.'

Pinorr crossed to the door. 'Then let the battle begin.'

Breathless, Sy-wen pushed into the room first. Master Edyll followed, assisted by Kast. Once everyone was inside, Sy-wen sealed the door.

'What is this place?' Kast asked warily, eying the cramped, unadorned room.

Sy-wen turned to the Bloodrider. 'We're in a pod on the underside of the leviathan.' She pointed to the room's only feature: a deep well in the floor. Ocean water could be seen bubbling a short way down the mouth of the narrow hole. 'We call this an *obligatum*,' she said, knowing the word meant nothing to Kast.

When the two had first come aboard the giant leviathan, the great seabeast had already surfaced, allowing Ragnar'k simply to alight on its wide back. Sy-wen had then hopped from the dragon's neck, breaking physical contact and returning Kast to his present form. From there, mer'ai guards had merely led them down into the leviathan's interior.

But to leave now in secret would not be that easy.

'An ob-obligatum?' Kast glanced down the well.

Nodding, Sy-wen explained. 'It's the way the mer'ai enter or leave a submerged leviathan. Also through this well, a dragon in the sea can extend its long neck and sip from a leviathan's air without having to surface.' Sy-wen studied the level of water in the throat of the well. 'Luck is with us. The leviathan does not swim too deeply today.' She turned to Kast. 'If it dives too far, the rising weight of the sea squeezes water up through the obligatum's throat and fills the chamber. It would block our escape.'

Master Edyll chuckled. 'It wasn't just luck, my dear.'

'What do you mean, Uncle?'

'When I heard you'd requested an audience with the council, I guessed your plans and ordered the leviathan to keep to the shallows this day.'

Sy-wen frowned. 'When Mother finds out, she's going to know you played a hand in our escape.'

'She will only *suspect*, but without proof . . .' Master Edyll shrugged. 'You see . . . my poor old ears were being bothered. I just needed a short rest from the pressures, so I ordered the leviathan to shallower depths.'

'Ah, I see,' Sy-wen said, grinning at his fabricated alibi.

'Now out with the two of you.' Master Edyll unhooked an egg-shaped gourd that hung on the wall from a trailing stalk and handed it to Kast.

The Bloodrider accepted the offered apparatus and studied it, turning and fingering its stalk. 'What is it?'

'An air pod,' Master Edyll said. 'You'll need it to breathe underwater. I think Sy-wen can hold her breath long enough.' He glanced significantly at his niece.

'Long enough for what?'

Sy-wen nodded toward the hole. 'Master Edyll is right. I can't call Ragnar'k forth in here. The large dragon won't be able to squeeze out this tiny hole. We're going to have to leave on our own and call forth the dragon while under the sea.'

Kast's eyes grew wide, but he didn't say a word. Sy-wen could see him fight to maintain his stoic self, even when faced with losing himself to the dragon again. Her heart ached for him.

Even Master Edyll seemed to notice his flaring tension. 'I should be going. The council will wonder where I'm at if I delay much longer.'

Sy-wen slid around the well and gave her uncle a tight hug. 'Thank you,' she said in his ear.

He returned her embrace. 'May the tides carry you safely,' he whispered. It was an old mer'ai farewell.

They broke their embrace. Master Edyll said his goodbyes to Kast and left, sealing the door behind him.

Now alone, the two grew quickly awkward. There was

too much to say, too much to admit. To Sy-wen, it was as if the leviathan now swam a thousand leagues under the sea. The very air seemed thick and hard to breathe.

She stared at Kast but could not meet his eye. He too avoided looking directly at her. 'We should go,' he finally said, his voice no more than a croak.

She nodded. 'I'll go first and wait for you just outside the leviathan.' She moved closer to him and silently showed him how to break the tip of the air pod's stem and suck fresh breaths through it. Standing close to him, she waved a hand over his body. 'When I'm gone, you should strip out of your shirt and leggings.'

He nodded. When the dragon burst free, anything he wore was simply shredded. 'You should be going,' he said.

Just as Sy-wen reached to hug him farewell, Kast stepped back, pulling his billowy shirt from his hard shoulders. She froze in midreach. He also stopped, his shirt half off, both immediately awkward. Even though Sy-wen had seen Kast naked before, she had never touched him unclothed.

She cast her eyes down and turned away. 'I . . . I will wait for you just outside the leviathan.'

'I . . . I'll be . . . right there.'

She stood at the well's lip, feeling the fool. She could not get herself to move. Seeming to sense her hesitation, strong arms suddenly circled her from behind. She tensed in the embrace for a single gasped breath, then melted back into the heat of his body. His lips brushed the tender hollow on the side of her neck. Neither spoke. Sy-wen dared not even turn around. They said their farewells with touches and soft noises.

At last, his arms withdrew, his fingers trailing down her bare arm as he stepped away.

She trembled as cool air traced over her flushed skin.

Without looking back, she dove smoothly into the sea, the cold water washing away the tears that had begun to well.

Once free of the leviathan, she arced under its belly and twisted around to face the opening. Sy-wen's inner lids had already snapped up, so she could see clearly through the crystal waters. As she waited, she fingered the spot where the Bloodrider's lips had touched her. Even in the chill of the sea, her blood warmed with the memory. She had no name for the flurry of emotions that stormed through her heart.

Sy-wen dropped her hand from her neck and kicked closer to the opening in the underside of the leviathan. She must not let her heart interfere with her duty. Kast was their forefather reborn. According to her uncle, the fate of her people rested upon Kast's shoulders. Kicking and paddling, she kept near the obligatum. It seemed forever until an explosion of bubbles marked where Kast crashed out of the leviathan's belly.

She kicked nearer. He was all flailing limbs and twisting body as he tried to orient himself. Once close enough, she realized he was blind in the water. He did not have the extra lids to keep the sting and blur of salt from his eyes. She could imagine his panic at being thrust into this cold, blind world, depending only on her for his survival.

She grabbed his hand, and his thrashings instantly calmed. He did not even grab for her but let her come to him, trusting her skill. With his chest bare and his manhood covered only by thin linen underclothes, she found it hard to look at him. The sight of his strong legs and chest made it difficult to keep her breath trapped.

She swam in front of him and drew him closer, keeping her eyes fixed on his face. She had to wrap her legs around his waist a bit to keep them both steady.

She touched his chin and turned his face to expose the dragon tattoo on his neck and cheek. He tensed under her, knowing what was to come. The emblem of Ragnar'k, a coiled black dragon with savage red eyes, stared back at her. She could almost feel the imprisoned beast urging her to release it.

Readying herself, she let go of Kast's chin. His face swung back to her, but his eyes were blinded by the salty water. A hand groped up and touched her own cheek, a signal that he was ready.

She reached for him, but not to his tattoo. She slipped the stem of the airpod from his lips. He did not resist, still trusting her.

She cast aside the pod and pulled him to her, pressing her lips to his. He startled a bit under her touch, then pulled her hard against him, their arms wrapping hungrily around each other. Through tight lips, they shared each other's breaths.

Time stretched toward eternity – but where hearts made promises that lasted forever, her air could not last that long. Before she could drown, her fingers reluctantly reached to his tattoo.

Good-bye, Kast, she sent silently to him. And for the first time, she allowed herself to add what her heart had known all along. *I love you.*

With her touch, the sea vanished in a rush of scale and wing. A roar filled her ears and mind as the dragon inside Kast broke free. Before the waters could clear, Sy-wen found herself seated atop the back of the monstrous creature, its wings like sails to either side, its neck stretched far into the blue sea.

Ragnar'k turned to face his rider. Ruby eyes glowed toward her; a hint of silver fangs glinted in the refracted light. *Sy-wen,* the dragon whispered to her, a throaty purr. *My bonded.* The beast's exhilaration at its freedom rolled over her, overwhelmed her; but under its thrill, she also sensed its hunger, a dark well that seemed bottomless.

Sy-wen brushed her fingers along Ragnar'k's thick neck, scratching under the hard scale to the tender flesh underneath. *Feed,* she sent to her mount, *we've still a long way to travel.*

Reaching forward, she slipped free the tiny siphon that let her share the dragon's air. She drew a breath, driving away the tiny sparks that had started to build from lack of air. It felt good to breathe again. But in her chest, an ache still remained. No amount of fresh air could dissolve away the sense of loss in her heart.

The dragon also freshened its own air by returning briefly to sip from one of the leviathan's obligatums. Once refreshed and its lungs full, the dragon twisted away and began its hunt.

Sy-wen settled closer to the dragon. Where in this great beast was Kast? With her thighs, she could feel the beat of the dragon's thundering heart. She let herself imagine that it was the Bloodrider's own heart. She leaned nearer, placing a hand over a thrumming vessel in the dragon's neck. She let her eyelids drift partway down as the dragon flew through the water, snatching yellowfin and angelwhites down its long gullet. The pleasure of its feasting blurred with her own memory of lips on skin.

They glided above reefs like distant mountain ranges. In the distance, she saw other seadragons darting like falling jewels through the blue waters. Fading behind now, she saw the massive bulk of the leviathan drifting away, an enormous mountain rolling through the sea.

She closed her eyes and just drifted in a haze of sorrow

and pleasure until Ragnar'k intruded on her thoughts. *Belly full. Where now?*

Sitting straighter, she slipped her feet into the folds at the base of the dragon's neck. *Up,* she sent to him, *up and away.*

A trumpet of excitement coursed through dragon and rider.

After tightening his neck fold to cinch snug her ankles, Ragnar'k swept his wings wide and dove deeper, then spun in a tight arc to gain momentum, coiling in on himself. Sy-wen had to lean against the pull of the water, her fingers latched to a scaled ridge of bone. Just before she thought she would be thrown free of Ragnar'k, the dragon's long tail snapped like a plucked bowstring. Ragnar'k sprang upward, his wings sweeping even with his body as he shot toward the distant light.

Sy-wen closed her eyes and held tight to the dragon's back.

She felt the rush as Ragnar'k burst from the waves. Seawater cascaded over her, trying to drag her back into the ocean, but the dragon kept her feet clamped in his neck folds. She clung by hand and nail.

Then it was over. The dragon pulled up under her and again she rode his back easily. She dared to open her eyes.

They glided above waves now, and breezes whipped dry her green hair. She stared forward toward the distant curve of the world. The ocean was a featureless plain before her. The bright sun hid behind scudding white clouds, giving the water a sheen of beaten silver.

The skies are angry, Ragnar'k sent to her.

'What?' Sy-wen yelled into the wind.

Suddenly a thundering crack exploded.

Craning around, Sy-wen saw the reason for the dragon's words. Behind her, a short distance away, the entire world was black clouds, sheeting rain, and lancing bolts of light. Again thunder rolled at them, the rumbling bellow of a savage beast.

Flee, she urged Ragnar'k. *We must not get caught in that storm.*

Ragnar'k swung to face the full fury of the tempest. The dragon opened its black maw and threatened the thunder with its own roar. Then it spun on a wing and swept away, sailing close over the waves.

Hurry, she pushed.

The crack of thunder and the scream of winds grew louder in her ears. She leaned close to Ragnar'k. The dragon sped onward, a fire building up under her seat as Ragnar'k fought to escape.

As they raced, Sy-wen began to realize that she and Kast may have been rash to seek the Dre'rendi on their own. She should have heeded her mother's counsel. Thoughts of returning to her people danced in her mind, but she pushed such ideas away and stared at the sea under her. Perhaps they could flee under the waves and let the storm pass over while they sheltered within the womb of the sea.

No, she thought savagely, bending lower over the dragon, urging him to greater speed. They had delayed too long already and dared not risk losing another day by hiding from the storm. Flying was not only faster, but free of the sea, their gazes could search from horizon to horizon. If the Dre'rendi were to be discovered in time, she and the dragon must outride this storm.

As if sensing her thoughts, a massive tangle of lightning burst behind them, casting the dragon's shadow upon the still ocean. The seas below grew flat and glassy as the sun's meager light was swallowed away by the savage squall.

The dragon spoke. *The fangs of the sky are upon us.*

With this thought, the black clouds rolled over the pair and blew forth with jagged spears of lightning. The boom of thunder pounded at Sy-wen's ears, and screaming winds threatened to tear them both from the sky.

They had lost their race.

The squall had caught them in its jaws.

Pinorr stood in the crowded commons of the *Dragonspur*. Half the crew had gathered to witness this battle between shaman and keelchief. The room served mostly as ship's galley, but this day the ale-stained benches had been shoved back, and a space had been cleared before the longest table. Though the reek of fish-belly stew still clung to the rafters, for the moment the galley had been transformed into a ship's court.

Pinorr studied his judges. Seated behind the long table were Jabib and Gylt, the ship's first and second mates. They were also Ulster's cronies.

Pinorr eyed the pair with distaste. Jabib, the first mate, was a giant of a man as gaunt as he was tall, with a misshapen nose sitting like a broken scow atop a pocked face. Gylt, his second, was short and stocky, his dark face frozen in a perpetual scowl.

Sheeshon would find no mercy from those two. From Ulster's smug expression as he stood alongside Pinorr, the matter of Sheeshon's attack upon the keelchief had already been settled. Supposedly a keelchief was the equal of any crewmember when a cause was brought forward, but here Pinorr spotted the veiled smiles shared between the pair of judges and Ulster.

Justice this day would be as blind as a mud crawler buried in silt.

As Pinorr sourly pondered his odds, Ulster stepped

forward to begin the proceedings. The keelchief bowed deeply to each of the two judges, as was custom.

Pinorr followed but only bowed his head – *once*. The crowd behind him muttered at his slight.

The faces of the two mates reddened angrily at Pinorr's lack of deference. Jabib opened his mouth to reprimand Pinorr, but Ulster cut him off, further proving who truly ran these proceedings. 'Shaman, your son's daughter should be present before the tribunal.'

Pinorr turned to his keelchief, keeping his voice respectful. 'I serve as her counsel here, as is allowed. I speak for her.'

'Counsel or not, she should still be present in this room.'

'Mader Geel watches her in my cabin, and your guards have the old woman and the frail child well in hand. Unless of course you fear the two might overpower your men. I could bring her here if you fear for your safety while the child is out of sight.'

Ulster began to bluster and redden.

Pinorr continued. 'We wouldn't want you to have to face such a dangerous swordswoman a second time, especially seeing as how she bested you once already.' Pinorr nodded toward Ulster's bandaged hand.

Again the crowd snickered, their faces averted so Ulster could not see exactly who laughed at the shaman's words.

Pinorr kept his features serious.

'Fine. Let her remain in your rooms. I would never want to be called unfair.'

Pinorr swallowed back a snort. 'Then let us settle this matter.'

Clearing his throat, Ulster stepped forward. 'I accuse Sheeshon di'Ra of an attack on a fellow crewman without properly declaring a challenge.'

Jabib nodded somberly as if considering his chief's words, then turned to Pinorr. 'How do you answer?'

Pinorr refused to step forward. 'This is a farce. My son's daughter could not declare a *tekra*, a blood challenge, because the word is meaningless to her. As all here know, Sheeshon is not hale of mind or body. She is but an infant in a young girl's body. To bring her before the tribunal as a full crewmember is the act of a craven man.'

The crowd erupted behind the shaman.

Ulster spoke into the uproar. 'You're mistaken, Shaman. I never claimed the girl was a crewmember. That is for the tribunal to decide. I only follow the old code of the Dre'rendi. The girl has passed ten winters, and she has broken our law. The code is clear. She must face the tribunal and trust them to find where justice lies in her matter.'

The crowd hushed to low murmurs.

Pinorr found the amused eyes of his judges studying him. It would be hard to fight the letter of the Dre'rendi code. Ulster had found a weak spot to exploit and now reveled in his sure victory here. But Pinorr was not finished. He knew that often a fire could only be met with fire.

'You speak much of code,' Pinorr said. 'But you have not read far enough back to remember one of our older codes: "He who stands accused can claim *jakra* of his accuser." '

'A blood *duel*?' Ulster's face paled, but soon laughter bubbled from his hard lips. 'You grow foolish in your tottering years, old man. Has the madness of *rajor maga* finally touched you, as it eventually claims all shamans?'

'I am not yet blinded by the sea gods' touch. My mind is still my own. And as counsel of Sheeshon, I declare *jakra* for her.' He pointed to the keelchief, a man with twice his muscles and half his age. 'I call you to a blood duel with Sheeshon.'

The shock on Ulster's face had wiped away all traces of smugness. Pinorr saw the man's mind working on the puzzle set before him. He could not fathom where Pinorr was tacking in this storm. No one of sound judgment would choose the path of *jakra*. The archaic code had not been invoked in over a century. All knew that it was far better to face the harsh decision of a tribunal rather than face a blood duel. The odds were against the challenger. He who invoked a blood duel had to face his opponent unarmed, whereas the other, the accuser, was free to choose any single weapon at hand. In the long history of the Dre'rendi, no challenger had survived the *jakra*.

'What is this game you play at?' Ulster hissed.

'Do you accept the challenge yourself, Ulster? Or do you wish to assign someone to take your place in the duel ring?'

Now that Pinorr had called the keelchief craven, he knew Ulster dare not refuse lest he risk losing honor with the crew. 'I accept the challenge,' the keelchief said warily. 'And I suppose you have someone in mind to stand up for Sheeshon who would be foolish enough to face me in the ring unarmed?'

Pinorr shrugged. 'Me.'

A gasp arose from the crowd. It was forbidden for a shaman to fight. Once the sea gods had called a man to the *rajor maga*, he was forced to untie his warrior's braid and wear only the robes of the shamans. Even carrying a sword was forbidden. It was considered the worst insult to the sea gods if a shaman should ever fight as a common warrior. It sullied the gifts that the gods had bestowed, calling ill fortune down upon a boat.

'You cannot enter the ring, *Shaman*.' Ulster declared. 'It is forbidden. Choose another to stand for Sheeshon.'

'The code is clear. He who invokes the *jakra* may choose

any willing champion. None can refuse him – whether shaman or not.' Pinorr turned to face Ulster. 'It is the code.'

Ulster now stood red-faced.

The silent Gylt raised his voice for the first time. 'But if you fight, you'll bring the sea gods' blight upon our prow,' he blurted out. Jabib just glowered beside his fellow tribune.

But the crowd echoed Gylt's sentiment.

Ulster noticed the panic rising in his crew. 'If you die,' he said with clear menace, 'the code of the *jakra* is clear. Sheeshon, as the one who is represented, must die also – by whip and ax.'

'I would rather have her dead than living on a boat cursed by the gods.' Pinorr turned his back on Ulster. He let the keelchief dwell on the predicament at hand. Ulster's craven attack on Sheeshon now threatened to bring the wrath of the sea gods down upon his boat, and even if Ulster was willing to accept such a doom, his crew clearly was not. If Ulster proceeded with the duel, forcing the shaman to fight, he would find himself with an empty boat. No Bloodrider would step foot aboard the decks of a cursed ship.

Pinorr waited until the moment was ripe and turned to face Ulster again. 'The only other option you have, Ulster, is to dismiss your accusation and end this tribunal now.'

Ulster's fists were clenched with anger. He knew he had been bested, tangled in the very code in which he had hoped to ensnare Pinorr. The keelchief's features squalled with frustration, brows dark with thunderheads, eyes flashing with lightning. 'You win, Pinorr,' he spat. 'I submit—'

'Wait,' Jabib interrupted. 'Before the matter is settled, we should bring Sheeshon before the tribunal.'

Ulster tried to wave away his first mate's objections.

But Jabib stood up. The first mate had always been

Ulster's schemer. Pinorr knew the man now had the seed of some new plot in mind. But what?

The first mate held up a hand. 'The tribunal has the right to question Sheeshon on her choice of champions. Let us see if she truly wishes to watch her grandfather die for her.'

For a moment, Pinorr's vision darkened. He began to understand the wiles here. He had left Mader Geel to drill Sheeshon, just in case the child had to name Pinorr as champion, but clearly Jabib meant to scare her into withdrawing his name. Even if they failed to wear Sheeshon down, they could always withdraw the charges and be none the worse. Yet if they should succeed, Sheeshon was doomed. The blood duel had already been called forth and could not be withdrawn by Pinorr – only Ulster could call it off by retracting his accusation. Sheeshon would have to call a champion who was willing to face the keelchief unarmed – which no one would do.

Pinorr's face drained of blood, and a coldness settled in his chest. With his own words, he may have doomed his granddaughter. He had let his pride and overconfidence blind him. Pinorr noted Ulster's growing smile.

A pair of guards left to fetch Sheeshon.

Pinorr cleared his throat. 'This is not necessary,' he tried futilely. 'She has already named me, and I accepted.'

Jabib scowled at him. 'That is a matter for the tribunal to judge, not you. We have the right to hear her choice from her own lips. It is the code.'

Pinorr knew it was futile to argue. As he waited, he prayed to the gods to protect his granddaughter. She did not deserve this punishment. He closed his eyes and willed strength to Sheeshon for the storm ahead.

After what seemed an eternity, the crowd, which had been mumbling and wagering the outcome among themselves, erupted with renewed vigor as Sheeshon was shuffled through the press of the crew. By now, even more of the ship's men and women had pushed into the cramped commons.

Sheeshon was led to stand before the long table. Mader Geel was with her. Jabib nodded toward the old woman. 'You are no longer needed.'

But Mader Geel eyed Pinorr and kept her place.

'Are you deaf to the tribunal's order?' Ulster asked. He waved to the guards, who reluctantly approached the old swordswoman.

'The child is frightened,' she said in defense, holding Sheeshon's hand.

Sheeshon stared around at the number of people, her eyes wide, her lower lip trembling. In her fear, the numb side of her face seemed to droop worse. Mader Geel was stripped from her side forcibly, leaving the girl alone before the table. Sheeshon tried to wander back toward Pinorr, but a guard held her by the shoulder.

Jabib, by now, had crossed around the long table. He knelt before Sheeshon with a smile and whispered soft words for her. Sheeshon listened but was clearly nervous, glancing frequently back at Pinorr.

Once he had her attention, Jabib raised his voice so the others could hear him. 'Now, Sheeshon, my little dear, do you know why you are here?'

Sheeshon shook her head slowly. A hand raised to suck a thumb, but Jabib guided her hand down.

'You must pick your champion. Do you know what that means?'

Sheeshon's voice was a wisp before a gale. 'Mader says I'm 'posed to point to Papa.'

'Oh, so you want your papa to die then.'

Sheeshon's eyes grew round; tears welled up. 'Die?'

Jabib nodded. He turned Sheeshon's face toward Ulster. 'That big man is going to slice your papa's belly open with a big sword if you pick your papa. Do you want to pick your papa?'

Tears welled up and ran down her cheeks. 'No,' she said in a strangled voice. 'I don't want Papa's belly opened up.'

Pinorr could stand no more of it. 'Leave the child be,' he said, his heart aching for his granddaughter. 'Please.'

Jabib patted Sheeshon on the head as he stood. His voice rang above the murmuring crowd. 'You have all heard her words. She declines Pinorr.'

Ulster stepped forward. 'She must choose a champion or face me in the duel. *Jakra* has been issued.'

Pinorr spoke up. 'End this, Ulster,' he said. 'Take me if you wish, but leave poor Sheeshon out of our squabble.'

'And kill a shaman? Bring a curse down upon my boat? I don't think the crew would stand for it.'

Pinorr just stared at Ulster. 'So you would slay an innocent child? Before your entire crew?'

'It was not my choice,' Ulster claimed. 'I had only meant to have her punished. Two lashes of my whip was what I planned – to teach both of you a small lesson. But you have set this new course, not I.'

Grimacing, Pinorr could not argue against the keelchief. The shaman had thought himself so clever, so wise in passing winters. 'If you take Sheeshon from me, I will find a way to destroy you. That I promise.'

Ulster shrugged.

Mader Geel was allowed back to console Sheeshon. The old woman hugged the girl and whispered consolation in her tiny ears.

Pinorr knew he had lost. He tried to join his granddaughter, but guards held him back.

Instead, Jabib knelt again by little Sheeshon. 'You must pick someone, my dear. You must find someone to fight for you.'

Pinorr had stopped listening. It was over. No one would agree.

Sheeshon pulled out of Mader Geel's embrace. Her eyes were glazed and far away. Fear had driven her to retreat inside. Sheeshon tilted her head toward the rafters of the galley. 'They're here,' she mumbled.

Suddenly a crack of thunder reverberated through the planks of the boat, as if the keel of the boat had snapped. Everyone jumped.

Jabib touched Sheeshon's shoulder. 'Choose,' he said impatiently.

In the throes of her madness, Sheeshon had the strength of a grown man. She shook free of Jabib and stumbled toward the crowd. The crew parted before her. No one would meet her eye. None wished to be forced to deny the child if pressed.

Jabib followed as Sheeshon began to run. The crowd stepped back, allowing Pinorr and Ulster to pursue at Jabib's heels. Sheeshon broke from the room and ran up the steps toward the outer deck. The crowd followed, surging behind Jabib, Pinorr, and Ulster.

As Pinorr stepped from the hot and cramped spaces below, the coldness of the air shocked him. Thunder again boomed. The skies to the south were a solid wall of black clouds stacked to the heavens. The sun, setting to the west, was already threatened by the storm's edge. Though the seas lay calm around them, they were unnaturally so. The waves were flat and colored like hammered iron by the dying sun.

In the distance, flashes of signal lights marked the other ships of the fleet. Sails were being reefed, and snatches of bellowed orders echoed over the still waters.

Pinorr turned to Ulster. 'You never sounded the alarm,' he said.

At least Ulster had the dignity to look momentarily guilty. His eyes, though, remained on the wall of storm.

But Pinorr knew he could not lay the entire blame at Ulster's feet. When confronted with Sheeshon's danger, Pinorr had forgotten the warning from the sea gods, too. They had both been fools – and now the entire fleet was in danger.

Sheeshon stood near the starboard rail and studied the building squall, searching the skies. Jabib was at her side. Ulster and Pinorr crossed to join them.

Jabib glanced to his keelchief. 'We must batten down the ship. This storm is not one we can run from. Our only hope is to lock up the ship and pray she stays afloat.'

Ulster nodded mutely. This was the first time the young keelchief had faced a ship killer, and it had stolen his tongue.

Pinorr took advantage of Ulster's fear. 'Only the sea gods will protect us this night. Release Sheeshon of the *jakra*, and I will beg a blood boon from the gods. Refuse and spout your own prayers. See how little the sea gods listen to ordinary men.'

Ulster spun on Pinorr. 'This is all your fault,' he growled, his fear lighting a fire in his chest. 'You have called this monster down upon us!'

Jabib tried to place a consoling hand on the keelchief's arm but was thrust away. The first mate stumbled back against the rail. 'We will need all the prayers,' he urged, 'especially the shaman's.'

Ulster grabbed Sheeshon roughly by the shoulder. 'Pinorr

has cursed us. Before this storm strikes, I will stab this traitor where he is most vulnerable.' Ulster tried to drag Sheeshon from the ship's rail, but she was latched like a barnacle. Ulster persisted, his face raging. 'The sea gods will know I follow the old code and will protect us.'

Jabib hovered near his keelchief. Pinorr could read his worries. The first mate knew it was madness that Ulster proposed. To shed blood on deck before a storm was the worst luck. Blood invited more blood. The crew would not stand for it.

'I call for the blood duel,' Ulster screamed. '*Now!*' He finally yanked viciously at Sheeshon, ripping her from her post.

A squeak of fear escaped her as she was swung around. 'Papa?' she cried, trying to grab at Pinorr.

Pinorr stepped directly into the path of the raging keelchief. Behind Ulster's eyes, the shaman could see the squall mirrored. It was called *storm fever*, when the might of an approaching gale destroyed one's reason. 'She must first choose, Ulster,' Pinorr said firmly. 'By code, she has until sundown to choose a champion or for you to retract your charges and end this matter.'

With these words, the storm clouds began to eat the sun. The light around them became a false twilight.

'End this?' Ulster waved a hand wildly. 'See? Even the skies tell us it is time. They drown the sun early, so the *jakra* can be held now.'

Jabib stepped beside Pinorr, shoulder to shoulder, facing Ulster. The first mate's words were firm. 'She must still choose, Keelchief.'

Frustration and fury fought across Ulster's face. He trembled a moment, then pulled Sheeshon up by the arms and drew her to his face. 'Choose!' he yelled.

She whimpered and struggled in his grip.

'Release my granddaughter,' Pinorr said coldly, 'or I'll take a sword to you right now.'

'You dare threaten me!' Ulster dropped Sheeshon. She fell like a broken doll at his feet, then crawled back toward Pinorr.

Jabib held Ulster and Pinorr apart. He towered over both of them. 'Enough!' he yelled. He faced Pinorr. 'The *jakra* has been called fairly, by your own mouth.' Jabib then turned to Ulster. 'And until this matter is settled, I am still tribune. So you will bow to my authority, or I will have the high keel strip you of your rank.'

His words seemed to dim the fever in Ulster's eyes. 'Then make her decide,' the keelchief ordered, backing a step away.

Pinorr glanced down to Sheeshon. Again her blank gaze had wandered to the roiling skies. She did not understand any of this. She pointed to the layer of black clouds sweeping overhead now. 'They're here.'

Pinorr found his own eyes drawn to where she indicated.

Suddenly a section of the thunderhead broke away. A fluttering piece of darkness fell toward them. Lightning chased it across the sky as thunder boomed in anger.

Other eyes spotted the oddity. 'What is that?' Jabib said.

Pinorr held his breath. His sea senses screamed in him now.

As they watched, the shred of blackness grew in size, darting between bolts of lightning. It was a huge creature, wings swept to either side. But Pinorr knew it was no ordinary gull or tern. He had seen Sheeshon's carving. 'Get back!' he yelled, hauling Sheeshon with him, but the child slipped free.

Sheeshon danced forward, arms raised toward the sky. 'They're here! They're here!' she chanted.

Ulster had his hand on his sword's hilt. 'She calls a demon to us!'

By now, everyone on deck had stopped their hurried preparations to secure the ship against the storm. All eyes watched the descent of the great black beast.

'Not demon,' Pinorr said, drawing Ulster's fury. 'Worse.'

'What?'

'Dragon.'

Thunder drowned out further conversation, booming, rattling the rigging. Overhead, Pinorr's statement proved true. The great beast sailed past the tips of the masts. Black scale reflected the lightning like oil on water. Suddenly it banked and turned on a single wing tip. Its red eyes held all the storm's fury.

Cries of terror spread throughout the deck. One man even jumped overboard in fright.

'Man the harpoons!' Jabib screamed, caught up in the panic.

Then it dove at them, dropping like a boulder from the sky. Pinorr's eyes widened. It aimed for the empty center of the deck – right where Sheeshon now stood, staring trans-fixed at the beast.

'Sheeshon!'

But Pinorr was too late. The dragon crashed onto the deck, wings braking and claws digging long gouges from the planks as it skidded to a halt. Once stopped, its hot breath steamed and fogged from its throat into the cool air. Red eyes stared at the men frozen on deck. Silver teeth longer than a man's forearm glinted brightly in the last glimmer of the sun. Suddenly it stretched its neck toward the folded sails and bellowed at the skies.

All across the deck, men fell to their knees, crying out supplications. Others ran for the hatches. A handful were brave enough to leap for swords and spears.

Pinorr waved the warriors back. Sheeshon was still out there. He stepped forward, palms raised, trying to indicate that he offered the beast no threat. The dragon bent its neck to study the approaching shaman. Pinorr ignored the menace in those crimson eyes. He cared only to see if Sheeshon was safe. Once close enough, he spotted a small drenched girl collapsed atop the back of the dragon, her green hair sluiced with water. Her skin was pale and ashen. Though he could see she breathed, the rider seemed near death.

What was happening here?

Suddenly Sheeshon stepped out from under the wing of the great beast. The dragon startled a bit at the child's abrupt appearance. It hissed and pulled back its wings.

Ulster and Jabib crept forward to shadow Pinorr.

Sheeshon wore a lopsided smile as the dragon towered over her. She pointed at the great beast. 'I choose him,' she said clearly, her voice ringing sharp across the silent deck. Even the thunder had quieted for the moment.

Pinorr turned to the keelchief. 'It's what you asked for, Ulster,' he answered grimly. 'Sheeshon has chosen her champion.'

15

Sy-wen heard voices and a familiar accent, deep and rich. *Kast* .She struggled through the black void back to a world of cold winds and rain. Where was she? She rolled her head and saw watery images, dark figures moving all around her. Lightning split the night and thunder roared, drawing back her memory. She whimpered as she recalled the rip of screaming winds and the dragon's flight through castles of black clouds. She pulled tighter to her mount. The sky opened up above her, and rain lashed down. But the heat of the dragon was like a roaring fire under her.

Bonded, Ragnar'k sent to her. The dragon's hunger was an ache in her belly. She shared its senses of blood and meat nearby.

She pushed a bit higher, pulling her cramped fingers from their stranglehold on the ridge of scale. Rain pelted her bare back in stinging bites. The dragon's hide steamed in the downpour, creating a thin, rising fog. She eyed her surroundings. Her vision had cleared enough to recognize that she and the dragon were on some boat. Overhead, a hastily tied sail had loosened a snatch. It snapped and cracked in the wind.

But all of Sy-wen's attention was on the figures around

her. A circle of hard men and women stood a wary distance from her, some kneeling, some armed. The lanterns swinging from yardarms and rail highlighted the sea-worn men. One feature was shared by all: the tattoo of a diving seahawk emblazoned on cheeks and necks.

'Bloodriders,' she mumbled. Kast's tribe.

One man stepped forward, his blue robe drenched and clinging to his tall frame. His hair was as white as Master Edyll's. As he stared up at her, his eyes held no fear, only awe. He reached out a hand, and a small girl wandered out from under Ragnar'k, her small eyes wide with wonder.

'He's big, Papa,' she said as the elder pulled the child to him, hugging his arms around her.

The robed man stared up at her. 'You are mer'ai.'

Sy-wen nodded.

Hungry, Ragnar'k complained uselessly. Sy-wen still sensed the dragon's burning belly. Ragnar'k leaned toward the two who stood nearest and sniffed at the old man and the child. *Not much meat, but taste good.*

No, Sy-wen sent him silently. *You will eat no one here. These are who we hunted for. They may be new friends.*

Don't need more friends. Need full belly. But Sy-wen sensed the acquiescence of the great beast.

Sy-wen cleared her throat, trying to mimic her mother's commanding voice and demeanor. 'I come seeking the Dre'rendi,' she said aloud. 'We call upon your ancient debt to serve us one last time.' Her attempt at dignity was ruined when a sudden gust of wind almost toppled her from her seat and she hastily grabbed at the dragon to keep from falling. She straightened and tossed wet strands of green hair back from her face. She did not feel like a herald of her people, but more like a drenched seal pup.

'I am Pinorr, shaman of this ship. I welcome you to the

Dragonspur,' the old man said, a ghost of a smile on his lips. Maybe it was just the resemblance to Master Edyll, but Sy-wen found herself instantly liking this fellow.

Two other men stepped forward and flanked the shaman. 'The ship's first mate, Jabib,' the old man introduced. 'And our keelchief, Ulster.'

Sy-wen eyed the second man. His face was stone, but his eyes glinted with suspicion. His hand rested on the hilt of a sword at his waist. 'Why have you come here?' he asked with clear anger.

The small child, still clinging to the shaman's robe, answered instead. 'They come to kill us all,' she said cheerily.

Sy-wen blinked at this outburst.

Pinorr patted the girl's head. 'My apologies, mistress of the mer'ai, but Sheeshon is a bit addled. She does not always know what she speaks.'

Sy-wen nodded. 'But perhaps she knows more than you suspect. For what I have come to ask of you may mean your deaths.'

'What is this you speak?' the keelchief demanded.

Suddenly a new burst of lightning and thunder drowned out all further words. Winds and rains tore at the ship.

Pinorr sheltered the child against this sudden onslaught. When the winds calmed for a breath, he glanced up to Sy-wen and yelled into the thunder. 'I don't know if your dragon can weather the storm atop the deck, but we cannot. The squall's fury is about to strike. I recommend we continue this conversation below.'

Sy-wen chewed her lower lip. Atop Ragnar'k, she felt little true threat, but she feared to be alone with them, even with Kast at her side. The crew easily numbered over fifty.

As if to goad her, a bolt of lightning struck the tip of the foremast with an explosive crack. Ragnar'k bellowed anger.

Blue energies danced along the rigging. Sy-wen studied the furious skies. No number of men, no matter how hard, could match the danger that thundered toward her.

She turned back to the others. The keelchief's narrowed eyes almost made her balk again. Sy-wen mistrusted him.

The shaman, though, drew back her attention. 'There is nothing to fear from us. I offer you full freedom of the ship. As shaman, you are under my protection.' Pinorr glanced at the keelchief as if his next words were meant more for that man than Sy-wen. 'None will harm you.'

Ulster's eyes twitched, but he lifted his hand from his sword and crossed his arms over his chest. 'May our hearth and keel keep you safe,' he said, his voice cold and formal, weakening the invitation in his words.

Pinorr seemed satisfied and turned back to Sy-wen. The old man missed the flash of hatred in the young keelchief's eyes. Clearly the storm above was not the only squall threatening this boat. 'Come,' the shaman said, extending his hand. 'Join us below.'

Sy-wen knew she needed to win these people to her cause, something she could never do atop the back of a dragon. Besides, she knew having Kast return to flesh would go a long way to earning the Bloodriders' trust. He was one of their people.

Sliding over the neck of the dragon, she slipped to the planks. She almost lost her footing and fell, both the slippery deck and her own weak legs betraying her. Sy-wen managed to keep one hand on the dragon. She did not want to lose contact just yet. She ran a hand along its neck until she reached its massive head.

Ragnar'k snuffled at her. *Bonded. Sweet in my nose.*

She rubbed at the ridge between the beast's flared nostrils. The dragon brushed her palm, its thick tongue pushing out to lick at her. Its glowing eyes stared into hers. *I don't want to go back,* Ragnar'k said sadly, almost a moan in her mind.

Her heart ached for the great beast. The dragon was a creature of simple pleasures but depthless heart. She hugged the huge beast warmly. 'Thank you for carrying me here safely,' she whispered at him. 'But I must send you back for now. I have need of Kast.'

Weak man, Ragnar'k said with a silent snort of derision. *I'm stronger than him.*

'I know, my big bonded, but some battles can't be fought with tooth and claw. I will call you back soon, and we will hunt the seas together.'

A feeling of trust and pleasure suffused through her. *You are my bonded. Go now. I'll dream of you . . . and fishes, many big fishes.* Dragon laughter echoed in her mind.

She smiled at him. 'Good-bye, Ragnar'k. Sleep well, my bonded.' Sy-wen lifted her hand from the wet scales and stumbled back a few steps.

Behind her, the crew gasped and fled farther away.

As expected, with the contact broken, the dragon began to fold upon itself. A twisting whirlwind of wing and scale, claw and tooth, spun down to reveal a naked man standing atop the deck. On his bare neck, the dragon tattoo glowed a bright ruby for several heartbeats, then died back down.

Kast's usual scowl deepened as he took a moment to orient himself. Sy-wen stepped closer, keeping her eyes slightly averted from his nakedness. The Bloodrider took her hand in his own as he studied those around him. 'You found the Dre'rendi,' he mumbled, slightly awed.

She nodded. 'They offer us shelter from the approaching storm.'

Speechless, Pinorr stepped forward, his mouth hanging open.

The small girl at his side was unfazed. 'That man is wearing no clothes, Papa,' she said matter-of-factly.

'Hush, Sheeshon.' Pinorr stopped before them. His eyes were on Sy-wen's companion. 'How . . . ? How could this be?'

Sy-wen tried to explain about Ragnar'k. 'On the island of A'loa Glen, we found a—'

Kast squeezed her hand, silencing her. The two men stared at each other for a moment, then Kast spoke. 'How fares my father, Pinorr?'

Startled, Sy-wen glanced up at Kast. So they knew each other.

'Your father died three winters past.' Pinorr's voice grew angry. 'On his deathbed, he called out for you.'

Kast remained quiet. Sy-wen felt his grip tremble in her palm, then grow calm again. 'I . . . I did not know.'

'You should never have left, Kast. After you fled with that mad shaman, chasing after dreams, something died in your father.'

'But what of my younger brother? He was to watch over the old man.'

Before the shaman could answer, the keelchief interrupted, pushing forward. The man had fled all the way to the rail when the dragon transformed. As he approached, his hand again rested warily on the hilt of his sword. He eyed Kast up and down sourly.

The keelchief glared at the Bloodrider defiantly, fists on his hips. 'What are you doing back here, Kast?'

Thunder crashed overhead as the storm's edge finally rolled upon them.

With rain sluicing over the hard planes of his face, Kast studied the smaller man. 'Ulster, after ten winters, is that how you welcome home your elder brother?'

*   *   *

Pinorr sat on the edge of his bed and shook his head at Kast's story. The Bloodrider and his ward, Sy-wen, had retreated to Pinorr's cabin while Ulster and the crew secured the *Dragonspur* against the storm. In a corner, Sheeshon played quietly with her scrimshawed carvings. Pinorr cocked his head and studied Kast's dragon tattoo. 'So this . . . this Ragnar'k . . . He's a part of you now? Sy-wen can call him forth anytime with a touch?'

Kast nodded, wolfing down fish stew and hard bread. He spoke around a mouthful of his meal. 'The mer'ai seek to join their might with the Dre'rendi in an assault on A'loa Glen. If we ever hope to drive the Gul'gotha from our seas, we must help the wit'ch reach the old mages' castle.' With the crusts of his bread, Kast wiped up the last dregs of stew from his third bowl. 'Is there more?'

Sy-wen, seated beside him and dressed in dry clothes, slid her bowl at him. 'Have mine.' Obviously, Kast's friend did not share the Bloodrider's enthusiasm for the meal. She had only nibbled at the bread. But at least the color had returned to her cheeks after getting dry and warm. Still, dry or not, the young woman was clearly nervous and frightened here. She jumped with each crack of thunder or crash of wave.

Pinorr met her eyes and nodded upward. 'Ulster may be a sour man, but the crew is experienced. We'll weather out the storm.'

Sy-wen glanced away, her words a shy whisper. 'Under the sea, the storms don't touch us. What rages above never bothers the leviathans. We just dive deeper, allowing the worst storms to pass overhead.'

'So the mer'ai have always done,' Pinorr said. 'And not just from squalls cast by angry skies. When the Dark Lord came to Alasea, they fled that storm, too. While protecting you, over half our fleet was vanquished by the forces of the

Black Heart. Thousands died so hundreds of mer'ai could escape. In old songs and tales, we still remember our dead, and we don't fondly reflect on your people, our ancient slave masters. It will be hard to convince the others to rally to your banner now.'

Kast spoke, coughing a piece of bread loose from his throat. 'It was not the mer'ai that slew our people. It was the Gul'gotha – and it is the Gul'gotha we intend to fight. That is what we must remind the Dre'rendi.'

Pinorr leaned back on his bed. 'The Black Heart has not disturbed our fleet in centuries. As long as we keep to the Blasted Shoals, his forces leave us in peace. But now you ask us to expose our throats again to the teeth of his monsters. For what end? So some snip of a girl can fetch some book?' Pinorr stared at Kast, who had finally pushed away his stew bowl. 'I'm afraid your journey here, Kast, will prove fruitless. I doubt the high keel will grant you his forces.'

'What if I can convince Ulster? My brother's position as keelchief may help sway the other chiefs.'

Scowling, Pinorr looked away. 'Ulster will not help. He is not the boy you left behind, Kast.'

'What do you mean?'

'After you left, Ulster bore the brunt of your father's ire. As the only remaining son and heir to your family name, he was driven hard by your father, his head filled with dreams of glory. Your father would brook no failings from him. Eventually something broke in the boy, and he grew into a hard man, bereft of compassion, a lover of easy cruelties. He is no brother to you now. Remember that.'

'I cannot believe these words,' Kast said.

Pinorr saw the mer'ai girl slip her hand into Kast's, comforting him. It seemed that more than magick bound these two. 'I'm sorry, Kast. I tried my best to guide Ulster after your father died, to mentor him in the ways of stewarding a ship. But I believe what broke in him will never heal. He now bridles against my counsel, turning his resentment for his father against me.' Pinorr went on to explain about the recent attack on Sheeshon.

Kast's face was red with anger by the time the story was finished. 'How could my brother grow so craven?'

Pinorr shook his head sadly. 'Let it go, Kast. It's over. With Sheeshon choosing Ragnar'k as her champion, I don't believe Ulster will press the blood duel now. He'll be glad to forget his threats.'

'For now,' Kast said grimly. 'But what of later?'

'We'll cross those rough seas when the winds blow us there,' Pinorr answered, waving away Kast's concerns. 'I only tell you all this so you will understand. The Dre'rendi are not likely to consider your request. There are few who will even listen to you.'

'But your people swore oaths,' Sy-wen argued and pointed toward the faded tattoo on Pinorr's neck. 'For your freedom, you promised to serve us one last time. Now is that time. We call you to honor your ancient debts.'

'Those are old oaths, faded and forgotten like the dyes on my wrinkled neck. None will place much strength on such vows.'

Kast's face remained ruddy with an inner fire. 'You're wrong, Pinorr. The Dre'rendi have no choice.' He related how the tattoos held magick in their ink, how Sy-wen had bent his will to her desires. 'The tattoos bind us to the mer'ai. If they have a need of us, we will be forced to serve. Trust me; I know.'

Pinorr fingered the old seahawk on his cheek, his eyes wide. 'So they would enslave us again.'

'That is not our desire,' Sy-wen persisted. 'Or even

possible. Each of the mer'ai can bond to only *one* of the Bloodriders. As I am bonded to Kast, I can command no others. Such a magick would not allow us to enslave your entire people. You outnumber us tenfold.'

Kast supported her. 'They'd rather have the Dre'rendi as allies, not slaves. The mer'ai have as little interest in us as we do in them. They only ask us to honor our ancestors' oaths and to unite against a common foe. Afterward, our two peoples can part ways with our old debts paid.'

'That is, if any survive,' Pinorr replied under his breath, remembering Sheeshon's words of doom.

Kast leaned closer to Pinorr. 'There must be some way to convince our people, to get them at least to listen.'

Pinorr sighed and contemplated their words. Kast, with his eyes afire and his brows fierce, reminded the shaman of the younger man's father, his old friend. The flame of the high keel still burned in this elder son. Pinorr had never been able to refuse the high keel anything, especially when the man's blood was aflame.

Rubbing at his chin, Pinorr mumbled softly. 'There may be a way.' He sensed that he was about to betray his people, to set them on a path of doom. Yet his heart told him to trust Kast.

'How?'

'It will take the dragon, the one named Ragnar'k. Are you willing to forsake yourself to him again?'

Kast nodded. 'If I must.'

Pinorr turned to Sy-wen. 'What I ask of you is much worse.' He told her what he needed accomplished. 'Only your hand can do this.'

The woman's eyes grew wide with horror, but she nodded her understanding.

'You must reach the high keel's ship before the morning,'

366

Pinorr finished. 'Otherwise, if the fleet regroups after the storm, you will need to face the full council of keelchiefs, and there are too many like Ulster for any chance of them listening. But the high keel himself is a just man. If you catch him alone in this storm, he will listen. Convince him and the battle is won. He must understand the truth of our two peoples' shared histories.'

'But what of the storm's fury?' Kast asked as thunder boomed through the planks, rattling the bowls on the table.

'We will have to trust the sea gods,' Pinorr said.

Sy-wen was clearly not as convinced, her eyes full of doubt. 'You place too much trust in gods and ancient stories of dragons.' Her gaze flicked toward the tiny child playing with her toys. Drool dripped from the slack side of the girl's lips. 'If either proves wrong . . .'

Pinorr stood. 'I know what I risk.' He crossed to Sheeshon and gathered his son's daughter up in his arms.

The girl smiled up into his face. 'Papa, where are we going?'

'You're going to fly, sweetheart. Fly with a dragon.'

Ulster sat hunched with Jabib and Gylt in the ship's galley. The storm rocked the lanterns on their hooks, waving their long shadows over the walls. Thunder rumbled in a continual growl through the boat, erupting occasionally into fierce booms that shook their mugs of Tulusian kaffee.

Every such burst caused Gylt to duck his head and glance nervously upward, as if he were about to be struck. 'May the sea gods protect us,' he prayed, then waited for the echoes to trail away.

Ulster scowled at his fears. 'The gods do not protect the foolish. Only a well-manned boat will survive this storm.' He turned his attentions back to his first mate. 'Who have you assigned to pilot, Jabib?'

'Biggin, sir. He's already lashed to the wheel. He's a good man in rough seas.'

'What about Hrendal?'

Jabib shook his head. 'He's a better navigator, but he doesn't have Biggin's sea sense.'

Ulster nodded, satisfied with his first mate's judgment. Jabib knew the crew's strengths and weaknesses better than he. 'Good. With the rigging secured and the decks cleared, we should steer right through this storm.'

Jabib's expression did not appear as confident.

'What's wrong?'

'The crew, sir. I've heard rumblings. They say your fight with Pinorr has brought this storm down upon the fleet. They believe the dragon was birthed by the skies to punish the ship and is being led by the spirit of your dead brother.'

Ulster snorted. 'That's ridiculous. Kast never died. He just ran off. The dragon and the girl are just some trick of his to rejoin the fleet. We'll deal with him and his green-haired whore after the storm.'

Jabib shrugged. 'It's just what I've heard. The men are scared by the storm's size and spooked by the queer happenings on the deck earlier. Their talk grows stronger. Rumors abound. I've even heard some of the crew whisper plans of casting the shaman into the sea to appease the gods—'

'*That* is not a bad idea,' Ulster grumbled.

'But I've also heard the same threats against you and your brother.'

Ulster pounded his gloved fist on the table. 'What are you saying? Is it mutiny they want?'

'It's just talk, sir. But a show of strength by you . . .'

Ulster pondered his words. 'What do you propose?'

'A demonstration of your love for the gods.' Jabib glanced

about the room, then leaned nearer. 'A sacrifice ... by your own hand.'

'And you think a spurt of goat's blood will still the tongues of these whispers?'

'No, but maybe something stronger will. The shaman's child – her twisted face, her ramblings. She makes the crew uneasy. Mader Geel is the only one who will even look after the girl.' Jabib looked significantly at Ulster. 'None will miss her.'

Gylt spoke into the silence, his voice cracking with fear. 'She is cursed. All know it, but none have dared confront Shaman Pinorr. Tales say the child was birthed from a dead belly. One just has to look at that half-frozen face to know the gods have shunned her.'

Jabib nodded. 'If you rid the ship of the child, the crew will see your strength and know you honor the gods. This will end their talk of mutiny.'

'But what of Pinorr?'

Jabib leaned even closer, his voice a hushed whisper. 'In storms, accidents can happen.'

Kast crept down the passageway. The deck rolled under his feet, seeking to topple him. Barefooted, he kept his balance and snuck upon the guard stationed near the hatch to the upper deck. His many winters at sea among the cutthroats of Port Rawl had taught Kast the art of the assassin. His prey was no challenge, his eye pressed foolishly to the peephole in the door as he watched the storm's first rally against the ship.

Beyond the hatch, winds screamed like tortured spirits, masking Kast's final steps toward the man's back. Without pausing, Kast struck the man a sharp blow to his neck with the callused edge of his hand. His prey collapsed at his feet.

Kast relieved the man of his sword, then hurried back five paces and waved the others forward.

Sy-wen, her eyes wide with fear, hurried toward Kast. Pinorr, his face red from both exertion and anxiety, held Sheeshon in his arms. 'We will not have much time,' Pinorr commented. 'You must hurry.'

Kast nodded. 'The storm is fierce. Stay close.' Turning to the hatch, he threw open the latch, but the door ripped away on its own, torn free by the howling gales. The fierce winds fought to drag the lot of them onto the deck, but Kast fought the wind's pull, legs braced, hands tight to the door's frame. Only Kast's strength kept the others sheltered within the opening.

Behind him, Sy-wen hung from his right arm, her cheek resting on his shoulder as she squinted at the storm. Her breath was like fire on his neck. 'I . . . I don't think I can do this. The rain . . . the winds . . .'

'You must,' Pinorr said.

A huge wave suddenly crashed over the rails, a monster of frothing foam and swirling currents. It tore loose a set of lashed barrels and sent them crashing across the deck. Kast scowled at such poor preparations.

He waited for the waters to sluice away and the ship to right itself. 'Now!' he yelled and sprang out, keeping a firm grip on Sy-wen's hand. Rain, whipped by the winds into stinging sleet, strove to hammer him to the deck. He sheltered Sy-wen under him. Before the fury of this storm, the small mer'ai woman would be nothing but a stray leaf.

Pinorr had remained in the doorway, Sheeshon in his arms. 'Hurry!' he called to them.

Once far enough out on the deck, Kast swung around, pulling Sy-wen into his embrace. 'Call the dragon,' he yelled as the wind tore at his words.

Sy-wen seemed frozen by the fierceness of the warring skies. Lightning played in jagged spears across the under-bellies of the black clouds. Thunder ached the ribs in their chests. 'We can't possibly fly in this—'

As she resisted, Kast drew her fingers to his tattoo. 'Ragnar'k can,' he said. 'The dragon and I are one. We will not fail you. Trust me. Trust the dragon's heart.'

Her eyes were moist from more than just the rain as she glanced up at him. 'I will trust my bonded,' she said, her words a whisper in the wind. 'Both of them.' She gazed into his eyes, and for a moment, the storm's howl vanished. It was as if they were alone on the deck.

In the silence between cracks of thunder, she placed her palm upon his cheek and leaned up toward him, her lips brushing his ear. 'I have need of you.'

With those words of binding, the world around him vanished.

Sy-wen sat astride the dragon's neck as Ragnar'k awoke to the storm. The great beast bellowed at the skies, its silver claws dug deep into the ship's boards. Sy-wen knew that no wind or wash of wave could dislodge the huge dragon.

Its massive head swung in her direction. Red eyes glowed at her. *Do we fly again?* it asked.

Yes, she answered silently. *We must make for the largest ship.*

Ragnar'k sent his willingness to her in a warmth of bonded loyalty. His thoughts drove away the storm's chill. He unfurled his wings.

Wait, she urged him. *We must carry someone with us.*

A rasp of irritation flooded her. *You are my bonded. Only bonded shares the winds.*

I know, my dragon, but I have a great need and it is only a short distance.

A grumble, the equivalent of a dragon's sigh, rose from his chest. Wings folded back down.

Sy-wen raised her arm toward the opening to the lower decks. Pinorr and Sheeshon were still sheltered in the doorway. She waved to the shaman.

Pinorr showed no fear as he scurried across the space between door and dragon. As the waves rolled the boat, he almost lost his footing on the slippery deck. Soon he crouched in the lee of the beast's bulk, protected from the worst of the storm. 'Can you manage?' he yelled up at Sy-wen.

She nodded. 'Ragnar'k will keep us both safe!'

Sy-wen leaned down and accepted the small child from Pinorr's outstretched arms. Sheeshon struggled and sobbed in fear, not of the dragon, but of the angry skies. Her eyes were wide as she stared at the lightning.

Sy-wen pulled Sheeshon into the space in front of her and wrapped both arms around her. 'Hush. You're safe,' she soothed, but in her heart, Sy-wen was not so confident. With her ankles locked in the dragon's folds, Sy-wen had to trust the strength of her own arms to keep the child atop the dragon.

Sheeshon glanced up at Sy-wen. The girl struggled for bravery in the face of the storm. 'Your big dragon has a funny name.'

'Yes, he does.'

'He's gonna eat me,' the child said calmly.

Shocked, Sy-wen stared as Sheeshon turned and patted happily at the dragon's scaled neck, her actions so incongruous with her words.

I will not eat her, Ragnar'k argued grimly. *She's too small.*

I know, my bonded. Ignore her words. She is addled. Still, Sy-wen shuddered. The child had spoken with such certainty.

Suddenly the roiling clouds unleashed their fury. A crash of icy hail pounded down from the black skies, pelting the deck with a roaring clatter.

Cringing from the stinging bites, Sy-wen leaned over the dragon's shoulder and found Pinorr staring up at her. 'Fear not, Shaman, I will get the girl safe to the *Dragonsheart*. Kast and I will convince the high keel of our urgency.'

His face was still lined with worry. 'You know what you must do.'

Nodding, Sy-wen pulled back, her lips tight. She clutched tighter to the child. *Sweet Mother, forgive me, but I do.*

Pinorr retreated, bent against the hail. He fled to the doorway and waved an arm in farewell.

Sy-wen turned toward the raging seas. *Fly,* she sent the dragon.

Ragnar'k obeyed, wings snapping taut in the strong gale, catching the winds. The dragon released his claws, and the storm took hold of him. Ragnar'k sailed over the rail. Away from the ship, whitecaps blew up from the sea, reaching for them, struggling to tear them from the skies. Some waves towered as high as mighty cliffs. But the dragon sailed above their grasps.

Lightning chased them across the sea.

Ducking away from the thunder, Sy-wen considered ordering the dragon to dive under the furious sea to escape the storm's brunt, but speed was essential. Flying was faster, and she feared the child's panic if they fled under the waves. Sheeshon could easily drown – and that must not happen. The success of their mission depended on the girl.

Sy-wen kept a firm grip on the trembling child. Sheeshon was mumbling something, over and over. It sounded almost like a child's song, rhythmic and repetitive. The wind tore away most of her words, but occasional snatches reached her. Sy-wen pieced them together in her head:

> *Dragon heart and dragon bone,*
> *only blood will shatter stone.*
> *Dragon dark and dragon bright,*
> *only pain will win this fight.*

Sy-wen pulled back, her mind working on the child's rhyme. What did it mean? Her skin prickled with the words. As with Kast's tattoo, she sensed old magick in the girl's chant.

Touching the child's cheek, Sy-wen drew her attention. 'What are you –?'

Suddenly the world exploded. Time froze. Pain seared Sy-wen's left side. Blind for an unknown length of time, Sy-wen came back to the world with a scream filling her ears. It took her a moment to realize that it was her own throat crying out. She stared in horror at the raging sea flying toward them.

Under her, the dragon dove in a spiraling fall, head lolling on a flailing neck. Sheeshon was still clutched in her arms. The child struggled an arm free and pointed to the left. Sy-wen glanced and saw the smoking tear in the dragon's wing. Mother above, Ragnar'k must have caught the edge of a lightning bolt! As she stared, other jagged spears pursued her injured mount.

Sy-wen concentrated on the dragon. *Ragnar'k, wake! I have need of you!*

Somewhere far away she felt a slight stir. She reached out with her senses and sent forth her urgency. *Awake! Help us!*

A faint thought came to her. *Sy-wen?*

She knew this was not the dragon. She did not have time

to ponder the miracle. *Kast! You must wake Ragnar'k!*

The dragon's body swept into a trough between gigantic walls of frothing waters. Instinct kept its wings wide, so they glided along the valley between the mountainous waves. But they had only another few heartbeats before the dragon struck the water.

Kast struggled. *I don't know how . . .*

Do what you must! Or the girl and I die!

Suddenly the dragon lurched under her. She was almost thrown from his back. The great beast wobbled, struggling with his injured wing. But finally his neck stretched long, scales slick with saltwater. His head swung side to side, surveying the situation.

A tower of water threatened to topple upon them, its top edge thrashed white by the winds. The dragon arched his back up, turned on his good wing, and fought to pull up from the trough.

Hurry! Sy-wen urged, watching the wave's crest begin to tumble toward them.

Muscle writhed under her; wings fought wind and rain. A roar of frustration and rage bellowed from the dragon as he dragged his bulk upward.

Sy-wen twisted her neck and watched the wave chase them. It snarled and gnashed at the dragon's tail.

Then it was over.

A final lunge and the dragon heaved above the monster wave. The waters crashed below, roaring their own frustration, missing the dragon's tail by a mere handspan.

Crying in relief, Sy-wen collapsed over the girl. 'We made it,' she moaned. Sy-wen rubbed her hand appreciatively along the dragon's neck. *Thank you, Ragnar'k.*

It wasn't just the dragon.

Kast?

I could not wake Ragnar'k. Sy-wen sensed the exhaustion and strain in the Bloodrider. *The shock and pain had driven Ragnar'k too deep. I was only able to reach his baser thoughts – his simple instincts and reflexes. But it was enough. With my will giving direction and purpose, the dragon's instincts and reflexes powered his body.*

But how . . . ?

The dragon tumbled downward, then caught itself. *It . . . it's too hard to talk this way . . . and control the dragon. Watch over the girl.*

Sy-wen sent her silent thanks and warmth to Kast.

Around her, thunder boomed as the squall's fury heightened. As they flew, the winds grew fiercer, forcing Sy-wen to lean closer to the dragon, sheltering the girl under her.

Suddenly out of the rain-swept darkness, a ship appeared. Triple masted and dragon prowed, it fought the waves with a fury that seemed almost alive. Sy-wen knew this ship from Pinorr's description. It was the largest of the fleet – the *Dragonsheart*.

Her mount must have spotted it at the same time. The dragon leaned his neck down, and his body followed, diving toward the ship. Sy-wen clutched the child as the ship grew under them. The tumble toward the ship's deck was not the artful glide of Ragnar'k in full control. *Kast must be struggling fiercely to fly the giant.* Wings beat and fought to both slow their descent and guide their aim. It was a close battle, the outcome uncertain.

The ship, rolling among the towering waves, made an unwilling partner. Its deck teetered, and the three masts stabbed at them like hostile spears.

The dragon roared at the stubborn boat, banking and twisting to match the ship's tumble.

As the ship's decks flew toward them, Sy-wen closed her eyes. It did no good to look. With her heart clenched in her throat, Sy-wen leaned and pinned the child under her, hugging the dragon tight. *Kast, do not fail me.*

A shuddering crash was her only answer. Sy-wen fought to keep her grip, but the impact was too great. Her ankles popped free from their footholds, and she and the girl slid up the dragon's neck. Gasping, Sy-wen willed her arms and legs to grip with every fiber in her small body. The screech of claw on wood stretched forever as the dragon skidded across the wet deck. Sy-wen waited for the snap of rail and the final tumble into the roaring sea.

It never happened.

The dragon settled to a trembling stop under her.

Sy-wen kept her eyes closed and sent a silent prayer to all the gods of the world. Slowly, she opened her eyes. The tip of the dragon's nose touched the rail. It had been close – too close. The great beast lay stretched across the deck, too exhausted to lift himself. His chest heaved in huge gulping blasts, steaming into the cold rain. Behind her, Sy-wen noted the deep gouges dragged across the deck. Pieces of broken silver nail littered the trail.

Sheeshon also surveyed their surroundings. 'This isn't Papa's boat,' she said. A trace of fear etched her words.

Sy-wen placed a palm on the child's cheek. 'It's all right, Sheeshon. You'll be safe here until your papa comes.'

A crash of wood sounded to the left as a hatch flew open. Sy-wen watched men rush out onto the storm-swept deck bearing spears and swords. When they saw what lay before them, they stopped, their faces mixed with fear and awe.

Sy-wen knew Kast should do the talking here. She lowered Sheeshon onto the deck. 'Stay by the dragon,' she urged the child.

Then Sy-wen, conscious of all the eyes upon her, followed the child off their mount, careful to keep one hand on Ragnar'k. Once her feet were secure under her, Sy-wen took Sheeshon's hand in her own and turned to face the growing audience.

Even the wicked storm could not keep the crew away. From among their midst, the tallest man Sy-wen had ever set eyes upon shoved through the crowd. Older, but still well muscled, he was as wide as he was tall. She heard a few whispered comments from the others gathered here. One name was spoken by all: *high keel*. The man stopped and stared at the two small women and the sprawled dragon. He wore a hard scowl; no twinge of welcome softened his features. His eyes were dark with suspicion.

Sy-wen swallowed. Kast was certainly the one to confront this man.

Stepping forward, Sy-wen removed her hand from the dragon, releasing the spell. She cringed away from the whirlwind to come – but nothing happened.

Glancing over her shoulder, Sy-wen saw the dragon still draped across the deck. Only his steaming breath gave sign he was still alive.

'Kast?' she called out.

A harsh voice drew her back around. It was the high keel. His glare promised pain. 'What manner of storm demon are you?'

As Pinorr returned to his cabin, worry gnawed at his belly. With his plan now under way, he was not as confident of his idea. It depended too much on the truth of ancient tales. If he was wrong, it could mean not only the failure of Kast and Sy-wen's hopes, but the death of Sheeshon as well.

He reached for the latch to his door, thunder in his ears,

lanterns casting twisted shadows. At that moment, a sudden lull in the storm saved his life. As the thunder's roar died away momentarily, Pinorr heard the faint scrape of heel on wood. It was enough to draw his eye.

Hunched a short way down the passage stood the stocky Gylt, a stained blade in hand. From his furtive posture and the sudden guilt in his eyes, the shaman knew the crewman meant him harm. After checking the rest of the passage, Pinorr turned to face the man fully. 'So you come to murder in Ulster's stead?'

The crewman still stood frozen in midstep, indecision wavering his determination.

'I see you draw the sea gods' wrath to your own shoulders, sparing Ulster. How brave of you to damn your own spirit.' Pinorr narrowed his gaze. He began to understand the keelchief's purpose here. 'Even though you may trick the crew and blame my disappearance on the storm's fury, do not think the sea gods will not know which hand wielded the sword. Even now, they watch you through my eyes. They stare at your heart.' A sudden burst of thunder shook the deck under their feet.

Gylt gasped and backed a step away.

Pinorr knew the man was easily cowed, especially when scared. He leaned closer. 'Hear how the gods call for your blood already.'

Gylt's eyes grew wide with horror. His sword trembled in his grip. 'I . . . I wasn't supposed to slay you, Shaman. Truly I wasn't! I w-was only supposed to make sure you returned to your cabin.'

Pinorr frowned at Gylt. He sensed the truth to the man's words.

Behind Pinorr, his cabin door suddenly swung open. He knew he had left his room empty. He had clearly stumbled blindly into an ambush. He had not thought Ulster could grow so craven – at least not this soon.

In front of Pinorr, a shadow cast from the room's lanterns spread on the far wall of the passage: *a man with his sword raised*. Pinorr watched the shadowy blade plunge toward his back.

Pinorr had no time to turn, only to duck sideways, raising an arm in warding. The blade sliced under his arm, just missing his chest and catching the edge of his robe. Pinorr saw the blade's tip thrust out from under his raised arm. At that moment, old instincts returned to Pinorr – under his shaman's robe still beat the heart of a Bloodrider. Though he had untied his warrior's braid long ago, a part of him remembered.

Crying a warrior's roar, Pinorr brought down his arm, trapping the flat of the blade against his chest. He clamped hard and twisted on a heel. As expected, his attacker was slightly off balance by his failed thrust. The clamped blade tore free of the other's grip. Pinorr did not pause. As he continued his turn, he reached for the freed blade. After forty winters, his hands again settled around the hilt of a sword.

Sweeping the weapon forward, he faced his disarmed attacker. A rage burst in Pinorr's heart. His vision narrowed to sharp edges.

Pinorr heard the gasp from Gylt on his left. 'You must not bear a sword. You must not shed blood. You're a shaman!'

Ignoring the man's outburst, Pinorr stared at his attempted assassin. He was not surprised to find Jabib standing before him, always Ulster's dog. The first mate reached for a dagger. Pinorr was faster.

The sword buried itself in the first mate's chest. Pinorr thrust deeper, stepping toward Jabib, until they were nose to nose, the sword's hilt lodged between their bellies. Hot blood washed over Pinorr's cold hand. He trembled with rage as he faced his attempted assassin. 'May the sea gods feed your spirit to their worms,' he spat as he stepped away, twisting the sword as he pulled it free.

Jabib gasped and fell to his knees. Blood frothed from his mouth and poured down his chest. Before the man could tumble onto his face, Pinorr grabbed the man's braid, holding him up by his corded hair.

Jabib raised his eyes in horror.

'I send you to the gods without honor,' Pinorr said coldly and sliced the braid away in one sweep of his sword. Unsupported now, Jabib crashed to the planks, his life's blood pooling under him.

Pinorr turned, sword in one hand, Jabib's braid in the other.

Gylt dropped his sword, eyes white with fear. 'You have cursed us,' he cried. 'You have soiled yourself with blood.'

'You have cursed yourselves,' he said. 'The sea gods warned me of your treachery, protected me. They silenced the storm so I might hear your tread. They cast Jabib's shadow on the wall, revealing his craven attack.' Pinorr stepped closer to Gylt. 'They bless me this stormy night, so I might seek their vengeance upon those who plot against the gods.'

Gylt shook his head, violently denying Pinorr's words. He slipped to his knees. 'No ... no ...' he moaned.

Pinorr towered over the sobbing man. 'Yes,' he said, his voice as harsh as the storm raging above.

Gylt must have sensed Pinorr's heart. He lunged for his sword – but it was too late.

Pinorr swung his own blade with all the rage in his bones. Blood sprayed over his forearms. Pinorr stepped over Gylt's body while the man's head still bobbled down the passage ahead of him.

With Jabib's braid dragging at his side, Pinorr continued deeper into the ship's bowels. He knew that for too long he had allowed a foulness to fester in this ship. Fear for Sheeshon, fear for himself, had stayed his hand. With Sheeshon gone, Pinorr knew it was time he acted. This night, tides of prophecy drew all the players together, allowing none to escape their destiny.

By morning, the Dre'rendi would either be forged into their final purpose – beaten into a weapon against the Gul'gotha – or sunk under the waves.

His people's final fate would depend on a shaman's cursed sword and the heart of a child.

16

With lightning ribbing the sky, Sy-wen faced the high keel. Raindrops pelted the decks in a constant, splashing rattle. Behind the man, the deck bristled with spears and swords. She ignored the other crewmen. All that mattered was the huge man standing before her. He was the leader here, the one she and Kast had been sent to sway. But nothing was going according to the old shaman's plan. Kast, as a fellow Bloodrider, was the one who was supposed to herald their cause, not her.

Glancing behind to the collapsed dragon, Sy-wen knew their plans needed to be hastily reworked, but she could not think clearly. Her thoughts worried on Ragnar'k and Kast. What had happened? Why hadn't the spell reversed itself? Was it the lightning strike? Was Kast forever trapped in the dragon's form? Her mind spun with the implications.

A small hand squeezed her own. Sheeshon tugged on Sy-wen's arm. 'That man's bigger than Papa,' she commented plainly, pointing to the high keel. The drenched child shivered in the wind.

Hugging the girl closer to keep her warm, Sy-wen turned. Even from a few paces away, Sy-wen still had to crane her neck to face the man. His eyes were shards of blue steel, his braided mane dark but silvered along the edges from passing winters. In his right fist, he clutched a whaling harpoon that towered over him. His eyes flicked between Sy-wen and the huge black dragon. With Ragnar'k behind her, he was cautious.

'Again I ask you,' he said, 'what manner of demon are you?'

Sy-wen finally freed her tongue. Silence was not going to sway anyone. 'I am no demon, High Keel of the Dre'rendi,' she said solemnly, bowing her head slightly in greeting. 'I am Sy-wen, emissary of the mer'ai. I have been sent by Shaman Pinorr to seek your counsel.'

His crew were too well trained to speak out of turn, but Sy-wen saw furtive glances pass among those who backed the high keel. Doubt and anger were mixed in their nervous stances. From their responses, Pinorr's earlier warning proved correct. The mer'ai name was not well received.

The high keel spoke into the stretch of silence. His voice cracked slightly from the shock of her announcement, but it soon returned to its commanding tones. 'Do you have proof for such wild claims?' he asked.

Sy-wen waved her free hand back to the dragon. 'If this is not proof enough,' she said as she pulled Sheeshon in front of her, 'Shaman Pinorr also sent his only blood as his seal of support.'

The high keel seemed finally to notice the small girl. He squinted at Sheeshon. 'I know this child . . .' he said hesitatingly.

Another man pushed forward, coming around the high keel's shoulder. He was blue robed like a shaman, but where Pinorr was weathered thin and hard, this man was full bellied, one hand resting on his ample paunch. He eyed the skies fretfully. 'We should take the captives below,' he said with a slight lisp. 'I fear this is but a calm before the storm's true fury strikes.' He glanced to the dragon, his gaze frightened. 'Bad omens still scent the winds.'

The high keel nodded. He waved for two guards to flank the pair of girls. The men bore sickle-shaped swords; lightning reflected off their wet blades. 'If you are not demons, then come with us. Tell us why you've come, why my old friend would send you.'

Sy-wen noted the raised blades. The high keel's statement was no request, but she nodded anyway. 'We appreciate your offer of shelter,' she said, then indicated the dragon. 'But my mount has suffered a grievous wound. I must first beg a boon from you.'

Thunder again began to build around them. 'What is it?' the high keel said impatiently.

'The dragon needs a healer.'

The Dre'rendi leader nodded to the boat's shaman. 'Bilatus is this ship's healer, but his arts serve men, not dragons.'

The portly shaman nodded his agreement vigorously, his eyes fixed on the steaming hulk of black scale and silver claw. 'I have no herbs or salves for such a beast. I could harm as easily as heal.'

Sy-wen's heart quailed at the thought of leaving the collapsed dragon unattended on the deck. What if a wave should wash him overboard? She glanced back at her huge companion. Twin streams of white billowed from his flared nostrils, but his eyes still remained closed.

A hand touched her shoulder, making her jump. It was the high keel; he had come so silently upon her. 'Fear not. Your dragon will remain safe, Sy-wen of the mer'ai. I have given my welcome. Until this matter is heard and judged, none will dare break my invitation. We will tether your mount with thick lines to mast and rail. Unless the *Dragonsheart* sinks, your beast will remain secure.'

'Thank you.'

The high keel stepped closer to the great dragon, reaching a hand to touch it.

'Careful, my high keel!' the shaman called out from behind them.

The broad-shouldered man ignored the warning and placed his palm upon a wet fold of scaled wing. 'I never imagined I'd see such a wonder.' He shook his head and pulled his hand away. As he returned to his line of men, Sy-wen spotted the whisper of a smile again on his face.

'Come,' he said as he passed her.

She followed this time, discovering a twinge of respect for the man. She now understood why Pinorr had placed such trust in the high keel. There was no question that steel flowed through his veins. But she found that a keen curiosity also shone forth from his eyes.

With Sheeshon clinging tight to her side, Sy-wen followed the high keel's back. Shaman Bilatus kept close to the man's shoulder, constantly glancing back at them as they entered the ship.

The high keel led the procession down a short stair and along a wide corridor. He pushed into a long room. Overhead, lanterns hanging from beams swayed with the roll of the boat. Tables and benches lined the floor. He faced the gathered crew. 'You all have your orders and stations,' his voice boomed. 'I don't expect my ship to sink in this storm because my crew turned into a bunch of slack-jawed gawkers. Be off to your duties!' He waved to one other fellow, a handsome man who stood almost as tall as the high keel. 'Hunt, accompany us.'

'Yes, High Keel.' His eyes lit up with excitement.

Suddenly Sy-wen recognized why the man seemed familiar. 'Is he your son?' she asked.

'And the *Dragonsheart*'s first mate,' the high keel said proudly. 'Come. We will retire to my cabin and speak of these matters in private.'

She nodded and soon found herself in a spacious room. The place was warm and inviting. Along one wall, shelves were crammed with weathered texts and crumpled scrolls. A desk stood nearby, a thick book spread atop its surface. Across the room, two goose-down chairs stood before an actual stone fireplace. A thick iron grate kept the burning logs within the small hearth during the storm's tumult.

The high keel waved Sy-wen to one of the thick chairs. She accepted the invitation, glad to get closer to the warm fire. The chill of their flight had set deep into her bones. The Dre'rendi clothes she wore dripped and clung damply to her skin. She wished she had kept her sharkskin breeches.

Once seated, she pulled Sheeshon into her lap. The girl raised her legs to heat the bottoms of her bare feet.

Bilatus was invited to the second chair, leaving the high keel and his son, Hunt, to stand. The two tall men flanked either side of the hearth. Side by side now, their distinct similarities were obvious: sharp eyes squinted at the corners, strong clefted chins, wide mouths made for easy smiling. Even their broad shoulders and stance were twins of each other.

Sy-wen found herself trusting these two and leaned deeper into the goose-down pillows.

'Tell us your story,' the high keel said simply.

Sy-wen cleared her throat and did as he asked. She explained about the coming assault on A'loa Glen, about the Gul'gothal forces fortifying the islands, about the hope of the lands placed in the hands of a young wit'ch. She related all she had shared with Pinorr – except for the secret of Kast and the dragon. She suspected none would believe her, and right now, she needed all the trust she could muster from these three men. 'So I have come to ask you to lend your ships and warriors to our battle.'

The high keel had remained silent during the entire discourse. Finally, he spoke. 'I believe you speak with a noble heart, Sy-wen of the mer'ai. I even believe your cause just and righteous. The Dre'rendi share no love for the Gul'gotha, but likewise we share no friendship with the mer'ai either. Why join old enemies to fight new enemies? What matter to us that the Gul'gotha torment the people of the lands?'

Sy-wen sat up straighter. 'The Gul'gothal lord will never be satisfied with just the land. Right now his eyes are turned toward the coast, but once that is fully subdued, his gaze will turn to you. Then who will be left to come to your aid?'

'The Dre'rendi are a free people. We call no lands our own. If the Gul'gotha push, we will give way. As long as there are seas to sail, we will never fall to another man's yoke.' He glanced significantly at Sy-wen. 'We remember too well when once we bowed to another's sword. We won our freedom with our blood then and mean to keep it now. Why should we join this battle and earn the enmity of the Dark Lord?'

'You are already an enemy of the Gul'gotha. Any who don't serve him are his foe.' Sy-wen swallowed hard. 'Is it truly *freedom* if you are on the run from the Gul'gotha? Are you on any less of a leash if his forces herd you this way and that? That is not freedom. It's blind cowardice!'

The fat shaman gasped. Hunt's hand dropped to his sword hilt. The only reaction from the high keel was a reddening of his cheeks. Then he burst out with a hearty laugh. 'No one can say you are not blunt, lass!'

Sy-wen blushed at his words. 'I meant no true offense.'

Again the high keel laughed.

'Father,' Hunt said. His face was dark red, but not with amusement. 'Will you allow such insult to the Dre'rendi?'

'What insult? The young woman speaks her heart. I would wish more would speak so plainly.' He waved to Sy-wen. 'Fine. I can see your point. The Dre'rendi should sail where the winds dictate, not the Gul'gotha. If we run from the Black Heart's beasts, we are cowards.'

Bilatus stared at this confession with wide eyes. 'The sea gods will protect us. We have no need to fear the Gul'gotha.'

The high keel shook his head, the humor fading from his lips. 'Spoken like a shaman. But I've learned that the sea gods protect those who protect themselves.' He patted his sword. 'This is the only true defense.'

Sy-wen could not believe her luck. The high keel warmed to her cause. 'So you will consider lending your forces?'

He stared at her silently for three long breaths, then answered. 'No.'

Sy-wen sat stunned. Her voice was meek when next she spoke. 'But why? This is the best chance to strike a blow against the Dark Lord.'

'Perhaps. But the Dre'rendi will never fight alongside the mer'ai. When last we battled the Gul'gotha, your people fled, leaving us to the teeth and axes of the enemy.'

Sy-wen bristled. 'But it was not as if we betrayed you. You offered your aid freely, allowing us to escape.'

'Still, it bespeaks your people's craven hearts.'

Now it was Sy-wen's turn to react to being called cowardly. 'What of your old oaths?' She pointed to his tattoo. 'Do you break your own vows? You promised to come to our aid one last time when we requested it.'

The high keel remained silent.

Bilatus answered. 'That was long ago. Since then we have come to worship the seven gods of the sea. Our hearts and spirits are bound to them, not to the mer'ai. We are slaves to you no more.'

The high keel slowly nodded his head. 'Whatever debts we owed your people are long faded to dust.'

Sy-wen wished she could show him how strong the tattoo's magickal bonds still remained, but she had already bonded to Kast and could not bring forth the magick of the tattoo in another. She sighed, knowing that only one chance lay open to them, the path Pinorr had suggested.

She glanced to Sheeshon, who had begun to doze in the warmth of her lap. Her heart went out to the small child. She had hoped to avoid Pinorr's full plan. Perhaps if Kast had been here . . .

She shook her head and raised her eyes toward the high keel. 'You place much on the differences between our two people – mer'ai and Dre'rendi.'

He shrugged.

Sy-wen's voice grew firmer. 'I will share with you a mer'ai secret, something to which even most of my own people are blind. I revealed this to Shaman Pinorr, and he sent his only granddaughter not only as proof of his support, but as proof of my next words.'

Bilatus sat up straighter at the mention of a fellow shaman.

The high keel narrowed his eyes. 'What?'

'We are not different people.' She stared intently at the high keel. 'Mer'ai and Dre'rendi are in truth one tribe.'

Their shock halted further discussion. Finally, Bilatus made a rude noise with his blubbery lips. 'Impossible.'

Sy-wen placed her palm atop the head of the napping Sheeshon. 'Here is the proof.'

The high keel glanced at the child, then back to Sy-wen. 'I see no clue here, only an addled child with a face that half droops.'

'You will.' Sy-wen clenched her fist. She hoped her words proved true. Glancing up at Hunt, she indicated Sheeshon. 'Can you carry her?'

After getting a nod from his father, the young Bloodrider lifted Sheeshon from Sy-wen's lap. The sleeping child only moaned a bit, then latched her tiny arms around Hunt's neck.

Sy-wen stood. 'To show you, I will need blood from the dragon.'

Bilatus had to push twice to extract himself from the chair. 'How do you propose to get –?'

Sy-wen slipped the long dagger from her wrist sheath. 'With this.'

The sudden appearance of twin swords at her throat quickly taught her the foolishness of such rash action. Sy-wen had not even seen the high keel or his son move. The tips of their weapons held steady in the hollow of her throat.

Sy-wen finally found her tongue again. 'I mean no one harm. I only need the knife to draw blood from my mount.' Sy-wen flipped the dagger in her hand and caught the blade, proffering the handle toward the high keel. 'If you'd feel better, please keep it. I will even allow you to stab the dragon to gain its blood.'

The high keel squinted at her, clearly trying to weigh the truth of her words and intent. Sy-wen did not waver from his hard gaze, though the dagger trembled a bit in her scared fingers.

Finally, the leader of the Dre'rendi lowered his sword and waved his son to follow his example. 'No, Sy-wen of the mer'ai. If anyone is to poke that slumbering beast atop my decks, I think it best be you.' Again the whisper of a smile flashed on his lips.

Sy-wen slowly slipped the dagger back into its sheath with a long sigh. 'I apologize for startling you all. I was not thinking when I bared my knife. I had only thought to clarify my purpose.'

The high keel sheathed his sword. 'And what purpose might that be?'

Sy-wen cowered a bit. After their reaction to her knife, maybe it would be best to leave Shaman Pinorr's theory unspoken. But all their eyes were upon her.

A sudden knocking at the door saved her from answering.

Bilatus opened the door to an excited crewmate. The man pulled off his soaking hat as he entered, his eyes excited. 'High Keel, sir. It's the *Dragonspur*. Word's come across the storm. Her mast's been lightning struck. You kin even see her sails aflame!'

Hunt glanced to his father. 'That's Shaman Pinorr's ship.'

Again Sy-wen found all their eyes upon her – and for the hundredth time, she wished Kast were here.

Behind Pinorr, cries of alarm echoed down the passageway. Shrill frightened voices mixed with barked orders. Pinorr ignored them and continued through the narrow corridors toward the ship's bow. The bodies of Jabib and Gylt must have been discovered. He quickened his pace, sensing that if he slowed, the fire in his blood would fade – and this was not a night for cool heads or wise counsel. What festered aboard this boat could only be cleansed with flames.

Suddenly, as if the gods had heard his thoughts, thick smoke billowed down from an open hatch somewhere behind him. Pinorr coughed. He smelled burned wood and again heard snatches of bellowing voices. His pace slowed. He turned back the way he had come. Past the smoke, a hatch slammed shut amid frantic calls for help. Overhead, the tread of running feet clattered as men fled the galley just above him.

The entire ship was being roused.

Pinorr could almost smell the desperation behind the smoke. Something was wrong, something more urgent than even murdered crewmen.

Pinorr glanced at his bloody sword and the limp length of braid in his left hand. Was this commotion a new trick of Ulster's? Something staged to distract the crew while the keelchief's minions disposed of the shaman?

He gripped his sword tighter; its hilt felt right in his fist.

Whatever alarm had been raised, for whatever reason, it was no longer his business. He was no longer the *Dragonspur*'s shaman, nor even her warrior. This night Pinorr was the gods' vengeance given form and steel.

Continuing toward the lone cabin in the forward section of the bow, he marched toward where, if Pinorr judged the keelchief correctly, the craven cur would be ensconced in his own cabin. Pinorr tightened his grip on his sword. He would enjoy seeing the keelchief's expression when the man learned his assassins had failed – though in all likelihood, the sight would be Pinorr's last. For whether justified or not, Pinorr had no misconceptions that he himself would be spared for his attacks. It was forbidden for a ship's shaman to touch steel, and it was death to draw blood.

Still, Pinorr knew his duty. Ultimately, the spiritual fate of the ship rested in his hands. He could no longer allow Ulster to befoul its decks.

Finally, Pinorr reached his destination. Stopping before a wide door banded and studded in iron, he waited a single breath. Then he raised his sword and pounded its hilt on the frame.

A voice snapped at him. 'I know of the fire! I'm coming!'

Pinorr blinked at this response. What fire? Before he could ponder the mystery any further, the door flew open. Ulster stood before him, pulling into a jerkin. Half dressed, the keelchief froze when he saw who stood in his doorway.

Neither man moved for several strained heartbeats.

Finally, Pinorr tossed Jabib's braid across Ulster's boots. It was the gesture of a warrior for a leader, a token of a kill done to protect the ship. The bloody tail slapped the planks like a length of soaked kelp. 'I believe this belongs to you,' Pinorr said coldly.

Ulster's eyes flickered toward the braid, but his gaze remained mostly on the sword. It was clear that the keelchief was more shocked to see Pinorr with a sword than he was concerned for his first mate's fate.

'What have you done, Shaman?' he asked with a note of horror.

'What I should have done long ago – cut away a festering canker before the disease spreads to the rest of the fleet.'

Ulster backed from Pinorr's sword. In his hurry, the keelchief had forgotten to don his own weapon belt. It hung from the back of a chair in the room.

Pinorr followed Ulster, step for step, words pouring out that had been bottled in his heart. 'I loved your father. It was only his memory that kept my hand in check for so long. But when your brother Kast arrived, I finally recognized how little of your father's blood runs in your own veins, Ulster.'

The keelchief spat bile to match Pinorr's fury. 'Not like my father?' Ulster laughed harshly. 'And you think these words insult me! The old man was more like me than you could imagine, Shaman. Were you at my side when my father lashed me bloody after my defeat in a sword spar with Zinbathi's son? Were you there when my broken ribs were wrapped after one of his savage beatings? Or how about when the burns on my arms peeled and cracked for an entire moon?' Ulster pointed to the doorway. 'Behind closed doors, men whose faces you think you know can change, Pinorr. Only I saw my father's true countenance, the one he hid from the rest of the crew.'

Pinorr stumbled a step at such lies. 'How dare you blaspheme your father's memory!'

'You were always blind, Shaman. Though you may have been gifted with keen sea senses, my father's heart was kept hidden from you.' Ulster's gaze narrowed. 'Or were you just too scared to look deeply? Did you suspect what lurked there, but feared losing such a skilled leader?'

Pinorr stopped his pursuit of Ulster across the cabin. As much as he would wish to deny it, Pinorr could not disavow how hard the old high keel had ridden his son. But he had never suspected such depths of wrath. 'But your brother –?'

'Kast?' Ulster snorted. 'The bastard escaped before the worst, leaving me to face our father's anger alone.' The fire seemed to die in Ulster, like a spent candle. 'I can never forgive him for that.'

Pinorr had to struggle to keep his own anger lit. 'Whether your story is true or not, what right do you have to wreak your father's old savageries upon my family?'

Ulster's eyes never left Pinorr's. 'Because you had the power to stop my father. He would have listened to you, Pinorr.' Ulster's voice cracked, then hardened back again. 'But instead, you only looked out toward the glories on the horizons, rather than at the evil that stood beside you. So do not seek sympathy in me.' Ulster turned and reached for his sword belt.

Stunned by his words, Pinorr could only watch numbly as the keelchief drew his weapon.

'No longer will I let you ignore the evil of my father.' Ulster faced Pinorr again. 'What it forged stands before you now.' With those words, Ulster lunged.

Pinorr barely had time to raise his own sword. Steel clashed steel. Luckily, Ulster's attack was guided by anger more than skill. Still, Pinorr fell back under the assault. The keelchief was younger and stronger of limb. It was only Pinorr's instinct from his warrior days that kept Ulster's sword from his belly.

Pinorr fought desperately. The furious fire that had ignited his blood earlier had waned to mere embers. How could he righteously despise that which his own hand had helped forge? Pinorr retreated. His left foot slipped on the discarded braid of the first mate. He toppled to the deck, his sword clanging out of his grip as he hit the floor.

Ulster towered over him now, sword raised. His eyes glowed red with rage, his breath ragged and panting.

Pinorr knelt up to face his death.

The keelchief looked him in the eye. 'You should have heard my cries, Shaman.'

Pinorr nodded once, briefly. 'You're right, Ulster. I'm sorry.'

The anger in the young man's face twitched with confusion. His sword arm trembled as he held the weapon poised.

Raising his face higher, Pinorr spoke quietly. 'But I'm also not your father, Ulster.'

The keelchief shook his head and stepped away, his brows tight, his gaze shaky. 'I know you're not my father . . .'

'It's not too late to try to heal what he wrought.' Pinorr saw the pain in Ulster's stance. 'I can help.'

Swinging toward Pinorr again with wild eyes, Ulster laughed and pointed his sword. 'You think you can help me? If you knew all, you'd curse me as resolutely as my father did during one of his rages.'

'I wouldn't,' Pinorr insisted, sincere in his words. He persisted in an attempt to reach the young man — not to save his own life, but to salvage what was left of Ulster's. 'Will you let me try?'

Ulster lowered his sword — but only slightly. His eyes had narrowed to slits. 'Do you know how your son died? Sheeshon's father?'

Pinorr flinched from Ulster's words. The keelchief touched upon an old wound that had never completely healed. 'He . . . he died during the Kurtish clashes. He took an ax in the brow.' Pinorr had no desire to revisit that memory. A black pigeon had brought word to Pinorr from the far coast as Sheeshon's mother had labored in birthing. When word reached the struggling woman, she wailed, and something broke in her. Blood poured over her thighs. She died shortly thereafter, almost stealing away the life of her daughter, too. 'Wh-why do you ask, Ulster?'

Ulster leaned closer. 'It was my hand that wielded the ax.'

Pinorr's eyes flew wide. 'No!'

Ulster leered. 'It was an easy thing. I thought little on it. During a skirmish aboard the *Broken Fang*, I discovered myself alone with your son. He turned to me, a smile on his blood-splattered face, the thrill of the battle bright in his eyes. But it was that *grin* — proud, boastful. I couldn't stand it. So I buried my ax in his face. But even as he fell, the bastard still smiled.'

The horror must have been clear on Pinorr's face. 'How . . . how could you?'

Ulster leaned nearer. 'Now that you know the truth, do you still wish to *heal* me, Shaman?' he asked with disdain.

A growl of pain exploded from Pinorr. He lunged at Ulster, knocking aside the blade, and tackled the man to the floor. Ulster gasped as he struck the planks. His head struck the wood with a resounding blow. Dazed, his sword fell free of his grip.

Pinorr did not wait. He snatched up the dropped blade, and using both hands, he raised the weapon and plunged it through Ulster's chest. The blade passed cleanly between his ribs and dug deep into the boards beneath. But Pinorr shoved even harder, his arms shaking with exertion. He drove the sword until its hilt was pressed hard into Ulster's chest. Dark blood welled around the hilt. Unable to push any farther, Pinorr fell atop the keelchief like a spent lover. 'How could you?' Pinorr cried in his ear, tears blurring his vision. 'He was like your own brother.'

Ulster choked on blood, but still he struggled to answer. 'That . . . that was why I killed him, Shaman.' The keelchief's gaze grew dull. 'He *was* like my brother – happy and proud. I could not stand to see that light in another's eyes.'

Pinorr shook with sorrow and rage. Sobs wracked his old frame as he rolled off Ulster's chest.

The keelchief's head lolled to face Pinorr. He spoke through bloody lips. 'I couldn't stand to see what was stolen from me.' Ulster's voice faded, but his eyes found Pinorr. 'You should have judged my father's heart as severely as you judged my own. You should have listened for a young boy's cries from behind closed doors.'

Ulster continued to stare at Pinorr. It took a long moment for Pinorr to realize Ulster had died. He reached with trembling fingers and closed the young man's eyes. 'You're right.'

Pinorr pushed slowly to his feet. He stared at the dead

man. His legs were numb under him. 'I will mourn the boy you once were, Ulster, but I still cannot mourn what you became. I cannot mourn that death.' Pinorr turned away, emptier than a hollow bone. He staggered from the room.

Shutting the door of the keelchief's cabin, Pinorr turned and traced his way back up toward the deck. He would blame all the bloodshed discovered here on mutiny. His lie would be believed. None would question a shaman too closely. None would dare look too deeply.

Blindness, he had learned this night, was often self-inflicted, a defense against what one wished not to see. He wiped the blood from his hands as he walked the corridors, rhythmically rubbing his palms on his shirt.

Pushing out the hatch, Pinorr found the decks awash in flame. The aft mast was a torch in the stormy night. As Pinorr looked on, crewmen with axes chopped the burning mast free and toppled it into the sea. Steam hissed and writhed as the fire was extinguished, and the charred section of mast sank under the waves.

A cheer arose from the gathered men and women. The ship had been saved from certain death, the danger cut away and flung into the sea.

Someone finally spotted Pinorr.

Mader Geel crossed to him, her gray hair blackened with ashes. 'I think the worst of the storm has struck. But that was too close,' she said with a tired grin. 'We almost lost the ship to the fire. But what a glorious sight it was! Flames leaping and dancing in the rain.'

Pinorr nodded slowly. 'Yes, evil often wears a handsome mask.'

Sy-wen stood at the rail of the *Dragonsheart*. The high keel conferred with his son, Hunt, on her left. On her right,

Bilatus grasped the rail with one hand in a white-knuckled grip while clutching his robe tight to his neck with the other. Wind bit at them. Rain stung exposed flesh.

'You can smell the smoke on the wind,' Hunt said. He still carried little Sheeshon under one arm. She clung to his neck.

'But at least they've put the fires out,' the high keel noted. He swung to another crewman. 'Order the pilot to swing us about. We should see how the *Dragonspur* fares.'

The crewman nodded and dashed off across the slick deck. Thankfully, the storm's fury seemed to be dying down. Lightning only flickered across the skies along the far horizons, and the roar of thunder had faded to a pale echo of its former fierceness.

Turning her back on the wind, Sy-wen saw that Ragnar'k still lay unmoving on the deck. Thick oiled ropes trussed his frame to mast and stanchions. Her heart ached to see such a majestic beast laid low and bound.

The high keel must have noticed her gaze. 'You mentioned earlier that dragon's blood will reveal how our two people are alike?'

'Not just alike,' Sy-wen mumbled. 'We are the *same*. We are one tribe.'

Bilatus huffed. 'Impossible. Look at you. Webbed toes, webbed fingers.' He shook his head in disbelief.

Sy-wen glanced at the three men. 'I had hoped that I could convince you, that you'd honor your old oaths. But Shaman Pinorr spoke wisely. He knew you'd doubt my words without actual proof.'

Hunt spoke up. 'What do you keep hinting at? What proof?'

Sy-wen chewed her lips. 'I'd best show you.' She crossed toward the slumbering black giant and slipped the dagger from her wrist sheath.

Once at the dragon's side, she ran her free hand along an edge of wing and sent a silent apology to her mount — and to the man inside. Before fear slowed her hand, Sy-wen stabbed the dagger into the beast's flank. She gasped as fire exploded in her own side. But she knew it was only a phantom pain, a whisper of shared senses with the dragon.

By now, the others had circled behind her, still keeping a wary distance. Only the high keel braved a step closer. 'Are you injured?' he asked with true concern, noticing her pained expression.

Sy-wen shook her head and pulled free her dagger. Dragon's blood welled over its blade. She flinched slightly and rubbed at her own side. The burn quickly subsided. Turning, she faced the others and held forth the fouled knife.

'So your dragon bleeds like any man,' Hunt said. 'How is this any proof of your claim?'

'It's not,' she answered. 'Not by itself.'

Confusion shone on all their faces.

Sy-wen felt a coldness settle over her. She suddenly balked at doing what Pinorr asked of her. The knife trembled in her hand, blood dripping from its tip. But she knew she must not fail here. Too much depended on her. She raised her face to Hunt. 'To prove my claim, I will also need Shaman Pinorr's granddaughter.'

The young first mate of the *Dragonsheart* glanced to his father. The high keel nodded. Hunt detached the small girl from around his neck. He crossed to Sy-wen and knelt with the girl in his arms. 'What purpose does this child serve?' he asked.

'Shaman Pinorr sent her as proof of his support.' Sy-wen raised the knife and plunged it into the girl's chest. 'And as *sacrifice*.'

Sheeshon cried out, her tiny arms spasming wide.

Hunt reacted quickly, jumping back and pulling the child free of the dagger. Before Sy-wen could move, she found a sword at her throat. She dropped the dagger; it clattered on the deck. With her role complete, the strength drained from her. Sy-wen dropped to her knees. 'I . . . I had no choice.'

The sword stayed at her throat, borne by the high keel. 'What foulness is this!' he bellowed at her, leaning over her. 'You come seeking a boon from us and think killing an innocent will win our hearts?'

Tears ran down Sy-wen's face as she looked up. 'It was Shaman Pinorr's idea.' Sy-wen watched Hunt carefully drape the child, now unmoving, on the wet deck. Bilatus crouched nervously beside the pale girl.

'You lie!' the high keel snapped. 'Pinorr would not order this. Stories of your people were always cruel! But I had never suspected the depths of your depravity.'

'Father!' Hunt called out. 'The child lives!' The high keel's son knelt over the girl. He had ripped open Sheeshon's shirt. With a scrap of the child's shift, he wiped away the blood from her pale chest. Her skin lay unblemished. 'There is no wound!'

Sy-wen sobbed in relief. 'It's the dragon's blood.'

Bilatus nodded his head. 'Blood from such a beast is valued for its healing properties. But it is forbidden for the Dre'rendi to use such a cursed balm. It is one of our oldest dictates. The sea gods forbid it.'

Hunt rubbed the child's wrists. Sheeshon still lay limp on the deck. 'But if the blood kept her from injury, why doesn't she wake?' he asked, concern in his voice.

All their eyes swung toward Sy-wen.

The high keel lowered his blade from her throat, but the fire in his voice was still present. He would not end her life until he had answers. 'What have you done?'

'I already told you. It was Shaman Pinorr's plan. He knew a blade drenched with dragon's blood would not kill his child. The magick would protect her from a mortal wound. But I don't understand . . .' Sy-wen waved to the limp girl. 'She should be hale, uninjured. I don't know why Sheeshon won't wake.'

'What was supposed to happen?' the high keel demanded.

Deaf to his words, Sy-wen stared at the pale child. 'Pinorr placed too much trust in the ancient tales passed down among our elders – stories of the birth of our people. The first mer'ai, our forefather, was said to have been forged by a savage mixing of Dre'rendi and dragon's blood. And to this day, dragon magick is still necessary to maintain our current forms.' Sy-wen waved her webbed fingers. 'Mer'ai who are banished from the seas eventually lose their unique features and become like ordinary men and women.'

'I don't understand,' Hunt said. 'What are you suggesting?'

Before Sy-wen could answer, a gasp arose from Sheeshon. The girl twitched on the deck. Her arms batted feebly at some unseen menace. Then her eyes fluttered open. Hunt helped her sit up. Sheeshon stared at those gathered around her, then down at her chest. She rubbed at the spot where the knife had struck. 'It tickles here,' she said.

Sy-wen let out a startled gasp of relief. 'Sheeshon! Thank the Sweet Mother.'

The girl's palm wandered to her face. 'It tickles here, too.' Sheeshon ran her fingers along her left eye and down her cheek to her lips. She smiled – a full grin, not lopsided. The side of her face that had been dead and slack had come back to life, also healed by the dragon's blood. Sheeshon must have felt the change. Her hands rose and cupped her cheeks, her eyes full of wonder.

A sudden gust of wind blew across the ship, and quicker than the flutter of a bird's wings, clear inner lids snapped up within Sheeshon's eyes, protecting the child's vision against the sting of rain.

Sy-wen gasped. She was the only one close enough to witness the event.

'What's wrong?' the high keel asked, noticing her startled reaction.

Sy-wen pushed off her knees and crawled closer to the girl. She was too stunned to hope, too shocked to articulate.

Hunt went to reach for his own sword in defense against Sy-wen's approach, obviously fearing she meant the child further harm. But the high keel waved him off.

Reaching the girl's side, Sy-wen tenderly picked up Sheeshon's hand. 'Pinorr was right,' she whispered.

'Right about what?' the high keel asked.

Sy-wen lifted the child's hand and spread her fingers wide. Small webs now traced from finger to finger. 'The blood of the dragon! It has made her mer'ai.' Sy-wen turned to the high keel. 'Here is the proof of our shared heritage. Dragon's magick can still transform Dre'rendi into mer'ai. We are one people!'

The portly shaman's voice filled with awe. 'No wonder the gods forbid us to touch dragon's blood.'

Sy-wen stood and pointed to the girl, who was now playing with the folds between her toes and giggling. 'Can you deny it now? Can you not see we are one people?'

The high keel glanced from the dragon back to the girl. His eyes were bright. 'It . . . it could be some trick,' he said warily, but his voice was unsure.

Sy-wen winced. What more could she do to convince him?

Overhead, the clouds parted, blown apart as the storm rolled away from the fleet. A bright moon shone down, almost as bright as the sun after the storm's gloom. Everyone glanced upward, bathing in the moonlight.

Nearby, Hunt suddenly moaned.

The high keel and Sy-wen turned his way. Hunt still knelt beside Sheeshon, but the tiny girl's fingers now brushed across the young man's cheek. The tattoo of a diving seahawk seemed to glow with her touch. Again Hunt moaned.

Sheeshon mumbled familiar words to Hunt, old blood oaths from the ancient past. 'I have need of you.'

Hunt stood, pulling the child up in his arms. 'I am yours to command,' he answered.

Bilatus stepped back. 'It's the ancient spell. The binding of our two people!'

Hunt began to drift toward the rail.

The high keel went to stop him. 'Hunt, what are you doing?'

The young man's voice was dulled by the magick. 'I must return Sheeshon to her papa. I have been ordered.'

Sy-wen touched the high keel's arm. 'Do not try to stop him. Once bound, he must complete his mission. After Sheeshon is back with the shaman, the spell will break, and your son will be free again.' Sy-wen recalled her own dealings with Kast. 'But in the future, I suggest that Hunt keep his tattoo covered when around the child. Or he will find himself running many errands for her.'

The high keel nodded, hesitant. 'Get a skiff ready for Hunt.'

With the storm dying down, the seas were still humped with swells, but the waves were not as fierce. Sy-wen glanced to starboard and saw that the *Dragonsheart* had already pulled near the fire-ravaged *Dragonspur*. Even from here, in the bright moonlight, Sy-wen spotted the familiar robed figure of Pinorr.

Sy-wen turned back to the high keel. 'Do you believe me now?'

He turned hard eyes on her. 'You leave me little choice.'

Relieved, Sy-wen sighed. 'So will you reconsider your refusal to aid the mer'ai in the battle to come?'

The high keel remained silent, glancing over the seas at the many other ships of the fleet. Moonlight turned the waves to silver around his boat. 'We are one tribe,' he said quietly, amazement thickening his voice. 'How can I refuse my brothers and sisters? That is not the Dre'rendi way.'

He turned to face Sy-wen and placed a hand on her shoulder. His next words were spoken firmly and solemnly. 'We will join you, Sy-wen of the mer'ai. We will honor our old oaths.'

Kast struggled through darkness back to the light. He blinked against the glare of the sun. The taste of the air, the scent on the wind – how long had he been asleep? He somehow sensed that more than a single night had passed.

A yell of warning burst out too loud, too near his ear. He felt a scurry of activity around him.

Wincing against the noise, Kast pushed up on one elbow. Where was he? Blinking away the sun's glare, he found himself naked and draped in wet ropes. He shook free of the slick cords. Overhead, sails billowed in a fresh wind. The smell of salt helped clear his head.

It took a moment for Kast to recall his last memory: the frantic flight through stormy skies and his struggle to control the dragon. He sat up as memories flooded back. The last he remembered was the tumble through the skies and the crash upon the deck of the *Dragonsheart*. But what of Sy-wen?

As if in answer to his heart's fears, a door flew open only a short distance away. Sy-wen stepped forth. She stared at him, a hand at her throat. Her face was deeply lined with worry and fatigue. A breeze caught her hair and blew it into a green sail about her face. Kast found himself choking in relief. Tears welled up in his eyes. She was safe.

Crying out, Sy-wen rushed toward him. 'Thank the Mother, you're all right.' Ignoring his nakedness, she fell into his arms.

'Wh-what happened?'

Two other figures crossed from the open hatch. One was the robed figure of Shaman Pinorr, but beside him hobbled another familiar silver-haired elder. 'Master Edyll?' Kast gasped with shock.

'I'm not sure this walking on hard surfaces is natural,' the elder grumped as he finally reached their side, but he wore a smile of amusement.

Pinorr studied Kast, cocking his head one way, then another. 'It seems you are correct. The blood of another dragon finally healed Ragnar'k and allowed the stunted spell to release.'

Master Edyll nodded. 'But I had not thought it would take so long.'

'Another dragon?' Kast's brow crinkled in confusion. 'I don't understand.'

Sy-wen pulled back, but she kept one hand on his shoulder as if afraid he would vanish like the dragon. 'You and the dragon were injured. You were both lost to us. But a draught of blood from my mother's dragon, Conch, was used to treat Ragnar'k. The injuries healed, but we still weren't able to revive you or break the spell to release you.' Sy-wen's voice cracked. 'I thought you lost forever.' She fell back into his arms, but not before striking him hard in the shoulder. 'Don't ever do that again!'

Kast hugged her tight. 'Gods willing, I've no intention

of ever leaving you again. But just where are we?' He pushed to his feet with Sy-wen's help. Someone tossed a rough blanket over his shoulders, but Kast scarcely bothered to draw it over his nakedness. He was too stunned by the sights he discovered around him.

All about their ship, the seas bloomed with scores of white sails, spread from horizon to horizon. It was the entire Dre'rendi fleet! But the true miracle was what else shared these same waters. Among the many boats, hundreds of dragons plied the waves, like jewels strewn across the sea's blue surface. In the distance, even the humped backs of the giant leviathans rose like living islands from the seas.

'We are only two days out from the Doldrums,' Sy-wen commented softly. 'We should just make the rendezvous with the wit'ch.'

'You did it,' Kast said in hushed tones, still staring at the spectacle before him. 'You brought our two peoples together. All the Dre'rendi. All the mer'ai.'

Sy-wen clung to his shoulder and pulled the blanket around them both. She burrowed tight to him, sharing her warmth. 'Yes, but I'm more relieved to bring this *one* Dre'rendi and this *one* mer'ai back together.'

Kast grinned down at her upturned face. Their smiles melted away as they recognized the passion in each other's eyes. He leaned down to her, his lips brushing hers. 'I have need of you,' he murmured, then kissed her deeply.

Book Four

SARGASSUM

17

Elena knelt in the hay. In the dimness of the ship's hold, the gray mare seemed more ghost than flesh. After six days at sea, the horse was still skittish, shying from everyone. Elena held out a slice of apple. 'C'mere, Mist. That's a good girl,' she urged in soft whispers. The mare refused to step nearer, even for her.

Sinking into the hay, Elena knew why Mist still balked from coming closer. Elena had grown a head taller and fuller of figure. She was not the same girl who had combed and curried the mare since she was a foal. The abrupt change in Elena's appearance and the strangeness of the boat all tweaked the small horse's edginess. The mare panicked whenever Elena neared, refusing even to recognize her scent.

From the neighboring stall, Er'ril's horse, the snow-dappled Steppe stallion, huffed and pawed at his hay. Of hardier stock, the larger horse had adjusted quickly to the roll and lurch of the *Pale Stallion*. And the tall beast knew that any apple refused by Mist would end up in his own feed bucket. So the stallion was more than happy to see Elena fail.

'I have enough for both of you,' Elena called out sadly to the other horse. Even her voice made Mist skitter back a pace. Elena sighed. For the sixth morning in a row, she had failed to coax the mare to her. Though she understood the horse's trepidation, it still upset her. Mist was a member of her family, and to be shunned like this wounded her deeply. The mare had always been there to comfort her when she was in pain.

And now more than ever, Elena needed to be comforted. The loss of Er'ril was still as raw as the day she had awoken aboard the ship, a dull ache in her heart that made the sun less bright and food bland and unappealing. Others tried to help, but no one understood. No words could ease this pain. The others thought Er'ril no more than her guardian, some knight who was more sword than man. They thought she had only lost some weapon, not a man who shared her heart.

Also, the others were all too busy with their own activities to offer any real compassion. Flint was constantly harried with running the ship and directing his sailors, the dark-skinned zo'ol warriors. Meric, though not as busy, was distracted by the appearance of his queen's sunhawk. His eyes were always on the horizon, and when Elena happened to catch his attention, he was stiff and formal with her. Even her brother, Joach, seemed more interested in discussing his staff's magick than in understanding Elena's pain. Only Tol'chuk and Mama Freda offered Elena any real warmth – but neither was family.

If only Aunt My hadn't left on her own quest . . .

Elena could use the woman's practical advice. Aunt My always knew what to say. For the thousandth time, Elena wondered how the others fared: Fardale, Mogweed, Kral. Now with Er'ril gone, too, it felt as if everything was falling apart.

Elena stared sadly at Mist.

The scuff of heel on wood drew Elena's attention around.

Beyond the stall's gate, a short man stood, peering in at her. His eyes glowed in the single lantern hung on the stall's post. Elena felt a flicker of fear, a shiver of tiny hairs. It was one of the zo'ol pirates assigned by their guild's leader to man this boat. The dark-skinned sailor, his chest bare, wore only a set of knee-length breeches.

'Can I help you?' she asked, her voice sharp and curt as she tried to hide her nervousness. Besides the two horses, Elena was alone in the hold.

Without an invitation, he swung the gate open, slipped in, and closed the stall's door behind him. Elena heard the latch click.

Quickly pushing to her feet, Elena brushed hay from her knees. With both her hands renewed with power, one from the sun, one from the moon, there was little she needed to fear from this man. She touched her magick, and it gave her the strength to straighten and face the intruder. 'H-have you come to change the horse's bedding?' Elena frowned at the crack in her voice.

The sailor held out an open palm. Elena backed a step away. Mist huffed at her movement.

Elena stared at the man. The zo'ol sailors understood her language but seldom spoke. He just stood there, arm out. The man had a shaven head, except for a tail of black hair that ran from the crown of his head down his back. Feathers of azure and rose adorned his hair. His eyes, lit by lantern light, shone a deep jade. But his most striking feature was the design of pale scars that crisscrossed his dark forehead. Each of the four black-skinned sailors were marked with a different design, their meaning known only to the zo'ol. This man's symbol appeared to be the edge of the sun peeking above a horizon, or maybe an eye just beginning to open. Elena found herself staring at it, transfixed.

Motion drew her eyes back to his raised arm. In his palm, there now rested a bright red apple. Elena blinked at the sudden appearance. Where had it come from?

The zo'ol, still expressionless, stepped toward Elena.

She moved aside warily, but he passed her without a glance. The sailor approached the nervous mare, a whistling tune flowing from his lips. Mist pawed at the hay, clearly ready to bolt away. The man continued his approach, slightly more cautious but still whistling softly. Mist's ears pricked at the tune, her head cocking slightly as if listening.

Soon the man had reached the mare and offered the apple. Mist sniffed at it, then pulled back her fat lips to nibble at the fruit. Elena could hardly believe the sight. No one had been able to approach the mare. Elena watched as the tension in the horse's withers relaxed. Even Mist's tail, which had been slashing back and forth, settled to a more contented swish.

The small sailor reached and rubbed the ridge between the mare's eyes. It was Mist's favorite spot to be scratched.

The man nodded for Elena to approach. She hesitated — not from fear of the man, but in trepidation at spooking Mist. Still, he persisted, his brow wrinkling with his demand.

Slowly, Elena drifted closer. One of the mare's eyes rolled to watch her approach, but Mist made no motion to bolt. Elena reached the horse's side.

The sailor shifted the apple toward Elena. Mist followed the half-eaten fruit with her nibbling teeth. He placed the apple into Elena's hand, and Mist continued her meal. With his palm now free, the sailor took Elena's other hand in his own and drew it up to replace the hand that scratched and rubbed the mare's brow.

Once Elena had taken over his role completely, he stepped away. Soon the apple, core and all, was gone. Mist sniffed at Elena's gloved fingers, looking for more. Elena glanced to the sailor. He indicated for her to remove her glove.

She did. Mist snuffled her bare palm. Then the mare seemed to tense. Elena braced for the horse to bolt, but instead, Mist pushed her nose firmer into Elena's hand. A soft whinny of joy flowed from the horse. Mist stepped into Elena, rolling her head into her chest, sniffing and rubbing. She was asking for Elena to hug her.

With tears rolling from her amazed eyes, a small laugh escaped Elena's lips. She hugged her mare, arms tight around her neck. Elena buried her face against the horse. Mist had finally recognized her, remembered her.

Crying now, Elena hung on the horse, almost too weak to stand. As her nostrils filled with the scent of horse and hay, she was home again, at least for a brief moment. She rubbed and whispered nonsense to Mist, sometimes laughing, sometimes crying again. In her heart, the losses she had endured recently were still present, but a small bit of healing had begun. The ache could be shared in the warmth of the mare, in the remembrance of family, in the whisper of home.

Elena finally turned to thank the zo'ol sailor.

But the stall was empty. He had gone.

Tol'chuk crouched by the ship's prow as the sun crested toward midday. Salty spray misted over the bow as the *Pale Stallion* rode the waves. Once again he raised his heartstone toward the horizon. In the bright sunlight, the chunk of crystal radiated sharply, but little else. He frowned, baring his fangs, and pushed up with one of his long arms. He slowly turned a full circle, the heartstone outstretched in his other arm. Still the jewel failed to do more than glimmer handsomely in the midday sun.

Sinking back down to the deck, Tol'chuk studied the faceted stone. Ever since the Heart had led the og're to Elena in the burning ship, it had begun to grow quiet – no, not just quiet, almost dead. Tol'chuk still sensed that the elemental power remained behind its facets, like the tremble in rock near an underground river. In the past, the stone had always guided him in some manner, given him some direction.

But now it was muted, dull.

Rolling the stone in his claws, Tol'chuk prayed to his ancestors for guidance. With danger all around him, why had the Heart grown so silent? Tol'chuk shook his head. Fingering open his thigh pouch, he began to burrow the stone inside.

'May I see your jewel please?' a voice said behind him.

Tol'chuk craned his head around to find the healer from Port Rawl standing at his back. The small gray-haired woman leaned heavily on a cane. The cool dampness of the ocean voyage did not seem to agree with Mama Freda's joints. She kept to her cabin mostly, wrapped in warm blankets, and only braved the decks when the weather was bright, like now. Though, in truth, her isolation was not as complete as it seemed. Her pet tamrink, Tikal, could often be found scampering through the rigging, nagging the sailors with its constant mimic. Tol'chuk knew that Mama Freda was listening and watching through the beast's eyes and ears.

'Please, may I just see your stone for a moment?' she repeated.

'It be nothing but a bauble to you,' he said with a trace of irritation. 'Why wish you to see it?'

Mama Freda turned toward Tol'chuk. Her lack of eyes made the bristles on his back quiver. Tol'chuk turned his gaze to her *true* eyes – those of the tamrink. Tikal perched on her shoulder, his fiery cowl of fur framing two rich brown eyes. The pet blinked at him, tail wrapped tightly around the woman's neck.

'Cookie?' it squeaked at him, digging at a large ear.

'Hush, Tikal,' the old woman scolded. 'You've already eaten.' Mama Freda turned her attention back to Tol'chuk. 'I would see your stone. I smell a corruption in it. As a healer, I find it draws me.'

Tol'chuk hesitated, then passed the stone to her. Perhaps the old woman might discover some clue to ridding the stone of the black worm in its heart. Tol'chuk explained the stone's history to her and its purpose in helping guide the spirits of his tribe on to the next world. 'But the stone be fouled by a creature called the Bane, a curse. The worm has trapped the spirits of my people and feeds on them to sustain itself. I go on this journey to find a way to lift the curse, to rid the stone of the Bane. Before rescuing Elena, the spirits in the stone guided me on my path, told me where I must travel ... but ... but now ...' Tol'chuk's voice trailed off.

Mama Freda had listened to his story in silence, turning the stone one way, then another. Tikal bent down from her shoulder to sniff and eye the crystal. 'But what?' she asked, obviously wanting him to continue.

'But now the stone has grown silent. It guides me no longer.'

She nodded sadly and passed the stone back to him. 'It is no wonder.'

Raising his eyes, his features tightened. 'What do you mean?'

She patted his thigh and remained quiet for a moment. 'I can sense traces of life force in the stone, but they are faint. The corruption – this Bane – fills almost the entire stone.'

She turned away and shook her head. 'I'm afraid that . . . these spirits of yours are almost gone.'

'What?' Tol'chuk clenched the stone as his own heart trembled. He suddenly found it difficult to breathe. He raised the stone in disbelief, but in his chest, he felt the truth of her words. In some small corner of his mind, he must have known this himself. It was what kept drawing him atop the decks to check the stone. With the healer's words, Tol'chuk was forced to admit that the pull of the stone had been fading gradually over the past moon, ever since the trials in Shadowbrook. He could no longer deny it.

The Bane was growing stronger.

Tol'chuk stared into the stone. His own father was one of the spirits trapped within the crystal. If the old woman spoke truthfully, Tol'chuk's father, along with the rest of his people's spirits, was now fading, consumed by the worm.

Mama Freda turned back to him, her expression pained, her voice a whisper. 'I had not thought to bring you such dire news.'

Tikal reached out a small paw and touched Tol'chuk's cheek. 'Cookie,' the beast said mournfully. 'Bad cookie.' Tikal pulled back his paw and sucked his thumb, pulling tight to Mama Freda's neck.

Mama Freda lifted an arm to comfort Tol'chuk, but something in his face must have warned her that no solace could ease this wound. 'I'm sorry,' she said and turned away.

Tol'chuk remained on deck, hunched over his stone as the sun shone brightly. If the spirits were fading, who would guide him now? He glanced to the horizons. Was there even a reason to continue this journey? With the Bane near triumphant, was there any purpose?

He stared up into the merciless sun. Tears welled in his eyes. His heart was as hollow as his stone. He silently cursed the trio of ancient og'res, the Triad, who had sent him on this futile mission. Had he not suffered enough already – born a half-breed and cursed with shame of his ancestor, the Oathbreaker? Must he now bear the loss of his people's spirits, too?

Tol'chuk raised the stone between him and the sun. He stared into the dark interior of the stone. Behind the glinting facets, he saw the true source of all his anguish – the slow churning of the black worm.

Growling deep in his belly, Tol'chuk squeezed the stone until its sharp facets cut into his palm. Blood dripped from his claws and down his arm to splatter on the damp deck.

Though no longer guided by the stone's pull, Tol'chuk would not forsake his journey. Even if he should fail to rescue the spirits of his ancestors, he promised himself one thing: Before he died, he would find a way to destroy the Bane!

That he swore on his own blood.

'We should reach the Doldrums by the next morn,' Flint announced. He glanced around the table in the small galley, studying the faces of his companions. Each evening, they all met to plan and discuss the upcoming day. 'I had hoped to hear some word already from Sy-wen and Kast, but we can only hope that they're on their way to the rendezvous point with the ships of the Dre'rendi.'

Joach glanced to his sister on his right, then back at Flint. 'What if the Bloodriders don't come?'

'Then we will continue the journey to A'loa Glen with just the mer'ai.' He leaned both fists on the table. 'We cannot wait. The Blood Diary must be retrieved before the Dark Lord gathers more forces.'

Elena spoke up. 'But only Er'ril knows ... um, *knew* where the book was hidden.'

'Not exactly,' Flint answered. 'All knew the book was hidden in the catacombs beneath the Great Crypt, but the tome is protected in a spell of black ice that cannot be breached without the proper key. It is that *key* that Er'ril has kept an enigma.' Flint's eye settled on the iron fist resting on the table. 'But I can guess Er'ril's secret. He placed much value on retrieving the iron ward. I believe its magick is the key to unlocking the spell that holds the book safe.'

'But you're only guessing,' Meric said from the other end of the table, disdain ringing clear in his voice. 'I say we wait until the queen's armada arrives from Stormhaven. With the elv'in warships—'

'Your queen will be too late,' Flint answered, cutting him off. 'Our best chance for success is a quick assault. We cannot let another moon pass, or the enemy will be firmly entrenched.' Flint drove his fist into the table. 'Whether we gain the support of the Bloodriders or not, we strike now or lose any chance for success.'

Sitting opposite Elena and Joach, the og're grunted his approval. It was the first time Tol'chuk had spoken during the evening's discourse. 'What be your plan, Brother?'

'A simple one. The mer'ai and their dragons will lay siege to the island, distract the eyes of the darkmages, while a small team slips past the island's defenses. I know of a hidden way into the catacombs, a passage known only to my sect. Gods be willing, it should be unguarded.' Flint stared at the others. 'But this night, we must settle who will accompany Elena and me to the island.'

Elena glanced around the table. 'I see no reason we need any others. Flint will guide me, and my magick will protect us. The fewer who come, the better.'

'I'm going,' Joach declared sharply. He turned to face his sister. 'Father told me to watch over you, and I will not let you walk into that nest of vipers without my staff to protect you.'

Elena shook her head. 'It is the darkmage's staff. He may sense when it is near, especially if you call forth black magicks. You will draw the mages to us like lodestone to iron.'

'I can give it my blood. Transform it into the blood stave before we leave. Your wit'ch magick will keep the staff's darkness hidden.'

Flint watched Elena's mind try to fathom other ways around this problem. Flint ended her consternation. 'Joach should come with us. His magick may help us forge a path to the book or cut a swath of escape. We dare not limit our protection.'

'For the same reason, I must also go with Elena,' Meric announced. 'I will not let the last of our king's bloodline end here. My skill with the wind will help keep her safe.'

'As will my strength of arm,' Tol'chuk added.

Elena stood, shaking her head. 'No. Too many will draw attention.'

'To guard you, four is not too large,' Flint said softly. He could read the fear in the young woman – not for her own life but for the others. He recognized the look of hopelessness in her eyes. The death of Er'ril had struck her too deeply. Flint rubbed his eyes. Curse the man for weakening the wit'ch when her strength was most needed. Why had he challenged that foul statue on his own? Sighing, Flint lowered his hands and crossed around the table's corner. He knelt beside Elena. 'We offer our lives not for you, but for Alasea. You have no right to tell us to sit on our swords while others struggle to throw the yoke of the Gul'gotha from our necks. Four is not too large.'

'Neither is five,' a quiet voice said at the table. All eyes swung toward Mama Freda. She sat straighter in her chair.

'My skill with healing may prove of more value than the sharp edge of a sword.'

Flint smiled and reached to pat the woman's wrinkled hand. 'I appreciate your offer, but I've seen you walk the deck with your cane. In this venture, speed will be vital.'

Mama Freda's lips turned hard and thin. 'Do not belittle me, *old* man. Here on this ship, I merely conserve my strength. But among my potions is a draught used by warriors of my home jungles to heighten their reflexes and stamina – an elixir combined from heartroot and hemlock with a pinch of nettlebane. Fear not. Its potency will keep me at your heels on any excursion.'

Frowning at her words, Flint nodded. He turned to Elena. 'A healer *would* be of aid. It could make the difference in saving one of our team.'

Elena waved her arm in submission, but she was clearly not happy. 'Fine. Let her come then.'

Flint settled back to his own seat. 'With that settled, we should all get a good night's sleep. Tomorrow will be a fateful day.'

'And let us pray,' Joach said as he scooted back the chair, 'that Sy-wen and Kast were successful in their search for the Bloodriders.'

Flint watched the others mumble amongst themselves and drift away. Only Elena refused to move. She still sat hunched over the table. Flint studied her in silence.

Finally, Elena raised her face. 'Have we lost already?'

'What do you mean?'

'Prophecies all said that Er'ril would be the one to take the wit'ch to the book – but he is gone. How can we succeed when even the tides of fate work against us now?'

Flint slid over to the empty seat beside her. 'Only blind fools trust prophecies.'

Elena's eyes grew wider.

He smiled. 'I know. Strange words coming from a Brother of the prophetic order of Hi'fai, but true nonetheless. Most prophecies are not chiseled in granite. They're often just the shadows flickering on the walls of caves, vague glimpses into *possible* futures. But the future is like ice. It may appear solid and unchanging, but with the slightest heat, it flows and pours into strange new channels.' He reached and squeezed Elena's hand. 'We are not without choices. It is our *actions* that will forge the future, not the words of some long-dead prophet. Only a fool bows his head to the fates and lets the ax fall – and you, Elena Morin'stal, are no fool.'

'But Er'ril –?'

'I know, child. He was a good friend of mine, too. But even he made his own choices when he decided to investigate the ebon'stone statue. Do not let his mistake take your future away. You are strong enough to forge your own path.'

'I don't feel so strong,' she mumbled.

He tilted her face until she met his gaze. 'There are depths to your heart that you are blind to, Elena, but that others can sense. That is why Er'ril cared deeply for you. You were more to him than just someone to guard.' The shock on her face drew a sad smile from Flint. 'For those who knew how to look, his heart was plain – as is yours, young lady.'

Elena twisted from his grip. 'I don't know what—'

'Do not deny what your heart cries loudly. If you are ever to heal from this loss, you must admit its depth. Only then can you move ahead.' He patted her hand and stood. 'It is late. Think on my words. Now is the time to grieve for all you've lost, grieve honestly. Only then will your heart be truly healed, only then will you be ready to move on. To forge a future, you must be staring ahead, not behind.'

Elena glanced up at him, tears moistening her eyes. 'I will try.'

'I know you will. Like Er'ril, I too sense the depth of strength in your spirit. You will succeed.' With those words, he strode away, leaving Elena to tend her grief.

Elena felt numb, as if her body were not her own. The old Brother's words burned in her mind. What had Er'ril truly meant to her?

In the past, she had refused to acknowledge her feelings. Even when his presence had fired her blood – the touch of his hand, the brush of his breath on her cheek, his crooked smile – Elena had dismissed her reactions as inconsequential, as something childish. How could Elena dare consider herself worthy of a man who had lived for over five centuries?

But Flint had judged her correctly; she could not deny her own heart. In the past, she had labeled her warm feelings toward the plainsman as merely the familial love for a father or a brother. But Er'ril had meant more to her.

Elena confronted her true heart for the first time in the empty room. 'I loved you, Er'ril.' Her voice caught on his name, cracking. By speaking those words aloud, something in Elena broke. Tears flowed down her cheeks, and wracking sobs shook her frame. Elena collapsed upon the table, face cradled in her two gloved hands.

It was as if a dam had burst within her heart. Walled-off emotions flooded her: sorrow for never speaking these words while Er'ril was still alive, shame at her cowardice, rage at Er'ril for leaving her too soon. But mostly a profound sense of loss washed over her. She could now admit that it wasn't just Er'ril who had died aboard the pirate's ship, but the secret dreams of her heart as well.

Finally understanding the nature of the pain that had

strangled her heart, Elena allowed herself to cry – not just for Er'ril, but also for herself. She hugged her arms around her chest, rocking slowly in her seat. Her sobs and tears flowed from her unchecked. She did not try to rein them in. For now, she let herself be weak.

The passage of time became meaningless as grief overwhelmed her. Her fingers found a pocket and pulled forth the length of leather cord. It was the scrap of dyed leather that Er'ril had once used to tie back his lanky hair. She pulled it to her lips. The scent of smoke and fire still clung to it, but under this reminder of his death there still remained a hint of Standish loam and the salt of his sweat. Taking the length of red leather, she slowly braided it into her long tresses. Silently, she said her good-byes.

It was time to release the ghost that had haunted her.

With her heart still bruised but healing, Elena wiped the last of her tears. She had lost any sense of the night's passage. It seemed that dawn must be near, but she was not sure. Slowly she became aware of soft music wafting though the open doorway behind her. It arose from somewhere on the upper deck. Her spirit was drawn to the mournful chords. It spoke to her own loss.

Elena straightened in her seat as the music wrapped around her. She knew the instrument that sang with such a sorrowful voice. It was Nee'lahn's lute, carved from the last of the nyphai's dying trees. Its notes reminded her of the other companions not here – Mycelle, Kral, Mogweed, Fardale. Without even knowing she had moved, Elena was on her feet. She was called toward the music like a moth to flame.

In the strum of strings and echo of wood, Elena heard the whisper of her deceased friend. Nee'lahn had given her own life, like so many others, to bring light back to Alasea, but death was not what the ghost mourned in the whisper of the strings. It sang softly of the wonders of life. It whispered of a cycle of death and rebirth. In the flow of chords, sadness and joy were mixed.

She stepped into the cool of a late summer night. The stars shone brightly, and the sails flapped sluggishly as they caught the occasional stronger breeze. Moonlight bathed the damp decks in silver. Near the prow, Meric sat, leaning against the rail, the lute in hand. He seemed to be staring up at the moon as he played. Near his feet, the young boy Tok sat mesmerized by the elv'in's music.

Under the stars, the power of the strings and wood swelled. Elena was lost in the wonder of its song. Where the reminder of Nee'lahn's death should have heightened Elena's grief, the opposite proved true. Elena's eyelids drifted lower. She let the music soothe her aching heart. Death was not an end, the lute sang, but a beginning. A picture of green life springing forth from seed bloomed in her mind's eye.

The music guided her feet toward the ship's prow. Tok mumbled something as she neared, but his voice could not break the spell. Elena soon found herself at the rail, staring out across the seas. In the distance, ghost trees seemed to sprout from the waves, as if the music had conjured a forest to appear.

Elena smiled at the sight.

Suddenly, under her feet, the decks trembled, and the ship lurched harshly. Elena came close to tumbling over the rail as the boat's course abruptly slowed. She clutched the rail with a gasp.

The lute's enchantment shattered as Meric flew to his feet. He joined Elena at the rail, searching the waters. He clutched the lute by its fragile neck and brandished it like a weapon.

Tok had clambered to the other side of Elena. 'What happened?'

In the distance, the ghostly forest had not disappeared with the lute's music. In the moonlight, it became clear that whatever lay ahead was as real as their own flesh. Elena stared at the tall boles sprouting from the seas. Their fronded tops waved in the silvery light. Thousands of trees filled the horizons. It was as if they were about to sail into some drowned forest.

By now, Tok had climbed atop the lower rail and was bent over the top rail to stare at the waters under the keel. 'Look at this!'

Elena and Meric joined him. The boy pointed below.

'What is that?' Meric asked.

Elena shook her head. To either side of the ship, the waters were thick with a red vegetation. It seemed to choke the dark waters all around them.

Flint suddenly appeared behind them. 'It is sargassum weed.' His voice was not fearful, but oddly bright. 'It grows heavy in this region, trapping many a boat. That's why few come this way. One must know the safe channels through the weeds or be forever lost.'

'So why are we here?' Meric asked.

Glancing over her shoulder, Elena saw Flint staring toward the ghostly forest. He seemed deaf to the elv'in's words. His voice was far away. 'Ahead lies the expanse of the sargassum forest. Only the foolhardy venture there.'

Elena's eyes narrowed. 'Where are we?'

Flint nodded toward the trees. 'The Doldrums.'

As he rested in the dark corridor, Greshym cursed the loss of his old staff for the thousandth time this night. He leaned heavily on the oily length of his new poi'wood staff. The fresh stick was still weak in its power. He had been too busy to bathe the rod in virgin's blood, sanctifying it for the blacker arts. Presently, it could hold only the mildest spells. The original, lost somewhere in the drowned bowels of A'loa Glen, had been honed for three centuries into a dire tool of black magicks, and over time, it had grown to be an extension of himself. Its loss wounded him deeply, as if one of his own limbs had been hacked off.

Scowling at the fates above, the bent-backed mage continued his trek through the crumbling heart of the citadel of A'loa Glen. He kept his route circuitous through its lowest levels. He did not care for prying eyes to know his comings and goings this morning. He had to be cautious, keep his true purpose hidden. But he was well accustomed to this game of masquerade. Just a moon ago, Greshym and Shorkan had disguised themselves in white robes and pretended allegiance to the Brotherhood hidden here. His centuries of subterfuge among those white robes would serve him well this morning among the black. Before the sun fully rose, he had two allies to meet; one who had already been forged to his cause and one who would still need convincing.

With his joints aching and his head pounding, Greshym finally reached the barred double doors that led to the Edifice's row of dank cells. He paused to rest, studying the iron door.

While the Brotherhood had held the island, the cells had been seldom used. Only the occasional drunken cook would be locked away until he sobered. But after the Praetor had wrested control, the dungeon had been reopened in all its bloody glory. Shorkan had collected all the white-robed Brethren and corralled them into the cells. Then he had gone to work on them. The screams had echoed from these shadowy halls for almost an entire moon. Those who couldn't be converted into ill'guard or bent to the Black Heart's will were fed to the demon spawn or spent as fuel for the creation of black spells. It seemed there were never enough hearts for all the spells Shorkan wished to cast.

Sighing, Greshym tapped his staff on the iron door of the dungeon. A small peephole opened. Eyes studied him. Greshym did not bother speaking. He was well known by all the dog soldiers who manned the key stations of the keep. Greshym had made sure of that. He heard the scrape of a key in a lock and the shift of bars. The door swung open.

As he passed through, he waved his hand before the guard's helmeted face. 'Forget all who passed this way. None entered the dungeon this night.'

'None entered . . .' the guard repeated dully. The quick spell of influence would keep the guard forgetful of his movements. It was a crude spell, but Greshym had already primed and worked on the key guards so that a small push was all that was necessary for them to do his bidding.

Greshym continued down the short stair. Let Shorkan busy himself with the bigger schemes. Let him gather dire forces and work black magicks as he prepared for the arrival of the wit'ch. With the Praetor diverted, Greshym devised his own small magicks.

In only four days, the moon would rise full again and the plot to unbind the Blood Diary would commence. Greshym must succeed before that happened. When in the company of Shorkan or that nefarious boy Denal, Greshym continued to voice his eagerness for destroying the book. He wet his lips and plotted along with the others. But in the blackest corners of his heart, he knew he must thwart them. The book must not be destroyed – not until he gained the magick to return his youth.

Anger built up in his chest. Both the boy and the Praetor had been gifted with eternal vigor and vitality. Neither was marked by the passage of centuries, unlike Greshym. Though he could not die like ordinary men, his body continued to rot from his bones. He shunned mirrors to avoid glimpses of his wrinkled and bent form. He was no more than a walking corpse.

Greshym shook his head. Only the Blood Diary could correct this injustice. With the cursed tome in hand and wielding a spell he had learned from ancient scrolls, Greshym knew he could return vitality to his decaying body. But if the book was destroyed first – if it was unbound – all would be lost.

He must not let that happen. If it meant betraying the others, so be it. He would have his youth back.

At last he reached the bottom stair and spotted his first quarry of the night. The slim figure stood nervously under the single lamp in the dungeon's empty guardroom. His brown limp hair and small mustache were familiar, though now his eyes bore a hollowness that had not always been present. The poor golem had been sorely abused of late.

Greshym pushed into the room. 'Rockingham. Did you have any trouble getting here unseen?'

'No.' Rockingham shifted his feet. He kept his arms wrapped around his chest as if his limbs alone could keep the Dark Lord from knowing of the treachery that was plotted here. Greshym knew the man was a dark conduit to the Lord of Blackhall. The golem had once carried foul creatures under his skin but had now been infested with an evil even fouler. In his hollow chest, the man's heart had been replaced with a chunk of ebon'stone blessed with the magic of the Weir. This tiny Weirgate was too small to allow the Dark Lord himself to pass here, but it was large enough for his black spirit to enter the man and peer through Rockingham's cracked ribs.

'Are we alone?' Greshym asked, nodding toward Rockingham's chest.

'He is not with me for the moment.'

'Good,' Greshym said. 'Now tell me what you reported to Shorkan.'

Rockingham's pale face grew whiter. 'You ... you said you'd give me a sample of what you promised.'

'After you tell me what you know,' Greshym said as he leaned in closer. He had bought this one's loyalty with a simple treasure. 'What have you learned?'

'The few sea goblins who did not flee after the death of their queen succeeded in following the wit'ch's boat. It has sailed south of the Archipelago's islands.'

'Do they seek to flee?'

'I don't know. Once they rounded the Blasted Shoals, the boat entered waters that even the drak'il fear entering, seas choked by a forest of floating vegetation.'

'Yes, the Doldrums,' Greshym commented. 'Wise move. It would be hard to trace them through the sargassum forest. But what of the mer'ai and their dragons?'

'No word.'

Greshym scowled. 'If only the wit'ch would attack before the full moon,' he grumbled. 'Any distraction would suit my needs well.' He turned to face Rockingham. 'Anything else?'

'Only one thing ... Something you will want to hear.'

Greshym's eyes narrowed. 'What?'

Rockingham tugged at his mustache nervously but shook his head. 'First what you promised.'

Greshym clenched his fist around his staff. He had needed an ear among those who plotted against the wit'ch.

After he had lost Elena's brother, Shorkan had cut him off from the main flow of information. Rockingham, his old companion, however, now filled that role. At first, Rockingham had balked at sharing what he knew, but every man has a price – and Rockingham's was cheap. Greshym bought information with information, an even exchange. Greshym wanted to keep updated on the whereabouts of the wit'ch, and Rockingham wanted the darkmage to fill in the gaps of his own memory. It seemed lately that Rockingham had been getting disturbing glimpses of a life he could not recall. Like bubbles rising to the surface, strange smells, snatches of conversations, and other bits and pieces of fragmented memories had been rising to the surface. Rockingham wanted Greshym to bring forth his memories in full. He wanted to know who he had once been.

'Please tell me,' he begged.

'I will give you one more piece of your past, but until I have the Blood Diary in hand, you will never know your complete heritage. Serve me well, and I promise you that all will be made clear.'

'Anything . . . Tell me anything.'

Greshym had to choke back a laugh at the man's desperation. 'I will tell you this, Rockingham. It was not without merit that the Dark Lord sent you as emissary to the sea goblins. In ways, you are not so unlike them.'

Rockingham scrunched up his brow. 'What nonsense is that? You give me riddles when I ask for answers.'

Greshym shrugged. 'That is all you will get. Bring me information that will put the Blood Diary in my hands, and I will sit and tell you your life's history in full. Otherwise, bring me scraps and that is all you will get in turn.' Greshym pointed his staff at Rockingham. 'Now tell me what else you've learned.'

Rockingham seemed hesitant, but Greshym stared him down. 'Do you never want to know the mystery of ... *Linora?*' the darkmage teased.

The woman's name had its usual effect. Rockingham jolted with its mere whisper. His eyes filled with agony; his fists clenched in frustration. Greshym waited. He knew the woman's hold on the fool's heart was still as strong as ever. Love truly blinded a man. Even when the physical memories were obscured, the emotion still remained to bind the heart with thorns. Greshym smiled at Rockingham's pain.

The golem's shoulders finally sank, defeated.

'So what else have you learned?' Greshym repeated. 'I won't ask again.'

Rockingham's voice was dull. 'Shorkan has moved the date of the book's unbinding forward by one day.'

'What?' Greshym could not keep the shock from his voice.

Rockingham shrugged. 'He has perused some ancient texts and determined that the stars are in better alignment on the first day of the full moon, rather than the second.'

Greshym's vision dimmed. All his careful plans would have come to naught if this vital piece of information had been kept secret. For a moment, Greshym wondered if Shorkan suspected his betrayal. But Greshym's vision cleared. Impossible. Shorkan had his nose too buried elsewhere to notice the bent-backed mage. No, this slight in not informing Greshym was just another example of the Praetor's lack of interest in the wrinkled old mage.

Greshym would eventually teach the fool how blindness kills.

Turning to Rockingham, Greshym waved him off. With a day less to plan, he did not have time to tarry with the golem. 'Keep your ears and eyes open,' he warned. 'If you have more information to trade, you know how to reach me.'

Rockingham stood another moment, wringing his hands, clearly wanting to beg for more substantial answers. Finally, though, he nodded silently, turned on a heel, and disappeared up the dark stair.

Greshym waited until the iron door above clanged shut, then turned to face the door that led to the prisoners' cells. He still had one more meeting this morning, one more ally to hire. But he did not worry overmuch. As with Rockingham, he knew this man's price.

Crossing the room, he pulled open the thick oaken door. The smell of human waste and dried blood assaulted his nose. He took a moment to choke back the rising bile in his throat. Once ready, he entered the dungeon proper.

As he walked, he passed rows of small doors on the left, so low that one had to crouch to enter. From beyond some of the doors, small moans and sobs issued. None slept in these cells. Terror kept one's eyes pried open. As he clopped by one door, something huge slammed into the wood; an inhuman mewl erupted from the beast. It had smelled his blood. Claws scraped at the wood. It was hard to believe that what lurked behind that door had once been a man. Greshym shook his head. Shorkan had grown in skills.

Greshym stopped before the next door. Here was his goal.

Bending with a slight groan, Greshym moved his staff to the crook of his stumped arm, freeing up his hand. He pointed a finger at the lock and twisted his wrist. The catch snapped open. Greshym smiled. He too had his skills. Shoving the door open with his staff, Greshym crawled into the cell.

'What are you doing here?' a voice inside growled.

Greshym straightened and kicked aside a rat. 'Your brother does not treat you well, Er'ril.'

The plainsman spat at Greshym but could do little else. Naked except for a soiled loincloth, Er'ril was trussed by chains to the far wall. Shorkan could not kill his brother; Er'ril was too vital to the unbinding spell. But neither did he care if his brother suffered until then. Fouled in his own filth, bruised from beatings, and smelling of disease from where the iron cuffs had cut into wrist and ankles, the once-proud plainsman appeared a beaten man.

Shorkan had ordered Er'ril strung up in chains mostly to restrict the man from killing himself. The Praetor could not let that happen – at least not until after the book was unbound.

Greshym leaned his staff against the wall and slipped a dagger from his robe. He himself had no such qualms. Er'ril's death would mean the book was forever safe from Shorkan's spell. Greshym watched as Er'ril eyed the blade, almost hungrily. But Greshym dispelled such hope. 'This is not for you, Er'ril. You are worthless to me dead.'

'You might as well kill me now,' Er'ril said hoarsely. 'I will never help you unbind the book.'

Greshym's eyebrows rose. 'Who said I wanted you to? I have less of an interest in seeing the book destroyed than you do. As a matter of fact, I come to make you a proposal.'

Er'ril's eyes narrowed warily. His lips cracked as he spoke, blood dripping down his chin. 'And what might that be, traitor?'

'I offer you your freedom.' Greshym waved his dagger about the rank cell. 'Unless you have grown fond of your accommodations?'

'Do not toy with me, foul one.'

'It is no idle offer, Er'ril. I want the Blood Diary for

myself, and you are the only one who knows the secret to unlocking the spell that protects the book. It's that simple. Free the book, hand it to me, and I will free you.'

'And why should I trust a traitor?'

'Because I am your only hope. In three nights, Shorkan will unbind the Blood Diary and kill you afterward. That much is certain. So what do you have to risk? Even if I betray you, you are none the worse off. But if I speak the truth, you will have your freedom – though the book will be kept from Elena. You can run back into the arms of your little wit'ch. And who knows? Maybe someday I will tire of the book and gift it to her. I have no love for the Black Heart. Let her take on the Gul'gotha. What do I care?'

Er'ril's brows darkened. Greshym knew the plainsman balked at joining in any such bargain with the enemy, but the man was no fool either. Danger or not, it was a chance to do something. Er'ril had lived as a warrior all his life. How could a swordsman decline an offer to shake free of these chains and at least attempt to fight for his cause? Greshym knew Er'ril's decision even before the plainsman's gaze confirmed it. 'What do you propose?' Er'ril asked, fire returning to his tired eyes.

Greshym smiled. Every man had his price.

Taking his dagger, Greshym sliced a small sliver from his new staff. 'Let me show you.'

18

At dawn, Elena stood with the others gathered along the ship's bow rails. The *Pale Stallion* drifted toward the sargassum forest, its bow parting the red seaweed before it. Elena's nose curled. The vegetation reeked of brine and decaying roots, and the odor grew more pungent as the ship delved deeper into the Doldrums. In the distance, from beyond the tree lines, gulls and nesting terns warned them back from the forest's edge.

Overhead, the sails had been reefed on Flint's orders. He had said the sea current would propel them from here. His words proved true. The pace was slow with the weeds choking their progress, but Flint seemed to know where the vegetation grew less thickly. Positioned around the boat, the zo'ol sailors called orders to one another in their foreign tongue. Manning the wheel at the stern, Flint listened and seemed to understand. He made tiny adjustments in the rudder.

As warning against any mistakes, the hulking ruins of ghost ships dotted the seas. Rotting behemoths, half submerged in the weeds, spread to all horizons. Nearby, a section of a mast poked through the red vegetation, a scrap of stained canvas flapping from its tip as they passed, as if begging for release from this choking death.

'It be a haunted place,' Tol'chuk grumbled.

Meric agreed. 'A long-neglected graveyard.'

About them, the chatter among the zo'ol sailors died down as the line of forest grew. A hush descended over the party. With the sun rising, the trees ahead lost their ghostly haziness. They towered twice the height of the *Stallion*'s masts, but their trunks seemed too thin to support the waving canopy of branching fronds.

'Look!' Joach said, pointing up toward one of the trees. Unlike the inland forests, these growths sprouted leaves the color of sunset, burnt orange and pale rose. A stray breeze fluttered the foliage. Buried among the leaves, delicate flowers were also revealed, so darkly red they appeared almost black. 'Those must be the flowers Flint told us about,' Joach continued. 'The ones his sect harvested for sleep powder.'

Elena nodded and stared as their ship slipped into a narrow channel through the wood. According to Flint, the forest was not exactly composed of trees. Each 'tree' was in reality a single shoot from the mass of red weeds, fronded growths thrust up to better catch the sun's light. But entering the forest now, Elena doubted his words. It was as if they drifted along a river that had only flooded its banks, swallowing the roots of the surrounding trees. The open seas seemed far away, a figment of some terrible dream. The world was now trees and water.

As if to enhance this effect, in the distance, hillocks of red weeds sprouted so densely that they appeared almost like land. Upon some of these matts, other flowering plants had taken seed. One tall hill was covered with what looked like yellow-petaled daisies. Elena even spotted a small furred animal scampering across one of these patches, its bushy tail sticking straight up. It darted up into a tree and vanished as their ship passed.

'It's hard to believe we're in the middle of the ocean,' Joach said.

Mama Freda nodded. 'It reminds me of sections of my own jungle home back in Yrendl. In some regions, the rainfall is so constant and heavy that the jungle has become swamped like this.'

'But is this place safe?' Meric asked grimly. 'We could be easily trapped here. Why did that old man pick this place to meet up with the mer'ai?'

'He must have his reasons,' Elena said.

Flint spoke up suddenly from behind, startling them. Their conversation had drawn him from his wheel. 'Fear not,' he said. 'For those who know the Doldrums, there is no safer place to hide a large force. This maze of channels, trees, and weeds has hundreds of exits and escape routes. But for those who don't know its paths, it can be a deadly trap.'

'And you know this forest well?' Tol'chuk asked.

'Aye, the sect of the Hi'fai, my order, has mapped these lands in detail. Besides the sleep powder, it is a bounty of botanical treasures.' Flint gazed at the surrounding trees. 'But there is another reason I chose this rendezvous spot.'

They waited for elaboration, but Meric grew impatient. 'Why?' he snapped.

Flint waved an arm to encompass the forest. 'These trees may appear like those that grow on land, but it's a deception. Each tree here sprouts from a common root – the sargassum weed. All around you are not individual trees but one single growth. This entire region – the submerged weeds, the entire forest – is all one creature.'

Elena stared out at the wide landscape. 'A creature?'

Flint nodded. 'In its own way, it is as intelligent as you or I. But it has a very foreign mind. It existed here before anyone stepped foot upon the shores of Alasea. It measures its life in centuries, as we measure days. The passing of a man's life is but a blink in its long existence. We are but gnats to this great giant.'

'So why are we here? How does this help us?'

'Long ago, centuries before the Gul'gotha plagued our shores, a Brother of the Green Order, Brother Lassen, made contact with the intelligence here. They conversed. Unfortunately, the forest thinks and speaks as it lives – over winters, instead of breaths. Just their initial greeting took one decade in the Brother's life. Their entire conversation consisted of four sentences and took six decades to complete. The entire time, Brother Lassen had to sit quietly in the heart of the Doldrums. Food was brought to him. He slept between syllables of the giant's speech. The poor Brother aged and died while saying good-bye and passing on his thanks.'

'What did they talk about?' Elena asked. 'It must have been important to cost a man's entire life.'

Flint shook his head sadly. 'No, their conversation consisted of a discussion of the weather. Nothing more.'

Meric scoffed. 'Foolish waste.'

'Perhaps, but the forest here respected the man's death. It seemed to sense the sacrifice the man made to simply acknowledge and pay his respects. Ever since, these lands have been a welcome haven for any of the Brotherhood. It has learned to be more responsive, listening for us. It now protects and cherishes us. There is no safer place.'

'How do you know it will protect us now?'

Flint pointed to beyond the ship's stern. 'It has heard my silent pleas, and even as we speak, it hides our path from those that might hunt us.'

Elena turned. The channel behind the ship had vanished.

Trees and matts of weed blocked their way back to open waters. They were now surrounded by the floating forest, swallowed within its belly.

Elena hugged her arms tight around her chest and gazed out at the landscape of draping trees and hills of weed. She tried to absorb all she had heard. So the forest was all one creature, some strange intelligence who viewed the lives of men as mere flickers of a candle's flame. Elena stared out at the endless spread of trees. It seemed to stretch forever. Elena was lost in the enormity of the beast's size and life span.

She glanced to her brother. Joach shared her same expression.

Flint's revelation had been meant to ease their worries.

It had failed.

Rockingham kept very still. Kneeling on the thick wool carpet in the Praetor's study, he tried to shrink into the background as the trio of darkmages argued. With his head bowed, he concentrated on the whorls of reds and golds in the rug under his knees. His calf muscle cramped, but he ignored it. He knew better than to massage the limb or even to shift to accommodate the cramp. A spasm of pain was nothing compared to drawing the gaze of the Praetor. So he sat frozen and listened as his fate was discussed.

He had brought word this morning from his drak'il spies. The wit'ch's boat had been discovered entering the sargassum forest of the Doldrums region, inhospitable waters even for the sea goblins. The drak'ils had refused to follow.

'We need further information,' the boy mage argued in his childish voice, sibilant and whining. Denal, a sandy-haired youth, lounged in one of the overstuffed chairs, kicking his heels against one of its legs.

'Denal is right,' Greshym agreed, grumbling a bit. 'We know they seek the mer'ai. If they should join—'

'There is only one thing the wit'ch seeks,' Shorkan said, interrupting starkly. His words frosted the air in the small tower chamber. 'She needs the Blood Diary. Let her scurry and gather scraps of supporters. I invite them all to come and dash their bones on our rocks. None can hope to penetrate the forces here. From the carnage, we will collect the Black Heart's prize, dead or alive, and deliver the girl to Blackhall's dungeons.'

Greshym dared to argue. 'Shorkan, as long as I've known you, you've always put too much trust in your power. Has the wit'ch not shown that she and her companions are devious? They've defeated drak'il forces and demon ravers. Only a fool would underestimate her.'

'Watch your tongue, old man.' The room's warmth suddenly chilled. 'Those were minor battles, meant only to hinder her progress.'

Out of the corner of his eye, Rockingham glanced at the combatants. The Praetor, dressed in white robes, towered over Greshym. Small flames of darkfire danced across the pristine whiteness of his robe as he threw back its hood. Rockingham could not mistake the kinship of this fellow with his brother, Er'ril – a rugged face built of hard planes, piercing gray eyes, and hair as black as a moonless night. Before this one's youth and vigor, Greshym appeared like some crippled beggar.

Still, the old mage stood steadfast before the gale of Shorkan's anger. 'But what about her blocking the shipment of the ebon'stone Weirgate?'

'Only luck played a role in her victory there. Who knew Er'ril's iron ward had the magick to activate the gate?'

'But luck or not, she still thwarted you.'

'She did not *thwart* us, only delayed us. We still have plenty of time to establish the Weirgate at Winter's Eyrie. It is only a minor inconvenience.'

Greshym scoffed. 'You describe the fact that she almost stumbled upon the Black Heart's ultimate design as *minor?*'

'They will never suspect – at least not in time.'

The boy Denal added his voice to the fray. 'What of the other Weirgates?'

Shorkan seemed to regain his composure, his back straightening, his spate of darkfire dimming. 'The gates at the Southwall and the Northwall are almost complete. Once the wit'ch is neutralized, either by killing her or unbinding the book, then none will have the strength to combat the Weir.'

'Perhaps,' Greshym argued. 'But do not turn your back on this wit'ch, or you may find her at your throat.'

'So what do you propose?' Shorkan finally relented.

'We attack her before she can gather her strength.'

Shorkan dismissed the idea with a wave of a robed arm. 'For now, she is too well protected. The forest will honor its pledge to our ancient Green Brother, Lassen. The sargassum weed will keep her hidden. We would waste forces hunting her in that watery maze.'

'Maybe not,' Greshym said.

Shorkan glowered at the crippled mage.

Greshym simply continued. 'Perhaps we could send an emissary whom the weed will take better to heart – someone the weed will trust more than the companions of the wit'ch. With the forest as an ally, it would be a simple thing to shred the defenses of our enemy and capture the wit'ch. With the right emissary, we could forge the weed into a tangled trap.' Greshym's gaze flickered toward Rockingham.

Rockingham cringed. He had caught the meaning in

Greshym's milky eyes. He was to be this emissary. A tremble began to build in his shoulders as he continued to kneel. What was the foul darkmage plotting?

Shorkan had the same concern. 'What is your scheme?'

Greshym seemed to enjoy the sudden attention and interest of the other two mages. 'If we sent our dog here out with a stick, a token of our affection for the sargassum, it might listen to our plea for aid.'

'Speak plain. Out with it.'

Greshym bowed his head in feigned obeisance. 'We must learn to use the resources that our ancestors conveniently stored here. Among the dusty relics of the Edifice's libraries and storerooms, there are many unusual items of worth.'

'Like what?' Denal asked, sounding like a child begging for a treat.

'Like the old staff of Brother Lassen,' Greshym answered. The old mage simply crossed his arms, as if this was answer enough.

'So you propose to send this lackey out to the weed bearing Brother Lassen's old staff as herald?'

'The weed will remember. Time moves oddly for the great beast. Though centuries have passed, it is only a handful of days to the sargassum. It will honor the man who comes bearing Brother Lassen's staff. It will do his bidding.'

Shorkan seemed to warm to this idea. He turned his back on the others and pulled up his hood as he contemplated. 'It is worth attempting. But our man here will need more support than a scattering of stray sea goblins. If we attempt this, we must strike vigorously. No more teasing and nipping at the heels of the wit'ch. This time we strike with full force.' Shorkan swung back to the others. 'Fetch Brother Lassen's staff,' he ordered Denal, then turned to Greshym. 'And you prepare your man for his role.'

Greshym nodded as he stepped toward Rockingham. 'And what will you do, Shorkan?'

Black flames again blew forth and coursed in rivulets of darkfire along the Praetor's white robe. 'I will loosen a legion of skal'tum from the island's defenses to go with the herald. We strike at nightfall.'

Though Greshym's lips spread into a wicked smile at these words, Rockingham quaked. He suddenly found it hard to breathe. He feared the winged servants of the Dark Lord with their poisoned claws and shredding teeth. To be accompanied by a hundred of such demons was a terror beyond reckoning.

Greshym reached Rockingham's side and nudged him with his staff. 'Come. We will retire to my room.'

Rockingham rose on numb legs and stumbled after Greshym.

The Praetor's room topped the westernmost tower of the Edifice. It was a long trek down. Once free of the chamber and upon the tower stair, Rockingham found he could breathe again. Denal, on his young legs, had long since disappeared into the descending gloom, leaving the crippled mage to struggle his way down on his own. Alone with Greshym, Rockingham finally felt free enough to speak. 'Wh-what is your real plan? I smell a plot behind the one you speak aloud.'

'Do not concern yourself with my plans,' Greshym wheezed. 'Obey me in this matter, and what you wish will be granted. You will learn your true past, Rockingham.'

'And there is nothing you are willing to tell me now?'

Greshym paused at a landing. He leaned heavily on his staff, exhausted already by the steep descent of the winding stair. 'I will grant you a boon. I will give you a question to ponder, a clue to your prior life.'

Rockingham knew the old mage wanted him to beg. He did not care. He was long past worrying about such minor concerns as dignity. There was only one drive that kept him from flinging himself from a tower, and that was to discover the mystery of his past. 'Please tell me what you know. I beg this of you.'

Greshym smiled. After dealing with the haughty Praetor, it obviously soothed the old mage's wounded pride to have Rockingham bow and scrape before him now. 'I will grant you a farewell gift then. A riddle to ponder on your journey to the Doldrums. There was a reason we dragged you from your shallow grave up in the mountains after the wit'ch defeated you the first time, a purpose in reinvigorating your corpse and making you our spy along the coast. But why? Why did we do this? What makes you so special? The answer is a clue to your past life.'

Rockingham had to restrain himself from throttling the man. What clue was this? How was he ever to answer this dark riddle?

Amusement shone in Greshym's eyes. 'The sea is where you will find the answer, Rockingham. The sea is your clue.'

'Wh-what do you mean?'

Greshym turned on a heel and continued down the steep stairs. 'Come. Half the day is already gone. By sunset, you must be off to set a trap for the wit'ch.' Greshym glanced back over his shoulders to where Rockingham still stood on the landing. 'And who knows what else may fall into our watery snare? Often the oddest things can be dredged from the sea.'

With rage building in his chest, Rockingham followed, fingering the closed scar on his sternum. He sensed the corrupt shadow that lurked at the edges of his awareness. He let his fingers drop. No matter what horrible deeds had haunted his past, this punishment was still too steep a price. No man should have to suffer this fate.

On leaden feet, Rockingham traversed the stairs and made a promise to himself. Before he left this world, he would know his true past, know why he had been cursed with such a burden, and have his revenge on those who had yoked him to such a fate.

This he swore.

By midday, Joach was alone on the deck, except for the strange black-skinned sailors who kept the *Pale Stallion* languidly gliding through the endless forest of red-fronded trees. His other companions had all retreated below to escape the sun's glare or to pursue individual goals.

Left alone, Joach had nothing but his own thoughts to occupy his time. He sat cross-legged in the shadow of the mast. His gloved hands kept rolling the dark staff across his knees nervously. He stared out at the passing forest's edge. After learning that the sargassum weed was intelligent, Joach could not escape the sensation that the forest was staring back at him. Joach wet his lips. It was as if a thousand eyes examined him: every hair, every patch of skin. The sensation worsened the deeper into the forest they sailed. Was this the true reason the others had fled below? Had they sensed the immense presence judging them?

Something touched Joach's shoulder. He gasped and rolled away, his staff coming to his grip. He found himself staring up into the face of one of the zo'ol sailors. This one was marked with a pale scar of a rising sun on his dark forehead. The fellow showed no sign of noticing the staff that Joach still held threateningly. Instead, he simply stared into Joach's eyes.

Feeling foolish, Joach lowered the length of wood. 'I'm sorry. You startled me.'

The fellow nodded and waved for Joach to follow him to the starboard rail.

Not understanding but afraid to insult the fellow further, Joach followed his bidding. 'What is it?' Joach whispered. With the sailor so silent all the time, Joach felt as if his own speech was loud and crass.

The dark-skinned man turned back to Joach. 'Eyes watch us,' he said, struggling with their language.

Joach's skin crawled with these words. So the sailors sensed the forest's presence, too. 'It's the trees,' Joach said.

The small man nodded. 'Many eyes ... but one heart.' He turned back to study the passing forest. 'It watches us as we watch it.'

'Brother Flint says it means us no harm. It barely knows we're here.'

The zo'ol made a noncommittal grunt. 'It knows,' he mumbled.

A long stretch of silence followed, each lost in his own thoughts as the forest grew more dense around them. The leafy limbs now spread high enough to filter out most of the sunlight, an arched bower overhead. It was as if they floated down some shadowy tunnel.

Joach glanced sidelong at his companion. He realized that, during the many days at sea, he had never learned any of the black-skinned sailors' names. They usually ate and lounged together, rarely socializing with the others.

The man turned to him. 'Names have power,' the zo'ol said plainly.

Joach could not hide his shock. It was as if the man had read his thoughts.

'No,' the man said, staring directly at Joach. The sailor

448

traced the pale scar upon his dark forehead with a single finger. 'I am a tribal wizen. I see only what is written on a man's heart.' The small sailor then reached and placed his palm upon Joach's chest. 'I read what is written here, not what is shadowed by thoughts.'

Joach's face scrunched up as the sailor removed his hand. 'You mean emotions. You can sense another's feelings.'

The man shrugged and moved his hand toward Joach's face. He traced a symbol on the boy's forehead, the same as marked the sailor's brow. 'You are wizen, too. I sense your hidden eye.'

Leaning away from his touch, Joach rubbed his forehead. He could still feel the trace of the man's finger. Joach realized the scarred symbol was not a rising sun, but an awakening eye.

The sailor continued to stare at him, waiting for an acknowledgment.

Joach found he could not deny the man's words. He knew the sailor would sense any falsehood. 'Yes. I have a talent . . . like you. I can read the truth of dreams, see paths of the future.'

The sailor bowed his head solemnly and remained silent for several breaths. Joach saw the man's lips move, as if in some silent prayer. Once done, he raised his face and lifted his arms openly. 'Fellow wizen may share names in brotherhood. I would share my name with you.'

Joach bowed his own head. 'It would be an honor.'

'Not an honor . . .' the man intoned. 'A responsibility. To take a name is to accept a burden.' The man slipped a hand into a pocket and removed a small object. 'I offer a gift for the weight of my name.'

The man held out his hand. Cradled in his palm was a rare black pearl the size of a robin's egg. Joach hesitated to

449

accept such a precious offering, but the sailor shoved his hand brusquely toward the boy. Joach sensed that it would be an insult to refuse.

Taking the pearl, Joach closed his fist around it. 'I accept your offering and your name.'

The man bowed. 'I am called Xin.'

As the sailor spoke his name, the pearl seemed to grow warm in Joach's fist, but it may have been just his own nervousness. He sensed that to this black-skinned sailor, a name was more precious than all the ocean's treasures.

Xin straightened from his bow and looked expectantly toward Joach.

Blinking, Joach realized he would need a gift to offer this sailor, too. He patted his pockets. Empty. He glanced at the staff. No, he was blood bonded to the length of wood. He could not part with that. Then he remembered. Pocketing the pearl, Joach reached to his throat and removed the dragon-tooth pendant that hung from his neck. It had been a parting gift from Sy-wen before she left to search for the Bloodriders with Kast. Joach did not think she would mind this exchange. It was done with honor.

Joach held out the dragon's tooth. 'A gift for the weight of my name.'

Xin nodded and accepted the offering.

Joach bowed, as the sailor had done. 'I am called Joach, son of Morin'stal.'

Xin placed the cord around his own neck, touching the dragon's tooth to his lips for a moment. The white tooth shone starkly against the black hollow of the man's neck. It seemed to belong there.

'We are brothers now,' Xin said. 'We bear each other's names in our hearts. Names hold power. When either heart needs the other, they must come.'

Joach reached and clasped the sailor's hand, understanding that a commitment was being forged here. 'We are brothers.'

A commotion suddenly erupted near the bow of the ship. Breaking their handshake, both turned to see one of the zo'ol sailors frantically point past the ship's bow. He chattered in the tribal tongue of the zo'ol.

Joach rushed forward with Xin.

Once at the bow rail, Joach saw the reason for the outburst. Ahead, the tree-lined channel ended in a huge expanse of open water. At first Joach had thought the ship had traversed the entire weed and that the ocean itself lay ahead. But he quickly realized his mistake. These waters were too still. Not a wave disturbed the glassy surface. As they floated closer, Joach spotted more forest through the mists on the far side of these calm waters.

It was not the ocean. It was a lake.

As Joach stared, the *Pale Stallion* drifted into the wide blue waters. Forest lay all around them, encircling their ship. With the channel closing behind them, soon there was no break in the continuous spread of weed, no path out from this weed-choked lake.

Joach sensed that they had just entered the sargassum's heart.

Beside him, Xin motioned for his tribesman to go belowdecks and fetch the others.

Joach stared up at the open skies. After almost the entire day hidden by the trees, the full sun seemed too bright. Joach suddenly felt exposed. A knot of edginess formed in his chest.

'Something comes,' Xin said behind him.

Glancing to the small sailor, Joach saw that Xin stared up at the skies, too. Joach followed his line of sight. At first he saw nothing but thin, scudding clouds high overhead.

Then the sun's glare seemed to wane, and he spotted the small dark speck against a white cloud.

Joach's staff responded. Small flares of darkfire trickled along its length. But Xin touched his shoulder, calming him. 'I sense no threat . . . only . . . only . . .' Xin shook his head. 'It is too far away.'

By now, others began to gather on deck. Flint crossed to them, Elena at his side. Joach pointed to the slowly circling beast up in the sky. He met Elena's glance and saw the matching worried look in his sister's gaze.

No one spoke.

Flint raised a spyglass to his eye and studied the interloper. 'Thank the Sweet Mother,' he said, relieved. 'It's the dragon.' Flint turned to one of the other zo'ol. 'Light the signal fire. Let them know it's us!'

Elena clutched Flint's shirtsleeve. 'Is it truly Ragnar'k?'

Flint smiled. 'And Sy-wen. They made it.'

Though relieved himself, Joach could not shake off the sense of unease. As a signal fire was lit among cheers from the others, Joach remained at the bowsprit. He stared at the circle of forest. Xin remained at his side.

Joach glanced to the zo'ol wizen. 'You sense it, too.'

Xin nodded. 'Many eyes still stare at us.'

Overhead, a roar cracked across the sunny skies. Ragnar'k had spotted their signal fire. Joach shuddered. It sounded like an approaching storm.

'Look!' It was Elena's excited voice.

Joach drew his eyes from the forest to stare at the waters around the ship. Bubbles rose all around, disturbing the waters' placid surface. It was as if the lake had begun to boil. Joach clutched his staff tighter. Soon hundreds of scaled heads surged forth from the salty waters. Dragons of every jeweled shade rose from hiding in response to the roar from

Ragnar'k. The entire lake filled with their twining necks and humped backs. Atop the dragons, riders waved to the boat in a salute of greeting.

Overhead, Ragnar'k swooped over the boat's masts. Another roar of greeting flowed from his black throat. The dragon slowly tilted on a wing above the gathered army; sunlight sparked off his pearlescent black scales as he turned. It was a wondrous sight. But just as a handsome face can suddenly reveal a malicious soul, Joach caught a glimpse of the horror hidden behind the jubilation.

Joach froze at the rail, his heart clenched in a knot. Sensing the boy's distress, Xin touched his arm, but Joach could not move. His sense of foreboding trapped him.

'I can read the fear in your heart,' Xin said.

Joach found no words to describe the claw of dread that pierced his throat. For the briefest moment, as Ragnar'k had banked over the mer'ai army, a phantom scene had appeared before Joach's eyes, overlaid atop the one before him now. He had seen the lake turn bloody, dragons writhing in death, the skies full of demons, the waters frothing with slaughter. But in a blink, the scene had vanished, leaving Joach frozen and bewildered.

He was no longer sure of what was real and what was imagined. Had the appearance of Ragnar'k somehow ignited his weaving talent? Had this horrible sight been a glimpse of the future? Ragnar'k, once a font of elemental magick as the dragon slumbered under A'loa Glen, was still potent with magicks. Even now, in the wake of the dragon's passage, Joach's blood tingled with flared energies.

But magick or not, Joach also remembered his false dream of battling Er'ril atop a tower in A'loa Glen. With that clear mistake, he had no confidence in his prophetic abilities.

Joach touched his forehead, confused.

Xin whispered at him. 'Share, Brother. Spread the fear to loosen its hold.'

The small man's calming words finally broke through to him. His voice trembled as he spoke. 'I . . . I saw a massacre. I think we were betrayed.'

Xin studied Joach for a moment, his head slightly cocked. Then he reached to Joach and again traced the awakening eye upon his forehead. 'You are wizen.'

The steadfast gaze as Xin traced the mark on Joach's brow helped clear the muddle in his mind, and Joach suddenly sensed the truth of his vision. He turned toward the others gathered around the rails. 'Flint was wrong,' Joach said, his voice growing as firm as his resolve. 'The sargassum weed is a trap.'

Voices argued across the crowded galley table. Elena listened, one hand resting in her brother's as they sat beside each other.

'The weed would not betray one of the Brotherhood,' Flint insisted.

A tall stately woman frowned from across the table. She encompassed both Flint and Joach in her displeasure. Her skin was the color of ivory, while her hair, hanging straight and long, shone like a cascade of sunlight in the glow of the chamber's torches. Elena recognized the similarity of features between this woman and Sy-wen, who was seated nearby with Kast. There was no question that this was their friend's mother. 'I entrusted half of the mer'ai forces to join you here in this sea of weeds. You promised it to be a safe haven. Now word comes of a trap.'

'Not word,' Flint insisted. 'A vision. Even if the boy's sight was truly prophetic, a weaving is only a *possible* view

454

of a future, not a certain one. The future is fraught with many paths.'

Elena heard the exasperation in the old seaman's voice. The brief moment of jubilation at the arrival of the mer'ai and their dragons had quickly ended when Joach had rushed from the foredeck to warn Brother Flint of some unknown menace in the forest. Joach had described his vision of the attack upon their forces here. With such threatening news, Flint had quickly called an assembly of leaders to discuss their options.

As a representative of the Council of Elders, Sy-wen's mother had been sent with the expeditionary force into the sargassum forest. She would speak with the voice of the mer'ai. Kast, on the other hand, had been given the aegis to speak for the Bloodriders by their leader, the high keel. Since the Dre'rendi fleet was too large and cumbersome to traverse the weed, the Bloodriders had anchored on the southern fringes of the Doldrums to await the others. So far, Kast had added no word to this argument. He had just sat silently, stone faced, as the others argued.

Everyone seemed split on what to do. Flint had suggested they wait until he could at least study Joach's vision to judge its veracity. Meric, though, had insisted that Elena was too vital, that they should leave the sargassum now. Sy-wen's mother had frowned even at the elv'in's plan. She spoke of not only leaving the sargassum, but of abandoning their planned assault on A'loa Glen entirely. It was as if all their careful plans were being shredded before Elena's eyes.

Glancing down the row of worried and angry faces, Elena knew that the fate of Alasea rested on what was decided in this room. Without a united army at her back, she would never retrieve the book from the clutches of the Dark Lord.

And if the Blood Diary was not retrieved, Alasea had no hope.

Elena knew she must somehow find a way to unite this group.

Kast finally spoke, clearing his throat loudly enough to draw the others' attentions. Since he had yet to speak, they all listened raptly, hoping the Bloodrider would add his support to one of their individual sides. Kast leaned forward. 'Are you all blind? We must not hide!' He turned to stare over Sy-wen's head toward her mother. 'Have we not fled for generations from the Black Heart of the Gul'gotha? Are you not tired of tucking tail and running? If we ever mean to shake these foul shackles, we will have to fight sometime. Yes, men will die. Dragons will perish. Did any of you come here expecting otherwise?'

Kast pointed to Joach. 'The boy has brought us a word of warning. I repeat: *warning*.' Kast glowered at Flint. 'I care not if his vision tests true. He has warned us of an attack. Instead of testing him, we should prepare. An ambush only works if the victim is blind to it. Forewarned, as we are now, we can pull the fangs from this beast, turn their ambush back upon themselves. Why flee?'

Elena's eyes grew wide with the Bloodrider's passion. She found herself on her feet. Here was the ally she needed. Kast had forged an opening, and she must break through it. She slipped the gloves from her two hands. 'Kast is right,' she said before anyone else could speak. She felt all their eyes upon her. 'If we flee, we run blind. Here, at least, we know what comes.'

'But what if Joach is wrong?' Flint said.

Kast came to his feet, adding his support physically to Elena. 'So? Then we move on. It costs us nothing to prepare.'

Flint nodded, clearly considering their case.

Elena persisted. She could not let the momentum slow. 'There is another view that no one has voiced,' she said. She glanced specifically at the cold countenance of Sy-wen's mother. From the woman's expression, the mer'ai elder had been little swayed by Kast's words. Elena pointed toward Joach's staff. 'My brother is already touched by black magicks. What if his vision itself is a trap?'

'What do you mean?' the elder said with disdain.

'What if the vision was sent by the enemy, meant to trick us into fleeing the safety of the sargassum? Maybe they know we're hiding here and hope to flush us out by sending visions of death if we stay. They hope to send us fleeing into their true snare.'

Joach stood, meaning to interrupt. Elena knew her brother meant to argue against her words, to insist his vision came from within himself. But that would just weaken her arguments. She glanced sharply at him and he held his tongue, adding his quiet support.

Elena went on. 'Joach's vision offers no clear path. Death can be awaiting us just as surely outside the forest as within. Kast offers us the wisest path: Proceed as if an attack is coming. Catch the enemy in its own snare.'

Flint stood. 'Elena makes a good point. With danger possible all around us, we might as well make a stand here as any other place.'

Though her countenance had paled, Sy-wen's mother remained unconvinced. 'There is *one* safer place,' she said. 'Under the waves. In the endless expanses of the Deep, the Gul'gotha will have a hard time finding the mer'ai.'

Sy-wen, red faced, pushed to her feet. 'Mother! Do you propose to flee once again? Do you expect these good people to lay down their lives so that we might once again run and hide? Are we fated forever to repeat our craven history?'

Sy-wen's shoulders shook. She grabbed Kast's hand in her own. 'I will not! Flee if you must, but I am staying!'

A flush rose in the elder's cheeks, angry or embarrassed.

'We will stay, too.' Elena glanced to where Meric and Tol'chuk were now standing.

The healer from Port Rawl slowly pushed to her feet. 'If you're all staying, I guess Tikal and I aren't goin' anywhere.'

This left only Sy-wen's mother still seated. She seemed little impressed by the assembled group standing around the table staring down at her. Elena sensed that the pressure here would likely just stiffen the stubborn back of this woman. Waving her hand, Elena indicated for everyone to sit. Chairs shuffled as she was obeyed.

Only Elena remained standing, staring at her opponent. She did not want to lose the support of the mer'ai during the coming assault. She spoke quietly, the fire gone from her voice. 'I've lost parents, uncles, aunts, friends. So I have the right to ask this of you – of all the mer'ai. Join us now. Heed my brother's vision and make it false. The future is not set in granite. After over five centuries, one thin hope for driving the Gul'gotha from these lands and seas now exists. I beg that you don't flinch from making the hard choices this day. The fate of freedom rests on the back of your dragons. Please do not turn away.'

The woman stared at Elena silently, lips pursed tightly. Slowly her face relaxed. 'For someone so young, you speak boldly, with perhaps too much passion. Over the years, I've learned passion leads to mistakes.' Her eyes seemed to turn inward. 'I've paid dearly for those mistakes and have learned from them. I now do not make decisions in haste.'

'It is not haste that—'

The woman silenced her with a single raised finger. 'I have not finished. Besides passion, you also argue well. Dare

I say that you would even do well seated on the Council of Elders?' She bowed her head slightly in Elena's direction. 'The mer'ai will stay. We will help set this trap. It is time the dragons rose from the seas and were heard again.'

Elena's knees weakened. 'Thank you,' she muttered. Elena found everyone's eyes upon her. She knew words were expected from her. Flint had told her yesterday that those assembled here gathered not for her, but for Alasea. Yet as she stared into the others' eyes, Elena knew Flint was mistaken. As much as she might object, she represented Alasea: *They were here for her.*

Still standing, she spoke as if to herself. 'My uncle once told me stories of Alasea's past: stories of cities whose magick-wrought towers scraped the clouds, tales of gilded streets and lands of plenty where creatures from every land gathered in peace. As I listened, I thought such tales were just myth, mere childish fancies. How could such beauty and grace have ever existed in this world?'

Elena lowered her hand slightly to stare at those gathered, tears in her eyes. 'I see that grace here now – and know such a world is truly possible.'

Before anyone could respond, the door to the galley burst open, startling them all. The young boy Tok rushed inside. He led one of the mer'ai, bare chested and still wet from the sea. Tok waved to the man. 'I told him you was discussing plans, but he says he has news you must hear.'

The mer'ai warrior gasped words between panting breaths. 'Something . . . in the water . . . It . . . it . . . !'

The elder woman's voice snapped at him. 'Bridlyn! Speak clearly.'

The man gulped for a moment, then swallowed hard. 'The channel we came through. It's closed. There's no way back.'

'What do you mean?' Flint asked.

Sy-wen answered. 'While Ragnar'k and I flew over the forest, the other dragons swam under the floating weed. They came up here through a hidden passage below the lake.'

Bridlyn nodded. 'We had sentries posted near the channel leading out from here. Just at dusk, the passage wove closed, weeds choking shut.'

Flint raised a hand, a scowl on his face. 'Calm yourself! The weed did the same to our channel here. It's only hiding our paths.'

Bridlyn looked at Flint with horror. 'It drowned both our sentries! Even their dragons were choked in weeds. Strangled!'

19

In the moonlight, Rockingham stood atop a hump of red weeds. His boots were soaked down to his cold toes. The bottom fringes of his green robe hung heavy with saltwater from his lone venturing into the edges of this drowned forest. With one hand, Rockingham drew the robe tighter around his neck. Greshym had insisted he wear the heavy garment – it was the raiment of the Brotherhood's old sect that communed with the green life. In Rockingham's other hand, he bore a long white staff whose end was topped with a carved cluster of wooden leaves. It was Brother Lassen's ancient oaken stave.

Rockingham continued deeper into the strange wood, the footing treacherous in the bobbing matts and hills of weed.

Earlier that day, he had been sent by swift ship to the Doldrums and unceremoniously dumped into this forest just before sunset. Once here, Rockingham had knelt at the forest's edge and performed the rites Greshym had taught him. He had begged the weed to hear him and to hold the wit'ch's group in its grip. Though Rockingham had not heard any acknowledgment from the sargassum, he had felt it. A weight, not unlike a wind, had rolled over him and hovered over the branch of oaken wood in his hand. Then the weight had vanished. Rockingham somehow knew the intelligence here had understood his plea.

His only role now was to act the part of the Green Brother, to wander this wet land until the legion of skal'tum arrived from A'loa Glen. Greshym had told him that he would have to traverse Brother Lassen's old steps and venture into the forest alone, bereft of any black magick. Greshym had warned that the use of the arcane arts risked overshadowing the faint traces of Lassen's spirit in the wood. If they were to maintain their ruse, they dared not touch black magick – at least not until the weed was won to their cause.

Afterward, once the weed had trapped the wit'ch, a quick strike should destroy the forces gathered here before the slowly dreaming forest could even realize it had been betrayed.

Rockingham peeked at the stars shining through the mesh of branches overhead, searching for any sign of the skal'tum. The legion should have taken wing just at sunset. It would not be long until the skies filled with their pale, scabrous wings.

Casting his eyes back to the forest's floor, Rockingham continued deeper into the wood, thankful for only one thing. Through the fabric of his robe, he rubbed the long scar on his chest. As long as he maintained this foolish masquerade, the Dark Lord was forced to vacate him, leaving him in peace. Yet Rockingham knew such a reprieve would be short-lived. Once the ruse was shed, Rockingham's chest would again swell with dark energies and burst open with the Black Heart's foul presence. He would again be swallowed in the immensity of that one's evil.

Tears, unbidden and surprising, rose in Rockingham's eyes. For the moment, he was somewhat his own man. Using the boles of the trees and his staff as support, Rockingham worked his way deeper into the forest. A part of him wanted nothing more than to disappear forever into this quiet and wet place. He would be glad to drown in these brackish waters. But he knew death was no escape. He had died twice already – once by his own hand and once while battling the wit'ch. And each time, death had failed him. He tried to grasp the reason for his first death. He recalled a tumble from a high cliff into a surging surf. He could not recall anything before that, no matter how hard he struggled to remember.

'Why?' he called out to the silent forest. 'Why can I never rest?'

No answer was offered. Sullenly, Rockingham climbed a larger hillock of tangled weed. As he reached the summit, a thrill suddenly trembled down the length of the wooden staff. Rockingham almost dropped the stave in fright, but he recognized where he stood. Before him, a small granite pillar topped this rise. Here was where Brother Lassen had sat for decades communicating with the great forest. Here was where Lassen had also died.

It was also where Rockingham was supposed to await the skal'tum.

Shivering, he strove to collect himself. He stared at the unadorned stone pillar, a monument to the ancient Brother. Rockingham knew some words were needed to acknowledge the site and the man's deed. He grumbled as he stood over the man's grave. 'Lucky bastard.'

With this utterance, the staff again trembled in his grip. Rockingham jolted. Against his will, his arm rose, reaching the staff toward the stone. As the carved leaves touched the plain granite, an explosion flung Rockingham backward. Catching a handful of weeds, Rockingham managed to keep himself from tumbling down the steep hill. Rolling up on his knees, Rockingham saw the staff hovering by the pillar. A hazy white cloud seemed to seep out from the stone and envelop the length of oak.

As Rockingham watched, the cloud swirled and shrank in on itself, coalescing tighter and tighter, until the mists seemed to gain substance. As it did so, a shimmering glow grew even brighter, and a figure was formed from cloud and light. It was a robed man. He held the oaken staff in his right hand. The mists swirled at the edges, but Rockingham could not mistake the face glowing from under the hood. He had seen the paintings when Greshym had instructed him in this duty.

It was Brother Lassen.

The apparition spoke, his voice echoing as if from far away. 'Who calls me?'

Rockingham sat frozen, unable to form words.

The ghostly eyes found his. It pointed the staff at Rockingham. 'Why do you disturb me?'

'I . . . I did not mean to.' Rockingham raised his arms in supplication. 'Forgive me, Brother Lassen. I did not know your spirit resided here.'

The coldness in the shade's eyes grew focused. 'I am no longer just Brother Lassen. You also speak to the forest. I have been communing with this wood for so long that the line between the two of us is blurred. I am the forest, and the forest is me. We are now one. The forest allows me to see time for what it is – an endless sea. I give the forest the ability see the beauty in tiny movements of time, to appreciate the flight of a bird across the sky, to value the span of a single day, to see life through the eyes of a man. Each is a gift to the other – to see the long and short in life.'

'I . . . I am sorry. I didn't mean to disturb either of you.'

'You are not to blame.' The shade lifted the green staff and examined its length. 'I can sense you in the wood. Your pain has drawn me from my slumber in the stone. There is a corruption in you that cannot pass my grave unchallenged.'

Cringing back, Rockingham feared the ruse of the darkmages was about to be exposed by this Brother of the wood. He dreaded the wrath of this strange forest and even stranger ghost.

But the shade continued speaking calmly. 'Do not fear. Though I sense the corruption in you, I also sense that your spirit rails against the evil inside. This is good. But in truth, it is no matter to me.' The shade's glowing eyes swung toward Rockingham. 'It is not revenge that drew me from my grave, nor wages of war. Neither the wood nor myself dwell any longer on the wiles of men's hearts. Here time is endless. Around us, cities rise, and kingdoms fall. It is of no matter. It is just another cycle of life. Instead, I come to you because your kindred nature calls to me.'

'I . . . I don't understand.'

'That is because you are blind. Though you do not know it, we are both the same – spirits entombed in stone.'

'Wh–what?'

'When I shed my body, allowing its substance to rot and nourish the roots of the sargassum, my spirit remained here to commune with the great forest. As the grave marker was erected, I bound myself freely to the stone.' He indicated the granite pillar. 'Stone does not rot. It is not a part of the cycle of life and death. In stone, a spirit may reside for eternity.'

Rockingham spoke before fear restrained him. 'But what does this have to do with me?'

'You are also bound in stone – but I sense the binding

was against your will. It is your pain that has called me forth.'

Finding it difficult to breathe, Rockingham dared hope. 'How? Why was I bound?'

'Why? I cannot see that far. I am no god to see into the mind of your tormentor. But I can see who stands before me now. I can see your heart and know it to be stone – a chunk of black rock from the land's bowels.'

'Ebon'stone,' Rockingham groaned, raising a hand to his scarred chest.

'There your spirit is entombed forever.'

'Is there no way to free me?' Rockingham asked, almost a moan.

'Ah . . .' The shade's lips drew into a sad frown. 'Here is your desire spoken aloud.'

'Can you answer it?'

'Yes, but once I do, I can answer no more. It is this need that has drawn me forth. Once I have answered, I can remain no longer. I do not belong to this world.'

Rockingham fought to voice his heart's most intimate desire. 'How? How do I free myself?'

The shade smiled, almost fatherly. 'It will mean your death. Your spirit has already been cast from your body and can never return to inhabit it. If freed of the stone, your spirit will simply move on.'

'I care not. I just want to be free.'

'Very well then. To unfetter your spirit, the stone must be broken.'

'But how can I –?'

'Shatter the black rock in your chest, and you will be free.' With these few words, the apparition slowly began to unravel, fraying at the edges first, then dispersing in folds of mist and cloud.

Still kneeling, Rockingham sank to his hands, hopelessness dragging him down. 'But ... but there is no way to break forged ebon'stone. Only the Dark Lord himself can do that.' Rockingham raised his face, begging for more of an answer.

But the stone pillar continued to draw the mists back into its cold embrace. Unsupported, the staff tumbled to the damp weeds.

'Please!' Rockingham cried to the empty forest.

A faint whisper answered him, a voice from an unimaginable distance. Brother Lassen's final words echoed out to him. 'There is a way, my friend. Only time itself is unchanging. Know yourself, and a path will open.'

With that, the hill grew silent. Only the pillar remained as if to mock him. He had come so close to answering the mysteries of his life, only to have more riddles cast at his feet. Rockingham pushed up out of the tangled vegetation. In the moonlight, the weeds were the color of dried blood.

Standing now, Rockingham stared at the pillar. 'Know yourself, and a path will open,' he said, repeating the shade's final words. 'Useless words for someone whose past has been stolen from him.'

Rockingham turned his back on the stone and stared at the skies. Greshym had promised to return his lost memories if he succeeded in his duty this night. '"Destroy the wit'ch, and you will have what you desire."'

Rockingham sighed. If the shade spoke truthfully, regaining his past could perhaps hold a key also to freeing his spirit. He pondered this realization. If true, was this the reason why his past had been kept from him? To keep him forever trapped in stone? But what mystery of his past life could break ebon'stone?

Somewhere, buried in a guarded corner of his memories,

a scent similar to honeysuckles and soft whispers still existed. It was a single rose growing in a barren field. He knew the name of this sweet flower – *Linora*. But there was nothing more, only that fragile memory he kept near his heart, protecting it from harm. *Who was she?* he cried in his head.

Rockingham shook his head at this useless quandary. There was only one way to answer the mystery. 'Destroy the wit'ch,' he mumbled to the stars.

As if he had been heard, the northern stars winked out one after another, swallowed away by an approaching storm. But it was not thunderclouds that rolled toward his position. Rockingham watched a single winged shape blacken the moon's glow overhead. His skin crawled at the sight.

The legion of skal'tum had arrived.

A crash of breaking limbs sounded off to his left. Swinging around, Rockingham saw stalked branches shatter as something large forced and clawed its way through the canopy. Rockingham fled back a few steps.

The pale-muzzled face of a skal'tum burst from the shredded foliage. It hissed at him, needled teeth shining in malign mischief. A long snaking tongue licked its lips, and its tall ears twitched this way and that. It tore itself free from its perch and crashed to the hill, knocking over the stone marker of Lassen's grave and snapping the Brother's staff under its claws. It stepped toward Rockingham. Its twin black hearts could be seen beating through its translucent skin. Behind its skeletal shoulders, wide pale wings shook and spread menacingly.

Rockingham stood his ground.

'It is time to cast assside our masksss,' it wheezed at him. The heat of the beast's skin steamed in the damp weeds.

Rockingham shrugged. He knew their masks were no longer needed. The wood, through the shade of Lassen, had already declared its neutrality. From here, each side would fight alone.

Stepping forward, Rockingham opened his arms to the foul beast. It had been assigned to carry him to the ship of the wit'ch. 'Let us be off,' he commanded the creature.

'Ssso eager,' it hissed at him, then scooped the small man up in its oily arms. 'Do you lussst so much for the blood-shed to come?'

As the skal'tum's leathery wings spread for flight, Rockingham answered. 'Yes. I am ready for death.'

It was now more than ever that Elena missed Er'ril. Alone at the rails of the *Pale Stallion*, she stared across the silent moonlit waters. She did not miss his sword or his strength. What she missed most was simply his quiet presence – how, whenever danger lay ahead, he would stand at her shoulder, speechless but never silent. His scent would whisper to her of his Standi plains, of home and peace, while his breathing, steady and unhurried, spoke of calm power and untapped vigor. Even his slight movements, the rustle of leather on wool, the scuff of boot, sounded like a stallion testing its bit, ready to explode forward with the slightest flick of a rein.

All this she would hear. And as he stood guard, a part of his iron would enter her. He gave her the strength to face even the worst horror. With Er'ril nearby, anything seemed possible.

But no more.

Elena glanced back to the empty decks and sighed. Other of her companions were also missing. Right now, Elena could use the stony calm of Kral, the flashing blades of Aunt My, the stout heart of Fardale. Even the tricky wisdom of Mogweed would be welcome now.

Across the ship, Flint must have noticed her melancholy. The grizzled Brother finished his discussion with the zo'ol sailors and crossed toward her. One of the zo'ol followed. Flint's face was grim as he joined Elena at the rail.

'Strange news,' he said. 'I just got word from the mer'ai guardsman, Bridlyn, that something has changed in the weed. The channels leading out from the lake have again reopened. The sargassum no longer holds this region clenched in its strangling grip.'

'But does it open a path for us to escape or open a channel so the enemy can reach us?' Elena asked.

Flint shook his head.

Surprisingly, the zo'ol answered. 'Neither. The forest no longer looks at us. I sensed its distaste for a moment, then nothing. It has abandoned us.'

'But why?'

The zo'ol simply shrugged and turned away, as if the question held no interest for him. The tiny man stared out across the glassy surface of the surrounding sea. At sunset, the dragons of the mer'ai and their riders had retreated beneath the lake's placid surface. Hiding in ambush, they lay in wait for any attackers. To any who would spy upon them, all that would be seen was the *Pale Stallion*, drifting alone in the center of the great lake.

Elena swung back to Flint. 'Maybe we should take the chance and leave? Should we reconsider our –?'

The zo'ol spoke again, talking to the empty seas. The black-skinned sailor raised a hand toward the northern skies. 'A sickness approaches.'

Flint pushed forward to study the dark skies. A few thin clouds obscured the stars, but otherwise the skies were clear of any enemy. 'Call the others to their stations!' Flint ordered the small man.

'What —?' Elena began to ask, but then she heard it, too: a distant flapping, like a large rug fluttering in a strong wind. At first it was faint; then it grew in volume and number. It sounded to her like the angry thrum of wings heard from a toppled hornet's nest. Something vile disturbed the night skies and flew this way.

Elena glanced to Flint. The zo'ol sailor had already left to raise the alarm. His other tribesmen lit signal torches along the boat's rigging. In the distance, Elena heard the soft splashes as some of the mer'ai sentinels who had been stationed in the branches of trees along the forest's edge dove down to alert the hidden army.

The grizzled Brother spoke to the skies. 'It is time.'

Elena slipped the pair of lambskin gloves off her hands. They were no longer needed; she dropped the gloves to the deck. From here, it was useless to hide her heritage. The wit'ch could no longer be denied.

Vaguely, the faint sound of drums carried on the wind. The rhythmic beat, though just a whisper, drove to the bones, shivering the marrows. It made Elena want to bolt.

Flint gripped her elbow. 'Dreadlords. Skal'tum,' he whispered. 'They sound their bone drums to unnerve their enemies.'

'How many do you think?'

Flint listened, then spoke with worry. 'I judge at least a legion.'

The hatch to the lower decks crashed open. Tol'chuk, bearing the d'warf warhammer in one huge claw, led the others atop the deck. Once the og're was out of the way, Meric and Joach pushed to the decks.

Joach clutched his staff under the crook of his arm. As he approached, he pulled off one of his own gloves with his teeth and spat it to the deck.

Before he could grip the length of wood with his bared hand, Elena touched his arm, halting him. 'Not yet. Save your blood until it's needed.' From the fire in her brother's eyes, she knew the magick called to him. The lust shone bright in his eyes.

Joach positioned the staff before him, still holding it with his one gloved hand. Small flames of darkfire coursed its length, drawing the warmth from the night. 'Should I try striking with black magick first?' He glanced to Flint.

'No,' the older Brother said. 'As your vision revealed, it is skal'tum that approach. Striking with black magick will only heighten the creatures' dark protections. Do only as we planned. Change your staff into a blood weapon and use its magick-wrought skills to guard your sister. Imbued with Elena's magick, your staff should strike blows that will harm the beasts at close range.'

'But how can we hope to defeat an army of them?' he asked.

'We must trust in our plan,' Flint said. He nodded to Elena.

She already had her silver wit'ch dagger in her grip. She sliced a small cut in each red palm, the hilt of the dagger now bloody. She then turned to Meric. 'Rein the winds to your will, but wait for Flint's signal.'

The elv'in nodded. 'I will stay at your side. None of the winged beasts will get near you.'

Elena gripped Meric's shoulder in thanks. He and Joach would be her bodyguards: Meric keeping any of the skal'tum from reaching her, and Joach guarding her back with his blood stave. Tol'chuk and Flint, along with the zo'ol, would man the stone-weighted nets along the ship's rails. Though the skin of the skal'tum could resist most attacks, the creatures were still beasts of the land. They could drown like any other. Their best weapon of attack this night would not be a sword, but the sea itself.

A tiny voice whispered above Elena's head from the rigging. 'Tikal, good puppy ... Want cookie ...' Elena glanced up to where Mama Freda's tiny pet clung to ropes high above and hid behind a fold of unfurled sail. Its dark eyes were huge as it stared at the skies, too. Mama Freda remained below with Tok. With the boy's help, she had set up a ward in the galley, her elixirs and balms already bubbling on the hearths in preparation for the injured. As she readied herself, Tikal was her eyes and ears above the deck.

'There!' Tol'chuk bellowed from near the bow. He pointed his d'warf hammer toward the northern skies. 'The stars vanish!'

All eyes swung to watch the black cloud sweeping across the night sky. 'Sweet Mother,' Elena moaned. It was as if the entire horizon swarmed with the beasts. How could they ever hope to survive this night?

Flint stood at her shoulder. 'Do not let their enormity overwhelm you. Battles are not fought across wide land-scapes. They are won at the length of your sword or flight of your arrow. Ignore all else around you but the foes within reach. Let the rest of the battle rage around you.' He then raised his voice as he stepped away. 'To your stations! The battle begins!'

Flint gave her a quick smile, a fire lighting his eyes that had nothing to do with magick. After so many centuries, the Brotherhood was once again on the attack. He strode toward Tol'chuk and the nets.

Elena glanced to Meric. The elv'in's eyes were partially closed, and his cloak billowed about his form, even though not a wind stirred this night. As she watched, he floated until the toes of his boots just brushed the deck. 'I am ready,' he intoned. He lifted one hand toward the slack sails, and Elena felt the brush of stiff winds on her cheeks. The sails filled, and the *Pale Stallion* drifted back from the approaching horde filling the sky. Meric would keep the boat tacking and turning across the lake, trying his best to keep the ship clear of the worst fighting.

Joach touched her shoulder, a question in his eyes. Elena nodded. Her brother gripped the staff with his bare hand. Elena saw his knees buckle slightly as his blood was drawn into the wood. Around his hand, the dark wood paled to a stark white. With each beat of her brother's heart, the darkness was driven from the wood, spreading from end to end. Vaguely, streaks of red, Joach's blood, could be seen coursing within the staff, fusing wood to wielder. Once the transformation was complete, Joach regained his footing. The staff was no longer a shaft of black magick, but a blood weapon bent to Joach's will.

With lips tight, Joach lifted the staff. He practiced a few parries and blows with the weapon. The flash of wood moved too fast for Elena's eyes to follow. Joach seemed satisfied and halted his staff's twirl. He met Elena's eyes. 'I only wish Father could see this,' he said quietly.

'He would be proud of you, Joach,' Elena said. They shared a sad smile for their lost family.

From the rail, Flint signaled her.

Swallowing hard, Elena turned away from her two bodyguards. She faced the cloud of winged death that now dove toward their tiny ship. Flanks of darkness spread to either side, meaning to encircle the small boat.

Sheathing her dagger, Elena raised her head and unfettered the magick locked in her heart. Her palms burst with flame; her right bloomed with the rosy flames of a sunrise, while her left burned with the cold blue of the moon. 'Let it begin!'

She thrust her arms toward the night skies, reaching for the two flanks of her enemy. Tossing back her head, she screamed as the magick ripped out from her very bones. Elena felt herself lifted from the decks by the burst of energies. Above her head, twin shafts of fire – one red, one blue – split the black night. Where the flames struck, the dark clouds were shredded. As Elena had learned in the streets of Winterfell so long ago, the dark protections of the skal'tum were no barrier against her blood magicks. All around the boat, pieces of blackness tumbled from the night sky to crash into the seas.

But even such an assault could not entirely block the horde of demons that flew this night. Drums beat at her ears, and winds whistled as Meric fought to keep the *Stallion* from the grip of the beasts. He tried to buy the ship as much time as possible.

Suddenly overhead, sails ripped. A yardarm snapped. Too soon, Meric had lost his chase. Distantly, Elena heard the thud of massive bodies striking the deck. Screamed orders echoed. She ignored them as Flint had told her. Her battle was with the mass of demons still flocking above. She cast her magick across the night sky, searing the darkness. But these were not dumb beasts she hunted; they were sly and learned quickly to avoid her flares of fire, banking and swinging away from her flames.

Elena noticed from the corner of her awareness that the decks had become a battlefield. Meric had given up maneuvering the ship and had turned his fight upon the winged creatures. He blasted the beasts as they tried to land, buffeting them into the seas. Meanwhile, those that did manage to land soon found themselves entangled in the weighted nets of the sailors. Tol'chuk would then heave the writhing creatures over the ship's rail and into the drowning depths. The og're's roar of blood lust echoed across the decks, drowning out even the bone drums of the skal'tum

While the battle raged, Joach danced around Elena, his staff a weapon of death. Christened with Elena's blood magicks, the stave penetrated the skal'tum's black magick and struck deadly blows. The heightened skill of the magick-wrought weapon forged Joach into a murderous force. But even skill and magick could be overwhelmed with sheer numbers. Elena saw the deep wound in Joach's shoulder. It steamed with poisons from a demon's claws. Her brother could not maintain his dance much longer.

Still, Elena fountained her power into the night sky, destroying and fraying the horde above. She knew she must not abandon her own post, not even to help her brother, or all would be lost. If she relented in her attack, the boat would be instantly swamped with winged beasts. Elena knew she was all that stood between the mass of the horde and this boat.

Finally, Flint yelled to Elena, giving her the sign. 'Now, Elena! The flock is all above the lake!'

Sighing in relief as the magick sang through her blood, Elena opened herself fully to the wit'ch. For the moment, she and wit'ch must be one. Bringing her palms together, she merged the coldfire of her left hand and the wit'ch fire of her right. In her heart, wit'ch and woman also fused into a deadly force. From these unions, Elena released her final weapon: *stormfire*.

From her joined palms, the frigid cold of the moon's ice exploded with the searing fire of the sun. A gale of winds mixed with hails of fire and spears of iced lightning tore up from her body. She gasped as a torrential whirlwind of energy coursed out to envelop the winged army.

Across the lake, the scream of her own magick was greeted by the bellowed roar of a dragon. It was Ragnar'k. The flare of Elena's stormfire had been the signal for the mer'ai to strike.

Elena fell to her knees as her magick continued to hurl skyward. Around her, the battle grew more fierce across the decks of the *Stallion*. Overhead, the moon and stars were still masked behind the wings of the demon horde. No matter how many of the foul beasts died, the flow of skal'tum seemed endless.

As Elena struggled with her own magick, she prayed the dragons would prove enough. But she still couldn't shake Joach's prophecy of doom – a vision of the dragons drowning in a sea of blood.

Sy-wen clung to the back of her dragon. Ragnar'k bellowed his rage at the demon horde as he flew toward the flock's underside. Off to the right, a torrent of flaming storm winds attacked the massive host of winged monsters and illuminated the ship far below. The boat seemed such a tiny target on the calm lake, a child's toy bobbing in a puddle. How could they possibly protect such a defenseless target from this blanketing host?

We must get atop the monsters! she sent to her mount.

Ragnar'k roared his answer, arcing on a wing and stretching higher.

Soon they were among the beasts. Wings, claws, teeth assaulted them. But Ragnar'k was no ordinary seadragon; he was the stone dragon of A'loa Glen, a font of elemental magicks. Once the great beast had faced the Praetor himself; the dragon's roar had blown back the black magicks of the Dark Lord's lieutenant, snuffing the flames of the mage's darkfire and leaving the man without a source of power. And now Sy-wen hoped the same proved true here.

As Ragnar'k attacked, he bellowed at the beasts and ripped at them with silver claws and daggered teeth. The dragon's roar washed away their dark protections. Skal'tum screamed, wings torn and shredded. They fell, fluttering and struggling with broken wings, to crash into the sea.

A single beast grabbed at Sy-wen. Even before she could scream, Ragnar'k was there. His head snaked back, snapped the monster's neck, and spat its flailing form into the roiling flock of its brethren.

Tastes bad, Ragnar'k complained.

Chaos reigned as the skal'tum realized the dragon's deadly potency. A hole opened in the flock, and Ragnar'k dove through the opening. Sy-wen knew there was no way Ragnar'k could significantly hurt the flock alone. There were too many. For every one the dragon killed, two more took its place. But conquest was not their plan.

We must get higher, Sy-wen urged.

Ragnar'k thrust upward, ripping his way clear of the flock. Soon he winged above the flow of beasts. Sy-wen glanced to the sky, appreciating the starlight and moonlight. It gave her some small hope to see the moon shining brightly. But she must not tarry. Glancing down, she prepared once again to assault the gathered host. Below her, the moonlight shone off the monsters' pale flesh, a sick sea of wings and claws that spread across the wide lake.

Sy-wen bit her lip against the hopelessness of their cause. But she gave Ragnar'k the signal: three thumps of her hand, her old signal for Conch to submerge. They must assault this foul sea.

Ragnar'k swung on a wing tip and dove toward the massive host. The dragon roared, and the flock fled from him, dipping lower to escape the dragon's wrath. But Ragnar'k persisted, sailing back and forth over the host, driving the beasts lower and lower toward the lake's placid surface. From the dragon's throat, a constant cry flowed. Occasional stragglers would attempt to attack Ragnar'k, but their broken bodies were soon tossed back into the pale sea of writhing forms. At times, Ragnar'k would reach with his silver claws and pluck one of the beasts out from its brethren, rip and tear at it, then drag its bloody corpse over the host, dripping gore over them as warning.

Slowly, as Ragnar'k wove a deadly pattern overhead, the sick flock was driven lower and lower. Like a herder's dog among sheep, the great black dragon forced the host toward the lake, nipping at its heels. Sy-wen knew that eventually the waters would pin the skal'tum and force them to deal with the dragon above, but Flint's assurance of the monsters' cowardice proved true. The demons had grown to depend on their dark protections and were not accustomed to fearing anything but their lord. When faced with a true threat, they chose to flee rather than fight.

Their cowardice here would prove their downfall.

As the flock was finally driven close to the lake's surface, Sy-wen sent a final message to her mount: *Now!*

Ragnar'k stretched his neck, and a trumpeting blare burst from the dragon's throat. The bright sound split the night.

Upon this signal, the entire lake erupted. Snaking heads of hundreds of dragons shot up from the water's dark depths and grabbed at the skimming skal'tum flock. Though not imbued with magick like Ragnar'k, the seadragons had their own weapons – fangs and sea. Across the lake, dragons seized limbs and wings of the flying monsters overhead and dragged them down into the lake. The lake became a frothing battlefield. Dragons screamed; mer'ai yelled;

monsters wailed. It became hard to say where the sky ended and the sea began.

Attacked from below, sections of the flock attempted to flee, but Ragnar'k was there with claw and tooth. Those few that broke past the great dragon were still not safe. They tried to band together, but the night sky was still afire with a magickal torrent arising from the boat. There was no safe haven. The lake was a bloody trap, and the skies were menaced by the black dragon and by flaming spears of magick. Though many of the beasts yet survived, perhaps enough even to swamp the ship, their ranks had been shattered. The skal'tum panicked among the chaos and fled toward the trees.

Sy-wen watched the tattered fragments of the foul army flap away but felt little cheer, numb from all the blood. A chorus of screams tainted the air. The battle still raged below. Sy-wen urged her mount lower to help her people finish the monsters trapped in the lake. Below, Sy-wen saw many dragons torn and lolling in the waters, most too far gone for even draughts of dragonsblood to cure. Mer'ai swam beside their dying beasts, offering what little comfort they could. Moonlight, now unblocked by the broken host, shone on the water like molten iron, the blue seas ruddy with the blood of the slain.

Tears rose to Sy-wen's eyes but were quickly blown away by the winds of their flight. 'Oh, Sweet Mother,' she moaned as more and more of the slain came into view, 'so many.'

Tol'chuk heaved the writhing form over the rail. Poisoned claws scrabbled at the entangling net, but it was too late. The screaming beast plummeted into the lake, and the stone-weighted net dragged it under the surface.

Straightening, Tol'chuk snatched up the d'warf hammer

and stared at the slaughter around the ship and in the skies. He knew the skal'tum host had been broken by their trap, but he also knew that now was the most dire time of the battle. The skal'tum would make one last furious strike at the boat.

Tol'chuk eyed Flint. The grizzled Brother panted, almost bent over with exhaustion. Across the foredeck, the four zo'ol masterfully teased and trapped another of the skal'tum in the net they carried. It wailed as it became fouled in the snagging ropes. Farther away, Joach held off two of the beasts with a blur of polished wood. Meric stood guard beside Elena, blasting demons from the deck with gales of wind, but the elv'in clearly weakened. Elena herself seemed lost to the battle, her eyes on the skies and her fierce sprays of magick.

Flint drew back Tol'chuk's attention by lifting the edge of a net in his hand. 'This is the last one!' From the old man's face, Tol'chuk knew Flint understood the situation as well as he did. Though the battle had been turned, it was hardly over yet.

As if reading his thoughts, a scream of rage tore above them. Four of the slavering beasts crashed to the deck, dividing Tol'chuk and Flint.

A pair of the skal'tum grinned at Tol'chuk, yellowish fangs glinting brightly. 'We've never tassted og're meat before,' one of them hissed.

A cry of pain arose from where Flint fought the other two beasts with his flailing net. Tol'chuk saw Flint stumble, his left leg torn and bleeding. Still, the man fought to keep the creatures from where Elena stood on the middeck; injured, he would not last much longer.

The og're raised the hammer in his claw. The lightning-wrought iron glowed like spilled blood in the moonlight.

The other eyed the hammer. 'So you think to ssslay those who can't be harmed with a stick, do you?'

Tol'chuk roared, leaping and swinging his weapon with all the might of an og're's back. Before the skal'tum's smile could even fade, the iron split the beast's crown and drove into the softer matter inside. Gore splattered out. Poisoned blood burned where it struck Tol'chuk's bare chest.

The other skal'tum froze, stunned by the damage to its companion.

Tol'chuk yanked his weapon free. 'This be no ordinary stick!' Turning, the og're drove the hammer into the face of the remaining beast.

Around him, more skal'tum, the final wave of the assault, crashed aboard the ship. Tol'chuk carried his fight to the two creatures who harried Flint. His gaze reddened as a growing fire stoked his blood. Tol'chuk hammered his way through to the grizzled seaman.

Once free of the two demons, Flint warned Tol'chuk, leaning on one of the zo'ol. 'We've no more nets. It is up to you to keep the monsters back.'

Tol'chuk only grunted. He was beyond words. The fire of the *fer'engata*, the blood lust of an og're, was upon him. Lifting his hammer, now steaming with blood poisons, Tol'chuk hewed a swath of death across the deck. All the strangling rage in his heart at the loss of his ancestor's spirits fueled his march. Guilt, anger, despair – all exploded out in raw savagery.

Unaware, Tol'chuk howled his clan's ancient war cry as he struck and bludgeoned his way throughout the ship. His sight became a red blur. One skal'tum swiped at his chest, gouging long burning tracks in his thick skin, but still Tol'chuk did not pause. He continued his deadly march. None would keep him from his revenge.

He sang his rage against the cruelties of fate. *Half-breed, orphan, cursed seed of the Oathbreaker* . . . Skal'tum now fled from him, leaping in the air and flapping away. Still, he continued his swath of destruction, leaping, hammering, even tearing at the beasts. If he was descended from a cursed heritage, then let him not deny who he was any longer. He howled his lust and rage and opened his heart to the monster within.

Suddenly, a small figure stepped in front of him. Tol'chuk struck at him, but the man darted to the side. As the iron slammed into the deck, Tol'chuk was jarred enough to realize he had almost killed one of the zo'ol.

From off to the side, words finally penetrated his grief and rage. It was Flint. 'Stop, Tol'chuk! Put down the hammer.'

The og're raised red-rimmed eyes toward the old Brother.

Flint limped closer, leaning on another of the zo'ol. About the ship, only two or three skal'tum still survived, but Joach and Meric dealt with them. Flint indicated the zo'ol pushing to his feet near the splintered deck. 'The man sensed you were about to lose all control, to become a larger menace than even the monsters here. He tried to stop you.'

The hammer fell from Tol'chuk's limp fingers, clattering to the deck. The og're sank to his knees. Tears finally began to flow, washing the blood lust from his eyes and his blood.

His heart felt as drained as the stone in his pouch.

Flint crossed to him, shooing away the zo'ol. He knelt beside the og're. 'Do not despair, my friend. I know from where this pain and rage arose. There is evil in this world, but trust an old man – it does not lie in your heart.'

Tol'chuk reached a claw to grip Flint's hand. 'Do not be so sure.'

* * *

As they flew, Ragnar'k rolled an eye toward Sy-wen. It shone brightly in the moonlight. Still, Sy-wen could sense her mount's growing exhaustion. Even a dragon's heart had limits. For an endless time, they had thrust themselves into countless skirmishes between skal'tum and dragon, slashing and roaring from above to slay the floundering monsters.

Little dragons die well, Ragnar'k sent to her. For once, the usual disdain of the great black for his tinier brethren was not present. Sy-wen sensed the sadness in his huge heart.

Sy-wen leaned and rested her cheek upon the scaled neck of her mount. She shared her grief with Ragnar'k. Below, the battle slowly died down. The skal'tum had no defense against the drowning sea. The cries of war dwindled to spates of shouted orders and the occasional pained trumpet from a dying dragon.

Little green one died well, too.

Sy-wen just rubbed her great dragon's scaled neck. It took her a few heartbeats for these last words to penetrate her grief. Her heart suddenly clenched. Ragnar'k could not mean —?

Pushing quickly back up in her seat, Sy-wen asked, 'Do you mean Conch, my mother's jade?'

Yes. Tiny green dragon, friend of my bonded.

Sy-wen's breath choked in her throat. Sweet Mother, no! Conch and her mother were not supposed to engage the flock, only direct and supervise. Conch was too old to fight. Ragnar'k must be mistaken. The black dragon had a huge heart but was not too bright. Ragnar'k must be wrong!

'T-take me to where you saw the tiny green dragon,' she said, unable to mask the pain in her voice.

The equivalent of a dragon's shrug was sent to her; Ragnar'k swung upon a wing and swept over the carnage below. Small pale mer'ai faces turned up to watch the great black pass overhead. A few raised an arm in salute, but most were as dull eyed and shocked as she was.

Too soon, Ragnar'k skidded onto the lake's surface, wings stretched wide to cup the air and slow their landing. Once drifting across the lake's surface, the floating corpse of a skal'tum bumped Sy-wen's knee. It seemed to claw at her even in death. Crying in disgust, Sy-wen kicked it away.

Ragnar'k worked through the bloody waters. Just ahead, Sy-wen saw the green hide of a jade dragon bobbing in the gentle swells. Its huge head lolled lifelessly. It was *not* Conch. Sy-wen was sure of it.

But as Ragnar'k neared, Sy-wen spotted her mother clinging to the far side of the dead beast's neck. As the black approached, her mother lifted a face whose usual cold countenance had broken into a mask of pain and grief. Wet locks of normally sun-bright hair clung damply across her face. Her eyes were sunken and hopeless.

'Oh, Mother,' Sy-wen moaned. 'No . . .'

'He . . . he tried to protect me.' Her mother's eyes drifted back to the body of Conch.

Sy-wen still could not believe this dead dragon was her dear companion. Where was the gentle humor that always seemed to cling to him? Where was the ever-present love in his eyes? With his spirit gone, this bulk of green scale and torn wing was not Conch. Still, Sy-wen could not move her eyes from the lolling form.

Her mother continued to moan the details of her story. 'One of the monsters broke free. Under the sea, the creature thrashed and twisted.' Her mother raised panicked eyes toward Sy-wen. 'I couldn't get away in time. It came upon me and attacked savagely.'

'Oh, Mother, where was your personal guard? Where was Bridlyn?'

She waved her daughter's question aside. 'Gone. Dead. I don't know. Only Conch remained. He fought back.' Her voice cracked with sobs.

'Leave it be, Mother. We'll talk of it later.'

Her mother did not seem to hear. 'But ... but the monsters are pure poison. They could not be harmed by a dragon's tooth or claw. All Conch could do was hold the beast away from me. But all the while, the monster tore at his neck with claws and teeth. It was horrible. The blood ... So much blood ...'

Sy-wen could tell her mother was near mad with grief and horror.

The woman droned on, eyes wide with the recent pain. 'Even after the skal'tum finally drowned, Conch clung to it, fearing it might yet attack. Even as blood flowed in thick rivers from Conch's wounds, he would still not let me near.' Her mother's voice broke into sobs. 'Only when his great heart finally ended, only then did he finally let the monster loose.' She raised her eyes up to Sy-wen. 'Wh-why did he do it? I might have been able to save him. If only I had been quicker.'

Sy-wen urged Ragnar'k beside the sobbing woman. 'No, Mother, you couldn't have. Conch loved you. You know that. He died to protect you. It was the way of his heart.' Sy-wen reached an arm toward her mother. 'Come, Mother, we must return to the ship.'

'No, let someone else go. I must stay here.' She wrapped her arms tighter to the jade dragon's neck.

The pain from the loss of a bonded dragon was known to cripple its rider. Sy-wen could not let that happen. She needed to get her mother away. A draught of numbweed tea and a warm bed was what her mother needed most right now – along with the love of her daughter.

Silently urging Ragnar'k lower in the water, Sy-wen was able to reach her mother's shoulder. Once close enough, a great black wing rose under her mother, scooping her limp form from the water. She struggled slightly, but her grief had made her weak as a babe. The dragon's wing slid the woman closer into Sy-wen's embrace.

Hugging tight, Sy-wen wrapped her arms around her mother and pulled her into the seat, cradling the crying woman in front of her. Sy-wen had not realized how small and light her mother was. It was as if the immense grief had not only broken the woman, but shrunk her also.

Sy-wen pressed her mother's head against her chest and gently rocked. 'I'm sorry, Mother,' she whispered as she stared at the dead and dying across the wide lake. 'I'm sorry for everything.'

She urged Ragnar'k toward the lone boat drifting amidst the carnage. In the distance, the boat still fountained with spears of flame. Sy-wen's brow crinkled with concern. What were they still fighting?

With the battle in the sky won, Elena fought to rein in her surge of stormfire. Upon the decks of the *Pale Stallion*, clashes still raged with the last handful of skal'tum who had crashed to the boat. Elena sensed her power and magick were no longer needed skyward, but here.

As Elena struggled to guide her magick, the wild energies began to break free of her control. When first she had unleashed stormfire, back in the swamps of the Landslip, she had had only the dregs of power at hand. The magick had expired almost as quickly as she had lit it. But now, almost at full strength, Elena found the magick had grown beyond her ability to control. It took both sides of her spirit, the light of the woman and the darkness of the wit'ch, just to keep the force of her raging energies directed upward.

Elena knew that even this meager control was about to be lost. With all her will, Elena fought the stormfire's wild bucking and writhing. Still, she could not keep her palms from beginning to slip apart. The spread of her hands, instead of weakening her stormfire, widened the scope of her magick. The larger force became impossible to harness.

Concentrating fiercely, she ignored the cries of those around her. As the stormfire spread, one of the ship's masts cracked near the top, caught by the edge of her gale of magick. It crashed near the stern and rolled into the sea, dragging two skal'tum with it, tangled in its ropes.

Elena's cheeks ran with tears, and not just from the strain. She had spotted one of the zo'ol sailors dragged overboard along with the pair of skal'tum. Elena had glimpsed the man's panicked eyes as he had rolled over the edge, a noose of rope around his neck.

Elena fell to her knees.

Grief weakened her control even more. Shouts of alarm rose from the deck as the others sensed that her magick was about to tear the ship apart.

Joach's voice barked near her ear. 'Elena, we've won! Stop!'

What did her brother think she was trying to do? She could not collapse the magick. It had grown too large. Her only hope was that her magick would burn out. Lost in the eye of the storm, Elena knew such a hope was futile. She sensed that her well of magick was still too deep. The ship would surely be demolished before the rage of stormfire ever blew itself out.

With her heart failing, Elena searched for guidance, for some means of chaining her magick. As if in answer, she suddenly sensed a presence nearby. She glanced over a shoulder. No one was there. But she caught a whiff of scent, a whisper of Standi loam. In her ears, she heard the rustle of leather. And from somewhere far off, someone called her name: *Elena*. It was Er'ril's voice, and the tone was clearly scolding. Her heart clenched. Elena knew it was no ghost that visited her in this hopeless moment. It was only her own memory. With her guard so weakened, a corner of her heart had stirred. She had thought herself just wit'ch and woman, but she now realized she had grown into something more. Somewhere along this journey here, Er'ril had become a part of her, too. The iron he had gifted to Elena in the past had not died with the man. It still remained – in her own heart.

Elena shoved back to her feet. She must not die. She would not let this tiny spark of Er'ril expire forever because she was too frail. Only by living could she keep his memory alive. Standing once again, she fought the raging magick with a furious passion, part iron, part spirit.

Slowly, she began to pull the magick back into check, drawing her palms together. She screamed with the effort.

Above her, the fountain of energies died down to a savage spear. Finally, with a last wrench of her will, she clenched her hands together, entwining her fingers, stanching the flow. The stormfire blew itself out.

Sagging with sudden exhaustion, she fell to the deck. One of the zo'ol caught her, and Elena stared at the destruction around her.

Nearby, Joach leaned heavily on his staff among the wracked ruins of several skal'tum corpses, his eyes wide with concern for her. Flint limped upon a leg torn and bleeding. Tol'chuk helped support the man, but even the og're was not unscathed. He bore deep scratches across his chest. Meric looked haggard and sunken, his spent magick wasting him.

A tiny call arose from the waters beside the boat. 'Help us aboard!'

Joach leaned over the starboard rail. 'It's Sy-wen and Ragnar'k. They have an injured woman with them.' He waved the others to help.

Flint, though, ignored the commotion at the rails and stared up at the skies. The stars shone brightly. 'It's over.'

'No,' whispered the zo'ol at Elena's side. His eyes were not on the skies, but on the dark forest around them. 'It's just beginning.'

20

From the bower of a treetop, Rockingham watched the slaughter across the lake with dispassionate eyes. Perched on a neighboring branch, his skal'tum lieutenant was not as calm. It hissed and worked its claws into the tree's bark, ripping at its rough surface with undisguised frustration. The beast quivered with rage, but it had its orders: *Stay beside the golem. Do its bidding.*

Rockingham glanced toward the beast, and it cowered back. Naked from the waist up, the wound in Rockingham's chest steamed with wisps of black fog. The Dark Lord had come here, and none dared disobey.

Satisfied, Rockingham returned to studying the dying army. He discovered no emotion connected with the annihilation of the skal'tum host. Not that he cared for any of the beasts. In truth, he wished them all dead. Still, their brutal massacre should have shocked him; the bloody lake and cold corpses should have sickened him. But the presence of his master dulled any such feelings.

With the stone gateway open in his heart, the man who was Rockingham had dwindled to a tiny spark, lost in the enormity of the black spirit that had squirmed and rolled out from the ebon'stone. The golem had had no say in what had happened or in what was to come. The orders had all risen from the darkness inside his chest, from a being who nested far away in the volcanic crèches of Blackhall.

From his mist-shrouded wound, a voice whispered out. The sound was an oily poison that ate at his sanity. 'Call them forth.'

Nodding, Rockingham raised an arm in the air. The Dark Lord could not be disobeyed. All around the lake's edge, a rustling arose from the tree line. A full third of his skal'tum army remained yet unbloodied by the previous assault. The master had sent the main mass of his host to draw out the enemy's fangs. It had succeeded. The wit'ch and her companions would be unprepared for the true attack.

'Now,' the voice ordered from his cracked rib cage.

Rockingham snapped his hand into a fist. From all across the lake, a pale force rose from the canopies, flocking into the air. Rockingham's lieutenant crawled atop him and grasped the man by the shoulders. With a rattle of bony wings, the skal'tum took flight, carrying Rockingham clutched in the claws of its feet.

As Rockingham flew across the lake, his host flanked him, a pale sickness spreading over the water toward the lone boat. While leading this final surge, Rockingham should have felt some sense of victory or revenge. But he felt nothing as the mer people and their dragons stared at the passing horde with shock and dismay.

The attack was so sudden and unexpected that no resistance was tendered. With skal'tum again filling the skies, dragons and their riders fled under the lake. As Rockingham swooped toward the deck of the ship, he watched men scramble over tangled corpses, seeking to retreat belowdecks – as if that offered any protection.

Still, Rockingham felt no emotion.

His lieutenant dove at the ship, throwing its wings wide to slow its dive, and settled Rockingham roughly to the deck. All around, sails ripped and rigging tore free as his hosts settled into perches among the masts and across the deck. Only a small section of the deck was left free.

Rockingham recognized most of those clustered before the hatch to the lower decks: the wit'ch's brother brandishing the darkmage's staff, the og're bearing a bloody hammer, the elv'in looking fierce but hard worn. Yet there were others who were strangers to Rockingham: a green-haired girl; the man beside her, a hulking, tattooed brute with a long black braid and an even longer sword; and a set of identical dark-skinned men who threatened with nothing more than broken oars.

Yet none of these mattered. His true target hid behind them, though in truth, Rockingham hardly recognized the woman. What strange magick had transformed the young girl into this comely lass of thick curled locks and hard countenance? Curiosity arose in Rockingham, but he sensed it was only because the same emotion welled in the Dark Lord. It was this oddity that gave his master pause.

'Come forth,' the darkness called to the wit'ch. 'You cannot win here. Give yourself freely, and the others will be allowed their freedom.'

'We would rather die!' Joach called back.

Unbidden, Rockingham's shoulders shrugged. 'If my beasts must dig the wit'ch from this boat, you will all wish for death. I can wield punishments far worse.'

As the skal'tum hissed in delight, Rockingham felt the others' eyes meet his own. He stood as an example of how much worse the Black Heart's punishment could be. The wound in Rockingham's chest spread wider. He saw the gathered faces blanch at whatever was revealed.

Elena, though, pushed boldly through the others, shaking

off restraining hands. 'You hide behind this flock of winged carrion,' she spat at him. 'And skulk in the hollows of dead men. Come out and face me! Let us end our battle here!'

A sound that could only be crudely defined as laughter answered her challenge. A flow of black energies rolled forth from Rockingham's cracked rib cage and pooled at his feet. From this dark well, screams echoed up. The voice spoke again. 'Then let it be!'

Elena stepped forward, thrusting her arms out and bringing her hands together. A tempest of searing flames and ice swept toward where Rockingham stood. Normally, Rockingham would have cringed and ducked, but even this instinctual fear was denied him. Instead, faster than his eye could follow, the pool at his feet burst upward in a black shield, blocking the flow of wit'ch magick before it struck him.

In the center of this conflagration, Rockingham watched the flames of dire energies cast by the wit'ch dash against his shield. Ice and fire roiled like living serpents around his barrier, seeking a way through the blockage. But it proved vain. The black shield was impregnable.

A cry of frustration arose from the wit'ch, and the torrent of magick flared brighter. Laughter answered her renewed efforts.

Beyond the shield, a harsh voice suddenly intruded, demanding and panicked. 'Elena! Pull back your magick! He only seeks to drain you!'

With these words, the flames instantly died away. In turn, the black shield dropped. Rockingham saw a gray, grizzled elder leaning on a crutch, his leg bandaged from ankle to thigh. A silver stud marked the man's ear. Agony was drawn in deep lines upon his face, but not all of the pain, Rockingham suspected, was from the injured limb.

Elena stood before the others. Her hands, still raised, were pale and white. 'It's too late,' she whispered.

A coldness spread through Rockingham, a touch of hoarfrost and ancient ice. Even under his master's control, Rockingham shivered. The black energies at his feet grew even darker. Rockingham knew more of the foul one's spirit had pushed through the ebon'stone gate in his chest. It was drawn by the despair of those gathered here.

Elena glanced to the gibbous moon overhead.

The Black Heart whispered with malign mischief. 'Renew, wit'ch. The moon's magick will do you no good.'

Needing little urging, the wit'ch raised her left arm toward the night sky. Bathed in moonlight, her hand vanished. As she pulled down her arm, her fist returned, rich again with ruby energies. Elena faced Rockingham, her words fierce. 'Useless or not, I will die fighting you with every scrap of iron and magick in my blood.'

From the black well, a hiss of amusement. 'Submit, wit'ch, and I'll still let the others live.'

Rockingham saw the girl hesitate, her staunch stance wavering.

The voice whispered now, trying to worm past the girl's own shield. 'There are none to save you.'

From beyond the others, a new figure shoved forth. A naked woman, eyes wild and hair tangled, burst free. The green-haired girl reached toward the clearly mad woman as she rushed past. 'Mother! No!'

The woman shook off the girl and ran at Rockingham, hands raised in claws. 'Y-you murdered Conch, you monster!'

Rockingham froze. The first image of the woman's face, wild and tear streaked, seared his mind, obscuring all else. He gasped and clutched his chest.

Something broke deep inside him.

In response, a howl of rage echoed out from his chest. But Rockingham ignored it. Old memories swamped him, drowning him. Emotions flamed through his core, swiping away even the black chains that bound him. A black stone the size of a clenched fist tumbled from his open chest and clattered across the deck.

Rockingham stumbled from the sudden release. Raising his head, he moaned the name that had been imprisoned in his heart for too long, the name of the woman who had burst from the doorway. '*Linora!*'

Speaking aloud, Rockingham felt his legs give out. He crashed to his knees.

His outburst struck the woman just as deeply. She halted her lunge and fell to her hands on the deck. Her eyes rose from Rockingham's wounded chest to his face. A look of recognition broke through her madness. She knelt back, covering her face with her palms. 'No! It cannot be!'

The small girl danced forward. 'Mother? You know this creature?'

Linora croaked, her voice lost. 'He's your father.'

Sy-wen dropped back in disbelief, her hand rising in horror. 'No!' Kast gathered the distraught mer'ai girl within his arms. She sank gratefully into his embrace. 'How could this be?' she cried. For so long, she had conjured pictures of her father in her mind's eye. He was always as tall as Kast, even broader of shoulder, but bore none of Kast's scars. She always pictured him with a perpetual grin and laughing eyes. Not . . . not this creature of nightmare dredged from the foulness of the Dark Lord's dungeons.

The golem lifted an arm in supplication. 'Linora?'

Before any further plea could be spoken, a screeching

howl blew forth from the stone at the man's feet. The noise tore at Sy-wen's ears and shook the sails like a wind. The roosting skal'tum scattered from their perches into the night sky like a startled rookery of starlings. Pale leathery wings flapped and sailed away from the ship's two masts.

Amid the chaos, Elena stepped forward, eyes on the retreating creatures, fist blazing with coldfire. Flint stopped the wit'ch with a touch and pointed down. 'Look!'

Sy-wen's gaze followed where the old Brother pointed. Upon the deck, the remaining pool of dark energies around the stone crackled with streaks of silver, matching the thin veins forking through the rock. It was as if the remaining splash of dark magick was in fact melted ebon'stone. As they all watched, the well of darkness drew back into the rock until only the chunk of ebon'stone remained. None dared draw near it.

Flint spoke. 'Free of its host, the Dark Lord has fled.'

Glancing back to the golem, Sy-wen noticed that only Rockingham and Sy-wen's mother seemed oblivious of the stone's transformation. Instead, the couple's eyes were locked on one another. 'I'm sorry,' Rockingham moaned.

Elena stepped as if to intervene, but once again Flint restrained her. 'Let them be. Though I might not be as rich in weaving magicks as your brother, I can sense when a flow of fate is best left undisturbed.'

Clenching her fist, Elena slowly backed away. Sy-wen could almost feel the hatred pulsing from the wit'ch. Sy-wen knew Elena's story. This man, her father, had once played a role in the murder of Elena's family.

Deaf to those around them, Linora and Rockingham knelt near one another. 'What happened to you?' Sy-wen's mother moaned. She reached to touch the man's face, but her hand faltered.

He looked away. 'You should have had me slain, like the others. I . . . I didn't deserve your m-mercy.'

Linora touched his cheek tentatively. 'I couldn't live with that. I barely survived your banishment. If not for Conch and the babe . . . your baby . . .'

Sy-wen realized they were talking of her, when she was a child. Sy-wen's heart roiled with emotions. Shock and anger, along with disbelief, confused her ability to sort out her feelings concerning this revelation. 'He cannot be my father . . .' This was the man who had killed Conch. How could her mother touch the creature with affection?

Kast leaned and whispered in her ear, reading her thoughts. 'We cannot always choose our blood. Ulster was my blood brother, but our hearts were different. Remember that. Even if this creature truly is your father in name, you do not have to take him to heart.'

Kast's words gave Sy-wen the strength to push free of his arms and step beside the two kneeling figures. She deserved to hear the truth finally. 'I don't understand. What happened, Mother?' she asked sternly.

Her mother would not look away from Rockingham. 'We were wed on a midsummer's eve. We promised to share the rest of our lives together. But then one winter, shortly after you were born, he tried to forge a pact with coast-landers. He broke the mer'ai code of silence.' A pang of anger etched her mother's features.

'I could not help myself,' Rockingham explained softly. 'I was so tired of our isolation. The world beyond the waves was so vast and varied. I wanted to bring these gifts back to the mer'ai . . . back to my newborn daughter.'

Sy-wen listened to his words and found her own heart responding. His descriptions sounded so much like her own cravings for new horizons, new experiences. She remembered the silent pull the coastlines had once had for her, too, when she and Conch used to sneak off and explore the Archipelago. Had she acquired this strange yearning from her father? 'What went wrong?' she asked.

Rockingham looked down, silent.

Her mother answered. 'Dragon blood proved too rich a prize to the lan'dwellers. Dragons were slaughtered, and for such a crime, the code was exact. As punishment, your father was to have been killed.' Suddenly her mother's voice cracked, and tears flowed. 'But I couldn't allow it. As an elder, I begged the older punishment instead: Banishment from the Deep.'

Rockingham took her mother's hand and held it between his own. 'But such a gift was no kindness.' The man glanced up at Linora. 'At first, I tried to live with my punishment. I wandered the coasts and islands until the webbing between my fingers dried and flaked away. Soon I walked like any other lan'dweller. Over time, I learned I could survive without the mer'ai.' Her father turned back to her mother, pulling Linora's fingers to his lips. 'But I could not survive without you. You were an ache in my heart. The ocean waves whispered your name to me every night. Rain on the water tinkled with your laughter. I should have left the coasts, but my heart bound me.'

He lowered Linora's hands to his lap, and his voice grew husky. 'One day, staring out at the seas from a high bluff, the pain was too great. I could stand it no more and sought to end my banishment.' Tears traced down his face as he looked into Linora's eyes. 'I stepped off the cliff.'

Sy-wen spoke, shocked. 'You sought to end your own life?'

Silently, her mother pulled Rockingham into her embrace as he dissolved into sobs. Her mother rocked him. Cradling the sobbing man, Linora held him until his wracking breaths slowed.

Rockingham continued, speaking between gasps. 'But . . . but there was an evil festering in secret along the coast. It sensed my despair and was drawn to it. By forsaking my own life, I exposed myself to its corruption. It d-did things to me, horrible things. Its only kindness was in binding my old memories of you in stone. That pain was finally gone, but so was the man you loved. I became only half a man. What I did afterward . . .' He pushed from Linora's embrace, facing her. 'Conch . . . all the others . . . Can you ever forgive me?'

She melted toward him. 'I can only love you. It was the evil that is to blame, not you.' She kissed him on the lips, then pulled slightly back. 'Now that I've found you again, I will never let you leave my side.'

Her mother's words only caused the man further pain. 'It cannot be, my love,' he said. 'I am dead. I know this. I can feel it in my flesh.' He nodded toward where the stone rested on the deck. 'Only the magick in the ebon'stone holds me here.'

'Then we will keep the foul thing safe.'

Rockingham shook his head slowly. 'No. The stone also binds me to the evil. The rush of old memories broke its cursed hold, but as long as it exists, they can always draw me back again, enslave me. It must somehow be destroyed. Only then will I be free.'

'No! I cannot allow it!'

Rockingham smiled sadly. He touched her cheek. 'Do you seek to keep me alive no matter the cost, as you did once before?'

Sy-wen saw her mother wilt. She crossed and wrapped her mother in her arms. Linora trembled in her grip. 'Hush, Mother, you know he's right.' The decision was not as hard for Sy-wen. She could not fathom that this man was her father. Kast was correct. To her, he was still a stranger.

Sy-wen raised her eyes to the man. 'How do we destroy it?'

His voice became hopeless. 'I don't know.'

'I do!' Elena's stern voice drew all their gazes. Sy-wen saw hatred burning in her eyes. Just as with Sy-wen, these newest revelations had failed to sway the wit'ch's heart. Elena saw only the murderer of her family. The wit'ch held no qualms about severing the man's ties to this world. Elena nodded to Tol'chuk and the rune-carved weapon he bore. 'The Try'sil hammer can smash ebon'stone.'

Rockingham pushed to his feet. With hope in his eyes, he faced the wrath of the wit'ch. 'I know of no way back to grace in your eyes. But please, if it's in your power, free me.'

Sy-wen saw how Elena hesitated. Was the wit'ch's hatred so deep that she would balk at even granting this final plea for death?

Flint spoke at her shoulder. 'We must be quick. The skal'tum have only been spooked by the loss of the Dark Lord's presence here. But in the skies, they already gather again. I think they mean to strike.'

Rockingham still looked with strained hope at Elena, his eyes pleading. 'Do this ... And if I am able, I will find a way to help you here.'

'What? By betraying us?' Elena said coldly.

Wounded, Rockingham remained silent, eyes cast down.

Sy-wen turned from where she knelt with her mother. 'Let my father go, Elena. Please.' Sy-wen turned and found Rockingham's grateful eyes upon her. 'I don't know this man's true heart any better than you do, but I know my mother's. Let the man who my mother married on a midsummer's eve die in peace.'

Elena hesitated, staring fixedly at her; then slowly the woman's shoulders relaxed. Wordlessly, she waved Tol'chuk forward. 'Do it.'

Rockingham seemed to shrink in relief. Linora pushed free of her daughter's embrace and climbed to her feet. Sobbing, she drew her lover into her arms. 'Let me hold you. I want you with me for every last breath.'

He drew her tight.

From over her mother's shoulders, Sy-wen met her father's eyes. He smiled sadly at her. Father and daughter. Two strangers.

Tears rose in Sy-wen's eyes, and her legs were suddenly weak. 'Father.' She moaned the word so softly that only her own heart heard. She slid toward the deck with grief, but Kast was there to catch her. His arms were always there.

Before she could even lean into the Bloodrider's warmth, a sudden thunderous crack exploded from nearby. Sy-wen jumped, glancing to where the og're was bent over his hammer. He swung the weapon again, and the fist of ebon'-stone was ground to dust under the magickal hammerhead.

Sy-wen swung her eyes toward her mother. Linora still held Rockingham in her embrace, but from the way his head lay slack on her shoulder, he was clearly gone.

'Mother . . . ?'

Linora suddenly shuddered. A scintillating fog blew forth from Rockingham and passed through her mother's form. She let the dead man slip from her arms, then swung around. The glowing mist swirled tighter to form a vague resemblance of the golem. He raised a hand toward Linora, but his fingers passed through her cheek.

'Good-bye, my love,' she whispered to the spirit.

The ghostly form stared a moment more, then turned to face the wit'ch.

Elena scowled at the shade wavering before her. Even just the wispy outline of the murderer set her blood afire.

Coldfire danced over her ripe fist. The mark of the Rose was now entirely masked behind spates of blue flame. Her shoulders trembled as the man's ghostly eyes focused on her.

When he spoke, his words were as insubstantial as his form, whispers from another world. 'Thank you,' he said. 'There are no words to beg your forgiveness nor acts that can wipe away my atrocities, but as I promised, I will seek an ally to help you in the fight to come.'

'I ask no boon of you,' she said with ice in her voice. 'Only that you truly leave this world and never return again.'

The shade bowed his head. 'So be it. But as I leave, I will still seek the shade of this watery wood and attempt to pry him from his eternal slumber.'

Elena did not understand any of this nonsense. She waved her fist of coldfire at the shade, but her fist passed through him with no effect. 'Go then. Do not sully these decks with your presence any longer.'

The shade bowed his ghostly head. His form began to dissipate, fraying at the edges in swirls of mist and roiling tendrils of glowing fog. Suddenly, though, the ghost of her parent's murderer grew more solid for a few breaths. 'One last word, Elena.'

She shuddered. Just her name on his tongue rippled disgust through her body. 'Begone, demon!'

But the ghost persisted, his voice just a hushed trace sounding from much farther off. 'You must know . . . The plainsman, Er'ril . . . he lives.'

Elena gasped. The blue flames flared brighter, then died away. A part of her quailed. Er'ril's death had almost torn her apart; it had taken all her strength to accept his loss – and now to think he might still be alive. She could not handle such a loss twice. Elena reached a hand and fingered the strip of singed red leather braided into her hair. 'H-he lives?'

The ghost wavered before her, fading away. 'He is a captive of the darkmages on A'loa Glen. In two nights, when the moon ripens full, they will use his blood to destroy the book. You must hurry.'

The shade again began to mist away into nothingness. Elena reached with both hands toward the fading spirit, trying to gather its glowing remnants back into the semblance of a man. He must not leave yet.

As her hands wove through his ghostly substance, her pale right hand vanished when it drifted through a small cloud of scintillating mist. Elena yanked her arm back as if stung, expecting some last bit of malice on the shade's part. Instead, as her limb pulled free, her hand returned, now aglow with a familiar rosy azure.

She raised the hand before her. Her palm and fingers were as insubstantial as Rockingham's shade. She could see the scurry of her companions through her palm. Elena had momentarily forgotten Aunt Fila's earlier lesson. Spirit light! When last with Fila, Elena had ignited this same magick while venturing too near the spirit world.

'Ghostfire,' Elena mumbled, naming the magick now imbued in her right hand. She raised her left hand still swirling with the ruby stain of coldfire and clenched her two fists. 'Both spirit and stone,' she said, bringing her two fists together, one ghostly, one solid. Whether the shade of Rockingham spoke truthfully, Elena knew that if Er'ril still lived, she would tear down the towers of A'loa Glen to free him.

A strangled voice drew her attention back to the decks. 'Elena?'

Lowering her hands, she saw Joach staring at her with his mouth hanging open. Tol'chuk and Meric stood at his shoulder, equally shocked. Elena glanced around the deck. Other eyes were also fixed on her. 'What?'

Joach stumbled a step toward her. 'Y-you're gone. I see your clothes, but your body's vanished.'

Elena glanced down at herself. Not again. She remembered when last she had touched spirit light. Her flesh had become invisible to the eyes of others. Only her clothes had remained visible.

Flint neared her, walking in a slow circle around her, studying her. Still, he kept a wary eye on the skies. The flock of skal'tum had gathered just at the lake's edge, but the pale cloud now swept slowly back toward the ship, circling in a closing spiral toward the boat. 'Perhaps it would be best if you disrobed, Elena. If invisible, you might survive the coming attack.' His voice sagged with a note of hopelessness. 'Afterward, you could perhaps still join up with the Dre'rendi fleet south of here.'

'No! I will not sit idle while the rest fight and die,' she insisted. Elena raised her hand and studied her insubstantial right fist. From her first dalliance with this ghost magick, Elena had learned to mask a dagger held in her palm by flaring out her magick. But what if the opposite was also true? Elena willed the rosy glow to draw inward, rather than flow outward. She drew the magick of her ghostfire down to a small bright ember in the center of her palm, draining it from her blood and body. As she worked, her fingers grew more solid. Elena could no longer see through them.

Joach's voice again gasped out. 'El, I can see you again!'

Elena ignored her brother. She must not break her concentration – not yet. Clenching her teeth, she bound the well of ghostfire in place, tying off the font of power until she was ready to release it again. Once done, Elena raised her face to the others. She knew they could all see her. She returned their stares, her gaze fierce. If the shade spoke truthfully – that Er'ril might still be alive – she would let nothing stand between her and the plainsman.

The pounding of the bone drums suddenly crashed into a thunderous cacophony. 'The skal'tum strike!' Flint called from the starboard rail. 'Ready yourselves!'

A flurry of activity burst across the deck. Tol'chuk swung the d'warf hammer to his shoulder and joined Flint at the rail. Joach and Meric posted themselves on the opposite rail. Even Mama Freda had abandoned the galley, leaving her brewing elixirs to the boy Tok's care. She bore some strange weapon in her hands: a long slender pipe into which she fed a feathered dart.

'Poison from the Yrendl jungles,' she explained. 'It will kill even these beasts if I can pierce their hides.'

Elena did not argue against the old woman arming herself. Every means of exacting death would be needed this night. They must survive until dawn, when the sun's light would weaken the dark protections of the demons.

A throat cleared nearby, drawing her attention. She found Kast and Sy-wen standing ready. Kast spoke. 'Should we call the dragon?'

'On my signal.' Elena raised her arm and faced the swarm of skal'tum. They now encircled the boat, sweeping toward them from all directions, low over the water but unfortunately not low enough for the surviving seadragons to reach them.

The ship grew hushed around Elena. No one spoke any further words. Only the beat of the bone drums disturbed the night. Still, Elena waited. She wanted the sudden appearance of Ragnar'k to startle the forefront of the legion, to perhaps cast them in disarray for a few critical moments.

As she held her breath, arm raised, Elena's heart quailed at the sheer numbers they faced. Everywhere she looked demons flapped and glided toward their lone boat. She fought against the hopelessness of their cause. Even if she should live, how many on board would die?

Suddenly a shivering scream of rage burst from the countless throats of the beasts.

Elena could delay no longer. Let the slaughter begin! She began to swing her arm down, but her limb was blocked by the hand of one of the zo'ol.

'Wait!' he snapped and nodded toward the seas. 'Something else comes!'

Elena twisted out of his grip. How much worse could this night grow? She stared at the leading edge of the skal'tum assault. They were only a stone's throw from the ship.

Then the world suddenly exploded around them.

All across the lake, a tangle of weeds burst out from the water, snaking far into the air, twice the height of the forest's towering trees. Twisting vines and coiled branches snatched the skal'tum from the skies, grabbing wing and limb, pulling the beasts under the lake. Nearer at hand, whipping roots and leafy snarls thrust up and ripped into the approaching flock. A few beasts managed to scrabble as close as the rail, but even these were quickly yanked away by snags of vines.

Elena stared at the decimation. It was as if the *Pale Stallion* had become trapped in a whirlwind of pale wings and frothing weed.

'It's the sargassum!' Flint called above the screams of the skal'tum.

The war raged around the boat. One skal'tum, crazed with fear, crashed into an unfurled sail, ensnaring itself in rigging and sailcloth. Its thrashing tore loose the sail, and the beast toppled into the sea in a net of its own making. That was the closest to the boat any of the skal'tum managed to get.

And as quickly as it started, it was over.

In the moonlight, the writhing red weed slowly subsided, sinking back into the sea, dragging the last of the demons down with it. None of the skal'tum had escaped its fury. Soon the lake was clear. Even the dead dragons had been whisked away.

No one spoke, just stared, too stunned.

Across the lake, a scatter of living seadragons and their riders emerged warily from the depths where they had retreated earlier. With the moon and stars so bright, Elena could easily spot the dragonriders' amazed expressions.

Around the ship, there was no sign of the night's carnage. The waters lay quiet and pristine. 'It's over,' Elena sighed.

Flint limped over to her. 'But why did the sargassum intervene?'

In her heart, Elena knew the answer. She glanced across the faces of her companions. All would live to see the dawn. Turning away, Elena stared across the lake, leaning both hands upon the rail. Tears of relief flowed from sore eyes. Alone, she whispered words she had not thought she could ever speak, words for the murderer of her parents. 'I forgive you.'

With her words, a scintillation of lights swirled up from the depths of the dark sea, like fireflies on a midsummer's eve.

Elena felt a presence appear beside her. It was Linora. The woman rested her hand on Elena's. 'Thank you,' Linora murmured to her.

Across the sea, the sparks of spirit light spread and faded until only the moon and stars were reflected on the lake's mirrored surface.

Book Five

TIDES OF WAR

21

Er'ril awoke in his dark cell on the last day of his life. Though there was no window to indicate the sun's rising, Er'ril knew dawn had come. After five centuries of living, the movement of the sun had ingrained itself into his bones.

Slumped in his shackles, Er'ril raised his head. Nearby, shadowy rats scurried through the hay and chittered angrily at each other, fighting for scraps of moldy crust left from last night's meal. On his bare legs were scabbed bites from where those same rats had investigated his sleeping form, sampling his flesh for when his corpse would be theirs.

From the neighboring cell, something cried and thrashed in its chains. The strangled howl of madness echoed down the cell row.

Er'ril tried to ignore the noise, but it rattled into his skull. Suddenly, somewhere down the hall, a door creaked open; iron scraped iron as a lock was undone. Then came the heavy tread of booted feet. Er'ril listened. He judged four men approached. Too many just to deliver the morning's gruel.

Straightening on his bed of hay, Er'ril strained his ears for some clue as to their intent. From the neighboring cell, the wailing creature had quieted. It, too, knew better than to attract the attention of any who ventured down here. Through the cracked mortar of the walls, only a soft mewling rose from the creature, like a dog about to be beaten.

But the beast need not have feared. The scuff of boots stopped before Er'ril's small door.

Er'ril quickly fingered the tip of slivered wood poking from the back of his neck. It was still in place. With only his loincloth as clothing, Er'ril's own skin was the best hiding place for Greshym's 'gift.' He had imbedded the staff's sliver under the skin at the edge of his hairline until it was needed.

The small door slammed open, and two men dressed in the black and gold of dog soldiers crawled inside. A torch sizzled in one man's fist. The sharp light stung. They scowled at Er'ril and crinkled their noses at his squalid accommodations. 'Smells like a privy in here,' one commented.

The other scrunched up his face. He had only one eye, the other orb lost in a long wicked scar. 'Throw in them leg shackles. Let's get out of these here dungeons before the contagion gets us all.'

A set of chains and manacles clattered into the cell, chasing the rats back into their black warrens. But the fierce vermin did not flee too far. Their red eyes glowed out at the guards, watching warily over their scraps left abandoned in the hay.

The one-eyed guard crossed and kicked Er'ril in the shin. 'Git yourself up. You're to be taken to the baths and cleaned.' He leaned down and leered in Er'ril's face. 'It seems the Praetor has plans for you.' He nodded toward where the neighboring creature still mewled. 'Maybe to make another pet out of you.'

The other soldier interrupted. 'Nock, quit goadin' him and give me a hand with these chains.'

Grumbling, the guard named Nock gave a final kick at Er'ril, then moved to take one end of the leg shackles. Both men quickly hobbled Er'ril's legs and ran a chain up and around his waist. They then unhooked his arm from the wall bracket and reattached it to a single shackle on his waist chain.

Once trussed up, he was led from the cell, wearing only a stained loincloth and flushed from a slight fever. The air in the hall chilled Er'ril's skin, raising a rush of gooseflesh. At wrist and ankles, the old shackles had left troughs of rent flesh, purplish with bruises and infection. He limped after the first two guards while two others, bearing spears and poking periodically at his back when his shuffling gait slowed too much, followed.

Soon he was escorted into a warmer room; steam and the scent of lye stung his nose. In the center of the room stood an iron tub. He was stripped of chains and loincloth and unceremoniously herded into the steaming water. He bit back a scream as the hot water burned his wounds.

'Clean yourself up and get dressed,' Nock commanded, throwing soap and a brush in with him. 'And be quick about it. We don't have all morn.' The guards backed to the room's door and clustered in the hall.

The stone room was featureless except for a fogged mirror and a single stool with a set of clean clothes laid out. Er'ril drifted back into the water's heat, letting its warmth drive away the dregs of his fever. Once his head stopped pounding, Er'ril took soap and brush to his wounds first. Clenching his teeth and struggling with his one hand, he scrubbed the filth and dried hay from the deep gouges. After the bath was red with his own blood and the wounds looked raw and fresh, he took the brush to his body.

As the water cooled, Er'ril let his thoughts drift to Elena and the others. In the days prior, he had purposefully kept his mind away from thinking about them. That path led to certain despair. Did they know he still lived? Had Sy-wen managed to bring the Dre'rendi to their cause? With the full moon rising this night, the darkmages would attempt the book's destruction at midnight. If they succeeded, all the Bloodriders and wit'ches in the world would be of no avail.

He covered his face with his one hand – not against this dreadful fate, but because he found himself strangely disconnected from any true feelings about the book or the destiny of A'loa Glen. He would attempt to thwart the mages' plot with every fiber of his body, but in his heart, there was truly only one concern. His mind conjured Elena's image in the shimmer of bath steam. Whether the Blood Diary survived or not, Elena must live.

'If you're done soaking, Your Highness,' Nock snapped at him from the doorway, 'git your scrawny arse out and dried.'

Er'ril pushed from the tub with his one arm and stepped onto the icy stones. Crossing to the mirror, he toweled himself dry and awkwardly dressed in the linen underclothes and fine gray breeches, taking care to wrap his wounds with the clean bandages left by the tub. Slipping into a white, billowed shirt, he inspected himself in the mirror.

Gaunt, with his cheeks and chin covered in dark beard, his gray eyes seemed shadowed hollows in his face. If he was to meet his brother, he would not walk to him a defeated man. He ran a hand over his rough neck and finger-combed his hair roughly in place. As he worked, his eyes grew hard with the flint of his homeland.

Nock and another soldier entered. Kicking the chain and shackles at Er'ril, Nock ordered him to truss up.

Er'ril barely heard his words, still staring in the mirror. He ran his fingers over the prickle of wood at the nape of his neck. Touching the sliver from the staff, Er'ril allowed himself a moment of hope. Black magick to fight black magick.

'Are you deaf? Git in those chains!'

Er'ril turned to face Nock. The guard saw something in the plainsman's eyes that stumbled him back a step, the pale scar on his face going white. 'Y-you heard me,' he squeaked out, glancing at his companion for support.

With a tired shake of his head, Er'ril bent and retrieved his shackles, then locked his ankles. Nock waved for the other guard to hook Er'ril's chains and wrist manacle in place. Er'ril stared at Nock while this was done. The soldier tried to meet and maintain the plainsman's gaze, but he glanced away and grumbled as he led Er'ril toward the door.

The trek to the westernmost tower of the great citadel, the Praetor's Spear, was a long one. Er'ril kept his back stiff and his gait unhurried. Now that he was dressed and cleaned, the guards with the spears no longer harried him. They seemed to sense that a new man had risen from the steam of the baths, one who would not tolerate such barbs, even when chained.

At long last, they reached the twisting tower stair. Er'ril sighed; after so long without proper nourishment, the climb would be interminable. Even his old leg injury, where the rock'goblin had stabbed him almost a winter ago, complained at the number of steps. By the time the group reached the top landing, Er'ril was gasping between clenched teeth.

Nock crossed to the two guards stationed before a pair of

huge, iron-bound oaken doors. Before he could speak, the doors swung open at his approach. The tower guards did not even register the movement, just stared straight ahead. Nock's single eye, though, grew huge. He bowed his head before the presence that seemed to flow from the opening portal.

Words trailed out to them. 'Tell my brother he is welcome.' The icy voice belied the warmth of the invitation.

Stepping aside, Nock turned to Er'ril and waved him forward. The plainsman even felt the slight poke of a spear's point in his back. It seemed the guards were more than eager to be rid of their charge.

Er'ril did not balk. Here was his quarry if he was to stop the book's unbinding. With a clink of chain, he shuffled past Nock and entered Shorkan's tower home.

As he stepped onto the thickly cushioned rugs of the study, the rattle of Er'ril's leg irons became muffled. Inside, he found the towheaded boy mage, Denal, lounging on a short couch, heels tapping the frame, and Greshym, smirking like a cat that just ate a pigeon, seated at a small cherrywood table. Only Shorkan, still robed in the traditional white of the Praetorship, had his back to Er'ril, indicating how little the plainsman's presence impacted him.

Shorkan stared out at the drowned city beyond his window as the sun's early rays bathed the toppled and crooked towers. In the distance, Er'ril spotted the glint of blue that marked the ocean and even a few humped islands. Shorkan spoke as if continuing a conversation that Er'ril had rudely interrupted.

'They come with full sails. The Bloodriders and the wit'ch will be at our doors before night falls.'

Er'ril could not help but smile with these words. So the Dre'rendi had been convinced to add their might to the assault!

Greshym spoke. 'With the loss of the skal'tum legion in the sargassum, how stand our remaining defenses of the island?' Er'ril caught the bent-backed mage's glance toward him. Greshym's lip twitched. 'Will they hold out until the ceremony at moonrise?'

Shorkan turned. Brother looked upon brother. Er'ril felt a momentary twinge of old memories: racing through fields, wrestling out behind the barn, manning snow forts on the windswept plains. But then Er'ril spotted the man's eyes, and any thoughts of a shared childhood evaporated into a foul smoke of blood and torture. Behind those gray eyes was no sign of the brother Er'ril had once loved. Instead, a presence that had little to do with men born of women lurked behind that gaze; it whispered of creatures hatched in poison and bred amid torture. Thankfully, the Praetor turned his full attention quickly away, fixing on Greshym.

'Will our forces hold out?' Shorkan mocked with clear disdain. 'We've still another two legions of skal'tum on the island and a fleet of ships that number in the hundreds, manned by ul'jinn-controlled berserkers. With an additional thousand dog soldiers ensconced in the peripheral towers with longbows and flaming pitch, you'll have no need to worry about the safety of your hide, Greshym.'

'Ah . . . But if we are so safe, why are two hundred d'warf ax warriors spread throughout the Edifice?'

'A mere precaution. I will not have this night's ritual in the catacombs disturbed by anyone.'

Greshym bowed his head, but not before once again glancing to meet Er'ril's eye. This litany of the island's defenses had been coaxed from the Praetor for Er'ril's benefit. The ancient mage wanted Er'ril to understand the current situation on the island.

Denal spoke up, his voice high and sibilant, a child's voice but with the boredom and malice of too many years. 'What of the golem Rockingham?'

'Gone,' Greshym answered. 'I sensed his spell's unraveling.'

Denal squirmed his face into a boyish pout. 'But I so wanted to play with him some more.'

'It is of no matter,' Shorkan commented. 'With the wit'ch and her army here, he was of no further use. He delayed her long enough for us to prepare our defenses. The wit'ch will find the island impregnable, and by dawn tomorrow, her armies will be nothing but shark chum. Now enough talk of the wit'ch's approach. Instead, we must make preparations for the ritual at sunset.'

Shorkan turned to Er'ril. 'It is time our roles were reversed, dear brother. Long ago, it was our blood that bound the book. To unbind it, the spell will require your blood this time, Er'ril. Unfortunately, we will require all of it.'

Er'ril shrugged.

Shorkan raised his eyebrows at this lackluster response. 'This does not concern you, Er'ril? Have the passing centuries weighed so heavily that you welcome your life's end?'

Er'ril spoke for the first time. 'I have no worries of death.'

'And why is that?'

'There is a traitor who stands amongst you, dear brother.'

Er'ril saw Greshym twitch in alarm.

Shorkan did not seem to notice the old mage's surprise. 'A traitor? And who might that be?'

Sighing, Er'ril shrugged again. 'Now if I told you, where would be the sport in that, *dear* brother?'

Aboard the *Dragonspur*, Kast stood beside Pinorr as the shaman studied the horizon, his eyes partially closed. Kast waited patiently, fingering the tattoo of the dragon on his cheek. It was best not to disturb a ship's shaman when he sought his *rajor maga*, his sea sense.

To the stern of the ship, the Dre'rendi fleet spread from horizon to horizon. The sails from over a hundred ships were like the billowing clouds of an approaching storm front. Mixed among the boats were the remains of the mer'ai forces, some hundred or so dragons and riders. Though a full quarter of the mer'ai had died in the sargassum forest, the presence of those remaining kept the spirits of the Bloodriders charged. The victory against the skal'tum had been sung on many decks this past evening.

Kast turned his attention back to his own vessel.

Elena and Flint stood nearby. Flint's head was bowed in quiet conversation with the ship's new keelchief. Hunt, the high keel's own son, had been assigned to the ship after the mutiny during the night of the storm. Kast's brother, Ulster, had been found slain upon the first mate's sword. Both the first and second mate were later also discovered dead; obviously the mutineers had fallen into some disagreement. Further investigation had turned up no other conspirators. Though Ulster had been no true brother, Kast still felt a twinge of anger at the man's death. He gripped his sword's hilt in an iron fist. If any others were involved ...

Finally, Pinorr straightened his stance by the rail. He cleared his throat. 'It is of no use.'

Kast tightened his brows. 'Can you read nothing of what awaits us?'

Pinorr turned his dark eyes on Kast, then swung away. 'The seas are dark to me now.' He reached for the hand of his granddaughter, Sheeshon, who sat on the deck nearby. But the girl ignored his offered palm, fiddling instead with the webbing between her toes.

Kast's eyes were drawn to the same. It was hard to fathom the transformation of the child. Even when faced with his people's shared heritage with the mer'ai, it was difficult to accept it fully. Kast turned his attention back to Pinorr. 'We're only a half day's voyage to the Archipelago. Does the evil entrenched among the islands resist your abilities?'

Pinorr grunted noncommittally.

Kast reached to the old shaman's sleeve. 'Do not fault yourself, Pinorr. If you can't read anything on the wind, then no one can. We will have to trust that the mer'ai outriders will bring back sufficient warning.' Kast's mind momentarily flashed on Sy-wen. She had returned with her mother to the giant leviathan that trailed the fleet. Linora sought the guidance of the elders in the battle to come.

Pinorr glanced up at Kast as if about to say something but then turned away. A certain awkwardness grew between them.

Before either could speak, Elena moved toward them. She knelt beside Sheeshon, giving Kast a quick smile. The wit'ch's other companions had been left aboard the *Pale Stallion* while the boat's damaged mast and sails were mended. As soon as the southern isles of Maunsk and Raib's Saddle came into view, the wit'ch and Flint would return to the *Stallion*. As the battle ensued, she and the others would take the smaller sloop west toward where Flint claimed to know a secret route onto the island. Meanwhile, it would be up to Kast and Sy-wen, along with the Bloodriders and the mer'ai, to keep the main forces of the island distracted.

Or so it had been planned. Kast only wished Pinorr had been able to ascertain some information about what lay ahead. The morning sun now climbed to midday; they would soon be in sight of the island and its drowned city.

'You sense nothing from the seas?' Elena asked Pinorr.

Sheeshon suddenly stood and waved her webbed hands through the air. 'Look, Papa! My hands are like birdies!'

Pinorr smiled sadly and pushed her arms down. 'Yes, little Sheeshon. Let's go see if Mader Geel has our meal ready.'

The girl wiggled in his grip, freeing an arm. She pointed out toward the northern horizons, toward the empty seas. 'That island over there has got big birdies flying around it. White ones with sharp teeth. But they're not nice birdies.'

Elena and Kast exchanged glances.

'More skal'tum,' Kast mumbled. He nodded to Sheeshon. 'Pinorr's granddaughter shares his gifts of the *rajor maga*. She can read magick and the seas, like her grandfather.' Kast leaned closer to Sheeshon. 'Do you see any other monsters around the island?'

Sheeshon scrunched up her face as if she had eaten something sour. 'I don't like that place. It smells like bad fish.' She turned her attention back to the webs of her hands.

Pinorr patted her head. 'She does not understand what she sees.'

'But at least she does *see* something.' Kast stared significantly at Pinorr.

'The *rajor maga* is a fickle gift, Bloodrider.'

Before the shaman could leave, Kast stopped him with a touch on the shoulder. 'Is there something you're not telling us, Pinorr? Since the night of the storm, you've grown quiet and withdrawn. Do you see something that you fear voicing? Do you know what will come this day?'

Pinorr shook free of Kast's grip and picked up Sheeshon. 'As I told you before, the seas are dark to me.'

'But why?'

Pinorr turned away from Kast. 'Some answers are best

left unspoken.' With those mumbled words, the old shaman crossed the decks. Kast watched him leave and knew it was more than the weight of the old man's granddaughter that bent his back.

Elena spoke from the rail. 'Those shadows on the horizons, are those storm clouds?'

Kast swung around and studied the sea and sky. 'No. Not clouds.'

'What are they then?'

'Islands. We've reached the southern edge of the Archipelago.'

Elena glanced over as Flint stepped beside them. His eyes were fixed on the horizon, too. 'We should be returning to the *Pale Stallion*, Elena. It is time we prepared for our own departure.'

'How long until we near A'loa Glen itself?' she asked.

Flint pointed to one of the dark shadows to the northeast. 'We are already there.'

From the rail of the *Pale Stallion*, Elena stared through a spyglass at the island. A chill breeze slipped past her woolen scarf and shivered her skin. After almost a full turn of seasons, her goal was finally in sight: *A'loa Glen*. As she stared, Elena felt no joy, only a cold dread that filled her belly. How could a place so fraught with darkness appear so bright in the midday sun?

Formed from three peaks, the island was roughly shaped like a horse's shoe. Its two arms seemed to stretch toward her, welcoming her into its embrace. Through the glass, Elena spotted the city itself, a bristling of towers and spires that climbed from the seas and spread up the slopes of the central peak. Atop this middle peak, like a crown on a king, stood a massive castle. Elena studied the structure's towers and knew somewhere beyond its walls was hidden the Blood Diary and the fate of Alasea.

Yet as Elena drew her gaze over the battlements and broken towers, her thoughts dwelled on one other prize hidden behind its cracked walls: *Er'ril*. If Rockingham spoke truthfully, the plainsman was trapped in a dungeon beneath the castle; by nightfall, with the rising of the full moon, he would be sacrificed in an attempt to destroy the book.

Elena lowered the spyglass. She would not let that happen.

Ahead of her, the massive ships of the Dre'rendi seemed to dwarf the *Pale Stallion*. The fleet filled the seas with sails and dragon-carved prows. With the sun shining directly overhead, the islands around them were no longer misty shadows but had grown into sheer red cliffs and towering green mountains.

'May I see?' Joach asked, reaching for the spyglass.

Elena numbly passed him the tool. All around the rail, her companions had gathered on the deck. With the fleet sailing toward the island, the *Pale Stallion* would soon be parting ways. They would drift behind the last of the Bloodriders' ships, and as the fleet rounded the isle of Raib's Saddle, the *Stallion* would slip farther west to the island of Maunsk. Flint knew of a back door to reach A'loa Glen in secret, a magickal gateway similar to the Arch of the Archipelago, but he kept the details a mystery.

Joach spoke, drawing her attention. 'I see watch fires in many of the drowned towers that edge the island. At least a hundred. They know we come.'

Flint took the glass from him and raised it to his own eye. 'They've known our every movement since we first entered these seas, and we will use that to our advantage this day. The fleet and the mer'ai will draw their gazes.

While they're blinded by our forces, we'll slip in a back door. With luck, we'll be in and out before they even know we were there.'

Tol'chuk grumbled nearby. 'Og'res do not trust luck. It be as likely bad as good.'

Flint patted Tol'chuk's arm. 'That is why we go with Elena. I do not trust fate any better than you, my big friend.'

Meric leaned on a cane with Mama Freda at his elbow. After the elv'in's recent injuries, the taxing use of his elemental gifts had left him wasted, but at least the fire had returned to his blue eyes. 'Fates be damned. We risk Elena needlessly here. We should leave her within the protection of the fleet and seek the book on our own.'

Flint shook his head. 'The book is bound in a spell of black ice. I wager it will take the ward's magick and Elena's power to free it.'

Elena added her support. 'I must go. If the Blood Diary is truly meant for me, I must free it.'

Meric scowled but let the matter drop, knowing he could not sway her.

The tiny fiery-maned pet of the healer clung to Mama Freda's shoulder. 'If you are all done admiring the island and plotting,' she said, scratching the beast behind an ear, 'I have prepared an elixir to ward off fatigue and sharpen the senses. We should rest and be ready.'

Flint nodded at her words. 'She speaks wisely. The zo'ol will man the sails and wheel. We will be striking on our own soon and—'

A sudden whoosh of expelled air and a spray of water exploded near the starboard side of the ship. All their gazes swung to the massive black dragon and its green-haired rider. Sy-wen spat out her breathing tube and raised an arm in greeting. 'I bring news from the mer'ai outriders!' she called and waved back toward A'loa Glen. 'A massive fleet lies in ambush on the lee side of the island, and flocks of strange, tentacled beasts lurk in the deep waters that border the sunken city. The Bloodriders fly ahead to flank both sides of the island, while the mer'ai have been ordered to hunt the deeper seas for the monsters!'

'Look!' Joach called out and pointed toward the island.

The small, sleeker ships of the Bloodriders, nicknamed shark hunters, had already sped forward of the main fleet. As they coursed nearer the edge of the city, racing the waves with full sails, a cascade of flaming embers blew out from the half-sunken towers and rained down upon the smaller ships. A few sails caught fire, flaring bright. Before the shark hunters could even begin dousing the flames, a barrage of boulders followed the trails of the fiery arrows, flung from catapults atop the towers. Even from this distance, the explosion of splintered wood and the concussion of striking rocks crashed over the waters.

Elena gasped at the slaughter. But she was not the only one to react.

Ahead, the larger ships of the Bloodriders dove forward, splitting into two flanks. They were a storm of sails upon the sea.

Suddenly, from around either arm of the island, foreign ships of every shape and size suddenly hove into view, ready to meet the Bloodriders.

Sy-wen called again from atop her huge black dragon as it glided the waves beside the boat. 'We must be off! Ragnar'k and I will coordinate the attack from the air.' With these brief words, Sy-wen swung her dragon around. 'You must leave! Now!'

'We're off! But be sharp yourselves! Watch for our signal fire atop one of the towers near sunset!' Flint called after her. 'If we get the book, we will need rescue from the island!'

Raising an arm, Sy-wen signaled her acknowledgment. 'We know! All eyes will be watching for you!' With these last words, the great beast surged away, wings rising from the water to either side. Striking out, the wings beat at the water and lifted rider and dragon from the seas. With a roar of war blasting from his throat, Ragnar'k climbed into the air, seawater sluicing from his scales. He angled over their ship, passing just above the tips of the masts. The *whump* of his massive wings beat down at them. In a flash of sunlight off pearlescent scales, he dove away.

Flint handed back the spyglass to Elena. 'We must not be caught in the edge of this fighting.' Flint waved Tol'chuk to his side and marched toward the stern wheel.

Elena raised the spyglass, unable to look away. She followed the dragon's course across the blue sky as horns of battle blared from the Bloodrider's ships. Spread out before them, the seas now frothed with cutting keels. Near the city, smoke from burning ships smudged the clear skies while pale tentacles rose from the depths to grab at rail and men as boats foundered.

Dragons rose, too, from the waves to tear at these blubbery beasts. Some of the seadragons also clawed aboard ships to protect their ship-bred brethren, while riders bearing swords attacked foe and beast alike. For the first time in ages, mer'ai and Dre'rendi were united in battle.

Near the island, a giant leviathan suddenly exploded to the surface. From the behemoth's belly, mer'ai surged out of countless openings. With daggers and swords, they joined the battle at the city's edge, climbing towers to attack the soldiers inside. Mer'ai, impaled on spears, toppled back into the seas even as others replaced those who had fallen.

Elena covered her mouth in horror, tears blurring her

vision. Everywhere she swung the spyglass, men and dragons died. It was as if the mer'ai and Dre'rendi were a fierce surf pounding themselves to death against jagged rocks.

The spyglass was suddenly taken from Elena's fingers. She did not resist; she had seen enough. Without the aid of the lenses, the battle now seemed so distant, almost like a bad dream. But sound carried different tidings over the water. Screams, horns, bellows from wounded dragons – all kept the immediacy of the battle raw in her ears.

Joach was at her side, pulling her away. He passed the spyglass to one of the zo'ol. 'Xin, take this. Watch the battle and keep us informed.'

'So much death,' she mumbled. 'All for a cursed book.'

Joach tried to soothe her. 'Not for a book, El. They die for the chance at freedom – and not just for themselves, but for their sons and daughters. They shed blood for a future dawn – a dawn only you can bring.'

Elena glanced at her brother. 'But when does a price become too high – even for freedom?'

'That is not for you to judge, El. It is a price each man must weigh in his own heart.'

Elena glanced at the war raging around the lone island and judged her own heart. What price would she pay for someone's freedom? She pictured the hard planes and gray eyes of Er'ril and knew her answer.

She turned her back on the death across the waves.

Some freedoms were worth any cost.

Meric opened the door to his cabin. He was greeted by the ruffle of feathers from the perch by his bedside. The sunhawk's snowy plumage flared brighter with the slight motion. Black eyes, unblinking, studied the elv'in as he entered the room, but the bird did not raise an alarm. The creature knew Meric. The hawk had been seated above his mother's throne in Stormhaven for the past sixteen winters.

Slipping a bit of dried beef from a pocket, Meric crossed to the bird and proffered the tidbit. The hawk cocked one eye at the strip of meat, then shook its mane of feathers, declining the offering with a flip of its hooked beak. Meric frowned at the insult. He should have known better. The bird liked its meat fresh and bloody, not limp and salted. Chewing the meat himself, Meric crossed to the small chest at the foot of his bed.

He needed a moment to himself to prepare for the battle to come. He ran a hand over the scars on his face. Memories of old tortures threatened to unman him, but he fought back such feelings, hardening himself.

He would not fail his queen. He had been sent to recover the lost bloodline of the elv'in king, and he must succeed. He would protect Elena with his own blood if necessary. Meric pictured the girl. Now grown into a woman by her magick, Meric recognized the subtle elv'in features in her: her tall, thin physique; the slight curving of her ear; the sharp corners of her eyes. There could be no mistaking their shared bloodlines.

Still, Meric had to admit that his concern for Elena had grown into more than just a desire to see the king's line continue. He again fingered the scars on his cheek. He had faced the horror that walked this land and knew she and the others fought in a just and noble cause. On their long journey here, Elena had demonstrated that her heart was as noble as her heritage, and Meric had no desire to fail her, either. Luckily, for now, his role as protector of Elena served both women in his life – queen and wit'ch. Elena must be safeguarded – not just for the preservation of the king's bloodline, but also for the hope of this land.

But as Meric eyed the stoic sunhawk, the symbol of his queen, he wondered how much longer the goals of these two women would share the same path. And if they should diverge, what path would Meric take?

Sighing, Meric pushed aside the question for now. From the sea chest at the foot of his bed, he removed a small stone. Rubbing its cold surface, Meric lifted it to his lips and breathed across it. A brilliant glow blew forth from its heart. Satisfied, he placed the windstone on his bed and removed another object from the depths of his sea chest. It was a long thin dagger. He ran a finger along the flat of the blade; his touch brought forth a crackle of silver energies along its length. Like the sunhawk, the ice dagger was a heritage of his family. More a relic than a true weapon, it would have to serve him on the journey ahead. He rested the ice dagger next to the stone. Next, he tenderly removed the last object from the chest, using both hands to carefully lift it free. It was the true reason he had returned to his cabin for a moment's respite.

He lifted Nee'lahn's lute from the chest and settled it in his lap. He studied the whorls of grain in the wood. It had been carved from the heart of the nyphai's tree as it died. Gently, he let his fingers strum the lute's strings. The sound was like a soft sigh, a whispered exhalation of relief at finally being able to speak again. Meric leaned into its allure, strumming through a few minor chords. He played softly to settle his heart for the battle to come.

As he let the lute's voice lull him, his mind returned to Elena's own quandary. Just what were they fighting for? Was it freedom, as Joach had insisted? Or was it perhaps something more tangible? In the music of the heartwood, pictures of Meric's own home, the cloud castle of Stormhaven, bloomed in his mind. These fond memories drew Meric away from battle and warfare, at least for a brief moment.

Suddenly, a scuffle of heel on wood disturbed his reverie. It came from just outside his door. The elv'in's fingers stopped their strumming. Silently, he crept from his bed, lute brandished like a sword, and crossed to the door. Meric listened for a moment. He heard no further sound, but he sensed that someone still stood at his doorstep.

Reaching to the latch, Meric whipped open the door to find a small boy cowering in the hall. Meric lowered the lute. It took him a moment to recognize the terrified figure of Tok. 'Boy, why are you slinking outside my door? Weren't you supposed to be sent to one of the leviathans for safety?'

'I ... I hid,' he said sheepishly. 'With the horses.'

Meric scowled at the boy. 'Not a wise choice, boy. You would have been safer with the mer'ai under the sea.'

'I didn't want to go with those others, sir. You're ... you're all the people I know in the world.'

Meric shook his head. 'Well, stowing away or not, why were you skulking in the hall just now?'

'Th-the music.' He waved toward the lute still in Meric's hand. 'I wanted to hear it better. It makes me feel good.'

Meric remembered how in the past Tok had always been underfoot whenever he played the lute. The boy had been constantly enraptured by its song. Meric settled back to his bed with the lute on his lap. 'Does the music remind you of your own home?'

Tok shrugged. 'I never knew no home, sir.'

Meric frowned. 'What do you mean you knew no home?'

Tok shuffled nervously in the doorway, clearly unsure whether to enter or not. 'I was orphaned on the streets of Port Rawl, sir. I took up with the boats to earn a keep. The sea's been my only home.'

Meric weighed this story with his own history. He could not imagine what it would be like never to know one's past, never to call any place home. He finally waved the boy to the sea chest beside the narrow bed. 'Sit.'

Tok's shoulders slumped with clear relief. He scurried to the chest and sat silently. His eyes grew wide at the sight of the sunhawk on its perch nearby. But the boy's gaze quickly returned to the lute, all but begging Meric to play.

'Then what do you hear in the lute's music, Tok? What draws you to it?'

The question made the boy squirm. When he finally answered, his voice was a whisper. 'It makes me . . . warm.' He pointed to his chest. 'In here. It's like . . . like it takes me somewhere where no one laughs at me or tries to hit me. I close my eyes, and in my belly, I think . . . I think I can finally belong somewhere.' The boy's eyes were bright with tears.

Meric's gaze drifted to the lute in his lap. He found it hard to stare at the boy.

'P-please play something for me,' Tok asked so hopelessly. 'Just for a little while.'

Meric did not move for several breaths. Finally, he handed the boy the lute. 'It is time you played for yourself, Tok.'

The boy held the instrument at arm's length, as if he clutched a writhing snake, horror clear in his eyes. 'I . . . I couldn't!'

'Put the lute in your lap. You've seen me do it enough times.'

Gulping past his terror, Tok did as he was told.

'Now put your left hand on the neck of the instrument. Don't worry about where to put your fingers. With your other hand, use your nails to brush the strings.'

Tok's fingers trembled, but he listened and obeyed. He treated the lute with a reverence that bordered on worship. When his fingers stroked the strings for the first time, the sound froze him. The chord hovered in the air like a frightened sparrow. Nee'lahn's lute spoke more with its own voice than with the skill of the player. Tok raised his eyes toward Meric, joy and wonder bright in his gaze.

'Now play, Tok. Listen with your heart and let the music move your fingers.'

'I don't know what—'

'Just trust me, Tok. And for the first time in your life, trust yourself.'

The boy chewed his lower lip and once again brought his fingers to the strings. He strummed lightly, almost apologetically. But soon his eyes drifted closed, and he let the music move through him. Meric watched the boy transform from a lowly urchin to something full of grace. Music flowed from the wood of the lute through the boy and out into the world.

Meric leaned back and listened. There was no art to the boy's playing; it was all heart, passion, and an ache of loneliness. It was the last song of Nee'lahn's blighted forest and the song of a boy who longed for a past that had been stolen from him.

Meric stared at the plumage of the sunhawk as it perched so imperiously upon its branch. In its stiff stance and unforgiving eyes, Meric saw himself – or at least the person he had been when he had first arrived on these shores – momentarily mirrored. Haughty and righteously indignant with all others. But was he still the same? Since coming here, Meric had experienced acts both brave and craven. He had beheld those of low birth shine with the majesty of kings and witnessed those of noble heritage crawl through mud to satisfy their baser lusts.

Glancing back to the boy, Meric noticed the streams of tears trailing down the lad's face as he conjured forth a home that he would never know, and suddenly Meric understood the lute's song. Here was what they should be fighting for – not the ancient honor of a banished people or the lost bloodlines of a vanished king, but simply peace.

Meric let the boy play, allowing him his moment of home and hope. And in this music, Meric also discovered a calmness of spirit.

Here was something worth fighting for.

Suddenly the sunhawk let out a piercing screech. Meric sat straight in his bed, and the precious lute almost tumbled from Tok's startled fingers. Both their gazes swung to the bird.

The hawk stretched on its perch, wings pinioned out. Its snowy plumage now flared with a brightness that stung the eye.

'What's wrong?' Tok asked.

Meric was already out of his bed, reaching for the bird. 'I'm not sure.' The bird leaped to the elv'in's wrist. Claws dug into his flesh, piercing skin. Meric swooned as images flooded him. He saw ships riding stormwinds, keels cresting through clouds. Sweet Mother, not now! He had thought to have more time!

With the bird on his wrist, Meric hurried from the room. Tok followed. Meric hurried atop the decks. Joach, Flint, and the black-skinned zo'ol were the only ones present. Their mouths dropped at the sight of Meric and the fiery hawk.

Meric raised his wrist, and the bird shot upward, sailing past the billowed sails and up into the sky. Lowering his arm, Meric stared out at the seas. The *Pale Stallion* had by now passed among the fringe islands of the Archipelago.

The Dre'rendi fleet and the raging war could no longer be seen except as a smudge of darkness to the east and an echoing whisper of horns in the distance.

Flint crossed to Meric. 'What were you doing? That cursed bird's brilliance could give away our position.'

Meric watched the hawk disappear into the glare of the sun. 'He's been called home. It seems other parties are being drawn to the battle here, like moths to the flame.'

'What do you mean?'

Meric glanced back to the grizzled Brother. 'If you want the Blood Diary, we must hurry. This war of the isles is about to rage more fiercely. My mother comes – Queen Tratal!'

Flint's brows rose with hope at the news. 'We could always use more allies. If we could get word to Sy-wen and coordinate—'

Meric clutched Flint's arm and hissed at him. 'You are not listening! She comes not to aid our cause, *but to end it!* She means to lay waste to A'loa Glen, to destroy everyone and anything on the cursed island.'

Flint blinked at his outburst. 'And . . . and she has such strength to accomplish this?'

Meric just stared at Flint. The elv'in's silence was answer enough.

Flint's eyes narrowed with concern. 'But what of the Blood Diary? It is meant for Elena. Why would your mother seek to thwart us?'

Meric scowled and turned away. 'Because I asked her to.'

22

The trio of mages led Er'ril through the Grand Courtyard of the Edifice. Two guards followed behind, bearing long swords. Not that Er'ril was much of a risk to anyone: Bound from ankle to shoulder with chains that limited his pace to a shuffle, he clanked with each small step. As he limped along the garden path of white stone, he stared up at the blue skies, squinting against the brightness of the afternoon after so many days buried in the dungeons of the citadel.

With the sun already drifting toward the west, the gardens of the central court lay pooled in shadow. Only the top branches of the huge koa'kona tree, the ancient symbol of A'loa Glen, stretched above the walls and reached the warm sunlight. But where the sight of the tree in the bright sun should have cheered him, the cries of battle from beyond the walls of the castle transformed the image into one of desperation. It was as if the dead limbs of the tree were struggling against its own demise, arms and fingers scrabbling against drowning.

To heighten this image, around the base of the tree's trunk, among the knees of its gnarled roots, a group of black-robed mages gathered, encircling the tree. Ten muscled men leaned on long axes nearby, their expressions dark. Er'ril could almost smell the menace from this swamp of evil.

But that was not all he scented: Smoke stung the nose and marred the skies, while all around the city, drums and horns blared stridently. At first the war sounded as near as the castle itself; even the occasional snatches of shouted orders could be heard. Then the clash of noises seemed muted, as if the battle had drifted far from here. But Er'ril knew neither was true. The seas played tricks with sound. In truth, the battle surged all around the island.

Earlier, he had viewed the launching of the attack from atop the westernmost tower. He had seen the ships of the Bloodriders and the dragons of the mer'ai collide with the forces entrenched here: Monsters had risen from the sea; ships manned by foul berserkers had cut into the ranks of Dre'rendi ships; showers of flaming arrows and boulders had harried the dragons and riders. The waves soon frothed with blood and gore. Husks of burned-out ships ran aground against the drowned edge of the city. Bodies of the slain – both friend and foe – floated amidst the wreckage. A few of the city's towers were now fonts of flame as the pitch and oil stored inside them were torched by the attackers. Everywhere one looked, carnage marked the seas.

During all this, Shorkan had merely stood at the window of his tower chamber and stared at the slaughter below. No emotion had marked his face. Finally, responding to some signal known only to himself, Shorkan had turned and ordered them all to the catacombs for the final preparations for the night's ritual. He had seemed little concerned for the battle raging below the city.

It was this lack of concern that unnerved Er'ril the most. If the fiend had gloated at the destruction, shown some sign of humanity, Er'ril would have felt better. This total disinterest in the slaughter demonstrated how far from human this creature who walked in his brother's skin was.

As they crossed the gardens, Er'ril studied Shorkan's back. The only rise he had managed to get from the man had been a narrow-eyed suspicion when he had suggested that a traitor lurked within Shorkan's party. But when Er'ril had refused to elaborate, the Praetor's concern had quickly died away.

Still, Er'ril had managed to spark that initial response. As much as his false brother played the role of the stoic demigod, Er'ril knew some of the old Shorkan still survived behind that cold countenance. Nothing noble or good, just the baser sides of his brother that Shorkan had once kept buried and chained.

When he was a young man, Shorkan's pride and confidence had sometimes overwhelmed his judgment. He had hated to be bested in a game of strategy. That childish rage still existed behind his white robe. Though the Praetor's face remained blank, Er'ril knew Shorkan's mind and blood roiled with thoughts of who the traitor might be. Er'ril had planted a seed of suspicion, and he trusted his brother's baser nature to grow this kernel into a true core of distrust. And a man who kept his gaze suspiciously fixed on those at his side might miss an attack from the front.

Or so Er'ril hoped.

With his ankles chafing and his old wounds complaining against the rub of the manacles, Er'ril was glad to reach the far side of the Grand Courtyard. In the garden wall, a gate of intricate ironwork molded and twisted in the shape of twining rose branches stood locked against visitors.

It was the entrance to the subterranean catacombs where, for the past centuries, the deceased Brothers of A'loa Glen had been interred. Its passages ran deep into the volcanic core of the island. Some said the tunnels below were once natural passages carved from the flows of molten lava when the island was first born. Now the halls bore little resemblance to natural structures. Centuries of scuffling feet had rubbed the black rock to a polished sheen, and the skill of the city's early artisans had worked the walls and roofs with carvings and facades.

Still, behind the worn sheen, Er'ril had always sensed the natural rock of the island. It was like the thrum of a heart as one rested one's head on the chest of a lover. It was always there, a sense of eternity.

Er'ril suspected it was for this reason that the site had been chosen as the burial crypt for the island. It was also the reason why Er'ril had entombed the Blood Diary here. In these subterranean tunnels, time seemed to have no meaning. It was a perfect place to preserve the past and protect the future.

Suddenly, the screeching complaint of ancient hinges drew Er'ril back to the present. He blinked away the old memories of the past. Even this close to the opening to the catacombs, the halls below seemed to draw him out of time's eternal step.

'Lock the gate after us,' Shorkan instructed the guard. 'None must disturb us.'

The guard nodded his understanding, but Shorkan was already past him and entering the catacombs. Denal followed next, while Greshym kept guard behind Er'ril.

Past the gate, a set of stairs climbed down into the first level of the catacombs. It was here that the most ancient Brothers were interred in narrow crypts sealed with engraved stones. A pair of torches flanked the opening. Denal took one of the torches; but Shorkan merely raised a hand, and a spinning globe of silver fire drifted out from his palm and floated before him as he led the way.

The group's steps and the clink of Er'ril's chains echoed hollowly along the passage. Their shadows danced on the wall to the hiss of the torch.

Greshym kept pace behind Er'ril's shuffling gait, guarding the rear. It was clear to Er'ril that the darkmage wished to speak but feared the others hearing. Yet it was also clear that fatigue plagued Greshym, keeping him from maintaining the pace of the pair of younger mages. When Er'ril glanced back, he saw the pain of protesting joints etched on the old mage's face and noticed how Greshym's single hand clutched his staff in a white-knuckled grip.

'Be ready,' Greshym breathed at him, his voice lower than the furtive whisper of a secret lover.

Er'ril nodded but did not answer.

The passage continued its wide spiral deeper into the island's heart. Other hallways branched and crisscrossed the main passage. 'It would be easy to get lost in here,' Greshym whispered between wheezes as they walked; the other two mages had drifted farther ahead. 'The extent of these tunnels has never been fully mapped. One could easily vanish down here.'

Er'ril only snorted derisively. Greshym was trying to suggest to Er'ril that escape might be possible. But of course, such a chance would only be offered after Er'ril freed the Blood Diary and turned the tome over to the ancient darkmage.

As their group wound deeper into the world of the dead, the etchings on the grave markers grew more legible as the age of the tombs lessened. Soon, they even passed a few open niches, graves awaiting future occupants.

'Still,' Greshym continued, 'it is something to ponder.'

Shorkan led them deeper, past the open graves to where

the walls roughened to natural stone. The depths of the cata-combs reached levels where the sea itself claimed the tunnels, but their group was not going that far. Shorkan led them without warning off of the main tunnel and into the narrow side passages. He continued without hesitation through the maze of crisscrossing passages and rooms, moving unerr-ingly toward his goal.

Finally, Shorkan followed a passage that ended in a blind chamber. Unadorned rock marked the walls to either side, but before them stood a sheet of black ice reaching from floor to ceiling. Its dark surface seemed almost to flow, as if the ice melted and refroze in an eternal cycle.

Shorkan approached the icy bulwark. In the glow of his flaming sphere, the solid barrier cast back their reflections. With a look of distaste, Shorkan turned his back on the sight. 'The mage who cast this spell for you, Er'ril, was skilled. For the past centuries, it has resisted my attempts to breach it.'

Er'ril shrugged. 'He had owed me a favor.'

'Do not mock me. Brother Kallon used his dying breath and the magick gifted to you from the book to forge this tomb for the Blood Diary. He died with the spell on his lips, taking its secret to his grave.'

Er'ril laughed sharply. 'Don't be so melodramatic, Brother. It is no great secret or arcane mastery. Brother Kallon was simply a better mage than you. You know this yourself. Before the book was forged, you complained many times to me of the old mage's immeasurable skill, how he bested you at every turn. It was for this reason that I sought him once I realized the road was no longer safe. He was better than you.'

Shorkan's face remained cold, impassive, but Er'ril noticed how the flames of his sphere blew brighter with his anger. 'Brother Kallon may have been more skilled long ago. But over the past five centuries, I have grown in power and talent.'

Shrugging, Er'ril nodded toward the wall of ice. 'Ah . . . true. But I see you are still not strong enough to defeat Brother Kallon. His spell stands, mocking you to this day, a testament to his superiority.'

Shorkan's countenance finally broke. A savage fury filled his eyes; his lips pulled back in a feral growl; his brow grew dark with a threatening storm. 'That will end this night! Brother Kallon's spell will be defeated by one of my own! His death long ago will have come to naught. Both the book and you will be destroyed with the rising of the moon.'

Er'ril remained calm in the face of Shorkan's fury, his words slow and deliberate. 'That is yet to be proven, my dear brother. Kallon has bested you before – and he will do so again this night.'

Shorkan glowered, anger choking him. He spun on Denal. 'Lay out the knives and prepare a mage ring!'

The boy mage placed his torch in a wall sconce and hurried forward. Bending down, he slipped two rose-handled knives from wrist sheaths and a long white candle from a pocket. Greshym joined the boy, setting aside his staff and collecting one of the knives. The old mage glanced at Er'ril, clearly worried by the plainsman's goading of Shorkan. Finding no answer in Er'ril's face, he returned to helping the boy. Denal lit the candle with a wave of his tiny hand and began dripping its wax in a wide circle before the wall of ice. They meant to recreate the setting when the Blood Diary was forged.

As the pair worked, Shorkan stepped nearer Er'ril. 'I will succeed,' he hissed. 'I will thwart Brother Kallon by destroying what he sought to preserve. And in doing so, I will watch your heart break as all your hopes and struggles are laid to waste before you. I will see you defeated!' Shorkan slipped a knife from his own sleeve and held it before Er'ril. 'Do you recognize this?'

Now it was Er'ril's turn to fail at feigning disinterest. His breath caught in his throat at the sight of the old worn dagger. 'Father's hunting knife . . .'

Shorkan leered. 'On the night of the book's forging, you gave it to me. Do you remember?'

Er'ril's face paled with the memory. Long ago, he had lent the knife to his brother for the spell of binding. He had thought the knife forever lost. But to see the piece of his father's memory now about to be employed for such a foul cause weakened his resolve.

Shorkan leaned over Er'ril. 'I know our father meant much to you, Er'ril. I will enjoy seeing his heritage help destroy all that you hold dear.'

Er'ril refused to cower before the vehemence of this other. He shot his words at Shorkan like arrows. 'Only if you first discover the traitor in your midst.'

Shorkan's left eye twitched toward the pair behind him. Er'ril kept his expression fixed. So his seed of distrust *had* found fertile ground.

Er'ril spoke clearly. If Shorkan thought to use their father's memory to dishearten him, he would return the favor. 'A traitor stands with you, Brother – in this very room. This I swear on our father's grave and eternal spirit.'

Shock and dismay bloomed on Shorkan's face. Enough of the old Shorkan remained for the fiend to know that Er'ril would not voice such an oath unless it was true. 'Why warn me then? What trick is this?'

'It is no trick. I tell you because the knowledge will do you no good. You are too late, Brother. You are trapped. If you don't find the traitor before the moon rises, you will be betrayed this night. And if you manage to destroy the traitor, you will be missing a key player in the spell of unbinding. Either way, the book will remain safe. There is no possible way for you to succeed.'

Er'ril leaned closer to Shorkan and drove his words deep. 'You have been outmatched, Brother.'

Shorkan trembled with rage. 'No!' He raised their father's dagger and plunged it toward Er'ril's throat. 'You will never win!'

'Stop!' The command burst from Greshym. 'Shorkan, if you kill Er'ril, the spell will never work. He deceives you with his oath. Don't listen to him. He only tries to trick you into killing him. He lies!'

The knife tip rested in the hollow of Er'ril's neck. Shorkan lowered the weapon and turned to face the pair of mages. His voice went cold. 'No. Er'ril spoke truthfully. There is a traitor amongst us.' He raised his free hand toward Greshym. 'I only threatened Er'ril to flush out the betrayer.'

Greshym raised his arm in a warding motion, but Shorkan spun on Denal instead. Darkfire shot out of his hand and washed over the boy mage. As magick poured forth, Shorkan spoke. 'Denal's silence revealed his mutinous heart. If I had killed Er'ril, it would have destroyed any chance of unbinding the book. Your timely warning, Greshym, proved your trustworthiness.'

With a twist of his wrist, Shorkan tied off his magick. Denal lay bound from scalp to ankles in wraps of darkfire, like a fly in a spider's web, unable to move, unable to speak.

Shorkan turned to Er'ril. 'You erred in your plot, Brother. I don't need this traitor's cooperation, only his living body. Bound and imprisoned, Denal will still serve his role in the spell. Afterward, I will kill you both.' Shorkan stepped back toward Er'ril. 'So you see, dear brother, it is you who have been outmatched.'

Er'ril kept his face blank. So far his plan was going perfectly. Shorkan had fallen into his trap like a blind rabbit. But Er'ril kept his hopes reined.

The moon would soon rise, and the final act was yet to be played.

Elena met with the others atop the deck of the *Pale Stallion*. Ahead, the towering cliffs of the isle of Maunsk filled the western sky. The sun had already descended past the twin peaks of the island. Under the shadow of the cliffs and mountains, it was as if twilight had already fallen. The seas became a midnight blue; the brilliant green of the island became darker with menace. Only the azure sky above promised ample time before the moon yet rose. Still, Elena hugged her arms tight over her chest. Evening approached too quickly.

From behind, Meric stepped to the rail beside her. His eyes were pained. 'I'm sorry.'

Elena glanced away, unable to face him. 'Why did you do it? Why did you call your queen's forces here? I thought I could trust you.'

Meric was silent for a long time. When he spoke, it was strained. 'Back in Port Rawl, I sent a small bird from Mama Freda's menagerie with a request for aid from my mother. I thought I was protecting you. I didn't want you walking into the darkmages' trap on A'loa Glen. If the island was destroyed first, I had hoped you'd finally put aside this banner of the wit'ch and end this war with the Dark Lord. Free of such a responsibility, I had thought you'd return to Stormhaven and claim your true heritage.'

'You know I'd never do that,' she said firmly. 'With the book or without it, I will continue to struggle against the evil here.'

'Yes, I've too slowly come to realize that. After the trials in Shadowbrook, I had thought escape was the best recourse. But on hearing the tales of the Dre'rendi and the mer'ai, I now know that was a fool's dream. You cannot turn your back on the evil here without losing a part of yourself, and even then the evil would still pursue you.' His voice became soft. 'But that is not the only reason I knew you would not forsake this struggle.'

She swung toward him, her voice harsher than she intended. 'Then why else?'

He raised bright eyes toward her. 'When Tol'chuk and I rejoined you, I saw how much you had changed – and not just in body. It went deeper, something that struck me to the core. I finally saw the elv'in in you – saw our king in you. I knew then that you'd never forsake Alasea and that I'd forever stand at your side.'

Meric turned away. 'I'm sorry,' he said quietly. 'I should have told you. I had hoped we'd have the book and be gone before she ever arrived.' He raised his gaze to the skies again. 'But with the flight of her sunhawk, our time runs short. Her warships will soon be here.'

Elena felt her knot of anger at Meric begin to soften. 'How long do we have?'

'No more than a day.'

Elena joined him in searching the skies. 'Then it probably won't matter. By dawn, we'll either be off the island with the book or we'll be dead.' She turned to Meric and touched his shoulder. 'Do not despair your actions, Meric. Sometimes understanding the truth in one's own heart comes too late.' Elena thought of Er'ril. 'I know this well.'

Meric glanced gratefully at her, his shoulders regaining some of their usual strength.

In silent forgiveness, Elena touched his arm, then turned to study the boat. Flint and the zo'ol were involved in guiding their craft through the treacherous reefs that ringed the isle of Maunsk. Orders were shouted back and forth, and slow corrections were made to the ship's progress.

'El, can I talk to you a moment?' Elena turned to find her brother crossing toward her from the ship's hatch. He bore his staff in a gloved hand.

'What is it?'

'It's about Er'ril.'

Elena fought to keep the wince from showing on her face. She had no desire to discuss the plainsman, but she could also not ignore Joach's worries. 'What about him?'

Joach stopped beside her. He ran a hand over the thin reddish beard that now fuzzed his chin and cheeks. Elena's heart jumped. Just then, his simple gesture keenly reminded her of their father. He too had rubbed his chin in exactly the same manner whenever he'd had hard words to speak. For the first time, Elena recognized the man in her older brother. He was no longer the boy who had run wild through the orchards with her. Now she saw their father's stern demeanor in his green eyes. 'If Er'ril lives, he has spent over a quarter moon with the darkmages.'

'I know this,' she answered sharply.

Joach sighed. 'I'm just suggesting that, if Er'ril still lives, he may not be the man you once knew. I know how their dark magick can corrupt and bend you to their will.'

'Er'ril will resist them,' she insisted, meaning to end this conversation. She feared Joach would renew her inner turmoil.

But Joach persisted. 'I hope you're right, El. I really do. But, please, I only ask that if you should come upon him on the island, perhaps it's best if you assume the worst until proven otherwise.'

Elena stared at her brother. He was asking her to distrust Er'ril. In her mind, she knew her brother's words were wise, but in her heart, she fought back the urge to slap Joach. Er'ril would never betray them!

Joach seemed to sense her anger. He spoke even more softly. 'Think on this, El. First, the black wyvern statue. Now Er'ril captured by the darkmages. It's almost like my earlier dream is coming true.' He raised his staff, and small spurts of darkfire played along its surface. 'Maybe it was a true weaving.'

'We already discussed this with Flint and Moris. Why bring it up again? Are you trying to scare me?'

Joach's eyes grew hard. 'Yes, El. I *am* trying to scare you.'

Elena began to turn away, waving a hand to dismiss him.

Joach grabbed her arm. 'Listen to me,' he whispered. 'I bring this to you now because ... because ...' He glanced around the deck to make sure no one else listened. 'Because just now I was resting in my cabin and ... and I had the dream again. The same dream! The wyvern attacking, the flash from my staff driving it off, Er'ril locking us atop the tower and coming at us with murder in his eyes.'

Elena shook her head. 'No—'

Joach squeezed her arm hard. 'At least be wary of him. That is all I ask!' He let go of her arm.

Elena almost fell backward trying to escape her brother's words. Before she could respond, a sharp call arose from the ship's stern. It was Flint. He stood at the wheel and pointed forward. 'The entrance to the grotto! We're almost there! Gather your gear and be ready to disembark!'

Elena stepped toward the ship's prow, meaning to watch their approach, but Joach stopped her. 'El?'

She could not face him. 'I know, Joach. I'll be cautious.' Clenching her fist, she stared back at the smudge of smoke that marked the distant island of A'loa Glen. 'But if Er'ril is corrupted, I will make them all pay. I will tear the island to its roots.'

Joach backed from her vehemence.

She ignored his distraught look. As much as it hurt, she knew Joach was right. If Meric could betray her, then why not the others? Had not Aunt Mycelle run off with Kral and the shape-shifters? Elena turned and surveyed her companions here. Who could she count on during the battle ahead? Tol'chuk stood glumly, lost in his own worries. She hardly knew Mama Freda. Even the steadfast Flint was only human; he could be tricked or controlled just as easily as Joach had been by Greshym. And what of her own brother? She glanced out the corner of her eye as Joach held the staff that had killed their parents. When would the black magick begin to taint him?

Shaking her head, Elena turned away. She pictured Er'ril's face and his quiet gray eyes. In her chest, a small piece of her heart died. She could no longer be the scared child who had trusted all others. In the days to come, she needed to harden her spirit.

Elena turned to stare one last time at the smudged sky marking A'loa Glen. 'I'm sorry, Er'ril.'

Joach watched his sister walk away. He knew his words had wounded her, but Elena had needed to hear them. She needed to be cautious. Though she appeared a grown woman, Joach had suspected that a small part of her still remained his wide-eyed younger sister. But now, as Elena walked away, Joach knew that was no longer true. The child in her, her innocence, was gone. Elena was as much a woman in spirit as in form.

Swallowing hard, Joach turned away, and for a brief moment, he regretted coming to her. But as he remembered how Greshym had once controlled him, locked him in his own skull, he knew his decision had been correct. He knew that Er'ril could be just as easily spellcast. And no matter what anyone else argued, Joach was now convinced that his dream was a true weaving, a glimpse of the future. Knowing this truth, he had owed it to his sister to warn her.

Resolute with his decision, Joach gripped his staff and crossed to join the others by the rail. They all watched their approach to the island.

As the ship rounded the isle of Maunsk, the cliffs opened up before them. A deepwater channel led into the heart of the island. Overhead, the ship's sails snapped as the craft heeled to the right. They now aimed directly for the narrow waterway. A soft shudder passed through the boat as its keel scraped a reef.

Flint called out from the stern. 'Don't worry! That's the last of the rocks!'

His words proved true. The *Pale Stallion* glided smoothly between the steep walls of the ravine. To either side, green falls of foliage draped the rock. Pink and lavender blooms lay open to the late afternoon warmth, their fragrances so thick that their sweetness could be tasted on the tongue.

No one spoke as the boat sailed down the channel that split the two peaks of the island. The channel's course curved gently to the left, then trailed in a long curve to the right. Finally it opened into a wide bay. As their ship drifted into the wider expanse, Flint called for the sails to be reefed. The boat soon slowed. Joach stared around. He saw no docks or beach to land the boat. In fact, the entire bay was surrounded by the same sheer cliffs as the channel. Looming over it all, the two peaks of the isle seemed to lean toward the boat.

Frowning, Joach drifted beside the zo'ol sailor he knew. 'Xin, do you know where we're going?'

The small man tied off a line, then straightened and shrugged. 'My men and I are to stay with the boat. The little one, Tok, will keep us company.'

'So where are we going then?'

Xin nodded toward the far side of the bay. A long narrow waterfall cascaded down from the heights to crash in a froth of spray at the foot of the cliffs. 'The old Brother says you go that way.'

Flint called out to them. 'I've dropped the anchor! We need everyone and their gear on deck! Now! We'll row to shore from here.'

Joach turned and saw the other two zo'ol freeing the tarp from an oared boat latched to the starboard side of the ship. He began to take a step away to retrieve his pack, but Xin touched his arm, stopping him.

Xin's green eyes seemed to shine slightly. 'As a wizen, I sense the fear and worry in your heart, Joach, son of Morin'stal.' Xin raised a finger to touch the pale scar of an awakening eye on his dark forehead. 'The fear arises from something your inner eye has seen.'

Joach's brow bunched. 'My dream . . . ?'

Ignoring him, Xin reached and touched Joach's forehead. 'Know this. Just as ordinary eyes can be fooled by illusion, so can the spirit eye of the wizen. You are young to your powers yet. Do not let them rule you.' Xin moved his finger to Joach's chest. 'You must learn to look from here, too.'

Confused, Joach did not know how to respond. 'I . . . I will try.'

Nodding, Xin slipped out an object from within his shirt. It was the dragon's tooth pendant Joach had gifted to him in exchange for his name. Xin clutched it in his palm. 'We have shared names and hearts. Remember this. If you need me, hold the black pearl and I will know.'

Joach frowned at his words. His hand drifted to the large smooth pearl in his pocket. Was this just native superstition of the zo'ol tribesmen, or was there truly power in their exchange of gifts? He touched the pearl and nodded to Xin. 'I will remember.'

Satisfied, Xin returned to his ropes.

Joach hurried to obey Flint's orders. Soon he had his pack over his shoulder and his staff in hand. He stood with the others. All were ready.

The oared boat had been lowered and now rested in the calm waters beside the ship. A rope ladder led down to it. Tol'chuk was already in the boat, holding the ladder stable. Flint helped Mama Freda over the rail.

In short order, the rest of them climbed down the slick rope and took their seats. Once all were aboard, Flint waved his arm; the rope ladder was pulled up. The three zo'ol and the boy Tok waved them off as Tol'chuk manned the oars near the stern. The og're's wide back and strong arms soon had the small boat moving quickly away from the ship.

'There should be a narrow beach to the left of the waterfall,' Flint instructed.

Tol'chuk grunted his acknowledgment and dug deeper with the oars. The low roar of the waterfall grew louder as they approached. Now even wisps of spray blew toward them. Joach glanced back and saw the *Pale Stallion* far behind. After so long aboard the small ship, it almost seemed like home. In his pocket, he clutched Xin's black pearl; then he turned back to watch as the tiny boat angled slightly away from the waterfall.

With only a few more strokes, the rowboat ground into the thin strand of beach. The roar of the waterfall was deafening. Communicating with hand signals, Tol'chuk climbed out into the shallows and pulled the boat higher on the beach. Joach blinked at the og're's sheer strength.

With their craft beached, everyone disembarked. The furious spray from the crashing waters soaked them all to the skin.

Flint yelled to be heard. 'Follow me! Stick close!' He led them along the narrow beach of coarse sand and rock toward the waterfall. As they neared, Flint pointed.

A gap between the cascade and the wet cliff face lay ahead. He led them there. Once near, a hollowed-out cave could be seen behind the waterfall. Flint waved them all to follow him inside.

They were forced to walk single file as they edged between the crash of waters and the rock wall. But once the cave was reached, they could gather again. Joach glanced around. The cavern ended only a few spans back. He had expected a secret tunnel or something. 'Where do we go now?' he yelled over the fall's roar.

Flint removed Er'ril's small iron fist from a sealskin wrap. He raised it for all to see. 'Like the Arch of the Archipelago, this is another site rich in elemental power. From here, the ward can open a path to the city.'

Joach glanced back to the black rock of the cave.

But Flint's graveled voice drew his gaze back around. He was pointing to the waterfall. 'We go this way! Join hands to form a linked chain!'

Leading them, Flint grabbed the iron ward with one hand and reached the other to Elena. She began to take his hand, but he shook his head. 'Skin to skin! You'll need to take off your gloves.'

She nodded and did so. In the gloom of the cave, Elena's two hands seemed almost to glow a soft ruby. She took Flint's hand, then reached for Joach.

Encumbered with the staff, he was forced to lodge the length of wood into the straps of his pack, then take off his own gloves. Once ready, he accepted Elena's hand. It was cold to his touch, as if he clutched the moon itself. He squeezed her palm in an attempt to reassure her. She offered him a slight smile, but it was as cold as her hand.

Turning away, he offered his other palm to Meric. Soon the party was linked, with Tol'chuk last in line.

Flint studied them, then nodded. 'Do not break the chain until we are through! I'm not sure where on the island we will end up. It takes a master mage to wield these wards with precision. So be ready!'

Swinging around, he lifted the iron fist and stepped toward the waterfall. As he neared, the sheet of crashing waters grew glassy. Stepping forward, Flint drew the others after him. As he reached out with the ward, the waters became as clear as fine crystal, but the wide bay and their boat were gone. The view beyond the falls was of buildings built of white bricks and towers that stretched toward the clouds.

It was the city of A'loa Glen!

Flint led them through the portal as if walking through an ordinary doorway. First the old Brother passed, then Elena. Joach followed next. He felt only a slight tingling in his skin as he stepped from the cave behind the waterfall and once again set foot onto the island of A'loa Glen.

But as Joach pierced the portal, the silent tableau of the city shattered. His ears were immediately assaulted by the screams and clashes of battle. Joach cringed from the noise. Smoke stung his nose, and the bellowing roar of dying dragons echoed all around him from the sun-scorched stones.

In one step, he had walked into the middle of a maelstrom.

Joach glanced behind him and saw Tol'chuk climb through the portal behind Mama Freda. The portal winked out behind them.

They now stood in the middle of a nondescript plaza in one of the higher levels of the city. Not far above, Joach spotted the battlements and towers of his old prison, the sprawling Edifice of A'loa Glen. His heart momentarily quailed at the sight. How could they ever hope to pierce the massive keep? As he stared, something struck him as wrong. He studied it a moment, then shivered as he recognized what was missing.

He raised an arm and pointed. 'The tree!' he shouted. 'The koa'kona is gone!' The dead branches of the mighty symbol of A'loa Glen normally sprouted out from the central courtyard to spread like a crown over the Edifice. But now it was gone!

Before he could even begin to fathom this portent, a voice arose from around the corner of a crumbled building. It was high and sibilant. 'We've been waiting a long time for you to arrive.'

Joach spun around. From every street, skal'tum clawed their way into the plaza. Even from the countless black windows overhead, pale faces leered down at them, razored teeth smiling at them.

Their group had entered a nest of skal'tum, an ambush.

A massive demon stepped into the plaza. It was the largest skal'tum Joach had ever seen. Its wings spread wide, striking an ancient pillar and shattering it. It leaned toward them with a hiss.

'Your delay hasss made us all very hungry!'

Sy-wen's arm burned with fire, but she ignored the pain. The injury was not her own, but the dragon's. She glanced to her mount's right wing. They had been sailing too near one of the city's towers when it had suddenly exploded in flames. The spout of fire and debris had caught Ragnar'k by surprise. Only a sudden dive and twisting turn had kept them from annihilation.

Still, the dragon's scales lay blistered and seared in a wide swath along the forward edge of his wing. Ragnar'k sailed in a long curve away from the city's edge. They now flew over the waves, aiming back for the beset fleet. Enemy ships fired arrows at their passing form, but their height was still beyond bow range. But for how long? Ragnar'k continued to weaken with his injured wing, losing altitude rapidly.

Below, the Dre'rendi fleet lay in chaos. Attacking ships, most smaller than the warships of the Bloodriders, plied among the fleet. Arrows flew across the waves, some flaming, some poisoned. Almost every dragon-prowed warship was harried by the smaller, swifter craft. Like remora on sharks, scaling ladders and boarding hooks had latched many of the enemy boats to the bigger ships' flanks. Battles raged across decks and rigging now.

Screams and shouted orders rang up from below.

But all was not lost. Among the adversaries' boats, the seas were not friendly. The mer'ai and their dragons surged from below to wreak havoc on the ships. Dragon claw and dragon fang ripped into keels and men alike. Ships foundered everywhere. Berserkers who were tossed into the water became dragon fodder.

Yet even the mer'ai were not safe in their own seas. Tentacled beasts snatched unwary dragons or riders. The worst of the undersea battle raged near the city's edge. A mountainous leviathan lay within a nest of the monsters. Flailing pale tentacles ripped at the giant. It was as if the leviathan drifted in a sea of pale, flickering flames. Dragons, mounted and alone, fought to free the creature, but even from this height, Sy-wen knew the seabeast would not survive its injuries. The waters around the sunken towers now frothed with blood. Wrecked boats and corpses clogged the narrow channels of the submerged city.

Wincing away the pain, Sy-wen sent an urgent plea to Ragnar'k. *We must make it back to the* Dragonsheart.

Ragnar'k tilted his head to flash one black crystalline eye at her. *I will not fail you, my bonded.* Hindered by the wounded wing, his body lurched under her as he fought for distance from the sea.

She leaned closer to his neck, running a hand along his straining flesh. She willed her mount strength. They must reach the high keel. 'Kast, if you can hear me,' she whispered, 'add your heart to Ragnar'k. I need you both.'

In her mind, she knew Kast was unaware of events that occurred after Ragnar'k took flesh. Still, her heart longed for him to hear her. Exhausted from the day of flying and fighting, Sy-wen allowed her eyes to close, just for a moment. With the wind whistling in her ears, the clash of battle faded to a dim roar.

Kast, hear me, she urged silently.

From somewhere deep inside, an answer arose. Sy-wen could not say for sure if it came from within her or the dragon. They seemed one spirit. *I am here, Sy-wen.*

Her eyes fluttered open. 'Kast?'

We are both here, my bonded. This was Ragnar'k.

How? she sent to them.

I think, after the lightning strike, the line between the two of us blurred, Kast answered. *I now see what the dragon sees, but only as if in a dream.'*

And you can speak to me?

It is hard for Ragnar'k to allow this. It strains his control of his own body.

Sy-wen sensed a silent agreement from the dragon, almost a disgruntled embarrassment. Ragnar'k never liked to admit a weakness.

Then we must end this talk, Sy-wen sent. *Ragnar'k must have his full strength. We must reach the* Dragonsheart *and the high keel.*

I know. I saw. Ragnar'k only allowed me a moment of shared union to bolster your heart. He wanted you to know I was here, too. Sensing your own despair, he sought to ease it, even at his own expense.

Sy-wen reached and rubbed her mount's flank. Warm sensations flowed back to her from the dragon. 'You both truly are my bonded.'

I must go, Kast sent back. *Godspeed to you both. Your knowledge must reach the fleet.*

Sy-wen sensed Kast slip away. Ragnar'k seemed to surge slightly in strength, the heat off his body intense. He angled across the battle below. Smoke marred their views, but the three-masted *Dragonsheart* could be seen far ahead. It kept mostly to the rear of the fighting. The high keel directed the fleet with horn and pigeon.

So far the battle was mostly a standstill, each force refusing to give ground. But not for long. The dark forces would win unless Sy-wen could reach the ship.

Their reconnaissance of the enemy's defenses had revealed two vital details, information that needed to reach the Bloodriders. First, they had spotted several roosts of skal'tum in the deserted city. Shunning the sunlight, the beasts had been hard to find. But the dragon's keen sense of smell had rooted them out. Sy-wen estimated that at least another two legions, maybe three, were still kept in reserve upon the island. She gritted her teeth. So many of the monsters still lived! She had hoped the battle in the sargassum forest had reduced their numbers more drastically.

Glancing back at the embattled city, Sy-wen knew speed was essential. The fleet needed to reach and subdue the docks before sunset. If they could at least gain a foothold on the island itself, their forces could use the crumpled buildings and tilted towers as a means of protection against the skal'tum. Upon the open seas, their fleet would be too vulnerable to the winged beasts. The tide of battle would quickly turn in favor of the enemy.

But word of the skal'tum legions was not the worst news she bore. Sy-wen watched their approach toward the *Dragonsheart*. They needed to hurry.

Must go lower, Ragnar'k said. The throb of pain in Sy-wen's right arm flared harsher. The strain of their flight was taking its toll.

Just get us there. Even swim if you must.

The war loomed greater as they sank toward the embattled seas. Soon the tops of masts skittered just under the dragon's wings. Arrows from enemy ships now reached them, peppering Ragnar'k's underbelly, but so far the dragon's thick scales protected him from harm.

In a few more swipes of his massive wings, they were beyond the worst of the battle and gliding low over the waves toward the rear of the fleet. The *Dragonsheart* lay just ahead.

Ragnar'k had to fight for additional height just to crest

the ship's rail. His landing atop the deck was more a crumpled crash. Silver talons tore into the deck, and his injured right wing collided with a mast. Agony shot down Sy-wen's arm, but they finally came to a rest. Ragnar'k sank to the deck.

Sy-wen straightened in her seat. 'Dragon's blood!' she called out. 'Bring us a draught now!' She dared not reverse the spell and call Kast forth yet, not with Ragnar'k so wounded.

Men who had fled from the crashing dragon now scurried about the deck. The high keel leaped from the stern deck and shouted for her to be obeyed. A cask was hurriedly rolled toward them.

No longer flying, Sy-wen got a whiff for the first time of the dragon's burned flesh. She fought her stomach. The smell warned how deep the damage was, more so than even the pain. She glanced to the blistered tissue. Black scale, now seared a sickly white, oozed a clear, yellowish fluid. Even bone could be seen through the rent tissue at the forward edge of the wing. Sweet Mother, she had not realized how badly Ragnar'k had been injured. How had the great beast flown such a distance?

She was answered. *Your heart, my bonded . . . I would not fail you.*

She leaned forward and hugged his great neck, then quickly straightened. Before the dragon's snout, a cask was rolled into position and tipped upright. The high keel himself stepped forward with ax in hand. With a single stroke, he chopped open the lid of the barrel.

'Drink!' he commanded.

Ragnar'k needed no urging. The scent of blood drew him. In Sy-wen, the hunger of blood lust almost overwhelmed the pain from the burn. Ragnar'k lowered his snout and drank the stored blood. In only a few heartbeats, the full cask lay empty.

Almost immediately Sy-wen sensed the healing property of the dragon blood. The throb of pain in her arm dulled, as with a wash of cool water. She almost sighed aloud in relief.

Ragnar'k nosed the barrel away.

'Do you need more?' Sy-wen asked.

No. Ragnar'k is strong. Blood from puny dragons was enough.

Sy-wen sagged in relief. If the dragon's haughtiness was returning, she knew he fared much better. 'Then I must seek the counsel of these others, my mighty bonded.'

Ragnar'k sent her a dismissive snort, as if such matters were beneath his attention.

Smiling at his growing arrogance, she slid from her seat to the deck, almost tumbling, her legs numb and tired from flying all day. Still, she managed to keep her feet with the timely aid of the high keel's supporting hand. 'Thank you,' she whispered to the tall chief.

With her palm still on her dragon's flank, Sy-wen turned to Ragnar'k. *Rest now, my bonded.*

Return soon. He swung and touched her gently with the tip of his snout. *I will miss your scent.*

'And I yours,' she said aloud and removed her hand.

Sy-wen and the high keel retreated a step as the spell reversed itself. Wing and scale exploded out wildly, then whirled back down until only a naked man crouched on the deck.

Kast straightened and stumbled a step forward. His right arm was seared a deep red from shoulder to wrist. But even as Sy-wen rushed toward him, the injury paled to a pink glow. She fell into his arms as the high keel waved a man to fetch a set of breeches and a shirt.

Sy-wen felt the heat of his bare skin against her cheek and wished to stay in his arms forever, but the urgency of their news required them pulling apart too soon.

Kast leaned next to her. 'I missed your scent, too,' he whispered.

Sy-wen glanced up to him, her cheeks burning now. He kissed her deeply, once. Her knees buckled under her, but his strong arms were there to keep her from falling.

Too soon, one of the warriors hurried forward, his arms laden with clothing.

Kast brushed his fingertips across her cheek and down her neck, then quickly dressed. He spoke to the high keel while slipping into his breeches. 'We must get word to the other keelchiefs. A change in the battle looms, and we must be prepared.'

'Come,' the high keel ordered once Kast was dressed. 'We'll retire to my cabin. I'd have Bilatus hear your news, too.'

Kast nodded. He embraced Sy-wen under one arm, and together they followed the high keel below. Sy-wen noticed that the war seemed to have energized the aging chief. He walked with vigor in his steps; even his eyes sparked with the excitement of battle.

In the chief's cabin, they found the portly ship's shaman poring over a set of tomes and maps. Bilatus raised his balding head, his cheeks rosy from the room's heat. He pushed to his feet with a small groan. 'Master Kast and Mistress Sy-wen, I had not known you had returned.'

The high keel stepped forward. 'Did you not hear the crash atop our decks and the commotion?'

Bilatus wore an apologetic expression as he waved an arm in the direction of the laden table. 'My books . . . When I'm studying, I'm lost to the world.'

The high keel clapped the fellow good-naturedly on the shoulder as he crossed to perch on a stool. 'I would have it no other way. That is the role of shaman. You stick to your scrolls and maps, and let us warriors handle the swords.' The tall man waved for Sy-wen and Kast to take the pillowed chairs near the small hearth.

Once they were settled, the high keel shoved off his stool and stalked back and forth across the room, his energy too large for the small chamber. Sy-wen sensed that the man longed to return to the deck and the smoke of battle. 'What news do you bring?'

Kast glanced at Sy-wen, but she nodded for him to tell. Kast quickly related their discovery of the skal'tum legions still awaiting release in the crumbled ruins of the city. 'Once the sun sets, they will take wing and attack. We must take the island before that happens. We'll need the cover of the buildings to wage a proper defense against the beasts.'

Kast's tale slowed the high keel's pacing. By the time Kast was finished, the chief had stopped, the fire dimming in his eyes.

'Dire news,' Bilatus said from near the table. 'So what you're saying is that we must direct all our forces in a full affront against the city's docks? If we can commandeer the piers, we may survive.'

The high keel clenched a fist. 'We must more than survive. We must win. The Dark Lord will not let us survive a half victory. If we don't wrest his forces from this island and take it over, there will be no safe seas anywhere for the Dre'rendi.' The high keel began pacing again. 'You have brought us vital news. I must alert the others and redirect our forces.'

He began to march toward the door, but Sy-wen stopped him. 'Before you act, we bring other news.'

The high keel turned, and in the man's eyes, Sy-wen could see the fire flaring within. Here stood a true man of battle. Talk and strategy were not as important as sword and pike. 'What else?' he demanded.

Sy-wen swallowed and spoke rapidly. 'We risked a flight over the city's castle to see what else may lie in wait. In a central court, we saw that the mighty tree there had been chopped down and its limbs were being axed to rubbish.'

'So?'

Kast answered. 'The tree had always been a font of magickal energies. This sudden action by the darkmages strikes me as suspicious.'

Sy-wen nodded. 'Also around the stump of the tree, we spotted a ring of black-robed men circling and chanting. Spread-eagled across the top of the stump, a young girl lay chained and writhing.'

The fire died in the high keel's eyes as he understood what they were trying to suggest. 'They strive to call forth some black magick to thwart us.'

'Yes,' Kast answered. 'So besides striking for the docks, we'd best be prepared for other surprises. I suspect the worst is yet to come.'

The high keel nodded more soberly. Now when he crossed toward the door, his stride was more urgent than excited. 'I must alert the fleet.'

As he reached for the latch, a sudden pounding on the door erupted from beyond. 'Sir! You must come atop the decks! Something is amiss.'

The high keel glanced back at them. Worry now replaced the fire in his eyes. They all rose to follow him. In a rush, they fled from the cabin, almost knocking aside the Bloodrider who had brought the warning.

Once atop the deck, Sy-wen knew instantly from which

direction the current crisis arose. Everyone on deck stared and pointed north toward the island. Sy-wen hurried to the rail along with the others.

Across the battlefield, a hush seemed to have fallen over the seas, as if the combatants all held their breath. In the distance, the island stood in sharp detail as the sun sank toward the west. From the central peak, from the Edifice that crowned its top, a black pall rose into the blue sky, a column of darkness that could never be mistaken for smoke. It was more like a black beacon, a spire of dark light cast up from the depths of some foul netherworld.

'What is it?' the high keel asked.

No one answered.

As they watched, the spear of darkness began to tilt like a toppling tower. It fell westward.

'Sweet Mother, no . . .' Sy-wen moaned. She knew the dire beacon arose from the magicked stump of the koa'kona, its last vestiges of white magick corrupted for this foul purpose.

The black shaft continued to fall until it pointed toward the setting sun.

'They cannot possibly wield such power,' Kast mumbled.

As they all watched, the end of the column of darkness bloomed like a foul rose and spread farther and farther across the western sky, pumping its blackness like spilled ink over the horizon. An eerie twilight descended over the seas as the sun was blocked. Sy-wen had only once before experienced such a strange quality to the light – when she was a child and had witnessed the moon eclipsing the sun. Such was the illumination now. Not night, but not day either, a shadowless half-light that weighed on one's spirit like the pressure of the deep sea.

'They steal the sun from us,' Bilatus stated. 'But why?'

Sy-wen knew. She glanced from the western sky back to the island. 'That's why,' she mumbled and pointed.

Kast, Bilatus, and the high keel all turned. Across the seas, a new menace arose from the island. In the strange twilight, flocks of winged creatures rose like a pale fog from the city, rolling out toward the fleet.

'The skal'tum take flight,' Sy-wen said.

The high keel studied the approaching menace. 'Then we are too late.'

23

In a lone plaza, deep in the heart of A'loa Glen, Elena stood in the center of a maelstrom of energies. Raw magick sang in her blood, but it was an old song. Instead, she bent the tendrils of energy to her will, striking out in all directions with spates of coldfire. Blue tails of flame lashed out and whirled in a tangled net around her. None dared approach too close.

When first confronted by the skal'tum ambush, Elena had quickly bloodied her hands and brought the attack to the monsters. The others had followed suit, moving in stride to bolster her attack. While she lanced forth with coldfire, freezing and slowing the beasts, the others had struck.

Joach, with his staff already bled into a blood weapon, skillfully kept step with Elena's dance of ice. What Elena froze, Joach shattered with a stroke of his stave. Meanwhile, Tol'chuk used the rune-carved d'warf hammer as an ordinary maid might use a broom. Directed by Flint, the og're swept a deadly path through the beasts.

'We must get free of this open space!' Flint yelled, striking out with a sword. With the sun yet out, the beasts were vulnerable to common weapons. But the monsters' strength, speed, and poisoned claws were still a serious threat.

Mama Freda also danced in the og're's shadow. Under the power of her herb, she was no longer a frail woman, but a whirlwind of death. Using darts dipped in venom and the keen eyesight of her pet tamrink, she showered the enemy with a rain of burning poison.

As they all fought the beasts in the plaza, Meric stood on the far side of Elena, matching her gale of energies with one of his own. His winds kept the skal'tum from attacking from overhead. Blasts of air caught wings and sent beasts tumbling into tower walls or crashing to the stone road.

While the others fought, Elena studied her quarry from her web of magick. Her team's initial furious attack had caught the skal'tum by surprise. Even though Elena was sure the creatures had been warned by the darkmages to be wary of them, the beasts had never faced any serious challenge in the past. They had counted on sheer numbers to intimidate any group.

This day the beasts learned a deadly lesson.

When Elena had first struck out with her magick, the huge leader of this group had fled, clearly panicked. Without guidance, the others had fought feebly and without coordination. So far, Elena's group had kept them at bay. But Elena watched as the massive skal'tum, their chief, hissed orders and began to marshal its forces. The beast's initial shock had worn off.

Now came the serious threat. Elena surveyed the remaining flock. While she and the others left a path of destruction, the plaza was still crowded with beasts. From windows and ledges above, more skal'tum threatened. The leader moved toward her tiny group, rallying the others to its side.

Unless something happened, her group was about to be swamped.

Another of their party must have realized the hopelessness of their situation. 'El,' Joach hissed at her. 'Release the spirit spell. Disappear and run.'

Elena knew that if she did that, the beasts would ravage the others. 'Not yet,' she answered her brother. She raised her right hand, the one whose Rose had been gifted by spirit light. Though she refused to use its glow to fade away from sight, Elena had another power still held in reserve: *ghostfire*. She had yet to call forth the spirit magick pent up within the Rose of her right hand. She had been hesitant on how to put it to best use.

Lifting her gaze, she found her eyes meeting the leering leader of this flock. It seemed to sense her attention, and its sick grin grew. A slithering red tongue slipped from between its fangs to curl like a hungry serpent.

Suddenly, far above the plaza, a spear of darkness sprouted from the citadel atop the hill. The sudden blaze of magicks was felt by all – beast and men alike. It was as if a bolt of lightning had struck nearby, a prickling of power that rose the tiny hairs on the back of her arms.

Everyone's eyes turned to stare at the cascade of black energies, even the monstrous chief skal'tum. When it turned to face them again, the amused glint had returned to its eyes. It stalked forward, claws gouging the ancient stone road.

Elena knew this was her only chance. Raising her left hand, she stanched her flow of coldfire and stepped free of her cocoon of blue flame. The beast slowed its approach, suspicious of Elena's strange new tack.

Elena took a step nearer the towering leader. The flock at its side shifted nervously. She raised her right hand. As she concentrated, silver flames blew forth from her sliced palm to dance along each finger.

The leader seemed little impressed. 'All the magick in

the world can't ssstop us all, little child. You will die, and I personally will eat your heart.'

'Wrong, demon. I will eat yours,' she said coldly. Thrusting out her arm, fire shot from her fingers, forming a claw of silver fire. It dashed into the chest of the skal'tum.

The leader wore a shocked expression, then glanced down to stare at the limb of fire thrust into its chest. Its skin did not burn. Raising its head, the huge beast cackled. 'It ssseeems your pretty magick is no danger to me.'

'Wrong again,' Elena said calmly and clenched her outstretched hand into a hard fist.

The skal'tum suddenly spasmed.

Elena yanked her arm back and tugged the beast's spirit from its body. The creature's carcass collapsed to the stone pavement in a clatter of bone and wing. Left standing was a phantom etched by ghostfire in the shape of the beast. The trapped spirit struggled in the silver grip of Elena's flaming magicks.

Neighboring skal'tum scattered away. Squeaks of fear and scrabbling claws sounded from all around. Overhead, startled skal'tum took flight from their perches.

In a few short moments, the spirit's writhing slowed and stopped. Her magick had succeeded in branding the ghost to Elena's will. 'Sssspread my touch,' Elena hissed, mimicking the skal'tum leader. She opened her hand.

Wings of ghostfire spread behind the phantom beast. It twisted and leaped at its nearest neighbor, diving within and ripping its brother's spirit loose. Now two spirits, burning with her will, stood upon the stone road. They leaped at others.

Before such bewildering magick, the other skal'tum panicked, leaderless and frightened. Some attempted to attack, but were quickly dealt with by Elena's companions.

Most of the others simply fled. Those that failed became fodder to the spread of her ghostfire. As with the ravers before, her magick swept through these beasts like fire through dry grass.

Soon the plaza and surrounding streets were littered with the discarded corpses of the skal'tum. Flashes of ghostfire sparked from farther down the avenues as her spirit dogs gave chase to the living.

Satisfied, Elena withdrew her magick from the hunters before they drained too much of her power. The handful of silver ghosts still visible vanished like the flames of spent candles. With the skal'tum weakened and scattered, her ghostfire army was no longer needed. With future battles ahead, preserving the last of her magick was more important.

Flint crossed to her side. 'Good work. I had thought us lost for sure.'

Elena ignored the compliment. 'How did the skal'tum know we would portal to this specific location? I though it was a random jump here.'

Flint frowned and answered, seeming not to hear the suspicion in Elena's voice. 'With Er'ril captured, the Dark Lord must have learned of his ward and set up a magickal net to snare our portal and bring us specifically to this nest of monsters.'

Elena frowned and glanced to the sky. She hated to think that Er'ril could have betrayed them in even this manner. In her heart, she would rather believe Flint had led them into a trap, that he was the traitor.

As she pondered Flint's words, a shaft of darkness began to eat the sunlight. A sick twilight settled over the city. 'What of this?' she asked.

Flint scratched his head. 'Perhaps some means to help

protect the rest of the skal'tum. To keep the sunlight from weakening their dark protections.'

As if to prove his words, legions of skal'tum took flight from roosts all across the city. They rose in massive numbers.

Joach moved beside them. 'We should get off the streets. I don't care to repeat this last battle.'

The others mumbled their agreement.

Flint responded. 'The hidden entrance to the catacombs is still much farther. We must reach the top city level, just below the Edifice itself. I'd guess almost a full league of travel still awaits us, so we should hurry.'

Flint then led them at a hard pace, up stairs and along narrow alleys. They passed sights both wondrous and sad. Statues as tall as towers stood everywhere. Some seemed to have weathered the centuries without blemish. Others lay toppled and broken. In one square, they had to cross under the stone fingers of a massive hand that rested from where it had broken off a statue high atop a tower.

They also passed areas where the seas seemed to bubble up from below, swamping entire sections of the city. As they skirted the edge of one such briny pond, something large and armored humped through the algae-slick waters. It reminded Elena of the kroc'an from the swamps. They gave the waters a wide berth.

Mostly as they fled, though, the city was just homes and buildings, long gone dark and empty. Winds whistled through the hollow husks of towers like the moaning cries of ancient ghosts. Elena found it hard to imagine that such a place was ever populated. But the city must have once housed hundreds of thousands of inhabitants. Tears suddenly rose in Elena's eyes. It hurt to see how much her people had lost.

Finally, Flint spoke, breaking the spell of timelessness. 'It

'. . . it should just be up ahead,' he gasped, winded from the long race across the city. 'Just around the next bend—'

As the grizzled Brother led them around the corner of a tulip-shaped building, he tripped to a stop. The rest of the team were too close on his heels to halt so fast. The group stumbled together in shock.

Crowding the next avenue, a squad of twenty squat creatures armored from head to toe stood guard. Though they stood smaller than Joach, each creature massed as much as Tol'chuk, all muscle and bone under the armor.

Elena named the squat soldiers' heritage. 'D'warves.'

The soldiers had clearly been awaiting them, axes raised, faceplates lowered. None moved, letting the enemy draw nearer. Not a single one shifted even a finger, as if they were a score of brass-and-steel sculptures. Elena sensed that these guards would not spook like their winged allies. From the cold stares and steady gazes, Elena knew the company would fight to the dying breath of the last d'warf. And with two hearts, each d'warf would be difficult to kill.

Pushing the others aside, Elena stepped forward, meaning to call forth her magick. Flint pulled her back. 'No, they wear spellcast armor. See how it glows?'

Elena stared closer and saw how an oily sheen roiled slowly across the breastplates and greaves of their armor in hues of a rainbow. Now that it had been brought to her attention, she could almost smell the magick here. 'What does it do?'

'I've read old tales of dealing with d'warf ax guards. Their armor is forged with elemental warding charms. Be cautious what you cast at them, Elena. It can dispel magick or reflect it back at its wielder. Beware using spells around such armor.'

Elena stepped forward, frowning, unsure what to do.

'Where is the entrance to the catacombs?' she asked Flint.

'At the end of this street.'

Elena's eyes narrowed. Again she wondered how the darkmages seemed to know their every move. Perhaps Greshym remembered more of the Hi'fai secrets than anyone supposed, and like Flint, he knew of this secret entrance and had set these guards. Still, Elena scowled at the forces here and at the suspicions that arose in her mind.

Without turning, Elena knew the team awaited her next move. Her group numbered too few to survive a battle of steel and muscle with this force. She pondered her choices.

As she studied her opponents, she recalled an old lesson, something she had once overheard her father tell Joach: Sometimes a fight was best won with wits rather than either sword or fist. With the odds against them here, Elena knew that just such a time had arisen.

They had only one small hope here. If she could weaken the black resolve of these guards, perhaps her group might survive this slaughter. From meeting Cassa Dar, Elena knew the d'warves had once been a noble people. It had only been the corrupting touch of the Dark Lord that had poisoned their hearts and bent them to his foul bidding. While her ghostfire might be unable to free their tainted spirits as it had the skal'tum, something else might hold such power, something that in a way was its own magick: *memory*.

Without turning, Elena called back to her group. 'Tol'chuk, Meric, come join me.'

The og're pushed forward with the elv'in at his side. Elena touched Tol'chuk's shoulder. 'Raise the hammer overhead for all to see.'

He did so.

Next, Elena glanced to Meric. 'On my signal, can you call forth a bolt of lightning to strike the hammer?'

'Yes, but without a natural storm brewing, I'll need a few moments.'

'Then prepare.' Elena stepped nearer the gathered ax guards and raised her voice so it rang down the avenue. 'I command you to set aside your weapons. Do you stand in the way of your own salvation?'

As expected, there was no response. Elena waved Tol'chuk forward. 'Do you recognize this relic? Have you forgotten your own heritage?' Elena raised her left arm and illuminated the rune-carved hammer with spurts of cold-fire flame. The weapon now seemed to glow with its own inner radiance.

A few of the d'warves in front shifted, and one even lowered his ax. Elena knew they would not fail to recognize the Try'sil, the Thunder Hammer of the d'warves, a cherished symbol of their people's past. But would the mere sight of it be enough to weaken the hold of the Dark Lord? Elena recalled how the memory of Linora had awoken Rockingham, breaking his black shackles. Could the same happen here? Was the Try'sil a powerful enough symbol? And if not, could Elena make it so?

One of the ax guards stepped forward from the rest. 'You seek to fool us with magicks of illusion,' he declared, his voice harsh. 'The Try'sil was lost ages ago.'

'No! On this night, the past lives again!' Elena signaled Meric forward with a sharp wave of her other hand. The elv'in seemed to sense his role here. He stepped from around the back of Tol'chuk, his magicks billowing his shirt and loose breeches. 'Forged by the elv'in, the Try'sil was a gift to your people.'

The d'warf leader stepped back, his eyes wide inside his helm at the sight of Meric. 'A Stormrider!'

'Yes! So it was before; so it is now! Remember who you

once were! The hammer has the power to break ebon'stone, to break the spell of the Black Heart! Let it free you of his chains now! Let us pass and open your hearts to the possibility of your homelands again ringing with the strike of your hammers and the roar of your forges. Remember your past!'

Elena nodded to Meric, and a bolt of lightning cracked down from the twilight skies to strike the raised iron head of the hammer. Thunder crackled along the street. Elena blinked away the blinding flash as the thunder echoed and died. 'Do you still doubt the power of your ancestors' relic?'

Several of the d'warves had fallen to their knees, but others still remained standing, including their leader. 'How did you . . . ? How did you come by the Try'sil? It was lost ages ago.'

Elena sensed that if she could sway this one d'warf, the others would follow suit. She lowered her voice, striving to pry trust from a hard heart. 'It was not lost, only *forgotten*. One of your people stood guard over it for centuries, waiting for someone to carry it back home. I was chosen! I swore a blood oath to return the hammer to your homelands. And so I will!'

'The pr – prophecy,' the leader mumbled. His ax slipped lower.

'Remember your past,' she whispered now. 'Remember who you once were.' She waved to Tol'chuk, who passed the hammer to her. With the rune-carved haft held in both her open palms, Elena stepped before the d'warf leader. She lifted it before him. 'Though your hearts were blackened by the Gul'gothal lord and your hands stained with the blood of the innocent, the Try'sil has the power to cleanse you.'

The d'warf warrior raised a mailed hand toward the weapon; his fingers trembled, and for a moment, he could not touch it. Then, he shook off his chain mail glove and, ever so gently, reached a single finger to the hammer's iron. Even this small connection to his people's past unmanned him. He fell to his knees with a crash of steel on stone. He tore off his helm and raised his wrinkled face to the skies. A cry of pain and sorrow flowed from his lips, as if he were casting out his own heart.

Elena stepped back, allowing the d'warf to face the pain of his lost past. She knew that no further words or demonstrations were needed. Still, she raised the hammer over her own head. 'There is salvation,' she whispered to the others.

Behind their kneeling leader, the others all fell to join him.

Lowering the Try'sil, Elena again met the eyes of the guards' chief. The well of pain behind his gaze was too deep even to fathom. His voice was strained to a small plea. 'Go,' he said. 'Free our people.'

Elena nodded. 'It will be done.' She led the others forward, still carrying the ax in both her palms. As she slowly passed among the kneeling d'warves, axes clattered to the cobbled pavement. Hands reached to touch the last symbol of hope for their people. She allowed each of the guards to connect with their ancient past, to remember for this brief moment their forgotten homes far across the cold seas.

Then she was past them all, and only an open street lay before her. Flint pushed beside her, his eyes full of wonder as he glanced back at the d'warves. 'You've walked us through fire,' he said, 'with only the strength of your word.'

Elena turned away. 'It was not my word. It was their own past.'

Tol'chuk accepted the hammer back as the others joined Elena and Flint. 'Where now?' Meric whispered.

Flint pointed forward. 'This way. It's just ahead.' The

old Brother led them down the avenue to a side alley.

As Joach entered the narrow street, he glanced skyward and almost tripped. Elena followed his gaze to see what had startled him.

Flanking the alley were two structures. On the right was a tower of reddish orange bricks the color of sunset. It rose to a small parapet high above. To the left was one of the massive statues that dotted the city. This one was of a gowned woman bearing a flowering sprig aloft in one hand. Joach's eyes met hers.

'The Spire of the Departed,' Joach said with a nod toward the tower, 'and the statue of Lady Sylla.'

Elena shrugged, not understanding the significance.

'This is where my dream took place, atop the Spire of the Departed.' He shifted his staff in his gloved hands. Without the touch of his skin, the wood had returned to its dark shade, a tool of black magick.

Elena remembered the details of Joach's dream and the role his staff had played in it – how its magick had driven off the black winged monster and how it had slain Er'ril. 'Are you sure this is the place?' she asked.

Joach only nodded, his eyes staring up at the distant parapet.

Not hearing their quiet words, Flint waved them all to the back of the alley, where a wall of red brick blocked their way. He began counting the bricks from the ground and the side.

As she waited, Elena shivered with her brother's words. It was as if his dream were coming true.

Ahead, Flint finally stopped counting and pushed three specific bricks. Each gave way and receded to the depth of a thumb. Upon pressing the third one, a sharp crack of an unlocking latch sounded from behind the wall.

Satisfied, Flint stepped back, then leaned both palms on the wall and shoved. A triangular section spun on an axis, opening the way into a dark tunnel beyond. He grinned at his success and waved them toward the opening. 'The catacombs delve deep into the heart of Mount Orr, the peak upon which the Edifice rests. This tunnel is an offshoot from the fourth level of the great spiral. We must reach the tenth level to retrieve the book.'

'Then let us hurry,' Elena said.

They all pushed inside, and Flint collected an oiled torch from a sconce. Once the torch was set to flame by a strike of flint, the old man shouldered the door closed. A staircase descended from the small landing here. 'Move quietly and cautiously,' he warned. 'More traps or enemies might be placed along our path. I suggest that we also leave a guard at this door to protect our escape.'

No one volunteered. No one wanted to abandon Elena. So Elena made the choice for them. She touched Tol'chuk's shoulder. 'If the d'warves have another change of heart or reinforcements are sent, the Try'sil may be needed to sway the enemy.'

The og're nodded. 'I will guard your backs.'

With the matter settled, Flint showed Tol'chuk how to work the door, and they proceeded down the stair. No one spoke for the hundred steps it took to reach the passages below. Flint led them quickly down a long winding hall to where it emptied into a wide passage. Here the rough rock was polished to a sheen and adorned with carvings and stone grave markers.

'The fourth level of the catacombs,' Flint whispered, raising his torch.

They continued deeper along this spiraling concourse. Mama Freda had her pet Tikal scamper ahead into the darkness to spy out any ambushes. But without the eyes of her pet, Meric had to help guide the old woman. Their progress was too slow for Elena's liking. Even though it was a false twilight above, Elena knew that true evening was not far behind.

Mama Freda suddenly hissed and dragged Meric to a stop.

'What is it?' Flint asked, pushing near the old healer.

'A light,' she answered. 'Through Tikal's eyes, I can see a glow reflecting around the curve of the passage farther ahead.'

Flint frowned. 'Someone else must be down here.'

'Can you get Tikal to creep nearer?' Elena asked.

'I'll try, but after the battle above, his fear runs high.'

Mama Freda leaned against the wall. She tired rapidly as her herbs began to wear off. 'I see ... I see a man! He crouches along the side of the passage. The light comes from a small lantern he carries.'

'Are there any others?' Elena asked.

'No, the passage is empty.'

'Strange,' Flint said. 'What does he look like?'

'He wears a ragged white robe and looks disheveled, as if he has not bathed in many moons.'

'Hmm ... The white robe suggests he may be one of my Brothers. There are many hidden passages and holes to hide from the evil here. If he's truly managed to avoid the dark-mage's forces, he might have valuable information.' Flint leaned closer to Mama Freda. 'Can you get Tikal to show himself? His response may give us some indication of his heart.'

'I'll try,' Mama Freda mumbled. 'But Tikal is shy of strangers.'

They all stood in silence as Mama Freda used her bond

579

to the tamrink to guide its actions. Elena glanced to her brother, who wore a worried expression. She also eyed Flint but could read no deception in him. Still, there had been so many traps. Could this be another?

Mama Freda suddenly smiled. 'The fellow seems normal enough. Tikal startled him at first, but after the initial fright, he called my little pet to him. It seems that even in such a dire situation Tikal is not above begging a cookie from a stranger. He is now perched on the man's shoulder enjoying a scrap of stale bread crust.'

Joach and Elena shared a glance.

'We should still be wary,' Flint cautioned, his face grim. 'Let's go and find out more about this odd denizen of the catacombs.'

Flint again took the lead. Joach followed with Elena at his side. Meric and Mama Freda kept up the rear. It did not take long until the glow that Tikal had seen became apparent. Flint passed Meric his torch. 'Let me go on alone. If it's a trap, let it only catch me.'

As Flint crept away, Elena nudged Joach. 'Go with him.'

Joach frowned at Elena, but something he saw in her eyes silenced any questions. Elena watched her brother join Flint. If the old Brother was the traitor setting these traps, Elena wanted someone else to bear testimony to what lay ahead. The pair disappeared around the curve of the corridor.

Elena held her breath. For too long, no sign of what might lie beyond was hinted. Elena bit her lip.

Suddenly a spate of mumbled conversation flowed around the corner, too low to make out any specific words. Elena glanced at Meric, then back down the passage. Suddenly, Joach popped around the corner. He frantically waved them to follow, a smile of relief on his face.

Elena and the others hurried after him. Once around the

corner, Elena saw Flint bent in whispered conversation with a ragged man. His once-white robe was soiled a deep gray, and his cheeks bristled with unkempt reddish beard, barely hiding the sunken, starved look to the man's face. Contrasting his beard, the pate of his head was bald as a newborn.

'Who is it?' Elena asked.

'Brother Ewan,' Joach answered in an excited hush, his words rushed with relief. 'He's a healer. He ... he was the one who helped treat Conch from his injuries. He stayed behind when we left the island before to see if he could be of help in defending the island from within. He is a Hi'fai, too, and knows all the secret byways. He's been hiding out in the maze of the catacombs for the past moon.'

Elena felt a burden lifted from her own heart. It was good to know someone could survive within the evil here. It stoked a measure of hope in her. Still, she remained cautious as she approached this stranger.

Flint waved Elena over. 'I want you to meet someone – a friend who knows several other ways in and out of the catacombs.'

Brother Ewan straightened from his crouch. He seemed embarrassed by his appearance. One hand went to smooth down his rumpled robe; the other tried to pull his beard into some semblance of order. Tikal still rode on his shoulder, noisily chewing on a crust of bread. 'So this ... this is your wit'ch, Brother Flint?'

Elena nodded her head. 'It's good to meet you.'

Brother Ewan grinned shyly and took a step toward her. His motion slightly dislodged the little tamrink. Tikal snatched at the man's ear to keep his perch but missed. The Brother's grin grew with the tiny beast's antics. He caught Tikal as the tamrink slipped.

'I'm sorry,' Brother Ewan said, holding back a chuckle. 'But I think this little creature has outlasted his welcome.' Brother Ewan lifted Tikal and, in one swift motion, snapped the tamrink's neck and tossed his limp form away.

Mama Freda gasped and fell back into Meric's arms. 'Tikal!'

The man's grin continued to spread into a foul leer. 'Now let me see this wit'ch of yours more closely.' Unburdened, he reached for Elena.

Too shocked to respond, Elena almost fell within his grip. Tikal's sudden, brutal death had frozen her heart and mind. But Flint thrust himself between Ewan and Elena. He fumbled for his sheathed sword but was too slow.

Ewan ripped the ragged robe open, baring his chest. Latched to his pale skin were hundreds of small purple leeches. He lunged and hugged Flint before the old Brother could raise his sword.

Joach grabbed Elena and dragged her back. She was still too stunned to think clearly. 'He's an ill'guard, El! We must get away!'

Meric hauled Mama Freda, now blind and broken, along with him, while Joach pulled Elena. As they stumbled back, Flint fell free of the ill'guard's embrace. He turned as he collapsed, his face and neck covered with the sucking leeches. In only a single heartbeat, the sick creatures swelled to the size of bruised fists, drawing more than just blood from Flint. His very form and substance seemed to be sucked into the writhing parasites. Flint crashed to the floor. As the creatures rolled off their host, bone shone through the wounds they had left. Still, Flint struggled to dislodge the monsters. One hand rose, quivering, then collapsed back down as he died.

The last sight Elena saw before she was drawn around the corner was Brother Ewan stepping over Flint's corpse.

His chest, now bare after hugging Flint, sprouted a new crop of the purple leeches, ready for the next harvest.

Then Elena was around the corner, and they raced away. As they ran, the horror slowly lost its paralyzing hold on Elena. She was able to think again and slowed to a stop. Joach tried to tug her onward, but she let out one sob and pushed him away. 'Go! Run!'

'El?'

Elena raised her right hand and unbound the spell that locked away the spirit glow. Her hand bloomed a rosy azure. She fed the magick into her hand and willed the glow to spread. Elena saw the effect in Joach's eyes as she vanished from sight. 'Take Mama Freda and Meric!' she ordered. 'Join Tol'chuk!'

'You can't face the ill'guard alone.'

Elena frowned and hurriedly shed her clothes. 'I'm not going to confront it. We don't have the time. But I must check on Flint and retrieve the ward, while you all lead the monster away from me. Can you do that?'

Joach nodded. 'What are you going to do?'

'I am going to get that cursed book!' She removed the last of her underclothes, then retrieved her wit'ch's dagger. She held it before Joach and blew forth her magick from her fist. In his eyes, she saw the knife vanish.

After a few moments, Joach glanced up and down the passage. 'El?' he probed tentatively.

Elena remained silent. She saw a look of fear and defeat grow on his face. He glanced back down the passage, thinking she had already left. 'Be careful, El.' But before he turned away, he added in a whisper. 'I love you.'

Elena did not fight the tears that rose in her eyes.

There was no one to see them anyway.

*   *   *

Er'ril stood between the wall of black ice and the darkmage's circle of wax. His chains, now bolted in place to iron rings in the floor, only allowed him a single step in any direction. He had been stripped of his shirt; black runes of power had been carved into his chest with the tip of Shorkan's blade, their father's hunting knife. Blood dribbled in hot trails down his belly, soaking into his belted breeches. Er'ril ignored the pain from the thirteen runes; his greater concern was on the final rites being performed within the mage ring. Half naked, his one arm bound to his waist, Er'ril felt a twinge of vulnerability. All his hopes would depend on the next few moments.

Denal stood within the ring wrapped in binds of dark energy, all but forgotten. Only his eyes shone brightly with terror and anger as, like Er'ril, he studied the final preparations of the other two mages.

Greshym spoke as he and Shorkan painted symbols on the floor along the inside edge of the mage ring with his own black blood. 'I sense the Dire Beacon has been lit. The skal'tum must already be in flight.'

'It matters not,' Shorkan said. 'With the number of traps set in and around the island, we have no need to fear intruders. By the rising of the moon, the island will no longer matter. With the book unbound, this city will be only a place of ghosts and lost hopes. We will have been victorious.'

Greshym met Er'ril's eye for a breath, then glanced away again. It was the signal. Er'ril cleared his throat. 'Shorkan, you will fail here,' he spat out. 'Brother Kallon's spell will defeat you ... again.'

Shorkan continued to work, undaunted and undistracted by his words. 'It was your blood that fed this spell, Er'ril. And it will be your blood that breaks it.'

'Are you so sure, Brother? I tell you that a piece of the puzzle yet escapes you.'

'And what might that be?'

'You were right. The spell did require my blood and part of the magick of eternity gifted by the book. It even took a part of the tome's power, too. But it took one last item, something you have never suspected. This missing element will be your downfall.'

'And I suppose you're going to tell me?'

Er'ril's eyes narrowed. 'You may have weaseled out my companion here,' he said with a nod toward the bound Denal. 'But this last secret I will never tell – not even to save the wit'ch.'

Shorkan shrugged and went back to his painting. 'I thought not. Well, I'll take my chances, dear brother.'

'You will die if you try, and there will be no coming back.'

Shorkan waved his words away. 'Enough, Er'ril. I know you grow desperate. Your protests only help support that I'm on the right path here.'

Er'ril frowned. He needed to get Shorkan to react, to abandon his painting for a moment. Greshym needed a distraction to complete his betrayal. Even now Greshym glared at Er'ril. Time was running out.

Er'ril's mind spun. 'Think back, Shorkan. From the times you've tried to pierce Brother Kallon's spell before, you know there is something unusual in the spell. Something that confounded you.'

Shorkan scowled but finally pushed to his feet. He stepped toward Er'ril, keeping the wax ring between them. 'Then tell me. What is it that you think my spell is missing?'

Even as evil flowed in waves from the darkmage, Er'ril kept his stance. He had to keep the man's eyes on him. Er'ril dared not even glance to see if Greshym was taking action. 'And what boon will I gain if I tell you?'

'I can make it so you survive this night,' Shorkan growled.

'And what of my freedom? Do I live in your dungeons?'

'That is up to you, Brother. Now tell me what—' Suddenly, Shorkan spun around on a heel.

Er'ril glanced to Greshym. The old bent-backed mage still knelt at the ring's edge.

'What are you doing?' Shorkan screamed. 'That is not the correct rune!'

Greshym did not answer, only stood with the aid of his staff and stepped out of the ring. Shorkan leaped at him, but Greshym reached within the wax circle with his staff and tapped the last rune he had painted. The symbol, two twining snakes, glowed with a reddish fire. 'The rune of entrapment is the right rune for *my* purposes, Shorkan!'

Shorkan's dive pulled up short of the ring's edge. He stumbled back from it. 'You!' He seethed at Greshym, his face as black as thunderclouds. He then glanced back to Denal.

Greshym waved a hand at the boy. 'Yes, Denal was always the loyal one, always the little pup.'

Shorkan stalked along the ring as if seeking a means of escape.

'You know the spell I cast,' Greshym explained. 'You will live as long as you don't try to cross the mage circle.'

Shorkan crossed back to glare at Greshym across the thin dribble of wax. 'Why?'

Thumping with his cane, Greshym sidled around the ring. 'I could not let you destroy the Blood Diary. It is the only hope of returning vitality to these hoary bones of mine.'

'Vitality? You already live forever! What gift could be greater?'

Now it was Greshym's turn to spin on Shorkan. 'I will tell you what gift is greater. You see it in the mirror each morning. *Youth!* Of what use is immortality if one continues to age and rot?' Greshym spat at Shorkan, but his spittle hit the invisible barrier above the wax and sizzled in midair.

Greshym continued around the circle until he stood beside Er'ril. 'Your brother and I made a deal.'

'You'd betray the master for such a small prize?'

'Master?' Greshym let out a rude noise. 'What do I care of the Black Heart's machinations? You were his pet, not me. As for this *small* prize, it is the least I deserve after serving the Black Beast for so long.'

'You will pay for your blasphemy, Greshym. This I promise.'

Greshym ignored Shorkan and turned to Er'ril. 'Now to complete our deal, plainsman.' Resting his staff in the crook of an arm, Greshym reached to the shackle imprisoning Er'ril's wrist. With a wave of his fingers, the irons opened, and Er'ril's arm was finally free. 'I don't know where you hid the sliver of my staff, Er'ril. But the magick in it is now active. It will unfetter your ankle chains and free you. It will also open any lock that stands between you and freedom.'

Er'ril reached for his neck, but Greshym stopped him with a claw on his wrist.

'But first, you promised to free the book. You claimed to have the power.'

Er'ril nodded. 'I do.' He did not know if Greshym's promise of freedom was true or not, but Er'ril had plotted his own defense against any betrayal by the darkmage. Yet it was a dangerous game each man played.

Turning, Er'ril stepped toward the wall of black ice. Over its surface, ageless energies still coursed. Er'ril could see a reflection of the room behind him in its glassy surface. He saw Greshym's hungry expression. He watched the old mage's fingers greedily clasp at the wood of his staff. Er'ril raised his own hand to the ice barrier, but sudden motion in the reflection stopped him.

Turning with a clank of chains, he saw Shorkan shove Denal and topple the boy mage backward. His small form sprawled across the wax ring. Instantly, the spell of entrapment punished its prisoner. Even through the bindings of dark energies, the boy's screams sounded. His tiny body writhed on the pyre of the wax ring. Smoke and the sizzle of burning flesh swelled in the small room. Denal's bindings were quickly eaten away, revealing a charred husk underneath. And still the boy struggled. A bleating cry flowed from his cracked and blackened lips, until eventually even this died away.

Shorkan waited no longer. Using the boy's charred corpse like a bridge, he leaped across the wax ring. But even through this weakened section of the barrier, Shorkan did not escape unscathed. A scream shattered from his throat as he landed in a crumpled pile. His white robe, now just ash, clung to his seared skin. Yellow blisters and large swaths of burned skin covered his body. Even his hair and brows had been burned away, leaving him looking as old as Greshym.

But Shorkan still lived! The mage rose slowly to his feet, tottering on limbs that still smoked. He stumbled a few steps toward where Greshym and Er'ril stood stunned. Shorkan's voice croaked at them. 'I . . . I will stop you.' Twin spouts of darkfire erupted from Shorkan's burned arms.

Greshym stepped forward and raised his staff, blocking the flow of force – but just barely. Er'ril saw how Greshym's arm shook as he held out his talisman against the might of Shorkan. The length of wood steamed and smoked in the old mage's grip.

Er'ril scooted away from the combatants to the full length of his chains. His bare back now touched the ice wall. He stared in shock at the show of force. For Shorkan still to be able to wield such strength after sustaining those burns spoke of the depth of his well of power. Er'ril's fingers scrabbled to his neck. He fished free the shard of Greshym's staff. If he was to help in this fight, he needed to be free.

Er'ril waved the sliver of wood over the locks that bound his ankles – but nothing happened. He even tried using the piece as a lock pick, digging at the keyhole. Still the irons remained bound as ever. Scowling, Er'ril straightened up. There was no magick in the shard of staff. It had been a trick. Greshym had played him well, giving him something tangible upon which to pin his hopes. Er'ril tossed aside the useless piece of wood and kicked at his chains.

Nearby, the spout of darkfire from Shorkan's arms began to wane and was soon sputtering, finally revealing a bottom to his well of black energies. Shorkan's arms dropped, and the flow ended. Using the last dregs of his power, he opened a swirling black portal under his feet and dropped away, but not before gasping out one final threat. 'I . . . I will get my revenge . . . on *both* of you!' Then he was gone.

Greshym still held his staff before him in a warding gesture, but with the disappearance of Shorkan, the old mage suddenly sagged. His staff fell to ash in his grip, crumbling away. Er'ril realized Shorkan had come to within a breath of defeating Greshym. Now nearly spent, the old mage had to support himself against the wall of ice and shuffle toward Er'ril.

'The book . . .' he whispered through cold lips. 'We must hurry.'

'Where did Shorkan go?'

Greshym shook his head and leaned in exhaustion against the ice wall. 'I don't know. Most likely to his tower. Or maybe he'll just flee. He may use the Weirgate that delivered you here to escape back to Blackhall.'

'A Weirgate?'

Greshym waved his arm weakly. 'That ebon'stone statue of a wyvern. It is a portal to the Weir. But none of that matters. Free the book!'

Er'ril knew now would be the only chance to gain information from this mage. He was weak and needed Er'ril's help. 'What is this Weir? And why were you transporting the statue to Winterfell?'

Greshym's gaze became more solid. His eyes narrowed with suspicion. 'It no longer matters. Free the book,' he commanded.

'Not until you answer my questions. As you said, time is running short.'

Greshym stared angrily at Er'ril, then sighed. 'You ask for a quick answer to a long tale.'

'Just give me what you know.'

Greshym sighed, his breath foul on Er'ril's skin. 'As you probably have learned from your dealings with the ill'guard, small pieces of ebon'stone have the power to trap and corrupt spirits.'

'This I know. But what does this have to do with the Weir and Weirgates?'

'It's complicated. When ebon'stone was first mined, four large pieces were sculpted by the d'warves into massive beasts: griffin, manticore, basilisk, and wyvern. These larger pieces of pure ebon'stone were found to hold an even greater power. They could trap not only spirits, but for those folks rich in magick, the ebon'stone could also trap the person themselves. This is what happened to you. Your ward's magick activated the ebon'stone, and you were drawn inside the dark dimension of the Weir.'

'I don't remember any of that.'

'The Weir has that effect unless you are prepared and

trained. And even then it's a danger. You can easily lose yourself in there. Even I wouldn't risk entering one of those gates. But once you entered the Weirgate, Shorkan sensed you and called the wyvern back here, bringing you to us.'

'But why were you hauling the statue to Winterfell in the first place?'

Greshym frowned. 'Some new plan of the Dark Lord. He had ordered three of the Weirgates – the basilisk, the griffin, and the wyvern – to different regions of Alasea. But I was not privy as to why. And no one questions the Black Heart's orders. Shorkan suspected it had something to do with strengthening the Weir.'

'You keep mentioning this Weir. What exactly is it?'

Greshym shook his head. 'I don't even think Shorkan could answer that. All we know is that long ago something fell within one of the gates and became trapped, but it was too large to be held by any one gate. It spread to all four, linking them forever and trapping itself for eternity.'

'But what does the Weir do?'

Greshym glanced to Er'ril, cunning entering his eyes again. 'Enough with this interrogation. I'll answer this last question only if you swear to free the book next.'

Er'ril frowned.

'Trust me. You will want the answer. It is one of the most guarded secrets of the Dark Lord.'

Er'ril licked his lips. He knew he could not keep the darkmage talking for much longer. One more answer would have to suffice. 'Fine. I swear to free the book. So what does this Weir do?'

Greshym leaned in close. 'It is the well of the Dark Lord's power, his sole font of black magick! The Weir is where he draws his power.'

Er'ril's throat clenched. Here was the answer to a mystery that had plagued the Brotherhood for centuries – the source of the Black Heart's strength! If only the Brotherhood had managed to obtain this information centuries ago, they could have perhaps devised a way to cut the Dark Lord from his magick. Greshym had not lied. This information was worth the price of his oath.

'Now break the spell and unleash the Blood Diary,' Greshym said eagerly, though he leaned heavily on the ice wall. The mage tired rapidly.

Er'ril nodded, still too stunned to speak. He twisted to face the wall of black ice and once again ran his hand along it. Finally he sensed the proper spot to unlock the barrier. Now to fit the key. Er'ril turned to lean his amputated shoulder against the ice one last time and faced Greshym. 'I told Shorkan that the spell required more than just my blood and magick.'

'Yes, I remember your ruse.'

'It was no ruse. The price was high.' Er'ril pressed his shoulder firmly to the iced lock in the wall. 'It also took my flesh.'

Searing pain shot into Er'ril's shoulder as bone, muscle, and fiber found their old home. All around, the black ice melted from the walls and ceiling, shrinking down toward where Er'ril stood.

As the wall vanished under Greshym, taking away his support, the old mage teetered and fell to his knees, his eyes wide at the transformation as the spell ended. He stared up at Er'ril as the last vestiges of the magick melted away. 'You were the key all along!'

Er'ril glanced to his scarred shoulder stump. An arm of muscle and bone now lay attached. It was no phantom arm, but his own, a limb he had sacrificed centuries ago to fuel the spell here. He bent the arm to his chest. Clutched in his hand was a book he had not seen in centuries, a battered black diary with a scrolled burgundy rose etched on its cover.

Greshym followed the book's path. 'The Blood Diary!'

Er'ril kept it from the mage's reach.

'We had a pact,' Greshym snapped. 'You swore an oath.'

'I swore to free the book. I have done so.' He then stepped with a clink of chains and rolled the sliver of staff he had discarded a moment ago toward Greshym. 'This is useless. You sought to betray me.' Er'ril ground the shard of wood under his heel. 'So any other promises we once made to each other are now void.'

Greshym fought to pull to his feet, but without his staff and weak from his fight with Shorkan, the mage was slow.

Er'ril pulled the book farther away from Greshym, resting it upon his own rune-carved chest. With its touch, his sliced skin drew together, and the foul markings vanished. 'You forget the book protects me – and not just with longevity.' About Er'ril's ankles, his iron shackles clanked to the stone floor. Er'ril shook free of the chains and stepped back. Free at last.

Greshym raised an arm, ready to lash out with the remains of his black magick, but Er'ril lifted the book between them. 'I think the magick in the Blood Diary will protect me, but if not, before your magick reaches me, it will destroy your only hope of ever obtaining your youth.'

The old mage's arm slowly dropped.

'Besides, I would suggest you let us keep the book. Elena and I will need it to destroy the Dark Lord. And after your betrayal here, you had best hope we succeed, Greshym. I do not believe the Black Heart will look kindly on your actions this day.'

Greshym's face paled as he realized the truth in Er'ril's words.

With a final searing scowl, Greshym waved his hand and opened his own portal. As the old mage sank away, he spat out a final warning. 'This is not over yet, Er'ril.'

Before Er'ril could answer, Greshym was gone.

Er'ril lifted the book before him. He didn't know what shocked him more, the reclamation of the book or the return of his arm. He ran a finger along the limb. A shiver ran down Er'ril's bare back, and gooseflesh pimpled his skin. After so many years, the arm seemed so unnatural, but at the same time, it felt like coming home. Odd memories returned, as if these recollections had been trapped in the stolen flesh and only now returned with his arm: memories of bal-ing hay in the fields, swinging a scythe in a two-handed grip, even hugging his father good-bye when he left for the last time with his brother, Shorkan. All memories of a simpler time, a more generous life.

Er'ril shook his head. Unlike his missing arm, that past was lost to him forever. No magick could bring it back.

His eyes came to rest on the Blood Diary. So many lives destroyed for this old battered book. He opened the cover and read the only entry, words that had first appeared on that fateful night long ago:

And so the book was forged, soaked in the blood of an innocent at midnight in the Valley of the Moon. He who would carry it read the first words and choked in tears for his lost brother . . . and his lost innocence. Neither would ever return.

Er'ril closed the book and thought of his brother and of the path of centuries that led to this room. Then too there

594

had been a ring of wax and the corpse of a boy. Er'ril shook his head and crossed from the room, grabbing the torch from the wall.

The book's words had proven too true.

Elena knelt by Flint. Naked except for her wit'ch's dagger, she felt particularly exposed and vulnerable, though none could see her. She kept her eyes averted as she reached over Flint's body. His face and neck were a cratered ruin. She touched his shoulder.

'I'm sorry,' she whispered and reached to a satchel at his waist. She felt like a grave robber as she fingered open the ties to his side pouch. From inside, she rolled out the small sculpted fist, the ward of A'loa Glen. The red iron glowed like fresh blood in the light from the discarded lantern.

Straightening, she weighed the fist in one hand and her wit'ch's dagger in the other. She needed to choose which to take; she was skilled enough to hide only one object with her magick. According to Flint's estimation, she would need the ward's magick to free the book, but she hated to leave the knife, abandoning her only other weapon.

As she pondered her choices, a small noise startled her. She clutched the knife in fright, dropping the ward. Rolling around, she raised her knife in menace. But nothing was there. Then the noise repeated: a small mewling almost too soft to hear. The sound stretched long enough for Elena to follow it to its source. In the shadows near the base of the wall, Tikal's crumpled form lay limp.

Elena crouched and slinked to the animal's side. The tamrink lay on its back, its neck twisted unnaturally. As she watched, Elena saw its chest softly rise and fall. She reached with a finger and touched the beast. A moan answered her probing. Elena winced. The little creature still lived.

Glancing back to the discarded ward, Elena knew she needed to hurry, but Tikal's small cries stirred an ache in her heart. She paused, unsure what to do. Elena clenched her fist around her knife and knew she could end Tikal's suffering with one thrust. She even lifted the dagger, but then lowered it again. She couldn't do it. Though her heart had grown harder on the journey here, it was not that hard. She had seen too much death these past days and could not slay this injured beast. But neither could she ignore it. Tikal was more than just a pet. He was also the eyes of Mama Freda.

Biting her lower lip, Elena made her decision.

She gently lifted the small tamrink, surprised at the softness of his fur. The cries worsened as she moved him. Cringing, she straightened his twisted neck. Bones grated. Tikal's mewling changed in pitch to a sharp whimpering. Elena cringed at the noise but did not stop. To survive, pain was sometimes necessary. This was one of the harsh lessons she had learned.

Finally, Tikal's neck was straight. Cradling the tamrink, Elena bloodied one of the beast's tiny fingers; then she did the same with her own. She remembered her old lessons. She must let only a small amount of her magick flow into another. Taking a calming breath, Elena lowered her bloody finger to Tikal's fresh wound. She kept her magick bottled inside her. She must let only a drop of her blood pass.

As her finger touched, Elena's thoughts bridged to the creature's for a brief moment. She merged with the beast, felt the raw ache in his neck, and sensed the dull awareness of the tamrink buried deep down. Then, for a single flash, she was somewhere else. She was stumbling in another's arm, racing, joints protesting, confused and blind. Blinking, Elena pulled back her finger. She was back in her own skin.

Elena knew that for that moment she had traveled along Tikal's connection to Mama Freda.

The brief contact reminded Elena of her duty. The others fled to lead the ill'guard away, and she was wasting her time reviving an injured animal. Elena settled Tikal back to the floor. The tamrink breathed much deeper now, and as she watched, Tikal's legs began to twitch and a small arm lifted to paw at an ear. From here, the tamrink would have to mend on its own.

Elena crossed back to the iron ward and retrieved it from the floor. This time she had no problem deciding which object to keep. She placed her knife near Flint and settled the ward in her right palm. After sensing the terror in Mama Freda, Elena knew she could face her own fears without her dagger. The ward was more important.

Decided, Elena stood straighter. As she paused, she heard the scuff of boot on rock. Swinging around, she realized it was coming from deeper down the catacombs. To confirm her suspicion, she saw light flickering from down the corridor. Someone else was coming!

Elena flattened herself against the wall. She pictured all manner of dangers: skal'tum, d'warves, ill'guard. What now? As she held her breath, the light grew. Shortly the flame of a torch came into sight around the curve of the passage. Elena tried to pierce the glare of the torchlight. The figure held the flame before him. Its brightness masked any details.

At least it was only one person. Still, she refrained from breathing, fearful of alerting the enemy to her presence. So when she finally caught her first glimpse of the newcomer's face, a trapped gasp escaped her. She could never mistake that sweep of black hair, the ruddy planes of his face, and those storm-gray eyes. It was Er'ril!

Elena stepped away from the wall. But, of course, Er'ril

could not see her. Instead, his eyes fixed on the collapsed form of Flint in the hall, outlined in the lantern light. Er'ril hurried toward the body.

Raising a hand, Elena thought to call to him. Then Er'ril lifted his torch higher and wiped at his forehead with his other hand. Elena stumbled back, almost stepping on Flint's body. Er'ril had two arms now! Nearly blind from shock, Elena dodged to the side as Er'ril rushed forward.

He tossed aside the torch and fell to his knees beside the dead man. His hands hovered over the corpse as if disbelieving what he saw. For the first time, Elena saw that Er'ril held something in his other hand: a tattered book. As he set the tome down, Elena took a small step forward. She spied the gilt-edged rose on its cover and blinked in shock. She covered her mouth to hold in a gasp. She recognized the book from Er'ril's description.

The Blood Diary.

'Flint . . .' Er'ril's voice drew Elena's attention. He reached and carefully turned Flint's head, exposing the silver starred earring. Er'ril covered his face with a hand, his fingers dark from the torch's soot. 'Flint, this is all my fault. I . . . I did this to you.'

Er'ril's guilt confused Elena. He sounded so genuine and heartfelt, but why? How exactly was he to blame for Flint's death? And what of those two arms? Joach's dream played in her head: Er'ril, with two arms, hunting her down atop a tower with murderous intent. Dare she trust this man? After knowing Er'ril for so long with only the one arm, this man with two seemed a stranger, especially bare chested, like now. It changed his whole physique.

Elena remained quiet. She was safe as long as she remained silent and hidden. She would heed Joach's warning and be wary – for now.

As she watched, Er'ril collected the book and pushed to his feet. While doing so, his toe nudged her abandoned wit'ch's dagger. He glanced down and spotted it. Retrieving the knife, he turned it over in his hands. Of course he recognized it. Er'ril glanced up and down the corridor as if seeking some answer. 'Flint, you fool, you brought her here.'

Er'ril held up the dagger, then shoved the blade into his belt. 'Elena,' he said roughly, his eyes bright, 'if you're here, I'll find you.'

Elena pulled back from the fire in Er'ril's gaze. She had never seen such heat in the plainsman before. In the past, he had always been warm, thoughtful, and supportive. But what Elena saw now went much deeper, a flame that arose from a depth that unnerved her. Like his new arm, Elena had never seen this side of Er'ril.

Where had it come from? Was it natural or unnatural? Was this new intensity directed at saving her or killing her?

As Elena weighed his words, Er'ril collected the ill'-guard's lantern. With a final glance at Flint, he started a fast pace toward the distant surface.

Elena leaned her head against the cool stone of the catacomb. Then she let out a long breath and began dogging the trail of this mysterious two-armed stranger. She would not give up the hope that Er'ril's spirit was still pure. She could not! Especially since he carried the salvation of A'loa Glen – the Blood Diary.

24

Pinorr paced the length of the keelchief's cabin. As the ship's shaman, this was his post during a battle: to pray to the seven gods of the sea and be ready with advice for the keelchief. But for Pinorr, this was an imprisonment, a torture beyond a man's ability to survive.

Above his head, the sounds of battle raged on the decks of the *Dragonspur*. Men fought and died while he cowered below. He had been informed of the magickal twilight and of the flight of the skal'tum. Even now he could hear the bone drums of the beasts and their cackling howls as men fought demons.

Pinorr clenched his fists. During past battles, he had never felt this way. He had accepted his position as shaman. But after the night of bloodshed during the storm, Pinorr knew his role was a mockery to the gods. He need only look down to be reminded of his crime. All the lye soap and scrubbing had failed to totally cleanse Ulster's blood from the cabin's planks. A brown stain marked the wood for all to see.

Pinorr covered his ears with his fists. Bad enough that he must stew while men died, but why must he wait here? He should be with Mader Geel and Sheeshon in his own cabins. For the thousandth time, Pinorr's eyes were drawn to the wide stain under his feet. He deserved whatever punishment the gods thought to inflict. He had taken a steel blade in hand, and he had taken a life. In the eyes of the seven sea gods, Pinorr was cursed forever.

Raising his eyes to the rafters of the cabin, Pinorr prayed with his arms lifted. 'Do not punish this ship! My hands alone have bloodied your gifts. Punish me, not those aboard this ship. Spare them of your curse! I will accept any punishment, any torture, to cleanse the *Dragonspur*!'

A sudden pounding on the cabin door startled Pinorr. Dropping his arms, he hurried to the barred door and lifted the latch; the door swung open before Pinorr could even step back. He had expected to see Hunt, the ship's keelchief, but instead he found Mader Geel rushing inside.

The old warrior woman's words were frantic. 'I turned my back on her for a breath! I swear!'

Pinorr clutched Mader Geel's shoulders in both his hands. Her eyes were wild. 'What is it?' Pinorr asked, dread clutching his heart.

'Little Sheeshon! I went to peek at the battle through the porthole and when I turned back, the cabin door was open and Sheeshon was gone!'

Pinorr released the woman. His legs grew numb under him. He glanced back to the rafters, trying to see the laughing gods above. No, this price was too high!

'Shaman?' Mader Geel asked, clearly sensing his inner turmoil.

Pinorr lowered his gaze but lifted his hands and began braiding the locks of his white hair. His fingers remembered the old pattern of a warrior's tail. 'I am shaman no longer,' he said coldly.

'What are you saying? What are you doing?' Mader Geel's eyes went wide with fright.

She reached for him, but Pinorr knocked her hand away. 'Curse the seven gods,' he spat. 'I am done playing their whipping boy. If they mean to wreak punishment, it will be on my head, not Sheeshon's.'

'Are you mad?' Mader Geel backed away.

Pinorr finished the last twist of his warrior's braid, then crossed to the wall where Hunt had hung an assortment of swords. He reached for the one that best suited his old skill, a long blade with a curve to its length.

'No!' Mader Geel cried. 'Don't touch it!'

But her call was too late. Pinorr grabbed the sword's hilt and swung it from the wall's hook. Blade raised, he turned to face Mader Geel.

Mader Geel fell to her knees. 'You damn us all!'

'That, I've already done. Now I must end it!' Pinorr swung around and stalked from the room. In the open hall, the sounds of battle worsened. Shouted orders echoed down from above, swirled with screams and wild laughter. Boots thundered overhead. Claws scraped wood. Pinorr hurried, half running down the passage. He met no others. All hands were on deck.

At last, he shoved through the hatch and into horror. Even fueled by his rage at the gods, Pinorr's feet stumbled to a stop. Blood and dead bodies washed the deck. The sails overhead were a shredded ruin stained with blood and gore. Torn corpses swayed in the rigging. It was all tainted by the eerie netherlight that had been described to him. Pinorr glanced to the west and saw the pall of inky darkness that masked the setting sun.

He shook his head at the ruin of the world. Everywhere he looked, men and women fought the winged demons. But without the sun, the beasts were invulnerable. The best the crew could manage was to hold the foul creatures off and use nets to tangle and shove them overboard into the seas.

Near the stern, a red seadragon roosted, claws dug deep into rail and decking. A small mer'ai woman, her eyes wide with fear, sat mounted on her beast and called orders to the Bloodriders around her. She urged the men to drive the skal'tum toward her, where her dragon would snatch at wings and throw the dark spawn overboard. But even from here, Pinorr could see the dragon bore countless scratches and deeper gouges from the monsters' fangs and claws. A greenish steam rose from these wounds, where poison met dragon's blood. The great dragon would not last much longer, and Pinorr suspected that the fear in the mer'ai's eyes was for her dragon, not herself.

Suddenly, Hunt's deep voice boomed over the chaos. 'Ragnar'k comes again! Be ready, men!'

All across the deck, the crew raised fists in the air, acknowledging their chief's order.

Pinorr pushed farther out so he could see atop the raised foredeck. Near the ship's prow, Hunt stood with five other Bloodriders, holding off a trio of skal'tum. Hunt, his face bloodied, a fire in his eyes, refused to give up the ship. The high keel's son was a true keelchief. For just the briefest flash, Pinorr was glad he had slain Ulster. If Ulster had still been keelchief, Pinorr suspected the ship would have been sunk by now.

Pinorr saw how Hunt's shouted orders seemed to revitalize the crew's spirit and strength of arm. All around the boat, men and women fought fiercely.

Past the keelchief's shoulder, Pinorr spotted the black wings of Ragnar'k. The great dragon swung toward their foundering ship, diving fast and low – too fast to land. What were Sy-wen and Kast doing?

Then almost faster than Pinorr could follow, Ragnar'k sped over their masts. His roar surged across the ship. Pinorr found himself ducking against the noise. It seemed to press at him. As he straightened, he watched as all around the boat, the crew hacked into the skal'tum. For the brief moment that Ragnar'k had roared, the dragon's voice had washed away the dark protections of the beasts. Axes and swords cleaved into flesh that a moment ago was impervious to blades. The screams from the score of wounded monsters followed the flight of the dragon across the twilight sky.

Pinorr watched Ragnar'k turn on a wing and dive toward a neighboring ship, spreading his deadly roar.

A small voice snapped his head around. 'I have need of you!' Atop the raised foredeck, Pinorr saw his granddaughter crawl from around an overturned barrel and push to her feet. She walked toward where Hunt and the others still battled the skal'tum trio.

The monsters were wounded now after the passage of Ragnar'k, but they were far from dead. With the fading of the dragon's roar, their dark protections had again returned. But it seemed the blades that had been bloodied during the last passage of the dragon could now pierce the dark protections. It was slow going, though; for every skal'tum slain, two others appeared.

Atop the foredeck, one of the beasts heard Sheeshon's voice and swung its fanged face around.

Pinorr scrambled up the ladder after his granddaughter, but Hunt also spotted the girl and fought his opponent more vigorously. Neither man would make it in time. Sheeshon still continued toward the grip of the nearest beast. 'I have need of you,' she called again to Hunt.

'Sheeshon! Get back!' Hunt called to her. Pinorr saw the

pain in the keelchief's eyes, but he was pinned down by his own monster.

One of the men at his side tried to break free and come to the child's aid, but he was cut down by one poisoned swipe of a skal'tum's claw. The man writhed for several breaths, then lay still.

By now, Pinorr had scrambled atop the deck. Sheeshon was only a step away from the beast. He would never reach her in time.

Pinorr met Hunt's gaze. The keelchief had spotted the shaman, and his eyes flew wide at the sight of a sword in his hand. But instead of words of warning like Mader Geel, Hunt yelled encouragement. 'Get Sheeshon back! Kill anything in your way!'

Having the keelchief's support instead of admonishment fueled Pinorr's heart, as if a great weight had been lifted from his chest. He leaped with a lunge of his sword. Old buried instincts again raged forth. His sword struck the outstretched claw of the skal'tum. It did no damage, bouncing off its protected skin, but it knocked the limb away from Sheeshon. Pinorr continued his roll across the deck, striking his granddaughter with his shoulder. Sheeshon gasped and bounced to the side.

Pinorr jumped to his feet, standing now between the beast and Sheeshon. He raised his sword against the monster's leer.

'You think to sssteal my treat, little man,' it hissed.

'You will never touch her, demonspawn!'

The skal'tum struck, lightning-quick. Pinorr danced back, barely in time, using a twist of his sword to parry a swipe of claws. But already the beast lunged with its other limb at the shaman's chest.

Pinorr was forced back. He now stood over his fallen

granddaughter. Sheeshon sobbed at his feet. The beast struck again. Pinorr spun a flurry of steel before him. Claws bounced back.

The skal'tum cocked its head and studied Pinorr for a moment. 'So the white-haired elder thinksss he hass fangs, does he?'

Winded now, his heart's fire was unable to maintain its ferocity for long. Pinorr's arm trembled.

Sensing the weakening of its prey, the skal'tum lunged once more. All claws and fangs, it leaped at him. Pinorr tried his best to fend the beast off with flashes of blade, but he tired rapidly.

A claw slipped past his defenses and ripped the robe across his chest. Then another's sword was beside his own. Pinorr did not have time even to glance at his savior, but he sensed it was Hunt. Back-to-back over the girl, the two men fought. It seemed an endless dance.

Then Hunt's voice boomed out again. 'Ragnar'k comes! Be ready!' In a lower voice, the keelchief added. 'Fight brave, old man. Just for a moment more.'

Pinorr tried his best to honor the keelchief's order. But relief at hearing of the dragon's return actually doused his heart's fire. He slowed.

Then the roar was upon them. 'Duck!' Hunt hollered in his ear. Pinorr dropped, his legs giving out anyway. He watched Hunt swing his sword with both arms. The head of the monster cleaved from its shoulder. It arced across the deck and rolled into the sea. The malignant body fell away like an axed tree.

With Pinorr down, Sheeshon crawled into the old man's lap. Pinorr dropped his sword to wrap the child in his embrace. 'Papa.' Sheeshon leaned her head to his chest. 'Papa, I love you.'

With his beast slain and a momentary lull in the battle, Hunt knelt beside them both. Pinorr met his gaze and straightened. 'I'm sorry,' he mumbled, nodding toward the sword.

Hunt shrugged. 'It's not as if it was the first time you picked up a sword.'

Pinorr blinked at these strange words.

Hunt's face was bloodied, but the fire of chiefdom still shone brightly through. 'You did the fleet a service by ridding the *Dragonspur* of Ulster.'

A gasp escaped Pinorr. 'You knew?'

'Do you think me a complete dullard, old man? There were clues enough for those who cared to look. But most would rather not see.'

Pinorr's voice cracked. 'But I cursed the boat. I broke my oaths.'

Hunt leaned a bit higher to keep an eye on the flow of battle. 'In these dire times, every warrior is needed, shaman or not.' He placed a hand on Pinorr's chest. 'I don't believe in the curses of gods, only in the strength of a man's heart. That is where the hope of the fleet lies. The world changes today. Whether it ends good or bad, nothing will be the same.'

Pinorr covered Hunt's hand with his own. 'Thank you.'

Hunt nodded and pulled his hand away. He glanced in shock at the blood that now covered his palm. 'Pinorr?' Hunt showed his stained palm.

Pinorr glanced to Sheeshon in his lap. A bright bloom of blood oozed through his robe over his heart. 'Take care of her, Hunt. If the ship survives, the next days will be hard for her.'

Hunt knelt lower, touching Pinorr's shoulder. 'I know. We already share a bond. I think she came up from below because she sensed my own danger. We will watch over each other.'

Pinorr hugged his granddaughter one last time, squeezing a lifetime of love into this one embrace. Then he placed Sheeshon's small hand into Hunt's. He glanced up to the young keelchief. He saw the strength, courage, and heart in the man. 'I made the right choice.'

Hunt nodded, his voice formal. 'You have served the fleet well, Shaman Pinorr. Go in peace.'

With tears flowing down his cheeks, Pinorr reached to touch Sheeshon one last time as battle raged all around. 'I love you,' he whispered as the poisons of the skal'tum finally reached his heart.

Sy-wen leaned over Ragnar'k's neck to view the spread of boats under them. Like steam rising from boiling water, screams and the clash of steel rose above the seas. All around the island, boats foundered and spats of skal'tum forces wreaked havoc wherever they flew. Sy-wen searched the island itself for any sign of the signal fire, some sign that the Blood Diary had been discovered. If the others were successful, she and Ragnar'k could wing to their rescue, scoop them off the island, and the battle below could end.

Tears flowed down her cheeks, but the winds quickly dried them. Her fingers were numb as they clutched a fold of scale. It seemed as if the war below had been raging for several days, not just an eternal afternoon. With the onset of the skal'tum attack, the tide of battle had turned. Fiery plans of taking the island had long gone to ash. Now the mer'ai and Dre'rendi fought just to survive. Each ship below was its own island under assault. Though the mer'ai struggled to help, with the strange twilight the skal'tum were almost impossible to vanquish. It was now a war to stay alive.

Sy-wen and Ragnar'k gave what little aid they could: diving toward ships when most needed and roaring away the dark protections of the beasts. But their main duty was still to watch the towers of A'loa Glen, awaiting the signal from the wit'ch. Until that time, the two protected the fleet.

'Over there!' Sy-wen yelled hoarsely. In her mind's eye, she sent an image of the ship she meant.

Ragnar'k sent his acknowledgment, and the dragon turned on a wing and began a long banking dive toward a ship's whose sails were ripped to rags and whose rigging was festooned with skal'tum. Sy-wen leaned against the wind. The heat from the dragon kept her warm, but still she shivered. As Ragnar'k swooped, roaring over the masts, Sy-wen closed her eyes. She no longer wished to see the carnage atop the decks of the ships; it wore at her heart. At least from the height of the clouds, such details were muted.

As Ragnar'k finished his run, Sy-wen felt an ache in her throat. The dragon's roar grew hoarse. This mode of attack would soon fail.

From somewhere deep down, words whispered up. *As long as we breathe, there is always hope.* Sy-wen opened her eyes and sat up straighter. It was Kast. She had not heard from him since they had initiated the transformation aboard the *Dragonsheart*.

'Oh, Kast, the deaths ... the screams ... the blood ...' Sy-wen sobbed.

Hush. Ragnar'k was right in allowing me forward. Do not lose heart.

'But, Kast, our people are being slaughtered.'

I see the deaths, my love. Sy-wen felt a warmth suddenly fill her that had nothing to do with the dragon's heated body.

It was as if Kast's arms had wrapped around her. He meant to comfort her, even as he spoke words that quailed her heart. *What occurs now is a price that must be paid. Both our people avoided this payment for too long. The mer'ai fled to the Deep. My people turned south and never looked back. If we are to find our own true spirits again, it will take such a cleansing flame. We've emerged after centuries of hiding. We've declared our loyalty to Alasea's future, and a line must be drawn here – even if it is in blood.*

Sy-wen again began to sob. 'I just want it to end. Either way, I want it to end.'

Come to me.

'What?' she whispered.

Close your eyes and reach for me.

'I don't understand . . .'

Just do it. Trust us both.

Sy-wen swallowed and did as asked. She closed her eyes and sent her thoughts toward him, sent her love and sorrow. The warmth she had felt a moment ago grew. Suddenly the warmth became two arms wrapped around her. She felt Kast's body pressed to hers. The boundaries between the three – dragon, man, and woman – grew blurred. For just this endless moment, three became one. No words were shared. In silence, three spirits comforted each other in an embrace of warmth and love.

Kast's voice finally whispered to her. It was as if he spoke at her ear, his breath brushing against her neck. *This is what we fight for.*

As answer, Sy-wen held Kast and Ragnar'k even tighter. She wanted to stay like this forever, but a thought – from Ragnar'k – intruded. *Something comes.*

Sy-wen opened her eyes, and the moment was gone. She felt those arms of warmth dissolve away and knew Kast had retreated deep inside Ragnar'k again. The dragon needed all his faculties to face this new threat.

Ragnar'k banked on a spread of black wing. Sy-wen now faced away from the island. The wall of inky darkness still marred the western skies, hiding the sun. The shaft of black energies continued to feed the foul construct.

At first, Sy-wen failed to see what had alarmed the dragon, but Ragnar'k had keener eyes. As the dragon passed over the rear of the Dre'rendi fleet, Sy-wen finally spotted strange aberrations in the wall of darkness. Her mind could not fully grasp what it was witnessing. It was as if huge white clouds billowed through the barrier, piercing the magickal wall.

Was this a storm front approaching? Sy-wen sensed that it wasn't.

Ships, Ragnar'k sent. *Many, many ships.*

Crinkling her brow at the dragon's strange words, Sy-wen could not understand the surge of excitement she received from Ragnar'k. What ships?

Then the strangest thing happened. Her vision shifted to that of the dragon's. Suddenly, she felt leagues closer to the coming storm. The wall of darkness swelled in her vision. What she had thought were clouds were actually billowing sails. She shook her head. How could this be? These ships sailed the air! Still, there could be no mistaking the timbered and masted boats under the huge sails. Through the dragon's vision, she even spotted small figures manning the decks of the strange flying ships.

As the vessels passed through the wall, Sy-wen was suddenly blinded. Like scores of arrows shot through a black sail, sunlight pierced the inky darkness, marking where each ship had thrust through the barrier. Bright shafts of sunlight outlined each ship. Sy-wen quickly counted. The aerial armada numbered twenty or thirty. Sunlight cast the ships in gold and set their sails ablaze.

Ragnar'k swooped and sped toward these strange intruders. Who where they? Friend or foe?

The ships flew higher than Ragnar'k, at least a quarter league above the island and seas. As they neared, Sy-wen saw that the keels under these strange boats were made of some peculiar metal that glinted under the columns of sunlight, a long rib of metal that glowed a bright red. Crackles of silver energy danced along the length of the keels.

Then Ragnar'k was among the wondrous fleet. The dragon swept between two of the boats, flying fast in case they proved enemies. But no arrows chased him. Sy-wen had caught a glimpse of a tall pale man standing in the prow of each boat, arms stretched to the twilight skies. Silver hair, longer than the men were tall, flowed behind each of them like a ship's banner.

As Ragnar'k swung in a tight arc for another surveillance run, Sy-wen pictured the men and suddenly knew who they were. She could not mistake their slender forms, the brilliance of their silver manes, even the spark of their blue eyes as they tracked the passing dragon. Though Meric's hair was only a sparse stubble, the resemblance of these men to the elv'in was clear.

Sy-wen remembered some mention of the arrival of a sunhawk and how it supposedly heralded the launch of the elv'in forces. Ragnar'k sped back toward the flying armada, gliding through lances of sunlight. The brilliance of the setting sun cheered her heart and fired her blood. She had not thought the elv'in fleet would arrive so soon!

She urged Ragnar'k to slow, tears in her eyes. Here was the salvation that Sy-wen had prayed for all day. Already the ships had rent holes in the wall of darkness. Sy-wen's gaze followed the shafts of sunlight to where they fell among the ships of the Bloodriders. She knew any skal'tum caught in the blaze of the setting sun would be vulnerable to attack.

Ragnar'k pulled up and maintained a pace to keep even with one of the ships. Sy-wen yelled a greeting to the boat, but none of the men or women aboard seemed to acknowledge her. They continued their duties atop the deck. She tried shouting again, but still they gave no response. The winds must be tearing away her words. A few of the crew glanced her way. She raised a fist in the air. They could at least see her signal. But they simply ignored her and went back to their duties.

Frowning, Sy-wen instructed Ragnar'k to bank away and try another ship. The dragon obeyed, but they had no better luck. Soon the elv'in fleet and the dragon were sailing over the war below. But the sky ships did not slow. They continued in force toward the island.

As they passed over the ships of the Bloodriders, Sy-wen saw faces turn upward in awe. Even the skal'tum were wary of these new intruders. Their attack paused as they pondered, along with everyone else, what these new ships intended. None of the beasts dared risk winging up to investigate.

Finally, Sy-wen noticed that one of the sky ships was much larger than the others – twice as large, in fact. It must be their flagship. She needed to get their attention, to ask them to aid the beleaguered forces below. Already time was running out. The holes in the twilight barrier were closing, healing the wounds.

By the time Sy-wen flew abreast of the flagship, the armada had reached the island. The fleet spread, encircling the city below. Five ships separated from the others and floated forward, over the city itself, to hover in a ring around the central castle. What were they doing? Sy-wen had a momentary gnaw of worry that perhaps she had judged them wrong. Maybe these were a new enemy.

She urged Ragnar'k to follow the flagship as it rose higher than the rest of the armada. Ragnar'k had to arc away then back to gain a matching height. The flagship now drifted above the center of the ring of five ships, taking up a post directly above the towered citadel.

In this thin air, Ragnar'k fought to maintain a matching position. At the prow of the flagship stood not a man, but a woman. She wore a long, flowing gown, its fabric so thin that Sy-wen could see her lithe form as easily as if she were naked. Her silver hair shone with a brilliance that had nothing to do with any ray of sunlight. The woman turned to her. As her gaze met Sy-wen's across the wide distance, Sy-wen sensed the energy that flowed from this woman: She was lightning given form.

The woman's lips moved, and Sy-wen heard the words as clearly as if the woman had been sitting beside her. 'Go. This is no longer your battle.' Then the elv'in woman turned away.

'Wait!' Sy-wen called, but the woman ignored her except to raise an arm in the dragon's direction.

Suddenly the skies were a whirlwind around them. Her mount fought to remain beside the ship, but his wings seemed incapable of catching wind. They fell in a spiraling plummet away from the flagship.

Sy-wen clung like a starfish as Ragnar'k tumbled. She was sure they would crash into the island. But then the whirlwind was gone, and the dragon's great wings caught the air. They pulled out of their dive and sailed smoothly again.

Ragnar'k flew with care now; their fall had put them among the towers of the lower city. Banking past the tilted statue of a man with an upraised sword, Ragnar'k took them up and out of the city.

Sy-wen twisted in her seat to monitor the circle of five ships. Ragnar'k began a slow turn around the island to keep the ships in view, but he dared not approach closer. And Sy-wen did not urge him, either. She had seen the look in the tall woman's eyes. It was like staring into a cold void. Sy-wen had sensed no hate or enmity in that gaze, only a profound indifference. It was as if Ragnar'k and Sy-wen were too small to warrant a second glance. They had been swatted away like a pestering gnat.

As Sy-wen continued her sweeping survey, she saw the crackles of silvery energy grow more violent along the keels of the five ships. Something was about to happen. The metal of the keels grew from a deep bloodred to a fiery pale rose, almost as if the ore were heating up. The crackling grew more intense, sparking now with small bolts of lightning, feathering out from the keels like jagged spears.

Ragnar'k flew too near one of the ships; Sy-wen's hair rose around her head, sparking with traces of power. The dragon swept away, sensing the danger looming here.

As her mount sailed over the city, Sy-wen watched the rage of energies now racing back and forth along each of the five keels. It was almost blinding. Sy-wen sensed that here was the power that propelled these great ships through the air, only *now* it was directed toward another purpose.

Even from this distance, Sy-wen could taste the energy in the air. The keels blazed with crackling power. Spates of lightning stabbed down at the castle but never quite reached. Suddenly it was as if the air around the castle were sucked away. Sy-wen gasped, clutching her throat.

Along the five keels, lightning bolts raced from stern to prow, jettisoning skyward in fonts of energy that struck the thicker keel of the flagship above. For a moment, a five-spoked star with the flagship at its center blazed in the twilight sky.

Then in a blink, the star vanished, and Sy-wen could breathe again. The five ships fell away from the citadel, drifting down and back, like spent lovers. Their keels were again a deep dull red. No energies crackled along their underbellies.

The same, however, was not true of the mighty flagship. It still hovered above the castle, ablaze with fire and energy.

Sy-wen's heart clenched with terror. 'What are they –?'

Then all the power trapped in the flagship's keel released. A bolt of lightning as thick as one of the castle towers struck straight down. It blew Sy-wen and Ragnar'k backward. Then the explosive boom followed, deafening, blinding them.

Even dazed, Ragnar'k helped keep Sy-wen in her seat, squeezing the ankle holds tighter as he tumbled away. Finally, their roll ended and Ragnar'k righted himself. They were over the seas again.

Ragnar'k sent his concern to her. *Do you fare well, my bonded?*

I'm fine, she answered, though in truth she was still dazzled by the bolt of energy. She could not blink the glare from her eyes. Then suddenly she sat up straighter. No, it wasn't the burn of lightning that still plagued her eyes! Sy-wen craned her neck all around her. It was the sun!

Sy-wen stared as the last of the inky darkness sank to the horizon, exposing the setting sun. She swung around. The spear of black energy was gone! In its stead, a pall of smoke rose from the castle's center. Its towers all stood, but Sy-wen knew that its central court must be a blasted ruin.

'They destroyed the source of the black barrier!' she said with a cheer in her voice. It was echoed from the seas around her. With the sun up, even a setting sun, the skal'tum were now vulnerable. Cheers and roars of blood lust rose from the boats and from the throats of dragons. The tide of battle had shifted! Victory could again be imagined!

Sy-wen, a weary smile on her face, turned to view the island and the armada overhead. She meant to wish them a silent thanks, but what she saw dimmed her smile.

Five new ships broke from the armada to rise toward the island, beginning to form a new ring under their flagship.

Sweet Mother, the elv'in were continuing their attack on the island!

Sy-wen feared for her companions. They must surely be down there already, somewhere in the castle or city. If these sky ships persisted, the island would soon be a smoking ruin.

Glancing over the hundreds of spires, Sy-wen prayed to spot the blaze of their signal fire. But there was nothing, only smoke and cold stone. Her friends could be anywhere. Maybe they were dead already. Sy-wen dismissed this last thought. She would not give up hope.

She glanced to the flagship far above and the cold woman who stood at its prow. 'Ragnar'k, we must stop them!' she called out.

Joach picked himself off the stone floor as dust continued to settle. He shook his head to clear the roaring inside his skull. Gods above, what had happened? He had been sure when the blast struck that the island itself was being torn apart. He had never expected to live.

Nearby, Meric rose to his feet with a groan. He bore a large bloody scrape on his forehead. He fingered the injury, then ignored it and helped Mama Freda up.

Without any eyes, the old woman's expression was difficult to read. But Joach guessed how she felt. Her hands grasped at Meric's arms like a drowning woman. Joach saw her lips move, but he heard nothing except the roar in his own ears. He gave his head another shake, and his hearing suddenly snapped back with a painful whine.

'—happened?' Mama Freda finished.

Meric glanced up and down the corridor. 'I don't know. But I expect it's some type of black magick.'

'Maybe it was a quake,' Mama Freda offered. She clung to Meric's arm. 'The volcanic islands around here are always giving us a good shake.'

Meric merely shrugged, but Joach was glad to hear some conversation from the old woman. These were the first words the old healer had spoken since their group had left Elena. At least the explosion had shaken her from the paralyzing shock of losing both her pet and her sight.

Joach moved closer to them as Meric retrieved the torch he had dropped. Luckily it had not sputtered out. 'I wouldn't count on it being a volcano,' Joach said. 'Some evil is at work here.' He glanced toward the lower passage. There was no sign of the ill'guard who pursued them. But how far back was he? Joach's thoughts went out to his sister. Could the explosion have been due to some effort of hers to free the book? If so, had Elena survived? With this worry nagging him, Joach nodded them all forward. 'We must keep going!'

Ahead was the side passage that left the main concourse of the catacombs and led toward the staircase where Tol'chuk was posted. Meric collected Mama Freda under an arm and led them into it. Here again the walls to either side grew cruder and rougher. They kept their pace quick but noisy. They wanted to stay clear of the ill'guard's grip but not so far as to lose him. Before long the stair appeared on the left.

Pausing to let Mama Freda catch a breath, Meric studied the steep stair. 'Once we reach Tol'chuk, we'll need to either make a stand or lead the ill'guard into the streets above.'

Joach shook his head. 'We make a stand. I won't leave with Elena still down here.'

Mama Freda spoke from beside Meric. 'It's too late. He's already here.'

Meric and Joach both swung back toward the corridor. Joach raised his staff, and Meric slipped a long dagger from a wrist sheath. But the corridors behind them were still dark.

'I see no sign of torch or lantern,' Meric whispered.

'He hides in the dark,' Mama Freda answered.

Joach fought a shiver down his back. Beyond the reach of their feeble torchlight, the passage was a wall of blackness. Joach had heard of how the blind were often gifted with heightened senses. 'Are you sure?'

The old healer simply nodded, showing no fear at her revelation. Instead, her lips were grim with anger. 'He listens to us even now.'

Joach waved to Meric. 'Take Mama Freda from here. I'll hold the monster off while you fetch Tol'chuk and his hammer.'

'You can't hold an ill'guard off by yourself – not for that long.'

'He's right, Joach,' Mama Freda said, shoving free of Meric's grip. 'I'll stay and fight alongside you.'

Joach bit back a retort. How did this old blind woman expect to help? In any fight to come, she would prove more a burden than an asset.

Meric seemed to agree. He glanced doubtfully from over the old woman's shoulder. Then he leaned his torch against the wall and turned to Mama Freda. 'If you mean to stay with us, you'll need a weapon.' He handed her his knife. Its long blade glittered in the torchlight. 'It's an ice dagger forged by my ancestors. If necessary, strike sure and deep. It will slice through bone as easily as air.'

Mama Freda awkwardly handled the knife. Her lack of sight hindered her. She almost cut her thumb on its blade. 'Thank you,' she said to Meric. 'This will do nicely.' She turned to face the black passage below them.

Joach followed her gaze. 'Why doesn't he come?'

Mama Freda slowly shook her head. 'He listens, hoping we will give him some clue to Elena's whereabouts.'

Seeming to hear her words and knowing his ruse was over, Brother Ewan pushed into their circle of torchlight. 'Right you are, my fine old woman. And before I slay you all, I will have my answer. Now where have you hidden the girl?'

Joach stepped forward to meet the ill'guard monster. He positioned his staff in front of him. His lips moved silently, and the length of wood blew to flame with spurts of dark-fire. 'Stand back!' Joach ordered.

Brother Ewan had stripped his robe to his waist. His arms, chest, and neck were draped with thousands of tiny purplish worms, each the color of a deep bruise. They seemed to reach for the darkfire of Joach's staff, their slender bodies stretching toward the flames. 'Young man, I see you've been touched by the black arts, too. So why do you fight when you should be joining me?'

Joach waved the staff before him in a warding motion. The leeches followed its motion, swaying in sync with his staff. 'Magick is only a weapon,' Joach said coldly. 'I wield it; it does not control me.'

Brother Ewan waved a hand dismissively, and a few

leeches flew from his fingers to strike the stone wall. 'You argue semantics. Touch darkness, and darkness touches you. Flint should have taught you that by now.'

Joach could not argue too fiercely against this one's words. In fact, Flint *had* warned him about the risk his spirit faced from wielding the staff's magick. An inkling of worry touched him, but he shoved it away. He would not be corrupted. Joach scowled at his enemy. 'Only the weak allow the darkness in them to eclipse the bright as you have.'

Brother Ewan's wan face grew heated. 'The master has not beaten me down. He has granted me a gift.' The ill'-guard raised his two arms, displaying the spread of worms. 'Leeches were always a tool of a healer. But no healer has been blessed with such a splendid crop as mine.'

Mama Freda slipped forward to Joach's right side, one hand on the wall to guide her. She could not directly find Ewan's face as she spoke. 'I'm the only healer here, Brother Ewan. You're a disease.' She threw Meric's knife at him. But without eyes, she did not even attempt to skewer him. She merely tossed the blade at the man's feet. 'Prove yourself still a healer. Cut the corruption from yourself!'

Her display brought a smile to Brother Ewan's lips. He nudged her knife aside and waggled a finger at her. 'Tsk, tsk. For such an experienced healer, you've made a terrible misdiagnosis. It is you who are the disease – and I am the cure!'

Joach inwardly groaned as he backed away. Why had the old woman wasted her only weapon? It was her last defense in case Joach and Meric failed to defeat the fiend. He moved Mama Freda roughly behind him in his anger. The old woman did not resist.

Brother Ewan stepped toward them.

Meric slipped forward in front of Joach, moving almost

too fast for the eye to follow. Already the elv'in's shirt billowed with his magick. Meric raised a hand, and a gust of wind blew forth from his fingertips. The whirling gale swept down the passage toward the ill'guard.

The man continued to smile. As the blast struck Brother Ewan, he remained standing. The tails of his robe snapped in the wind. His smile grew as the winds whipped at him. The leeches upon his body flailed in the gusts, but instead of being ripped from the fiend's skin, they stretched and grew. Soon the man's pale skin was draped with leeches longer than a man's forearm.

Brother Ewan's laughter echoed out from the center of the magickal gale. 'Send me more power, elv'in!'

Mama Freda pulled at Meric's sleeve from behind. 'Stop! I know about these ill'guard. Elemental magick feeds their darkness. You only strengthen him with your own magick. You must stop!'

Meric stumbled backward as he withdrew his magick.

Joach took his place. Where elemental magick failed, black magick might prevail. Joach raised his staff.

Brother Ewan grinned and suddenly lunged out with an arm. Joach blocked with his burning staff but realized too late that his move was just what the ill'guard wanted. Ewan grabbed the end of his staff. Leeches flowed onto the wood.

Joach yanked his staff away in disgust, managing to free it of the fiend's grip, but not the leeches. The purplish worms clung to the wood, bathing in the darkfire, writhing in what could only be described as pleasure. Joach stumbled away. He watched in horror as the leeches on his staff swelled further in size. In only a single breath, they stretched and grew to the size of huge jungle snakes.

'Shake them off! Now!' Mama Freda yelled. 'They feed on your magick, too!'

Joach obeyed and struck the butt of his staff against the wall, hard enough to sting his hand. The giant leeches fell in a tangle to the cold stone – all except one tenacious beast that lunged at Joach's hand. Fire flamed up his arm, and Joach fell to his knees.

Suddenly Mama Freda and Meric were there, tugging Joach back by his shirt. Their quick movement saved his life. He was dragged backward just as more of the monstrous leeches lashed out at him, quick as mountain adders. Still, the beast attached to his hand burned and swelled.

Joach's vision began to blacken.

Meric used his boot to kick the staff from Joach's grip, knocking away the leech attached to it. Immediately, the fire in his hand ended. Joach glanced down to see his two smallest fingers and part of his palm gone. Blood spurted and flowed.

'Move!' Meric yelled. 'If you wish to live, boy, then help us!'

Joach raised his eyes in time to see more of the leeches already at his heels. Ignoring the pain in his wounded hand, Joach scrambled away on hands and feet. In a tangle of limbs, the trio retreated.

All the while, Brother Ewan pursued, step for step, following with his writhing pack of monster leeches. 'Why run? Tell me where the wit'ch hides, and I will let you live! Or stay silent, and take your medicine.'

Joach's face paled. How could they fend off such a monster when their magicks had failed them? What hope did they have to survive?

Suddenly, Mama Freda stopped her own flight. She stepped between Joach and the fiend. She spat at Brother Ewan. Her aim was deadly accurate. Her spittle hit the fiend square in the face.

Joach rolled to his feet, cradling his wounded hand.

Brother Ewan wiped his face, leaving a few leeches clinging to his cheek. His laughter died with the strike of spittle. 'You will pay for that,' he said coldly. His giant leeches writhed around his ankles.

Mama Freda faced Brother Ewan squarely. 'I'm not finished.'

Joach glanced askance to Meric. Something slowly dawned on Joach. Mama Freda had warned them about the magickal growth of the worms; she had even pulled him away from the striking leeches and spat in the ill'guard's face. 'Mama Freda . . . ?'

She ignored Joach. 'I have one more gift for you, Brother Ewan!' She pointed a finger at the fiend. 'Death!'

Brother Ewan's lips spread into a grin. Laughter bubbled up. Then suddenly Ewan tensed in midstep. His smile faded into confusion, and his cackle strangled in his throat. Blood dribbled from the man's lips.

Brother Ewan toppled forward, crashing to his face on the stone floor. He spasmed a moment, then lay still. Dead. Impaled in the center of his back was the hilt of Meric's ice dagger. Small crackles of silver energy danced out from the blade and skittered across the fiend's skin. As they looked on, the leeches dissolved into clots of blood, steaming slightly on the cool floor.

'How . . . ?' Joach's mind was too full of questions. Then he saw the answer. A small furred creature scrambled from around the man's legs and scampered toward Mama Freda.

'Good boy, Tikal,' Mama Freda said warmly. She bent and hauled the creature into her arms and up to her shoulder.

Tikal wrapped his tail around Mama Freda's neck and gently licked her cheek. 'Cookie?' Tikal asked in a frail voice.

She patted him and scratched behind his ear. 'You'll get all the cookies in Port Rawl after this.'

Tikal closed his eyes and leaned into the woman's neck, clinging tight.

'But ... but your pet was killed,' Joach said, pointing uselessly at Tikal. Blood flowed from his wounded hand. Reminded of his injury, Joach swooned to the floor.

Mama Freda rushed forward, kneeling before the boy and pulling bandages and a vial of elixir from various pockets. She explained as she cradled Joach's hand in her lap and worked on him. 'I, too, thought Tikal had been killed. When I first began to receive visions from him again, I thought I had become deluded, wishing so strongly for him that my mind made it so.' Mama Freda reached and touched Tikal once more with clear love. 'I can sense the magick in him. Someone healed him.'

'Elena?' Joach asked weakly.

'Who else?' she said as she applied a cooling balm that washed away Joach's pain with a single swipe. 'Tikal has her scent about him. Elena must have found him on her way back down the catacombs. Her magick strengthened him enough to survive and follow. But, like you, he will need more healing.'

Meric spoke up from where he stood over the corpse of the ill'guard. 'Why didn't you tell someone?'

Mama Freda's expression grew embarrassed. 'I wasn't sure the visions were real. It was only after Tikal came upon the ill'guard on our back trail that I knew it was true. By that time, the ill'guard was already listening to us, so I kept silent. I hoped Tikal's stealth would prove useful.' Mama Freda nodded toward the knife's hilt. 'And so it has.'

Joach stared at the old woman, eyes wide. He had secretly considered Mama Freda a burden to this venture. But now he knew better than to judge by appearances. The old woman had just saved his life.

Mama Freda finished wrapping his hand in a snug bandage. 'Dragon's blood mixed with root of elm should save the rest of your hand.'

Joach raised his arm, almost afraid to look. He cringed at the sight of his half hand, but he flexed his remaining fingers and felt no pain. The wrap was even clean of blood. It was as if the injury were months old, rather than mere moments. Joach swallowed and glanced to the old healer. 'Thank you, Mama Freda. I'm in your debt. If you had not—'

An explosion suddenly ripped through their world. Joach and Mama Freda again found themselves tossed roughly to the floor. Dust billowed, and stones groaned. Joach's skull rang with the force of the concussion. He pushed to his feet even before the ground had finished rumbling. He helped Mama Freda up. Tikal still clung to her neck.

Down the passage, Meric shoved himself off the ill'-guard's body, his face a mask of disgust. Suddenly, through the wafting dust, a monstrous figure rose behind the elv'in.

Joach opened his mouth to warn Meric, but a familiar graveled voice spoke. 'What happened?' Tol'chuk asked. The og're waved through the dust cloud and crossed toward them, eying the fallen ill'guard.

Joach crawled to his feet, then helped Mama Freda stand. 'What are you doing down here? You're supposed to be guarding the door.'

The og're surveyed the scene one more time, then spoke. He pointed absently above his head. 'The island be under attack from ships that fly the clouds. I came to fetch you away from these crypts before the castle lands on all your heads.' Tol'chuk glanced around. 'Where be Elena?'

'Gone for the book,' Joach answered as he retrieved his staff from the floor. He examined the length of wood for damage but found none. 'What is this about flying ships?'

Meric interrupted, his face pale. 'Did they have keels that glowed?'

Tol'chuk nodded his head. 'And lightning bolts danced below them.'

Meric groaned. 'The Thunderclouds, the warships of my people – they're already here. If they're attacking, they probably saw the sea battle and assumed their windships had arrived in time. They won't know we're here.'

'What're they trying to do?' Joach asked.

Meric covered his forehead with his palm. 'They mean to tear down the island. And if we don't stop them, they'll take us down with it.'

Joach shook his head. They had survived skal'tum, d'warves, and ill'guard, only to be threatened now by one of their own allies. 'Meric, you must find some way to stop them. Take Tol'chuk and Mama Freda with you. Get your people to call off their attacks.'

Meric nodded. 'What are you going to do?'

Joach nudged his staff toward the deeper catacombs. 'With the ill'guard out of the way, I'm going to search for Elena. If you fail to stop the warships, then book or not, I must get her out of here.'

Meric reached and clapped Joach on the shoulder, holding his grip tight. 'Be careful. And be quick.'

Joach returned the clasp. 'And you do the same.'

Tol'chuk moved forward with Mama Freda at his side. 'Meric does not need us. But more eyes in these dark passages will find your sister quicker.'

Joach touched the og're's elbow. 'Do not fear, Tol'chuk. I will find her. But it will do me little good if the catacombs collapse atop us. Go with Meric. Guard him from the dangers that must be raging up there by now. He must stop those warships.' He then turned to Mama Freda. 'And you must use your wiles and your pet's eyes to find them both a safe path.'

Tol'chuk grumbled, clearly not entirely convinced, but he bowed his head. 'I will not let the elv'in fail.'

The og're turned away, and Joach found Mama Freda facing him still. She raised her chin as if examining Joach down her long nose. 'You send us all away for another reason. Something is hidden in your heart.'

Joach sighed. He could not lie to her. 'My destiny lies here,' he said quietly. 'This next path I must walk alone.'

She nodded, seemingly satisfied with the truth of his heart, and turned to join the others.

In short order, Joach found himself alone in the catacombs. Even the tread of his companions' boots faded behind him as he marched with staff in hand into the bowels of this subterranean crypt. As he walked, his blood stirred with the gift of weaving. His words to Mama Freda had not been a lie. He sensed the culmination of forces and circumstance pulling him toward one destination, one fate.

What came next was between Joach, Elena, and a plainsman from Standi. Joach pictured the sunset tower, the Spire of the Departed, and gripped his staff in an iron grip.

In this last battle, he would not fail his sister.

25

Elena continued to follow Er'ril and his lantern. She willed him to a faster pace, but after the second blast from above, he had grown even more cautious. Contrary to the plainsman's wariness, the explosions made Elena want to race blindly ahead. Worry for Joach and the others inflamed her fears. Had these blasts something to do with the ill'-guard? She forced her feet to keep pace with Er'ril. She could not flee his side, not as long as he still clutched the Blood Diary.

As she matched his pace, mindful of the floor under her, she became fixed upon the play of light and shadow across the muscles of his back. She had seen Er'ril bare chested before, but never with two arms. At first, she had trouble reconciling this new physique with the old one in her mind. There was a symmetry of form now that had been missing before. She found her gaze riding over his shoulder to his new arm. No scar separated the two, yet a clear delineation could be seen. His shoulder and back were deeply tanned from the summer's sun, and though his new arm was also a coppery hue, it did not share as deep a bronzing. Where the old Er'ril and the new met could be distinctly noted.

Elena licked her lips as she followed, her mouth dry. How

she wanted to run a finger along that fine line between copper and bronzed skin, to find out for sure if this was the same Er'ril who had been snatched from her. If only he would offer her some clear clue, something that would let her run into his embrace once again. She shivered in the cool air of the catacombs. It had been too long since she had felt the heat of his skin on her cheek. *Please,* she begged him silently, *give me some clue to your true heart.*

Elena clutched the iron ward to her chest. Its cold touch reminded her to be wary. Now was not the time to let her guard down. But even the scent of his sweat trailed behind him, reminding her of times when he had held her close. Elena held the ward in a white-knuckled grip. She was no longer a little girl to moon over a knight; the fate of Alasea depended on her caution and control. She must hold steadfast.

Suddenly Er'ril stopped in front of her.

Lost in her own heart, Elena almost collided into his backside. She pulled up short, so near she felt the heat off his body, her naked skin so close to his bare back. A flush traveled from her legs to her face. His scent filled her senses. She tensed, afraid to move, afraid to breathe, lest he hear her.

Slowly Er'ril crouched and moved away, taking his heat with him. Elena sighed silently, both relieved and disappointed. Though no one could see her, Elena crouched also, instinct still making her follow Er'ril's lead.

She spotted the source of Er'ril's sudden caution. A flickering light played out from a side passage ahead. As she crouched with Er'ril, Elena suddenly realized it was the same passage that led to Flint's secret staircase. She had not thought they had traveled so far. Her worries and concerns had befuddled her sense of distance.

Er'ril dimmed his lantern's flame to a trickle. He placed the lantern on the floor and drifted across the hall to crouch in the shadows near the curve of the wall. As he bent down, he reached behind him and slipped the Blood Diary under the belt of his pants at the base of his back, keeping it hidden. He then removed Elena's wit'ch's dagger and held it before him.

Elena found herself momentarily transfixed by the gilt rose on the book's cover as it poked from under Er'ril's belt. The rose seemed almost to glow in the feeble lantern light nearby. She had only to reach out and grab the book. Her fingers stretched for it, but she clenched a fist. It could be a trap. She pulled back her arm and crouched alongside Er'ril. She would wait to see who else shared these halls ahead.

Taking the lesson from Er'ril, Elena knew the only certain safety lay in staying unseen.

As she waited, Elena listened to the plainsman's breathing, a wolf on the scent of a deer. Soon the tread of boots grew louder from the side passage, and a figure appeared outlined by torchlight. Elena was sure it was the ill'guard returning to his roost. But as the figure stepped nearer, Elena saw that it was not the ill'guard who approached, but her own brother.

She came close to calling out Joach's name in relief, but after staying cautious for so long, she controlled this sudden urge. Maybe here, hidden and listening, Elena could discover some answer to Er'ril's loyalty.

Joach approached, staff in one hand, oblivious to the wolf in the shadows. Er'ril could easily slay her brother, but instead he straightened and stepped clear of the shadows. Her brother startled backward. 'Er'ril!'

Elena spotted the bandage around her brother's right

hand. What had happened to him? And where were the others?

'Joach, what are you doing down here alone? It's not safe.' Er'ril returned the dagger to his belt.

But Joach's eyes seemed blind to Er'ril's moves. The plainsman could have stabbed Joach, and her brother would not have seen it. His gaze flickered between Er'ril's two hands. 'Your . . . your arm,' he finally mumbled. Joach broke from his stunned stupor and raised his staff against Er'ril. Flames of darkfire bloomed along its length.

Er'ril refused to back from Joach's display. He raised his new arm. 'Do not fear. It was the key to unlocking the Blood Diary from the spell that protected the book. My arm was fuel for the spell, and with the release of the magick, it was returned. Now where is Elena?'

Joach shook his head and took a step back into the side passage. His face was a mask of disbelief, his eyes glazed. Elena knew her brother's sight was obscured by his recurring dream. 'I'll never tell you! First the ill'guard tried to find out and failed. And now you appear. I'll not let you near Elena!'

'What . . . what ill'guard?' Er'ril snapped angrily. 'What are you rambling about, Joach?'

Joach raised his staff higher.

Eying her brother's response, Er'ril choked back his anger. He took a deep breath and started again. He lifted both his arms. 'I know how this must appear. It was the reason that I encouraged you to come along with us. Flint and Moris thought your dream was a false weaving, believing it an impossibility for my arm ever to return – but I knew better. Still, to keep the book safe, I had to remain silent.' Er'ril's voice grew firm and sure. 'Look at me, Joach. I am *not* corrupted. I don't know what will happen next.

But understand and believe me, Joach, I mean your sister no harm. I . . . I care deeply for her.'

Elena's breath caught in her throat. She swallowed back a sob. She longed to step forward and reveal herself, to end this charade, but what might happen next could reveal the truth of Er'ril's words.

Joach lowered his staff slightly. Er'ril's words had removed the glaze from her brother's eyes. 'How can I trust you, Er'ril? You know how my dream ends.'

'Dreams, even weavings, can fool. But I know that that is no answer that will convince you.' Er'ril reached behind him. 'Maybe this will.'

Joach backed a step warily.

Er'ril slipped the book from his belt and held it toward Joach. 'Here is the Blood Diary.'

Joach's eyes grew wide.

'It has been my responsibility for five hundred winters,' he said. 'But I want you to take it now. I sense that my role in guarding the Blood Diary is ending. If you will not let me near your sister, then you must get the book to her.' Er'ril stepped forward and placed the tattered tome at the entrance to the side passage. He then moved back. 'Take this burden from me.'

Elena stood stunned by his act. Surely this was a clear sign of Er'ril's loyalty. A creature of the Black Heart would never relinquish the book.

The same thought appeared to course through Joach's mind. But where Er'ril's offering made Elena hope, it only made Joach more suspicious. Her brother's eyes narrowed as he set down his torch and slipped closer. He hovered over the book with his staff raised, eying Er'ril with clear distrust. Joach slowly bent, then snatched the book from the floor and darted backward, away from Er'ril.

But the plainsman made no move against Joach.

Elena's eyes remained on Er'ril. Joach's continued suspicion held her back from revealing herself. Though the release of the book seemed contradictory to anything a dark minion might do, Elena knew her only safety lay in the spirit spell that hid her.

'Take the book to her, Joach. The duty I swore so long ago is over. From here, Elena has no need of me.'

Elena carefully circled in front of Er'ril, studying him as he spoke these last words. Sorrow and relief were mixed in his eyes. But what did these emotions mean? She stood there, only an arm's length away, searching for an answer in his face. A single tear rolled down his cheek. Her fingers rose to wipe it away. In her heart, she suddenly knew the truth. Er'ril was not corrupted.

Then Joach spoke behind her. 'These pages are all blank.'

Elena lowered her hand and glanced over her shoulder at Joach. Her brother held the book in one hand and rifled through its pages. Even from here, Elena could see the clean white pages.

'This is not the Blood Diary,' Joach spat out. 'It's a trick.'

Elena turned to see Er'ril's eyes flash with anger. This sudden change was like a flare of wildfire, burning away the sorrow from a moment ago.

Elena stumbled away. She cursed herself for being so blind. Why had she not even considered that the book might be a fake?

Er'ril's voice was rough. 'It is *no* trick, boy.'

Joach still held the book up by its cover. 'And I am to take your word on this? You who step from my dreams with two arms?'

Er'ril shook his head, the fire dying to ash in his eyes. 'Believe what you want, Joach. There is nothing I can do to

634

prove my heart more than giving you the book itself.' Er'ril stepped away and returned to his lantern. 'Take the book to Elena. That is all I ask.' He lifted the lantern and turned toward the ascending spiral of the catacombs. 'My brother is somewhere up there, weak now. I will take my war to him since my usefulness to Elena is at an end.'

Joach danced back as Er'ril moved past the entrance to the side passage. Once Er'ril was marching away, Joach slipped the book inside his shirt, grabbed his torch, and darted down the throat of the side passage, escaping from whatever threat he imagined in Er'ril.

Elena, though, waited at the crossroads. She watched Joach's torchlight fade down the side passage while Er'ril's lantern glow disappeared around the curve of the catacombs' hall. She stood fixed in place, unable to move. Which path should she take? She clutched the ward to her belly, begging it to reveal some sign.

More than ever, she wished Aunt My were here. Right now, Elena could use the swordswoman's wise and practical counsel.

Finally, Elena took a step toward the side passage. Surely here was the wisest path. Even if the book was a trick, it was best to rejoin Joach and the others. Even Aunt My would approve such a pragmatic decision.

Or would she?

Elena's feet froze at the threshold. Long ago, back in Shadowbrook, Aunt My had warned her that there must be a reason that a woman, rather than a man, had been destined to carry the banner of freedom. Aunt My had explained her own personal belief: that ultimately the fate of Alasea would depend not on the capacity of *magick* in a woman, but on the strength of her *heart*.

As Elena pondered her aunt's words, the two sources of

light faded completely. Gloom descended on her. In the darkness, she pictured the single tear on Er'ril's cheek, shining like silver in the torchlight.

Elena stepped away from the side passage and turned to the dark catacombs. Her mind attempted to justify her decision. Surely she should pursue Er'ril in order to discover the truth of his allegiance. But Elena needed none of these justifications for her decision. Her feet were already treading up the spiraling concourse, moving faster and faster. She had been won over already. Her heart would not let her leave Er'ril's side.

And for now, that was enough.

Through the streets of A'loa Glen, Meric rushed ahead of Tol'chuk and Mama Freda. Around them the city lay in chaos. Trails of smoke scarred the horizons. Cries and screeches echoed off the stone walls. The citadel atop Mount Orr still rumbled as bricks and sections of wall tumbled from the heights to crash and rattle into the lower streets. Overhead, the bloated bellies of warships hung in the skies, slowly circling like so many vultures. Under the pall of smoke, the sharp tang of lightning flavored the air, radiating from the ships above and from the recent pair of assaults.

'They mean to strike again!' Tol'chuk called to Meric. 'One more blow and the castle be rubble.'

Meric pulled to a stop and glanced overhead just as a score of frantic wings swept past. More panicked skal'tum. Since fleeing the catacombs, Meric's group had spotted many such fragments of the skal'tum army. Torn into frightened scraps, the beasts sought to escape the arrival of the elv'in warships. So far none of the beasts had attempted to assault the trio. Meric suspected the monsters' eyes were fixed on the skies above.

Once the skal'tum had flown past, Meric saw that Tol'chuk's assessment proved accurate. Another five Thunderclouds were beginning to ring the top of the hill. The *Sunchaser*, his mother's flagship, still hovered over the smoking castle heights. He cringed at the sight. This was all his fault. 'We must move faster!' Meric cried out above the din of battle.

Tol'chuk crossed next to him. The og're's face was purplish with exertion. He had carried Mama Freda most of the way. He pulled forth the Try'sil, the d'warf hammer, from its sheath on his back. 'We be close enough. Let's find an open plaza and try it.'

Meric shook his head. 'They'll never see. Not unless we are right under their noses.'

Tol'chuk pointed to the ships moving into position. 'We either try now, or we lose everything.'

Meric sighed loudly. He knew the effort would prove futile, but the og're was right. They at least needed to make the attempt. He could not let the land's hopes be dashed without first trying to signal the fleet, to warn the ships away. Meric studied the skies for some clue, some way to redeem his mistake. His heart ached with the pain of his betrayal.

Mama Freda spoke from near Tol'chuk's elbow. 'Tikal has found a long plaza up and to the left. We could be there in moments.'

'Let's go,' Meric said and ran ahead.

Tol'chuk slung Mama Freda under one of his large arms and loped after him. The old healer called out directions, and soon the trio reached the open court. They were almost under the very cliffs upon which the citadel perched. The square was in full shadow from the setting sun. Tol'chuk set Mama Freda down so she could grab her pet tamrink and retreat to the side of the plaza.

Tol'chuk followed Meric to the center of the square. 'Hurry, elv'in.'

'I know, og're,' Meric snapped back; but then his eyes apologized for his harshness. Tol'chuk was only expressing all their concerns. 'Raise the hammer high. I will do my best to create a good show.'

Tol'chuk grunted and lifted his arms toward the skies, bearing the hammer aloft.

Meric touched his magick and gathered winds to his frame. Once insulated, he mixed dry and moist winds, creating a crackle of energy from their frictions. He gathered more power from the air. With the warships overhead, the winds were rich with energies. Soon his clothes snapped and danced with scintillating sparks. 'Be ready!' Meric called out. 'Hold the hammer steady!'

Hands raised high, Meric gathered energy to his fingertips. It built into a sphere of lightning that slowly spun and shone in the shadowed plaza. But Meric knew such a feeble glow would attract few eyes. He needed more of a show. He fed more and more power until his whole frame tremored with the power overhead. All the hairs on his body stood on end, quivering. A sheen of sweat glistened his face and arms. His fingertips began to burn from their proximity to the sphere of lightning. He had meant to shout one final warning to the og're, but it was too late.

He shifted his eyes to stare at Tol'chuk. The og're met his gaze.

In a final wrench of shoulders and power, Meric threw his lightning at the hammer. Its ball of energy smashed into the iron. The Try'sil had been forged by lightning. It could withstand the force. It remembered its origin and shouted it skyward.

From the head of the hammer, a brilliant silver-blue bolt

shot toward the ships above. Thunder cracked across the plaza. Tol'chuk was thrown backward, his arms scorched to the elbows.

Meric, protected by his winds, was buffeted backward also, but he kept his feet. He watched the bolt shoot between two of the warships overhead. 'See it,' Meric prayed. 'Look down.'

Tol'chuk scrabbled off the cobbles with a groan, but Mama Freda was already at his side, smearing a balm over the og're's singed and smoking skin. Tol'chuk seemed more annoyed than comforted by the old healer's attention. 'Did it work?'

Meric tried to watch the ships above him. He saw no sign that the vessels had recognized the bolt as a signal. With the dance of lightning among the many keels, the crews must have thought little of Meric's display. 'No,' he said sourly. 'My people are too much creatures of air and cloud. It takes more than my little spark to get them to look down.'

Tol'chuk rolled to his feet. 'Let us try again.'

Meric shook his head. 'I used almost everything in me. I would need to rest at least a quarter moon to repeat even the same show.'

'Then it be hopeless.' Tol'chuk's tired eyes swung to the five Thunderclouds as they gathered around the crown of the peak.

'We should return to the catacombs,' Meric said. 'Try at least to get the others away.'

'We'd never make it—'

A sudden rumbling roar shattered across the plaza from behind them. The trio spun around in time to see a massive black-winged shape skirt around a tower's top and dive toward them. It roared again, silver claws wide as it lunged toward the square. Meric and the others ran out of its way.

With a snap of its scaled wings, it slowed its descent to land with a screech of nails on stone.

Meric spotted the tiny rider atop the beast's back. 'Sy-wen!'

The tiny mer'ai woman seemed haggard and exhausted. It was almost as if she had lost substance during the day's horrors. 'Thank the Sweet Mother! I saw your flash and could only hope it was you!' Then she glanced around the square. 'Where are the wit'ch and the others?'

Meric rushed forward, ignoring the swing of the dragon's head in his direction. The beast's large black eyes seemed to drink him in. 'We have no time to explain! Can you get me to that large ship above the castle?'

Sy-wen frowned. 'I've been trying to reach it since the fleet arrived, trying to get them to stop their assault. But between the lightning and that cursed woman's winds, I've made no headway.'

Meric finally glanced to the dragon. 'If your mount will allow it, I can get us there.'

Sy-wen turned to her dragon. A silent exchange passed between them. 'Ragnar'k will allow it. But we must hurry.' Sy-wen nodded above.

Meric turned. Already the five Thunderclouds were gathering energy to their keels. He swung back around to see the mer'ai offering her hand from the neck of the dragon. 'Climb behind me.'

With a brief nod of thanks at the dragon, who still stared at Meric with clear disdain, Meric crossed and took Sy-wen's hand. In the moments it took to settle and wrap his arms around Sy-wen's waist, the dragon spread its wings, pushing up on its stout legs.

'Hang tight!' Sy-wen called.

Then the world swept out from under them. Ragnar'k

leaped upward, wings snapping, pulling them from the square.

Tol'chuk's voice bellowed from below, wishing luck and speed, but most of the words were lost as the dragon's wings fought to drag them into the sky. Ragnar'k climbed above the highest towers, then banked to the west, circling around the cliffs atop Mount Orr. The bellies of the warships were just overhead. Meric smelled the lightning wafting from them.

Ragnar'k swung farther out, fighting to gain more height. Slowly, too slowly, he scaled higher and higher into the sky. Glancing behind, Meric saw that the keels of the five Thunderclouds now raged with energy. 'Hurry,' Meric moaned, both to himself and to the dragon.

Ragnar'k must have heard. The dragon suddenly wheeled back, tilting frighteningly on one wing tip. Meric saw the spread of city and ocean far below. As Ragnar'k swooped around, the dragon's wings caught a sharp updraft and shot skyward. Soon they sailed above all the armada except the *Sunchaser*, the flagship. It hovered directly ahead. Ragnar'k banked and aimed for it.

Sy-wen bent low over the dragon's neck, forcing Meric to crouch, too. Ragnar'k sped faster. 'Just get above the ship!' Meric yelled into Sy-wen's ear.

The dragon was now near enough to the ship that Meric could spy the members of its crew. At the stern wheel, he spotted one crew member with a characteristic streak of copper in his silver hair. It was his older brother, Richald. As they neared, Meric saw the tall woman manning the prow of the ship. Her silver hair already glowed with power.

'Mother,' he whispered.

She seemed to have heard him. She glanced toward the dragon, but the expression she wore was not one of welcome.

Fire blazed in her eyes even from there. She snapped a hand at them in clear irritation. Winds suddenly assaulted them.

'She does this whenever we draw near!' Sy-wen yelled into the winds as Ragnar'k fought fiercely to hold his position.

Meric slipped one hand from around the mer'ai girl's waist and lifted his palm against the winds. He cast out his magick, weakening rapidly, and thrust against his mother's assault. The winds abated, but only slightly. From the back of the dragon, Meric saw his mother's expression of surprise.

'Go!' Meric urged Sy-wen, pulling back his magick.

Ragnar'k used the break in the gale to sweep at the ship, driving just over their masts. Once above the vessel, Meric released his other arm from around Sy-wen and rolled off the rear of the dragon. He tumbled toward the ship below as Sy-wen yelled in surprise.

Under him, the five Thunderclouds suddenly blasted forth with flows of power, a brilliant star dawning below. Meric fell toward the center of this fiery display.

Stretching out his arms, Meric shoved down with his magick to slow and guide his fall. His body straightened its rolling pitch. Meric swung his legs under him and slipped past rigging and sail. He landed hard on the decks of the *Sunchaser*, pain lancing up his right leg. The limb crumpled under him. He crashed to his knees, broken bone slicing through his thigh. He bit back any complaint; he had been lucky to live.

Meric raised his face, lines of agony marring his features.

He was already surrounded. One man shoved through the others. The man bore a long thin sword but lowered it when Meric met his gaze. 'Brother,' the man said with calm surprise.

'Richald.' Meric nodded as if this were an ordinary meeting of brothers on a sunny day.

Richald glanced up and down his brother's body, his nose slightly curling at what he saw. Burned, scarred, and now broken limbed, Meric knew he hardly resembled one of the royal blood of their house.

Meric spoke into his brother's appraisal. 'You must stop Mother. She must not strike again!'

Around them, the star of power winked out. Meric could sense the energy now stored under the keel of the *Sunchaser*. It trembled the deck beneath his knees.

The crowd of elv'in opened before Meric, and a woman shining with power stepped toward him from the prow. Her skin glowed, and her eyes shimmered too bright. His mother had linked to the storehouse of energy below. Her voice quavered with the suppressed might. 'Why should I stop, my son? Is this not what you asked?'

Meric attempted to stare up at his mother, but the blaze in her gaze stung. 'I was wrong, Mother. The fate of these people depends on what happens next on the island below. We must not interfere.'

'I care not about the fate of these people.'

Meric cleared his throat, his voice sharp. 'But I do.'

His mother waved a hand as if to whisk away his statement, crackles of energy playing across her fingers. 'You have been walking in the dirt for too long, my son.'

'Yes, I have. So I am the best judge to decide if these people are worth saving.'

His mother lowered her hand, pondering his words.

Meric pressed on. 'And what of our own bloodlines?'

His mother cocked her head slightly. 'What are you saying, Meric?'

'If you care so little for these people, then consider our

own. The last of our lost king's heirs struggles below. Destroy this island and you destroy half the heritage of the elv'in.'

These words finally reached her, but she showed little emotion. She simply turned on a heel and nodded to Richald. 'Pull back the *Sunchaser*. We will discharge our load into the sea.'

'No! Wait!' Meric called to her. 'I know where this energy can be best spent.'

His mother glanced back, eyes blazing. 'Where?'

Meric did not answer. He waved for Richald to assist him to the rail. Meric stifled a cry as he was pulled to his feet. In the distance, he saw the black-winged form of Ragnar'k swing around and sail back toward the ship. Once close enough, Meric waved an arm to Sy-wen. He wind-spoke to her so she could hear him.

'Lead us to the battle in the sea! Scout for the worst skirmishes that still rage! It's time to end this! We will use the might of the *Sunchaser* to smite the last of the attackers!'

Once he received acknowledgment from Sy-wen, Meric sagged against the rail. The pain of his broken leg and his weakened state finally overwhelmed him.

His mother slid beside him, still cool and passionless. 'You care this much for these people of the land?'

Meric turned to her, this time not even flinching from the blaze in her eyes. 'Yes, Mother, I do. I would give my life for them.'

Reaching to her son, Queen Tratal rested a palm over his hand. She gave him a quick squeeze of affection, then raised her other arm. On her signal, the *Sunchaser* heeled around and followed the dragon. 'Then as you said, let's end this.'

Somewhere among the rubbled streets of A'loa Glen, Greshym leaned against the wall of an ancient distillery. His breath rasped and wheezed from between lips clenched with pain. The creation of the portal so soon after battling Shorkan had taken its toll on the ancient mage. As a creature sustained by black magick, to empty his well of power so thoroughly wasted him physically as well. At the moment, he felt every one of his over five hundred winters. Even the air itself felt too thick to breathe.

In the shadows of the crumbling old building, Greshym leaned his head against the cool brick. He had only been able to leap as far as the city. At full strength, he could have created a portal strong enough to transport him all the way to Blackhall, not that he would have dared. Er'ril's last words to him were true. Once Shorkan passed word of his betrayal to the Dark Lord, he was a marked man. Every demon hound and netherworld beast would be hunting him.

Greshym eyed the Edifice far above. The second strike by the flying ships had taken out the easternmost tower. The spire had been aptly named the Broken Spear due to its cracked parapet. Now it was just a smoldering pile of blasted stones. *It'll have to be renamed the Smoking Heap,* he thought sourly.

'A shame it wasn't Shorkan's tower,' he groused aloud. If the ships had struck the Praetor's Spear, most of Greshym's problems would have been solved. With Shorkan dead, Greshym's traitorous actions in the catacombs could have remained a secret. But today the gods had not smiled on him. All his careful plans had not only failed to bring the book into his grasp but had doomed him as well.

Greshym pushed off the wall and moved down the avenue. He needed to get free of this island, but first he needed an infusion of magick. But from where? He crouched for a moment where the street of ancient ale houses ended in a wide square. He watched for any skal'tum. All that remained of their immense legions were ragged bands of panicked beasts. In his weakened state, without even a staff, he would be easy prey for the monsters. Since he was one of the darkmages who had sent them to this slaughter, they would not treat him kindly.

Greshym sidled around the corner, sticking to the deepest shadows cast by the setting sun. As he hurried, he caught a whiff that stirred his withered heart. He stumbled as the scent struck him to the core. He leaned his stumped wrist against the wall, panting. Dare he hope? Had it been his imagination? Once he collected his breath and calmed the clamor in his heart, Greshym lifted his nose like a hound on a scent. His eyes closed with the pleasure of the tang in the air.

If he had not been so starved, he might have easily missed it. He sniffed again. He knew what he smelled. Black magick! Somewhere nearby someone or something reeked of power, raw and untapped. Greshym thought of Shorkan, but quickly dismissed it. Not only would the Praetor avoid the streets, but after crossing the mage ring and enduring their short battle, Shorkan did not have the amount of magick he sniffed now.

But where was it coming from?

Revitalized by the scent, Greshym shoved from the wall and began to hunt the trail. Pausing at every corner to sniff the breeze, the old mage tracked the whiff of magick. His legs began to hurry along the dusty streets as the scent grew richer and more potent. Famished, his weak sight blurred further, but he continued on, drawn by the smell. His nose became his eyes, leading him onward to the source.

Finally, he scurried along a narrow street on the highest level of the city. Though the air was still fouled by smoke from the castle above, the tang of magick could not be obscured. Its source was just around the next corner. Caution slowed his feet. With the power he sensed, he could escape this tortured island.

Greshym dragged himself along the square base of a tall statue, creeping carefully. Once at the corner, he closed his eyes and focused himself with a rattling breath.

First, he needed to discover what lay ahead. Leaning forward, straining his old back, Greshym peeked around the corner. What he saw in the alley beyond almost tumbled him out of hiding. But he managed to pull back, one hand rising to throttle a shout of surprise and delight.

It was the boy! His boy! The wit'ch's brother! How could he be so lucky? Maybe the gods were smiling on him after all!

The view around the corner still burned in his mind. The lad stood in the center of the alley, staring up at the neighboring tower, lost in thought. But that was not all Greshym had spied. In the boy's grip was a staff. And Greshym would recognize that length of poi'wood anywhere. It was his own staff! He had thought it lost forever. The boy must have retrieved it.

Greshym closed his eyes and drank in the scent of ripe magick in the staff. He licked his lips. He would have it again. *He would have them all again!* – his staff, the boy, and his magick! But first he needed a plan.

Greshym's mind spun with various scenarios. He could not just snatch the staff from the lad. It was clearly bound to him. Greshym had seen the spurts of darkfire skittering its surface. He clenched a fist in frustration. He had forsaken the staff, and to retrieve it now, the staff must be handed back to him freely. But how? How could he get the boy to relinquish the staff?

The darkmage sent his thoughts probing around the

corner and grinned when he discovered that the old strings of his woven spell remained in the boy's mind, frayed but still there. The boy had never had them removed, but then again how could he? There were no mages left with the skill to do so. It would be a simple thing to retie those old knots and trap the boy again in his mind, making the lad a slave once more. But even that would not help much. To take the staff in this manner would be the same as snatching it from him. To keep the magick potent in the staff, it must be given freely from the heart. Otherwise, it was just an ordinary stick.

Greshym coiled his thoughts around the puzzle. He needed to hurry lest more of the wit'ch's companions should appear. But how to get the boy to trust him? Then, like a light dawning after the blackest night, the answer appeared in his mind. He could not coerce the boy by enslaving him, but he could still use the fragments of magick imbedded in the lad's mind.

Greshym knew what he needed to do. It would take only the slightest touch of magick to reach to those familiar strands and tug on them. Maybe he couldn't get the boy to dance for him like a marionette, but he could tug hard enough to move the boy's heart.

Knowing what he must do, Greshym reached out with the last dregs of his power. In his weakened state, even this small bit of magick weakened him as if he had cast a major spell. Greshym stumbled around the corner. He did not need to fake the groan as he fell to the cobbles in the alley.

Joach swung around at the sound, eyes wide with threat. The staff burst with darkfire. To Greshym, the magick wafting from the staff was like heat from a hearth in the middle of a winter storm.

Then as quick as the flames had appeared in the staff,

they died away. Joach ran at Greshym. He fell to his knees beside the old mage. The boy's eyes were bright with concern and worry as he reached to help him.

'Elena!' the boy called out. 'What happened to you? How did you get out here?'

Greshym smiled as he pulled and tweaked the various strands of magick to maintain the illusion in the boy's eyes. 'I don't know,' he said feebly, not needing to feign weakness or confusion. Greshym knew that his voice sounded like the boy's beloved sister's in Joach's ears.

'We must get off these streets,' Joach said, reaching under his shoulders to help him up.

'Yes. Yes, we must hide.' With the boy's aid, Greshym allowed himself to be led, half carried in his depleted state. His fingers secretly brushed the poi'wood of the staff affectionately. *Soon,* he thought silently.

Joach spoke, words tumbling from his mouth. 'It seems Meric was successful in getting the elv'in fleet to pull back. We need to get atop a tower and signal them.'

'To escape?'

Joach nodded, gathering Greshym tighter to his side. 'Save your strength, El.' As they limped across the alley and headed toward the door of the neighboring tower, Joach's eyes met his own, a tired grin on his lips. 'It seems we cannot avoid our fate,' he said, then nodded to the doorway ahead. 'We must go up.'

Not understanding the boy's cryptic words, Greshym craned his neck to stare at the parapet of the tower. He wrinkled his brow. Why did the boy think they needed to climb the Spire of the Departed?

His heart heavy with despair, Er'ril shouldered aside the warped iron gate to the catacombs. He stared at the destruction in the central courtyard. Rubble and smoke filled the square. Fires still burned, mostly from the smoldering ruins of the ancient koa'kona tree, now a cratered ruin. Er'ril winced at the destruction of the mighty tree.

But like himself, the tree had lived long past its usefulness. Both of them were just hoary and ancient remnants of Alasea's past glory. With the Blood Diary free, his duty to the centuries was finally completed. From here the fate of these lands would now rest on shoulders younger than his. It would be up to them to wrest the Dark Lord from his seat of power. And if prophecy held true, the wit'ch and the book were the land's only hope. He would offer what strength of arms he could, but in the greater schemes of prophecy and destiny, the wit'ch must walk alone from here.

At this thought, a sharp pang clutched his chest. He ground a fist against his ribs. He blamed the pain on the searing heat and smoke-filled lungs, but he could not entirely fool himself. He had come to define himself as Elena's knight, and some of this ache was from knowing that he would never share the same closeness with her again. He sensed that the book would replace his role. From this day forward, he would be as useful to Elena as the smoldering limbs of the dead koa'kona.

He stared at his new arm for a moment and swore a silent curse. He had gained so little and lost so much.

Sighing and girding himself to continue onward, Er'ril studied the open court for any dangers or foes. Overhead, he spied a huge flying ship retreating from the citadel. Lightning danced along its iron keel. Er'ril guessed this was the source of the destruction here. Silently, he thanked the unknown allies. Their aid had broken the mages' control of the island. Ahead, the castle itself now seemed dead and deserted. Er'ril only hoped that Shorkan had not been driven away just yet.

He eyed the towers as he stepped from the cool stone of the catacombs. The heat of the court instantly smote his bare skin, raising a sheen of sweat. From here, Er'ril surveyed the full destruction of the eastern tower. Through part of the shattered wing of the castle, he looked upon the city and ocean beyond. Even from here, Er'ril could see the ships embattled below. The war still raged in the seas surrounding the island.

Only able to wish them luck from here, Er'ril turned away. His own goal was closer at hand. He faced the westernmost tower, Shorkan's lair. Atop its crown, in the last rays of the setting sun, Er'ril spotted a black figure perched among the tower's parapets. At first he thought it a living creature, but then he recognized it. It was the ebon'stone statue of the wyvern. And if Greshym was to be believed, it was also one of the four Weirgates that opened to the source of the Dark Lord's power.

Stopping to collect a long sword from the blistered corpse of one of the catacombs' guards, Er'ril entered the courtyard. If he could not find Shorkan, he could at least topple that statue off its perch. Maybe a fall from such a height would crack the cursed sculpture.

Passing the edges of the crater in the center of the courtyard, Er'ril avoided several dark-robed corpses that lay blackened on the blasted stone. He scowled at them. Disciples of the darkmages.

As he moved on, he thought he heard a stifled gasp and the sound of something striking the stones a few paces back. He swung around, crouching, eying the nest of corpses. But nothing stirred. Er'ril straightened. The winds and the crumbling castle must be playing tricks on his ears.

Studying the bodies for one more breath, Er'ril swung away. He hurried across the remainder of the open courtyard, fearful of any eyes in the hundreds of dark windows. But no arrows were shot at him, nor were any shouts raised against his intrusion. Soon he pushed through the charred and shattered grand doors to enter the castle proper.

As Elena watched Er'ril disappear into the dark castle, she rolled to her feet, rubbing the knee she had twisted after tripping over a loose stone. A moment ago, Er'ril had come so close to catching her. When the plainsman had swung around, Elena had panicked and frozen like a startled rabbit, her face just a handspan above one of the blackened corpses. Even now the stench of charred flesh clung to her nose.

Straightening, Elena took a step toward the castle. Her knee protested strongly, shooting lances of pain up her thigh. She could walk, but only slowly. Elena studied the looming mass of the Edifice, the ancient citadel of A'loa Glen. Its black windows stared back at her nakedness. Though none could see her, she felt exposed. Sighing, she knew there was no way she could follow the plainsman, not as fast as he was moving now. Already he must be lost deep within the castle. She would never find him. If only she had paid more attention to her own feet a moment ago . . .

Biting her lip against the pain of her injured limb, Elena hopped back. She craned her neck. Where was Er'ril heading? He said he sought his brother. But was this true? She swung her gaze to the tower that had captured Er'ril's attention when he had first entered the court. The setting sun's last rays painted the western tower's parapets in gold.

Far above the blasted court, she spotted what had drawn Er'ril's attention. Atop the spire stood the familiar black-winged figure of the wyvern, the ebon'stone statue of the darkmages.

As she stared, a stray breeze shivered her bare skin. Elena wrapped her arms around her chest, trying to hug away the dread that had settled under her ribs. Though not certain of his true heart, Elena still feared for the plainsman.

Tears suddenly rose in her eyes, blurring her vision. After almost losing Er'ril once already to the black magic of the statue, Elena could not face such a loss again. The wounds were still too raw. She watched the tower for some sign of the plainsman, some clue to guide her.

'Be careful, Er'ril,' she whispered as winds sighed through the blasted courtyard. 'Come back to me.'

In the empty halls of the Edifice, Er'ril increased his pace. Well familiar with the Edifice, he knew the shortest path to the Praetor's Spear. His feet led him quickly toward his goal while he stoked the fires in his heart. In a battle with his brother, he must not let despair slow or weaken him. With Shorkan's black magick currently at an ebb, here might be his last chance to rid the lands of his evil.

Er'ril leaped up steps three at a time and raced along dark halls. In short order, he found himself mounting the winding tower stair. He slowed his pace just enough to snatch glimpses from the slitted windows along the steep stair. He surveyed the battle around the island. By now, the sun had sunk into the western horizon, blazing the skies with fire. Below, the war in the seas continued.

As Er'ril passed another window higher in the tower, a flash of brilliance caught his eye and stopped his feet. What was this? Twilight had begun to settle over the seas. In the growing gloom, Er'ril watched as bolts of lightning struck out from one of the large flying ships. Lances and spears of radiance blasted amidst the warring boats and dragons, taking out ships and flocks of skal'tum. The ship glided languidly through the air, reaping a harvest of destruction from the enemy under its keel as it crisscrossed the battlefield. The rumble of thunder trailed its path.

Thanking these unknown allies once again, Er'ril allowed himself to imagine victory. The despair in his heart lifted slightly. He mounted the steps with renewed vigor and soon reached the top of the staircase. The doors to the Praetor's tower chambers lay open. Er'ril slowed and clenched his sword tighter in his fist. He did not trust such an open invitation.

Cautiously, he slipped past the threshold into Shorkan's study. It was empty, its hearth cold. Holding the blade before him, Er'ril crept through the neighboring rooms. The small bedroom was also empty, as was the bathing chamber. He sensed that neither had been used in a long time. Maybe Shorkan had not come here after all. Ending back in the central chamber, Er'ril studied the room. He paused in the middle of the bright rug and strained to listen for any sign of the darkmage.

He both saw and heard it at the same time. Along the floor, a section of the wall's tapestry fluttered slightly with a whisper of bird's wings. Er'ril crossed toward it, careful to keep his tread silent. He used the tip of his sword to shift the length of silk to the side.

Behind the fold of tapestry stood a small oaken door, partially cracked ajar. Through the narrow opening, Er'ril smelled the ocean and smoke. Pushing the door wider, Er'ril discovered a secret stair leading up toward a trapdoor overhead. Light trailed down. Er'ril knew where it led, and his heart thudded louder in his ears.

Not risking the creaky old hinges, Er'ril slid through the

gap and mounted the stairs. He climbed one stair at a time, careful where he placed each foot. Overhead, a trapdoor lay flung open to the sky. Er'ril crept up to it and held his breath for a moment. Rolling the hilt of his sword in his right palm, Er'ril also loosened the dagger at his belt.

Once both fists were armed, Er'ril leaped through the trapdoor and rolled across the stone roof of the tower. He shouldered himself upright and jumped to his feet, quickly taking in the scene.

His brother, burned and blistered, stood on the far side of the tower. This high above the sea, the sun's light still bathed the spire's top. The stones of the parapet glowed golden, starkly outlining the ebon'stone statue from its perch behind Shorkan. Above his brother's head, the ruby eyes of the statue glowed in the sun's fire. Wings of ebon'stone rose to either side of Shorkan's shoulders, as if the wyvern were about to take flight.

When his brother spoke, no fear etched his calm words. 'Er'ril, it seems we meet one last time.'

Er'ril raised both sword and dagger. 'It *will* be our last!'

Shorkan eyed his weapons with disinterest but cocked his head and glanced back and forth between Er'ril's two limbs. 'So that was the secret of the book's protection spell. Flesh.' Shorkan shook his head. 'I had never imagined old Brother Kallon could stomach such a sacrifice from you, Er'ril. No wonder it has confounded me for so long.'

Er'ril shrugged, circling around the trapdoor toward his brother. He eyed the wyvern statue warily. 'What are you planning to do with the Weirgate, Shorkan? What is the Dark Lord plotting with the other statues?'

Shorkan's brows rose as Er'ril approached. 'It seems a little bird has been singing in your ear, my brother. You seek answers to questions that are beyond your ability to understand.'

'According to Greshym, the same could be said of you.'

Ire flashed in Shorkan's eyes. 'Since you are my brother, I will give you one answer – something to keep you up at night.' Shorkan waved his hand toward the wyvern statue. 'The Weirgates pose more of a danger to Alasea than does the Black Heart. You fight the wrong enemy, Er'ril. You have all along.'

'You lie. Greshym already told me how the Weir is the Black Heart's source of black magick.'

Shorkan shook his head. 'You understand so little. It truly saddens me. Was this the paltry information for which you traded the Blood Diary? If so, Greshym bought the book cheap. But he will pay for his treachery.'

'Greshym doesn't have the book,' Er'ril said, raising his sword higher. 'It is on its way to the wit'ch as we speak.'

These words twitched the blackened skin around his brother's right eye. 'Then where is Greshym?'

'He's fled.'

Shorkan eyed Er'ril's sword as it flashed in the last rays of the sun. By now, Er'ril was only a few paces away. 'Then so must I, my brother.' Before Er'ril could move, Shorkan reached behind him and touched the wyvern statue. A spatter of darkfire played about Shorkan's fingers, and then the statue became a carving not of stone, but of shadows. Sunlight disappeared into its depths. Shorkan stepped backward between its wings and into its dark well. 'Good-bye, Brother.'

Er'ril lunged after him, but he was blasted backward by a force that deafened him. Only the stones of the parapet kept him from a long fall to his death. His head cracked the stones with a resounding blow. Ignoring the pain and dazzle from his bruised skull, Er'ril rolled to his feet. He searched the tower roof. It was empty. The statue and his brother had vanished.

Standing, Er'ril crossed to the edge of the tower and searched the skies. Sunlight basked the towers of the citadel and a few of the tallest spires of the city. Where had Shorkan gone?

Then, in a blink, an inky stain appeared just an arrow's shot off the western edge of the tower. It was the shadowy wyvern, alive and gliding toward the golden spires of the city below. Er'ril now understood how he himself had been transported here. Just the thought that he had once been swallowed and transported within that darkness shuddered his spirit.

'Curse you, Shorkan!' Er'ril called out to the retreating form.

Suddenly, as if his brother had heard his cry, the wyvern seemed to twitch in the air and bank sharply around. It dove back toward the castle, sailing closer to one of the sun-touched spires of the city.

Er'ril squinted to see what had so attracted Shorkan from his flight. Then he spied it, too: two small figures atop a spire nearby. Across the distance, Er'ril recognized the staff and the red-haired boy who bore it.

Joach.

As he recognized Elena's brother, Er'ril's vision suddenly twisted queerly; a strange sharpness tweaked his sight. This was Joach's dream. He had thought that by leaving Joach's side he could turn fate's path. But even now, it was coming true.

Er'ril leaned both fists on the stone parapet. He studied the other figure atop the spire. From Joach's description of his dream, it had to be Elena. But as Er'ril studied Joach's companion, his heart climbed into his throat. It was no woman that stood beside Joach. He saw the way the man's back was bent. Sunlight shone on his bald and leathered pate. But mostly Er'ril recognized the dark robe the man wore. 'Greshym!'

Er'ril's legs suddenly weakened under him as he remembered that he had left the Blood Diary with the boy! What was Joach now doing with Greshym? Had the boy been a traitor all along?

Er'ril stumbled away from the tower's edge. Twisting around, he dove for the trapdoor. Something was direly wrong.

He had to stop them!

Er'ril tore through Shorkan's study and flew down the tower stair. As he ran, he knew the fate of A'loa Glen depended on his speed, but he also recalled Joach's other revelation from his dream weaving: Upon the tower, Er'ril was doomed to die in a blaze of darkfire.

Despite knowing his fate, Er'ril raced on.

It seemed destiny was not done with him yet.

In the courtyard of the castle, Elena clutched a hand to her throat. A moment ago, a whooshing blast had drawn her eyes upward, and she had seen the wyvern statue vanish from its tower perch. Now it had reappeared, gliding and circling just past the walls of a castle.

What had Er'ril done? Was this his doing?

As her heart pounded in her throat, Elena could not help but remember Joach's dream. Her brother had insisted his nightmare was a prophetic weaving, and from Joach's description, the first part of his vision was of an assault by a black shadowbeast. Elena stared as the wyvern banked away.

The dream was coming true.

Somehow Er'ril had unleashed the beast. Whether he had triggered it with malice or by accident, Elena did not know.

All she knew for sure was that Joach's nightmare was beginning. She backed across the courtyard toward the entrance to the catacombs. She could wait no longer. She knew where she had to be. Fate called for her to fulfil her role atop the Spire of the Departed. She must be at Joach's side.

Overhead, the wyvern beast opened its black beak in a silent scream and dove beyond the castle wall, disappearing out of sight.

It had begun.

Elena turned and ran as fast as her injured knee would allow. Though Er'ril was somewhere in the castle behind her, Elena knew she was not abandoning him. In a way, she was running toward him. They were fated to meet atop the neighboring tower, and she would not miss this rendezvous!

Joach's dream played over and over in her head. She knew how it was destined to end: with the murder of Er'ril. Elena clenched her fist around the iron ward and ran harder. If their fates were set in granite, Elena meant to shatter that stone with her own magick. She would not let Er'ril be slain if he was still true of heart. This she swore.

As determined as she was, a part of her still quaked with fear. How would she know for sure? How did one judge another's heart with certainty? Elena cast aside her doubts.

She must find a way.

26

Joach stood amidst the sunset's blaze. To the west, the skies were still awash in a final fiery display as the sun dipped below the horizon. As Joach watched from the parapet, the sights below the tower trapped his breath in his chest. The oceans beyond the city lay cast in deep shadow, a promise of the night to come. All around the island, elv'in warships glided above the seas. Occasional spears of lightning shattered the gloom, reflecting off the waves, highlighting the sails and rails of their many ships.

Meric had succeeded. He had turned aside his people's attack on the island and directed their might to the war below. Upon the seas, victory was near. But what of the island itself?

This sobering thought drew his eyes back from the views. He found Elena staring at him. She eyed his staff. He knew what she must be thinking. According to Joach's weaving of this day, his staff would protect her atop the tower. It was up to him to make sure Elena remained safe.

Even with her hands ripe with ruby magick, Elena was clearly too weak to defend herself. The climb up the tower stair had wasted her. He had never seen her so weak.

On the way here, he had been unable to get Elena to talk

much. She refused to speak of what had happened to her after they had separated. It must have been horrible, and she was too raw to discuss it yet. Still, he had to ask one more thing of her.

'We need a signal, Elena,' he said as he crossed closer to her. 'Do you think you have enough magick to blaze a sign for Ragnar'k?'

His mention of the dragon jolted her from whatever reverie she had fallen into. 'No, not now.' She waved a hand limply at him. 'Maybe your staff . . .'

'I dare not waste its magick,' he said. 'You know of my dream.'

His words only seemed to raise a look of confusion on her features. She reached weakly toward his staff. 'Let me try.'

Joach pulled away the length of poi'wood. 'You are stubborn, El. You know this burden is mine.' He shook his head at his sister's bravery and her willingness to sacrifice herself. This was her fourth attempt to take this responsibility from him. But he would not let her. It was his destiny.

Holding the staff in his bandaged hand, he ran his glove along its length and drew the magick to the wood's surface with his touch. Trickles of darkfire ran in small rivulets along the staff. He must be ready. Again he scanned the skies. Still no sign of the shadowy beast.

From the corner of his eye, Joach saw Elena watch him manipulate the staff. Longing and anger were bright in her eyes. After wielding so much power, Elena clearly still refused to yield to the inevitability of fate.

Joach spoke in an attempt to distract her. 'I know what distresses you, El.' He glanced at her, then away again. 'It's Er'ril. I know how much you wish him to be pure. But I met him.'

Elena startled beside him.

'I'm sorry, but I didn't want to tell you. You were so exhausted, and I had hoped to keep this from you. But maybe it's better you know. Er'ril has been turned. He now serves the darkmages.' He swung to face her. 'So when I kill him, do not grieve. The Er'ril you knew would rather die than harm you. It must be done.'

'Er'ril? You've met Er'ril?'

'Yes.' Joach hated to hear so much hope in her voice. He lowered his voice as he revealed his last. 'And he has two arms. He even tried to trick me with a fake copy of the Blood Diary. He foolishly thought such a prize would blind me to his treachery.'

Elena stumbled toward Joach. 'The book . . . ?'

Joach patted his shirt where the tattered old diary still rested.

Elena's hand rose to snatch at him, but a keening cry split the skies. Joach swung around, shoving Elena behind him. She landed hard on her backside with a curse on her lips. He did not have time to apologize.

From behind the neighboring citadel, a monstrous black shadow swept toward him. He stared into the ruby eyes of his enemy. 'Now it begins . . . and ends,' he said and stepped away from where Elena crawled toward him. This was not her battle. Joach lifted the staff over his head and called the magick in the wood to a full blaze. 'Come to your death!' he screamed in defiance. 'I will not let you near Elena!'

As the beast dove toward them, Joach saw the shape was indeed a wyvern. The black hooked beak, the glowing crimson eyes, wings of razor-sharp pinions. But he did not quail from the sight. He swung his staff and pointed its end at the streaking shadow. He recited the dream-cast words.

His lips grew cold with each utterance. As he spoke the

incantation, traceries of frost skittered outward through his heated blood to reach for the wood in his gloved hand. As the last word fell from his lips, a shaft of darkness jetted out from the end of his staff. Balefire! Crackles of energy danced along this spear of darkness.

Joach grinned at the power. He would let no one harm his sister. He had given his promise to his father. He would not fail!

The lance of balefire struck the beast full in the chest, halting its dive, holding it in the sky above the tower. Its sharp cry changed to an almost human wail of agony. It writhed, impaled on Joach's spear. The shadowy beast began to lose form; its edges blurred as the darkfire tore into it.

A harsh laugh exploded from Joach's chest. He sensed when his magick was about to vanquish the beast, like a storm about to burst. Joach's lips ached as they stretched into a wide grin. He had never felt such power.

Then something broke in the beast overhead. Joach sensed it.

In a blink, the shadowy wyvern became stone again, a statue once more. And like any stone, it plummeted toward the streets far below.

Joach dashed to the parapet to witness the end result of his handiwork. The statue tumbled toward the ground. 'Die, demon!' he screamed after it.

But the monster held one more trick. Just before it struck the cobbles, a brief flash flared in the shadows at the foot of the tower, and the statue vanished. The streets below remained empty.

Pulling back, Joach raised his staff and searched the skies around the parapets, but nothing tried to attack again. In truth, he knew he would not be assaulted by the beast again. Joach sensed that the wyvern had jumped far from here.

But more significantly, in his dream, the beast had only struck the one time and was driven away.

'Joach?' Elena still crouched in the shadows of the parapet.

He recognized the relief in her voice, but he held up a hand to hush her. It was not over. There was one more participant yet to appear. Joach swung to face the tower door. He spun the staff between his fingers. With a smile of triumph and a heart iced by his taste of magick, he waited.

'Come to me, Er'ril.'

Atop the long stair inside the Spire of the Departed, Elena stood with her hand hovering over the latch to the tower door. She braced herself.

Earlier, while racing up the stairs, the screeches and the sounds of battle had echoed down to her from above, firing her urge for speed. She had been determined to burst through the doorway and face whatever was attacking the tower and her brother. But as she had climbed the last few landings, the sounds had suddenly stopped. Beyond the door, she heard nothing. Caution again gripped her heart.

According to Joach's dream, she herself was fated to be beside her brother, not climbing these endless steps. So what had changed? Her hand touched the iron latch. There was only one way to find out.

Just before she shoved into the door, a hurried stamp of boots echoed up from below. She snatched back her hand and stared down into the tower's gloom. She carried no torch or lantern. Only the occasional window along the staircase had lighted her way.

Sliding away from the door and down a few steps, Elena tried to pierce the shadows. But in her heart, she knew who came. She pressed herself against the far wall of the stairway and waited for Er'ril, holding her breath and clutching the ward between her breasts.

Up from the darkness below, like a rolling storm, he came. Er'ril clutched a long sword in his right fist. His breath gasped between clenched teeth. His eyes shone with anger; the muscles on his arms and chest bunched with suppressed might. He almost glowed with an inner rage.

Elena hugged herself tight to the wall, but Er'ril was blind to all but the door above. Even without the spell, she imagined he would not have seen her, such was his haste.

He swept past Elena, so swift that the heat off his body was like a slap in her face. But he paused at the top of the stairs. Elena moved one step closer. He raised his sword's hilt to his brow, using its steel to cool his forehead. Elena moved closer still. She saw the pain behind his anger. He lowered his sword and took a deep breath. His eyes told her all she needed to know. Er'ril knew his death lay beyond the door but that he still must go.

He grabbed the door's latch, his fist tightening on his sword. 'Damn you, Joach. I'll kill you for betraying your sister!'

Elena froze, shocked by his words. He meant to kill Joach!

Somehow Er'ril must have sensed her presence. He glanced behind him, his expression suddenly confused. Then, with a shake of his head, he tore at the latch and shoved the door open.

After the gloom of the long stair, the brilliance of the sunset sky blinded her. It must have done the same to Er'ril. He raised his free arm to shade his eyes and stepped out onto the tower's roof.

Elena followed, slipping around his back and moving to his side.

A voice cracked out from beyond the doorway. 'I've been waiting for you, Er'ril!'

Elena's eyes blinked away the glare. She saw her brother standing just a few paces back. He bore his staff in his half hand. But this was not the sight that startled a gasp from her throat. She spotted the crouched and robed figure of the darkmage Greshym behind Joach.

Er'ril's angered words as he locked the tower door covered her own startled gasp. 'Joach, you traitor! You would forsake your sister for mere power!'

These words had little effect on Joach.

Her brother was preternaturally calm, especially with a darkmage at his back. Joach warded the mage away with his other palm. 'Stay back, El. This must happen!'

Joach twisted his staff, and Elena felt the surge of power.

Elena's eyes twitched to the darkmage, then flew wide. She suddenly understood the illusion behind Joach's dream. She leaped between her brother and Er'ril just as both men struck at each other.

She felt Er'ril's sword pierce her back at the same time as Joach's spear of darkfire struck her between the breasts. She cried out at the agony as the blade scraped against her ribs. Bones broke. But even this was but a pinch compared to the flaying burn of the black magick's touch. Her skin burned; her breasts were charred to cinder.

The touch of black magick blasted away the spirit spell. She saw the horror in Joach's eyes as she appeared. The font of black energies died instantly, and he flew toward her.

But her brother was too late. Elena fell back into Er'ril's arms. The plainsman crashed to his knees under her – not from the heaviness of her body, but from the weight of his horror. He cradled her in his lap. 'Oh, Elena, no . . .' His voice was like nothing she had ever heard. He sounded like such a lost boy. 'What have I done?'

Elena stared up into his eyes. 'It ... it was my choice, Er'ril. Let me have this blame, not you.' She reached toward him, though the pain almost blinded her. She wiped away a tear that was not on his cheek. The horror of the moment and the shock had not allowed the plainsman any tears yet. But she remembered the glistening single tear on his cheek at the crossroads of the catacombs. She had known even then that it was for her. She wished to erase it.

Er'ril leaned into her touch. 'I can't live with this,' he sobbed, tears finally breaking forth. 'Not after so many winters. Not after ... after ...'

Joach interrupted them. 'Elena?'

She lifted her face toward her brother. He stood a step away, his eyes stricken. She knew that expression. His mind was in shock. He glanced from her, then back to the dark-mage behind him.

'It's a trick,' the darkmage hissed. 'They only seek to deceive you, Joach. You know I'm your real sister! They only strive to steal the book.'

Joach stepped away from both of them. His gaze still shifted between them, almost panicked by his confusion. 'The Blood Diary?'

'Yes,' Greshym spat. 'Bring it to me! I will use it to destroy their illusions.'

Elena coughed at the darkmage's deceitful words. 'J-Joach ...' But she had not the energy to argue.

Er'ril did. He shifted under her. 'Don't listen to him. It's Greshym that lurks at your back, Joach. He is the one masked in illusions of your sister. It is he who seeks the book.'

Joach continued to back away from both sides. 'I don't know who to believe.' He held his staff before him, threatening both.

Elena added her voice. She knew how to convince her brother. She lifted an arm toward Joach. 'Remember ... remember, Joach ... the staff.' She reached farther toward him, but this was too much.

Darkness rose from the edges of her vision and swamped over her. She fell limp in Er'ril's arms and heard his cry of anguish. Elena struggled toward Er'ril against the rising tides of darkness, but she lost her battle. The currents here were too strong.

She was carried away.

Joach stared as Elena's singed and naked body sagged in the plainsman's arms. Surely this was not his sister. He could not have just slain Elena. Joach stared at the other twin. This one was clothed in the same light shift and leggings that his sister had worn to the island. This had to be his true sister. Did it not?

Still, the earnestness of this other Elena seemed so real. She had begged him with her eyes. In the past, he had seen that same expression in his sister's face. 'Remember,' she had insisted. But remember what? Something from his past? Some detail only brother and sister would share? Joach crinkled his brow as Er'ril grieved over the fallen girl. Joach saw that her chest rose and fell, but her breathing was ragged and faded fast.

Joach turned to the other. 'If you are truly my sister, tell me why I was punished to shovel our family's barn every morning for a full moon.'

Elena smiled sadly. 'Must you test me? But considering the nefarious scheme being played here, I guess I can understand. The answer to your question was that you were punished for feeding a berry pie to Tracker.'

Joach's tense shoulders relaxed with relief. He smiled at

Elena. He had been right all along. Here was his true sister. He glanced at the wounded woman, glad to know she was not truly Elena. He did not know if he could have survived the guilt of slaying his own sister.

Er'ril, though, interrupted his relief. 'Answer the boy, darkmage!'

Joach turned to Er'ril, lifting his staff. 'Stop this charade, plainsman. Elena just gave me the correct answer.'

Er'ril scowled. 'He plays your mind like a fine instrument. No words were just spoken. He plied you with a trick to make you think you heard the right answer.' The plainsman nodded toward the fallen twin of Elena. 'Here is your sister, Joach. Not that monster. Even now she dies. If you love her, bring the book to me. It may yet hold a chance to save her.'

'Don't, Joach!' Elena insisted. 'He struggles to trick you.'

By now, Joach's mind spun in dizzying circles. Whom to believe? If Er'ril meant to harm him, why did he still cradle the girl? None of it made sense. He clutched his staff in both hands. How was he to discover the truth?

Er'ril looked up at him, not in anger but with eyes that beseeched him. 'Her death nears, Joach. You must decide.'

'But my dream . . .' he mumbled.

'Dreams are difficult to judge, Joach, and weavings are even more so. In your vision, you saw yourself defending Elena, but in truth, it was this sorcerer disguised as your sister. Dreams are fraught with illusions.'

He pondered Er'ril's words. The plainsman's argument sounded familiar and struck Joach to the core. Had not someone just given him similar advice? But who? Then Joach remembered. He dropped his injured hand from his staff and fished in the pocket of his pants. It was still there.

He palmed the object and drew it forth. Opening his

fingers, he stared at the large black pearl, the one Xin had given him. The zo'ol wizen had promised its power could connect them when the need was great. Joach closed his fist over the treasure and spoke his friend's name. 'Xin!'

Nothing happened.

Joach opened his fist and stared at the pearl. He was a fool.

Then words rose from the jewel's blackness. *Joach, son of Morin'stal, I sense a storm in your heart.*

Words tumbled from his lips in a rush. 'Xin, my dream . . . I can't tell what is real and what is false. Can you help me?'

Elena interrupted. 'Joach, what are you doing?'

Joach ignored her and listened. 'I cannot help you from here,' Xin answered. 'But, Joach, your own heart can.'

'How?'

'Ignore what your skull tells you. Listen with your heart. There is where all truths lie.'

Joach had no words to answer Xin. He returned the pearl to his pocket. How could he follow advice he did not even understand? He glanced to the clothed Elena. Her face, her voice, her mannerisms all spoke true. She reminded him of home and farm, all he had loved dear. Here was the sister from his past. He felt nothing wrong about her.

He then turned to the dying girl. What did he feel about her? He looked past her battered body. In her face and words, she had demonstrated bravery, selflessness, and a love that could even forgive her own murder. This was a woman Joach hardly knew. She was *not* from his past.

The truth of the situation then dawned in him, almost blinding him with its clarity.

Xin had been right.

In Er'ril's arms was not the sister of his past, but of the

present. The other Elena was a figment of old memories – familiar and comfortable memories – picked from his mind. But that was not who Elena was anymore. Joach hardly knew the woman whom Elena had become on her journey here. In his mind's eye, he still considered Elena just his younger sister, someone he had to protect. But that was true no longer. Elena was no longer just a girl of the orchards. The strange woman in Er'ril's arms was his true sister.

Still, Joach needed to be sure.

He glanced down to his staff and remembered Elena's last words to him: *Remember the staff*. Even in this matter, his sister had surpassed him. Though in agony and near death, Elena had given him the key to the truth: *the staff*.

Joach raised his eyes toward the false Elena. If Er'ril and Elena spoke truthfully, there stood Greshym, the man who had tormented him for almost six moons, enslaved him, debased him. Joach was tempted to use the staff one more time and slay the monster, but after harming Elena, Joach could not bring himself to touch black magick again. He just wanted to be rid of the foul talisman.

But before he did that, the staff had one more duty.

Turning, Joach tossed the staff toward the one who claimed to be Elena. One of her arms snatched the staff greedily from the air. She brought it down to her side. Even disguised as Elena, Joach could see how well the poi'wood staff fit this figure. It was as if it were another limb.

'Good, Joach,' the false Elena encouraged. 'I knew you wouldn't fall for Er'ril's tricks. Now bring me the Blood Diary.'

Joach slipped the book free of his shirt. 'Er'ril . . .'

The plainsman raised hopeless eyes toward Joach. Er'ril did not say a word, clearly thinking himself defeated.

Joach tossed the book to Er'ril. 'Save my sister if you can.'

Er'ril deftly caught it, eyes wide with surprise.

Cursing, Greshym shook free of his illusions. Elena's features fell away, and Joach found himself staring at the wrinkled, bent-backed fiend. The darkmage glanced between the two men as Joach stepped closer. 'How?'

'Elena could not handle the staff. It seems the two magicks – black and blood – repel one another.'

Greshym sneered and raised his staff. He pointed it at Joach's chest. Darkfire bloomed along its length. 'Your cleverness will cost you your life.'

Instead of ducking away, Joach stepped even closer. When he was within an arm's length of the dire weapon, he shook off his deerskin glove and grabbed the end of the staff with his bare hand.

Greshym laughed. 'You've grown bold, boy. You think to challenge me in the black arts?'

As Joach grasped his end of the staff, his blood entered the wood. The staff grew pale around his hand and spread down the length of the wood, dousing the spats of darkfire as it flowed. 'I don't challenge your skill at the black arts, mage,' Joach said with ice in his voice. 'I will fight you with my own blood.'

Greshym stared as his staff paled. Joach saw the darkmage tighten his hoary grip upon his end of the poi'wood. The flames of black magick grew taller and thicker, washing against the paleness like an angry black surf.

Joach lost some ground, but not much. His blood continued to feed the hungry wood. White and black staff fought in its center. To continue to hold back the wall of darkfire, more and more of Joach's blood was needed. The usual small red rivulets in the pale wood grew in number and size. Now thick torrents of crimson pumped through the staff. Joach's heart beat like thunder in his ears. His vision focused down to a point. His entire world became just the staff. It was both his body and his spirit.

Across the length of wood, Greshym fared no better. Sweat ran down the mage's face, and his breath grew ragged.

Joach knew something must give soon. Either he would faint from lack of blood, or Greshym would collapse in exhaustion. What actually happened startled both combatants. The staff exploded between them in a spray of stabbing shards.

Joach fell backward, as did the darkmage.

Both men eyed each other, bloodied by stabbing splinters. The staff was gone. Its entire length was just so much kindling scattered on the stones.

Eying the scraps, Greshym pushed off the wall. The flare of black magick from the destruction of the staff had revitalized him, but he still wobbled a bit on his feet. Their battle had taken its toll. Greshym spat in Joach's direction. 'You will pay for this, boy. We will meet again.' With those last words, Greshym waved a hand, and a portal appeared behind him. The darkmage stepped back into it, falling away and vanishing in a blink.

Joach suddenly sagged, wasted and suffering from loss of blood.

Suddenly Er'ril was at his shoulders.

Joach could not even look up. He just glanced to where Elena lay sprawled on the stone. 'I'm sorry.'

Er'ril's voice was gruff, but not unkind. 'Her blood is on both our hands, Joach. We were equally deluded by fears of treachery.' Er'ril gathered Joach under his arm and pulled him toward Elena. 'It's time we put aside the past. If we are to have any chance of saving your sister, we must act quickly.' Er'ril then gripped Joach's arm, hard. 'And we must work together.'

Joach raised his eyes and met Er'ril's gaze without flinching. 'What must I do?'

With Joach's help, Er'ril spread Elena across a thin blanket from the boy's pack. Though the sun had set and the full moon had begun to rise, the stones remembered the day's heat and kept her warm. Her flesh, naked and bared to the stars, seemed carved of ivory. She was so pale. The seared circle in the center of her chest was like one of the dark-mage's black portals.

Er'ril touched her cheek. She was so cold. Her breathing was so shallow that Er'ril found himself holding his own breath between each rise and fall of her chest. She should be dead already, but her magick sustained her. Er'ril glanced to her hands. Only the softest pink hue remained of the deep ruby Rose; only a dribble of magick remained. When that ran out, Elena would die.

'What now?' Joach asked.

Er'ril glanced to the boy's handiwork. As instructed, Joach had finished applying a bandage made from the boy's shredded shirt over the sword wound. Its rough cloth should help clot the flowing blood. Er'ril stared at the bandage, suddenly reminded that it was his sword that had stabbed into her. He could not look away.

'Er'ril?' Joach touched his elbow.

Leaning back, Er'ril shook his head. He had no time to dwell on his own guilt. It would do Elena no good. 'We're ready,' he barked hoarsely. 'Grab the ward.'

Er'ril knelt nearer and placed the Blood Diary atop the blasted circle upon her chest. The gilt rose shone in the growing moonlight.

Joach fetched the small iron fist from the stone floor and handed it to Er'ril.

Er'ril shook his head. 'I must not touch book or ward from here.'

'What are we trying to do?' Joach finally asked, but his question ended in a sob. His resolve was deteriorating. Er'ril could not blame Joach. After bandaging the deep wound, the boy's hands were fouled with his own sister's blood, and the air reeked of her charred flesh: harsh reminders of what he and Er'ril had done to her.

'I'll try to explain.' Er'ril waved for the boy to kneel on Elena's other side. 'When the book was first forged, the spell was incomplete. The boy mage, Denal, never infused his spirit into the book. Still, the presence of Shorkan and Greshym were enough to ignite the magick and bind me to it. To this day, the Blood Diary heals me and sustains me. If we can add Denal's spirit to the book, then the spell will start again. When it ends this time, Elena must be the one bound. The book's magick will then be available to heal her and protect her.'

Joach nodded, but his eyes had filled with doubt and fear. He lifted the ward. 'And the boy Denal's spirit is trapped in this iron fist?'

'Not trapped. Stored. Denal gave his spirit freely.'

Joach studied the ward. 'What do I do with it?'

'Just place the iron fist on the book. If the spell ignites, there will be a flare of white light, and the book will be flung open. We must each then take one of Elena's arms and guide her hands to close the book and complete the spell. Neither of us must touch it.'

With shivering hands, Joach reached across his sister's prone form and bobbled the tiny iron fist atop the book's cover. It kept rolling off until Joach found the right balance. Once done, Joach leaned back. 'Now what?'

'We wait.'

And so they did. The passing of time grew agonizing. All they could do was watch Elena's breathing grow more and more shallow. Er'ril noticed Joach eye his sister's hands. Both were as pale as her arms now. Neither man spoke of it.

As they waited, the moon continued to rise, full and bright.

Once the moon crested the parapets and the light shone fully on the book, the fist began slowly to open, like a midnight rose basking in the moon's glow.

Joach glanced to Er'ril and held his breath. Er'ril found himself doing the same, afraid to disturb what was happening.

Soon the fist had opened fully and rested palm down on the gilt rose. Er'ril remembered how, long ago, the three mages had placed their palms upon the book, just as this iron hand did now. Er'ril could almost hear a whisper of chanting from far away. It was not just one voice but three.

Winds kicked up around the tower. The book trembled slightly.

As Er'ril watched, eyes unblinking, the small fist began dissolving away, sinking into the book. As it did so, the winds picked up, and the book's trembling worsened. The chanting grew louder. Er'ril met Joach's gaze over Elena's body. He willed the boy to be ready. Joach seemed to sense his thoughts and nodded his head once, very slightly. Both feared to move.

Soon the ward was but a vague outline, a ghost hand; then it disappeared completely. No sign of the iron fist remained. Denal had joined the book.

With the act complete, the book settled on Elena's chest, and the winds died. Er'ril's brow crinkled. Was that it? He continued to wait, but nothing happened.

Joach finally released his trapped breath in a moan of sorrow.

Then, as if this were some mysterious signal, the book suddenly jumped from Elena's chest to float a handspan above her blackened skin.

Joach tumbled back upon his rear. 'Sweet Mother,' he swore.

Its covers split open, revealing the empty pages within. From the white parchment, a blaze of brilliance shot high into the night sky. Er'ril glanced away from its blinding radiance. He was sure it lanced high enough to strike the moon. Under his knees, the tower shook.

'Er'ril?' The boy's voice was edged with fear.

'Now's the time, Joach!' Er'ril commanded sternly. 'Grab your sister's wrist and bring her hand to the book!' Er'ril demonstrated with Elena's right limb, while Joach matched the movements with her left.

The two brought her arms under the book, palms toward the covers.

'On my count, we use her hands to close the book. Then make sure you get clear.' Er'ril recalled the last time he had performed this act. It had thrown him across the inn's room.

Er'ril counted, and on *three*, they slapped the book shut with Elena's palms. Both men quickly rolled away. They were lucky they did. The blast that followed split the night. Er'ril was thrown into the tower door, while Joach was tossed to the stones of the parapet. The boy ended down on his belly, his arms over his head.

Er'ril did not hide his face. Rolling to one elbow, he saw Elena lifted from the stones of the tower. Still limp and unmoving, she hung in the air, bathed in a light that stung the eyes. It came from the book still caught between her two palms, a star fallen from the night sky. Elena blazed in its glory. From such a height, the sight would be visible all the way to the coast.

'Joach! See this!'

Slowly Joach lifted first his head, then his body. He sat up to bask in the glow.

Elena's form slowly twirled in the brilliance. As Er'ril watched, he saw her stir. One hand moved from the book to rub at her face, as if she were simply awakening from a nap. Slowly the glow receded into the book. Elena's legs drifted lower until her toes touched the tower's roof. She settled to her heels, pulling the book to her chest in wonder. Her eyes were wide and reflected the remaining glow of the book. They were so alive! Even her hair was a drape of fire down her back.

Er'ril had never seen her so beautiful.

Elena turned to him, her lips curving in a gentle smile of relief and welcome. She lifted the book in both hands. The gilt rose on its cover still blazed sharply, but even this was fading. 'The Blood Diary.'

Er'ril bowed his head slightly, crossing his arms on his chest in the ancient honor of a liegeman for a mage. 'The wit'ch and the book are united at last.' For all his postured reverence, he could not hold back a grin.

To his delight, Elena matched his expression.

As she lowered the book to her side, Er'ril's smile faltered. The blackened circle of charred skin remained on her chest. His gaze drew Elena's eyes. Frowning slightly, she fingered the damage. It came apart under her fingers, flaking away to expose soft and perfect skin.

'I'm healed,' Elena said in amazement.

'The book will protect you from here,' Er'ril said softly, not able to completely hide his regret. Mixed emotions stirred his heart. Though he would not change anything, Er'ril knew that from here Elena would no longer need him. Er'ril's honor to her a moment ago was also his good-bye. From this day onward, Elena would not age, while he would. The passing of the book marked the end of Er'ril's immortal life.

As Joach moved forward to greet his sister and offer her a thin blanket, Er'ril raised his hands before him. He stared at the bones and veins of his hand. Already he could almost feel the weight of time descending on him.

As brother and sister reunited, he hardly heard their whispered apologies and absolutions. Tears glistened on both their cheeks. Joach hugged his sister tight, needing to heal as badly as Elena – and Er'ril knew the boy would heal with time.

Er'ril lowered his hand. *Time.* From here on out, his own was no longer limitless. He would age like any other man. After five hundred winters, he had no right to complain of time's inevitable march. Still, as Er'ril stared at Elena, she met his gaze and smiled at him in the moonlight.

And for once, Er'ril prayed that time would stop.

Elena pulled free of Joach's grip and handed him the book. With her arms free, she took the thin blanket from her shoulders and wrapped it around her torso, tucking and cinching it in place. Elena felt foolish with this bit of modesty after running throughout A'loa Glen as naked as the day she was born. But as the fire of their trials died down, she sensed both Joach's and Er'ril's discomfort at the sight of her bare skin.

Once she was done, Joach offered her back the Diary, but she shook her head. 'Could you hold it a moment more?'

'Are you sure?' Joach asked doubtfully, holding the tome out as if it were a poisonous snake.

'I trust you, Joach,' she said with a slight laugh.

He returned her smile, then studied the Diary's cover.

The golden rose still glowed softly in the night. 'When do you think we should open it?'

'Later. Another day.' Elena had had enough magick and surprises for two lifetimes. 'We should wait until everyone is gathered. It's something they all deserve to share.'

Joach nodded and carefully tucked the book under his arm. He crossed to the parapet to watch the end of the war below. Elena stared out at the seas for a moment, too. With the darkmages gone, the island's defenders fled from all fronts. The remainder of the fighting was more housekeeping than battle. By sunrise, the War of the Isles would be over.

Turning her back on the sight, Elena found Er'ril studying the moonlit skies and city, wary of any new threats. Always the guardian. In the moonlight, shirtless still, he seemed a bronze sculpture.

She crossed and stood beside him, silent for a breath. 'Er'ril,' she said softly.

'Hmm . . .' He did not turn, keeping up his vigil.

Elena reached and touched his bare right shoulder. She did what she had wanted to do in the catacombs while following him. She traced the tanned line where his restored arm met his shoulder, where the new Er'ril merged with the old. She knew that from here, nothing would be the same between them. He had completed his task, and she sensed that in the future the book's power would grow between them. Her heart ached at such a thought. Was there not some way to keep the new Er'ril and still not lose the old?

The plainsman shuddered under her touch.

Elena lowered her hand to grasp his wrist. Gently she turned him from the parapet.

'Elena?'

'Shush,' she scolded him. Taking his left wrist in her other hand, she lifted his palms toward her. She studied them for

680

a moment, like an oracle in a village fair seeking some vision. Here were the new and the old. But they both looked the same. Who was he really?

Er'ril turned his wrists in her grip and held her hands now, gently, tentatively. 'I . . . I thought I had lost you.'

'And I feared the same for you.' She leaned toward him, tears in her eyes.

Always her protector, Er'ril slid his hands up her bare arms and wrapped her into his warm embrace, two arms circling her, holding her against the horrors of the day. She leaned against his broad chest. As her cheek touched him, Er'ril tensed for a moment, still a sculpture in bronze; then she felt him relax against her, melting into just a man. They held each other silently, both knowing that their embrace meant more than mere consolation but neither speaking of it, fearful of ruining the moment.

Elena sank into his warmth, wrapped in both his arms, and she knew here was her answer. Two arms circled her completely. She could not say where one started and another ended. In his embrace, there was no *new* or *old* Er'ril. There was only one man. And she would not lose him – not even for the book's promise of immortality.

Er'ril held her tighter.

Thoughts of war and wit'chcraft seemed far off as she listened to the beat of his heart. Time slowed to a stop at that moment. The stars halted their endless dance; the moon froze in the night sky. For now, there was just the two of them. And for the first time since leaving her family's orchard, Elena knew she was home.

Suddenly, from behind them, a roar shattered the peace of the moment. Elena and Er'ril twisted around, still in each other's arms. A black winged shape skated from below to rush overhead.

681

Across the roof, Joach swung to face them, his eyes bright with excitement. 'It's Sy-wen and Ragnar'k! The blaze of the book must have summoned them!'

Elena and Er'ril slowly pulled from each other's embrace. The world beyond called for them, trumpeted from the throat of a dragon. But before Er'ril turned away, Elena touched his chin, stopping him. She leaned and softly kissed his cheek, where once a single tear had glistened.

She raised her face to his. 'Thank you.'

They turned together and watched the dragon circle above. With the war ending here, Elena's thoughts turned to those friends unable to share this victory: Mycelle, Kral, Mogweed, Fardale. How did they fare this night?

Elena stared at the stars, praying they were safe.

As the sun's last glow faded to the west, Mycelle led her gelding down the final switchback of the mountain pass. The others in her party were draped along the trail behind her, moving slowly along the slick rocks. The Pass of Tears had been named for the glistening droplets sprayed on the boulders alongside the path from the nearby cataracts of the Mirror River. The rumble of the river had been a constant song for three days and nights. By now, the noise had set Mycelle's teeth to aching. Even the tiny jungle snake around her wrist seemed agitated, writhing in slow circles around her wrist as if it sought some escape from the rumble.

She soothed the paka'golo with a finger as her gelding, Grisson, cautiously traversed the rocky terrain. Ahead, the forests of the Western Reaches spread across the landscape, stretching from horizon to horizon, an endless sea of green. As foreboding as the dark wood appeared, it was still a welcome sight. Not only did Mycelle look forward to leaving behind the roar of the mountain pass for the quiet of the forest, but those woods had also once been her home. Lost under the green bower were many strange creatures and odd folk, including her own people, the si'lura.

Mycelle held up a hand and willed her flesh to flow. Her fingers responded, spreading and twisting in the moonlight like the tendrils of some nocturnal vine. With her shape-shifting abilities returned, she felt a renewed kinship to her own people, and it soothed her heart to know that she was about to reenter her forest home. But a homecoming with her tribal clans would have to wait. First, she must honor her oath and join Tyrus in his fight against the Grim. Only after Castle Mryl was recovered would Mycelle's oath and debt be paid. Willing her hand back to its previous shape, Mycelle lowered her arm.

Once they reached flat ground, Mycelle kicked her mount to a faster clip toward the woods. Though night had descended, Mycelle refused to set up another camp within earshot of these roaring cascades.

She scouted ahead of the others. Fardale kept her company, loping through the brush and scrabble like a dark shadow. Behind her, Mogweed rode alongside Prince Tyrus. Kral and the trio of Dro women guarded their rear flanks. Their party had spoken little since passing the wellspring of the Mirror River. After the many days of hard travel, everyone was saddle sore and exhausted; tempers were short and attitudes sour.

Except for Prince Tyrus.

The former pirate seemed little fazed by the long trek. Even now, Mycelle could hear his laughter echoing down the trail. While the others were worn down, the man seemed to thrive on the hardship of this march. His spirits seemed to grow with each league that brought him closer to his ancestral home, Castle Mryl, overlooking the Northwall.

Scowling at his bright merriment, Mycelle snapped her

reins to move Grisson faster. The mount rounded a section of cliff face, and it was as if she had entered another world – a world of whispers and hushed noises. Blocked by the cliff, Tyrus' laugh and the falls' roar were instantly muffled. Mycelle sagged in relief. She let Grisson slow to a leisurely walk. Fardale wandered closer to the edge of the forest, leaving Mycelle a moment of rare solitude.

As she enjoyed the peace, Mycelle drifted away from the wolf. She encouraged Grisson to follow the wood's edge. Oaks and alders predominated here, a mixture of mountain and valley trees. A few maples were even scattered among them. Mycelle drew in a long breath, taking in the scent of the forest: loam and leaf, bark and moss.

Her eyelids slipped closed as she inhaled. Lost childhood memories returned, buoyed by these smells of the forest. As Grisson walked, tears flowed down Mycelle's cheeks. She sniffed and wiped at her eyes, surprised by the depth of her reaction.

Then, from somewhere ahead, a whisper of music arose. It took a moment for the sound to reach her consciousness. It seemed to sing more to her heart than to her mind, wrapping its notes and chords around the ache in her spirit, drawn to the pain of her lost childhood and home. Mycelle cocked her head, unsure for a moment if the soft sounds were real or merely old memories. As she listened, straining for the melody, Mycelle seemed to recognize this mournful tune.

But where had she heard it?

Grisson continued along the forest's edge. Around a corner of the forest, Mycelle found her answer. Standing in a small glade, outlined in moonlight, was the singer. Cloaked and hooded in a patchwork of hues, the figure stood as still as the trees. Only the sweet voice rising in song from inside the shadows of the hood suggested life.

Mycelle knew this figure. She had encountered the singer once before, in the coastal wood on her way to Port Rawl. Mycelle knew that it was no man or woman who sang from within that motley cloak, but some shade or ghost.

Slowly, Mycelle slipped from her saddle and waved for Grisson to remain. She feared startling this apparition away. She wanted to discover why this ghost haunted her. As she slipped into the moonlit glade, the figure finally shifted in her direction with a rustle of leaves. As it kept its head bowed in shadows, a single arm lifted toward Mycelle, beckoning her.

Near enough, Mycelle saw that the cloak was actually an intricate patchwork of green and autumn leaves. Even the shade's hand was gloved in foliage. Not a speck of skin showed. But Mycelle knew no skin could show. Under the leaves was nothing but a hollow shell.

Suddenly, from behind Mycelle, a low whine arose. She glanced over to find Fardale standing at the glade's edge. His amber eyes were huge and aglow with an inner light.

The melody of the song ended.

Mycelle swung around, fearful that the wolf's appearance had chased the apparition away. But she found the singer still standing in the glade's center, silent now, but with an arm still stretched toward Mycelle, palm up as if begging for a copper.

Unsure what to do, Mycelle turned to instruct Fardale to fetch the others. But instead she found Fardale wagging his tail with a strange whine flowing from his throat. Mycelle stared into the wolf's amber eyes and opened her mind to him. She begged Fardale to tell her what his wolfish senses perceived. He might have some clue as to why this ghost persisted in haunting her trails.

She only received one mental picture from the wolf: *a black acorn*. She blinked at this response, remembering the sprouting oak seed she had found in the discarded piles of leaves after she had first met the singer. Was the wolf trying to tell her that the apparition wanted it back? Frowning, she turned to find the singer still frozen with an arm outstretched.

Fardale whined again, deep in his throat.

Mycelle backed to her horse, refusing to look away. 'Fetch the others,' she ordered the wolf.

Fardale hesitated, then spun away.

Mycelle searched her pack. How did Fardale or this apparition know she had not discarded the acorn? Mycelle had thought of doing just that many times, but the tiny green shoot peeking from under the acorn's cap had always stopped her. It was a living thing, and Mycelle could not simply cast it to the stone or into the trash.

But where was the cursed seed now?

As Mycelle searched, she kept glancing back at the leaf-shrouded figure. The mysterious singer had not moved.

Fishing through a side pocket of a pack, her fingers found the familiar shape of the smooth and oddly warm seed. Mycelle slipped it free just as the others of her party came thundering around the forest's edge. She held a palm out to slow them, then waved them off their horses.

Once they dismounted, she led the others toward the glade.

Kral's gruff voice was ill suited to whispering. 'Who is that?'

Mycelle shook her head and stepped forward. Once near enough, Mycelle reached out and placed her acorn in the foliage-wrapped palm. It shone brightly, limned in moonlight for all to see.

Mogweed spoke from behind her, shock in his voice. 'That's the acorn I gave to Elena! From the sp-spider forest!'

The shade's fingers closed over the seed. The apparition raised its fist to its chest, head bowed over it. Again the song

686

began – but its mournful overtures now ran with traces of hope.

No one moved.

As they watched, a soft glow arose from the figure as the song continued. Mycelle stared and knew it was not the outer cloak that shone, but something inside. Its internal glow shone out from between the patchwork of leaves, like a distant hearth seen through trees.

'What's happening?' Tyrus asked brusquely.

Mycelle hushed him.

The song grew stronger and richer, less ethereal. The glow also grew sharper, almost blinding. Mycelle lifted a hand to shield her eyes. Then, in a single heartbeat, the song ended; the brilliance winked out.

It took a moment for the dazzle to fade from Mycelle's eyes. She saw that the figure still remained in the glade, a sculpture in leaves.

Suddenly, a sharp gust blew into the glade. The figure shuddered as if it found the breeze chilling. With this small movement, the apparition's cloak fell to the forest floor, scattering into leaves that whirled a bit in the wind. This time the singer did not vanish with the breeze.

Among the discarded foliage stood a woman of simple beauty. In the moonlight, her skin was the color of cream. Her bowed face and upper body were draped modestly in long tresses the hue of warm honey.

Posing in the moonlight, the woman's fist still lay clutched to her throat. Slowly she lowered her arm, opening her hand. The acorn was a hollow shell, split into halves. The singer dropped it to the leaf-strewn floor, then raised her face toward them all. In the starlight, her eyes were the deepest violet.

Mogweed coughed and stumbled away. 'Nee'lahn!'

27

Two nights later, Elena stood before a full-length looking glass and frowned. For the victory celebration, she had been primped and dressed like some porcelain doll. Her hair had been woven and pinned atop her head, with just the barest trickle of curl allowed to dangle alongside the small diamonds that now studded her earlobes. She was bound in a gown of soft green velvet with a deeper green sash and matching gloves. Her hem draped full to the woven rug and completely hid her silver slippers, which were each adorned with a single silk rose.

Behind her, two wasp-thin women appraised her with pursed lips. Their silvery hair had long gone gray. According to Meric, these were his two aunts. The pair were also the ones to blame for Elena's current predicament.

'This will have to do,' Ashmin said with clear dissatisfaction.

Carolin smiled slightly at the other. 'You judge too harshly. You just need to see it move.' The older woman waggled her fingers at Elena, and a small breeze blew into the castle chamber and billowed the gown around her. 'See? The dress is meant to move.'

Ashmin sighed loudly. 'If we were back in Stormhaven . . .'

'Of course, Sister, then I would hide my head in shame to present even a servant girl in such attire.'

Tapping a finger against her chin, Ashmin tilted her head. 'Maybe we should try the pale rose gown again.'

Before Elena could scream, a knock at the door interrupted the aunts. 'Elena!' a voice called out. It was Joach. 'Everyone's been gathered in the hall now for almost a fortnight. I've been sent to escort you.'

Elena thanked the Sweet Mother for her salvation. 'I'm coming now!' She glared to her two torturers, daring them to object.

Ashmin threw her hands in the air. 'It will just have to do.'

Carolin grasped her sister's hand. 'She looks lovely. You have worked wonders.'

Elena rolled her eyes and proceeded to the door. She wanted to run, but the gown and slippers forced her to a shuffling walk. She reached for the latch, but Ashmin was already there. Elena frowned at the magickal quickness of the woman's elv'in feet.

Ashmin lifted the latch and pulled the door wide. It was not done in courtesy or in respect for Elena's lineage to their ancient king, but for a more practical reason. 'You mustn't soil those gloves. Keep your hands folded under your bosom as we showed you. You are an elv'in princess, child.'

Elena frowned but obeyed. The old woman's tone was too motherly to ignore.

Beyond the doorway, Joach stepped forward from the hall. So far, he had remained speechless. His mouth hung open as his eyes traveled from her slippered toes to her pinned hair. 'You're beautiful!' His words would have been complimentary if they had not been spoken with such sheer disbelief.

Still, Elena smiled. She *was* a princess after all. 'And I see they scrubbed you enough to find a man under all the usual filth.'

Joach straightened his shoulders proudly, posing slightly to showcase his attire. His hair had been oiled and combed out of its normal tangle. The small reddish brown beard he had started to grow had been clipped and contoured. If Elena had not known better, Joach could have passed as some rich lordling. His pants were a hue of green so deep they appeared almost as black as the boots he wore. Tucked into a thick black belt was a shirt of spun silver overlaid with a sleeveless green jerkin.

Elena shook her head slightly. Joach's outer garment was the same hue as her gown. Clearly the two aunts had had some hand in his attire. If Joach was to be her escort, then of course the two must complement one another.

Ashmin bowed, stiff from the waist. 'My prince,' she said, formal and warm. 'You are looking most handsome. My niece will be well pleased.'

Joach returned her bow, then slipped an arm under Elena's elbow. 'Thank you, ladies. But our guests await.' Joach guided her away.

At a safe distance, Elena leaned to Joach's ear. 'What did you do to win a civil tongue from Lady Ashmin? What was that about her niece?'

Joach smiled, though his lips had a twist of exasperation. 'Since these elv'in learned that, as your brother, I also share the blood of their lost king, every elv'in mother with a daughter has found her way to my door.'

Elena squeezed his arm in sympathy. 'I'm sorry, Joach. But at least I'm no longer the sole heir to half the elv'in heritage.' She grinned at her brother. 'Believe me, I'm glad to have you share this with me.'

'Thanks, El,' Joach said sourly.

Too soon, they reached the double doors that led into one of the many halls of the Edifice. This room had been chosen for the ceremony due to its lack of damage from smoke and bloodshed. But the rest of the castle had not fared as well. It would take many moons to repair a tenth of the damage.

Elena sighed at how much work still lay ahead. But once done, it would be well worth it. The island would become a foothold against the Gul'gotha. For the first time in five centuries, A'loa Glen would once again be a bastion of hope. And they meant to keep it that way!

Around the island, three forces kept constant guard. The seas themselves were watched from below by mer'ai outriders who searched and questioned any ship that neared. Closer to the island, the remaining fleets of the Dre'rendi rode the waves in armed patrols, daring anyone who challenged their dragon-prowed might. Above the city itself were the ever-present warships of the elv'in, plying the clouds and watching the skies for threats from above. For now, the island remained secure.

Meanwhile, word of their victory had already spread. Boats from many lands were beginning to investigate. Elena had heard that a trading ship from the distant jungles of Yrendl, the old homeland of Mama Freda, had even docked at the island to share information. The captain had heard tales of the return of A'loa Glen and had come to see for himself.

At the castle itself, men and women had labored for the past two days and nights to prepare for the coming celebration.

A feast had been planned for this night, to raise mugs and voices to their victory. And to mark the beginning of the festivities, Elena had a role to play. With the rising of the moon, she was to open the Blood Diary for the first time and read the prophetic words written therein. Supposedly her magick had the power to bring the blank book to life. But that was yet to be proven. So much was based on the words of long-dead prophets. Who knew for sure if it would even work?

As the doors to the great hall were swung open before her, dread at what might be revealed by the book suddenly constricted her chest. Elena found it difficult to breathe as the music in the cavernous hall washed over her. Distantly, Elena heard someone announce their arrival.

Gentle clapping greeted their appearance.

Joach led her inside. She was overwhelmed by the press of people. Walking arm in arm, the two passed down a narrow aisle between tables laden with wines and ales, cheeses and herbed breads. And a more sumptuous feast was still to come.

At long last, the aisle emptied into a central court. Elena glanced around. Framing the four sides of the open space were long dining tables of polished mahogany. Seated at each table were the representatives of the various parties who had come to her aid.

On her right, Elena nodded to Meric, who sat beside his mother, the elv'in queen. Meric's older brother, the regal Richard, sat stiffly on the queen's other side. Elena met Queen Tratal's eyes for a moment. The silver-haired woman bowed her head slightly, not with any warmth, just as one woman of the royal blood acknowledging another. Elena smiled more warmly at Meric, quietly thanking him for saving the island by bringing the warships to their aid.

Elena turned next to the more boisterous table on her left. Kast sat with Sy-wen among a party of Bloodriders who were well into their cups of ale. Elena recognized one member, a striking man named Hunt. He had come to the castle to represent the Dre'rendi fleet. The man's father, the high keel, had been gravely wounded in the battle and still rested in Mama Freda's ward. From this table, Sy-wen smiled at Elena, as did Kast. But Elena noticed how the two held each other's hands. She sensed the pair's pleasure lay more in the company of each other than in this feast.

As Joach led Elena to the center of the open court, she noted that the table across from her was only sparsely occupied. It seemed that even a feast could not lure many of the mer'ai from the sea. Among the few here, Elena recognized only one. She nodded to Linora, surprised to see the elder present for the feast. Elena had heard that Linora still sorely grieved the loss of her bonded dragon and the passing of her husband. But from the way her gaze kept flickering to her daughter, Elena could guess the woman's reason for coming. Through the cloud of sorrow behind Linora's eyes, a glimmer of joy shone as she watched her daughter discover love. Elena left the mer'ai woman to her tiny island of happiness.

As Elena drew near the last table, a full smile bloomed to her lips, and tears rose to her eyes as she greeted her friends. Tol'chuk sat in the center, hulking and towering over the others. Someone had managed to outfit the og're in finery that ill fitted him. He seemed ready to tear the linens from his body at any moment, but so far had refrained. As their gazes met, Tol'chuk rolled his eyes but grinned, exposing his fangs. Elena waved a hand across her own elaborate finery, indicating her understanding of his discomfort. They shared an amused smile.

Beside the og're sat Mama Freda; her pet tamrink sat crouched atop a wheel of cheese on the table, nibbling at his perch. The three zo'ol sailors sat on Tol'chuk's opposite side with the boy Tok among them. The small lad's eyes were wide at the pageantry of the night. Elena thanked them all with a nod. The zo'ol and Tok had sailed the *Pale Stallion* to the island after the war, delivering her mare, Mist, to a makeshift stable beside the docks. Elena visited the horse each morning with a bit of dried apple. The mare seemed happy to discover solid ground under her hooves again.

Elena moved farther down the table. As she spotted the empty seats and settings, her smile faded and tears flowed anew. Places had been prepared for Flint and Moris as a remembrance to the two Brothers' sacrifice. This castle had once been their home. They had given their lives to turn it over to her and the others. Swallowing back a sob, Elena had to turn away from the empty chairs.

As she swung around and wiped at her tears, she saw one last figure step forward from the opposite aisle of the court. Er'ril carried the Blood Diary in his hands. But his hands might as well have been empty; Elena was blind to anything but the man himself. His hair, combed and curried like a stallion's after a run, shone with the rich hues of a raven's wing. His skin was ruddy from the heat of the hall, almost aglow with the hues of the setting sun. Under a midnight-black jerkin, he wore a silvery gray shirt that matched his eyes. As he moved toward her, Elena watched how the silk slid over the firm muscles of his shoulders and arms. Not even this handsome attire could hide the man's power; he was something raw and wild.

Er'ril crossed to stand before her. He suddenly knelt and offered her the book. The rose on its cover glimmered in the hall. 'Accept your birthright, Elena.'

She took the book, then his hand. She pulled Er'ril to his feet. 'Only if you swear to stand beside me, Er'ril, for all times. In the past, a mage needed a liegeman at his side, to keep him honest, to keep him humble.' She stared into his eyes. 'Be my liegeman.'

Shock froze his face, as if her words had stung him. His own words were strained. 'Y-you do not know what you ask.'

She touched his hand. 'I think I do,' she whispered.

He looked into her eyes, silent, as if about to say something. Elena suddenly knew he would refuse. He had already sacrificed five hard centuries of his life. He had earned his freedom. What right did she have to beg him to stay? She opened her mouth to rescind her offer, but then Er'ril knelt again on one knee.

He reached to her hand and held it between his two palms. 'My heart made its oath to you long ago. If you will have me, I will always be at your side.'

Tears again rose in her eyes. She pulled on his arms. 'Rise, my liegeman.'

Er'ril stood and moved to his place at her shoulder.

Elena found the others' eyes all staring at her expectantly. It was time. She lifted the book and took a step forward. She had delayed long enough. If Er'ril was strong enough to oath-bind himself to her once again, she could at least face her own responsibility.

The dread she had felt before entering the hall was gone. With Er'ril at her shoulder, she could face anything – even the Blood Diary. Slowly she peeled off the green gloves, revealing her two hands ripe with the Rose. Her palms seemed almost to glow in the torchlight.

A murmur rose from the crowd at the sight.

Elena ignored the onlookers and glanced to the book. In her bared hands, she felt the Diary's power, a warm coal in her fingers. Before she lost the iron in her heart, Elena snapped open the rose-engraved cover.

She gasped, stumbling back.

In her grip, the book flared from a warm coal to a fiery agony, as if she clutched a flaming brand by its burning end. But she did not let go. She knew this pain. It was the same as when she had grabbed Joach's staff. She felt blood magick rip from her palms, feeding the book. Still, Elena hung on. She sensed that to let go now would spell disaster. Tears ran down her cheeks.

'Elena?' Er'ril took a step nearer.

'No,' she choked out. 'Stay back!'

At her words, a sharp brilliance flared from the open pages, blinding her, searing into her mind. Then, as quickly as it came, the light vanished, taking the pain with it. Elena blinked away the residual glare. The book became a cooling balm in her hands. Relieved, Elena straightened, glancing down into the Diary.

What Elena found within the tome so startled her that she almost cast it away. Er'ril steadied her with a touch on her shoulder, then leaned to gaze with her into the book. She heard his sharp intake of breath. Elena spoke to the plainsman, hoping he had an answer. 'Er'ril, where are the pages?'

There was no book between the tattered covers – there was another world. The open book became a window to a landscape of black voids, dense-packed stars, and clouds of gases in a rainbow of sharp hues. Suddenly an insubstantial figure composed of foggy light swept up and through the window and into this world.

All around the room, chairs toppled as the celebrants retreated back. Weapons were drawn, but none dared approach.

Er'ril pulled Elena back.

Oblivious of their panic, the foggy form settled calmly to

the hall's marble floor, swirling and spinning with an inner glow that whispered of moons and stars. Slowly, the mist drew tighter, fog becoming substance. Arms and legs stretched out, ablaze with the same fire that had marked the rose on the book's cover. The misty light grew even denser until actual features could be seen.

Before the transformation was complete, Elena recognized the stern expression of the apparition. Soon what was once a glowing mist of scintillating light became a sculpture carved of moonstone. The apparition from the book faced Elena and the others.

Elena's heart eased. She knew this woman: the thin, unforgiving lips; the small nose that tilted slightly up at its tip; the hair bound in a severe braid, woven out of harm's way while its owner labored at baking. Elena named their visitor. 'Aunt Fila?' After so much strangeness, this familiar face was most welcome.

Then the shade spoke, and all sense of family and old homes shattered. The voice was cold, echoing up from some distant plane. Behind the words, stars died, and worlds were burned to ash. As Greshym had hidden behind the face of Elena a few days back, now something larger and even stranger hid behind Aunt Fila's face.

'We are Cho,' the figure said, cocking its head and studying them as some bird might examine a spider for a meal. *'The void has been opened,'* she stated with a nod toward the book in Elena's hand, *'and the bridge has been sacrificed.'* Her other hand indicated the form she wore.

Elena raised a fist to her throat. 'Who are you? What have you done to Aunt Fila?'

The apparition bent its head. *'We are Cho. We are Fila.'* The words were spoken with finality, as if this should be clear enough. Then the woman cocked her head as if she was listening to something from far off. *'We understand.'*

Somehow Elena knew this last statement was not meant for her. As she watched with Er'ril at her shoulder, the carving of glowing moonstone seemed to relax, almost as if something warmer had entered the sculpture.

When the apparition next spoke, Elena knew it was her dead aunt. Even Fila's familiar tired smile appeared. The eyes wandered up and down her niece's form. 'Elena, honey, you've grown since last we talked, but you'll have to explain how that happened later. Right now, I must be quick. Healing you earlier took most of this moon's power.'

Elena shook her head, trying to shake one of the thousand questions loose from her skull. 'What . . . ? Who was that other?'

As usual, Aunt Fila sensed her confusion. She raised a hand. 'Calm yourself. Not even I can explain everything yet. But I can answer your question. Cho is the being who has granted you your power. She is a creature of neither form nor substance. She is light and energy, magick and power. As we live on this world, she lives in the void between stars and travels among them.'

Elena's eyes grew wide.

'I will give you more details later, my dear. For now, I must be brief. The book is your only link to communicate and understand Cho. And my spirit is the bridge between the Blood Diary and this being. She shares my spirit and uses it to travel from the stars to the book. But there are limits to even this, rules you must follow.'

'Like what?'

'First, you ignited the book under a full moon, so the path can only be opened during one of the three nights when the moon is most ripe. Otherwise, during the day or any other night, it is only a font of power. It will help protect

698

and heal you, but only to a point. It is not limitless. Even on the night of a full moon, it takes power to maintain this connection. For this cycle, we used much of it to heal you, so now we must be brief until the next cycle of the moon. In the coming moons, Cho and I will use these nights to teach and train you for what must come next.'

'And what is that?'

'For now, just rest. You have done much. Use the autumn and winter moons to firm this foothold in the Black Heart's domain. It will be needed.'

'But what is to come after that? When do we take the fight to Blackhall and the Gul'gotha?'

Aunt Fila glanced around the room at the gathered forces. Elena sensed that she was leaving much unsaid, especially in front of so many eyes.

'What is it, Aunt Fila? What are you holding back?'

'There is much I still don't understand. Cho has just joined me, but she is so foreign that not all is clear. When she thinks about Chi, there is much I don't understand.'

Er'ril stepped forward, his voice bitter. 'What of Chi? What have you learned?'

Aunt Fila squinted and scratched behind one ear thoughtfully. 'It's confusing. Cho and Chi are somehow part-nered. They are familial, like brother and sister or husband and wife ... but then again not. They are also opposites. Man and woman, white and black, positive and negative. It's all very strange.' Fila glanced to Er'ril. 'All I know for certain is that Cho returned to this world to find Chi. It took her five hundred of our winters to return here after first sensing Chi's disappearance.'

Er'ril scowled. 'Then she came a long way for nothing,' he commented sourly. 'Chi is gone.'

'No, Er'ril. One thing is clear from Cho: Chi never left.

He is still here *somewhere*. That is why Cho has returned and why she has granted Elena her power. The wit'ch was forged to be Cho's warrior upon this world, while the Blood Diary is Cho's eyes and ears.' Aunt Fila's shade blew forth with a fiercer light. 'This is Elena's true purpose! Not to fight the Dark Lord, *but to find Chi!*'

Elena shook her head, confused. 'I don't understand. How —?' Before Elena could question the woman further, Aunt Fila's form began to dissipate into a fog.

'I can speak no longer. The connection wears thin for this cycle.' Aunt Fila reached to Elena. 'You have done well, child. Rest now until the next moon. We will talk more then.'

The shade of Aunt Fila became mist and seeped back into the book. The glow spread over the Blood Diary, obscuring the view into the starry landscape. As the light faded, Elena found herself staring at blank pages in a tattered book. She closed the tome, flipping the cover up. Even the rose on its cover was dull, no longer shining with any inner fire. It was just plain gilt, flaking at its edges.

Elena turned to Er'ril. The plainsman's face had grown pale. 'How are we supposed to find Chi?' she whispered.

He shook his head. 'We'll ponder such mysteries later, Elena.' He waved to the crowd. 'For now, a party awaits.' The banquet minstrels began tentatively to strike up their instruments.

Elena frowned. Right now she wished nothing more than to be left alone. Too much had happened, too much to digest. Still, she took Er'ril's arm. Duty called to her even this night.

As midnight passed, Er'ril stalked down the crowded passageway outside the great hall, searching for Elena. She had slipped away from him and vanished while he was momentarily distracted by a toast. But Er'ril could guess where she had gone. After the endless stream of courses during the feast, the hall had grown stifling. He had noticed how flushed and melancholy Elena had grown by the time dessert was served. Maybe she had sought fresh air.

Finally reaching the renovated doors to the central courtyard, Er'ril pushed through. It was a warm evening, but after the press of bodies, the open air still felt refreshingly cool. Er'ril searched the court. Though the worst of the debris had been cleared from the yard, it would be a long time before even a glimmer of its former beauty could be restored. In a corner lit by torches, a foursome of minstrels played quietly. Since the residual reek of smoke in the yard was too potent a reminder of the war, the musicians had only one listener in attendance.

Er'ril approached the single spectator. His large bulk appeared like a boulder fallen from the castle heights. The og're did not turn as Er'ril approached, but he did speak. 'If you be looking for Elena . . .' He pointed an arm toward the westernmost tower. In his raised claw was his tribe's heartstone talisman. It shone like a faded rose in moonlight.

Tol'chuk lowered his arm, cradling the stone again in his lap. From the og're's slumped shoulders, Er'ril sensed his melancholy. He knew the source of the og're's distress. All the past day's victories – winning the war, recovering the book, retaking the island – had failed to help the og're in his one goal: to free the Heart of his people from the Bane. His people's spirits continued to fade in the stone.

'Tol'chuk . . . ?'

The og're turned more of his back toward Er'ril. 'I be fine, but she needs you, Er'ril. Go to her.'

Er'ril glanced to the tower's parapets. Far above, moonlight outlined a small figure leaning on the stone's tower.

'She shouldn't be up there alone.'

Tol'chuk grunted, half in amusement. 'You don't need an excuse, Er'ril.'

He blinked. 'Wh-what do you mean?'

Tol'chuk just shook his head, exasperated. 'Humans.' Tol'chuk waved an arm. 'Go!'

Er'ril's feet were already moving. He needed to make sure she was safe. He reentered the castle and wound his way toward the western tower.

As he climbed the long stair, he thought back to the last time the two had been atop a tower together. He recalled the long embrace they had shared and cursed himself. He shouldn't have let his emotions rule him then. Er'ril touched the hilt of the silver sword in its new filigreed sheath. This is all he should be to her – her liegeman and nothing more. It was time to dig out these other feelings that had taken root in his heart. They were weeds that would weaken him, choke his ability to protect her.

He must be her sword, nothing more.

With this new determination in his heart, he followed his way to the tower's roof. The trapdoor was open. He paused before stepping out. A sharp breeze flowed down the throat of the staircase. Er'ril took a moment to appreciate the fresh air. From the tower's height, the winds carried no smoke or banner of war. Er'ril closed his eyes and allowed the winds to rush over him, cleansing him.

Once ready to face Elena, Er'ril climbed the last steps to the roof. Elena did not hear him. She just stared out to the skies beyond the parapet. Moonlight bathed her in silver, while starlight danced along her gown.

Er'ril suddenly could not breathe.

Sadness and loneliness shone from her as bright as the moon.

His heart ached. At that moment, he knew he could never be content with being just her sword. He wanted to be her moon and stars, her sun and sea. He wanted to be everything to her.

Er'ril gazed at her in wonder, and he knew he must lock away these desires forever. Elena had the weight of worlds on her small shoulders. He could burden her no further. But from here, he could no longer deny his own heart either. He loved her. It was that simple.

Though he would never speak of his deeper feelings, he would strive to be more than just her sword, her liegeman. He would do his best to protect her – even from the despair he saw in her now.

Still dressed in her finery, Elena stood atop the tower once called the Praetor's Spear. Already it had been renamed the Wit'ch's Sword after the sole occupant of its highest chamber. Overhead, elv'in ships glided silently by, blocking the stars, then moving on. She stared at the sky. The moon was on its descent. Midnight was well past.

Still, the sounds of revelry echoed up to her from the streets and castle below. The whole city was in celebration and would be until dawn. She eavesdropped on the merrymakers: the strike of drum, the strum of lyre, the bawdy songs of men glad to be alive. But under it all, there remained a vein of sorrow. The laughter from below had a strained edge to it. Even the calls of the celebrants were often tearful.

Done with her duties, Elena had retreated to her rooms as soon as possible, taking the Blood Diary with her. She needed a moment of quiet to contemplate Aunt Fila's story of the twin spirits, Chi and Cho, whose destinies intersected with her own. She shook her head. It was too much to ponder for one night. She would simply take Aunt Fila's advice to rest and wait for the next full moon. Hopefully then she would learn more.

Glancing to the Blood Diary in her hands, she traced a finger along the twisting stem of the rose to the warm blossom in the center. So many lives had been lost for this.

A voice spoke behind her. 'Elena?'

She turned to find Er'ril standing behind her. How long had he been there? He still wore the earlier fineries of the evening, but his eyes shone with a new light, something she could not name. The breezes atop the tower had loosened his hair, fluttering it over his face.

'I'm sorry to disturb you,' he said, his voice quiet. 'But Tol'chuk noted you from the courtyard below. It's not safe to expose yourself alone to the night like this.' He moved near her. 'As your liegeman, I should always be at your side when you venture out.'

Sighing, Elena turned away. She glanced to the stars. 'Can't we ever have a normal moment, Er'ril?' she asked sourly. 'Listen. Music is playing, and the night is bright. Must we always act as if we are about to be attacked? Can't I just have a moment to pretend I'm not a wit'ch? Pretend that the fate of Alasea does not depend on where I take my next step?'

She turned to find him staring sternly at her, all iron and solidity. Under his gaze, she instantly felt like a churlish child. What right did she have to complain when so many others had lost so much more? She lowered her eyes. 'I'm sorry . . .'

He simply stepped toward her and held out one arm.

She was unsure what he was offering.

'May I have this dance?' he whispered softly to her.

Elena failed to hide the surprise on her face. Only then did she hear a familiar Highland tune rising on the winds from street minstrels below. It was a common dance from her own lands.

A smile haunted Er'ril's lips as he suddenly recognized the tune, too. 'It seems Tol'chuk sensed the heaviness of your heart, too.'

Elena's cheeks flushed as the plainsman stepped nearer. Er'ril stood over her, arms out. The night's breeze carried his scent to her, warm and familiar. Before she could balk, Er'ril took her hand in his. He guided her gently into his arms. Tentatively, they began to move to the music. The first few steps were awkward as they danced cautiously across the stones.

Soon, though, they found their rhythms and began to move in step, quicker and more joyous now. Elena allowed herself to be led, circling and turning in unison with the larger man. Er'ril's palm blazed like a flame at the base of her back as he guided her, teasing her to keep up.

As he pulled her into a tight spin, a small laugh escaped her lips. The sound surprised her.

'For a wit'ch with the fate of Alasea riding on your next step, you're awfully light on your feet,' he said with a sly grin.

Soon Elena could not stop laughing in his arms. They spun and spun with the stars whirling overhead. The world beyond the parapets faded away. There were just the two of them, the music, and the moon.

Then, after a final giddy twirl, with both dancers breathless, the music's cadence slowed to something more languid but no less passionate. Elena's laughter quickly died.

Er'ril still held her, but again the awkwardness rose between them.

He began to step back, but Elena tightened her grip on him. She did not want him to step away, not this night. He relented and moved nearer.

As the music grew, Elena reached and pulled the pins from her hair. She shook out her fiery curls. For this one night, she no longer wanted to be a wit'ch or a savior. She let all this drop away with the pins to the floor. She would just be a woman.

Er'ril pulled her near, and they slowly swayed to the music from below. Elena did not know when she began crying, but Er'ril offered no words. None would have helped. He just held her close to his heart as the music played long into the night.

And so as Er'ril and Elena slowly dance toward dawn, I must end this section of her story. With the War of the Isles won, it is time for the land to heal and prepare for the coming days of darkness – and, trust me, those days will come.

So allow our friends a moment of well-earned peace. Pick a partner. Stroll the streets. Raise a mug of ale to their victory, and join the celebration. For it won't last long. Soon the dogs of the Black Heart will be loosed from their ebon's-tone shackles to ravage the land.

And the gods themselves will learn to scream.

Read on for a preview of

Wit'ch Gate
Book Four of
THE BANNED AND THE BANISHED

The cloaked figure crouched motionless in the murk of the keep's courtyard. Her slender form was but another shadow amid the piled rubble of stone and twisted iron. She had been waiting, motionless, since midnight, spying on the play of lights atop the wit'ch's tower. She had watched the dragon alight on the stones of the parapet and vanish. Still she had not moved. Even when the glow of moonlight had faded from the tower heights, she remained frozen in her hiding place. Patience had been taught to her by her Master. Those trained in the deadly Arts knew that victory lay in the silence between battles. So she had remained throughout the night.

Drops of morning dew collected in the folds of her midnight green cloak. A cricket crawled across the back of her hand as her palm rested in the dirt. While she watched the castle battlements, she felt the small insect scratch its hind legs together, heard a whisper of cricket song. The promise of dawn. Now was the time. She moved smoothly to her feet as if she had only paused to pick a flower from the newly planted garden. Her motion was so swift and smooth that the cricket remained on the back of her steady hand, still playing his last song of the night.

She raised the hand to her lips and blew the surprised insect from its perch. If only her current prey were so unsuspecting ...

Without pausing, she moved from her cubby of fallen

stones and fled swiftly across the courtyard. None would know she had passed. She had been trained to run the desert sands without disturbing a single grain. The main doors to the central castle were guarded. She could see the backs of the guards through the stained glass windows. But doors were for the invited.

As she ran, she flicked her wrist, and a thin rope shot out from her fingers and flew toward the barred windows of the third landing. The trio of hooked trisling teeth, fastened to the end of her rope, wrapped around the bars. Without stopping, she tugged on the rope and tightened her grappling. The rope was strong, woven of braided spider's silk. It would hold her. She flew to the wall and up it. No one watching would have even suspected she was using her rope. The ancient stone was full of pocks and old battle scars; climbing was as easy as scaling a steep stair.

Without even raising a sweat on her brow, she reached the barred window of the third floor. From a pocket appeared a vial of blackfire. She smeared the oil on three bars, top and bottom. The stench of scorched iron wafted briefly, but no glow marked the work of the blackfire oil. *Nothing must draw the eye:* one of the first lessons taught apprentices.

She ticked off the time. At the count of ten, she grabbed the bars and yanked them free. The blackfire oil had eaten fully through. Carefully, she rested the free iron rods on the window's granite sill. She couldn't risk someone hearing the clatter of iron on stone if she merely dropped them.

Reaching through the opening, she flicked her wrist and a thin steel blade appeared in her fingers. She passed it through the window's casement and slipped the latch. She tested the old window hinges. An immediate rasp told her this particular window had not been opened in ages.

Frowning at even this tiny noise, she reached into a pocket and oiled each hinge.

Satisfied, she pushed the window a finger-breadth wide, and used the polished surface of her steel blade to study the reflection of the hall. Empty. Without waiting, she squeezed through the narrow opening and rolled into the hall. She was on her feet and in the shadows within a single heart-beat.

Still she did not pause. She raced down the passage and slid down two staircases, never even leaving a footprint in the dust. In a short time, she had reached her goal – the doors to the Grand Court. She crouched. A dance of tools and the lock was open. She cracked the door just enough to squeeze her lithe form past the threshold. At least these hinges were already well-oiled.

Once inside, she hurried to the long ironwood table. At its head was a tall chair on a raised step. Its high back was carved with twining roses. As she approached, a trace of misgiving threaded through her veins. Here was where the wit'ch sat. Her feet slowed as she walked down the long length of the table and neared the seat of power. She could almost sense the eyes of the wit'ch upon her. She knew such thoughts were nonsense, but still she shivered.

Cringing slightly, she sidled around the table's edge and stood at its head. With her back to the tall chair, she reached inside her cloak and withdrew her weapon. In the dimness of the hall, the long black blade almost glowed. Her hand trembled slightly as she held it. 'Don't make me do this,' she whispered to the empty hall.

But there was no retreat now. She had come too far, given up too much. If there was to be any chance, this cowardly deed must be done.

Raising the long black dagger high in both fists, she

prayed for forgiveness and drove the dagger down into the table. Its sharp point pierced smoothly through the iron-wood, as if it were only warmed butter. Still a shock spiked up her arms as the hilt hit the table. Gasping loudly, she pulled her hands free and ground her palms on her cloak, trying to escape the feeling.

She stared at the impaled blade. Its hilt protruded from the center of the handprint burned into the table – the handprint of a wit'ch.

As she watched, crimson blood welled up from the wood, spreading along the table's surface. The pool ran over the table's edge and flowed in rivulets to the stone floor. But that was not the worst. As she stood frozen, a distant cry of pain and shock rose from the spreading pool.

Raising a fist to her throat, the cloaked figure backed away. *What have I done?*

Turning on a heel, she fled out the door and into the maze of halls. But even the shadows could not hide her from the echoing cry of a wounded wit'ch. *Gods above, forgive me!*